THE STEALING OF THE SAHARA

© 2017

Sam T.K. Neel

"The Western – or, until now, Spanish – Sahara is a small place. Its decolonization and the fortunes of its mere 75,000 inhabitants do not attract instant or prolonged public attention. Nevertheless, or, perhaps, in part for that very reason, the disposition of the Sahara case by the United Nations has been monumentally mishandled, creating a precedent with a potential for future mischief out of all proportion to the importance of the territory."

Thomas M. Franck, *The Stealing of the Sahara*, The American Journal of International Law, Vol. 70 , No. 4 (October 1976).

Global Directives LLC
New York
2019

ACKNOWLEDGEMENT

Few stories illustrate the heights to which people will go to achieve their aspirations for freedom – or the depths to which the political forces of the world will descend in order to deprive them of their hopes and dreams – as well as the epic 16 year war between the Sahrawis and Morocco to rule Western Sahara, the former colony of Spain – the last remaining colony in Africa.

This is a story of their struggle, based on actual events, as told through the eyes of those who lived it. It is a story of hope, patience and pain, of promises and betrayal, but most of all, it is a story of courage. It is dedicated to all those whose lives were destroyed by a war that would never have begun if the international community had adhered to the lofty ideals that so easily roll off their leaders' lips and are so seldom followed in practice. It is dedicated to those who died in the battles of this war – the Sahrawi men who sacrificed all they held dear for the attainment of an ideal, men like Hammada El Ouali, Said Sgheir, Sidi Hiduk, Sidi Haidougue, Mohammed Chadad, Hadad, Najem Tahil, Ali Ahmed Zein, Bachir Saleh, Brahim Alati, Ami Ahmed Mkhailil, Mehd Zergua, El Haj Badadi, Maichan, Zel Alia – and, of course, first of all El Ouali Mustapha Sayed – as well as others too numerous to name. It is also dedicated to the men and women who "disappeared" during the war, or who died during the bombings of the civilians who tried to flee the war, or who perished during the scourges that plagued the women and children in the refugee camps while their men were off to war.

And it is also dedicated to the young Moroccan men who fell fighting far from their homes for a cause that they didn't fully understand and which was not of their making, as well as the Mauritanians who never wished for this war in the first place.

But as one of the world's greatest leaders once said, in a larger sense with mere ink we cannot do justice to the story of those who have fallen or who have sacrificed so much to achieve justice. The brave men, living and dead, who struggled in the battles depicted in the book and those

i

who perished while aiding them have told with their blood a story far above our poor power to add or detract with words.

I want to thank all of those who sat patiently with me through the three years it took me to write this book imparting their wisdom and knowledge: Mohammed Abdelaziz, Brahim Ghali, Bachir Mustapha Sayed, Mohammed Lamine Bouhali, Mohamed Akeik, Mohamed Salem Ould Salek, Mohamed Beisat, Mouloud Zaid, Boukhari Ahmed, Emmad Khaddad, Bana Baha, Mohamed Lamine Ahmad, Khadija Hamdi, Aminatou Haidar, Fatma Mehdi, Babiya Chia, Mohamed Bachiri, Melanine Moustafa Aouinat, Mohamed Ouadadi, Brahim Lili, Hdaya, Sid Ahmed Tayeb Beri, Ounaina, Mouloud Didi, Bachir Abdallah Sidiya, Mohamed Salem Dkhil, Cheikh Allal, Abdeslam Omar, and Mohamed Ouilida – to name just a few. And I wish to give a special thanks to Bachir Mehdi, my indefatigable interpreter cum escort, without whose painstaking attention to factual accuracy and dogged review I could never have understood and written the myriad details that are contained within it, and Khatri and his crew at the guest house in Rabouni, who took care of me as if I were visiting royalty. I hope that this book will be part of the archives that form a lasting testament to the history of their people for themselves, their children, their children's children and the future generations of Sahrawis to come.

And just as Abraham Lincoln said about those who died in the fields of Gettysburg in an equally tragic conflict, it is up to us, the living, to ensure that the sacrifice of those who died was not in vain, and that the long struggle of the people of the last colony in Africa to obtain justice will end in victory.

Sam T. K. Neel

ii

CHAPTER 1
1974

October 20, 1974. Somewhere in the desert . . .

Rain was both a blessing and a curse in the Sahara. For months the arid and scorched soil blistered under the sun in temperatures that could exceed 120 degrees Farenheit in the summer. Nothing but a few strains of hardy grass, barren bushes and the occasional acacia tree could provide sustenance to the animals that the nomads relied upon. Here and there, usually hundreds of miles apart, were tiny oasis where underground streams suddenly burst to the surface, providing the only source of water. If it were not for these oasis humans could not survive in the desert.

However, every once in a while nature attempts to disrupt this balance by opening its skies and allowing liquid refreshment to descend. At first, this manna from above is gobbled with gusto by the plants and animals, and by the humans that depend upon them. However, the parched earth, unaccustomed to such largesse, can absorb only a fraction of what falls, and soon rivelets of water in the sand turn into streams, turning the crevices of the hills into enormous shallow lakes of water and sediment as thick as quicksand, trapping all who venture near and wiping away any settlements that stand in their way. Then the rain stops, and after a few, short weeks in which flowers cover the landscape, the desert reverts back, leaving scarcely a memory behind. Except for those who stood in its path. Hundreds of people have died in Sahara floods.

On October 20, 1974, a Land Rover wound its way through a bumpy desert terrain. It had started to rain and pellets had bombarded the contents of the open Land Rover and covered everything they touched with a slippery film. Nothing but desert was visible for miles. In the Land Rover a young woman wiped moisture from her brow and strained to see something in the distance before looking at the map on her lap. The tire marks that had marked the dirt path she had followed from the main road had started to be erased by the rain, and she was lost. She was in trouble, and she knew it. She had lived in El Ayoun since her parents had brought her there from Spain four years ago and knew that rain only meant trouble for those outside the tiny enclaves of Spanish Sahara. Already it was getting difficult for her to navigate through the mud filled desert paths. As she tapped the gas ever so lightly she said a silent prayer in Spanish. *Por favor, Virgin Maria, don't let me get stuck here*! But the car had not heard her prayers and her right rear wheel started spinning in the

1

mud, refusing to budge. The more she tried to move forward, the deeper into the mud it sank. She put the car into four wheel drive and rocked it gently back and forth, as she was taught. But the ditch was too steep and slippery, and for every inch she moved forward she slid back another four inches until, exhausted, she got out of the car to examine the damage.

It was then that she saw him. He had been able to approach unnoticed, the noise of the rain and the motor of the Land Rover masking his approach. Even now, a few yards away, she could only make out his shape, his features blurred by the rain that slammed into her eyes. Fear swelled inside her. Who was this man, out here in the desert, alone? A robber? A nomad? She said another silent prayer, hoping against all odds that he was a Spanish soldier, a member of the garrison that protected El Ayoun.

But all hope of this disappeared as he reached her. He was dressed totally in black: black pants and shirt, with a black scarf around his neck, and his head and face were covered by a black turban masking all of his features except for his eyes, which were dark, and penetrating, and somewhat annoyed. He surveyed the situation and yelled something in a language she could not understand. Suddenly three other men appeared out of nowhere, and together they pushed her Land Rover out of the ditch and onto level ground.

She wanted to say something, but she did not know how to make herself understood. She muttered the few words in Arabic she had learned from her maid. At least she knew how to say "Thank you."

Finally, he turned to her and in a perfect Castillion accent, somewhat crossly said, "You must be crazy to be out here in the desert, alone, in the rain. What on earth do you think you are doing?"

She was startled and could barely compose herself to respond. When she did it was with the imperiousness bred into Spanish ladies of her class. "I am out here doing research on the archaeological finds", she said, and then added, "if it is any of your business!"

He just shrugged his shoulders and started talking to the other three. Finally they motioned to her to get into the car, on the passenger side. She did not know what to do. "Can you take me back to El Ayoun?" she finally blurted. What she had said must have been funny, for the three men accompanying him started to laugh. "I thank you for your help, but I think I can make it on my own now", she forced herself to say. Actually, she was scared stiff of trying to navigate her way back to El Ayoun, but she was even more frightened of getting into the car with four strange men. "You would never make it back to El Ayoun on your own," said the man with the Castillion accent, "and, unfortunately, I do not think we would be welcome there." She looked at him more carefully. Behind him, a few yards, she could make out the silhouette of a car, a Land Rover. In the rear an assortment of large cans and the tip of a rifle of some sort protruded from beneath a rain soaked blanket. She understood. They were guerillas. Guerillas had been fighting the Spanish for a year, trying to oust them from the territory. But it was her car, and she had no intention of becoming a hostage – or worse. She walked within a couple of feet of the man and gave him her most ferocious look. "This is *my* car," she said imperiously, "and I insist that you just go back to wherever you came from and let me go on my way."

He had been fiddling with the instruments, but now he looked up. "I don't have time to discuss this," he said, "It will be dusk soon and you will never find your way back in the rain. We can't leave you out in the desert, so I'm afraid you will have to go with us until we can figure out somewhere to leave you. So get in." and with that he opened the door to the passenger seat. But instead of getting in, she backed up a couple of paces and shouted "No!" He was obviously losing patience. He took a couple of paces towards her, lifted her over his shoulders and unceremoniously dumped her in the passenger seat. Then he took control of the car and started to drive. She attempted to get out, but the door was jammed. "If you insist on trying to get out I will just have to tie you up, which will be quite uncomfortable in the rain, I can assure you," he said, unwinding the scarf that was around his neck. "Here, this will have to do for now," he muttered, handing her the scarf and gesturing to the others to follow. The three men who had accompanied him had been laughing with amusement at the spectacle of their comrade and his guest, but at his command retreated to where the Land Rover was waiting for them.

She looked at the scarf that lay in her lap, then wrapped it over her head. It had a musky smell that reminded her of the camel drivers who appeared at the market in El Ayoun each Sunday to sell or trade. "Who are you?" she finally said.

He looked at her, his black eyes flashing, but said not a word.

But he didn't have to. She knew who he was.

Polisario

October 20, 1974. Later that Evening.

The rain had stopped as quickly as it had started, leaving the desert floor dewy, with a damp odor. The sun had dipped over the horizon and shadows were beginning to fill the crevices. The young men made their way slowly through the desert. It was now getting dark and only faint lights of El Ayoun in the far distance separated the sky from the earth. Soon the stars would appear in their full glory, transforming the sky into a jeweled tapestry. But in the twilight only dark shadows pierced the gloom.

They inched their way over the pavement, recognizing each stone, each indentation of the earth. About thirty minutes into their journey they were greeted by the hum of a second engine – and a second Land Rover silently joined them. There, in the middle of nowhere, they waited.

Soon dusk turned to dark and in the sky a swath of tiny glimmering lights began to emerge from the total blackness that enveloped them. At some self appointed hour they renewed their journey. The lights of the town gradually receded until they disappeared entirely. The two cars deftly navigated the crevices and gullies that dotted the landscape. They were far from any source of electricity. Together they navigated the terrain through instinct, silently, with only the stars as their companions. After a few minutes they parted company, the first car turning in the direction of the ocean, the other in the opposite direction.

The young men in the first car inched forward in total silence for another ten minutes. Then, in the far distance, a pinprick of light appeared, growing ever larger as they approached. Soon they were able to discern the shape of a building faintly illuminated by two or three solitary lights, and the whirring of a large generator broke their solitude.

They stopped their Land Rover a fair distance from the building and turned off the motor. The men quickly withdrew the cans and equipment in the back and without uttering a word advanced towards the building, their flashlights searching for the door. It was locked. One of them held a crowbar, and began prying at the metal door. After a second or two, another of them gave the door a swift kick, then another and a third, until the hinges of the heavy door began to crack. Finally an opening appeared. The room was filled with machines and control panels, their blinking lights of red and green sparkling like Christmas ornaments. One of the men walked quickly to a machine at the far side of the room and switched a few buttons. The lights went off. He then gathered three or four pieces of the wood that covered the electrical wires and placed them on top of the machines. Two of his companions then entered with cans, poured the contents of some of them over the equipment, and placed others in the corners. Outside, someone painted a word on the walls. Then, as quickly as they came, they lit a match and retreated.

Suddenly a fire erupted, spreading so quickly through the building they scarcely had time to retreat, sending shockwaves through the night air, ripping through concrete, twisting iron, and hurling flames skyward like an angry volcano, until the whole earth seemed like one large ball of fire. The inferno could be seen for miles across the desert, and as the little band made its way to their homes they could still see for hours the light of the fires that burned and the smoke that obscured the stars.

October 21, 1974. The Morning After.

General Federico Gomez de Salazar, the portly Governor-General was livid. He had been enjoying his Sunday morning coffee at his villa when the knock came at the door. It was around half past eight in the morning. The Boucraa mine – the lifeblood of the territory – was out of commission. Early that morning saboteurs had broken into two of the stations that controlled the conveyor belt, sprayed gasoline over its sophisticated control equipment, lit fires and vanished into the night, leaving behind several million dollars' worth of damage.

A large section of the conveyor belt was now just a piece of twisted metal and the control stations smoldering ruins. The Polisario! He had quickly formed a police unit to hunt for the culprits, but he knew they would have little luck. They were ghosts – striking in the darkness then melting back into the desert. They had staged attacks before, but nothing like this. They had gone too far this time, he fumed!

Several hours had now passed and he was pacing impatiently in his office near the Church that served as the headquarters for the Spanish government in El Ayoun. El Ayoun, or "the source" in Arabic, was one of only four outposts of civilization in the Spanish colony. Three of these – El Ayoun, Boujdour and Villa Cisneros – bordered the Atlantic facing the Canary Islands, about 200 miles apart. The fourth – Smara – was a hundred or so miles inland southeast of El Ayoun. Together they formed what was considered the "useful" triangle of Spanish Sahara, the part rich in phosphates and fisheries and worth possessing. Beyond the triangle was just rocky desert and sand dunes, appealing only to the nomads that inhabited the region – the Sahrawis.

But here in El Ayoun the Spanish had the creature comforts of home – or at least some of them – and could etch out a reasonable living waiting for their tour of duty to end. At least that was what the majority of Spanish soldiers thought. But Salazar was different. He was a romantic. He looked around him each morning and saw the glory of Spain and its historic role in the world. He considered the ragtag Sahrawi goat herders who assembled each week to sell their wares children of the empire whom he was there to protect. His paternalistic demeanor was at the same time amusing and repugnant to the Sahrawis who were his servants. After all, it was *their* country.

"Do you have any idea who the culprits are?" a voice proclaimed, shattering his momentary reverie.

Salazar turned from the window and looked at the distinguished, but weary looking gentleman sitting in an armchair beside his desk. "No, not yet," he said slowly, "but whoever they were they knew what they were doing. They managed to dismantle the TT40 device that transmits data to the central control station, the only station that is manned, so that we would have no notice of the fire for sufficient time for them to escape, and we know they were the Polisario, they were brazen enough to paint the word "Polisario" on the wall!"

The man in the armchair stifled a smile, not wishing to add insult to the indignant feelings of his friend and colleague. He had to admit a grudging admiration for the audacity of this group of miscreants. But Salazar had not noticed.

"This reminds me of the trouble we had a few years ago with the so-called "Army of Liberation," the man said, settling back in the armchair and reaching for the cup of coffee that lay on a table beside it.

"The *Army of Liberation*," Salazar said with a sneer. "They disbanded quickly enough when we joined forces with the French! But these new groups . . . first Bassiri and now this." He looked at his guest and shook his head. "They are proving to be as slippery as eels!" He turned to face the window once again, muttering *wily bastards* under his breath.

His thoughts wandered to the developments that had plagued the colony in the last few years. A resistance movement had sprung into being four years before he had arrived – a group of young natives led by an intellectual, Bassiri. This group was different from the tribal warriors who had led the independence movements that had sprouted in the 30s and 50s. Inspired by the philosophy that had won the independence of India, Bassiri at first preached non-violent political action to win both economic and social reforms and political independence for the colony. Salazar smiled wryly. Bassiri had been naïve to think that the non-violent approach that worked so well against the British could be effective against the last remaining fascist dictator. When he was bold enough to organize protests in Zemla, the Sahrawi ghetto in El Ayoun, his predecessor had had him and his followers arrested.

However, although Bassiri had been unsuccessful in achieving his goals, his movement had set the stage for a group that was proving to be more difficult to disband – the Polisario. This was no movement led by irascible but largely itinerant tribal elders, more accustomed to navigating through the dunes of the desert than the corridors of the UN, or idealistic dreamers easily deterred by the point of a sword. No, he thought, this group had at its core a handful of young, college educated Sahrawis, who seemed to be learning fast the *realpolitik* of the day --- and they were complemented by just enough savvy and seasoned military and political veterans to give their movement a biting edge. Their spawning grounds had been the cafes of Morocco, Mauritania and the Canary Islands, and from carefully concealed cells they had organized rather successful raids on the more isolated Spanish garrisons. *Wily bastards*, he again half muttered, shuddering at the image of a cadre of young Bedouins sitting at the knees of radical professors lapping up their socialist dogma. It was lucky for Spain that only a handful of them had been able to get an education!

It was now several hours after the attack and still no arrests had been made. As Salazar continued to pace nervously in his office, lost in his thoughts, he was barely aware of the conversation that surrounded him.

Colonel Luis Rodriguez de Viguri y Gil, the Secretary-General of the provincial administration, had entered the room and was engaged in a heated conversation with the man in the armchair. "I simply do not understand it. Why in heaven's name he agreed to expedite the date for this referendum is beyond me. Just when we were putting all our efforts into convincing the local population to accept the autonomy proposal."

Salazar's thoughts were again interrupted. He turned to face the newcomer. The man who was standing beside his desk was a tall, aristocratic looking gentleman of obvious breeding, who always managed to make Salazar aware of his rough edges. "Colonel de Viguri," he began sweetly, "you know as well as I do that the Generalissimo had no real choice. Hassan forced his hand. We will just have to see to it that the results of this referendum support our interests."

De Viguri stopped his tirade, gave his host an exasperated look, and, with an audible sigh of resignation, sat down on a couch. There were important matters to discuss. The Polisario attack had indeed been troublesome, and it would cost the government a pretty penny to repair the control stations and belt, but the larger menace was this looming referendum. If they did not do something quickly to ensure that any new government in the territory was conducive to Spanish interests their entire investment in the colony would be lost.

The gentleman in the armchair had been quiet, listening with one ear to the conversation around him. But, at the mention of the word 'referendum' his expression turned serious. "Miguel, have you identified a possible leader among the natives?" he said, trying to take Salazar's mind off the events of the previous evening.

The Governor-General stopped pacing and turned once more to face his guests. Perhaps they were right. Perhaps he should concentrate on these political matters, and forget, for the time being, these young upstarts. After all, with a friendly government in place in the territory, they, not he, would have the problem of taming them.

When he spoke his voice had become calm. "I have spoken with a number of persons, both among the Djemma and the few younger men with an education, and I believe I have identified a leader. He has agreed and, with the help of my officials, has begun to form the nucleus of a Sahrawi "pro-independence" group . . . I think he has baptized it the Parti de Union de National Saraoui or 'PUNS' for short." He looked gravely at the two men sitting before him before continuing. "I am sure you are both aware of the importance of promoting this group, and I will be counting on you to give me your support."

The two men nodded in agreement. De Viguri, looking pensive, reached for a cigarette. "Colonel de Viguri," Salazar said, casting a serious glance at his guest, "I will assist you in every way possible, but I will leave the organization of this group in your hands."

De Viguri returned his look. "I will do the best I can," he said, his tone somber. "The sooner we get this group organized, the better it will be. Tell the leader of this group to contact me as soon as possible." Then he rose and took his leave. When he had left the room Salazar turned to his other guest.

"Don Cardenas, as a highly educated man and a member of one of Spain's oldest families you command a certain respect among the natives. I am relying especially on you to help me with this campaign. The future of our relationship with the territory depends on it."

Don Cartenas took one last sip of coffee before responding. When he did his words were carefully measured. "You know you can count on me to do my best, but it won't be easy. Resentment of the Spanish is running high – especially after that Bassiri incident." He rose from his seat and started towards the door, but before entering the hallway he turned. "By the way, I understand he hasn't been seen for months. Has anyone found out what happed to the man?" he asked.

Salazar hesitated before responding, looking intently at his guest. "No, it seems to be a mystery!" he finally said, looking away, his voice betraying no emotion.

"Yes, a mystery." Don Cartenas repeated with a puzzled look before walking out the door.

When his guests had left, Salazar once again turned to the window, his gaze falling upon the steeple of the Church that rose proud and defiant from the sand. . . . the symbol of everything he cherished. *How long will it stand there?* he thought wistfully. The Old World Order – the Order he had served so diligently and which he believed in so fervently – the Order which had assumed that the countries of Europe had a God given right to assert supremacy over the peoples of the Third World, was crumbling. One by one France had lost its colonies in North Africa – first Morocco in 1956, then Mauritania in 1960, and finally, Algeria in 1962 after a long and bloody war. Only Spanish Sahara was left, a remnant of the glory of Spain the Old Caudillo had tenaciously held onto.

But the ground was slipping under the Generalissimo's feet. By the 1960s the principle of self determination for colonial peoples had emerged as a pillar of the United Nations, and upon joining the United Nations in 1955 he had been asked to report to the organization the status of Spain's colonies. He immediately proclaimed Spanish Sahara a province of Spain and reported that Spain held no colonies. This fooled no one, however, and in 1966 Spanish Sahara was added to the United Nation's list of "non-self governing territories" to which the principle of self determination applied. At the same time the newly created states of Africa combined to form an organization, the Organization of African Unity – later called the African Union – dedicated to the emancipation of the many remaining colonies on the continent. The political will of these two institutions formed a potent force on the international stage. Gradually the winds of change that had unshackled most of the other colonies in Africa and the Third World began to erode the iron determination of even one of the most tenacious of European dictators.

Salazar looked away from the window. This was the beginning of the end, he thought sadly. Reluctantly, Franco had finally acquiesced in the idea of self determination for the inhabitants of the territory – but only when they were 'ready' – and for a number of years he utilized every means at his disposal to convince the outside world that his subjects in the territory were not yet 'ready' – that they were too 'backward', too 'ignorant' to be able to exercise their rights properly. He even went so far as to create a consultative committee of elderly tribal sheikhs, called the Djemma, to whom he gave all the trappings – but none of the substance – of power, who dutifully supported his position at the United Nations.

Salazar sat at his desk and poured himself another cup of stale coffee. It was normal that Franco would feel a special attachment to Spain's North African possessions, he thought to himself. After all, it was from a base in the Canary Islands that he had led forces from the Spanish Foreign Legion in North Africa into southern Spain to fight the Republicans in the Spanish Civil War. He might have felt obliged to let Morocco have some land to the north that Spain had considered a "protectorate" rather than a colony, but he had no intention of losing his grip on "Spanish Sahara," Spain's only true colony in Africa. But by 1973, the pressures of the international community and the growing rebelliousness of the natives had caused him once again to modify his strategy.

The plan he had announced last year was simple, and at first Salazar had thought it would succeed. He would transform the territory into an 'autonomous region' and grant the inhabitants of the territory a modicum of self government as a precursor to an eventual vote on their future through a referendum. This, everyone hoped, would be sufficient to mollify the international community and grant him time to cultivate a cadre of leaders who, after independence, would preserve Spanish interests in the lucrative fishing off the coast facing the Canary Islands and the phosphates at Boucraa.

That was where Salazar had entered the picture. Five months ago Franco had appointed him, a career officer, as Governor-General, and a month later, a colonel in the Engineers, Luis Rodriguez de Viguri y Gil had become Secretary-General of the provincial administration. Both he and Viguri were initially charged with implementing a "Statute of Autonomy" for the territory and promoting hand-picked members of the native population to act as their representatives.

However, this announcement had ignited a storm of protest from the territory's northern neighbor – Morocco – who for years had claimed that the territory had been under the dominion of the Sultan of Morocco in pre-colonial days and should be returned to the "motherland", and before either of them had had a chance to put this plan into action Franco had changed course and come to the conclusion that it might be wise to set an early date for the long-promised referendum.

So, two months ago, eight years after first being urged to do so by the UN General Assembly, Franco informed Kurt Waldheim, the UN Secretary General, that he would agree to hold a referendum under UN auspices during the first six months of 1975. Salazar had been placed in charge of organizing this referendum. Just as importantly, he had been placed in charge of grooming a cadre of Sahrawis to take the reigns of government following the independence of the territory – a group that would ensure the continuation of Spanish interests.

Salazar sighed. It was a grave responsibility, but one which he was determined to fulfill with honor. And, after taking one last sip of coffee, he put aside all thoughts of the evening's events, sat at his desk, and began the work of planning the colony's future.

October 21, 1974. Don Cartenas.

As the distinguished looking man in khaki dress wound his way through the streets of El Ayoun in the early hours of the morning, he stood out among the handful of turban clad men and brightly robed women who stood in the doorways, peering out at him. Even though he had been in the country for four years – travelling from Spain with his family to direct the archeological digs – he still felt like an outsider, like someone who was trespassing on property belonging to another.

When he, a renowned amateur archeologist, had finally agreed to come to the territory after reports of significant pre-historic cave drawings and marine fossils in the hinterlands, he had wondered what he would find. This tiny Spanish foothold in Africa was the last fragment of a vast Spanish empire that had once dominated the civilized world. Sadly, the glory days of the Spanish conquistadors and adventurers had long since passed when a few solidary Spanish traders first landed on its shores in 1884, set up a trading post at a place they named Villa Cisneros, and claimed this desolate strip of barren land in the west coast of Africa for Spain. The baton of colonial empires by this time had passed to Britain and France, who greedily dissected the rest of Africa and at the Berlin Conference of 1885 had left the crumbs to its neighbors Belgium, Portugal – and Spain. The territory that they had graciously ceded to Spain was an area slightly larger than Great Britain, a tiny island amidst a vast French empire that included a Moroccan "protectorate" to the north, and the colonies of Algeria to the east and Mauritania to the south. Except as a transit point for slaves, gold, salt and other riches from the south through the few, tiny, Spanish enclaves along the coast, the territory for a long time had appeared useless – a vast desert wasteland inhabited by nomads unwilling to be brought into the civilized world.

For decades the relatively laissez faire attitude of the Spanish had promoted a sort of peaceful co-existence with these nomads – so he had been told -- a peaceful coexistence that might have continued indefinitely if it wasn't for the French. *The French!* he thought, ruefully. Not content to dominate the resources of their territories, they were intent on dominating the lives of their subjects as well! Needless to say, this didn't sit well with the irascible and independent nomads who populated the region. In the early years of the 20th century members of some of the native tribes had formed alliances with tribes in the French colonies to oust the French from Mauritania, often attacking isolated pockets of French soldiers in lightning raids, which they called *ghazzi*, only to retreat just as quickly into the vastness of the desert. At times they would stage these forays into French territory from hideouts in the Spanish colony. By the mid 30s, under pressure from France, Spain had felt obliged to install garrisons in the interior of the colony to curb these anti-French activities. That was when the trouble began. The nomads, used to their independence, began to chafe under Spanish domination.

Don Cartenas emitted a half audible sigh. The large stucco building that he called home was now in sight, its rooftop illuminated by the sun. He quickened his pace.

The Old Caudillo *still* could have handled the situation, he thought to himself, had it not been for the so-called "Army of Liberation."

Beginning in the 50s a rural partisan movement in the Rif and Atlas mountains had mounted a guerilla campaign dubbed the "Army of Liberation" to oust the French from Morocco and gain its independence. France, already neck deep in battles with an Algerian independence movement, and wishing to avoid fighting on two fronts, quickly decided to return to the Moroccan throne its ruler -- Sultan Mohammed V -- whom it had arbitrarily exiled to Madagascar two years earlier. Then, after assuring itself that the Sultan would protect its interests, in 1956 it granted its Moroccan "protectorate" full independence.

But there the story got complicated. The French had miscalculated the ambitions of the natives. Instead of celebrating victory, leaders of the Army of Liberation turned on the Sultan and mounted a campaign to eradicate French influence in the country from cells deep within the Draa valley and anti-Atlas regions. Others simply went south to organize a campaign to oust the French from Mauritania – this time with the assistance of hundreds of nomads from the Spanish territory. Together they formed roving hoards of guerillas, fighting the French from bases in northern Mauritania, and escaping into the Spanish Sahara desert.

He shook his head again, and quickly walked the few yards to the ornately carved wooden door that he had brought from Spain to serve as the hacienda's entrance.

"If it wasn't for the bloody French we might not be faced with this problem today," he muttered aloud. What happened next he remembered all too well from the stories he had heard when he first arrived. The guerillas eventually turned on Spanish targets as well as the French and Franco had considered it expedient to join forces to crush the movement. The Sultan of Morocco, now calling himself a "King," bowing to pressure from his neighbors to the north and concerned over his own political future, joined forces with the Spanish and French to destroy them. In return for his help in crushing the guerillas – and to curry favor within the halls of the United Nations for his claims to Gibraltar -- Franco retroceded to the King in 1959 the portion of Spanish Sahara that had been considered a "protectorate" of Morocco under the Algeciras Franco-Spanish convention of 1912. This included a swath of desert north of the Zini mountains as far as Agadir. However, he stubbornly refused to relinquish control over the territory that had been designated a Spanish colony in the Convention of the Canary Islands between Saharan notables and King Alfonso 13, later supported by the Berlin conference of 1884. This was the Saguia el-Hamra and Rio de Oro – otherwise known as Spanish Sahara. By 1960 displaced Sahrawi members of the Army of Liberation, joined by others from Spanish Sahara escaping the droughts that had beset the region, had fled northwards to the territory newly ceded to Morocco, eastward into Algeria, and southward into Mauritania, in the tens of thousands, inflating the towns and villages of Tan Tan, Lemseid, Lebouirate, and Tindouf, and creating a diaspora that continued well into the 70s. Many of the refugees who went north were enticed to join the armed forces of Morocco.

Even then, he said to himself, contact between the roving Bedouins and the Spanish settlors on the coast might have remained minimal if it hadn't been for the discovery of phosphates. In 1947 a Spanish geologist, Manuel Alfa Medina, had been surprised to stumble on large deposits of phosphates only about 70 miles southeast of the coastal hamlet El Ayoun. But it took nearly a quarter of a century before exploitation of these deposits began. A year after Don Cartenas arrived a mine had opened with the construction of the world's longest conveyor belt – over 100 miles between the mine and the coast -- and exportation from these mines, named Fosboucraa, or "Boucraa" for short, started challenging those of the Moroccan OCP to the north. The Boucraa mine quickly became the center of economic activity in the region, and was largely responsible for the migration of many Sahrawis to the towns and, for many, their first significant encounter with Spanish civilization.

As he fumbled in his pocket for a key he shook his head. This recent encounter between the natives and the Spanish officials had not been a happy one. The natives were treated not like subjects but rather like a group of unruly teenagers needing a father's watchful eye. This paternalism extended to their schooling, their medical needs, their economic rights. The natives were encouraged – sometimes forcibly so – to settle, and when they did they were offered jobs – jobs in the schools, in the offices, and, most importantly, at the Boucraa mines -- the kind of menial jobs the Spaniards didn't want.

He turned the key in the lock, trying to suppress the troubled thoughts that had invaded his mind. Despite the best efforts of Spanish officials they had not been able to suppress the spirit of freedom that had bubbled slowly to the surface, he thought to himself, reflecting, sadly, upon the brutality with which the Francoist government greeted any manifestation of dissent. This spirit of freedom managed to erupt into violence from time to time, like some unwelcome guest. The group that called themselves the Polisario were just the latest manifestation of this violence . . . and who could blame them . . . for years suffering under the domination of foreigners in their own country?

His thoughts returned to the looming referendum. This group that Salazar is grooming. . . the PUNS . . . will the people really accept them as their leaders, or see them for what they really are, Spanish puppets? He felt more than a slight tinge of apprehension. But this new group . . . the Polisario! He had read their manifesto. They were not merely fighting for the independence of the territory, they were struggling to change, fundamentally, the social fabric of their people . . . to drag them into the 20th century from a mentality that was centuries old. But were their people willing to accept such change? Could a society for so long tied to ancient customs and ways of thinking change overnight? Certainly the elderly among them . . . the aged sheikhs in the Djemma . . . and the few prosperous individuals . . . would see their revolutionary ideas as a threat. But the younger ones? He shook his head again. Revolutions had always been. . . and always will be. . . the province of the young. And so it will be in the Sahara.

He heaved a sigh as he pushed open the heavy wooden door. There was no telling what would happen in the future. The one thing that was certain was that he and his kind would no longer play a part in it. He stepped quietly inside the courtyard, closing the door and turning his back, at least for a moment, on the troubles outside.

Meanwhile, 1,500 miles to the north, King Hassan of Morocco was putting into place his own plans for the territory. The events of the past month had abruptly shaken him from the lethargy that had enveloped him in the past few years and had catapulted the issue of Spanish Sahara to the first item on his political agenda.

No one ever accused Hassan, the absolute monarch of Morocco, of being naïve. Nor was he ever accused of being idealistic or adhering to lofty principles. To the contrary, the world leaders who reluctantly or not had to deal with him considered him to be the consummate crafty politician – a wily Machiavellian only matched in current times by the likes of Henry Kissinger, for whom he shared a grudging respect.

He was able to recognize an opportunity for the advancement of his power and prestige when one was presented, and such an opportunity had clearly been presented by the idea of the "Greater Morocco." It mattered little that the thought did not originate with him, but rather with one of his arch rivals. Indeed, the idea sprouted during his father's reign, from the mouth of the leader of the Istiqlal party, the party which had lobbied for the return of his father to the throne.

In a burst of patriotic fervor, Allal El Fassi, the ambitious dreamer and political upstart -- emboldened by the role his party played in the return of Hassan's father from exile and the protests that led, finally, to the independence of Morocco from French rule -- had embarked upon a new crusade. On June 19, 1956, in the midst of the nationalist fervor which had followed independence, he declared "If Morocco is independent, it is not completely unified. The Moroccans will continue the struggle until Tangier, the Sahara from Tindouf to Colomb-Bechr, Touat, Kenadsa, Mauritania are liberated and unified. Our independence will only be complete with the Sahara! The frontiers of Morocco end in the south at Saint-Louis – an – Senegal." Dubbed the principle of the "Greater Morocco," it quickly created converts among leaders of the opposition parties.

Hassan's father, sensing that this doctrine might serve to bolster the prestige of the monarchy (and not wishing to appear less patriotic than his main rival) quickly adopted the principle as his own, but it was Hassan who attempted to put rhetoric into practice and for a number of years embarked on a fruitless campaign to "recover" land ostensibly belonging to the Kingdom in pre-colonial days. First, an unsuccessful attempt to wrest Tindouf from Algeria by force in 1963, then a losing diplomatic battle to keep Mauritania from being recognized at the United Nations and the OAU. By 1974 all that remained was the territory controlled by the Spanish – a few enclaves in the north and Spanish Sahara – and Hassan could not afford to lose that battle.

As long as Spain had been determined to hold onto its territories he could be content to wage a war of words – condemning Spanish rule on the international stage and asserting Morocco's claim, but doing neither forcefully. But this past summer Spain seemed to be caving in to UN pressure to hold a referendum in the territory, and Franco's shift in position required a new strategy. All at once the notion of a referendum, to which everyone gave lip service but few thought would ever materialize, seemed a distinct possibility. He could not allow a Spanish puppet state to be installed in territory that should rightfully be Moroccan. He realized that if he did not stop or at least postpone this referendum, the territory might be lost to Morocco forever. It was time to act or risk another humiliating defeat.

And a defeat on this issue might just be the straw that would break the back of his regime. He had never felt secure on his throne. Indeed, it seemed that each day brought another crisis, another problem that could only be solved by astute political maneuvers. He had become adept at fending off political challenges by pitting his rivals against each other – a talent he also put to use when dealing with foreign governments. Indeed, it seemed as if the imperatives of the "Cold War" was tailor made for his benefit. By carefully maneuvering within the labyrinth of political intrigues this feud among the major powers presented, he not only survived, but thrived on the international stage.

However, his Achilles heel had been his own military. Twice his most trusted Generals had betrayed him. On July 10, 1971 a group of cadets, at the instigation of several powerful Generals, had burst into his palace at Skirhat during his birthday party and opened fire on his guests, narrowly missing him. Then, on August 16, 1972 he had another close scrape when a group of air force officers strafed his private plane as he flew home from a vacation in France. He had only managed to survive that attempt by the crafty manipulations of the pilot, who convinced the attackers that the King was dead. The purges that followed these attempts had decimated the ranks of his armed forces. Nine of the country's sixteen Generals were put to death after the 1971 coup attempt. After the 1972 attempt two hundred twenty members of the air force were arrested, and eleven of them were executed. Oufkir, his Minister of the Interior, committed suicide by shooting himself in the head – twice. He felt obliged after the second coup attempt to take personal command of the Air Force.

But Hassan was a man of letters, not the sword. His greatest strength was on the political battlefield and it was on that battlefield that he decided to wage his war to regain the Sahara. He had taken a calculated risk by inflaming the population with the lust for additional land and his campaign had generated its own relentless force, like a "locomotive with a terrific head of steam ready to go rattling down the track," as one foreign journalist had remarked. Retreat was now impossible. So, just when it seemed that a referendum through which the people of Spanish Sahara would be able to gain their independence was a *fait accompli*, he hit upon a scheme that would pull the proverbial rabbit out of his hat – a request that the referendum be postponed in order for Morocco to prosecute its claims to the territory before the International Court of Justice! How could they refuse, he thought wryly? At the very least this would buy time for him to pursue the backdoor intrigue that was his bread and butter; and if the decision was in his favor the naysayers in the international community would not have a leg to stand on.

However, in order for the plan to work, he would have to hold his breath, bite his lip, and romance the leader of the colony's southern neighbor, Mauritania.

Mauritania! The word stuck in his throat even today, years after he was finally forced to abandon his crusade to prevent the independence of that French colony and its admission to the United Nations. Led by that puppet of French colonialism, Mokhtar Ould Daddah, who had the nerve, even before he was formally sworn in as President, to suggest that the Saharan tribes join their fellow *beidan* to the south in creating a "new Mauritania." He wasn't sure whether Ould Daddah really believed that the Spanish colony should be integrated into his country or whether it was really a ruse to thwart Morocco's claims. Either way it was a threat that he had needed to counter.

So, he had decided to reach out to his arch enemy, and during the Arab League conference three years earlier had secretly knocked on his door at midnight and amid copious shots of Black Label had casually proposed dividing the territory between them at some future date. Ould Daddah, after recovering from his shock, had cautiously agreed. But events had overtaken them. The referendum that no one had really taken seriously was looming before them. Now was the time to put their plan into action, and the best time to discuss that was at the October Arab League conference that was conveniently being held the next day in Rabat.

That evening, as he sat in his lavish office, he called for his scribe. "Sit down," he said, "I want to dictate a note to be hand delivered to the President of Mauritania when he arrives."

October 29, 1974. Arab League Conference.

Ould Daddah sat in the ornately gilded room in Hassan's palace mulling over what the King had just proposed. He had just arrived to attend the Arab League Conference that was being held that year in Rabat when he received a diplomatic note from Hassan requesting a nighttime meeting. When the King finally got around to discussing why he had summoned him, he was at a momentary loss for words.

Ould Daddah, the first Mauritanian to receive a university education, was no fan of Hassan's, and he had only contempt for the "Greater Morocco" idea that had fueled many of his speeches since he succeeded his father as King in 1961. After all, fewer than 15 years ago Morocco had used that same argument to lay claim to Mauritania, and when Mauritania finally obtained its independence from France in 1960, Hassan had tried to block its admission to the United Nations and had refused to recognize his government for a decade. However, during the 1971 Arab League Conference, when Hassan had proposed a secret agreement to bisect the territory between them he hadn't wanted to dismiss Hassan's proposition out of hand. He knew that besides the tiny coastal town of Villa Cisneros the southern portion of Spanish Sahara was mostly an empty wasteland devoid of usable natural resources. However, if Hassan's suggestion could somehow pass muster with the international community it might give him the opportunity to create a buffer zone between the present northern

15

border of Mauritania – along which the major resources and towns of the country lay – and the Moroccan state. The last thing Ould Daddah wished to see was the Moroccan flag within spitting distance of the iron mines at Zouerate, or the major coastal hub of Nouadibou. Besides which, hadn't he told the three thousand Saharan members of the Army of Liberation who had surrendered to the French in 1958 that they had been right to give themselves up because, as *beidan*, they were Mauritanians, not Moroccans? So shortly after Hassan had finally granted recognition to the Mauritanian state the two leaders had exchanged a written agreement to divide the territory between them which had remained secret for the past three years.

All these thoughts swirled in his mind as he sat silently pondering Hassan's latest proposal. He knew that if it was to work, the plan to divide the territory would need the right catalyst, and to be revealed at the right time. While Franco had remained determined to hold onto the territory they had both been content to let the plan remain dormant. But the political climate had now changed, and when Hassan had started revving up political fervor over the issue a few months ago he had followed suit and had reasserted Mauritania's counterclaim. He had arranged for the Foreign Minister to issue a broadcast in August reaffirming Mauritania's ties to the territory. That had prompted an exchange of angry words between the two leaders, well planned for public consumption. But nothing had been proposed to put the plan into action. That is, until he received Hassan's note the previous evening. So, now the ball was in his court, and adopting what he hoped was his most convincing smile, with some trepidation he turned to the man sitting before him.

"Let me get this straight. You are suggesting that we jointly petition the General Assembly to convince Spain to postpone the referendum in Spanish Sahara in order to allow us to file a claim to the land before the International Court of Justice? Am I getting this right?"

Hassan languidly reached for the pack of cigarettes he had placed on the table before him and casually lit one before turning his eyes to his guest. "Yes," he responded, coolly. "I think it is time to put our plan into action, and this is the way to do it." He stared at his guest, suddenly turning very serious. "Let's look at it this way," he said slowly. "We have nothing to lose by filing a legal claim, and a lot to gain. Neither of us really wants to see a Spanish puppet state created in the Sahara, and you know that this is Franco's intention. If we do not do something now to prevent this referendum from taking place – or at least to stall it – we may lose forever our chance to reclaim the territory."

Ould Daddah thought for a moment. Yes, a Spanish puppet state would not be good, but the annexation of the colony by Morocco would be even worse, and if he didn't go along with Hassan's plan . . . .

"But what about the inhabitants?" he said after a long pause. "Won't they object?"

Hassan placed his cigarette in the ashtray and gave his guest a withering look. "Do you think anyone really cares what they think?" he replied with a contemptuous note in his voice. "Besides which, that is the beauty of the idea!

They have no standing to oppose us before the International Court of Justice!"

Ould Daddah looked at him long and hard before staring out the window. He had to agree. He was new to this diplomatic game, but he had quickly learned that history did not always uphold the rights of people, especially groups of poor, uneducated desert nomads. Didn't the long struggle of his own people tell him this? It would be a gamble, especially without obtaining the blessing of Boumedienne in Algeria, but it just might be a gamble that would work.

So he turned once again to his host, and with an air that betrayed a hint of quiet acquiescence, told him, "I will think it over."

After Ould Daddah left, Hassan summoned a tall, dark haired man with a mustache to his chambers.

"I think he will agree," he quietly whispered. "Now is the time for us to discuss plan B." And with that the two men commenced a conversation that, accompanied by several packs of cigarettes and a bottle of scotch, lasted well into the morning hours.

A month after the Arab League Summit, Hassan and Ould Daddah formally petitioned the General Assembly to pass a resolution authorizing a postponement of the UN sponsored referendum in Spanish Sahara in order to permit them to obtain an advisory opinion from the International Court of Justice concerning their claims to the territory. Despite the protests of many third world countries the General Assembly passed this resolution in December, and Franco was pressured to accede to its request.

But at the same time the General Assembly arranged to send a mission to Spanish Sahara to ascertain the wishes of its people.

This didn't phase Hassan in the least. Behind the scenes he had already put into motion "Plan B." In July he had appointed Colonel Ahmed Dlimi, his former Chief of Military Intelligence, as the Commander of the Southern Military Region bordering Spanish Sahara, with full civil as well as military powers, and he had entrusted Driss Basri, Dlimi's aide and his newly appointed Director of Interior Affairs, with a secret dossier.

December 20, 1974. Mauritania.

Somewhere in the expanse of desert in northern Mauritania a small group of men sat beneath an acacia tree sipping tea and chatting. It was the waning days of 1974, nearly two months after the sabotage of the Boucraa mine, and the high spirits that had accompanied that raid had long been replaced by an increased sense of concern. A tall man in his mid 20s with a dark complexion, piercing black eyes, and a mass of curly, unruly black hair waited for them to finish their pleasantries before calling the meeting to order.

They were the top echelon of an eclectic group of young students, former military officers and remnants of Bassiri's movement. In the spring of 1972 they had organized themselves into a clandestine movement dedicated to the liberation of the territory of Spanish Sahara from Spanish rule – the Polisario. Its leader had been a student attending a university in Rabat, El Ouali Mustapha Sayed.

17

Ouali, as he was called, was one of the few Sahrawis lucky enough to receive a higher education. Born in 1949 somewhere in the Spanish Sahara wilderness, to nomad parents, he was brought at the age of 10 to Tan Tan, a year after that region of the Sahara had been retroceded to Morocco by Spain, among thousands who had migrated northward after the defeat of the Army of Liberation. He managed to gain a government scholarship to attend the Groupement Scolaire Mohammed V Lycee in Morocco, and after receiving his baccalaureate in 1970, he immediately entered the Mohammed V University in Rabat, where he delved enthusiastically into the study of law. At that time he was one of a handful of Sahrawis – all men – who were granted the privilege of acquiring a higher education at universities in Morocco.

Education, however, is a two edged sword. It can prepare a person to be a productive member of society, but it can also open a person's eyes to the injustice around him. And so it was with Ouali. He had watched with interest the student revolts that had shaken Paris in 1968, and the civil rights movement that had swept the United States in the same decade. He had read about the exploits of revolutionaries such as Che Guevara and had witnessed, first hand, the victories of the liberation movement next door in Algeria that had expelled the French from Northern Africa, and the struggles of the other liberation movements that were changing the map of the continent. The 50s and 60s had been decades of upheaval throughout the continent. One by one the colonies were getting their freedom. Soon it would be Spanish Sahara's turn. And he was determined to help make it happen.

He had drawn at least one lesson from history, as well as from the failure of Bassiri's concept of non-violent resistance: only an armed struggle would succeed in liberating the territory from foreign domination. What has been taken by force can only be recovered by force he was fond of saying. What was it that Franz Fanon said? *Decolonization is always a violent phenomenon.*

Several of his fellow Sahrawi students at the university felt the same way. In the summer of 1971 three of them spent a month in El Ayoun to assess the feelings of their fellow Sahrawis. Encouraged by their response, they organized meetings of students and others in Morocco to press for the liberation of the colony from Spanish rule.

However, the Moroccans had their own problems to deal with. The revolutionary spirit that had propelled others on the continent to revolt against authoritarian rule had not entirely bypassed the Kingdom. Social unrest was rampaging the cities, where large numbers of people -- about a quarter of the urban population – had found themselves relegated to shanty towns by the 1970s. The year 1965 had seen violent rioting among the poor in Casablanca. The universities had been almost continually plagued by strikes between 1969 and 1973.

The King had retaliated with an iron fist. Thousands of Moroccans were arrested during the late 1960s and early 1970s – aptly named the "years of lead" --on political grounds. So, by the time Ouali and his group had begun to organize meetings of students to press for the liberation of Spanish Sahara,

Hassan was in no mood to tolerate another revolutionary group. In March of 1972, Moroccan officials broke up an anti-Spanish demonstration at the yearly *moussem* camel market in Tan Tan and arrested several of the students – including Ouali. Their cries for help from the Moroccan opposition parties went unanswered.

So, Ouali decided it was time to move on. After the Tan Tan incident the group of students met to discuss their future. Those who wished to continue their studies would be able to do so, but those who were willing to "take a leap into the dark" would form a movement dedicated to the emancipation of the Spanish colony -- by force if necessary. The members of the original student group who initially formed the movement dispersed to population centers inside the territory and in adjacent areas to preach their dogma, while Ouali traversed the globe seeking support from friendly governments. The following year the core group from Rabat joined with a handful of members of Bassiri's movement and others at a secret location in Mauritania to plan their next move.

The former students included Mohammed Lamine Ould Ahmed, and Mohammed Ali Ould el-Ouali, and, joining them later, Mohammed Ould Sidati and Mohammed Ould Salek – El Ouali's classmates from Rabat -- as well as his younger brother, Bachir Mustapha Sayed, who was at the time enrolled as a lyceen in Agadir. Last, but not least, was Mohammed Abdelaziz, the brother of one of Ouali's classmates, who had been studying in Morocco to become a doctor.

Joining the former students were a number of young men who harkened from the "university of the desert:" M'hammed Ould Ziou, a veteran of the Army of Liberation in Morocco, who had settled in Mauritania after the 1957-58 war; Ahmed Ould Qaid, a fellow member of the Army of Liberation, who had joined Bassiri's movement and then, after its disbandment, had been jailed in the Canaries and Dakhla until his deportation to Mauritania in 1971; Mahfoud Ali Beiba, the mastermind of the Boucraa attack, who had also been a member of Sahrawi resistance groups in Spanish Sahara under Bassiri; Brahim Ghali Ould Mustapha, who had served six years in the Spanish territorial police administration and had been Bassiri's right hand man; and Mohammed Bouhali, the scion of a nomad family from the eastern part of the territory whose mastery of military tactics was second to none.

On May 10, 1973 somewhere near the border of Western Sahara and Mauritania, they christened their group the Frente Popular para la Liberacion de Saguia el Hamra y Rio de Oro, or POLISARIO. On the day of its inauguration the group issued its first manifesto, declaring that it was a "unique expression of the masses, opting for revolutionary violence and the armed struggle as the means by which the Saharawi Arab African people can recover total liberty and foil the maneuvers of Spanish colonialism." But the young revolutionaries were not content merely to wrest their homeland from foreign domination, they wished to tear down the artificial barriers of tribe, race and caste that had divided their countrymen and establish a society based upon the principles of democracy and equality. "There are no more Ulad Delim, Reguibat, Larosien," Ouali proclaimed. "Despite multiple nationalities, multiple tribes, multiple societies, we are one people, one identity, one nation. We are Sahrawis." After this meeting they all went their separate ways. Some went to organize cells in the territory, others went to neighboring countries, and other were sent on diplomatic missions. They established offices in Zouerate and Tindouf.

By 1974 the group had gained ever increasing numbers of converts among the Sahrawi diaspora in Mauritania, Algeria, southern Morocco and France. Then they had concentrated on activities within Spanish Sahara itself, quietly and surreptitiously under the noses of the Spanish, educating the masses and winning the support of groups of men and women in scattered enclaves throughout the territory.

By the time they met under the acacia tree in Mauritania at the end of 1974 they had mushroomed into a highly effective clandestine organization. Though they had sympathizers in nearly every corner of the territory, as well as among the Sahrawi diaspora, no one but the most senior members knew who these sympathizers were. Followers would be organized into "cells" of no more than five members. Only the leader would be able to communicate with the next on the chain of command. Messages would be sent by code – mostly by word of mouth -- along a closely guarded chain of command. Everything had to be done below the radar of the Spanish and other authorities. Although the top leaders – the ones responsible for planning and carrying out guerilla attacks – were all men, the responsibility for organizing most of the political activities, as well as disseminating information about the group, soliciting recruits, money, food and other necessities, had rested on the shoulders of the Sahrawi women, who, in many ways had greater revolutionary zeal than the men.

The bones that the Spanish government had begun tossing to the population in 1974 did little to placate them or the other Sahrawis. In their Second Congress, held in August of that year, shortly after Salazar's arrival in the territory, they had denounced the proposed Spanish "autonomy plan" and referendum as "a maneuver to save colonialism in a state of weakness, an attempt to dupe the people in order to continue its domination over our land and our national wealth." They were savvy enough to see through Franco's attempts to create a puppet state, and had nothing but contempt for the group that was being groomed by Spain to eventually rule the territory, the PUNS, who were opposed to nearly all the social changes they were advocating. They declared that the Sahrawi people had no alternative "but to struggle until wresting independence, their wealth and their full sovereignty over their land."

By the end of October they had shown that they should not be taken lightly. They had already successfully attacked small Spanish garrisons in Khanga, Gal Lehmar, Aghzoumat and other isolated regions of the territory. Their political *coup de grace*, however, had been the sabotage of the Boucraa mine by Mafoud Ali Beiba, Mohamed Akeik and a handful of carefully groomed followers. This would hit the Spanish where it hurt the most – in their money belt.

So, as Ouali rose to call the meeting to order and thought about the road that was behind them, he was pleased. Yes, they had come a long way. But they still had a long way to go. And in the back of his mind there was a nagging sense of foreboding, a feeling that he could not put into words.

"We cannot let the Spanish dupe the international community into thinking that the people will accept to be governed by that group of Spanish apologists," he said, snapping his mind back to the business at hand. "We must assert ourselves. It is no good winning small skirmishes with the Spanish military only to lose our fight in the corridors of the UN." The others nodded in agreement.

"What about Morocco?" one of them said quietly, voicing a concern that many had on their minds.

Morocco! That nagging sense of foreboding began to rise to the surface, but was engulfed in a wave of anger. He felt no animosity towards the people of Morocco; indeed, many of the students at the university had become his friend. But the King! Mohammed V had been no friend of the Sahrawis, turning his back on his father and many others when the French and the Spanish joined forces to crush their dreams of liberation in the 50s. And his son Hassan had been no friend of theirs. Yes, he had been able to go to school in Morocco, but that did not mean he considered himself a Moroccan. And he had only disgust for the feudal monarchy that held the people in chains. No, the people of the Sahara had never kow-towed to a King in the past, and they certainly would not wish to do so in the future. His dream was the dream of many others who became of age in the 60s – a government should serve the interests of the people, not the other way around.

Ouali shot a glance at the men squatting in the sand around him. "Hassan claims that some of our people once pledged allegiance to the Sultan of Morocco in the days before the Spanish arrived and because of these "historic ties" Morocco owns the Sahara. Hassan should study history. If he did he would know that the Almoravids – our ancestors – conquered Morocco before going on to conquer Christian Spain in the 11th century, and that Ibn Tashfin, the man who founded Marrakesh and crossed the Straits of Gibraltar in 1086 to defeat the army of Alfonso VI of Castile at Zellaka was a Sanhaja! Perhaps, then, we should claim the territory of Morocco as part of "Greater Sahara!"

The group laughed, but underneath their laughs was uneasiness. That feeling of foreboding swelled in Ouali again, but he dismissed it.

He continued, this time in a voice teeming with emotion. "What are we, puppets to be pushed around first by Spain and now by Morocco? Are we to have no say in the future of our own country? No, we must speak up – and make sure our voices are heard! The UN is sending a mission to "ascertain the wishes of the people." Let us make sure our voices are loud and clear!"

Reflections on a Dream.

After the meeting ended Ouali walked towards the west, where the setting sun was already casting hues of red and gold over the sands. This was the Sahara of storybooks – undulating waves of sand rising gently from the earth, slowly melting into the horizon. He found a place atop the highest dune and sat, just staring at the horizon to the west and north. Four hundred miles from where he was sitting the earth would meet the sea and above that point would be the land he called home.

He sat there, watching the colors of the sand gradually change, and thinking about the future.

Ouali was a true child of the 60s, and the forces that shaped his philosophy reflected the tumult of the times in which he lived. As a student in those years, like so many young people around the world, he had admired the Kennedys and had embraced the principles that had propelled the United States into the leadership of the free world. He could still remember some of the words that had inspired him. "Those who make peaceful revolution impossible will make violent revolution inevitable." Yes, John F. Kennedy seemed to understand.

But like so many young Africans, his enthusiasm began to wan when he saw how these lofty principles were translated into action. For some reason he could not fully understand the United States seemed to support every totalitarian regime on the continent – pitting its might behind the expansionist apartheid regime in South Africa and the murderous regime of Mobutu in Zaire -- and that was just in Africa. Anyone who tried to organize the population to rise against their leaders was dubbed a "terrorist" – even such mild mannered revolutionaries as Nelson Mandela. And instead of applauding the efforts of people under the yoke of colonialism to free themselves, the United States stood beside the regimes of Portugal and France that had held the people in chains for so many years. Strange actions for a country that itself revolted against the colonial dictates of a King a bare 250 years ago, he thought to himself. All in the name of combatting "communism."

Communism! The West seemed to be in the grip of paranoia about communism . . . justifying any act, no matter how unjust, that might seem to combat it, and tarnishing with the communist label any group that even hinted at a revolutionary goal. It is true that for a while he had flirted with the idea, but he had quickly realized that what sounds good on paper does not always translate well into practice. Yes, he agreed with the proposition that the beleaguered classes needed to be freed from the oppression of the rich and powerful, and admired those who struggled to liberate the third world from colonial domination. But that was all. As an economic theory it was doomed to failure. The only way true communism can work is if all property is owned by the state and all important decisions about a person's life are made by the state. He laughed when he tried to imagine telling a Sahrawi that he could not own private property and that he must live and work where some government official dictated. No, the Sahrawis would never accept that. And he held no admiration for how communism had been interpreted and implemented by countries such as China and the Soviet Union – or how they treated the people of other countries who had been unfortunate enough to come under their aegis. Just another form of dictatorship. Just another form of colonialism, he thought. No, he would not be lured into their fold. So, while he held great admiration for the type of socialism practiced in countries such as Sweden, he felt no affinity with the major communist powers of the day.

But if the Polisario insurrection was to succeed they would need support, and he didn't have the luxury of being choosy over where that support came from. So, he had met with leaders on both sides of the cold war divide -- with anyone who would listen.

In early 1973 his efforts had been rewarded when Libya's Muammar Khaddafi, always eager to support an anti-colonial regime on the continent -- particularly one within the Arab fold -- permitted Tripoli to become the headquarters of Polisario's external relations committee. Indeed, to his amusement, Khaddafi had considered him to be a sort of "younger brother"—a desert fighter who might one day follow in his footsteps as a world leader. For his part, Ouali considered Khaddafi a man not quite suited to his time, a visionary whose dreams of pan Arab unity propelled him precariously beyond the tiny plot of earth that was his domain. Such men have to be treated with caution, he thought, for they could either become the most inspiring leaders of their generation or the most despicable of despots. In his eyes, as of 1974 the verdict was still out on Khaddafi.

His efforts with other leaders on the continent, however, had been less successful. Mauritania's president, Ould Daddah, a timid man propelled into a difficult role by the French, was not a born leader. Walking a diplomatic tightrope, he was willing to turn a blind eye to the group's activities in his country as long as they did not seriously jeopardize his relationship with Spain, but would offer no support. His suggestion of a possible future alliance between the two countries had been rejected. For his part, Algerian president Boumedienne remained suspicious of his group. Many of the member states of the Organization of African Unity, while willing to give encouragement and political support, were reluctant to get involved militarily.

Outside Africa they had fared little better. Some of the smaller states recently emerging from their own revolutions – Cuba and Vietnam – gave them some encouragement, but little in the way of aid. And the big powers? It was useless to ask the United States for aid, and despite the group's revolutionary rhetoric they had refused to become puppets of the Soviet Bloc, making them the only liberation movement in Africa that did not gain the military or diplomatic support of the Soviet Union.

Yes, it had been tough going. And just when it seemed that their efforts had produced some fruit the spectre of Morocco had appeared. Until recently the King of Morocco had done little more than mouth the "Greater Morocco" tantra of the Istiqlalians, and he had thought that his speeches were just attempts to take the wind from the sails of El Fassi and the opposition parties. But Franco's plans to permit a referendum seemed to have ignited a dormant

23

volcano. Four days after Franco's announcement Hassan had declared that he would not tolerate a "puppet" state "in the southern part of our country," and he had appealed to his subjects to make 1974 "a year of mobilization at home and abroad to recover our territory." And this was just the beginning. In speech after speech he continued to assert a claim to the territory, inflaming his subjects with an almost messianic zeal to reclaim their "lost" lands, and he topped that by sending emissaries to the four corners of the world to preach his propaganda.

By the autumn of 1974 Hassan had been riding high on a groundswell of patriotic fervor, as television, radio, and pro-government newspapers poured out a continuous stream of stories painting the King as the country's savior, and the reunification of the Kingdom a goal of the greatest importance.

The King's remarks had not been lost on Ouali or the others. After the Polisario's Second Congress he had sent a letter to Hassan warning him not to engage in an "expansionist war against a small people which has few resources but is deeply devoted to its country and its defense." And just how had the King responded to that letter? By calling on the Spanish government to curtail the "secessionists" – in particular Ouali. But this was just talk, his *coup de grace* came when he proposed that the referendum planned for the territory be postponed and that the International Court of Justice rule on Morocco's claim.

At first Ouali and the other Polisario leaders had been shocked at Hassan's *hubris*. Since when did the King care about international law? Surely the officials at the UN would see through this ploy. And what about the wishes of the Sahrawi people? Were they to be ignored? Surely their wishes would be considered more important than what had transpired two hundred years ago – even assuming that Hassan's claim was credible, which it was not. But once again Ouali found himself dumbfounded by the machinations of the international community. The UN had acquiesced. The referendum was on hold. And a case had been instituted at the International Court of Justice to rule upon both Morocco's and Mauritania's claims to the territory – a case in which the Sahrawis would have no say. *International "law," indeed!* he thought wryly. *What about international justice?*

Dusk was now descending on the desert, and the warm hues of red and gold in the sand had been replaced by deep shadows of blue and purple. As he stood to leave he took a last glimpse of the horizon to the northwest. "We will not be forced to accept the will of foreigners in our own land!" he shouted, the wind carrying his words far into the distance. "We will fight until every last drop of our blood is spilled . . . until we can call our land our own . . . I swear it by everything that is holy!" With those last words he turned and walked slowly back to the campsite.

CHAPTER 2
1975

With the planned referendum now on hold, Morocco and Mauritania busied themselves putting together their claims to the territory before the International Court of Justice – claims that were based on allegations that there were historic ties linking the territory to them prior to the Spanish occupation. The existence of these 'historic ties' was hotly contested by Spain and Algeria, both of whom were given leave to file briefs by the Court. The inhabitants of the region – the Sahrawis – on the other hand, were not permitted any say in the proceedings.

While all eyes were on developments at The Hague, Salazar quietly proceeded with his efforts to shape the leaders of the PUNS into effective representatives of the population for the upcoming visit of the United Nations delegation.

And, just as quietly, the leaders of the Polisario laid their own plans for the visit . . .

May 12, 1975. The Visit.

It was 8:00 a.m. on the morning of May 12, 1975. General Salazar got into a heavily guarded car at the military compound at El Ayoun and, followed by a fleet of smaller cars, started the 20 minute drive to the airport. With him was Colonel Sanchez, cradling a bundle of official looking papers on his lap. As they silently winded through the back streets of the town toward the main road he was pleased to observe small groups of mostly Sahrawi women and children on the sidewalks, carrying neatly inscribed placards all claiming "PUNS" and "Solidarity." Interspersed among them, and at a discreet distance, were the faces of some well known members of his platoon.

As he turned onto the main road these numbers increased and included a greater number of men and boys, all carrying the same placards. They smiled and waved as the convoy passed. He waved and smiled in response.

"You did a good job, Sanchez" he finally remarked. "I think we will impress upon our UN visitors the fact that the people support our plan."

Sanchez smiled, but his smile was a bit nervous. He had worked for weeks to organize mass rallies of Sahrawis in the towns of the territory to demonstrate in support of Franco's proposed plan for the region and the sympathetic Sahrawi leaders that his commanding officers were backing to lead the local population. It wasn't easy. Franco's decision to put on hold the referendum

25

didn't help. The people were there, all right, lining the streets as commanded by his officers and hoisting flags and banners proclaiming "PUNS" as they had been told, but he suspected that their support for the Spanish initiative was paper thin.

But none of that really mattered. What mattered was that the visiting UN delegation would see a show of support for Spain's plans for the territory, and *that* he would deliver.

They were nearly at the airport now, and could already see the large UN cargo plane used to transport UN personnel in inhospitable regions taxiing to the one room shack that served as the airport of this tiny, provincial outpost.

Inside the airplane was the delegation sent by the General Assembly to report on the wishes of the indigenous people. As they descended the aircraft they were met on the tarmac by Salazar and his delegation. The head of the UN delegation, Simon Ake of the Ivory Coast, was swiftly ushered into Salazar's car; the other diplomats from Cuba and Iran relegated to the following sedans. In a slow procession they started the journey back to the city and the Parador, the hacienda like hotel reserved for notable guests, where they would be staying and where they would be meeting with a group of hand-picked Sahrawi leaders.

As they passed the crowds waiting to greet the delegation, however, suddenly a boy dropped his flag and turned his placard to the other side where the words POLISARIO were clearly visible. As if by command, each Sahrawi bordering the road did likewise, until there was a sea of placards each proclaiming the words POLISARIO. Almost in unison the crowd started shouting POLISARIO, louder and louder until the orders of the Spanish military guards were completely obliterated.

Salazar was dumbfounded and for a split second did not know what to do. The UN representative took the initiative.

"It looks to me like there is considerable support among the people for this group "Polisario", he commented sanguinely, ignoring the obvious distress of his host. Salazar regained his composure. "Only among certain groups, Your Excellency," he finally responded. "The Polisario are a terrorist organization that we have outlawed. You will see that the majority of the people support the PUNS, who are a law abiding group that truly represent the wishes of the people."

But even as he muttered those words the supporters of the Polisario seemed to grow with waves of placards proclaiming POLISARIO flying above the heads of the crowd. The waves of placards, banners and flags, all proclaiming POLISARIO seemed to merge until the entire route to El Ayoun was covered by thousands of people waiving placards and shouting chants in support of the group.

In El Ayoun itself thousands of Sahrawis had formed in the squares around the Parador and other major spots, waiving Polisario banners and shouting slogans. The police, greatly outnumbered and not wishing to create an incident before the eyes of the visiting UN delegation, held back helplessly and watched as the PUNS signs they had so carefully distributed were discarded in bulk for homemade signs reading Polisario.

Salazar herded the delegation quickly inside the gates of the Parador, and ushered them into a room for a private conversation. There he introduced the members of the delegation to Khalihenna Ould Rachid, the leader of the PUNS.

"I want you to meet a leader of a group that represents the native population," he said, attempting to ignore the shouts from the crowd outside that could still be heard through the thick walls.

Ake gave him a hard, appraising look. "And what about this group. . . the Polisario? Are they being represented by anyone? They seem to have a number of followers . . ."

Before he could finish, Ould Rachid interrupted. "The people do not really believe in what that group stands for . . . their leaders are extremists . . . they wish to eradicate Sahrawi society . . . our traditions . . . our customs. . . and replace it with some sort of socialist egalitarianism. The people don't really want that."

"Well, it seems that a number of people *do* want that!" Ake said, with a frown.

"They don't really understand what that group intends to do!" the young man replied, his voice becoming shriller. "Our group intends to preserve our traditions and create a government based on Western values that can work with other friendly governments to create a strong economy and future for the people."

"And Spain will be one of these 'friendly governments'?" Ake asked.

The young man blushed slightly. "Of course we will wish to work with our Spanish friends," he stammered.

Ake paused for a moment. Then he turned again to his host. "And there are no groups in favor of integration with Morocco or Mauritania?" he asked, his voice becoming serious.

"I can assure you, Your Excellency, that the Sahrawis reject any attempt to integrate the territory into any other state. They have been clamoring for independence for some time now," Salazar replied in an equally serious tone.

Ake stood silent. Outside the building the cries of the people grew louder, with shouts of 'libertad' filling the air. Then, turning once again to his host he asked, "And you are sure that the majority of the Sahrawi people are in favor of this group, the PUNS, Governor? I would hate to think that the government of Spain would attempt to impose upon the people a government that does not reflect their wishes." Salazar, who was momentarily flustered, quickly regained his composure. "I can assure you that the Spanish government's only desire is that after independence the people have the government that they choose."

Suddenly a voice was heard from the back of the group. It was Marta Jimmenez, the official from Cuba, who had been listening quietly to the conversation. "Yes, Governor," she said in a firm voice, staring directly into his eyes, "I will see to it that they do!"

May 14, 1975. Soukeina.

It was two days following the arrival of the UN delegation and one day after a mass demonstration in El Ayoun of over 15,000 Sahrawis in favor of independence and the POLISARIO, and Soukeina was quickly burning the placards that she had carried the previous day before hurrying off to the school in El Ayoun. The school, one of the few in the territory, was manned by Spanish teachers and Spanish administrators, and created to teach Spanish children and the few children of nomads lucky enough to be allowed to get an education. While a few Sahrawi families across the border in Morocco had been able to give their sons a high school education, the education of Sahrawi boys in Spanish Sahara was rare. The education of Sahrawi girls was practically nonexistent. She was one of the few Sahrawis even permitted to work in such an elite environment, and, like the others, she was relegated to the menial tasks the Spanish did not care to perform.

The school that day was abuzz with commotion – much of it having to do with the visit of the UN delegation and the demonstrations the previous days. As she swept the floor, two Spanish ladies in the next room began a heated conversation.

"I tell you, it was mass hysteria!" proclaimed one of them emphatically, "Everywhere you looked there were rows of Sahrawi women blocking the sidewalks, thick as fleas. At first nothing seemed to be amiss – the gendarmes were standing by just in case – but suddenly, without any warning, they all began to chant something in their dialect, and from beneath their robes they raised placards with the words "Polisario" and "libertad" written on them. Those who had been carrying signs supporting the administration either dropped them or turned them around to the back, where they had scrawled Polisario slogans. For a while it was sheer bedlam – I honestly didn't know what to do! Yesterday it was even worse. The streets were so jammed it took me almost an hour to get here. And I heard on the radio that the same thing is going on today in Smara! I cannot believe that the natives really support that band of terrorists! Why, we still haven't been able to get the Boucraa mines in operation after their last attack. And as for their demand for "independence" -- do they really think the administration is just going to walk away and give them our land?"

"Its their land too," the other said in a quieter tone of voice. But quickly added, "I agree with you, though. Generalissimo Franco would rather give freedom to the Basques than abandon the Sahara to a group of terrorists. You know what he did to the communists when they tried to take over the country!" She was thinking of the long and bloody civil war in Spain in the late thirties that resulted in the death of thousands of her countrymen.

Soukeina stopped and for a fleeting moment their eyes met. Their remarks were nothing new to her. She had heard them before – the patriotic gibberish of well brought up Spanish ladies, coddled from birth to death in a fairy tale vision of the world spoon fed by the Spanish media and government officials. Their land, indeed! Inside her she was raging to tell them off, to throttle them until they realized that they had no right to be here – that this was HER land, the land of HER people.

Soukeina, like most of her family, had been born in the desert, somewhere east of Smara. Her family moved from season to season with their large black tent, a few goats and even fewer camels, seeking the best pasture lands, but never venturing too far to the north or east. Two years ago her father had moved the family to El Ayoun and had become a watchman at the Boucraa mine – all the better jobs had been taken by the Spanish -- and her family found quarters in Zemla, the section of town that had become a Sahrawi ghetto. She was 18 and, except for some rudimentary lessons the government had provided in her early years, had never gone to school. But, then again neither had any other of the Sahrawi girls she knew, or most of the boys for that matter. They were forced to watch while the Spanish built schools, and hospitals, and mansions to live in, and they wondered whether they would ever again be able to call the territory their own.

And then came Bassiri. Like a sweet Spring breeze he and his small band of followers swept through the settlements, engaging in peaceful political activities in order to get the Spanish to pay attention to the inequities they were forced to endure. They paid attention, all right. On June 17, 1970, his followers demonstrated against the Spanish plan to integrate the territory into Spain as a province. The Spanish reacted by firing upon them. The next thing anyone knew many of them were imprisoned – or worse – and he mysteriously disappeared. Now, five years later, they still had no word about his fate.

Just as things seemed the darkest, however, came El Ouali.

He had also come from the North, and like all the others he had been born in the desert, to nomads. Also, like many other Sahrawis, his family moved into Moroccan occupied territory after the defeat of the Army of Liberation and settled somewhere near Tan Tan. When he returned as a university graduate it was with stories of liberation movements and the great men who had led them, of great writers who had championed the right to freedom and democracy, of new movements and institutions dedicated to the emancipation of all peoples from foreign domination. He told the people of their right to establish their own government and be free from the Spanish. He also told them that it was now the dawn of a new age. That men had walked on the moon. That there was no longer a place for the tribal rivalries and separations of the last century. That the only way the people of the territory could regain their freedom and their rightful place in this new world was to unite.   And to fight for their rights – in the political arena, if possible, but if that doesn't work, in the streets.

Soukeina could only begin to imagine the things he had been able to see, and the things he had been able to do. She was one of the lucky ones. She had been able to get a glimpse of the world out there – there was a television set at the school where she worked and on rare occasions, when the teachers took a break and turned it on, she would steal a glance, and for a fleeting moment she was transported to the world of cars and movies and ice cream cones, of stern faced news reporters speaking about wars and civil rights and women's lib. She would sometimes listen in on the classes taught by the Spanish ladies and try to memorize the lessons – the alphabet, the mathematics, the geography – but she yearned for a real education. The kind that El Ouali had received.

So, when El Ouali spoke to them it was what he symbolized as much as what he said that had galvanized her mind. His words had spread like wildfire across the wide expanse of desert, imbuing the inhabitants of the outermost regions as well as the small towns with a renewed vigor and sense of purpose. Like desert flowers after a rainfall, small cells of followers began to spring up until the entire landscape was dotted with Sahrawis suddenly united for the same purpose. Libertad!

After her work was done, buoyed by the events of the previous days, she virtually skipped home, only stopping to purchase a few ripe dates for her great-grandfather.

He sat alone in his room, perched on a heap of rugs, Sahrawi style.

"Soukeina, is that you?" the elderly man muttered as she quietly entered the room.

"Yes, Doda," she replied, gently approaching him and giving him her hand to hold so that he could recognize her. He was over 90 years old now and cataracts had gradually darkened his vision. He grasped her hand and held it to his chest. Her eyes glazed over as she remembered the tales she had been told at his knee – tales of warriors with names like Limam Mohammed Mamoun, Ali Mayara, Ismael Bardi, Ahmed Hammadi, Ould Souiyeh, Ould Machenan, and a slew of others. Warriors on camelback who would descend upon enemies in lightning raids from long distances through the desert, capturing livestock and disappearing as quickly as they had appeared. Warriors who led the fight to expel the French from Mauritania and keep them from advancing northward, spurred on by the words of the great poet Dkhil Sidi Baba: "You Sahrawi. You who consider yourselves leaders of your people. You who think that your words are important. Don't think only of yourselves. Involve yourselves in the affairs of your people. Take precautions before the flood enters your tent, for once it arrives the strongest swimmer will not be able to resist it."

She remembered proudly the story of how as a young man her great-grandfather had been a disciple of one of the foremost religious leaders of the time – Sheikh Ma el Ainin — who, besides encouraging his followers to resist foreign occupation, was the author of a number of scholarly religious treatises and the founder of the city of Smara as a center of learning. And Sheikh Mohammed Elmami, who authored the Book of Kitab el Badia, which extolled the religion practiced by the Saharan tribes and suggested that they should not be expected to conform to the religious norms practiced elsewhere. She remembered hearing about how the French subsequently sacked Smara and destroyed its hundreds of books, dealing a blow to Sahrawi culture from which it had not yet rebounded. Ma el Ainin's son, Ahmed Al-Hiba, had been one of the most illustrious Sahrawi revolutionaries, until he, too, was defeated at the end of the First World War. Even then it took the combined forces of the French and the Spanish in the mid 1930s to finally put an end to their insurrection.

Her great-grandfather's eyes always gleamed when he told her these stories. He was a sheikh of a large subfraction of the Reguibat el-sahel tribe, and it always amazed her how he would be able to tell her the history of each of its members, going back five generations, including where and when they were born, where they were living, their marriages and deaths, and all other pertinent information – totally from memory, for he could neither read nor write. It was sad to see this proud, distinguished, elderly patriarch huddled with the other members of her family in the small house they now occupied in Zemla, at the edge of the "native" section of El Ayoun.

"Here, Doda," she said, softly, I brought you some fresh dates.

The old man reached out his hand, and she placed two pieces of fruit into his palm.

"I have a meeting to go to now, but I will be back this evening," she said, kissing his head and walking to the door. The visit of the UN Mission was over and it was time to plan their next move.

May 14, 1975. Warning.

The young girl swiftly darted through the back streets of El Ayoun, avoiding the passers-by, stopping only to extend a brief hello to a neighbor or friend. Finally she reached her destination and knocked. The heavy wooden door widened a crack, and two dark eyes peered at her from the dark. Then it opened, and the girl was quickly ushered inside.

The room was packed. As she made her way slowly through the crowd she recognized the faces of many of her neighbors as well as a number of others she didn't know. She managed to find a spot to sit on one of the rugs that had been hastily spread on the floor. The room was abuzz with commotion – people speaking excitedly, mostly about the recent events. Above the din she could barely hear someone speak her name.

"Soukeina!" It was her next door neighbor. He made his way to her side and sat down. "I'm glad you could make it!" he whispered in her ear.

"I got a message to come," she replied, her voice straining to be heard. "But I don't know why."

"He's in El Ayoun, that's why, and he wants to speak to us. El Ouali himself!"

Before she could reply a hush came over the crowd and she could see a tall figure with a mass of black curly hair standing in the center of the room.

"My friends," he began in a soft, clear voice, "I thank you for the support you have shown during the visit of the UN Mission to El Ayoun. We have shown them where the wishes of the people truly lie. With us. With the Polisario." At the last word the members of the crowd began to shout, but he beckoned them to be silent. When it was again quiet, he resumed his speech.

"The leader of the PUNS -- that puppet – this very day has fled to Morocco, and we have been invited by the Spanish to a meeting – a meeting which can only be for one reason, to discuss the transfer of administration from them to

31

us once the UN plebiscite is over. " Once again he silenced the crowd.

"We have won a great victory, but the fight is not over. Even now our neighbors to the north and south are plotting against us – plotting to make us once again servants in our own land. The action they have instigated at the International Court of Justice is just the first step. I fear that the King of Morocco will stop at nothing to take our land – whatever the Court decides and whatever arrangements we may make with the Spanish. So, while we hope for the best, and prepare ourselves for these talks with the Spanish, we must prepare ourselves for the worst."

This time he didn't have to silence the crowd. . . .

Soukeina made her way quietly through the streets, unaware of the people and places she passed, her mind a million miles away and her thoughts troubled. When she told her mother and brother what transpired at the meeting, they, too, became silent.

Finally her mother broke the silence. "Perhaps it would be best to form some sort of alliance with Spain. That might keep Morocco and Mauritania at bay," she said, quietly.

"Yes, and make us puppets once again," her brother quickly interjected. "No, not after all we have struggled to achieve. If we must fight Ould Daddah and Hassan, let it be!"

The old woman looked at him with eyes that seemed weathered by the world. "Don't be so quick to take up arms," she said softly, shaking her head. "What will you use for a weapon? This old hunting rifle?" She pointed to a long piece of metal gathering dust against the wall.

He looked at her, his eyes becoming hard as steel. "I will fight with only knives if I have to!" he growled.

And so the discussion continued, well into the night. What should they do? What choices did they have? Compromise with Spain? Run to the UN? Seek help from friendly countries? Prepare to fight?

Soukeina listened to all of it in silence, not knowing what to think. Her mother was right – they were not prepared for a fight with Morocco and Mauritania -- but so was her brother.

And for the weeks to come this same discussion was repeated in house after house throughout the land, with no solution in sight.

August 14, 1975. Algiers.

Houari Boumedienne, the President of Algeria, had watched the unfolding drama in Spanish Sahara with interest. It had only been a dozen years since Algeria wrested control of its territory from France, after a long and bloody war that had left lasting diplomatic scars on both nations. Since then Algeria had gained enormous prestige in the third world for having hosted the fourth nonaligned summit in 1973 and for having spearheaded the South's efforts to secure a better deal from the industrialized North at the special session of the UN General Assembly on raw material prices. Algeria also prided itself on being the major supporter of liberation groups throughout Africa in their struggle against similar colonial oppression. For that reason alone Boumedienne was inclined to support the right of the native population of Spanish Sahara to choose its own destiny.

But there was another, equally strong reason why he was inclined to support a Sahrawi liberation movement and disinclined to support Morocco's attempts to annex the territory. Morocco's claim to the Spanish colony was based upon the very same argument of "Greater Morocco" that had caused a newly crowned King Hassan to attempt to seize a chunk of Algeria by force in 1963, when Algeria had just gotten its independence and Boumedienne was the head of the Algerian Armee de Liberation Nationale. Indeed, it was only after the intercession of Egypt's president that a war between the two countries had been averted, and Hassan had still not agreed to the demarcation of a boundary between the Kingdom and Algeria that had been drafted in 1972 after many years of arduous negotiations. Unlike Algeria, the Moroccan king had maintained a cozy relationship with the country's colonial overseer, France, and – in Boumedienne's eyes -- had become an African Uriah Heep for the Americans, who were in the habit of espousing lofty principles while supporting nearly every tyrant on the planet. He had cultivated a dislike for the King on a visceral level. Indeed, in his eyes Hassan and Kissinger were two of a pair: Machievalians who would employ any means to achieve their ends. King Hassan's self serving proclamations of religious authority also irked him -- a strong supporter of a secular state. Besides, his security agents kept him well informed of the King's peccadillos; a devote Muslim he was not. Nor was he noted for his respect for international law or international institutions.

So alarm bells rang when Hassan decided to enflame the Moroccan population a year earlier with the jihad of reclaiming their "lost southern provinces." Later, when Hassan petitioned the United Nations to request Spain to postpone its planned referendum for the colony so that Morocco and Mauritania could obtain a decision of the International Court of Justice on their alleged "historic ties" to the territory, Boumedienne smelled a diplomatic rat. The stench grew stronger when he got reports of an accumulation of thousands of Moroccan soldiers on Morocco's southern border. He had felt in his gut that Hassan was up to something, and whatever it was, was not in the interest of the inhabitants of Spanish Sahara – or Algeria. He was determined to counter him with every diplomatic card he possessed.

But all this would amount to naught if the Sahrawis themselves did not have the will to fight for their right to self determination and if there was no Sahrawi group capable of representing them. Emissaries of groups purporting to represent liberation movements in the territory had presented themselves to him for several years. He had even allowed representatives of one group – the "Blue Men" – to install themselves in Algiers in 1973 until he discovered a year later that its leader, Edward Moha, had no following in the territory and may, indeed, have been an agent sent by the Moroccan regime to undermine any legitimate representatives of the population. He was in no hurry to embroil himself in another such fiasco.

33

So, in the spring of 1975 when emissaries of the Polisario presented themselves to him, he studied them carefully. There had been emissaries from them before – in 1972 the leader of their movement met with representatives of the FLN and military commanders in Bechar, Tindouf and Oran. Then in 1973 a young former doctoral student named Abdelaziz and his companion, Mohammed Lamine Ould Ahmed, a cool and diplomatic spokesperson with a distinguished air, had come to solicit support from Jeloul Malaika, the head of the Department of Liberation Movements of the FLN, and their verbal jousting with Edouard Moha had revealed the latter's incompetency. The Algerians had considered them sincere, but somewhat young and inexperienced in the ways of the world. Diplomacy is a game not well suited to idealists, Boumedienne had said at the time. So he had sent them away with his good wishes but little else. They had come again later that year. By that time their group had waged a number of small, but significant, attacks on Spanish interests in the territory and had won the right to call themselves a legitimate liberation movement. But Boumedienne had still wished to play his cards close to his chest. This would be an important gambit on the part of Algeria – confronting its neighbor to the west and an influential European power on behalf of a population of natives that all together wouldn't even fill the casbah of Algiers. He had to be sure that any group he backed had the support of the people and the will and skill to uphold their rights, not only on the battlefield, but in the corridors of power.

But it was now the summer of 1975. The planned referendum for the territory had been placed on hold, and while Morocco and Mauritania were waging a war of words at the International Court of Justice, the mission of the United Nations that had been sent to the territory to determine the wishes of the people had been met with huge demonstrations in favor of independence. The diplomatic stew was simmering. And a month earlier the Spanish Minister of Foreign Affairs had met with the leader of the Polisario in Algiers to discuss details of a truce, the exchange of prisoners, and a political rapprochement. And now, just as things were coming to a boiling point, another emissary had arrived – this time a tall, lanky, bushy haired youngster in his mid-20s, who looked more like a refugee from a left wing university than the leader of a serious political party.

Boumedienne spoke first. "I was impressed with the support your group seems to have received from the people when the UN Mission visited last spring.   And I have read your Manifesto. It seems somewhat familiar . . ." He smiled wryly, thinking about similar statements that he and others had made at the outset of their rebellion against French rule. "But I am still not convinced that you have the stomach for a fight. You may be able to reach some sort of accommodation with the Spanish, but Morocco will not be easily deterred." He gave the young man a long, hard look. "Your fighters are not trained in modern, sophisticated warfare, and you have no weapons except for a few hunting rifles. Do you really think you can take on the Moroccan army if it comes to that?" His voice was deadly serious.

The young man interrupted him. "Do we have a choice? How many more years are we supposed to submit to being governed by outsiders? To be forced to work in menial occupations while foreigners control our land, our resources? For how long are we to be denied our freedom . . ."

Boumedienne interrupted him with a wave of his hand. "You do not have to lecture me on the injustice of colonialism. That is not the issue. The issue is do you have the will and the stamina to fight for your rights against a modern army – against the army of Morocco and quite possibly also the army of Mauritania, and do the people back you?"

The young man rose from his seat, stood quiet for a second then, leaning on Boumedienne's desk, his eyes a few inches from his host's, responded, with a firm voice. "The answer is yes on both counts."

Boumedienne looked at him intently for a second. His demeanor was firm and calm.

The young man's lips tightened. "The people do not want to be governed by some "king." In the long history of our people we have never been governed by a king. Nor do we want to be governed by a group of tribal sheikhs that are puppets of Western powers." He paused for a moment before continuing. When he did, his eyes were as cold as steel. "Nor do we want to be manipulated by a foreign regime like the Soviet Union intent on dictating how we should rule. We do not want any government to intervene in our affairs – including Algeria." He turned away for a moment, and when he turned once again to face Boumedienne, his voice was low and calm. "Look, all we want is a country where the people can decide how they are to be ruled and by whom."

Boumedienne gave him another long look. That was easier said than done, he thought, thinking of the trials and tribulations of his own country. Yet, wasn't that the goal that had propelled the revolution against the French? Was he getting old? Perhaps a revolution needs a younger generation – one that takes for granted their right to determine their future. It was the mid 70s and Hassan was still governing like a feudal tyrant. How many more years would it take for his people to wake up and feel the breath of change on their necks? Perhaps that was why he was grasping at Spanish Sahara so desperately. His world was ending and theirs was just beginning.

He paused for a moment before speaking. "What do you want from Algeria?" he finally said.

"More than any other thing we want the support of the Algerian people," Ouali said quietly. Then he leaned closer, looked Boumedienne straight in the eyes, and in a barely audible whisper added "but we also need the support of the Algerian government. Spain has agreed to withdraw from the outlying areas of the territory in preparation for a handover of administration to us. We intend to occupy these areas. We want you to support the accord we have reached with Spain and help us if Morocco attacks."

Boumedienne paused for a moment. "I understand you have already gotten some support from the Libyans," he said, scowling. "You had better be careful with Khaddafi!" he muttered, shaking his finger at his guest. "He can be dangerous!"

"We have told him the same thing I am telling you . . . we will be grateful for his aid, but we want no meddling in our internal affairs . . . we do not intend to fight one colonial master just to become the servant of another!" the young man said.

Boumedienne turned to the window, deep in thought. When he turned again to his guest he spoke, slowly and deliberately. "I will take a gamble on you, and I will help train your fighters – -- but if you want any other help you will need to prove to me that you are capable of leading a movement that will have to confront not only Morocco, but Mauritania and possibly Spain."

The young man smiled. "You will see. Just wait."

August 14, 1975. Commander of the Southern Region.

600 miles to the west a tall, heavy set, mustached man was quietly nursing a drink. Colonel Ahmed Dlimi was nobody's fool. He had managed to maneuver through the labyrinth of Moroccan politics since before he graduated to the officer corps. He then quickly rose through the ranks becoming General Oufkir's right hand man until, after attempting a coup against the King in 1972, Oufkir was unceremoniously killed – some say by Dlimi's own hand. He had then been appointed chief of the military's intelligence service – that shadowy cadre of officials who answered to no one but the King. In Morocco the Army was politics at its finest and most corrupt level. The King held absolute power, and held it close to his chest, but the Army had the guns. More than one Sultan had been deposed by his loyal army units in the history of the Moroccan empire, and the King knew his history well. It paid to keep the Army well paid – and occupied, preferably far from Rabat. And what could be a better way to occupy the officer corps than to send them on a patriotic venture deep into the Sahara to regain the lost lands of the Empire?

It was already over a year since Dlimi had been appointed the commander of the military region bordering the territory, with full civil as well as military powers. Since that time he had quietly mobilized the forces at his command until they numbered over 20,000. Dlimi chuckled to think of the glee the King must have felt as he sent the bulk of his army south, retaining just enough men to ensure his personal safety. Yet, such ventures are a double edged sword, he mused, for reputations are made from such ventures, and glory on the battlefield can quickly turn to fortune in other areas as well. It was not by chance that the richest men in Morocco – other than the King himself – were Generals.

So here he was, approaching the prime of his life, entrusted with the secret mission of amassing troops at the edge of the Sahara, ready to infiltrate the Sahara and demobilize any resistance from the civilian population so that the transition from Spanish to Moroccan control – with or without Spain's acquiescence -- would seem effortless to the outside world. In reality, he did not expect it to be effortless at all. He knew Franco's sentimental attachment to the colony and he was well aware that there would be resistance by Sahrawis insisting on their "right" to self determination. His gut was telling him that the majority of Sahrawis did not want to submit to Moroccan control.

Yet that thought did not disturb him. Years of austerity and self denial had honed his temperament. He was no stranger to the King's flashy soirees, filled with half dressed girls and Black Label. But he was a complicated man, and his moods changed as often as his female companions. He could often be found at night, in his room, nursing a drink, with only his thoughts as companions. Neither his family, nor his associates held any particular value for him other than their usefulness as means to gain even more power. If he held any political convictions – any convictions of any sort – he kept them well hidden. It was not useful to betray any emotion. Yet, beneath this frigid exterior one could sense an ember just waiting to burst into flame.

He had a favorite method of dealing with dissidents: they would simply "disappear" – like the exiled opposition leader Mehdi Ben Barka, leader of the left wing Socialist Union of Popular Forces, who simply vanished in Paris in 1965. He smiled when he thought of that episode, and how effectively he had sidetracked the police investigation. Cruelty did not phase him. Indeed, he seemed to get some perverse pleasure out of personally inflicting punishment on his enemies. His favorite method, which he had learned from Oufkir, was to pierce the chest just between the ribs with a short knife and twist it until the prisoner passed out from pain. Then a quick thrust through the heart would finish the deed.

Franco was gasping his last breath, and his successor, Juan Carlos did not have the stomach for a fight with Morocco over the interests of a few thousand nomads. No, Spain would be no problem, he mused. And the natives? A few itinerant Bedouins with hunting rifles would be no match for his troops. Just let them try something . . .

And with that thought he emptied his glass of scotch and turned out the light. He had already moved his contingents close to the border. Tomorrow he would begin the preparations for Plan B.

September 8, 1975. Elena.

The table was set with meticulous care, with ornate sterling silverware surrounding Limoges plates, topped by glasses of the finest baccarat crystal on top of the embroidered Madeira linen table cloth. In the center of the table was a tureen of freshly cut flowers. When Elena's mother entertained, it was in the grand Spanish style of her generation. Elena herself was decked out in her finest apparel, befitting a co-host. At 11 in the evening the guest arrived and was warmly greeted. The company at once withdrew to the drawing room where cocktails were served. At precisely half past 11 the maid announced that dinner was served.

Salazar usually enjoyed the opportunity to mingle socially with the higher echelons of Spanish residents in the territory, and he was exceptionally fond of the Cartenas family, especially their spirited daughter, Elena, who always seemed to keep a social gathering from becoming a bore. This evening would be no exception, for he had a request to make of her.

As they were seated he proposed a toast to the health of their leader, who had just recently recovered from a major heart attack. They quickly raised their glasses, then returned to the amiable chit chat that consumes most of the time in such gatherings.

When they were half way through their meal he judged that it was time to raise the subject.

He turned to Don Cartenas and spoke in a serious tone. "We are expecting envoys from the Polisario tomorrow to discuss the future of the territory." Elena's mother gasped and dropped her fork. The room suddenly became quiet.

Salazar, ignoring the obvious distress of his hostess, continued. "Our Foreign Minister already met in secret with their leader in July, and now we will be discussing the details of a possible handover of the government to them." He paused to let the information sink in. "I hope I will be able to count on your cooperation."

Don Cartenas was somewhat surprised. Several months had passed since the visit of the UN Mission and much to their embarrassment the leader of the PUNS had immediately fled the territory to Morocco. He had heard rumors of a possible rapprochement with the Polisario, but had dismissed them as idle gossip. After a brief pause he responded in an even voice, "The Polisario? That group who sabotaged the Boucraa stations last year?"

Salazar sighed. "I am afraid that after the mess the PUNS made during the visit of the UN delegation the Spanish cabinet has concluded that we have no choice but to deal with the Polisario. Perhaps they can be made to listen to reason. As a gesture of goodwill, we have decided to release some of them whom we have taken prisoner – including some of the ones who sabotaged the mine." Then, turning in the direction of the young lady on his left, he smiled. "Elena, I have a special favor to ask of you."

Elena had let her thoughts wander during his speech to her encounter with the tall man with the piercing black eyes that rainy day in October – the same day the Boucraa mine had been attacked. She still chafed at his impertinence – tossing her over his shoulders like a sack of potatoes and forcing her to let him drive her car, then abandoning her and her car without so much as a farewell when they reached the tarmac road leading to El Ayoun. They may have been the ones who sabotaged the mine, she thought with alarm. But for some strange reason she hadn't told her parents – or the officials – about her encounter. Was it because she didn't wish to alarm them? That must have been the reason, she concluded, her thoughts once more drifting back to those piercing eyes. But at the sound of her name she snapped back to attention.

"Yes, Your Excellency, of course. What would you like me to do?

"I need someone to help me take care of the delegation tomorrow when they arrive. They will be staying with their families, but I want someone I trust, a civilian, to accompany them around town – to be my eyes and ears so to speak – to report their movements and conversation to me and to make sure that they do not get into any trouble. Someone they would feel comfortable around . . . someone they would not suspect of being a spy. Would you be willing to do that for me?"

Elena for a moment did not know what to say. She was not accustomed to dealing with unkempt, itinerant herdsmen. What kind of conversation could she possibly have with them? If they were at all as impertinent as the one she had met last year she would have very little to say, indeed! And they were murderers. Just a few months ago they had attacked yet another Spanish outpost and killed several soldiers. To make matters worse, she had heard that they were communists! These thoughts whirled in her head, but were quickly overcome by her curiosity.

"Why of course, Your Excellency," she finally said, smiling her most ingratiating smile. "I would love to give you whatever assistance I can."

"Your Excellency, are your sure she will be safe?" her mother asked anxiously, "Escorting a band of ruffians . . . a young lady of her age . . ."

But before her mother could finish her sentence, Elena interrupted. "I am sure I can handle any problems that might occur . . . after all, I am not a child, and they wouldn't dare try anything here, where they are surrounded by an entire Spanish garrison!" she said, emphatically. Then turning to her guest, she added, "And I am sure His Excellency will be watching from afar!"

"I can assure you, Dona Cartenas, that she will be perfectly safe," he said, stifling a smile. Of course they would be watched from afar.

Relieved that the issue was settled, the Governor General settled back to enjoy the rest of an excellent meal.

As he was putting on his jacket to leave that evening he beckoned his host aside.

"I didn't want to speak in front of the ladies," he whispered, "but there are some developments I think you should know about. I have heard rumors that Navarro, Solis, and others in the Cabinet have started to question once again the wisdom of continuing the General's policy. As you know, when the Generalissimo suffered his first attack in July and handed the reins of government to Prince Juan Carlos, the Prince and Navarro had held secret talks with Hassan to discuss a possible handover of the colony. I vigorously protested at that time and, thankfully, when Franco recovered he put a stop to such nonsense. But he is an old man and if he should go…"

Don Cartenas took a deep breath. "But surely the visit of the Foreign Minister must be a sign that they are still following the plan!"

Salazar sighed. "Yes, I would think so, but I do not trust the intrigue that goes on at the palace. Besides, something else is troubling me. There has been a recent movement in the Moroccan military. I have gotten reports of a major buildup of troops just over the border. I think something's up, I can feel it in my bones!"

Don Cartenas hesitated before speaking. "Spain is no third-rate power to be bullied by the likes of Hassan. We can handle anything the Moroccans throw at us. Surely they can see that. If we give our word to these people we must follow through. Spain's prestige will be at stake. I'm sure you are worrying for nothing, my friend."

"Yes, I suppose you are right," he said in a low whisper as he slowly walked through the door.

September 9, 1975. The Parador, El Ayoun.

The following morning at 10 o'clock sharp Elena walked into the halls of the Parador, up the steps to where the delegation was scheduled to meet. Before she entered the room she could make out bits and pieces of a conversation. The men were all speaking Spanish, and besides Salazar's voice, she recognized the voice of de Viguri. The others she did not recognize.

As she entered the room, the men rose from their chairs.

"Ah, here is Elena," the Governor said in a genial voice, taking her arm. "My dear, I would like to introduce you to our guests." Then turning to a tall, wiry man with dark hair and a thick, black mustache, dressed in khaki trousers with a black headband wrapped neatly around his head, he said, "This is Senior Brahim Ghali." The man nodded his head, politely. Then, turning to a slightly shorter man with dark curly hair, also dressed in khaki, with a scarf draped nonchalantly around his shoulders, he added, "And this is Senior Mafoud Ali Beiba. They are the representatives of the Polisario who will be joining me in discussions over the next week or two." He then turned to a young man standing at the far side of the room, and added "Oh, and they will be joined by a member of their group, Mr. Salek Zaid." Smiling, he turned towards Elena and announced, "And I would like to introduce you to Senorita Elena Cartenas, the daughter of one of Spain's most eminent archeologists. She will help to make your stay here a pleasant one."

Elena managed to mutter a few words of greeting to two of the strangers, but her eyes rested only on the man in the corner, the man named Salek, a tall man with piercing black eyes. When his eyes met hers a glint of recognition seemed to pass over them, but he spoke not a word.

Elena politely asked them what they would prefer for their meals. Although this was their home country – and perhaps even their home city -- they would be treated as "guests" of the Spanish government and their movements carefully monitored. But they politely declined, preferring to fend for themselves. Just as well, thought Elena, as she prepared to leave for home.

She didn't know whether to be irritated or pleased that the man had not spoken to her, and as she made her way along the dirt street that would lead her to her house, she was unaware of the piercing black eyes that had watched her every move.

September 10, 1975. Zemla district, El Ayoun.

The following day Elena donned her most attractive outfit and made her way through the back streets of El Ayoun, trying to find the addresses that were scribbled on the crumpled piece of paper she held in her hand, and trying to ignore the stares of the men and women she passed on the street. She was in the "native" part of town and the streets were as unfamiliar to her as were the gypsy caves in Granada. She was only a few steps from the door of the first house when something she heard caused her to stop in her tracks. Coming from somewhere inside the compound the strands of a guitar had pierced the stillness of the morning hours. She strained to hear better, but could not believe her ears. Yes, it was a guitar, and the music made her heart skip a beat. She listened to the music, transfixed, not wanting to utter a sound lest the spell be broken. The chords carried her away to the gardens of Spain, to her childhood in the storybook enclaves of Castile, to the sounds and smells of that faraway land that she called home. But who could be playing that tune, so effortlessly and with such finesse? In the native district, no less? She had to find out. The heavy wooden door was slightly ajar, so she gently pulled it back and peeked inside.

There, squatting on a stool in the middle of a courtyard with his back towards her was a man, dressed in khaki, with a black turban tied around his head, and in his hands a beautifully adorned classical Spanish guitar. He seemed not to notice her presence, but kept on playing. Finally, after putting an end to the tune, he turned his head in her direction.

For a moment they stood looking at each other in silence. She was the first to speak.

"Where - how -- did you learn to play that way?" she managed to blurt out.

He placed the guitar gently by his side. Then, returning her gaze, he spoke in a low tone. "When I was a child, my father used to bring wool and meat to an elderly Spanish gentleman who owned a store in El Ayoun. I used to accompany him. One day I saw a guitar that he had stored in a back room. It had belonged to his son, who had died. I asked him to teach me a few chords, and he did. I guess I must have reminded him of his son, for on each visit he took me aside and taught me a few more chords. Then he taught me this tune. He also taught me some Spanish." He looked away for a moment, as if remembering some fond scene. Then his eyes turned once more to hers. "He died two years ago, and left me his guitar. He named it Esmeralda."

She averted her eyes. They were the same black, piercing eyes that she remembered.

He looked at her closely for a moment. "You didn't tell the authorities about me when you had the chance. I suppose I should thank you," he said slowly.

She stiffened slightly. "I didn't think it mattered anymore, now that the government is trying to work out some sort of accommodation with your group," she began in a somewhat imperious tone. Then, looking at him again, she added, "Although why the government would wish to collaborate with a band of terrorists is beyond me!"

He paused for a second before speaking. "Is that what you think we are? Terrorists?"

"Well, what else would you call a band of ruffians who blow up buildings and attack our soldiers?" she asked, the tone of her voice rising an octave.

"How else do you expect us to liberate our country?" he asked in a similar tone. "The Spanish government wouldn't just give it to us." He stared at her, his eyes glowing. "Remember, *we* didn't start the bloodshed, the Spanish did, when they killed those of us who tried to protest peacefully!"

41

"They are willing to give it to you now," she replied, her teeth clenching.

"But not because we asked nicely," he quickly retorted.

She paused for a second, somewhat flustered. Then, pulling herself up to her full height, she declared "I still think you could have relied upon international law principles. Why even now the United Nations . . ."

Before she could finish he interrupted her. "You mean the same United Nations that asked us to postpone the referendum it promised so that the Moroccan king and Mauritania could lay claim to our country in a proceeding before the International Court of Justice – a proceeding in which we have no say? And since when has the leader of your country ever paid attention to principles of international law – or do you really think you are living in a democracy?" he sneered.

She wanted desperately to answer him – to defend her country – to defend the principles she believed in, but the words would not come out. Instead she blurted out "At least the Spanish under his rule did not succumb to communism!"

"Oh, so now we are communists, is that it? We believe in a government that is of the people, by the people and for the people. Does that make us communists, or Abraham Lincoln? We believe in a society without barriers due to race or class or tribal affiliation. Does that make us communists or Mahatma Ghandi? We believe in a country where all people can freely express their views and vote for whatever candidates for office they wish. Does that make us communists or John F. Kennedy? When are you people going to learn that those who fight to liberate their country are not all cut from the same cloth? Maybe all we want is the chance to run our own country our own way!" He stopped, finally out of breath.

"Don't give me that line!" she shouted, her eyes flashing, "I have read your manifesto . . . your proclamations . . . straight out of Karl Marx!"

"Oh, and which part didn't you like?" he sneered, "Perhaps it is the part where we support freedom of expression and equal rights for women . . . you could do with a little of that in your own country, you know!" he said, a note of contempt creeping into his voice. "You are ruled by a dictator who tells you how to live, what to wear, what to think . . . you are afraid to utter one word in disagreement with anything he says . . . admit it! And as far as women's rights are concerned, there aren't any . . . you can't get a divorce . . . you can't even get contraceptives . . ." He looked at her and shook his head. "Women in your country are little more than chattel to be used first by their fathers and then their husbands . . . they have no control over their own money and they have no say in political life . . . they cannot be professors . . . they cannot be judges. . . they can't even testify at trials! You could do with some of the changes we are advocating!"

"And I suppose you are free to criticize your leaders . . . and Sahrawi women can do all those things!" she blurted out angrily.

He looked at her intently. "Our leaders would not be our leaders long if they tried to stifle our freedom to speak our minds. . . and as far as our women are concerned, well, Sahrawi women can choose their husbands. They can get divorced, and if they choose to divorce it is easy for them to remarry . . . there is no stigma attached. And they have complete control of their money. And when we come to power we will see to it that they can be any profession they choose. . . and that they will get the same education as men. He stopped for a moment and leaned towards her. "You see, unlike your government, we "communists" want women to be equal!" he whispered in her ear.

She stared at him for a long moment, trying to find the words to rebut his tirade, but they didn't come. So finally, she just quietly took her leave.

She walked briskly back to her house, her mind seething. Why did she find this man so irritating, she wondered? But try as she might she couldn't erase his words from her thoughts or find a way to contradict them. She had never been comfortable with the authoritarian policies that had ruled her existence, and suddenly wafting before her was the soft breeze of a type of freedom she had never known. Yes, they were an unruly, unkempt lot devoid of the niceties of civilization as she knew it, but they were free in a way she wasn't – and were willing to fight and die to make their dreams of liberty a reality. She remembered the look of contempt on the Sahrawi woman's face at the schoolhouse when her compatriots had spoken about "their" territory – and the embarrassment that she had felt upon hearing their remarks. Yes, it wasn't their territory, it belonged to the Sahrawis, and she, for one, was glad that her government had finally agreed to give it back to them. At least *that* was something she could be proud of.

October 16, 1975. Rabat.

King Hassan sat at the head of a long, ornate table at the Skhirat Palace in Rabat, flanked by three nervous looking high ranking officials. None of them wished to speak before the King, so they all waited anxiously for him to start. It was just before noon on October 16, 1975, and earlier that morning the King had gotten word of the release of the long awaited Advisory Opinion of the International Court of Justice. Within hours of the release of the Opinion he also received a copy of the Report of the Mission of the UN General Assembly to Western Sahara. Neither of them contained good news. Finally, taking one last puff on his cigarette, he addressed the waiting ministers.

"I see no reason to alter our plans," he said in a low, but firm voice.

"But, Sire," the man closest to him, a short but powerfully built man, replied, "the Court is quite clear." Reading from the papers before him he quoted, 'the information before the Court does not support Morocco's claim to have exercised territorial sovereignty over Western Sahara', this is stated not only once but at least three times in the document."

"Yes, I know, responded the King, but the Court admits that there were certain ties between the Kingdom and some of the inhabitants of the region. I will just concentrate on those portions of the text and ignore the Court's ruling on the sovereignty question."

Around the table the aides looked at each other nervously. Finally, one of them cleared his throat. "Sire, what are we to do about the report of the UN Mission?"

Hassan frowned. The UN Mission had traveled to all the main centers in Spanish Sahara and had even visited Sahrawi enclaves in Tindouf, Algeria, Mauritania, and southern Morocco. It had reached the conclusion that the indigenous peoples of the territory wished to be independent not only of Spain, but also of Morocco and Mauritania. Worse still, it cited popular support for a bunch of young radicals, led by a student from a university in Morocco, which had organized mass demonstrations of support wherever the Mission visited, noting that the movement, although underground, "appeared as a dominant political force in the Territory" and commenting that it believed that its visit had brought into the open "political forces and pressures which had previously been largely submerged. . ." The recommendation was that "the General Assembly should take steps to enable those population groups to decide their own future in complete freedom and in an atmosphere of peace and security . . . ."

"Rubbish," he yelled, "What does it matter if a handful of UN officials with no knowledge of the history of this part of the world deduce from a few days' visit that the people are against returning to the motherland? Are we going to let a handful of UN bureaucrats deter us in our plans to regain our southern provinces? Do we or do we not believe in the destiny of our country to regain the lands that were taken from us by the colonists? I do not intend to let El Fassi's group own this issue." He paused for a second before continuing. "As for the inhabitants of the territory, since when did we have to take into consideration their wishes? A group of ignorant Bedouins who only recently learned how to wear socks? Spanish Sahara was part of my Kingdom and will always be part of my Kingdom!" And with that last vehement statement, the room became silent, for no one wanted to contradict the King.

"Besides which," the King added after a long pause. "It is time to implement Plan B." And with an imperious gesture the King barked an order: "Send a message to our mission at the UN and get the Minister of Communications on the phone. I want to address the nation."

Within hours, the King was broadcasting live on Moroccan radio. His address was brief and to the point.

"The opinion of the Court can only mean one thing. The so-called Western Sahara was a part of Moroccan territory over which the sovereignty was exercised by the Kings of Morocco and the population of this territory considered themselves and were considered to be Moroccans. Today, Moroccan demands have been recognized by the legal advisory organ of the United Nations. The whole world has recognized that the Sahara belonged to us for a very long time, and I intend to recruit three hundred and fifty thousand civilian volunteers to march into Western Sahara to rejoin our kinsmen. This march, which I will call the Green March, will express the unanimous will of the Moroccan people and print a new page of glory in letters of gold in our nation's history."

Far away, in Agadir, a tall black haired man with a mustache wearing a colonel's uniform listened to the King's announcement and smiled. Preparations for the Green March had actually been begun by him two months earlier, in August of 1975. By the time of the Court's opinion, he had already moved several units of the army, including all thirty-five of Morocco's T-54 tanks in the Southern Command, to the Western Sahara border, and had commenced the logistics preparations to move thousands of men, women and children to the border – or beyond. He smiled, poured himself a drink, and sat back in his chair relishing the moment. He was ready to strike at his leader's command.

October 17, 1975. Madrid.

In Madrid, as word of the King's speech filtered down, Generalissimo Franco was livid. Hassan had gone too far this time, threatening years of a de facto détente on the issue of Spanish presence in North Africa. Now the General would be forced to make a public rebuke. As he took his seat before his cabinet officials, he surveyed his audience. Bureaucrats, all, he mused wryly – not one with the guts to do anything forceful. They had reluctantly supported his policies for years, afraid to mutter any dissent lest they foment his displeasure. But yes men were preferable to enemies, at least when you can control them. And for years he had controlled them with great agility. But now he clutched his heart when he climbed the stairs, and he felt the heavy breath of mortality breathing down his neck. He was no longer the young, brash military man who had seized power nearly 40 years ago and whipped a reluctant country into shape. He had already suffered a heart attack that caused him to be bedridden and forced him to transfer authority temporarily to the Prince, Juan Carlos. While he was in the hospital Hassan had apparently approached the Prince and members of his cabinet to dissuade them from holding the referendum. He had put a stop to this talk when he resumed his position at the end of August and had told Salazar to put the army units in Spanish Sahara on high alert. He also dispatched his foreign minister, Pedro Cortina y Mauri, to hold talks with the Polisario leaders to see if they could come to some sort of accommodation.

He was in command again, however he was beginning to wonder how long he would have the strength to control the squabbling factions within his government. The vultures had already circled and he could smell the rancid stench of death in their breath. But this Sahara thing was important. His mind drifted to the glory days of old, and sighed. Even though the territory was useful only for its phosphates and fish, it was important that he defend it. It was a matter of principle, a matter of the prestige of Spain, a matter of his own personal honor. The territory was just as important to him as to that pipsqueak, Hassan. And so it was that two of the most stubborn dictators in the world squared off across the Mediterranean like gunslingers at the OK coral.

He stared at the cabinet members for a long minute, then spoke.

"We cannot let Morocco simply dictate the policy we are to follow in the Sahara. I do not care how many people he sends on his jihad, we will not be pressured into giving them the Sahara! They had their chance at the International Court of Justice, and they lost. We never wanted to give the issue to the Court to begin with, but we went along with it when the members of the General Assembly insisted. Now, after insisting on postponing the referendum in the Sahara to obtain the Court's judgment on their claims they want to ignore it and pressure us into just giving it to them outright! Never!" he said, pounding the table with his fist to emphasize the last word.

There were times when his fist would have shaken the table and sent quivers up the spines of his listeners, but no more. His strength was waning, and his punch barely jostled the coffee cups that littered the table. But his mind was as alert as ever.

Carlos Arias Navarro, the Prime Minister and head of the cabinet, was the first to speak, and he measured his words carefully. "Your Excellency, it is of course important to maintain the prestige of Spain and not appear to be caving in to the demands of a third rate monarch." He said the last words with an audible sneer. "But we have already agreed to terminate our presence in the colony," he hesitated, then added, "at least our official presence, so we gain little from embarking on an armed confrontation. Remember, until last month these very same natives that you are trying to protect were slaughtering our soldiers and demonstrating against us. Why we should care one whit what happens to them is beyond my comprehension!"

"But I agree with His Excellency" chimed the foreign minister, Pedro Cortina y Mauri, enjoying the opportunity of siding with the Generalissimo. "We cannot let that upstart Hassan push us around. We would become the laughing stock of Europe!"

"What do you suggest?" Navarro responded somewhat wearily.

"At least take it to the UN. Force them to face the problem. We should be able to muster enough votes to force Hassan to back down. He wouldn't dare defy us if we had the backing of the UN."

Franco paused to consider the suggestion. The United Nations was no friend of his. For years they had snubbed or openly opposed him, calling him a 'despot' and condemning his regime as 'authoritarian'. It didn't help matters that he was considered closely aligned with the Fascists in the last war. He refused to bow to such criticism – who were they to dictate how he governed his country? As if he were the only leader who ruled with an iron hand. Hypocrites, he muttered under his breath. Yet, they could be useful hypocrites if channeled into the direction he wanted, and no one he knew of approved Hassan's last gambit. Indeed, they had recently heaped praise on him for finally agreeing to let the people of his colony have their independence, even if he would see to it that it was an independence closely bound to Spanish interests.

Mustering the sternest look he could, he barked an order. "Get me our mission in New York on the phone."

And with that, diplomats were sent scurrying through the halls of the

Palace and, a continent away, through the corridors of the UN.

When all was quiet Franco sat back in his arm chair, his thought drifting to things in the past – memories of people, places, exploits. He was tired. The meeting had exhausted him. He would retire early that night.

At the end of the day he ate a hearty meal, drank more than one glass of wine, and retired for the evening. It was a sleep from which he would not awaken.

October 17, 1975. Washington, D.C.

While Franco was quietly slipping into a final coma, two of the most powerful men in the world sipped coffee and planned the destiny of nations. Secretary of State Henry Kissinger was meeting with the President of the United States in the oval office. It was only two days after the International Court of Justice had published its opinion rejecting Morocco's claims to the territory and hours after the King had announced his intention to assemble the Green March. Kissinger was not pleased. Earlier that month he had been warned by the CIA of the buildup of Moroccan troops in the region of Tan Tan and of the likelihood of some sort of Moroccan incursion into Spanish Sahara in the near future. *"King Hassan has decided to invade the Spanish Sahara within the next three weeks . . . a serious conflict could develop"* leading to the *"downfall of the present government in Rabat"* as well as to *"a political crisis in Madrid"* if the fighting went on for too long.

Another ally doing something stupid – requiring him to take time from the more serious matters that crossed his desk, such as keeping the Soviet Union and the Chinese at bay, and battling the communist backed rebel groups that had gained ground in Guinea-Bissau, Mozambique and Angola following the leftist leaning military coup in Portugal the previous year. Now – in addition to all that -- he had to handle the pesky issue of Spanish Sahara. Normally he wouldn't give a damn about what happened to an insignificant dot on the earth on the other side of the world, but arguments over this insignificant dot might lead to the downfall of a regime that was vital to U.S. interests.

Hassan had become a useful pawn in the fight against communism in Africa – providing a counterbalance to two of the most important client states of the Soviet Union in the region – Algeria and Libya. On more than one occasion the King had offered to help the United States out of a tricky situation. Now that the President was officially prohibited from engaging in military actions in foreign arenas without the approval of Congress, Kissinger had turned to some of the country's allies – including Morocco – to fill the void. Already Morocco was providing aid to the UNITAs in Angola – backed by the apartheid regime in South Africa as well as the United States – in their war against the Marxist leaning MPLA guerillas. And the King was one of the government's few supporters in the Arab world. Yes, it was important to keep his regime in power.

He had sent Hassan a letter asking him to avoid drastic measures, and Hassan had responded assuring him that he would not attack Spanish interests.

47

Nonetheless, he went ahead with plans to organize this mass demonstration at the border of Western Sahara, deliberately antagonizing the Spanish.

Now the United States Secretary of State would be forced to devise a means to diffuse the crisis that Hassan had instigated.

He turned to the President and announced "Morocco is threatening a massive march on Spanish Sahara." Then, parroting the King's quixotic interpretation of Morocco's legal rights he added: "The ICJ gave an opinion which said sovereignty had been decided between Morocco and Mauritania. That basically is what Hassan wanted."

President Ford was baffled. Why such drastic action if their claim could be legally supported? But he knew enough not to expect logic from state leaders.

"What do you suggest we do?" he finally responded.

Kissinger already had a plan in mind. "I will send another letter to Hassan, asking him to avoid escalating the situation and to let diplomacy take its course through the UN. And I will send a cable to Moynihan to make sure that the UN is kept in line. But I think it is time to send a personal envoy to Hassan and Navarro to underline our concern and attempt to diffuse the situation behind closed doors. And I know just the right man."

And with that the subject of Spanish Sahara was closed.

October 19, 1975. Emissary.

If he had a dollar for every mile he travelled on a plane, he'd be a millionaire several times over, he mused as he sipped one of the generous alcoholic beverages they served in first class on flights over the Atlantic. Walters was used to packing his bag at a moment's notice and flying to some remote part of the world on a secret mission. He had prepared the groundwork for Kissinger's secret mission to China in 1971 and the Paris peace talks with the Vietnamese in 1972, as well as a host of other missions he would not care to disclose. Ever since he served as an Army intelligence officer in Morocco during the Second World War, and offered a ride in his jeep to a young Prince Hassan, they had been close friends. Indeed, so close was the friendship between Hassan and himself that he was considered in some CIA circles to be practically the King's case officer.

He had visited the palace on innumerable occasions – weddings, state visits, vacations – and had been able to forge a close relationship between Hassan, now King of Morocco, and the United States government. Among these accomplishments was permission for the United States fleet to use facilities at Moroccan ports and to base military personnel in the country – a major coup considering that nearly every other Arab country had slammed its doors to the United States in light of its position on the Palestinian issue.

Now, as Deputy Director of the CIA, he had been able to forge additional, less public bonds. Indeed, he had convinced the King to allow the CIA to set up an office in the Kingdom from which it would monitor and attempt to control activities throughout Africa. Below the radar, of course.

But this was no pleasant, sightseeing trip. He had to convince a very stubborn friend to abandon a course of action that might result in armed conflict between Morocco and Spain, and would most certainly drag the United States and Europe into the conflict besides leading to the downfall of his regime.

The collapse of his regime would not be acceptable to Washington. He knew why the King was doing it – for years he had diverted his subjects' attention from problems at home with a patriotic campaign to recover Morocco's "lost" territories. He had worked them into a fevered pitch over the subject, and could not back down now that Spain was finally sending signals that it was prepared to withdraw. But Spain also had its reputation to uphold, and relations with Spain were also important to Washington. The four huge U.S. military bases built in Spain during the 50s and 60s had been invaluable to the U.S. Air Force as refueling stops for its emergency airlift to Israel during the 1973 Arab Israeli war. The lease for these bases had run out in September 1975, and Washington was anxious to renew it.

So, in Washington's eyes Spain and Morocco were on a diplomatic collision course that the US would have to prevent. It was a tense situation. Morocco's target date for the Green March was October 26, so he would have to act fast.

But diffusing tense situations was his forte, and he had no doubt that with a deft combination of carrot and stick he would be able to convince the King to alter course. Besides, he had a very attractive carrot to offer.

As he deplaned he searched for the limousine that would take him directly to the palace. There he was immediately ushered into one of the ornate rooms that were reserved for discussions with high level officials. He didn't have to wait long. Hassan, appearing through another door, walked swiftly to him and warmly took his arm.

"Welcome, *habibi*" he said, using the familiar Arabic term for friend.

And with that they embarked on the usual polite chitchat that precedes any serious discussion between friends. But they both knew what this meeting was all about, and after a polite interval, Walters came to the point.

"My friend, the White House is acutely aware of the problems you face keeping a lid on the opposition, communists and other extreme elements in your country, and the President is worried that this position you have taken about the Sahara is an enormous risk that could exacerbate these problems. To be blunt, we think you were ill advised to make the Sahara issue such a personal endeavor. It could easily backfire and if it does . . ."

"But it will not backfire, my friend," the King said with some assurance.

Walters took a deep breath. "Do not underestimate the Spanish pride. They don't care a whit about Spanish Sahara, or anyone's right to self determination, but they cannot be seen to be pushed around by you any more than you can be seen to back down on this issue by the Istaqlalians. I am afraid you are both backed into a corner on this unless you let me help you find a compromise."

The King reached for a cigarette. After a few puffs, he turned to his guest, a serious look on his face. "I cannot compromise on this – you of all people know that!" he said, slowly, "and I know my people, they will back me on this jihad to recover our ancient lands." He paused and, placing his hands on the table, leaned towards his friend until their eyes met. "I am willing to take the gamble that when the Spanish are faced with 350,000 unarmed civilians crossing the frontier with the Holy Koran in their hands they won't dare start shooting – especially with a force of 25,000 Moroccan soldiers behind them for "moral" support!" he whispered.

Walters stared at him for a moment, then shook his head. "You are playing with fire," he growled. "One misplaced shot can start a bloodbath. You are lucky that Franco is in no position to call the shots on this one. Navarro seems to be in charge. He is a lot more flexible. He has assured me he doesn't want to go to war over Spanish Sahara, but he may be forced to defend the territory if you invade. His hands are tied." Then he paused before continuing. "But there may be a way out of this . . . ."

Hassan's ears perked up. His friend was notorious for pulling diplomatic rabbits out of diplomatic hats. He smiled.

"What do you have in mind?"

October 21, 1975. Madrid.

Salazar fidgeted nervously in the anteroom of the reception hall. He was tired after his long journey and somewhat miffed at being kept waiting so long, even though it was for an audience with the head of the Spanish cabinet. He would have greatly preferred Franco himself, but the aged ruler had slipped into a coma four days ago, and just that day had suffered a heart attack and was now in the emergency room of the Madrid hospital. No telling when – or if – he would recover. So he was forced to deal with Prime Minister Carlos Arias Navarro and Minister Jose Solis Ruiz.

The developments were disquieting. Before he left he had received word that thousands of Moroccan civilians had converged upon Tarfaya, only 5 miles from the Spanish Sahara border, waiting to invade the territory on October 26. Moreover, throughout the summer thousands of Moroccan troops had been quietly amassed under Colonel Ahmed Dlimi's command in the same area. He estimated that Dlimi had twenty five thousand men there. He knew that the Spanish army had as many men on its side of the border as Dlimi had on his – and they were much better equipped. But he also knew that ever since the mutinies of the Tropas Nomadas and the success of the Polisario during the visit of the UN Mission in emasculating the Sahrawis that he had hand picked to lead a new government, Navarro and others in the Cabinet had started to question the wisdom of continuing Franco's policy. He had been relieved when the Spanish Foreign Minister, Pedro Cortina y Mauri, held secret direct talks with El Ouali to discuss the economic and political ramifications of independence. It had seemed as if Spain and the Polisario might be able to reach some sort of accommodation. However, now, just when things had reached a critical stage, Franco had lapsed into a coma, and Navarro and the other nay-sayers were calling the shots. He had quickly called together a meeting at the "Casino" in El Ayoun of officers of the Spanish Legion in the territory and they were unanimous in opposing any compromise with Morocco. Navarro and Ruiz were not of the old school. But he hoped that he could reason with them. Spain's honor demanded it.

At long last the great wooden door opened and an aide ushered him in. Navarro stood gazing out a window, his back toward him. Ruiz was sitting at a long, ornate conference table. Salazar, a military man, not a diplomat, got straight to the point.

"Your Excellences, I am here to present to you a petition that has been signed by officers of the armed forces in El Ayoun urging you to oppose vigorously this so-called "Green March" planned by Morocco. I implore you to give me permission to order our troops to resist any attempt by Moroccans to enter into our territory. The Moroccan army is no match for our soldiers and we have at least as many men as they do stationed along the border. There are no groups in the territory which support this Moroccan ploy. Every one of them – the Polisario, the sheikhs, the ordinary citizens – they are all up in arms about it. If we do not take immediate steps to stop it, I am afraid there will be violence."

Navarro was well aware of the sentiments of the people. Just three days ago the Polisario had published an appeal to the Spanish people to "press the Madrid government to take measures to defend our territory", and the most senior sheikh in the territory vowed publicly to "fight to the death" for independence. But he was not worried about the sentiments of the people in the Sahara. They had cut their ties with Spain. He was more worried about international opinion, and about the criticism he would get at home if one drop of Spanish blood were lost trying to defend a population which, for the last twenty years, had done everything possible to make life difficult for the regime. Franco might feel some paternalistic sympathies for these Bedouins, but he was not so romantic. Besides, if the Polisario succeeded in establishing a government it might tempt other separatist movements to move against the regime – and for a number of years Spain had had to cope with Basque separatists and an independence movement in the Canary Islands. And yet, Salazar was right – the regime could not appear weak, especially with Franco in a coma. There had to be a way around this impasse.

He had suffered a number of sleepless nights. The date set for the march – October 26 – was quickly approaching. And then out of the blue the American had appeared. They had talked long into the night in secret about options and finally settled on a solution. Yesterday he had sent an envoy to Hassan to urge him to postpone the march and to enter into discussions. The American would intercede with Hassan to convince him to go along. It would not be what Franco would want, but Franco was in a coma and he was in charge now. Anyway, Franco was the ancient regime, it was time for a new way of thinking about Spain's position in the world, it was time for him to lead.

But if these discussions were to succeed they would have to be held in complete secrecy. And if they should fail . . . He needed to keep his options open.

So, after listening politely to Salazar's fervent pleas, he turned to face him and declared with a firm voice. "I assure you, General Salazar, that I am just as interested in maintaining the prestige of our country as you are. I understand that you have invited the leaders of the Polisario to El Ayoun tomorrow to continue discussions about the ramifications of independence. Good. You should continue these discussions. But in the meantime I don't want you to do anything to antagonize the Moroccans. Keep your units on alert, but away from the border. We will handle this problem diplomatically."

And with a wave of his hand, Salazar was summarily dismissed.

October 22, 1975. The United Nations.

The tall, distinguished diplomat leaned back in his leather armchair and casually flicked back a lock of his longish, grey hair. He had just come from a long discussion with the Secretary. U.S. Assistant Secretary of State for Near Eastern Affairs, Alfred Atherton had just finished a meeting with Hassan in Marrakech. He had come away with the impression that Spain and Morocco had already achieved some kind of understanding and that the Green March would be symbolic only. Good. That would make his job easier. Jaime de Pinies, the Permanent Representative to the UN from Spain, four days earlier had presented to the Security Council a letter in which he claimed that the Green March "threatened international peace and security" and had asked for action by the UN. Costs Rica, supported by a number of other states, had drafted a resolution which would call on Morocco to "desist from the proposed march on Western Sahara." It was his job to see that this proposed resolution got nowhere. Two weeks earlier, at a high level meeting in Washington, he had been given his orders. It was not in the interests of the US to place Hassan in a difficult political position that might jeopardize his hold on power. The State Department wanted him to remain on the throne – at all costs. They would handle this issue behind closed doors. So, instead of the stern warning suggested by his colleagues, he had proposed a resolution that merely called for "restraint" from all sides of the conflict and requested the UN Secretary General to enter into consultations with the parties - and he had lined up his ducks to see to it that this resolution would pass. He smiled. After all, he was very effective at his work.

Two days after the General Assembly passed Moynihan's resolution -- the same day that the Moroccan Minister of Foreign Affairs Ahmed Laraki met with Spanish officials in Madrid -- the Moroccan government announced that the date for the Green March had been postponed to October 28. The following day the date was again rescheduled for November 4 – 6. By the date of this announcement 145,000 civilians had already positioned themselves at the border ready to cross at their leader's command.

October 27, 1975. Betrayal.

As soon as she saw the look on his face, Elena knew that something was up. The jovial greeting that usually accompanied his visits to the household was replaced by a solemnity she had never before seen. In a voice that betrayed a note of irritation he demanded that the man servant announce his presence to her father. Upon her father's arrival he was quickly whisked into the drawing room and the door shut behind them.

Elena stood silently by the door, her ears poised to pick up any fragment of the conversation she could. But she needn't have bothered. In a highly agitated voice Salazar began his tirade.

"This is outrageous! An insult! Do they have any idea what they are doing to the image of Spain in the eyes of the world! Behind our backs . . . and just when we had nearly reached an agreement with the Polisario. To forfeit all our work – we will look like idiots!"

"Calm yourself," her father said in a tone intended to be reassuring, extending a small glass of brandy to his guest. "What exactly have they decided?"

Salazar took a sip, and in a tone just slightly less agitated, answered. "They have reached some sort of tentative agreement with Morocco. I don't know the details, but two days ago the Moroccan march was again postponed, and I have been ordered to withdraw our troops from the outlying areas and place a curfew on the cities. Apparently they are expecting trouble."

Don Cartenas pondered this for a moment before speaking. "Do you think the Polisario know?"

"I don't know, but I don't think so. Their delegates that arrived last week -- Brahim Ghali and Mafoud Ali Beiba – as well as Salek Zaid, are still in the city. We were scheduled to have another round of talks tomorrow."

"What do you intend to do with them?"

Salazar paused for a long moment, as if pondering a great question. Then he slowly muttered, "They must now be considered enemies. Tomorrow, when they come to the meeting I will place them under arrest. And I will order my men to arrest all known Polisario sympathizers."

Then, after a slight pause, he continued. "And you, my friend, you must begin at once preparations to leave. I have orders to evacuate all Spanish citizens by mid January. . . ."

Elena did not wait for the conversation to end. Wrapping her shawl around her head, she quietly slipped out the back door and made her way through the alleyways to the part of town that was the Sahrawi ghetto. For days now Salek had chosen to eat his meals with his family, and on more than one occasion she had met him there to escort him to meetings. The irritation she had first felt in speaking with him had gradually been replaced by respect – respect for his honesty, his ideals, his love of country – as they spent the long hours together. He often entertained her with his guitar, and their mutual love of music forged a bond between them. She felt that she could tell him things she wouldn't dare share with her family – her dream of becoming a lawyer and fighting for justice in the world – a dream that she knew she could never achieve in her country, where well brought up Spanish ladies were relegated to a future of marrying well and settling down to a life of producing children and

53

officiating at grand dinner parties. She had smiled when he told her his dream of becoming a classical guitarist – of playing in the grand halls of Madrid. But there would be no such conversations today. She quietly made her way to the familiar house, avoiding the surprised stares of the few men on the streets. It was after midnight and Spanish ladies did not venture into the ghetto alone, not at this time of night. She knocked at the door and a girl in her early twenties opened the door, her eyes wide in astonishment.

"Can I please speak with Salek?" she said in a low voice.

The girl, sensing something important had happened, invited her in and asked her to wait in the small area that served as a place to entertain guests. She didn't bother to sit. Within a minute Salek appeared. Before he could extend a greeting Elena spoke.

"Salek, you must leave El Ayoun at once – tonight!" she blurted, almost out of breath.

"Calm down, Elena," he said, in a soothing voice. "Tell me what has happened."

Elena sat on one of the low lying couches and began. "Governor Salazar was at our house tonight. The negotiations with you are over. The officials in Madrid are colluding with the Moroccans to hand over the territory. Salazar has been ordered to place a curfew on El Ayoun tomorrow and to prevent anyone from leaving." Then she said in a lower voice. "And he intends to arrest you and the others in your group tomorrow." With those last words she paused to catch her breath.

Salek was silent for a moment. It all made sense. The continual postponement of the march. The shenanigans at the UN. Had they ever been serious about negotiations with the Polisario or was it just a ploy to distract them from what was going on? Perhaps he would never know. In any event, the important thing was to tell Ghali and Ali Beiba and get word to the others.

He turned to look at her again. His eyes began to soften as he spoke. But the words he wanted to say just wouldn't come out. Instead he just said "I want to thank you for coming to warn me. It was very kind of you."

She averted her eyes from his. She was just doing the right thing, she tried to convince herself. No more than that. And as she turned to the door she stammered "I . . . I just couldn't let them do this to all of you. It just isn't fair."

Before she could leave Salek spoke a few words to his father. He quickly wrapped a turban around his head and met her at the door.

"It is not good for you to walk at this time of night alone. My father will accompany you back to your house."

She turned to look at him once more, a long look as if to burn the image of his face into her memory. He looked at her as well, and for one brief moment there was no one else in the world.

October 28, 1975. The Last Act.

Governor General Salazar sat slumped at his desk, where he had been most of the night, lost in a whirlpool of thoughts and a bottle of brandy. He thought about the turmoil that was enveloping the United Nations as international diplomats scrambled to address the growing menace of a potential conflict between Morocco and Spain. He thought of the brazen threats of Morocco's king and how he had completely ignored the findings of the International Court of Justice on Morocco's claim to the Spanish territory and had twisted the court's words beyond recognition for public consumption. He thought of the people of the territory, duped into believing that they could trust Spain and the international community to enforce their "right" to self determination.

But today these were just afterthoughts. His main thoughts turned to events in Madrid, where Generalissmo Franco was barely hanging on to life. The Old Man had a soft spot for his African colony, as did Salazar. He would never have kow towed to Moroccan demands. Never.

He felt betrayed. After Franco succumbed to a coma on October 17, 1975, Prime Minister Carlos Arias Navarro and Minister Jose Solis Ruiz, had cut a secret deal with Hassan behind the back of the foreign minister, Pedro Cortina y Mauri, and despite his fervent pleas and those of Secretary General Colonel Luis Rodriguez de Viguri y Gil. More than perhaps any other government official he knew that the Sahrawis were nearly unanimous in their desire for independence.

Juan Carlos and the ministers had given him orders, but they stuck in his throat like lumps of lead. He was in charge of over 25,000 troops located in the territory, with another 2,000 waiting to be deployed in the Canaries. The strength of the Moroccan army was no match for his troops, and he knew it. Yet he was ordered to stand back and let the motley crowd of civilians amassing on his borders march into the territory, the Moroccan flag held high. It was a disgrace, even if they were to be halted before they could reach El Ayoun.

But those orders did not bother him half as much as the others. He called his lieutenant. "I want you to send a communiqué to the commanders of all of our garrisons east of Smara, including Mahbes, Jdiriya, and Housa. They are to withdraw at once to our garrison at Smara. Tell the commanders of the troops at La Guera, Awsard and Tichla to withdraw to Villa Cisneros."

The lieutenant, startled, hesitated for a moment.

"Well, what are you waiting for?" Salazar barked.

"But, Your Excellency," blurted the young man, "this will mean that there will be no Spanish presence in most of the territory!"

Salazar heaved a sigh. "We have been ordered to pull our troops back to the main towns," he replied, wearily, gazing out the window. The soldier turned and prepared to leave, but before he got to the door, Salazar turned to face him and with a voice dripping with bitterness, added, "And we have been ordered to place a curfew on El Ayoun. No one will be allowed to travel at night. I want you to place guards at the roads leading out of town, and cordon off the native quarters with barbed wire. Henceforth no one will be authorized to leave the city without permission, and gas stations will be prohibited from giving gas to any Sahrawi vehicles." The lieutenant was startled as the implications of these orders set in. As he turned once more to the door, Salazar stopped him. "And one more thing," he said, staring gravely into his half filled glass of brandy, "I want you to dismiss and disband the Tropas Nomadas. Send them to their homes and families – without their weapons!" The lieutenant stopped for a moment as if to speak, then turned and silently disappeared.

The deed was done. He sat down at the large ornate desk and sat quietly for a long, long time.

Two days later the Moroccan Minister of Foreign Affairs, Laraki, revealed that three joint Spanish-Moroccan-Mauritanian commissions had been set up to examine the political, military and economic dimensions of Spanish withdrawal. That same day, because of Franco's deteriorating condition, Carlos Arias Navarro activated Article 11 of the Spanish Constitution which provided for the temporary transfer of the head of state's powers to Prince Juan Carlos. By that time all Spanish troops had been removed from outposts east of Smara, and the Polisario quickly took control of three fourths of the territory.

October 29, 1975. The Invasion.

It was the evening of October 29, one day before Morocco announced the creation of a joint Spanish-Moroccan commission to draw up plans for the future of the territory, and a week before the planned Green March of civilians into the Sahara. Dlimi smiled his most self congratulating smile. He had managed to orchestrate the perfect decoy for his activities. While all the press and the rest of the international community were focused on the fanfare taking place in the west, he would quietly, just before dawn, infiltrate the territory from the east and establish his troops in the smaller military outposts abandoned by the Spanish. He had quietly moved part of his army from their stations near Tarfaya past Lemseid, ready to move at a moment's notice.

He scrutinized the map carefully. The Spanish territory was shaped like the state of Florida, only backwards, with its longest portion along the Atlantic coast. The northern border was almost a straight line from the coast to the Algerian border. From there it was again virtually a straight line south before it turned sharply due west until it reached a point just slightly west of a tiny enclave called Amgala. From there it ambled southwest past the oases of Guelta Zemmour and Mudraiga and the tiny outposts of Mjek, Awsard and Agwanit, until, just shortly before it reached the hills surrounding Choum, it turned west again, and skirted the town of Tichla, until it reached its final destination: the Atlantic ocean just north of the Mauritanian city of Nouadhibou. Besides Morocco, it bordered Algeria and Mauritania. But its border with Algeria was only a few hundred miles. By far its longest border was with Mauritania.

He smiled when he thought of the misconceptions so many people had about the part of the Sahara desert that bordered the Atlantic. Yes, in the south there were a fair number of the sand dunes that most people think of when they think of the Sahara, but they did not fill the entire area. Indeed, the majority of the territory of the Spanish colony consisted of a flat, rocky surface, occasionally punctuated by an acacia tree or small bush, broken in places by crevices and small hills. These crevices and hills become more prominent the farther northeast you traveled from El Ayoun. Indeed, there was a natural barrier between Morocco and the colony that had shaped the relationship of the peoples of these regions for centuries. Although it was possible to access Spanish Sahara from the north along the Atlantic coast, where the terrain was largely flat and rocky, just a little farther to the east the plains gave way to rocky crevices, semi-dry river beds called *wadis*, and the Zini mountains to the north. There was only one pass through these crevices, down from slightly east of the coastal Moroccan city of Tan Tan through the Zini mountains past the tiny enclave of Lemseid, then, farther south to the plains that would lead to Housa and Jdiriya and southwest to Smara. Southeast of Lemseid was the Ouarkziz escarpment, rising gently to a peak from the south, then cascading precipitously to a valley below like some diminutive version of the Grand Canyon. This escarpment extended eastward along almost the entire length of the border between Morocco and Spanish Sahara. A few miles north of the escarpment were another series of hills providing only one pass through their eastern most perimeter, called Lengueb, guarded by a small fort built by the French foreign legion at a place called Zag. Nestled in the valley between the escarpment and the hills was the tiny enclave of Lebouirate. Beyond this, the eastern boundary of Morocco where it intersects with Algeria, as far as the Anti Atlas mountain range to the north, was protected by another group of mountains. The southern fork of the Oued Draa, a 550 mile long river flowing from the Atlas mountains in Morocco to the Atlantic, formed part of the desert's natural northern frontier.

He examined the map more closely. Extending southeast from El Ayoun almost to the Algerian border was the Saguia el Hamra, a *wadi,* and its tributaries, where along their banks trees and other vegetation were able to flourish. Not far from these *wadis* was the town of Smara and the tiny enclaves of Housa, Jdiriya and Farsia. Farther east was the *hammada*, a flat barren swath of land that began in the eastern part of the territory and stretched to the Algerian frontier and beyond. This area in the summer was the domain of the irifi, a searing sandstorm, blown by powerful winds from the southeast, that becomes hotter and drier as it sweeps across the *hammada*, enveloping everything in a cloud of sand and reducing visibility to a few yards. Nestled in the *hammada*, only a few miles from the Algerian border, was Mahbes, a small military outpost guarding the eastern frontier.

In the center of the map, along the coast he found the town of Boujdour and to its northeast, slightly south east of El Ayoun, the mines of Boucraa. From Boucraa east the terrain was flat and rocky until you reached the outskirts of Amgala, just slightly north of the Mauritanian border, a small settlement surrounded by hills on three sides. Farther east in the hills along the border was Mharis and beyond that, where the southern plateau began to drop precipitously into gullies and ravines, was the tiny enclave of Tifariti. Farther

57

east, across the plateau, was Bir Lehlou and just across the Mauritanian border from Tifariti was Ain Ben Tili.

As his eyes moved farther south, to the east he could see another group of hills where the Zemmour massif, began to form, hiding small oases called gueltas in its belly, and to the west the outpost of Bir Enzaren and finally Dakhla. Moving farther south, near a chain of hills called Choum, just north of the Mauritanian border, sand dunes began to appear, often obstructing the passage east to west in Mauritania from Zouerate to the coastal city of Nouadhibou, making travel by vehicles in this part of the desert next to impossible.

He smiled. It was no wonder that the Spanish limited their presence to a few small enclaves along the coast, abandoning the vast interior wasteland to the marauding caravans of Bedouins.

It was important that his troops slip across the border without raising the suspicions of the journalists who had gathered at Tarfaya to cover the Green March. He decided to send a contingent of troops, armed to the teeth with tanks, artillery and air support, south from Lemseid, and another south through the Lengueb pass about two hundred miles to the east. From there they would head for three of the eastern outposts evacuated days before by the Spanish.

He called for his aide de camp and gave the orders. That evening two columns of infantry and tanks quickly moved forward, under cover of darkness.

October 31, 1975. The Battles Begin.

Jdiriya was a small outpost bordering the Saguia el Hamra riverbed in the northeastern part of Spanish Sahara, just a few miles south of the Moroccan settlement at Lemseid, in the valley north of the escarpment that formed the northern boundary of the territory. On the last day of October in 1975, the rains that came with the winter months and provided needed nourishment to the desert valley had come early, and had begun to coarse through the veins of the river, swelling its tributaries. The Spanish troops that had occupied Jdiriya had just been evacuated, transforming the tiny settlement overnight into an eerily quiet ghost town. The small contingent of Moroccan soldiers sent by Dlimi to occupy the position waded through the stream a few hours north of the settlement, followed by an assortment of trucks and tanks, with helicopters buzzing overhead.

The Moroccan commander was young and not accustomed to the rugged terrain of the Ouarkziz escarpment that they had been obliged to traverse, encumbered by heavy artillery. He was looking forward to arriving at his destination, where a long, cool bath would await him. But when his troops were knee deep in water, attempting to cross the stream, his thoughts were suddenly interrupted by a sharp blast. He froze. Then another blast. Snipers! He quickly ordered his men to take cover. Most of the soldiers and vehicles managed to scurry up the embankment but one of the tanks found itself stuck in the mud, unable to move. Under fire from unseen assailants, he ordered a handful of his soldiers to re-enter the stream and attempt to dislodge the tank. It wouldn't budge. They tried again. Same result. He ordered his troops to take cover as best they could and sent a scout back through the hills to Lebouirate to request reinforcements.

For hours, until dusk finally forced both sides to quit, his men shot in the direction of incoming fire across the stream, rarely seeing the men behind the rifles, while the helicopters buzzed helplessly above. He did not dare leave without the tank. The image of Dlimi's scowling face sent shivers through his veins. During the night they took turns resting, standing watch in total darkness, unable to light a fire lest it reveal their positions. The next day, it commenced again. Over and over, for almost a week his soldiers would enter the stream and push and shove at the tank to no avail, all the while under fire from snipers they could not see.

He was getting low on ammunition, and his casualties were mounting. Finally, after almost a week of being pinned down unable to move, he awoke to find the snipers gone. In the distance he could hear the rumbling sound of advancing troops. Reinforcements from the garrison at Lemseid. Within a day the tank was pulled from the mud, and with the help of the reinforcements the small unit finally reached Jdiriya. But at a heavy cost. Besides the wounded and dead, an officer, Tahiri Taher, had been captured by the enemy. The first prisoner of war – but not the last.

Farther to the east a column of 70 soldiers, accompanied by helicopter gunships, was slowly advancing towards Farsia, another recently abandoned Spanish outpost. The commander was in a good mood. They had managed to traverse the Lengueb pass on the first day of November and advanced to within ten miles of the settlement without incident. But his mood did not last long. Without warning, they suddenly found themselves engulfed in a sea of bullets. They took cover where best they could – behind their trucks and armored vehicles, in the gullies and crevices, behind whatever acacia trees were within reach, and the helicopters dotted the landscape with craters – but the blasts were coming from all directions, from ever moving, invisible assailants. A truck soon burst into flames, casting a veil of smoke over the nearby troops. In the dust and confusion, the soldiers – young and inexperienced in guerilla warfare – could not see or hear their commanding officer and began to panic. One by one they ran in all directions, trying desperately to find the tracks that would lead them back through the pass.

The snipers followed, emerging like cicadas from the ground, engaging them in hand to hand combat. By the end of the day six more prisoners of war were escorted back to the guerilla base camp. The remainder either lay dead on the desert floor or were wandering somewhere in the hills. Either way they would pose no problem – at least for the time being.

Back at his headquarters in Agadir, Dlimi sat at his desk, his face revealing no emotion. The lieutenant who stood at his side nervously fingered a paper in his hand. The reports from the troops sent to occupy the eastern positions had been filtering in during the day, and they were not what was expected.

59

The troops had met resistance every inch of the way. From the sound of the gun fire the commanders estimated that the attackers possessed no more than low caliber hunting rifles, and were on foot. Gnats attacking a bumble bee. They were no match for the Moroccan army, but they had managed to inflict casualties and – to Dlimi's chagrin – had even managed to capture some Moroccan soldiers.

Dlimi ordered the lieutenant to leave and sat for a long time, alone with his thoughts. Is this the way it was going to be? Sniper fire, quick assaults, and then retreat into the desert? *Just a bunch of itinerant Bedouins*, he thought to himself. *They won't be able to keep this up for long.* But the resistance had been stiffer than he had expected and he began to feel a sense of foreboding, a strange feeling that annexing the Sahara would not be as simple a task as the King had thought – that it might not be a question of days, but of weeks, and possibly even months.

He rose from his seat and stood at the window, gazing at the reflection of the sun upon the rooftops of his compound, and beyond them, the bright blue of the ocean. When he returned to his seat, his expression was grave. *All right,* he thought. *If you want to play hard ball, so be it!* He yelled for his lieutenant and soon a bevy of officers were seen scurrying through the compound.

November 3, 1975. Washington, D.C.

Meanwhile, on the third of November a slightly balding older man wearing a White House badge scurried along the corridor inside the White House to the Oval Office. Inside, totally unaware of the clashes that had commenced two days earlier between Moroccan troops and the Polisario, the President was meeting with Henry Kissinger and Brent Scowcroft. The balding man barged in, obviously agitated.

"He's gone ahead and done it, the damn fool! Despite what we told him! Couldn't he wait? What does he think he is going to gain, sending marchers to the borders of Spanish Sahara. My God! According to the press there are over 300,000 of them!"

Kissinger did not move. With a limp gesture he bade the intruder to be quiet. The bald man sat down and waited. Finally, in the growling voice that was his trademark, Kissinger spoke.

"Relax, Charlie. Its taken care of!" With a perplexed look on his face, the bald man started to respond "But . . ." but was quickly silenced.

"Just go back to the desk people and tell them to make no comment if they are contacted by reporters. We will handle this from the oval office." And without a further word, the bald man departed.

Kissinger sighed a quiet, barely audible whisper of a sigh. It was the day after the so-called "Halloween Massacre" when the President had summarily fired two of his more moderate Cabinet officials – CIA Director William Colby and Defense Secretary James R. Schlesinger – and replaced them with the more conservative George Bush and Donald Rumsfeld. This was a welcomed change. He expected more support for his plans in the future. And he would need it. Things were heating up in Africa's southern colonies, and Kissinger was livid. For months he had been carefully nurturing a possible thawing of relations with Cuba, but in what could only be interpreted as a diplomatic slap in the face, on October 20 Castro had sent three Cuban navy vessels carrying troops to Angola to support the MPLA guerillas. And he feared that this would be only the beginning.

Who did that pipsqueak Castro think he was, meddling in his African plans? But there was no denying that he had thrown a corkscrew into the Secretary's well rehearsed designs for the continent – and now Kissinger was more determined than ever to avoid a catastrophe in Morocco. He had already sent his trusted envoy, Vernon Walters, to smooth over the situation and had instructed Moynihan to keep the wolves at the UN at bay. Despite Walter's efforts, however, Hassan had persisted in plans for this so-called "Green March." Again, two weeks ago he had sent another message to Hassan asking him to avoid escalating the situation and to let diplomacy – code for his maneuverings -- take its course through the UN. The previous day he had sent a third message to King Hassan warning him of the Spanish government's concerns that if the Green March involved incursions into Spanish territory it might force Spain to respond. Kissinger urged him to wait until the "bilateral and multilateral" efforts he had initiated could bear some fruit. He already had the Security Council under control. The previous day Moynihan had managed to outmaneuver critics of the march at the UN once again, and instead of issuing an order to "cease and desist," they had merely appealed to all the parties concerned to avoid "any unilateral or other action which might further escalate the tension in the area" and requested the Secretary General to "continue and intensify his consultations" with them. Moynihan later wrote in his memoirs "[t]he United States wished things to turn out as they did, and worked to bring this about. The Department of State desired that the United Nations prove utterly ineffective in whatever measures it undertook. This task was given me, and I carried it forward with no inconsiderable success."

Moynihan's machinations were highly effective. The tepid response of the Security Council towards the Green March had Washington's desired effect -- Spain had found it prudent to resume direct talks with Morocco. Things had been going as planned. The fly in the ointment was Algeria. Boumedienne had begun to put pressure on Navarro which had caused him to blink. But Kissinger was confident that he could bring him in line – if Hassan would only cooperate. Hassan, however, was obviously in no mood to take direction from the White House, and his intransigence was beginning to grate on Kissinger's nerves. Perhaps It was time to play hard ball.

When the three were alone once again, Kissinger turned to the President.

"On the Spanish Sahara, Algerian pressure has caused the Spanish to renege. We sent messages to the Moroccans yesterday." He paused a moment before continuing. "Frankly, I think we should get out of it. It is another Greek-Turkey problem where we lose either way. We could tell Hassan we would entirely oppose him; that might stop it but it would make us the fall guy.

Or we could force Waldheim forward."

The President did not hesitate for a moment. "I think the UN should take on more of these problems. God damn, we shouldn't have to do it all and get a bloody nose!"

Kissinger smiled. "The UN could do it like West Irian, where they fuzz the 'consulting the wishes of the people' and get out of it."

They both knew what he meant. In 1949 at the end of the Indonesian National Revolution the Netherlands agreed to recognize Indonesian sovereignty over the territories of the Dutch East Indies with the exception of Western New Guinea, whose population, Papuans, the Dutch claimed were ethnically different from the Indonesians and entitled to self determination. For years the Dutch government continued to administer the territory, preparing its inhabitants for self-rule. However, in 1962, due to pressure from the Kennedy administration and its desire to keep Indonesia as an ally in the Cold War, the Dutch were pressured to relinquish the territory to United Nations administration – with the caveat that a plebiscite would be held by 1969. However, instead of conducting this plebiscite itself, the UN allowed the Indonesian military to organize it, and the vote was by a show of hands by a hand-picked group of less than 1% of those who should have been eligible to vote. Not surprisingly, the vote was in favor of integration with Indonesia, and has fomented discontent ever since. But the United States got its way – Indonesia remained in the Western camp.

The President returned the smile. "Let's use the UN route."

Kissinger was pleased. If he could manage to pass the buck to the UN so that it would seem that the international community, not the US, was calling the shots, he could prevent the White House from being blamed for what would develop while still pulling strings behind closed doors.

"Yes, let's use the UN route," he replied, with a smile, and as he left the room a nascent plan had already developed in his head.

However, if Kissinger believed that he would be able to use the United Nations to diffuse the crisis that Hassan had fomented, he soon found that he was mistaken, for two days after his meeting with the President he was called into a top level emergency meeting with his deputies Atherton and Arthur Hartman, head of European Affairs, to discuss the crisis in the Sahara. He was growing even more impatient to get this issue settled. The previous day Castro had dispatched an additional 650 troops to Angola and just that morning the British had sent troops to Belize. He had more important things to do than hold hands with Hassan. But things were quickly getting out of control in the Sahara. The Secretary General of the UN was getting nowhere in negotiations with Spain and Morocco and the number of Moroccans lined up at the Spanish Sahara border was increasing daily.

When they had assembled Atherton spoke first. "Things are continuing to move towards the crunch in the Sahara. Tomorrow is the outside day on which the march will probably start. There is a lot of diplomatic activity. The Moroccan Prime Minister flew into Madrid. We have a report in from Wells about the Spanish account of this, in which the Spanish seem to have made a fairly reasonable suggestion, but there is no indication . . . .

Kissinger didn't wait for him to finish. Didn't they agree just two days ago to hand the issue to the UN?

"Just turn it over to the UN with the guarantee it will go to Morocco!" he snapped.

Hartman shook his head. "But there will be a problem if the marchers go into Spanish territory!"

For a moment there was silence. Then Atherton spoke up. "Why don't they let the marchers go into it ten miles, with maybe a token number going all the way to El Ayoun, and then having done this turn around and go back. And then do all they can to see to it that the UN self determination procedure comes out in favor of Morocco." He paused for a moment. "This suggestion has already been carried back to Hassan. Hassan's problem is that if he seems to cave very much, he is in difficulty at home, of course."

Kissinger looked at him intently. "But he is going to get the territory, isn't he?"

Atherton quickly responded "Well, he wants it 100 percent guaranteed. I think he is getting less than that – but he is getting probably the most he can hope for now in the position that the Spanish have taken."

Kissisnger looked at him. "He is getting the most he can hope for?" he repeated.

Atherton continued. ". . . in the way of a promise that it will come out in the end the way he wants, after going through the UN procedure." He stopped to take a breath. "It isn't a 100 percent guarantee. But I don't see that there is any more he can hope for or will have any support for from anybody else."

After a moment of silence Hartmen spoke up. "If it makes a difference -- the Spanish government was very explicit about what they would do in influencing the referendum for Morocco."

The three men were again silent. When they left the office they were confident that they could persuade both the King and the UN to tow the line.

When the UN Security Council convened the following day in an emergency session at three in the morning to address the deteriorating situation in Spanish Sahara they finally called on King Hassan to stop the march. But by that time it was too late. The die had already been cast.

November 5, 1975. The Green March.

Hassan's gambit to whip up the religious and patriotic fervor of his people in support of his "holy crusade" paid off. Within days of the King's speech more than half a million Moroccans volunteered to join the "Green March" – so many that the authorities had to choose the marchers by lot, weighing them heavily in favor of ignorant or semiliterate peasants from the countryside to the north, where loyalty to the King was the greatest, and who could be easily manipulated into obeying whatever orders he might desire. This was no time to risk a negative backlash by the opposition or from the residents of southern villages whose sympathies might lie with the Saharans. By October 28, a motley crowd of more than 145,000, carrying little more than the large, green Korans they had been issued by the government, had arrived in Tarfaya, a tiny outpost in south Morocco, in a region that had been part of Spanish Sahara prior to 1958, when Spain was "persuaded" to cede the northernmost strip of its territory to Morocco in return for Moroccan help in defeating the Army of Liberation. The logistics needed to transport, feed and clothe the marchers were daunting. All regular public transportation was halted so that special trucks could shuttle marchers to Marrakesh, where they would be transported by truck or bus the remaining distance to the south. The Moroccan air force dropped sacks of grain, and the army trucked in carloads of food, water and fuel. Soldiers herded marchers into a rapidly expanding tent city just south of the town. There they waited each day for orders to proceed -- waited and waited, hungry and growing restless with the passage of time, in the middle of nowhere, far away from home.

Two men, obviously Westerners, also waited -- sitting under a makeshift tent at the fringe of what appeared to be a large crowd of Moroccan peasants, interspersed with men in army fatigues barking orders and doling out meager scraps of food. It was the early morning of November 5, 1975 at a campsite located somewhat to the south of Tarfaya, and the Westerners had obviously been staying under this tent for some days, judging by the grime that had accumulated on their khaki safari outfits. They glanced languidly at the feeding frenzy, then settled back to polishing their camera equipment. They were obviously journalists.

"I heard rumors that today was the day" one of them finally said. "It looks like they are packing up some of their equipment. That's a good sign."

"I certainly hope so," replied the other, continuing to polish his equipment without looking up, "We've been stuck in this hell hole now for over a week. I wonder why Hassan decided to postpone the march in the first place."

His companion gave him a bemused look. "Dunno" he finally said, shrugging his shoulders, "Probably some backroom political maneuvering. I understand he is good at that. But I wish he would get a move on. My paper is clamoring for something to fill the front pages and you can't get anything juicier than hundreds of thousands of civilians marching on a holy crusade to reclaim their historic lands – straight out of the Bible."

"Or Cecil B. De Mille" added the other, with a slight laugh. "I wonder how many of these crusaders know that the International Court of Justice ruled that Morocco did not have any historic claim to Spanish Sahara. Most of them do not look like they can read or write."

"But they all listen to the radio," the other said, "Did you hear Hassan's radio speech when the ICJ opinion was issued? "We now have confirmation from the highest judicial authority that Spanish Sahara is and has always been Moroccan" or something to that effect. I couldn't believe my ears! Did he read the same opinion I read, or did I miss something?"

"They bought it, didn't they," the other said, shaking his head and gesturing to the crowd. "That's all that matters."

Their conversation was abruptly interrupted by the blare of a loudspeaker. The words were barely intelligible, but the speaker was obviously excited.

"Hey, Mo." shouted one of the journalists, beckoning to a dark haired companion a few yards away, "What's going on?"

Mohammed Lamri, the translator hired to accompany the journalists, was in no hurry to respond. He strained his ears to make sense of some of the words. Finally, with an air of satisfaction, he announced "The King just made an announcement over the radio from Agadir. He told the marchers that today was the day . . . they were to march to the border, and wait for a signal. When they crossed the border they were to kneel down to pray . . . ." He tried to continue but his words were being drowned out by the sound of dozens of motors being revved up, the shouts of a handful of soldiers, and the cheers of the crowd. The marchers quickly set about gathering their belongings. By noon the trucks and buses were packed to the brim and ready to roll. After one last check by the security guards, they began the trek southward.

The journalists quickly packed their belongings and waited impatiently in their Land Rover for the start of the journey. When the convoy started to move they took up the rear. Hour after hour they passed nothing but open rocky terrain, bereft of even modest shrubbery, the road more a path in the gravel then a proper highway. After about four hours of a journey that left their backs in agony, the caravan stopped a few hundred yards from the old border post at Tah, which the Spanish had abandoned just a fortnight earlier. There they set up a makeshift camp. All through the day and well into the night people arrived, until, by dawn, there was a crowd of thousands aimlessly milling to and fro, impatiently waiting for some signal.

The signal finally came at 10:40 a.m. On the morning of November 6, Ahmed Osman formally inaugurated the march by walking through a hastily erected arch of iron scaffolding, ornate with flags and portraits of King Hassan. With him were a score of cabinet ministers and official delegations representing three of Morocco's most conservative third world allies, Saudi Arabia, Jordan and Gabon. Trailing him at a respectful distance was a hoard of civilians chanting "Allahu Akbar" and "The Sahara is Moroccan" and waiving the Moroccan flags, portraits of the King and paperback copies of the Koran they had been issued. It made a colorful spectacle for the press, who hungrily grabbed every photo opportunity. Once across the border they fell to their knees in prayer in orchestrated waves and then were quickly hustled to the sidelines by the gendarmes. After a few hours the amassed throngs were directed to the waiting busses that shuttled them south along the single lane road in the direction of El Ayoun. The long caravan finally halted about six miles south of the frontier, and, at the direction of the gendarmes they pitched their tents in a large salt pan known as Oum Deboaa, the "mother of hyenas." In the distance they could see the column of Spanish soldiers that had cautiously and discretely tracked their movements. Forty thousand camped there the first night. By the night of November 7 this number had swelled to 145,000. That same day another 25,000 crossed the border about forty miles to the east and set up a second camp to the north of Hagounia. A third column began a march fifty miles to the east, to the north of Smara. There they waited, and waited, and waited . . . .

It was early in the morning again, but three days had passed since they had crossed the frontier, and the journalists were getting restless.

"This is silly," one of them finally said, breaking the monotony. "I thought we were going to El Ayoun. It is just a hundred miles south west of here, it wouldn't take more than a day to get there, even with a few thousand people in tow. I wonder why we are stuck here."

"Must be some political wrangling going on," murmured the other, fiddling with a coffee cup and not even bothering to look up. "Stands to reason. I couldn't believe that the Spanish would just let the Moroccans invade their territory without a protest. Did you see them?" he finally looked up and gestured to the small hills just to the south of the camp. "They are just over that ridge. I would guess a full column. Makes me kinda nervous."

The other one sipped his coffee and looked pensively at the horizon. "I've gotten reports that Dlimi has amassed thousands of soldiers not ten miles from here, although their location is off limits to reporters. By the way, don't you think it is curious that Dlimi was absent from the festivities the other day?"

The other one sneered. "I bet something's up. Franco may be dead by this time, for all we know, and Juan Carlos has no stomach for a battle. I wish we could get some decent news out here." He cast a disparaging look at the senior officer in charge, who was conversing with some couriers who had arrived that morning. "All we get is Moroccan propaganda. I guess we'll have to wait until we get back to New York to find out what is really going on."

But they didn't have to wait for long. A loudspeaker began blaring a message and the crowd gathered around it straining to hear the words. Suddenly there was commotion and a lot of discussion among the marchers. An officer tried to silence them, but he was having some difficulty. Another officer arrived and fired into the air. The crowd fell into silence and he started to address them in crisp military fashion.

"Now what?" muttered the journalist, half to himself. Mohammed joined them and blurted the news. "We've been ordered to retreat!"

The journalists were stunned. They were even more stunned when they read the announcement that Mohammed handed them. It was the Moroccan version of a press release, in English, complete with misspellings. King Hassan had addressed the marchers over the radio and had announced that the march had achieved its purpose and that they should return to the base camp.

"There is an understanding and an accord is in sight" read the press release. The long retreat began later that day. The date was November 10.

November 10, 1975. Washington, D.C.

At the same time that Hassan was evacuating civilians from the borders of Spanish Sahara, Kissinger once again met with the President and Scowcroft in the Oval Office. It was the morning of November 10, and

Hassan, following suggestions from the White House, had pulled back the Green March's incursion into Spanish Sahara to a mere symbolic gesture. A major confrontation between Spain and Morocco had been averted. Vernon Walters had earlier convinced Juan Carlos and some members of the Spanish Parliament that Spain's interests were not served by seeking to maintain a foothold in Spanish Sahara, especially since it was clear that if the UN conducted a referendum the population would choose a government under the Polisario, not the PUNS leaders who had been carefully cultivated by the Spanish government. Why not withdraw gracefully, he asked, especially if Spain could retain some economic interests? Walters had also been able to convince Hassan to postpone the march to let the Spaniards deliberate. When an agreement had been reached he had hastily returned to the capital to make his report: Spain would allow Hassan's marchers to enter the territory, but only for a few miles. That way they could both save face. Then they would withdraw and the Spanish and Moroccan governments could pursue talks behind closed doors on how to satisfy each party's interests. There would be an eventual transition of control to Morocco, but it would be done legitimately, through a United Nations process steered in the right direction by the United States. And so, Hassan had complied. But now it was up to the U.S. to follow through on its promises.

When Kissinger sat down in the Oval Office he came directly to the point. "Hassan has pulled back in the Sahara. But if he doesn't get it, he is finished. We should now work to ensure he gets it. We should work through the UN to ensure a favorable vote." That was all he said, or needed to say on the subject. The following day, he warned the President : *"It has quieted down, but I am afraid Hassan may be overthrown if he doesn't get a success. The hope is for a rigged U.N. vote, but if it doesn't happen . . ."*

By that time Kissinger had become fully aware of the negotiations that were being held in secret between Navarro and Hassan. He would have preferred to work through a referendum conducted by the United Nations to get Hassan what he wanted, but the King was wary of the United Nations. Its members were unpredictable -- and so was a referendum. He wanted a 100 percent guarantee, something Kissinger could not give him. So Hassan opted for the direct route -- pressuring Madrid for concessions. Well, if it worked, OK. Franco would never have gone for it, but Navarro and the Prince -- well, they were neophytes in this business. Walters could be trusted to keep a close eye on developments.

And so, as diplomats in the United States were putting plans for a UN referendum on hold – at least for the time being -- thousands of miles away other diplomats were putting the final touches on an agreement that would trump any action that the UN might take, and unbeknown to most of them, the first volleys had been fired in what was to become a long, grisly war.

November 14, 1975. The Madrid Accords.

For weeks the residents of the towns and villages in Western Sahara had been on edge, confused and not knowing what the future would bring. Ever since Salazar had withdrawn the troops from the outlying area and had placed a curfew on the towns the anticipation of some future catastrophe had mounted. Residents – both Spanish and Sahrawi – walked zombielike through the streets in ghostly silence, waiting for the final shoe to drop. Reports of fighting in the eastern district had started filtering in – first small skirmishes, then large scale battles with troops invading from the north.

Then, on November 14, an eerie silence descended upon them. The morning radio broadcast was filled with news: earlier that day the governments of Morocco, Mauritania and Spain had issued a joint communique unveiling an agreement they had reached behind closed doors about the future of Spanish Sahara. They had announced a "declaration of principles" which stated that Spain would withdraw from Western Sahara by the end of February 1976 and in the meantime it would institute a "temporary" administration in the Territory in which Morocco, Mauritania and the Djemma, the council of Sahrawi sheikhs appointed by the Spanish, would also participate. No mention was made of what would transpire after this "temporary" period and there was no reference to a referendum.

According to the broadcast it was widely believed that under this agreement -- dubbed the "Madrid Accords" -- Spain had agreed to withdraw from the territory in return for an interest in the Boucraa mine, as well as certain concessions on fishing rights off the Saharan coast. Despite the fact that the agreement officially referred only to an "interim administration" there was no doubt in anyone's mind that power would be transferred permanently to Morocco and Mauritania.

The bewildered residents at first couldn't believe their ears. Spaniards, their eyes brimming with tears, spoke bitterly of their government's humiliating capitulation; Sahrawis, equally bitter, complained of their betrayal. And rather than acquiesce in the partition of Western Sahara by Morocco and Mauritania the Djemma dissolved itself. Most of its members fled to the areas controlled by the Polisario, and in a document called the "Guelta Declaration" pledged their allegiance to the cause.

But their complaints were to no avail and could not stem the legions of armed men from the north and south that began pouring into their territory.

November 20, 1975. Resistance.

Somewhere in the region of Tifariti a hastily assembled group of men sat among the rocks and crevices that littered the area. As soon as they had gotten word that Salazar would be placing a curfew on the towns and trying to prevent the residents from leaving, members of the Polisario knew that it would be suicide to remain – the Spanish had put together a list of the leaders and they and many of their followers would be sure to be arrested. Mafoud and Ghali were helped by sympathetic Spanish soldiers to leave El Ayoun.

Many of the others who were on the list also managed to escape – sometimes by foot – into the desert, and had scattered among a number of tiny enclaves spread sparsely throughout the territory, leaving wives, mothers, fathers and children behind. There they were joined by many members of the now defunct Tropas Nomadas.

After the publication of the Madrid Accords, Brahim Ghall had sneaked back into El Ayoun to contact the members of the Djemma and convince them to join the rebellion. As a result, many of the members of the now defunct Djemma had made their way to a meeting with Polisario leaders in Bir Lehlou to pledge their support for the cause. At the same time a number of "solidarity" demonstrations had been scheduled throughout Algeria by Boumedienne.

Throughout this period the Polisario leaders had tried every means possible to halt the invaders who had begun creeping into the territory from both north and south. From hideouts in the hills and desert they had begun to carry out a hastily organized campaign of military resistance.

In the south, Sahrawi fighters had begun attacking Mauritanian troops early in December, crossing the border and battling them at Ain Ben Tili, Bir Moghrein, and Inal within Mauritania. They had managed to halt their advance until mid December. But when thousands of Mauritanian soldiers landed near La Guera, the coastal city at the tip of the border between Spanish Sahara and Mauritania, attacking inhabitants of the town by air and sea, they could resist no longer. One hundred or so resistance fighters barricaded themselves in the town's police barracks and factories and managed to fend off the Mauritanians for a week, but by December 19 the town had fallen. However, the Sahrawis were still putting up stiff resistance at Tichla and volunteers had poured into the tiny enclave of Argoub to block their approach to Dakhla.

When Moroccan troops began their advance towards the small settlements that bordered the Saguia el Hamra in the north, fighters under the command of Mohammed Abdelaziz began to harass them as much as they could with the few weapons at their disposal – mostly small gage hunting rifles and a few heavier rifles members of the Tropas Nomadas had managed to keep from being confiscated – and mostly on foot. On November 3, after being blocked for several days, a Moroccan battalion with 600 soldiers had managed to come within a few miles of Jdiriya. However, Polisario foot soldiers had followed them and had placed land mines in their path preventing them from moving forward. Then they had attacked. The Moroccans fired at them with mortars and machine guns, and paratroopers had descended upon them from helicopters. But the guerillas decimated the paratroopers and were only dislodged the next day when Moroccan units with 20 tanks, hastily dispatched from Lemseid, came to their comrades' rescue. Two days later the guerillas destroyed 10 trucks and 4 tanks and downed 3 helicopters in the Farsia area, and helicopters had to be deployed to evacuate the Moroccan wounded.

Their clashes with the Moroccan and Mauritanian troops went largely unnoticed by the outside world – the press had been hypnotized by the histrionics of the "Green March" and had failed to notice what was transpiring elsewhere.

69

However, the battles had not gone unnoticed among their fellow tribesmen. The image of these small groups of fighters, mostly on foot, defying hoards of heavily armed Moroccan and Mauritanian invaders did more than anything else to solidify a sense of fellowship among the members of the various Saharan tribes. The strong sense of *asabiya* or blood ties among members of these tribes, regardless of where they lived, would cause many thousands from southern Morocco, northern Mauritania and southwestern Algeria, to make their way to the Polisario camps by the end of the year. They would be joined by almost all the eighteen thousand or so Sahrawis who had settled in the Tindouf region of Algeria in the early seventies. Several thousand more would arrive from northern Mauritania and from southern Morocco, including practically the entire populations of Zag and Lebouirate.

But by the third week of November, the Polisario could count on only several hundred men. As El Ouali stood to address the newcomers, his emotions were mixed. There, before him, were men of nearly every Sahrawi tribe, mingling together, with one voice, one aim in mind. They were as young as 15 and as old as 65. They had no equipment, no provisions, and for the most part carried no more than hunting rifles. Most of them had traveled to the spot on foot, for few were able to bring along vehicles of any kind. But what they lacked in material goods they more than made up for in determination.

His words were brief and to the point. "Do they really think they can just hand over our territory without our consent? After all the rhetoric in the United Nations about our "right" to "self determination"? After Morocco and Mauritania for years had proclaimed their support for our rights? After Spain had promised us a referendum? After we had shown the UN Mission that the people wanted independence, not integration with another state? After the ICJ had determined that there was no legal basis for Morocco's or Mauritania's claims to the territory? After all the patience we had shown in the past few months in talks with the Spanish authorities, and all the promises they made? This! Without any attempt at all to consult with the people?"

"They can't do this legally, can they?" interjected a voice from the rear.

"I don't think so," he replied, "but we cannot rely upon "law" to support our rights."

"Do you think the international community will go along with it?" interjected another.

"Who knows?" he responded, somewhat wearily, "but we cannot wait to find out. We must show them that we will not surrender until every last inch of our territory is returned to us. We must fight them any way, and with any means we can. Spread the word – each man must carry out his own jihad. Look for their weaknesses and strike them where they are the most vulnerable. We cannot fight them with tanks and rockets, but we have one thing they do not have – we are fighting for our wives, for our children, for our very existence, for our country!"

But Ouali's words never reached Rabat, or if they did they were drowned out by the self-congratulatory applause of hoards of followers, for five days later, on November 25, in a press conference, Hassan declared the Saharan dossier "closed." That same day the first Moroccan officials, accompanied by troops led by Colonel Dlimi, reached El Ayoun. By December 10, 5,000 troops had reached the capital.

December 10, 1975. Moynihan.

As Dlimi was solidifying his army's control over El Ayoun, the Permanent Representative of the United States to the United Nations was solidifying his control over the United Nation's General Assembly.

The corridors of the United Nations had been buzzing with activity the whole month of November. Moynihan found that it was becoming increasingly difficult to keep members of the General Assembly in line with the U.S. position, and ever since the announcement of the Madrid Accords the representative of one country in particular – Algeria – had been a thorn in his side.

Algeria had become a powerhouse in the General Assembly. The Algerian popular uprising against France – as bloody as that which had engulfed France itself in 1789 -- had been a turning point in the relationship between colonists and the people they ruled and had given hope to oppressed populations throughout the African continent, and indeed throughout the world. Algeria quickly assumed the mantle of the principal backer of independence movements throughout the continent – aiding FRELIMO in Mozambique from 1964 until its independence in 1975, helping the rebels in Guinea-Bissau snatch independence from Portugal in 1974, and most recently enabling the MPLA in Angola to gain ground against the UNITA front supported by apartheid South Africa. In all of these endeavors Algeria had pitted itself against the United States and its allies, earning Boumedienne's government the enmity of several U.S. Presidents, not to mention Henry Kissinger.

And now they found themselves on the opposite side of the table with respect to Spanish Sahara.

Kissinger would have preferred going through the UN route. But as they say, "all roads lead to Rome" and now that the Accords were a *fait accompli* he would see to it that the "road" led to the same destination. So Moynihan was given his instructions.

Algeria had immediately sprung into action at the UN when the Madrid Accords were announced. It sponsored a resolution in the General Assembly which strongly reaffirmed "the inalienable right of the people of Spanish Sahara to self determination" in accordance with "the free and genuine expression of their will" and underlined the responsibility of Spain to see to it that the decolonization of the territory was accomplished in accordance with the General Assembly resolution. It was clearly meant to deny any legitimacy to the Madrid Accords. Rather, the UN Secretary General was requested "to make the necessary arrangements for the supervision of the act of self determination" and all parties were urged "to desist from any unilateral or other acts outside the decisions of the General Assembly on the Territory." The resolution was quickly getting support within the United Nations, particularly among the former colonies of the third world.

It was Moynihan's job to dilute it, and if he could not dilute it, to introduce a more "neutral" resolution – one that would recognize the Madrid Accords and lay the groundwork for a "West Irian" type solution to the "thorny" issue of "self determination."

So the same day as the General Assembly passed Algeria's resolution, it also passed a second resolution on Spanish Sahara – this one sponsored by the United States – which took note of the Madrid Accords and merely requested that the interim administration in Spanish Sahara "ensure" that the Saharan population would be able to exercise its right to self determination "through free consultations organized with the assistance of a representative of the United Nations appointed by the Secretary-General." Of course, he smiled to himself, he would see to it that this "representative" also represented the interests of the United States.

It never occurred to him in those days to doubt the wisdom of what he was asked to do, or to question why the people of Spanish Sahara had been given no say in the future of their territory. Indeed, it had never occurred to him to question the rightness of the deception and dissimilitude that had driven US policy on the issue of Spanish Sahara. Later in life, the Irish Catholic school demons of his primary years would torment him and he would apologize for his actions, calling them "thoroughly dishonorable," but these were the waning days of 1975, the Cold War was at its apex, and the world was either black or white, so when the Ambassador finally fell asleep that night after a hectic day, he slept soundly, convinced that he had once again struck a blow in support of the free world.

CHAPTER 3
1976

By the end of 1975 an invading army from the north had poured into El Ayoun and Smara like a swarm of ants, and Spanish troops had begun to withdraw. The Moroccan troops initially made an effort to cultivate good relations with the native population, distributing livestock and other supplies. However, after fighting with the Polisario intensified, they retaliated with a vengeance – by poisoning wells, machine gunning herds, looting civilian populations, removing civilians from the countryside and forcing them into the cities, mistreating captives, and staging public executions, in an effort to intimidate the Sahrawis. As a result, by the second week of January, 1976 at least 40,000 Sahrawis had fled their homes.

And the major towns of the territory began to resemble ghost towns.

January 5, 1976. The List.

It was the first week of January and Soukeina was helping her mother prepare dinner. Platoons of Moroccan soldiers had already arrived -- thousands of them in tanks and other military vehicles, carrying large guns that she had only seen on television. By mid December El Ayoun had become a military camp, surrounded by barbed wire. The Spanish sentries had gradually been replaced by Moroccans who constricted every movement of the native population.

The streets of El Ayoun were now nearly deserted. Hundreds of her neighbors had fled in advance of the invasion. She had wanted to flee as well, but did not dare to leave her mother and her elderly great grandfather unprotected. But the news she heard from her cousin that day chilled her to her bones. The Moroccans had compiled a list of Polisario supporters and had been going door to door, rounding them up, one by one. No one knew their fate.

It was then that they heard the knock. Soukeina froze, her blood stiffening. Her mother looked at her, her eyes wide with terror. Her brother barked an order. "Go to the door and delay them," as he ushered her quickly into the small room at the back of the house where they kept provisions. There, heaps of burlap bags filled with rice, beans, and other foodstuffs lay strewn helter-skelter on the ground. He told her to lay down and quickly covered her with bags until she could barely breathe. Then he returned to where his mother was excitedly explaining to a Moroccan private that her daughter was still at the school.

The private, a boy barely out of his teens, gave her a contemptuous sneer, then turned to face Hamed, a suspicious look crossing his face. "Who are you?" he barked.

"I am a neighbor, Hamed Ould el-Bashir," he lied. The private stared at him for a moment, then looked at a piece of paper he was carrying. No, there was no Hamed Ould el-Bashir on the list. "Do you have your identification papers?" he growled. A year earlier the Spanish had conducted a census of the population and had given the Sahrawis identity cards. "No," he replied, managing a small smile, "I was not yet 18 when the Spanish conducted the census."

The private stopped to think. He would have liked to pursue this matter – 18 year old Sahrawi males were not to be trusted – but his orders were to find this girl, Soukeina. So, without saying a word, he marched into the adjoining room, and then into the rooms that served as bedrooms, looking carefully around for any sign of the missing girl. When he came to the store room, he paused at the heap of burlap bags. "What's in the bags?" he demanded. Soukeina's mother spoke quickly, "They are just bags of grain and other provisions." The soldier approached the bags. There were tracks on the floor where bags had been moved. Smiling, he drew his saber and thrust it through the top bag until it touched the floor. Immediately, a stream of rice poured out. Soukeina's mother found her voice. "Are you satisfied?" she demanded, "I tell you she is not here!"

The soldier turned and walked briskly through the house, not bothering to look behind him. When he had left, Soukeina's mother collapsed on the pile of pillows that served as a couch. Hamed raced to the bags and gently removed them, one by one. There, huddled in a fetal position, lay Soukeina, half suffocated, her face inches away from the slash made by the sword.

Soukeina rose to her feet, wiping the grains of rice and dust from her clothes and shaking them from her hair. She knew that it was only a matter of time before they returned to search for her. She had to leave. But where could she go?

Hamed had the answer. Dakhla.

Gradually news from the south had reached the capital. Despite heroic resistance from Sahrawi fighters La Guera and Tichla had fallen. However, the Mauritanian forces had not been able to get to Dakhla, where her aunt lived. The Sahrawis were putting up stiff resistance at the tiny enclave of Argoub, a few miles south of the town, and Hamed was preparing to join those forces.

"Hamed is right. Go with your brother. He will leave you with your aunt in Dakhla. Stay with her – and wait until it is safe to return!" her mother implored. "Hurry, there is no time!" she added, pushing her into her room. There her mother helped her gather a few pieces of clothing and place them into a large canvas bag. She then put together a basket of bread, a canteen of water, a tin box containing tea, a small kettle and some morsels of food, and placed it in her hand.

Soukeina hesitated a long moment at the door before leaving. She had already said goodbye to her cousins and her mother, but she somehow could not bring herself to bid farewell to the elderly man who stood silently in the door frame. She stood for a long time just looking at him, etching the details of his face in her heart, not being able to speak. She began to feel a wetness on her cheek and realized that she was crying. She kissed the elderly patriarch one last time, on his forehead. Her mother held her in her arms for a brief moment, and then she turned away.

As she left the house she turned one more time to wave to the two figures at the door. She didn't realize then that she would never see them again.

January 5, 1976. The Escape.

It was late at night and there was no moon to illuminate the sky, just a pinprick of stars. Soukeina and her brother, turning off the headlights of their Land Rover and pushing the car slowly, had managed to evade the guards that patrolled the Zemla district of El Ayoun. Avoiding the main roads they finally reached the outskirts of the city. There, however, they faced another barrier – a barbed wire fence with sentries posted along the only road south towards Dakhla. Hamed crept slowly and silently to the barbed wire enclosure. There he quickly cut a hole through the wires big enough to permit a car to exit and returned to the vehicle. Holding their breath they pushed the car slowly through the hole into the open desert. After a few hundred yards, they turned on the motor and quickly darted south through the rocky terrain, avoiding the main road, with headlights off, guiding themselves by the stars and the tiny compass Hamed was wise enough to put in his pocket before leaving.

It was daylight before they managed to reach the outskirts of Boujdour. Moroccan troops had already cordoned off the town and posted sentries along its perimeter. But there were no Moroccan troops in the open desert, and Soukeina and Hamed were able to speed through the flat, open space unhindered.

By the end of the day they were able to see the lights of the tiny hamlet of Villa Cisneros – or Dakhla, its Arabic name – in the distance. Not knowing what they would find, they thought it prudent to wait until dark before trying to enter the town. They placed the Land Rover beneath an acacia tree and covered it with a tarp. Then they waited. When dusk had descended, they quietly crept on foot to the outskirts of the village. There they could see the silhouette of Spanish sentries and the Spanish flag waving on top of the town's main hacienda. Good! The Mauritanians had not yet arrived.

The Spanish garrison at Dakhla was preparing to vacate the city by January 12, and the soldiers were not seriously trying to control the movement of the population. Soukeina and Hamed were easily able to sneak pass the sentries, and once in the town they proceeded calmly to the house of their aunt.

When she saw them at her door, she screamed with joy and ushered them into the house, where they were quickly surrounded by relatives and friends anxious to hear about their escape – and to get news about El Ayoun. All night long, until her hosts mercifully permitted her a few hours sleep, Soukeina talked about the events that had forced her to flee. She finally fell asleep, as the first rays of sun announcing a new day began filtering through the windows.

January 6, 1976. Argoub.

After leaving his sister in the arms of their aunt, Hamed returned to the Land Rover and proceeded under cover of darkness to the tiny enclave of Argoub, about 20 miles south of Dakhla. There, positioned in the town as well as in hastily dug trenches protecting its southern border were a number of Sahrawi fighters. Facing them, across the desert, was a column of Mauritanian conscripts, hurling at them from time to time a barrage of bullets. Hamed quickly took up a position in a trench occupied by three other Sahrawis. They were Oulad Delim – he could tell from their accents. The Oulad Delim was the predominate tribe in this part of the territory, and he smiled inwardly as he recalled previous encounters between their tribe and his own – the Reguibat. Their great-great grandfathers had probably fought each other, he mused.

The others were probably thinking the same thing, for all at once one of them, with a broad grin on his face, yelled, "What's a Reguibat doing this far south?"

Hamed laughed. "I came for the climate," he retorted, "I got tired of seeing vegetation!"

The other laughed as well. The desert in this part of the territory was mostly barren rock and soil, and a little farther south, near the Mauritanian border, mountains of sand dunes stretched as far as the eyes could see.

"You are welcome, *habibi*," he replied. My name is Bachir, and these are my brothers, Mustapha and Lahbib.

"How long have you been here," Hamed asked, after extending the long, Sahrawi greeting.

"Five days," Bachir replied, offering the other a cigarette. "We had been fighting the troops near Tichla, but finally decided to retreat and concentrate our forces here."

"How many men are here?"

"More than at Tichla. Maybe 200 or so. It is difficult to tell, since we are spread out, and each day brings us newcomers – like you – and costs us others." Hamed couldn't help noticing the pool of blood at the far side of the trench.

"And how many Mauritanians are there?"

"Maybe a thousand. Who knows? After a couple hundred I stopped counting."

Hamed tightened his grip on his rifle. Then he slouched down into the trench.

"What do we do now?" he finally asked.

"Wait," was the reply.

January 8, 1976. Flight to Mudraiga.

Soukeina's rest did not last long. Two days after her arrival her aunt rushed into her room.

"Soukeina," she said, nearly out of breath, "I have just gotten word that Moroccan troops have been sent south. They are expected to reach Dakhla tomorrow!"

"Moroccan troops?" she asked, somewhat astonished. "I thought this part of the territory had been given to Mauritania!"

"Yes, that was the agreement," her aunt replied, "but the Mauritanian troops are bottle necked at Argoub, and apparently Hassan is worried that they will not reach Dakhla before the Spanish troops withdraw."

Soukeina sank into her chair, her thoughts racing. She had to think quickly. Once the Moroccans arrived they would undoubtedly cordon off the town, making it difficult to escape. Her best bet was to leave this evening. But where to? And with what, now that Hamed took the Land Rover?

Her aunt broke her reverie. "Soukeina, I have gotten word that the Polisario has established a temporary camp a few miles east of Bir Enzaren where they are collecting civilians for evacuation to Mudraiga and Glaibat el Foula. I have arranged for us to join a family that will be leaving tonight for the camp at Bir Enzaren."

So, once again, Soukeina gathered her few belongings and prepared to escape, her final destination unknown. Within a few hours she and her aunt had joined a procession of cars and trucks that were leaving the city, under the indifferent noses of the Spanish guards, towards the abandoned enclave of Bir Enzaren, 100 miles to the northeast of Dakhla, in the middle of nowhere.

January 11, 1976. Bir Enzaren.

The sun was now at its zenith, scorching the earth and turning the desert into a furnace. In the trenches surrounding Argoub the men tried their best to cover themselves. Water was scarce, and the few provisions they had managed to squirrel away were treated like manna from heaven. Hamed and the others had tried to take their minds off the heat by swapping stories – stories of ancient battles, stories of the exploits of their ancestors, stories of the Arabs from the east who had married the Sanhaja of the territory and had formed the tribes they called the Sahrawi – of Beni Hassan for whom the dialect of Arabic they spoke – hassaniya – was named. They knew these stories by heart, for they were passed down from generation to generation by word of mouth, for few of them knew how to read and write.

But their brief hiatus did not last long. Shots – first one, then a barrage, suddenly whizzed over their heads. They responded in kind, and soon the air was filled with the bursts of gun fire. After a few minutes the firing stopped.

Bachir rested his shoulders again against the wall of the trench, casually reloading his rifle.

"Why have they stopped?" Hamed queried, somewhat puzzled.

"Oh, they are probably reloading – or taking tea – or taking a nap. They are in no hurry. They can wait until we run out of ammunition – or starve," he said, matter-of-factly.

Hamed slumped into the trench, his thoughts whirling. It was true. The ammunition they had wouldn't last more than a few days, and as for the food and water . . . .

He looked at his friend's eyes. They were clear and calm. The eyes of someone who had made peace with himself, with the world. The eyes of someone who knew that he would die.

The hours passed slowly. From time to time bursts of gunfire descended upon them from the desert, but for the most part there was just a horrible waiting. That night Hamed could not sleep. He lay there, just staring at the stars.

Before the first glimmer of daylight had had a chance to break through the darkness of night he heard a sound and reached for his gun. Someone was approaching the trench. He crouched lower and aimed the rifle in the direction of the approaching footsteps. Suddenly a figure was visible. He cocked his rifle and prepared to fire. But before he pulled the trigger, a voice called out, in a low voice "Bachir?"

When Bachir heard his name he reached up and pulled the figure towards him, hugging him and crying out, "Souilem!"

He was his third brother, and he was a welcomed sight, for he brought with him a canvass bag filled with food, a tureen of water, and, most important of all, several rounds of ammunition.

When the hugging was over, they settled down to hear the news. It was not good. Moroccan troops had landed in Dakhla and were sending soldiers towards Bir Enzaren – towards scores of refugees who had been assembled at a camp not far from there for transport to Mudraiga, where a hastily built refugee camp had been erected. They were expected to reach the outpost by the end of the day.

Hamed nervously figeted with his rifle. Bachir could see that he was disturbed. "What is it *hermano*" he asked in a soft tone.

"I left my sister and my aunt in Dakhla," he finally said.

"They have probably been moved by this time," Souilem interjected, his voice somewhat cheerful, "Polisario brigades have been evacuating the city for days. They may have even reached Mudraiga by this time! And I have gotten word that Sahrawi fighters are racing to Bir Enzaren to block the Moroccans to give the remaining refugees time to escape."

But his words did nothing to ease Hamed's mind. Bachir gave him a long, hard look. Then, in a determined tone, he whispered, "Go to them, Hamed. Go to Bir Enzaren. Souilem can show you the way. We can manage here."

A look of excruciating tenderness passed over his face as he stared into his companion's eyes. "I will not forget you," was all Hamed whispered as he scampered over the trench. No sooner was he on open ground then the bullets started flying. But somehow, through luck, or a miracle, or maybe

both, neither he nor Souilem were hit, and they quickly ran out of the range of
the firing and into the open desert, in the direction of Bir Enzaren.

January 11, 1976. Oum Mudraiga.

The motley procession proceeded into the open desert, travelling at a snail's
pace. The small Spanish cars used by most of the inhabitants were useless in
the desert, and although some of them had managed to get their hands on a
Land Rover, there wasn't room in them for all the people wishing to leave, so
many had to walk alongside on foot. At nightfall they stopped to rest, and
pitched the small, white tents most families carried for emergencies. They
quickly lit fires to brew tea and boil a little rice, which they passed around first
to the hungry children, then to the elderly, and finally to the women and the
few men driving the vehicles. Soukeina was glad to drink a little tea and eat a
morsel of food, for she didn't know what she would find at the Polisario camp.
When dawn arrived they had already packed their belongings and were ready
to proceed. By noon they reached the outskirts of Bir Enzaren, a tiny enclave
that used to host a garrison of Spanish soldiers. It was empty now, and scouts
were sent ahead to see if they could find any remnants of food, clothing or
weapons. They returned with a few sacks of grain that had been abandoned,
and some discarded clothing, but the garrison had left few pickings behind.
By nightfall they had reached a sprawling city of tents in the middle of the
wilderness, where guerillas were busy loading people and provisions onto
trucks for an evacuation to the nearest water hole – Mudraiga. The following
day a procession of trucks and cars, filled to the brim with men, women, and
children and their belongings, set off through the desert. By nightfall, empty
trucks returned, to begin the process anew the following day.

Soukeina and her group patiently waited until it was their turn. Finally,
one of the Polisario leaders in charge of the evacuation gave a signal, and her
group, joined by a hundred others, slowly started the final leg of the voyage.
They needed to hurry now, because they had just gotten word that a column
of Moroccan troops had been seen in the vicinity of Bir Enzaren, and that
a convoy of Polisario troops had gone out to prevent them from going any
farther.

By nightfall Soukeina was able to see the outline of hills in the distance,
and knew that they were close to their destination. Oum Mudraiga, a spot
about 50 miles southwest of Guelta Zemmour, the largest guelta in the area,
was the site of a well in an area surrounded by hills to the north, close to the
Mauritanian border to the east. Here, in three camps nestled among the hills,
the Polisario had established an impromptu tent city for thousands of civilians
escaping from towns in the southern part of the territory. It was here that they
would find shelter, food and water.

<h1 style="text-align:center">January 12, 1976. Toucat.</h1>

While Soukeina and the other refugees from Dakhla were slowly making their way through the desert, 500 miles to the north a tall young man with unruly black hair and a mustache to match was busy pondering his next move. When he was a young student, Mohammed Abdelaziz had never dreamed of being a soldier. No, he wanted to be a doctor, and when he entered the university it was with this aim in mind. But destiny has a way of interfering with one's dreams, and here he was, in his mid 20s, commanding a rat-tail bunch of goat herders and camel drivers in an epic battle to attain an even greater dream. He was from Smara and knew well the area where the territory intersected with Morocco. So, when the war started El Ouali had asked him to take charge of groups of volunteers who had gathered in the hills near Farsia, the desert near Mahbes, and the towns of southern Morocco, to fight the advancing Moroccan army and cut their lines of communications. They possessed no more than three vehicles. His first battle was at Jdiriya, where he and his small band had been able to impede the invading troops for days. Then his troops proceeded to harass them along the entire Saguia el Hamra corridor, shooting down the first Moroccan plane and a few helicopters in the process. But he hadn't stopped there. He sent small *kateebs* to engage Moroccan troops based in the towns and villages of southern Morocco – Lemseid, Tan Tan, Goulimene, as far north as the anti-Atlas town of Assa, at times carrying their supplies on the backs of camels. And he took pains to cultivate the support of the inhabitants of the region, who were only too glad to provide him with information about troop and convoy movements. By January he had established a base camp in the Saguia el Hamra *wadi*, at a place sheltered by trees and vegetation called Toucat.

It was now the morning of January 12, and he had just settled down for his second cup of tea when a messenger approached. He looked closely at the boy. He must have been no older than 15 – barely old enough to shave. He was one of the volunteers who had rushed from Tan Tan to join his forces when the fighting started – one of dozens who had come from southern Morocco. He was still wrapped in the blanket he used for warmth in the freezing nighttime temperatures and on his feet were the remnants of what used to be shoes. He was one of the fighters stationed near Farsia, and he had obviously run the entire distance to his camp with some news. Abdelaziz looked at him tenderly.

"Sir," he began, somewhat breathlessly, "We have just seen Ben Othman and a column of Moroccan infantry with tanks leave their camp heading in your direction!"

Colonel Ben Othman was one of the highest ranked officers in the Moroccan military, in charge of the battalion that had been dispatched from Lemseid at the beginning of the conflict and had finally installed itself at Housa.

Abdelaziz calmly invited him to join him for tea and beckoned for one of his lieutenants. Soon scores of men began taking positions among the crevices and trees that dotted the landscape. Then they waited. . . .

It wasn't long before a slight rumble announced the arrival of a column of men, followed by a half dozen tanks and artillery, winding their way slowly through the hills to the north of the *wadi*. But when they approached the edge of the dried river bed they ran into a field of land mines and sniper fire, forcing them to retrace their steps and take cover in the crevices and hills above it. They returned the volley and soon, as in a scene from some Hollywood movie, the air was filled with flying bullets, ricocheting off the hills and trees. At first the Moroccans assumed an air of defiant superiority, taunting the guerillas, taking comfort in the tanks that lumbered perilously close to the precipice edge. But when a projectile suddenly hit one of the tanks, blasting a hole in its side, the Moroccan troops began to silently slither away.

But not for long. The following day they returned, this time accompanied by helicopter gunships which blasted huge craters into the sand. The fighting was fierce. Several times the Moroccans seemed close to entering the *wadi*, but each time they were repelled by guerillas on foot, engaging them some times in hand to hand combat.

And so it continued, day after day. Only the curtain of night permitted rest for the weary.

January 18, 1976. Prelude.

The fighting had quickly gained momentum in the early days of 1976. As Abdelaziz and his small group of irregulars waged battles against Moroccan troops in the north, small units of guerilla fighters at Argoub, Bir Enzaren and elsewhere in the territory did everything they could to impede the enemies' advances into the territory.

But the guerillas quickly found their attention diverted by the mass exodus of Sahrawi citizens who began fleeing the towns in droves as the Moroccans and Mauritanians approached.

Refugees from Dakhla and the south had been directed to a camp established by the Polisario at Mudraiga. At Mudraiga they would wait until they could be ferried to Tifariti or Guelta Zemmour.

Refugees from El Ayoun and the north – if they had a vehicle -- could either follow the asphalt road east to Boucraa and then down to Mharis and from there to Amgala or Tifariti, or make their way farther south to Guelta Zemmour, the largest guelta in the territory. But many of them did not have a vehicle, or were afraid of being intercepted by Moroccan troops along the asphalt road. For them the journey was a long trek on foot through the Saguia el Hamra *wadi*.

By mid-January Boumedienne had offered help to the Polisario leaders in evacuating the refugees to safety in Algeria. The major staging point for the evacuation of those fleeing from the northern towns was Amgala, a point in the dry river bed nestled among small hills about 250 miles from the Algerian frontier. Several hundred Algerian troops had been sent there, under the command of Commander Radwan, bringing food and medicine and offering transport.

And their activities had not gone unnoticed.

January 20, 1976. Operation "fateh" ("opening").

Back at his command post in Agadir, Colonel Dlimi sat in his armchair pondering his next move. Ould Daddah's ineptitude had forced him to send a contingent of soldiers to Dakhla, to ensure that the rebels would not be able to take over the town before the Spanish were able to hand over the keys to the Mauritanians. It was only on January 12 – with the aid of relief forces sent by Dlimi -- that Mauritanian troops were finally able to reach Dakhla. By that date, the majority of Spanish forces had been evacuated to the Canary Islands and the main towns were under the control of the Moroccans and Mauritanians. But although he had managed to exert control over the major hubs of the territory, small groups of guerillas were still staging surprise attacks on his troops in the outlying regions, and on caravans carrying much needed supplies. He had increased the number of troops and supplied them with enough tanks and artillery to wipe out several regiments -- and on a number of occasions he had flown to the front lines by helicopter in person to direct their assaults. But to no avail. Much to his chagrin they had not been able to defeat the elusive enemy. And to top it all, the guerillas had managed once again to attack the Boucraa mine. By January 20 they had sabotaged the belt as well as the power pylons running alongside it and one of its control stations, putting the mine once more out of commission. The belt was to remain out of commission for six years and although the Moroccans would be able to carry some stockpiles by truck to the coast, no additional mining would be attempted.

And then there was the problem of the fleeing civilians. It was quickly becoming an embarrassment for the King. Once Dakhla was in the hands of the Mauritanians he had sent his troops on a mission to intercept the refugees escaping from the vicinity. He would force as many of the women and children as possible back into the confines of Moroccan held territory, and as for the men . . . well, they were the enemy, weren't they? But stiff resistance from the rebels had thwarted their advance and while they were bottle necked east of Bir Enzaren most of the refugees had managed to make their way to a watering hold called Mudraiga. Farther north, refugees were still hemorrhaging from El Ayoun and Smara and finding their way to Polisario camps in Tifariti, Amgala, and Guelta Zemmour despite his efforts to confine them. And Boumedienne's meddling didn't help. Who did he think he was, giving aid to the Polisario and sending troops into the territory to ferry the civilians to camps in Algeria?

He would not let these activities go unpunished, he thought to himself. He would put together a force that would sweep through the territory, mopping up any resistance and teaching Boumedienne a lesson. A force he would lead himself. He would stop this resistance once and for all.

January 21, 1976. Convoy.

It was early in the morning of January 21, and a platoon of soldiers leading a convoy of tanks followed by 60 trucks was slowly winding its way through the valley that formed the southern flank of the Lengueb pass towards the Western Saharan border. The march was slow going – the winter rains had swelled the small tributaries in the *wadi* and the trucks often found themselves stuck in the soft mud. Once on dry land the Moroccan commander assembled all the trucks and surrounded them with the tanks and armed guards. They would stop for an hour or two in order to make some necessary repairs and he was taking no chances. As he looked around him he could see nothing but a few small hills and gullies – nothing out of the ordinary, nothing to create an alarm. Only the cry of a solitary crow broke the stillness of the desert.

What he didn't see were the eyes peering at him behind those hills and gullies.

After eleven days of intense fighting Ben Othman's troops had withdrawn from the vicinity of Toucat and returned to their base in Housa, only engaging in sporadic exchanges between the troops at Jdiriya and the guerillas. Abdelaziz and his men had been enjoying a brief respite from the battles when a patrol informed him that a Moroccan convoy had passed through the pass. Now he and three of his men in two Land Rovers had come out to intercept it. With his binoculars he could see a circle of tanks in the near distance, surrounded by troops. He gave a command and suddenly the stillness was shattered by blasts of gunfire. The Moroccan commander quickly took cover and ordered his men to fire back. They did, pummeling the hills with lead, creating large craters in the sand, sending swirls of smoke several yards into the air. The fire fight was still in progress when Abdelaziz beckoned to one of his men.

"I think it is time to use our new weapons," he shouted over the din. The man ran to where three large metal objects rested on the ground. They were small hand held bazookas, ones that had been sent to them only a few days earlier by headquarters, the only ones they had. The man nervously picked one up and ran to Abdelaziz' side.

"Aim for one of the tanks," Abdelaziz shouted.

The man brought the weapon to his shoulder, aimed and fired. But he missed his target, and the projectile instead struck the side of a hill, sending splinters of rock into the air. He looked at Abdelaziz. "Try again," he said. So, he raised another bazooka to his shoulder and fired. But it bypassed the tanks, striking something on their other side. Suddenly, an enormous blast filled the air, sending shrapnel in all directions, covering Moroccans and guerillas alike with a blanket of dust. Soon that blast was followed by another, and then another, until an enormous fire ball blackened the horizon.

The guerillas, totally dazed, stared at the fireball in disbelief for a moment before advancing to where an equally dazed and frightened group of Moroccans lay prostrate on the ground. It was only then that they saw what remained of the trucks.

"What do you think happened?" the guerilla asked Abdelaziz, his eyes wide with astonishment.

"They must have been carrying ammunition in those trucks and after you hit one of them the fire spread to the others," Abdelaziz replied.

The man shook his head, his eyes surveying the debris. "I wonder where they were heading?"

Abdelaziz didn't wait to respond. Instead, he made his way through the dust and smoke to where the Moroccans were squatting in the sand. He found the commander.

"Where were you heading with all that ammunition?" he shouted.

The man at first said nothing, but when Abdelaziz grabbed him by the arm and asked the question a second time he spit out a word. . .

"Amgala"

January 21 to 27, 1976. Amgala.

On the evening of January 21, Salek and a group of his comrades had hidden themselves among the hills just east of Smara, where a huge Moroccan garrison had recently been stationed. Two units of guerillas were at that time helping to evacuate to safety the refugees at Amgala, roughly 60 miles to the south. After having led the initial battle against Moroccan troops at Farsia in the autumn of 1975, Bouhali had been sent to Algeria to bring back Sahrawi troops that had received additional military training in Algeria. Then he and these troops had been sent by El Ouali father south, to the region bordering the Mauritanian frontier, and for days had been battling Mauritanian troops across the border at Ain Ben Tili. Fighting at Ain Ben Tili had been so fierce that Ould Daddah had called upon the Moroccans for air support, and the previous day the guerillas had shot down one of their F-5 jet fighters. By January 21, Bouhali had returned to Mharis from days of chasing Mauritanians fleeing south to Bir Moghrein, and El Ouali, with Brahim Ghali at his side, was circling the region coordinating activities as best he could.

Salek was asleep -- dreaming of peaceful days in El Ayoun surrounded by his friends, cheerfully discussing the ordinary details of life – the price of camel milk in the market, the merchant who sold the best *zatar*, the weather – the thousand miniscule items that occupy a day of peace, when a fly began to circle his head. He swatted at it, but it would not go away. Instead, it dove at his head, buzzing in his ear. Soon it was joined by another fly, and then another, until at least a dozen flies seemed to be circling his head.

He sat upright, jolted quickly from his slumber. He could hear a faint, but steady buzz, and a noise that seemed like the sound of distant thunder. But there were no thunder storms in the Sahara at this time of the year. He could feel his heart pounding. He had heard that sound before, at Tafoudaret when they waited in ambush for the column of Moroccan tanks to approach.

He pulled his covering off him and raced to the top of a hill to get a better view of the valley to the west. Others had heard the noise too, and were barking orders. The Moroccans were on the move. During the previous day Moroccan forces from Smara and El Ayoun had joined forces at a place between them called Oum Abaduz. Now they were on the move again, approaching the troops that had hidden themselves in the hills that skirted Smara to the east, their destination unknown.

"We won't be able to hold them off for long," Salek shouted to his companions, "I am going to run to the troops stationed at Amgala to warn them," and with a departing good bye he was off.

He ran quickly through the valley in the direction of the *wadi* where dozens of refugee families had recently been camped. A small Polisario band was there with the Algerians trying to evacuate those that remained. Salek quickly spread the word through the camp, and at once a mass exodus began, with hoards of refugees loaded on the Algerians' trucks and whisked quickly eastward through the *wadi*. Meanwhile, word of the Moroccan troop movement had been sent ahead, and by the evening of January 21 Bouhali and his men were racing to blockade them.

By the morning of January 22 a column of Moroccan infantrymen, followed by Land Rovers and troop carriers carrying cannons – an enormous force -- had camped at Khang Ramla, on the western side of the hills, and Bouhali and his men had reached Amgala. At 11:00 that morning the Moroccans started moving south, parallel to the hills.

But sandstorms had erupted that morning, quickly enveloping the territory in a cloud of dust, making it difficult to pinpoint exactly where the Moroccan troops had gone – or whether it was their intention to go south to buttress their beleaguered comrades in Bir Moghrein or to go north to invade Amgala, where at least 200 civilians remained to be evacuated.

During the evening of January 22 Bouhali was in his tent assessing the situation with the commander of the Algerian forces, Captain Radwan, when he was surprised to see El Ouali's Land Rover approach his location from the south. Ouali had astonishing news. He had been stopped for questioning by a contingent of Moroccan soldiers – a tiny fragment of a much larger force -- at a point near Douikat, about 15 miles southwest of the *wadi*, but had dashed off before they knew who he was. Luckily, they had not tried to follow him. So they now knew where the Moroccans were, but where they were going was still a mystery.

It wasn't a mystery for long. The morning of January 23 saw fog envelop the *wadi*. But as the fog lifted with the rising sun, the mystery surrounding the Moroccans' intentions also began to lift. They were marching north, and in a few hours would reach the *wadi*. There were still over 100 civilians left to be evacuated. Ouali immediately raced off to accelerate the evacuation efforts, while Bouhali planned a way to halt their advance.

At 8:40 a.m. the following morning the first shots were fired. Dlimi, who was leading the Moroccan troops, at first tried to move his infantry into the *wadi* ahead of the armored vehicles. But they were shelled mercilessly by the guerilla troops in the hills, and forced to stop about a mile south of the *wadi*. The shelling continued throughout the day and by 6 p.m. the Moroccans were forced to withdraw and reorganize.

Meanwhile, Bouhali sent word to a unit of his troops stationed at a point approximately 5 miles south east of the *wadi* called Gara Foug Gara, to harass the Moroccan forces as much as possible and prevent them from advancing north for sufficient time to evacuate the remaining civilians.

The following day – January 24 – was decisive. The Moroccan infantry, unable to advance more than 2 miles from the *wadi*, continued to be shelled by Polisario forces in the hills, while the bulk of the Moroccans' main force – including all their armored vehicles – traded gunfire with both the Polisario units in the hills to their north and the units of guerilla fighters at Gara Foug Gara to their east. The shelling on both sides was fierce and lasted for more than two hours, with the guerillas continuously blocking the Moroccans' advances. Then the aerial bombing began. Moroccan helicopter gunships swooped over the *wadi*, blanketing the area with craters and masking the sky with clouds of dust. Finally, at 11 in the morning the shelling became more sporadic and the Moroccans decided to stop their advance.

At 1 p.m. that day Captain Radwan informed Bouhali that he had received instructions to return to his base in Algeria, and by 4 p.m. that day a convoy of trucks carrying the last civilians and supplies, with a number of men, women and children marching alongside on foot, left the *wadi*, escorted by the Algerians and Bouhali's troops. By midnight of January 24, with all the remaining civilians evacuated, Bouhali and his men withdrew from the hills north of the *wadi* and returned to Mharis.

January 24, 1976. The Rescue.

By the evening of January 24, Bouhali had regrouped his men near Mharis. Most of the Algerian troops had departed with the remaining civilians to Algeria. However, some of the Algerian troops, including one of their lieutenants, were unaccounted for, and later it was learned that a few of them had gotten lost in the *wadi* and marched right into the waiting arms of the Moroccans.

Bouhali motioned to three of the figures who were busy unloading provisions. "I need two of you to go back to the *wadi* and make sure we have accounted for all the civilians." Then he turned and said to the third -- a short, slim guerilla, covered from head to toe in camouflage fatigues – "I need you to go to the *wadi*, find the missing Algerian lieutenant, and bring him and his troops here. Do you think you can do that?" The guerilla smiled and nodded.

Soon they were off.

During the battle the missing lieutenant had tried to escape in his truck with several of his soldiers, but, being unfamiliar with the terrain, and with their tracks covered by the sandstorm that had enveloped everything around them, instead of going towards the *hammada* they had traveled deeper into the *wadi* and had quickly become stuck in the soft sand that filled the dried river bed. The more they tried to extricate themselves, the more their tires spun out of control and the more desperate they became. By nightfall the exhausted troop had given up all hope of escape and had resigned themselves to capture by the Moroccans.

Then, out of the dark, a figure appeared, clothed in camouflage fatigues, with a face covered by the green headdress of the guerillas.

"Quick, move over!" he shouted to the driver of the truck. The man obeyed, moving into the passenger seat. The guerilla took the mats that covered the floor of the driver's and passenger's seats and placed them behind the back wheels of the truck. He then turned to two of the other soldiers. "I will rock the truck back and forth, and when I give you the signal, push."

With that he climbed into the driver's seat and gently tapped the accelerator. After the truck moved an inch or two forward he released the accelerator, put the gears into reverse, and repeated the step. The truck began to rock back and forth in the sand. When it had done so three or four time, the guerilla yelled "push" and placed his foot firmly on the accelerator. The soldiers at the front shoved with all their strength, and gradually, for what seemed like an eternity, but was in reality less than a minute, the truck hauled itself out of the hole. When it was freed, the driver barked "Get in quickly" and the soldiers eagerly complied.

Once the truck was able to move he told the Algerians to keep their headlights off and to follow him as quietly as they could. With no headlights he navigated deftly through the darkness, using only a cigarette lighter for the Algerians to follow. They were not far from two large contingents of Moroccan forces to their south. A Moroccan column had camped less than half a mile to their left, and he could see distinctly the lights of their campfires. Another column was not far off to their right. The driver led the truck slowly through the soft sand until they reached firmer ground. Once they were on firmer ground he raced towards the northern hills and the relative safety of the Polisario command post a few miles away.

It took nearly two hours to reach the Polisario camp, and at the first sight of the camp, the Algerians shouted with joy. The sight of a truck approaching was also like a gift from heaven to the waiting Polisario guerillas, as they turned out in numbers to greet it.

When the truck had stopped, surrounded by guerillas who began hugging the Algerians with cries of joy, the driver stepped out of his vehicle.

As he unwound his headgear, flocks of long wavy hair descended past his shoulders. A hush came over the crowd. The Algerians stared in astonishment. He, or rather *she,* quietly approached the commander, who was speechless.

"Commander Bouhali. I hope you can use another truck!"

January 27, 1976. Dlimi's Mopping Up Campaign

Three days after the Polisario withdrew from the area, Dlimi and his troops at last marched into the now deserted Amgala *wadi*. Dlimi then left his troops and returned to Agadir. Breaking the back of the resistance was proving to be more difficult than he had thought. But the mopping up operation would continue. His troops would remain in Amgala only two days. Then, after sending most of their equipment back to Smara, the bulk of his forces would push forward to occupy Tifariti, Bir Lehlou and Mahbes. Others would be sent to eradicate the guerilla forces based at Toucat. However, rather than engage the Polisario units in a frontal assault, he would move the troops from Amgala southeast so as to reach Tifariti from the south, and he would send reinforcements from Smara to circle Tifariti from the north, boxing them in. Other units, carrying supplies, would reach Mahbes – the gateway to Algeria – and points north from platoons he would send south through the Lengueb pass.

Following his orders a portion of the Amgala force went south and camped a few miles from Tifariti, and a small contingent of Moroccan soldiers from Smara tried to approach Tifariti from the north. But Bouhali had moved the majority of his troops to a base camp slightly east of Amgala at a place called Motlani, where there were copious hills and caves to provide cover and he could protect access to the town. The Smara forces were intercepted by his men and forced to join their comrades to the south. The Moroccans remained three days in the vicinity without ever occupying Tifariti or Bir Lehlou, before heading for Mahbes and points north.

And much to Dlimi's irritation, his troops were not able to eradicate the guerillas in Toucat. Instead of engaging the Moroccan forces advancing towards Mahbes, Abdelaziz simply took his troops west, into southern Morocco, and attacked their rear guard in the vicinity of Lemseid, Tan Tan, and Goulimine, cutting their supplies and lines of communication.

But you would have never learned any of this from the Moroccan media. A day after their assault on Amgala, Moroccan radio announced that Colonel Dlimi had overcome the enemy in an operation code- named "fateh" or "opening", named after a famous battle of the Prophet Mohammed, following a skirmish which lasted more than one day, and in the process of which had "killed dozens of Algerian soldiers" and captured twenty nine. The captured Algerians – the troops that had been lost in the *wadi* and wandered into the Moroccans' arms -- were displayed on television and Hassan offered them as proof that Algeria was behind the armed conflict.

A few days later, in a video made for French and Moroccan television, Colonel Dlimi, dubbed the "desert fox" by the press, took film makers on a tour of Amgala, showing off the small arms that had been captured, and bragging of the prowess of his forces in his "mopping up" operation.

Sidimi.

After the commander of Polisario's units in the area had gotten over his initial shock at seeing the woman who had delivered the Algerian soldiers to his headquarters, he asked to see her. When she appeared before him he gave her a closer look. She was at an age, not young but not ready to be old, when some women appear their most beautiful. She had discarded the headscarf and had washed the dust off her face, but she still wore the men's camouflage pants she wore when he first saw her. He could barely hide his curiosity.

Sahrawi women did not wear men's clothes, nor did they drive cars, let alone trucks.

Before he could say a word she spoke up.

"My name is Sidimi," she began. "I am from El Ayoun, and I have been trained as a nurse. You have a number of wounded men in your unit. I believe I can be of some assistance."

"Where did you learn to drive a truck?" he blurted.

She blushed slightly. "My brothers taught me to drive and in my spare time I taught others."

"Other women?" he asked. "No, just men." she replied.

He paused and looked at her again. The Algerians had sheepishly told him of their difficulty getting the truck out of the *wadi* and how she had come to the rescue. They were the only Algerians who had managed to escape. The others had been captured by the Moroccans.

She broke the silence. "Do you have any medical equipment here?" she inquired. Managing to overcome his shock, he regained his composure. There were indeed several wounded men in the camp, and one of the soldiers had been looking after them as best he could with the meager supplies they had been given by the Algerian Red Crescent. But no one at the camp had any real medical training.

He decided to put his questions aside for the moment and called for one of his assistants. "Salek, this lady is Sidimi. She is from El Ayoun and she is a nurse. Bring her to where we are keeping the wounded and see to it that she gets any medical supplies we have – and ask Ahmed to follow her instructions."

Sidimi smiled, offered a curt "thank you" and exited the area.

He sat down and slowly sipped the cup of tea that had been placed before him, savoring the warm sugary liquid. For what seemed an eternity, despite his best efforts, he couldn't get the image of this strange woman out of his mind. But finally, the pressing needs of his soldiers filtered in, he put aside the tea and turned to the business of fighting a war.

February 10, 1976. Bir Enzaren.

While the Polisario forces in the north were still recovering from Dlimi's sweep through the territory, five hundred miles to the southwest Hamed removed the branches that had camouflaged his Land Rover, and he and Souilem quickly began to race in the direction of the approaching Moroccan column in an attempt to prevent them from reaching the refugee camp at Mudraiga, roughly 74 miles northeast of Bir Enzaren. But, no sooner had they gone a little over 50 miles than they ran out of fuel and had to proceed on foot. It took them several hours to reach the outskirts of Mudraiga and the scores of Sahrawi fighters who had amassed there, traveling hundreds of miles on foot, armed only with their hunting rifles, to attempt to repel the invasion. By that time the Moroccan troops in advance of the column were only hours away. Hamed and a number of his comrades decided to prepare an ambush, and hid themselves in a ravine close to where the troops were expected to approach.

89

Then they waited.

Finally they heard a distant rumbling that grew louder with each passing moment and saw the huge columns of dust that began to cloud the skies. The Moroccans were close – perhaps less than a mile away. Soon they could hear muffled voices along side the rumble of engines. They quickly scrambled up the ravines and began firing at the troops. At first, the Moroccans, thoroughly surprised, didn't know what to do. Then, someone barked an order, and they began firing back, sending clouds of dust swirling among friend and foe alike. For an hour shots streamed in both directions. Hamed was quickly running out of ammunition. He shouted to Souilem to pass him some bullets, but there was no response. He turned and touched his shoulder, and that was when he saw it – the bullet hole that had pierced his breast, the blood that was seeping into the sand. He reached out to cover the wound, but it was too late. Souilem stared at him with empty eyes, the grey shadow of death on his face. He lay him softly on the ground and grabbed the rifle that had fallen to his side. It was then that it hit him, knocking him to the ground, blood spurting from a hole in his shoulder. He found himself unable to lift the gun and his right arm began to feel numb. Mustering all his strength he clambered once again over the ravine, half hidden by the swirling dust. From there he ran in the direction of a crevice, which provided some cover. After a few minutes the shooting stopped. The Sahrawi guerillas, after inflicting as much damage as they could, had retreated to the desert, and the Moroccans were in the process of looking for the wounded and dead. He could hear the footsteps of a soldier just a few yards behind him and was sure that within minutes he would be captured – or worse. But suddenly someone barked an order. The commander had told them to return to the column. He was in a hurry to make up for lost time. So the soldier turned and returned to his troops and within minutes the entire column had left the scene.

Hamed was in the middle of the desert, without water or other supplies, and badly wounded. He decided to walk as far as he could eastward, towards the refugee camps. But before long he began to fee faint from loss of blood and in the searing sun he started to become disoriented. Finally he collapsed.

When he regained consciousness he felt he must be dreaming or dead. Staring down at him was the face of a woman – or was it an angel – with large, beautiful eyes that seemed to glow in the semi-darkness. He tried to move, and the pain he felt in his shoulder told him that it was no dream. "Don't try to move yet," the woman said softly, "Let your wound heal for a few days. Here, try to eat some soup. It will give you strength." She dished out a bowl full of harira, the traditional soup of the Sahrawis, which he eagerly drank. When he had finished he was full of questions. Where was he? Who was she? Where were his comrades? What happened to the refugees going to Mudraiga? She patiently listened to his tirade and then began to answer his questions one by one.

Her name was Miriam. He was in the tent of her family, part of the Oulad Delim tribe, who had camped in the desert with their camels, goats and sheep a few miles south of Bir Enzaren. They had heard the sound of the battle and had waited until the Moroccan troops had departed to see whether there were any survivors. Her father had found him unconscious in the desert and had brought him to their tent where she had tried to wash and bind his wounds. He had remained unconscious or semi conscious for several days and they were not sure whether he would survive. But Allah had been merciful.

When she had left the tent an old man entered and squatted on a rug next to him. "Welcome," he said in the long Sahrawi custom, "My name is Salama Ould Rashid. I am Miriam's father. We are the only ones here. Her brother has gone off to war, and her mother is dead."

Hamed thanked him for his courtesy and tried once more to move, but the pain forced him to lie down again. "I am afraid it will take a little longer for that wound to heal," the old man said softly, "But you are welcome to stay as our guest for as long as it takes."

A shadow passed over his face. He was itching to return to the conflict. It was difficult for him to remain idle while others were fighting and dying on the battlefield. And he was eager to learn the fate of his sister and aunt, and what had become of Bachir and the others at Argoub.

"Have you managed to get any news about the refugees? About Argoub? I met some kinsmen of yours there. Bachir Ould Bouhari and his brothers," he said, and then, with his voice lowered, added, "His other brother, Souilem, died when we were fighting the troops approaching Mudraiga." The old man cast his eyes to the floor. Miriam, who had entered the tent, quickly tried to change the subject. "There will be time to get news from the outside world later. But for the time being, you need to tend to your wounds," she said in a business like tone. But her eyes avoided his when she spoke, and something told Hamed she knew something – something she did not want to tell him. He looked at her more closely. She had averted her eyes and was fidgeting with the blanket that covered him. "What is it, Miriam, what is it that you are hiding?" She murmured "nothing" but refused to look at him. Finally the old man turned to face him, his eyes filled with sadness. "You have a right to know," he said softly. Then, in almost a whisper, he spoke. After a standoff of more than a week Argoub had fallen. The fighters had put up a stiff resistance, holding back the Mauritanian forces for as long as they could. But they ran out of ammunition. Bachir and the other two hundred fighters were all dead.

The news pierced Hamed's heart like a thunderbolt. He immediately shot up as if to grab his gun. But he could not move his firing arm and the effort made his head spin. So, he slumped back on the rugs and after a few days of rest tried to make himself as useful as he could, as the days of January slowly receded into the past.

Sidimi's Choice.

The men who had followed Bouhali to his hideout in the hills near Lemgassem were scattered among the caves and crevices of the area, with Bouhali and a small contingent occupying a makeshift headquarters in one

91

of them. Close to this headquarters was an area reserved for the wounded, where Sidimi and a couple of men assigned to assist her occupied their days tending the wounds of those fallen in battle and relieving the suffering, as best they could, of those who had succumbed to the harsh winter elements.

One day, as she was wrapping a bandage around a soldier's leg, a boy, no more than 18 cautiously approached her, a nervous look on his face.

"What is it, Abdati?" Sidimi asked when she had caught a glimpse of his expression, "You are as white as a ghost!"

The boy cast his eyes to the floor.

"Well, spill it out, Abdati," she said, after a pause.

The boy raised his head and looked at her. "I heard that Bouhali has received orders to send you to the camps," he blurted. He knew that the news would not be well received.

And he was right. Sidimi sat upright, her eyes glowing, her mouth firm. "Abdati, I am not going. That is all there is to it!" she declared in a low growl.

"But, Sis," the boy pleaded, "It is too dangerous to remain with the troops, and besides which they need you to take over the emergency aid operations in the camps. I heard that the director of medical operations himself asked Bouhali to send you."

"Well, he will just have to make do without me!" she declared, putting down the bandage and reaching for a piece of paper and pen. She quickly wrote something down, and then, with a determined look, stormed up the hill, entering the cave that served as the command post for the purpose of doing battle with an equally determined personality.

Bouhali was reviewing troop movements with one of his officers when she stormed into his makeshift "office." Ignoring the other man present, she came straight to the point. "Commander, each day more and more wounded arrive from the battlefields and many have wounds that have become infected. Others have lost so much blood that it is a miracle when they survive. We are losing dozens of our men on the battlefield, too seriously wounded to be transported. I believe I could save many of them if I could give them treatment at an earlier stage." She paused for a second, held her breath, then continued. "Commander, I want to stay here and accompany the troops to the front lines."

Bouhali at first didn't know what to think. He had received orders from headquarters to send her to Tindouf to help organize medical facilities there. And a woman at the front lines? They had trained women as soldiers, but they had been used primarily for logistics tasks, like preparing food and ammunition for transport to guerilla units buried in isolated posts in the desert. The front lines were reserved for the men.

As he turned to face her, his face betrayed no emotion "Sidi, you know you are needed in the camps. . ." but before he could finish the sentence, she interrupted. "There are others who can take over duties at Tindouf. They can manage without me."

He then tried to continue, "and the front lines are too dangerous. We cannot afford to lose you . . ." But once again she would not let him finish. "I am fully aware of the danger, but I simply cannot stand by and allow our men to die on the battlefield when I know I can prevent it." She paused and looked at him squarely in the eyes.

"Sidimi," he said gently, "do you have any idea what it is like out there? Our men sleep under the stars, in remote hideouts for weeks at a time. They march for hours each day through the desert, constantly changing their position. There is little food, and nowhere to wash. You have seen them when they return – their bodies covered with fleas, their clothes filthy. It is no life for a woman."

But Sidimi would not be convinced. She waited for him to finish, and then said calmly, "If the men can endure it, so can I. I am determined to go, Commander, and nothing you say will deter me! Rather than return to Tindouf I will take a rifle and join you as an ordinary soldier! Here, I have prepared this letter for the Chief Medical Officer," and with those last words she placed a handwritten note before him. He read the note and sighed. He had fought in hand to hand combat with Moroccan soldiers. He had led guerilla raids against the Moroccans and the Mauritanians. He had suffered wounds that at times made his entire body ache. He was tough. But in Sidimi he had found his match.

He couldn't help admiring her courage, and he had to admit, he liked having her around. He had had no lack of feminine companionship in his life – young, pretty things that would occupy his thoughts for a day or two. But she was like no other woman he had ever met. Besides which, she was right. He could certainly use medical aid at the front lines, and unless the central command was willing to send someone else. . .

After a moment's hesitation he turned to face her, his face stern and frowning. "All right, Sidi, I will tell you what I will do. I will send your letter to the Chief Medical Officer and I will write to the central command informing them that I require someone to move with my troops to provide medical aid, and that if they are not prepared to send someone else I would request permission for you to stay . . . ." Then he paused, and in a tone as if he were chastising a child, he added, "I just hope you won't regret this!"

Sidi returned his look. "I won't, I promise you," she said curtly.

She left as quickly as she had come, never noticing the smile that had begun to cross the commander's face.

February 10, 1976. Grim Assessment.

Meanwhile, reports of the invading troops and Dlimi's "mopping up" sweep through the territory continued to filter in to the Polisario leaders.

El Ouali already knew what had transpired. He also knew that as a result of the seizure of the Algerians at Amgala, Boumedienne had quit sending troops to help evacuate refugees and had limited Algeria's involvement in the conflict to the provision of training, weapons and supplies. Henceforth, the evacuation of civilians, as well as all other tasks, would be carried out by

Polisario soldiers, severely constraining their ability to fight the ever advancing Moroccan and Mauritanian forces.

Moroccan superiority in numbers and firepower had already enabled them to entrench themselves in the main towns. Polisario fighters could do little more than snip at their heels. Meanwhile, in the south, Moroccan troops advancing eastward from Dakhla had reached the abandoned outpost of Bir Enzaren in the third week of January. From there they had tried to follow the stream of refugees to Mudraiga but were blocked by Polisario units. On February 8, Mauritanian troops finally managed to dislodge guerilla units at Awsard, the small administrative center protected by craggy hills 125 miles east of Dakhla that had been occupied by the guerillas since the war began.

In the first months of the war Ouali could rely upon only 500 or so fighters with scant previous military experience and few weapons. Their armaments had increased once Libya and Algeria began providing aid, but even with this aid they lacked heavy artillery. By the second week of February they had only two trained battalions, one led by Abdelaziz in the north, and the second led by Bouhali, based in the central region. Every unit of these battalions had only one or two Land Rovers – and no trucks or other vehicles. Other than that the soldiers were on foot.

The war was now in its fourth month and both El Ouali and Brahim Ghali were even thinner than usual – both had spent most of this period without sleep looking for new weapons and supplies of ammunition and trying to organize and train new units of fighters.

Later in the evening, in the hills near Lemgassem, two of Bouhali's troops huddled for warmth. It was the middle of the winter, and the harsh, cold, nighttime winds and freezing temperatures had numbed their fingers and toes. They could light no fire for warmth in the evening, lest it reveal their location to the ever marauding Moroccan planes, and the one blanket they shared was riveted with holes. So during the day they lit a fire with the brush they had collected and dug trenches into which they put sand that had been warmed by the fire. Then during the night they huddled in the trenches trying to divert their minds from the shivers that coursed through their limbs.

"How long do you think it will be before we move out?" one of them asked. "It is easier when we are on the move . . . we don't feel the cold as much."

His companion shifted slightly. He also much preferred fighting to waiting in the cold. "I don't know, but I hope it is soon. The Moroccans obviously think they can get away with anything," he began slowly, "So far we have been just treading water. The people in the camps are putting up a brave front, but I can tell that they are demoralized . . . I guess Ouali is waiting until we have some more recruits and supplies."

"Well, I hear that a number of fighters have joined Abdelaziz in the north and that Beni Baha has amassed some volunteers to try to head off the Mauritanians in the south," the other said, drawing the blanket closer.

"Yeah, I heard that too," his companion replied. "And I also heard that Ouali has arranged for us to get some more supplies from Algeria or Libya."

"I hope these supplies come soon," the other responded, "My shoes are worn so thin I can see through them . . . and as for ammunition . . ."

He didn't need to finish the sentence. They carried only a few small caliber rifles, and barely enough ammunition to put a dent into any Moroccan forces they might encounter.

"Well, we are getting new recruits daily," his companion answered, "But the additional aid we are getting from Algeria and Libya probably won't arrive for a few weeks, and the new recruits will likely be escapees from the towns or desert dwellers who will need some training if they are to be any use to us."

"So, for the foreseeable future it is just us and our hunting rifles on foot, is that it?" asked the other in a weary voice.

"Well, let's hope that the Moroccans are bad shots!" his companion said, trying to dispel the cloud of seriousness that had enveloped them.

The other laughed slightly and before long the soft blanket of sleep finally descended upon them.

February 12 to 15, 1976. Amgala 2.

On the evening of February 13, Bouhali had just returned to the base camp at Motlani that he had established shortly after the first Amgala battle, when the lieutenant he had left in charge of the camp suddenly appeared at the entrance to the cave that served as his barracks with an important message.

"What is it now?" he asked, somewhat startled.

"Sir, a large column of troops – maybe a battalion or larger – moved today from their base in Smara and are now occupying the guelta at Amgala," he blurted.

"So they have moved at last," Bouhali muttered to himself, thinking out loud.

A day earlier he had gotten word that a column of Moroccans from their base near Boucraa were on the move, heading southeast, in the direction of Amgala. Later he had gotten a second message: instead of continuing in the direction of Amgala that force was heading south. They had camped at a place approximately 10 miles southwest of Amgala, their destination unknown. It was the chance he had been waiting for – to intercept the Moroccans on the move, outside the garrisons they had established at Laayoune, Boucraa, and Smara. So, without further hesitation he had set out with his infantry that morning and engaged them in a battle that had lasted the entire afternoon. He had just returned to his base – with a handful of Moroccan prisoners in tow – when he had gotten the latest news.

But another large force – headed in the same direction? What could it mean?

He thanked his lieutenant for the news and walked to a clearing where a small group of Moroccans sat glumly beneath a tree.

"I am going to ask you something, and I want a true answer," he asked, in a tone that demanded respect. "Where are your troops heading?"

The men averted their eyes and squirmed somewhat uneasily. All but one. He looked at Bouhali with weary eyes.

"South, that is all we know."

". . . to meet up with troops from Smara?" he asked.

"Maybe. We don't know. All we know is that Dlimi wants to attack and occupy some targets in the south. . . . where refugees have gathered. . . . and block their escape. . ."

Bouhali stood still for a moment. After pumping the soldier for as much information as possible he quickly sent for his lieutenant.

"Get my car ready," he barked. "We are going to find Ouali."

As he walked swiftly towards his cave he passed Sidimi, who had been busy carrying supplies to her makeshift clinic.

She grabbed the lieutenant's arm. "What's wrong?" she asked, noting the grave look on Bouhali's face.

"He's just been told that a large column of Moroccans may be heading to Mudraiga and Guelta Zemmour," the man said in hushed tones.

The smile on Sidi's face disappeared in an instant. Mudraiga and Guelta Zemmour were filled with thousands of refugees.

It took Bouhali less than an hour to reach the impromptu headquarters where El Ouali, with Brahim Ghali at his side, had been spending days and nights trying to direct troop movements, parcel equipment and ammunition, and coordinate the evacuation of the thousands of civilians camped in scattered locations in the territory. As soon as he arrived he requested an urgent meeting. The leaders had been discussing for weeks their next move . . . whether to try an attack on the garrison at Smara or the "fateh" troops Dlimi had sent to Mahbes. Now there would be an answer.

"We know that there are Moroccan troops at Bir Moghrein," he began. "We can't be sure where the troops from Boucraa are going, but the prisoners think their destination is Mudraiga. And Dlimi's plan is to have half the force from Smara go southeast and meet up with troops coming from Bir Moghrein to block the route from the east of Amgala to the south . . . while the other half heads for Guelta Zemmour."

He stopped for a second to let the gravity of the situation sink in. "You know what they plan to do if they find the civilians, don't you?" he started to say, slowly, "Just today we managed to rescue a young man who told us that the Boucraa troops killed a dozen members of his family and buried them in a mass grave in the desert . . . and if they are able to block the Amgala road south so that we cannot come to their aid   . . . and they cannot escape . . ." He shook his head. "There are several thousand . . . at least two battalions . . . and they are well armed with heavy artillery and armored vehicles. . . and we would need to fight them on two fronts . . . but I think if we take them off-guard . . . and if Allah is on our side . . . we might succeed," he said quietly.

The three men looked at each other. Each knew what the others were thinking. They had only one trained battalion in the vicinity, a handful of Land Rovers and a few trucks – and no heavy artillery. If they attacked it would be mostly by infantrymen on foot with their rifles – against well armed forces with tanks and aircraft to protect them. They would be risking everything –

the lives of their men, and maybe the future of their country!

Finally, El Ouali spoke.

"I don't think we really have a choice," he said, somberly. "We cannot allow them to reach the refugees at Mudraiga and Guelta, and there is no way to ferry them out in time."

Brahim Ghali looked passed him, deep in thought. Finally he turned to the others and without uttering a word, nodded his head.

That evening Bouhali sent word that his troops, which had been stationed in scattered locations throughout the area, should rush to his headquarters. When they had assembled he looked at their faces – men as old as 60 and boys as young as 15, most armed with nothing more than rifles and a grim determination to fight or die for their land. How many of them would live to see another full moon, he thought, but quickly banished that thought from his mind. When he turned to address them his words were grave. "Tomorrow we will face the enemy – the enemy that has invaded our land, imprisoned our brothers, bombed our women and children, and told us that we are no longer free men but must bow to a new master – the enemy who intends to annihilate our people, and take the riches of our country for themselves. Tomorrow we will choose whether to die as free men or to live as slaves. Tomorrow will tell us if we are to survive as a people or be consigned to the dustbin of history. We have not chosen this fight – it has been thrust upon us. But fight we must until every last drop of our blood has been spilled on the field of honor. There can be no turning back. As our ancestor Ibn Ziyad once said 'Before us is the enemy, behind us only the sea!' We have only Allah in the sky and the refugees in the camps!" As he finished cries of "Sahara libre" filled the air, and with those cries still in their throats, the fighters he commanded set out on what they all knew was a battle that would determine the fate of their movement, if not their people.

By the morning of February 14 a column of guerillas had been dispatched with a somber mission: to prevent the Moroccan column that came from Boucraa from advancing any farther towards Mudraiga . . . or die trying. Meanwhile, Bouhali led a second column to Amgala to engage the Moroccans coming from Smara that had arrived the previous afternoon and were camped in the *wadi*.

After canvassing the area he decided to attack the Moroccans from the east, where there were small hills that could provide cover and which could be traversed easily on foot. To the southwest of Amgala were larger hills that would be more difficult to mount. The Moroccans camped at Amgala did not expect an attack and concentrated their forces, with most of their artillery covered by tarps.

The guerillas approached stealthily in the dark, as quietly as possible. Their Land Rovers, which were blue, had been covered in mud for camouflage and their roofs and glass had been removed to make them lower to the ground and not reflect the sun. Perched on the Land Rovers were machine guns or bazookas – allowing the weapons to be used in rapid, mobile assaults -- a

97

technique devised by the Polisario and one that would change the dynamics of this, as well as every other desert conflict, forever. But most of the troops would advance on foot from the hills through the *wadi*. They would attack at dawn.

Salek had paid close attention to Bouhali's speech. As they approached the outskirts of Amgala under cover of darkness a few of them steered their vehicles to the north and to the south. He was part of the infantry that would attack from the east, with Bouhali at the lead.

In the early morning hours a blanket of fog had descended upon the area where the Moroccans were sleeping. The fog was so dense that their aircraft had been grounded, and the Moroccan soldiers were lying in scattered positions on the ground. Salek and his companions, approaching quietly on foot before daybreak, crept within feet of them without being detected.

But their peaceful slumber did not last long. Suddenly, out of nowhere the guerillas descended upon them, like a swarm of ants attacking a locust. Before they had time to man their heavy artillery the Polisario infantry overran their ranks, engaging them in hand to hand combat. In the gloom of fog it was difficult to differentiate friend from foe, and the attackers appeared so suddenly that many of the Moroccans thought they must have parachuted from the sky. It was sheer bedlam.

The Moroccans, now with the enemy in their midst, and not knowing the size of the force they were facing, became confused. Some Moroccan soldiers, unable to see more than a couple of feet before them, and frightened by the blasts of guns from unseen assailants, ran away without their weapons or ammunition. Vehicles were abandoned as they ran helter-skelter in every direction, chased on foot by the guerillas.

Salek raced up to an enemy soldier and fired. But the gun jammed. The startled soldier then reached for his weapon and the two started struggling to get hold of it. They rolled together in the sand, covering their clothes and faces in a layer of dust and sweat. After a minute Salek managed to pin the soldier to the ground and was able to wrest the weapon from his hand. As he turned the weapon towards his face and prepared to fire a wave of fear shot through the Moroccan's eyes. For a split second Salek hesitated. The soldier was a boy, barely 18. Far from his home, fighting for a cause he didn't even understand. For some strange reason Salek couldn't shoot. He loosened his grip on the boy and like a caged animal suddenly freed, the boy sprinted off without a backward glance, into the fog. "Run," shouted Salek after him, "Run back to your family, back to your country, and leave our land!"

All day long the guerillas fought, pursuing Moroccan troops through the desert, then returning to fight again.

Sidimi had followed the infantry in a Land Rover filled with as many torn rags and bottles of medicine as she was able to gather from the supplies that they had managed to salvage from those that the Algerians had brought to Amgala. As the infantry was preparing their assault she chose a spot under an acacia tree in a tributary near one of the hills that surrounded the spot and told the men that they should bring the wounded to her there. Then she quickly unloaded the provisions and waited. It wasn't long before she heard the shots and shouts that announced the battle. Soon she saw a man, the pants of his left leg covered in blood, slowly limping towards her with the help of another soldier. She ran towards them.

"Ahmed, you can leave him with me now," she said as she reached for his arm. The other soldier nodded and darted back towards the battlefield.

She tore off his pant leg to the thigh and inspected the wound. A bullet had torn through his thigh, and blood was quickly oozing from it. She quickly constructed a tourniquet to stop the bleeding. She then heated the pen knife she carried. She tried to comfort him, telling him to be as still as possible and to think of his wife and children for it would hurt and she had no anesthetic. Then she wiped the dust from the hole as carefully as she could and with the pen knife cut into the wound. The man gasped in pain and uttered a moan, but did not move. When she had removed the bullet, she washed the wound with the alcohol she used for an antiseptic and wrapped a piece of cloth tightly around his leg.

"There, this will have to do until we get back to the camp," she said, matter of factly. By this time two more soldiers had appeared, their head scarfs covered in blood. Then two more, with chest wounds, carried to her. And so it went, minute by minute, hour by hour, day after day, until, finally, at about 2 o'clock in the afternoon on the second day, the noise diminished, and finally stopped.

By that time at least two dozen guerillas lay on blankets near her Land Rover. But more lay on the battlefield, unable to move. Sidimi then began the grisly task of searching the battlefield for survivors. With the help of some of the soldiers she transported the wounded and dying to her clinic in the sand and helped them as best she could. The ones she could not help were quickly buried by their fellow soldiers fully clothed, following the custom prevalent in Moslem societies for burying the dead in battle. After she had tended to the wounded guerillas she turned her attention to the captured Moroccans.

By 10 a.m. the guerillas had been able to occupy the hills surrounding Amgala. They had killed at least a hundred Moroccans and had taken nearly another hundred prisoners. The rest had fled into the desert, with guerillas close on their heels. They pursued some of them nearly all the way to Smara. Two Moroccan battalions had been decimated.

When the fog lifted and Bouhali was able to survey the scene around him, his eyes widened. The landscape before him was dotted with trucks, Land Rovers and tanks abandoned by the Moroccans. Moreover, the Moroccans had left behind enough ammunition to last them through a number of battles. As Sidimi peered into one of the trucks she gasped. In the back, half obscured by weapons, was a tin box with a large red x painted on it and in the box were neat rows of bottles, rolls of bandages and other medical supplies. She ran to a second truck. It also contained a box. Every truck was supplied with a box of medical supplies, and the command unit itself had a large trunk of such supplies. It was indeed a god send – whatever they contained – since, not being able to read French, she could not decipher the labels.

However, to Salek, the most important items the Moroccans had left behind were now gracing his feet. Shoes! His old ones had worn out weeks ago from the constant marching. And by the end of the day the caravan of exhausted, but happy soldiers, disappeared once again into the desert.

February 14, 1976. Dlimi's Riposte.

At his command post in Agadir, Dlimi had just gotten off the phone with a very irate Commander of the Faithful. He was fuming. It was the evening of February 14 and the King had just gotten word of the fiasco at Amgala. It was only a few weeks since he had posted that video, an interview with reporters in which he had triumphantly declared victory over the rebels at Amgala and was able to parade a host of captured Algerians for all the world to see. He now had to face those same reporters and explain why it was that his army – equipped to the hilt with heavy artillery and protected from the air by the Moroccan air force, and numbering in the thousands – could find themselves routed at that same place by a couple hundred Bedouins armed with no more than rifles and a few dilapidated cars. It was humiliating in the extreme.

The King had taken to the airwaves ranting about how two of his battalions had been destroyed by troops well trained in hand to hand combat techniques too sophisticated to be mastered by itinerant Bedouins and calling it further evidence that it was the Algerians who were masterminding the attacks on his troops.

The King was furious, but not as furious as Dlimi, who considered this a personal slap in the face, a challenge that he would not leave unanswered. He called his second in command and barked an order.

And while the fighting was still raging in the north and the guerillas were still pursuing remnants of his troops in the desert near Amgala, Dlimi unleashed his revenge.

February 18 – 22, 1976. Oum Mudraiga.

It was a beautiful day in the middle of February. The sun's reflections off the hills encircling the makeshift tents glistened in rays of red, blue and gold, and somewhere way above the hills could be seen the outline of a solitary bird, making one last effort to catch a meal before the heat of the noon day sun made any such foray impossible.

But the two men in the grey camouflage suits had not noticed. "I am worried," one of them said in a low tone so as not to be overheard. "Mafoud told us last week that the Moroccans had bombed the camps at Tifariti, and that we might be next, and we asked the people to stay in the hills, but look at them." And with his last words he gestured to the scores of tents that littered the *wadi*.

"It is that fool Omar," the other said, shaking his head. "He has been going around telling the people they have nothing to be afraid of since the

Moroccans have broadcast a plea for them to return to their homes, and so far the planes that have passed by have ignored us."

"Still, I don't like it," the first one said, casting a wary eye towards the horizon.

Far above them, in the northernmost camp, Soukeina had been awake for hours. Although she had no watch, she could estimate from the shadows on the ground that it must be close to 11 in the morning – time to rouse the sleepyheads around her for morning tea. Not that she blamed them. The march had been grueling, particularly for the young ones and her 70 year old aunt. They had barely had time to recuperate from it. It was almost a shame to wake them.

Carrying a tin box she quietly stepped over the sleeping bodies in the tent to a corner where a small tin pot and a few small glasses were neatly stacked besides a gas burner. As she started the burner the fumes of gas began wafting through the tent, causing the bodies that were huddled together for warmth in the other corner to begin to stir. She began to pour the contents of the tin box into the pot and added some water from a small plastic container – very carefully, in order to protect every last precious drop, for no one could predict how long it would be before they could get any additional supplies. Then she added some sugar from a pouch she had hung from the center pole of the tent and reached into a plastic bag to extract two tiny lumps of crystallized powder. She smiled. This was the "secret ingredient" that made the Sahrawi tea special – she had no idea what its formal name was, but the Sahrawi called it *el alek*, roughly translated as "Arabic gum." By the time she added the last ingredient the pot had started to bubble, and after a minute or so, she started pouring its contents into one of the glasses, holding the pot high above the glass so that the liquid became darker and frothy in the glass. She repeated this several times until she was satisfied that the tea had just the right consistency.

By the time she had finished this ceremony, the rest of her group had awakened and were in the process of freshening up the clothes that they had been sleeping in. They had left so abruptly that they were able to bring only a few garments with them, so they had to make due with the items that were on their back for a few days.

"Hassan, go ask Mohammed Bachir and his family to join us for tea." Soukeina ordered. It was a custom among the Sahrawis to have tea together in a communal setting, and they were prone to do so several times a day.

Hassan, who had driven them from Dakhla, quickly complied, and within a few minutes Mohammed Bachir appeared at the opening of the tent. But instead of climbing over the portico into the tent, he hesitated, as if remembering something. Then he raised his head and peered at something in the sky. There was a faint humming noise in the background, as if someone were using an electric razor. Of course, no one could be using an electric razor in the camp. But the noise grew louder . . . .

Mohammed Bachir's figure became rigid. "It's a plane . . ." and before he could even finish the sentence they heard the explosion. It was the dispensary, and it had been bombed.

Soukeina stood up, uncertain of what to do. She ran to the opening of the tent to look out and saw smoke and flames rising above the makeshift tent that had served as a dispensary for those injured in the flight from the cities, and on the ground a sea of hot sand the color of the sky. She also heard the groans and screams.

By this time people had begun to stream out of their tents, running in all directions. Many were screaming and crying. Babies lay dead in their mothers' arms from the sheer heat of the explosion. Others crawled helplessly with limbs twisted and black. A few brave ones ran to the dispensary to offer help. It didn't help much, because before they could even reach the tent, the next bomb fell, this time blowing to bits a swath of tents close to where Soukeina stood. There was no time to grab any belongings. There was barely enough time to grab the children and help her aunt. She ran instinctively deeper into the hills. But her aunt could not walk as fast and lagged behind. Another bomb fell, this time landing so close to her that her ears ringed with its vibrations. She looked behind her to where her aunt had been. There was nothing but smoke and rubble and a large trench. She cried out, but there was no answer. She looked down to where tents had stood. There were no tents. Instead the camp was filled with potmarks and its sand seemed to glow. She told the people near her to run ahead, to go anywhere they could in the hills and to look for shelter. She walked back, looking through the smoke and ash for any sign of her aunt. There was none.

Suddenly there was a hand on her shoulder. A man was beckoning her to join the others who were heading towards the hills. She felt numb and somewhat nauseous. When she looked down she saw that her foot was bleeding. She managed to hobble along with the rest and after a few minutes the group reached an inclination in the hills where they stopped to rest. After an hour they could hear in the background the drone of another plane, and the blast of another bomb, and then another . . . She had no idea what they were bombing – surely nothing remained of the tent camp.

Finally, there was silence. Soukeina looked around her. Clinging to the rocks, as if they could provide some meager protection, were a dozen or so men, women and children. Some were bleeding. Others seemed numb and confused. The women were quietly trying to calm the children, whose tears seemed endless. Soukeina quickly approached a man whose leg was badly shattered and tore off a portion of her *mefhla* to create a makeshift bandage. He grabbed her hand and held it for a long while before slipping off. She didn't know where they were, or where any of the other refugees had gone, or how many of them remained. There was no food or water, or medicine to dress the wounds or to stifle the pain of the wounded. She did the best she could, tearing at her *mefhla* until her knees showed and her head was bare. To hell with modesty.

Finally, after what seemed an eternity one of the men who had been leading the caravan scrambled over the rocks to where they had positioned themselves.

"Listen, all of you, the bombings have stopped, but the plane may return at any time. We must move from this location quickly. Please follow me," he said. With that he grabbed the shoulder of one of the injured and helped him to his feet. Slowly, and with great pain, the rest of the injured tried to get to their feet. With the help of those who were not injured they formed a single line which slowly followed in the footsteps of the leader. After half an hour they reached a spot where a number of the refugees had been collected. Those who were badly injured lay on the ground on blankets, tended to by a few of the women. There was a truck. After a while there was another, and some medicine and bandages started to reach them.

Soukeina had had no training as a nurse, and the sight of all of the wounded and bleeding bodies around her sickened her to her stomach. She wanted to vomit, but there was no food inside her stomach. She hadn't eaten for nearly a day. A man beckoned her to where a man lay on the ground, a bloody bone protruding from what was left of his left leg. The man stared at her with eyes that were beyond pain. She had no more dress to use as a bandage, but the man who stood over her handed her something and quickly, almost in a daze, she began to unravel the tightly wound piece of cloth and wrap it around the man's leg, tight to keep the bone in place. Around her the people on the ground lay moaning, or praying, or just staring into the sky in silence. She counted twenty or more, and more were being placed on the ground as others, who had finally found peace, were removed.

Soukeina had been too busy tending to the wounded to ask questions, but now she was curious. What had happened to the camp? How many had survived? Where were they, and more importantly, where were they going? They had all assumed that Mudraiga would offer safety, would be so far from the towns of their country that the Moroccan army could not reach them. They had not counted on the airplanes, or on the desire of the Moroccans to annihilate the civilians who had streamed out of the cities rather than submit to Moroccan rule. She wondered what was happening to those left behind. Would she ever see her mother again? All they could do was wait – wait for help, wait for answers.

The second day after the attack the leader who had been barking orders was approached by another, older man. Together, they walked a few steps from where the group had gathered. Soukeina could see them talking excitedly, but could not make out any words.

The leader returned to the group. "Get you things together. We are going to move." And with that, the men who were still able to walk began to help the others to the trucks that had been parked a few yards away. The most seriously wounded were placed carefully into the vehicles. The others had to walk or remain hidden in the hills. No one had any idea where they were going, but they followed the leader, slowly and with great pain, as he led the group farther into the belly of the desert.

Soukeina, with great effort, managed to drag herself to the head of the convoy. "Do you know what happed to the rest of the people?" she asked, a quiver in her voice. The leader looked at her, then turned his gaze sharply away. "The Moroccans returned again this morning and tried to bomb the last camp, but their bombs struck the hills, and the people had already fled the hills. But they may return, that is why we are leaving," he said in a somber tone.

Soukeina and her group marched for what seemed an eternity. They eventually stopped to rest at a point where the hills gave way to a rocky, barren plateau. But not for long. Dusk had arrived, and the leader was shouting for them to continue. So they marched, and marched, until Soukeina's feet were bleeding from blisters and every movement was painful. They stopped only when the sun began to rise. They were now deeply into a barren plateau that offered no cover should they be attacked from the air. In order to camouflage their location they covered themselves with pieces of cloth cut from their tents. They hadn't eaten for over a day, and were exhausted with hunger. The leader began to distribute a few items of food. Soukeina remembered the story a Spanish missionary had told her about Jesus feeding a multitude with two loaves and two fish. She wished that Jesus were there. There was not enough food to go around, so the most seriously wounded were fed first. Soukeina had to wait. But there was a lot to do to keep her mind off food. She had to tend to the wounded. She had to help bury the dead.

The march continued for two more nights. For two more nights the tiny band marched across an open and hostile desert, under the constant threat of attack from the air. A number died along the way and were buried in unmarked graves in the desert. Families were decimated. Children were orphaned. No one knew what had happened to their parents.

The motley group, most on foot, the sick, the old, the wounded, huddled in the rear of the trucks or dragged on makeshift stretchers, slowly inched their way eastward at night through the desert *hammada* – that huge expanse of arid wasteland that stretched eastward for miles across the Sahara from the coastal regions of Western Sahara to the tiny settlement of Tindouf in Algeria, and for miles beyond. She had done her best to comfort the sick and wounded, but water was in low supply and medicine nonexistent, and the moans of the wounded and dying filled her head and caused a dull pain in her heart. All the resolve she possessed could not stifle the sounds or eliminate the stench of rotting flesh.

By day fall on the third day they were met by a couple of Land Rovers from the east, carrying some much needed food and water. A few miles farther they saw the outline of the outpost just over the Algerian border. There they would be safe from attacks from the air; there they would finally be able to rest.

Tindouf had been a major trading hub in the Sahara for centuries and had lodged a garrison of the infamous French Foreign legion in the days when France ruled the desert. Just like in the movies, it was in the middle of nowhere, with only barren land stretching as far as the eyes could see, and beyond. The few provisions that reached the outpost had to be airlifted from Algiers or trucked over 1000 miles through the desert. Water was scarce, and animals of all sorts found it difficult to survive the summers, where temperatures reached beyond 120 degrees Fahrenheit and the soles of rubber shoes would melt in the sand.

The little band marched a few miles from the outpost. There was nothing but rocky soil for miles around. The sun had risen an hour ago. Soon it would be too hot to work. It was time to pitch what remained of their tents and tend to the wounded. This would be their home -- for how long they had no idea.

Later they learned that Moroccan aircraft had strafed a column of refugees, numbering at least 10,000, at the largest oasis in the territory – Guelta Zemmour – a *wadi* which was surrounded by steep hills about 22 miles west of the Mauritanian border, and the only area in the territory still occupied by the guerillas. As in the case of Mudraiga, many of the refugees were able to escape through the *wadi*, but many others were killed or forced to hide for weeks in the hills without adequate food, water or shelter. It took over two months before all the refugees were evacuated from the hills of Mudraiga and Guelta. During that period, raids by Moroccan aircraft using napalm would continue to kill scores of refugees in those areas and isolated outposts throughout the region. Only Mahbes was spared.

Later that month – well after the Polisario had departed the area with much of their supplies -- Moroccan troops crept back into Amgala, but without the fanfare that had accompanied their initial onslaught. Indeed, the Minister of the Interior made sure that not a word would be spoken in the international press about the defeat of the Moroccan army in the second battle at Amgala, or about the bombing raids on civilians at Mudraiga, Guelta Zemmour and other spots across the territory -- and the hundreds of bones of old men, women, and children that lay, scattered across the sands, glistening in the sunlight.

February 25, 1976. Somewhere in the Desert.

If ever there was a man born to fulfill the role destiny had in store for him it was Mohamed Lamine Bouhali, the commander of the 2nd military region. Born to a family of nomads whose patriarch had stubbornly rejected the allure of the cities, he had spent his adolescent years in Smara, raised by his aunt, when by chance a young, bushy haired Sahrawi student from Tan Tan had traveled the countryside preaching his vision. For some strange reason he could not really understand he had found himself drawn to this stranger, and when he had asked him to join his movement he had followed him. He quickly mastered the art of guerilla warfare, for which he seemed to have a natural aptitude, and was entrusted with greater and greater responsibilities, directing a number of the attacks against Spanish garrisons in 1974 and 1975. By the outbreak of the war with Morocco and Mauritania he was one of El Ouali's most trusted lieutenants, directing the battle against Moroccan troops at Farsia in the first days of the war, shooting down a Moroccan jet and capturing a number of prisoners. Ouali had then entrusted him with the command of the guerilla forces in a swath of territory in the central region that included some of its most important settlements. A man who commanded the respect

105

of his troops, he was the consummate field marshal, never rushing headlong into battle like some military figures were wont to do. No, he would probe the enemy's weaknesses and only when he had mapped a strategy thoroughly in his mind would he strike, always in the midst of his troops. He was admired by men and women alike – although, perhaps, for different reasons. So, when the ladies of the camp learned that Sidimi would be spending countless days and nights in the company of the dashing commander, more than one of them felt a tinge of envy.

On Sidimi's part, if she ever thought of the commander as more than the brilliant leader of his troops, she never showed it. And as the weeks passed he, the man who led his men on the battlefield, and she, the women who healed their mangled bodies when they returned, grew to admire and respect each other.

On an evening in late February, a lone figure sat atop a dirt mound at the edge of the camp, her blanket wrapped tightly around her and her gaze fixed on the sky. Ahead of her was a vast emptiness. It was after midnight and all the creatures of the camp had retired, one by one, to a welcomed slumber. He had watched her from a distance, hesitant to break the silence that surrounded her like a comfortable cocoon.

As quietly as he could he came up beside her. Her gaze never shifted. For a moment there was silence.

She was the first to speak.

"I never stop marveling at the stars in the desert sky," she said in a quiet voice. "Nothing on this earth can compare with it."

He was startled. For what seemed like an eternity his life had centered around battles. For countless nights he had marched beneath these same stars, scarcely giving them a thought except as a way to calculate the time and direction for his troops. Now he was looking at them with different eyes. Yes, she was right, above him as far as he could see was a magnificent canopy of twinkling diamonds thrown nonchalantly on a carpet of the darkest black velvet. Somehow the clean clear air of the desert polished them to a perfection never reached in the towns and cities of the civilized world.

"When I was a child in El Ayoun I would often go to the roof of our house just as the sun was beginning to set and wait for the stars to begin to appear. My favorite was the star that first appeared over the horizon, a star so bright you could even see it before the sun had set. It seemed to be saying, "You can go now, sun, the stars are coming!" She smiled. "Of course, later I was told that it wasn't a star at all, just a lowly planet, like ours, condemned to forever circle the sun. Yet it shines brighter than any star and the ladies in the hospital told me that the Romans found it so beautiful that they named it after their goddess of love."

He turned his gaze from the stars to her face. She was still wearing men's trousers and her uncovered hair rested on her shoulders in soft, dark ringlets.

He wanted to ask her a thousand questions. But instead he merely muttered, "I never had a chance to thank you for the truck."

She smiled in that mischievous manner that ladies sometimes use when they know full well what is really on a man's mind.

"I suppose you are curious to know why I learned to drive," she interjected matter-of-factly. "Well, that is simple. I needed to use a car in El Ayoun to get to the hospital, and I couldn't be bothered to wait for someone to drive me. And a truck is just an oversized car." She made it sound so simple, as if anyone would be able to extract a truck from a sandpit in a war zone.

He found himself stifling a smile despite himself. He was used to high spirited independence in Sahrawi women, but Sidimi was in a class by herself. He wondered what else she knew how to do. Launch anti-aircraft missiles?

"And how did you learn about medicine?" he asked. "I didn't think the Spanish would allow a Sahrawi to get a medical education . . . especially a woman!"

Sidimi smiled again. "My father worked for the Spanish . . . as a construction worker, and one day he was killed when a building collapsed on him. The Spanish decided to compensate our family by giving me a job. So I began working at the hospital . . . and one thing led to another. Of course, they wouldn't let me study medicine formally . . . or study to become a doctor . . . but I watched . . . and I learn fast. . . and I think I would be able to perform most operations as well as any doctor." Then she turned again to look at the stars. "I guess we will find out fairly soon," she murmured in a low voice.

He decided to change the subject. "Did any of your family besides your brother come with you from El Ayoun?" he asked.

A cloud seemed to pass over her face at his question, and he wondered if he had raised a painful subject.

"My cousin came with me," she replied, quietly. "He has joined the troops in the northern region."

"And your husband?" he asked in a tone that tried to be nonchalant.

She looked at him and laughed. "I have no husband. Not now, that is. I was married but when I decided to join the Polisario it became difficult for him. So, we decided to divorce."

He looked at her intently. "Do you have any regrets?"

She sighed. "No. I have no regrets. He was a good man, a kind man, but he wasn't willing to fight for what is right – our liberty, our land. I could not live without fighting."

He looked at her a long while without saying a word, and for a moment she returned his gaze, but then she abruptly rose to her feet. "Its getting late. I think I will try to get some sleep," she said, and started walking slowly back to the dark hollows where the sleeping soldiers lay.

He was left in the dark, with just the stars as his companions. Tomorrow he would meet with Ouali to discuss troop movements. But this evening he had other matters on his mind. For several long minutes he sat, beneath the stars, in total silence. Then he looked into the distance to where Sidimi had disappeared, smiled, and slowly made his way back to the camp.

February 25, 1976. El Ayoun.

Meanwhile, farther to the west a figure in the darkness groped its way cautiously on the rocky terrain. He had spent his entire life in the vicinity of this town and considered himself lucky that he was familiar with the crevices and bits of vegetation he was now crossing, for there were no lights to guide him. Only the stars. When he came to the barbed wire barrier that stood between him and the city outskirts he withdrew a long blade from under his belt and slowly, ever so silently, began sawing through. Once he had passed through he skirted the edge on the lookout for flicks of light that would indicate the presence of a sentry. When he was satisfied that there were no sentries present he darted quickly towards the lights of the city. But he was not yet free – a Land Rover filled with soldiers on patrol was passing dangerously close, blocking his way. He was forced to wait for what seemed to be hours as they stopped someone. He could hear someone arguing in a loud voice, demanding to see identification, and someone else complaining and fumbling with something in his robe. This went on for some minutes before the pedestrian was allowed to continue his journey. He knew he couldn't afford to be stopped – it would mean prison for sure, and probably torture as well.

As he proceeded down the dirt alleyway his heart began once again to beat louder. He did not know what to expect. For weeks now there had been no real communication with those who remained behind, and there had been stories – horrific stories of imprisonment, torture, or worse for the families of suspected Polisario guerillas.

He knocked at the wooden door of a small, stucco house and waited.

Inside an elderly man huddled with his wife and pregnant daughter, fear etched across their faces. The Moroccans would often come without warning, often in the middle of the night. The next morning their neighbors would come to find their house empty. Whole families would disappear overnight, without a trace, without any explanation.

He went to the door and opened it cautiously. When he saw who stood before him, he stifled a cry and put his arms around him. The young man quickly entered the room and closed the door behind him. By this time the woman and her daughter had come to the door to greet him, with muffled sobs.

The old man could barely speak. "How did you get through, there are armed guards everywhere!" he finally blurted.

"I sneaked through the lines – they do not know the desert the way we do. I had to come. I had to see if you were safe. We have been getting reports . . ." His voice trailed off.

"Yes," the old man said, shaking his head, "Just yesterday I went to give some goat meat to the Ould Salek family, and they were gone – simply disappeared, with no one knowing where they went. The Moroccans won't give us any answers if we ask."

Salek's face turned white. "And what of the others . . ." he started, and proceeded to name the others in the troop with families in the capital, all eager to learn news of their loved ones. What he heard made his heart heavy.

"And the Spanish?" he asked somewhat hesitantly. The old man smiled. "She is still here. Her father decided to stay until the rest of the civilians were safely evacuated. The soldiers left long ago." Then he added, somewhat nonchalantly, "But I think they are preparing to leave . . . perhaps tomorrow."

Salek grabbed him lightly by the shoulders, looking intently into his eyes. "You must leave at once, it is not safe for you here."

The old man looked at the young man with eyes that had seen too much. "I cannot leave your sister in her condition," he finally said, with a gesture towards the young woman who by this time had reclaimed her chair. She was nearly eight months pregnant. "He is right, father," she said softly, "You should go. I can take care of myself here. There are others who can help me." But her eyes were downcast when she spoke.

The mother, who had been quiet during this exchange, quickly spoke up. "You must go, my son, but we must remain here with Layla."

The young man started to protest, but he knew it was no use. They were right. Layla would never be able to endure the arduous trek through the desert on foot, avoiding the security guards at every turn.

He turned to look at them, holding back the tears that were forcing their way down his cheek. He hugged each one of them in turn, whispering a farewell. At the door he turned to look at them once again, and then he was gone, as quickly as he came, into the cold clear darkness of night.

February 25, 1976. Farewell.

It was the evening of February 25 and Elena stared glumly at the sky. The stars sparkled as usual. But tonight she was immune to their charm. She stood on the deck of a ship that would soon take her far from the place she had grown to love. As she stood there her thoughts wandered back to the many nights she had stood at her bedroom window marveling at the tapestry that filled the night air in the desert, and wondered whether she would ever see such a magnificent display again. Tomorrow at dawn she and her family would depart for Spain. Later that day the handful of Spanish administrators who had remained would officially turn over administration of the territory to the Moroccans. The governor and viceroy had already left, refusing to witness the last day of Spanish rule. The family's trunks had already been sent ahead, and she had only a couple of suitcases to accompany her in exile – for that was exactly how she considered it. She walked desolately back to her bunk and climbed in, but for all her trying she could not fall asleep. The tears that rolled down her cheek didn't help.

The following morning, as the ship was preparing to hoist anchor, she heard a knock at her door, and opened it to find one of the crew standing before her, something large in his arms.

"Ma'am," he started to say, holding out the package for her, "A man gave me this to give to you. He said it was important. And he gave me this note." The young man handed her a folded piece of paper. When she read it, she emitted a short cry, and raced to the front of the boat. The ship had just begun to leave the harbor, and on the shore scores of men and women had gathered to wave goodbye. She scanned the faces intently, but could not find the one she was searching for. Desolately, she returned to her room, the folded piece of paper clutched in her hand. She read the note once again. "I will not be able to use this where I am going. Take care of it for me until we meet again – when the Sahara is free!" She unwrapped the package carefully, and smiled. In her arms was Esmeralda.

And in the shadows of the port a young man with piercing black eyes stood for a long time staring at the ship as it slowly disappeared over the horizon.

February 27, 1976. The Sahrawi Arab Democratic Republic.

Nothing, not even the bombing raids unleashed by Dlimi, could dampen the spirit of the refugees after their victory at Amgala. Most of the vehicles and equipment that the guerillas seized at Amgala were distributed among the various military units. But some of the captured equipment was sent to Tindouf where it went on display for the people to see. There talk of the battle filled every tent, and the hoards of bedraggled and poorly fed old men, women and children, bereft of possessions, and far from home, felt a sense of pride and began to believe that they were capable of defeating the invaders.

And gradually an impressive military apparatus began to emerge. When the Polisario withdrew from Amgala to the hills northeast of the outpost they began to regroup and re-form their military units with the addition of nearly a thousand soldiers from the Tropas Nomadas. None of the new recruits was able to bring any arms or vehicles with him – for that they would have to wait for supplies from Libya and Algeria – but while waiting they established a training center where they trained all the civilians in military techniques.

From the battle of Amgala onward the military commanders adopted a strategy of procuring arms from the enemy rather than relying solely on arms given to them by friendly states. Attacks on Moroccan and Mauritanian convoys and shipments of military materials increased sharply, and after each successful battle caravans of looted materials were whisked away to desert hideouts.

On February 26, in a poorly attended ceremony in front of the Parador, a group of glum looking Spanish officials symbolically handed over the territory of Spanish Sahara to what was officially declared a "tripartite" administration of Morocco, Mauritania and the Sahrawi Djemma -- although the Djemma had disbanded in protest and most of its members had joined the Polisario. No legitimate Sahrawi representatives were present.

The day after the transfer, at a night time ceremony near Bir Lehlou, attended by thousands of Sahrawi guerillas and refugees as well as 30 foreign journalists, M'hammed Ould Ziou, the President of the Provisional Saharawi National Council, stood to survey the crowd. Besides the group in the tent there were a number of men and women sitting on blankets outside, watching intently the events that were unfolding.

"The Spanish have withdrawn their administration from the territory of Spanish Sahara and have left. They have declared that they have ceded the territory to Morocco and Mauritania. But it is not Spain's to cede, it is not their territory, it is ours." The last words were greeted by a wave of shouts.

"This territory is the land of our fathers, and their fathers before them. It belongs to us, the people of the Sahara. We claim it in the name of the people!" Again, the crowd shouted in approval. "The Sahrawi people have no alternative but to struggle until wresting independence, their wealth and their full sovereignty over their land."

"We hereby declare the birth of a free, independent, sovereign state, ruled by an Arab, national, democratic system of unionist, progressive orientation and of Moslem religion, named the Saharawi Arab Democratic Republic, as the one and only government of what was once called Spanish Sahara!" With those last words the new state's flag was then hoisted on a makeshift pole and the crowd got to their feet. The shouting lasted for minutes.

When the shouting died down, El Ouali stood to address the audience. "Ours will not be a government of kings. Ours will not be a government of dictators. Ours will be a government dedicated to the principle of democracy, equality and the rights of man. We are not only fighting for liberation, we are fighting for a government that reflects the will of the masses. We reject the tribal jealousies that have divided us in the past, and all forms of discrimination and exploitation." Looking straight at the women who crowded the entrance, he added, "We will struggle to reestablish the political and social rights of women and to open up all possibilities for them."

Then, with a glance at the elderly men who were huddled in a corner of the tent, he added, "We will strive to achieve a fair distribution of resources, to overcome the differences in economic opportunity between the countryside and the towns. We will see to it that there is adequate housing and health care for everyone and ensure that everyone gets an education, regardless of social standing or wealth." At the last words the women in the group in particular shouted in approval.

The speeches lasted fewer than fifteen minutes, but the applause and shouts that followed it echoed in the desert for nearly an hour, as one by one the members who were present pledged their allegiance to the newly formed state.

In the back of the crowd two reporters quietly surveyed the scene. "Do you think they have a chance?" one of them said quietly. "Dunno," the other responded in a whisper, "I've heard it all before – all this revolutionary stuff – and it is one thing to say it and another to put it into practice. But I would like to think that the good guys can win every once in a while."

"You're a dreamer," said the other one, shaking his head. "They are just a small band of youngsters not even old enough to remember the Second World War. And they want to take on the big powers?"

"Well, we did it once, didn't we?"

The other laughed. "Well I guess we did. We didn't want to be ruled by a king either. Well, all I can say is that I wish them luck – they will need it!"

111

And with those parting words they entered the trucks that would take them to Algiers and the planes that would ferry them across the ocean.

And five hundred miles away, scarcely aware of what was transpiring to the east, the Moroccan flag was raised over the roof of the Parador in El Ayoun – henceforth renamed "Laayoune" – removing the last vestiges of Spanish presence in the newly re-christened Western Sahara.

March 1, 1976. Captives.

By the end of February Hamed was able to use the fingers of his right hand and the wound in his shoulder had healed enough that he would soon be leaving to join his comrades. Miriam and her family had moved north towards the largest guelta in the region – Guelta Zemmour. They had reached a spot only a mile or two away from the guelta when they heard the sound of explosions, and later learned of the bombing that had taken place there. When they reached the guelta they saw the remains of the tents, utensils, and vehicles that had once been part of a huge encampment, and the bones of camels, sheep and goats that lay scattered on the ground. They decided to camp away from the guelta, far away from any known outpost, where they might find some relative safety.

One day, when Hamed was out rounding up the camels, he returned to find a vehicle parked near the tent. As he entered the tent the worried faces of Miriam and Salama turned in his direction. Miriam at once went to greet him and told the two men in uniform who were squatting near her father that he was her brother, Hamed.

The two men paid little attention to her at first; they were busy enjoying the morsels of meat and rice that had been placed before them. But when they had finished their meal one of them, who was obviously the senior in rank, gave him a closer look.

"How old are you, Hamed?" he asked inquisitively.

Hamed just stared at the man. "18," Miriam said quickly.

The man said nothing, but Hamed could see what he was thinking. He was wondering why he was not with the guerillas.

The soldier had indeed found it strange to have found Hamed there. His unit had swept the area for a week now, rounding up any stray Sahrawi they could find for encampment in the cities, and so far all they had found were women, children and old men.

"Let me see your papers," the man growled.

"Papers?" Miriam repeated.

"Yes, the identification papers given to him by the Spanish!" the man exclaimed, turning to face her.

"He doesn't have any identification papers," Miriam quickly interjected. "He was too young at the time."

The man stared at Hamed, who was standing motionless a few feet away. "Can't he speak for himself?" he asked, giving him a closer look.

"He's a bit slow, that's all. Ever since the accident with the camel," she said, drawing next to Hamed and putting her arms around him as if to comfort a child.

The man sneered. A Sahrawi imbecile. That's all we need, he thought to himself. But he didn't question him further. All he said was that they should take down their tent and be prepared to move.

At his order Miriam and her father began the job of rolling up the rugs and dismantling the tent. When Hamed failed to help Miriam lift one of the posts, the soldier shouted at him "Hey, you, imbecile! Are you going to let your father and sister do all the heavy work?" Miriam started to protest, but the soldier told her to be quiet, that this was not women's work, and ordered him to help lift the posts of the tent, "Like a man!" Hamed moved to the far corner and slowly lifted one of the posts that held the tent in place. But when he went to lift the second a small trickle of blood seeped through his jacket at his shoulder. He turned away, trying to hide the blood from the soldier's eyes. But it was too late. The soldier ordered him to stop and remove his shirt. When he failed to comply the soldier grabbed his jacket and pushed it down below his shoulder.

"How did you get this?" he asked, pointing to the wound.

Miriam spoke up. "A camel kicked him," she said quickly.

The soldier shot her an angry glance. "A camel with a rifle?" he said, sarcastically. "This is a bullet wound!" Then he moved closer, and, within inches of Hamed's ear, yelled "Where did you get this?"

Hamed remained silent. When he failed to respond the soldier sneered, "Never mind, there will be time for this later," and barked an order to his companion. Before long Miriam, Salama and Hamed were herded into the back of the Land Rover, their possessions abandoned, their animals left to wander the desert, and their destination unknown.

April 13, 1976. In the North.

Farther to the north and east, the skirmishes between Abdelaziz' forces and the Moroccans had continued unabated for months, like some enormous cat and mouse game. The guerilla units along the Saguia el Hamra corridor and in Moroccan territory were posing a constant threat to Moroccan caravans carrying supplies – not to mention their troops -- and had forced Dlimi to keep many of his forces in southern Morocco. Dlimi had developed an almost fanatical desire to see these bands of guerillas eliminated and had used every conceivable means to accomplish this. The battles near Toucat in the early days of January had lasted more than 11 days. Moroccan troops in the hills north of the *wadi* had constantly tried to invade it, carpeting the area with cannon fire and bursts of artillery, but each time were repelled by the guerillas' land mines and snipers. Finally, they had been forced to retreat to Housa. When Dlimi had begun his "fateh" campaign he had sent forces south from Zag to Mahbes, hoping to coax the Polisario leader into a confrontation. However, Abdelaziz had refused to take the bait, instead taking his troops northwest to

113

Lemseid and Goulimine in his own "fateh" campaign, battling the Moroccans at Abatih, Zalya, Ghera Lahmar, Ghreizima, Lagtaifa, and as far north as Tan Tan.

By the beginning of March, Abdelaziz had returned to Toucat, and Dlimi, eager for another chance to confront his troops, had quickly sent reinforcements to his battalion at Farsia. On March 18 this battalion attempted a two pronged assault – with one column approaching the guerilla hideout from the hills north of the *wadi*, while a second approached it from the hills south of Housa. But Abdelaziz had been waiting for them, and after two days of battle, the Moroccans had been driven back to Farsia.

It was now the middle of April -- nearly a month after that last confrontation -- and Abdelaziz had been enjoying a brief respite from the battlefield when a messenger once again interrupted his tranquility.

"Moroccan troops have left Farsia heading west through the hills north of the *wadi*," was the message.

"How many?" he asked.

"It looks like most of the troops stationed there."

Abdelaziz stopped for a moment to think. Then he ordered his men to break camp. They were going on a journey.

To the northeast of their camp a column of Moroccans wound their way silently westward through the hilly terrain. Their planes had pinpointed the guerilla camp and, at the pace they were going, they should reach a point slightly north of their camp in a few hours. The commander's hands twitched nervously and he continuously darted his eyes left and right, scouring the hillside and the gully below for any sign of snipers. By three o'clock in the afternoon they had reached their destination, so far without incident. The commander chose two soldiers and they quietly and cautiously began the descent into the dry river bed. Within 30 minutes they returned. They had found signs of a camp, but it was deserted. The commander followed them. Within a few minutes he saw a clearing, the burnt out ashes of a fire and marks in the sand where blankets had been laid. He also saw footprints leading farther into the *wadi* and up the embankments. He quickly dispatched a handful of men to scout the area to the south. Within an hour the men returned – no sign that guerilla units had passed that way. The commander was perplexed. Where had they gone?

While he was pondering his next move a messenger arrived, out of breath, from the troops he had left behind in Farsia. Guerillas had stormed the barracks and rampaged the town. Their troops had fled into the hills. He must return at once!

It was dark by the time he reached what was left of his compound in Farsia. Most of it was destroyed. Tanks lay in burnt out hulks. Vehicles were missing. Ammunition gone. Abdelaziz and his men had occupied the town for hours, and then had vanished as quickly as they had come.

Once again the mouse had escaped the trap, and back in Agadir Dlimi was left to contemplate another humiliating riposte.

Shortly after she had arrived at the camp Soukeina surveyed what was around her. Besides her little group, others had managed to make their way to the camp. She counted nearly a thousand people, half of whom were injured, most of whom were seriously dehydrated. There were a handful of cars, a number of goats and a few dozen camels.

By the time the sun had reached its zenith, four large new tents had been erected, providing shade for the wounded in her group and many of the children. The others squatted on blankets on the ground, covering their bodies to shield the rays. They were lucky. It was winter. During their march it had often been so cold at night that they had to huddle together for warmth, and several of the injured and elderly died from simple exposure. But now the winter temperatures worked in their favor, making it possible to work during the daylight hours, pitching tents, tending to the animals, preparing food.

In the camp the 20 or so men assigned to help resettle the arriving refugees set about distributing the little water and food rations they had been able to coax from the Algerian government. They faced enormous logistical problems. Very few of the refugees had been able to bring any livestock with them and there was sparse land in which to pasture animals. Firewood had to be fetched from about two hundred miles away, and canvas tents had to be obtained for most of the families since few had been able to bring the traditional *khaimat* with them.

The water was the main problem – there was a natural spring near the headquarters, the only one for miles, but from there all potable water had to be carried by truck in cisterns to the various camps. As soon as they arrived the women sprang into action, forming groups called "Popular Committees", one assigned to erecting tents, others to cooking and distributing food, still others to caring for the sick and wounded. Soukeina and the other women took turns disinfecting wounds and tying bandages, working from the first light of dawn until well into the night.

Inside the tents the wounded lay on row after row of makeshift stretchers. Some were white with pain from wounds infected and swollen. There was no medicine to relieve their agony. As the days progressed, and other stragglers began to arrive, their numbers increased until the tents were filled to capacity and the less serious wounded were placed outside on stretchers with only strips of canvas to protect them from the sun and wind. Within a few days medicine began to trickle into the camp in boxes marked "Red Crescent." She was glad, especially for the morphine.

After a week or so large green tents began to be distributed and were quickly converted into makeshift hospital wards. Finally there was some protection for the wounded from the glare of the sun, the fierce *hammada* wind, and the bitter cold of the winter nights. Any tents that remained sheltered dozens of refugees.

At first the survivors of Mudraiga and Amgala formed the core of the refugee camp. But stragglers continued to arrive on a daily basis, escaping on foot or through whatever means they could from the advancing Moroccan armies. Some from Smara; others, like Soukeina, from as far away as Dakhla.

Except for the few men who drove lorries filled with medicine, food, water and other supplies to the camp on a weekly basis, and the sick, the wounded or the elderly, there were few men in the camp, and most of the management of the camp rested in the hands of the women.

By the time the Moroccan flag was being hoisted in Laayoune, the influx of casualties from the war and the Moroccan bombing of fleeing refugees caused the population to increase twofold. By the end of the first four months of 1976 this number had again doubled. There were so many of them that they were divided into several separate "camps" each one named after the town in Western Sahara where they were from.

A grass roots government called the Base Congress had been formed, with women at the helm. The Base Congress had organized the women into committees in charge of food distribution, health, sanitation and all the other tasks that would permit the camps to run as efficiently as possible. For a month now members of the Congress had sent delegates to officials of the Algerian Red Crescent and other relief organizations to beg for as much aid as they would be willing to give. They had managed to obtain a trickle of supplies – but it was never enough – and the first few months of the camps saw widespread outbreaks of tuberculosis, bronchitis, and dysentery that felled men and women, young and old alike.

And these scourges had been followed by one that was even worse.

It was a Friday, the day the women in the camp had set aside for a communal gathering to cook whatever meager food was available and share it among the women and children – Soukeina remembered it well. When she looked around her, she had noticed that several of the women were absent. Taking care of sick children she had been told. She had not been worried – the children in the camps were frequently victims of colds and flus, especially in the cold winter months. But after the meal she had decided to visit her friends and bring them some of the food that had been prepared.

When she entered one of their tents she saw a woman bent over a small boy who lay quietly on a rug, rubbing him gently with a wet cloth. She started to approach but stopped suddenly, the canvas cloth filled with food dropping from her hands. Red blotches covered the boy's face and chest. Measles!

The epidemic had spread like wildfire through the close quarters of the camps. Within days children began dying in the dozens and an urgent plea had been sent to the Red Crescent for aid. It took another couple of weeks before a shipment of vaccine arrived. By that time nearly a hundred people – mostly children, but some of the elderly as well – had died of the disease. Within the next few days scores of children had received the vaccine. But the vaccine had to be refrigerated, and there was no refrigeration in the camps, so after the first week the vaccine had become useless. For three months the scourge plagued the camps. When it was over more than 500 children had perished.

Soukeina's job had been to count the dead, help to bury their little bodies, and give nourishment to those who survived. A grisly task, and one that had filled her nights with anger and despair.

So, she had spent her remaining hours on the one project that could relieve her pain. For years Sahrawi women had stood and watched silently while the Spanish invaders had held all important positions in their land, relegating all Sahrawis to second class citizens. Education had been out of their reach. The Spanish had begun, hesitantly, to offer education to the boys, and a few of the boys who had migrated with their parents to Tan Tan and other towns in Morocco in the mid 1960s had been lucky enough to get at least a primary education. A handful of them – such as El Ouali -- had even been able to attend Moroccan universities. But these opportunities were reserved for the men. The women – with such notable exceptions as Sidimi -- remained illiterate, without even a rudimentary education.

So it was with great joy and determination that Soukeina had embarked upon her project when she reached the camps.

It was now three months after she had arrived and as she walked through the tents to a clearing at the far side of the camp, the somber veil of hardship seemed to have lifted. There a small group of women, ranging in age between 18 and 40, with their children at their side, sat squatting in the sand. Soukeina advanced and joined them. Then she smoothed the soil before her and, with the tip of a metal spoon, wrote a character in the sand. "This is the letter 'a.'"

April 19, 1976. Disappeared.

The refugees had managed to carve an existence out of the desert in Algeria, but for the people left behind in Western Sahara life became filled with terror. Occupying forces encircled towns with barbed wire and eliminated all movement beyond their perimeters for the majority of those who had not managed to escape. The civilians were penned in like animals. Then the brutality began.

In the days following his son's escape the old man sank into an ever deepening sense of despair, only occasionally relieved by the birth of his first grandchild.

Most of his friends and neighbors were gone, and those who remained lived in constant fear. Rumors circulated that Moroccan soldiers had butchered hundreds and perhaps thousands of Sahrawis, including children and old people, who refused to publicly acknowledge the King of Morocco. He had seen women whose faces were battered, and he had heard rumors that a Moroccan commander, angry at the death of one of his comrades at the battle of Farsia, had thrown a group of Sahrawi prisoners from his helicopter. He had even been told that entire families had been buried alive in the desert.

But Morocco's favorite tactic was simply to make dissidents "disappear." Relatives of known Polisario leaders, as well as anyone suspected of being a sympathizer, would simply disappear, never to be seen again. Their neighbors would go to visit them and find their houses empty, their possessions still in place, their food still on the table, rotting. No note left behind. Nothing. If they were lucky they would simply be killed. If not they might be placed in one of the secret detention facilities, Kalaat Magauna or Derb Moulay Cherif, that were rumored to exist at Agdz and Ouarzate in Morocco, or the "black prison" of Laayoune. He, like all other Sahrawis, lived in constant fear of a knock on the door.

On the evening of April 19, 1976 he had just sat down to dinner with his wife, his daughter and her baby when he heard such a knock.

The following morning, one of the old man's cousins came to give him some fresh camel milk for the baby. The door was ajar, and when he entered the room he saw plates on the table encircling a bowl of cold stew and bread. He looked around but the house was empty. He would never see them again.

April 20, 1976. The Black Dungeon.

After an hour in the Land Rover, Hamed, Miriam and Salama were crowded with a number of other Sahrawis in a pen, where they spent the night. At dawn they were taken in truckloads northward, towards Laayoune. There they were separated into groups. The women and children were taken in one group, the old men in another. But they had a special welcoming for Hamed and the few Sahrawi militants they had been able to capture.

Hamed soon found himself dumped with a number of other prisoners into the basement of a large stone edifice somewhere in the heart of Laayoune the prisoners called "the black dungeon." There they squatted for hours in the semi darkness, barely able to move. At intervals one or two of them would be taken by guards to nearby rooms, and then the screaming would begin. When they would return, hours later, their bodies would be bruised and bleeding, and they would often be unconscious.

They could never be sure what to expect. The Moroccans liked to be adventurous and somewhat experimental in their investigative techniques, at times merely beating inmates with stones, whips, chains and metal rods until their flesh was covered in blood, at other times holding their heads under water until they nearly passed out or partially asphyxiating them by stuffing rags soaked in bleach into their mouths. At other times they took their amusement by stripping them naked and suspending them by their hands so that only their toes touched the ground, causing severe swelling of the extremities, beating them as if they were a piñata.

After two days of suspense the soldier came for him. He was led to a small, dimly lit room. Two men in uniform, one carrying a whip, sat on chairs. He was forced to stand. One by one they asked him questions. "Who were your comrades?" "Where are they hiding?" "Who gives you instructions?" He pulled himself up as erect as he could and said nothing. After a few minutes one of them, a small, balding man whose breath reeked of stale cigarettes, approached him, a lit cigarette dangling from his fingers. He gave a command

and the soldier pinned Hamed to the wall. The man then tore open his shirt. "What is this?" he asked, noticing the wound on his shoulder where the bullet had been removed. Hamed did not answer. After a minute, the man smiled, took his lit cigarette, and forced it into the wound. Hamed cried out in pain but said nothing. The man asked him again his questions, and when Hamed refused to answer he dug his cigarette into Hamed's arm until the flesh turned black. He did this again and again until he became tired of questioning him and returned to his seat. Then the man with the whip left his chair and stood behind Hamed. Soon a sharp pain cursed through his body and streaks of blood trickled down his back. Then another, and another. The man in the chair repeated the questions. Silence. Then another sharp pain.

It could have been an hour, it could have been two hours, it could have been twenty minutes. The pain continued until he lost all sense of time. Then nothing.

When he finally regained consciousness he was back in his cell, lying on his stomach on the concrete floor. He could feel the breath of someone behind him and turned his head. A tall man in his early 40s was bending over him. He was gently washing his wounds with a few drops of water he held in a plastic cup. Hamed tried to sit up.

"Relax," said the man, gently pushing him again to the ground. Hamed was too weak to resist. The man continued washing the wounds for another minute. Then he took off his shirt and covered Hamed's bleeding back as best he could.

When he saw the burnt flesh on Hamed's arm, the older man shook his head. "That devil of a prison warden loves to torture his prisoners like this. Most of us here have souvenirs of our 'talks.'" Hamed, from where he lay, could see the round brown marks that covered the older man's arm. "We call him 'the Hyena.'"

"Try to sleep," he said gently, "It will lessen the pain."

"Who are you?" Hamed asked. "Mouloud," he replied, seconds before Hamed fell into a deep sleep.

It took days for the wounds to finally heal. In the filth and excrement that covered the floors of their cramped compartment disease rapidly took hold. Infections became rampant, and since they were given no medicine to stop their spread, limbs began to rot and flesh began to crawl with maggots. Septicemia would claim a number of lives, and viruses would claim others. Each day the newly dead would be extracted from the herd and dumped into trucks to be carted to unmarked mass graves.

This went on for days and days – too many to count – and in the semi darkness where time stood still, one could not know how many days had passed. Only the length of their beards gave some indication of time.

Hamed and Mouloud quickly become friends. Mouloud had been a storekeeper. He had tried to escape with his family from Smara and had managed to get some of them out of the city. But when he returned for the others he had been arrested and carted off to this jail with others who had tried to escape. Women and children had been arrested as well. He had no idea where they were being held, and shuttered to think of the fate that had awaited them.

New prisoners were dumped into their cell each day. Newcomers were a cause for celebration, for it was only through them that they had any news of the outside world.

He had learned from such newcomers that several months had passed since his capture, and that in February there had been several great battles at Amgala, where Polisario forces had decimated an entire division of the Moroccan army. He learned of the bombing of refugees at Mudraiga, and the resettling of thousands of refugees across the Algerian border in Tindouf. But he didn't get the information he most wanted – information about the fate of Miriam and her father. Were they imprisoned as well? Were they still alive? And what about his sister, Soukeina, and his aunt? Had they been some of the victims at Mudraiga? He grilled each new inmate for an answer, but none came.

As the days and weeks passed, he became numb to the pain and could block out the screams. Only the hope of seeing his family and Miriam and her father again kept him alive.

April 30, 1976. The Ghazzi.

By mid-April the Polisario forces had battled Moroccan troops for nearly half a year. But their strategy had never been to hold onto territory. So, Dlimi had gradually been able to secure a hold over Farsia, Mahbes, Jdiriya, Housa, Amgala and the other small outposts in the territory. Guelta Zemmour, the largest and most strategic oasis in the territory, was the last to fall, on April 19 after a series of bombing raids. By that time Morocco and Mauritania had also successfully expelled the majority of the Sahrawis from their homeland.

However, by September of that year there were few attempts by the Moroccans to engage the Polisario in large scale "mopping up" endeavors. Rather, besides attempting a number of small scale forays into guerilla held territory, the Moroccans' strategy shifted to an essentially defensive war.

And the conquerors violated one of the basic rules of army combat summarized by Frederick the Great: "He who attempts to defend too much defends nothing." In an attempt to control every inch of the Sahara, Moroccan forces were spread thinly in isolated units throughout the region. Mauritanian troops, much fewer in number and with a much larger border and desert regions to patrol, were spread even thinner.

The vast emptiness beyond these towns and outposts, however, was the domain of the guerillas – and the *lelamaia*.

Nestled within the *wadis* of the Saguia el-Hamra, the crevices of the Zemmour massif, the Ouarkziz escarpment, and the sand dunes of Mauritania, a network of small, scattered guerilla bases, usually numbering no more than a couple hundred men, had blossomed. From these bases Polisario fighters would conduct daily ghazzi styled rapid assaults (which they called *lelamaia,* the Arabic word for "blind") using a weapon they had first unveiled at Amgala – gasoline propelled Land Rovers topped with machine guns -- mostly captured from the enemy. The tops of their vehicles would be discarded to make them closer to the ground, and headlights and all glass would be removed to prevent reflection from the sun. During the nights they would crawl through the desert silently in total darkness, navigating by instinct through the terrain, and in daylight they would propel through the desert at top speed covering huge distances. At the sound of a plane they would split up, hiding among the nooks and crannies of the desert, or under an accommodating acacia tree. They would pounce upon unsuspecting targets and, after decimating the enemy forces and looting their equipment, they would evaporate into the desert sands.

During this period they targeted a number of the garrisons and Moroccan troops. On April 26, for instance, Bouhali staged a daring raid on two Moroccan garrisons and their headquarters based near Laayoune, killing or injuring over 300 Moroccans, and raids by his guerillas on any Moroccan troops attempting to traverse the desert were common. In the north Abdelaziz and his men continued to harass troops in both Western Sahara and southern Morocco, particularly targeting the vulnerable locations in southern Morocco where large numbers of Sahrawis lived. And in the south, guerillas from the third military region frequently attacked the smaller army outposts along the Zouerate – Nouadhibou corridor.

But the guerillas didn't have to target military installations or troops to be effective. What was it that Napoleon was rumored to have said? That an army marches on its stomach? Perhaps the most effective raids were not the ones designed to kill the enemy in battle, but those calculated to starve them into submission.

During the first year of the war the guerillas concentrated most of their efforts on attacking the caravans that carried food and ammunition to the Moroccan and Mauritanian troops, confiscating their cargo, and cutting the lines of communication between their headquarters and their rear bases. Specialized units were created just for this task . . . and they did their job well. Moroccan convoys were frequently attacked en route to isolated garrisons in the interior, or along the main supply route to Laayoune from the north. A favorite target was the bridge over the Oued Chebeika, between Tan Tan and Tarfaya, and convoys were sometimes reaching Laayoune weeks late. Eventually supplies had to be airlifted to the capital or shipped by boat. In order to defend Bir Moghrein, Ould Daddah had to air lift a battalion of troops with tanks and artillery in C-130 transport planes, and supply it from the air.

Through all these battles Sidimi had doggedly followed the troops. For her the year 1976 was the year in which her feet knew no rest.

By the end of April the equipment they had pilfered from the Moroccan and Mauritanian troops combined with the arms and equipment that had

121

tricked in from Libya and Algeria had made their troops better equipped. They travelled with a few Land Rovers and trucks, with machine guns, bazookas and a few surface to air missiles loaded into the backs, but most of the soldiers still marched on foot. Initially Bouhali had offered to let her ride in one of the few available Land Rovers, but at times she marched with the men, and she marched, and marched, and marched, until the soles of her shoes were bare and she could feel the sharp sting of pebbles attack her feet as she walked.

Bouhali's troops usually moved during the day, approaching as near to the enemy as possible without being detected. Then his troops would race through the desert during the night, when they could navigate the empty desert without being detected, to pounce upon the enemy at dawn in a surprise attack. When they stopped to rest, or to regroup after a battle, they would lay well worn blankets on the ground, camouflaging them as best they could. Their meals were often small clumps of rice hastily steamed over small fires. It was a luxury when they could get a cup of camel's milk or a piece of mutton from people returning from Tindouf. It was even a greater luxury when they were able to wrest provisions en route to Moroccan garrisons from passing convoys.

Sidimi camped with the men, ate with the men, shivered in the cold with the men and languished in the heat with the men.

The thing that bothered her the most about the conditions they were in, however, was not the constant moving, not the sleeping on hard ground, not the lack of food, not the frigid winter nights, nor most of the harsh conditions that would test the perseverance of most humans. It was her hair. The little water they carried was needed for cooking and drinking, and little was left over for washing their bodies. Thankfully, the dry desert air absorbed sweat like a sponge, and made possible weeks without bathing. But her hair became matted, and dirty, and infested with the flies and sand fleas that pester livestock and humans alike in the desert. Finally, she decided to do something about it, and one day she took her knife and after a half dozen strokes her long, black tresses lay in lumps on the desert floor.

The Mauritanian Campaign – the Beginning.

As far back as the time of the creation of the SADR in February, the Polisario leaders had come to a strategic decision to concentrate most of their initial efforts at defeating Mauritania, which they considered by far the weaker enemy.

Mauritania's agreement to the Madrid Accords had taken the Polisario leaders by surprise. There were large numbers of ethnic Sahrawis in Mauritania and a number of the other tribes had links to the Sahrawis through blood relations, and Ould Daddah's decision to take up arms against their neighbors was not popular with these groups or with the members of the armed forces who would have to fight against them. Until 1974 Mauritania had given lip service to the right of the Sahrawis to self determination, both at the United Nations and in the Organization of African Unity, and Ould Daddah's decision to join forces with the Moroccan King to invade the Sahrawis' homeland by force was widely viewed as a betrayal and as a desperate maneuver to keep the Moroccans at bay – a maneuver that could easily backfire.

Mauritania was by far the weaker of the two allies both in terms of resources and expertise. Moreover, it was in a vulnerable position geographically. The Mauritanian state circled the territory both to the south and to the east, interposing itself between Western Sahara and Algeria along most of the territory's border, allowing the territory to touch Algeria for only a few miles near Tindouf. With more than 3,000 miles of border and an area nearly twice the size of France exposed to attack, Ould Daddah could do little more when the war began than transport his army – which numbered fewer than 3,000 soldiers in 1975 -- to strategic posts within Mauritania's section of the territory, leaving vast areas of its desert borders with Western Sahara and Algeria virtually undefended. In early 1976 he established three regional commands. The area around Awsard and Nouadhibou was under the command of Colonel Viah Ould Mayouf. The area around Zouerate and as far east as Bir Moghrein and Ain Ben Tili was under the command of Lieutenant Colonel Ahmed Ould Bouceif. Lieutenant Colonel Ahmed Salem Ould Sidi was in charge of the Dakhla region.

The Polisario refused to make their job easy. At the beginning of the year the guerillas' resistance to the invading Mauritanian forces had slowed down the Mauritanian advance to such an extent that Ould Daddah's troops had almost failed to reach Dakhla before the January 12 deadline set by the Spanish for the evacuation of their last two thousand troops from the city, and Colonel Dlimi had been forced to rush Moroccan troops south from Laayoune. Mauritanian troops only broke through to the city the day before the Spanish were set to withdraw. At the end of January Polisario fighters were dislodged from Awsard, but they almost immediately recaptured it and were not driven out again until a week later. Ain Ben Tili – just over the eastern border of Western Sahara -- came under renewed attack in mid-January, and guerilla troops occupied it until they were finally dislodged in mid February. Bir Moghrein was under daily attacks in early 1976.

They were like a swarm of tsetse flies; no matter how many times Ould Daddah would swat at them they would return to bite him in the rear.

Then, in what seemed like a nightmare come to life, the attacks against the rail line linking Zouerate and Nouadhibou -- the lifeline of the nation -- began.

May 1, 1976. The Rail Line.

As he started on his journey from a camp near Awsard, Salek chuckled to himself. He had become an expert in these types of operations – sabotaging the Boucraa conveyor belt and power installations twice in the last year. When this was all over he could put on his resume: "demolition expert." That should get him a job! But this time it was not a mining installation in his homeland, but a rail line next door in Mauritania.

123

Just as important, he mused. One of the main objectives of the leaders was to bleed the economy of Mauritania by attacking the iron mines at Zouerate and the trains that brought iron ore from the mines to the coast. The iron mines accounted for 80 percent of Mauritania's foreign revenue and were operated by the Comptoir Miner du Nord (COMINOR), a government regulated corporation with heavy French investment. Indeed, the French essentially ran the place – and got a lion's share of the revenue. They had sabotaged the power station that fed the iron mines within a month after the Madrid Accords was announced. But the railway was a much more convenient target. Skirting around the Western Sahara frontier, the railway, 419 miles long, was as easy to attack as it was strategic.

But he had never been to Mauritania, therefore Brahim Ghali, who had been appointed the coordinator of military units in March, had asked the commander of the southern region to provide him with a partner who knew the territory. So here he was, sitting in his Land Rover, chatting amiably with Ahmed, a fighter whose family was from the vicinity.

"What made you decide to join Ayoub Lahbib's troops?" he asked, nonchalantly.

"My family." Ahmed replied. "Two of my cousins live near Ain Ben Tili. Others are in Nouadhibou."

"What do they think of this war?"

Ahmed heaved a sigh. "They are disgusted. They met El Ouali when he traveled to Mauritania before the war started, and liked him and what he was preaching. They have no desire to fight him or their brethren over the border. They tell me that many of the colonels are equally disgusted – you know that Heydalla and Boukhreis are Sahrawis themselves! And Ahmed Baba Miske, the special advisor to the President, used to be a member of the Polisario! They know why Ould Daddah is doing this – he doesn't really want part of the territory, especially one with no real resources. But he wants to keep the Moroccans away from the iron mines and Nouadhibou – far away."

Salek laughed. "Well, if that is what he wants he has a strange way of getting it. Already he has had to ask Dlimi twice to come to his aid."

"Yeah, I know, and his army are mostly young men from the black tribes who have no interest in fighting a battle among the "arabs.""

Salek grinned. The tribes in Mauritania with predominately black blood, the znaga, had little in common with the ruling classes, who were predominantly drawn from the mixed arab-berber tribes which had infiltrated the territory from the east.

As they got closer to Zouerate, Ahmed led them on a route through the desert that would bypass the Mauritanian units that were heavily patrolling the area. When they were about halfway between Zouerate and Choum he directed Salek to a gully where they stopped to rest. It was nearly dusk and they had been driving for over a day. They could use some sleep. At daybreak they proceeded the few miles to where the rail line stood – a glistening rope of metal snaking its way through miles of empty space.

Salek quickly unwrapped the plastic explosives and placed two of the packages carefully below the center rail. Then he repeated the step 100 yards down the line. He uncoiled the umbilical cord attached to each package and, when he was safely at a distance, he pulled the trigger.

Immediately a blast sent shock waves through the desert and flying bits of iron and wood were sent spiraling into the air in clouds of dust and sand. After it had quieted down once again Salek and Ahmed surveyed the damage. A line of track over 200 yards long had been ripped apart, and turned into a jagged mass of iron, the ground where it had stood forming a large, sandy pit. That should hold them for a while, he mused, as they turned the Land Rover around and headed into the desert.

May 31, 1976. The Plan.

It was a peaceful night on the last day of May. The moon was nowhere to be seen and the heat of the day had given way to a warm, slumbering evening. Not a sound could be heard for miles over the vast desert. From the rocky hills to the north of the camp one could count literally thousands of stars. There was no electricity to blunt their brightness, nor any light at all as far as one could see. The serenity of the night, however, was soon broken by the hum of engines.

When they had arrived at the designated spot, El Ouali got out of the Land Rover, followed by three companions. Waiting for them were three other men seated on blankets spread neatly over the rocky soil. After the usual protracted greetings, the ensemble settled down for tea. They were curious to hear what he would say. He had called for a meeting of leaders to discuss something important. After one last sip of tea, he began.

"We need to do something to focus attention on the conflict, to show that we are capable of winning. It is not enough to raid their troops and capture their equipment. These tactics will help us get the weapons we need, but they will not impress the Mauritanians or the Moroccans – or their supporters – or make us front page news," he said. Then he slowly added, "and we need to get the attention of the international community."

The group pondered his words for a moment. They had been frustrated for months by the lack of attention their movement had received from the international press. No matter how daring their attacks on convoys, no matter how many times they had put Boucraa out of commission, no matter how many times they had sabotaged the rail line, there was scarcely a word about them or their struggle in the newspapers.

"What exactly do you suggest, Ouali," someone asked. "Our forces lack the weapons to launch a major frontal assault, even against the Mauritanians. Guerilla tactics are all we have."

The group fell silent for a moment. It was true. The guerillas did not have the force to launch a frontal attack against either the Moroccans or the Mauritanians. Nor did they have the resources to take and hold territory. But without doing either they risked being discarded as an insignificant force, like

125

so many other revolutionaries throughout history who fought for years in vain to have their voices heard. The man pouring tea stopped for a moment, and glanced around the room. "I agree with El Ouali. A war of attrition won't win us back the territory. We can bleed the Moroccans and the Mauritanians for years, and still not force them to withdraw. We need a decisive battle, or at least an incident that shows our determination."

"I agree," replied another, "We need something that will convince not just the Mauritanians and Moroccans, but the United States and France, and the rest of the world that we are a force to be reckoned with, not just some insignificant group of rebels. Hassan was able to gain a lot of media attention with his "Green March" gambit. We need something that will gain the same sort of attention."

"Yes," responded one of them, his voice bitter, "But for months we have been fighting – the entire territory has been blanketed with battles – and we have managed to capture a number of prisoners and destroy a number of convoys, not to mention the troops we have battled, and still, not a word of any of this in the newspapers! Instead, just a bunch of Moroccan and Mauritanian propaganda. According to them, the annexation of the territory is a fait accompli."

They fell silent, their frustration seeping through. Then a man sitting quietly at the rear of the group spoke up. "The OAU will be holding its conference next month. They have been calling for a withdrawal of Mauritanian and Moroccan troops and a referendum, but so far it has been only words. This would be the time to stiffen their resolve by doing something dramatic."

"But what?" asked someone, desolately.

Ouali half smiled, paused for a second, then spoke.

"That is why I called you here. I think I may have a plan."

June 3, 1976. The Great Expedition.

The sun had just cast its last rays upon the desert floor, forming shadows on the rocks and transforming the sand into hues of purple and blue. Overhead a solidary crow winged its way back to its nest for the night and the desert switched to slumber mode. It was about 140 miles southwest of Rabouni at a camp near Bir Lehlou. The day was June 3, 1976. Camped in the desert was a gathering of guerilla fighters. Most of them were young and inexperienced; many of them came from Guelta Zemmour after the Moroccan forces bombarded and took control of that area the preceding April. Others, like Salek, were veterans of the campaigns at Amgala. There were about 100 fighters in all, who had among them no more than 10 Land Rovers and a few trucks. Each vehicle was outfitted with some meager provisions. The glass was removed from the windshields and headlights to avoid glare that could be spotted from the air, the roofs of the vehicles were removed and the sides were covered in mud for camouflage. And perched in the rear of each vehicle was a machine gun. At El Ouali's command they formed a loose line and began heading westward, across the desert, at top speed. At a point near Ain Ben

Tili, just over the Western Sahara border with Mauritania, they slowed their pace. It had turned dark and they lit matches from time to time to identify their location. There was no road, no guideposts and no maps. Just open desert.

In the lead car El Ouali gazed intently at the stars. His father had been a Bedouin, herding sheep and goats in the desert, guided only by these same stars. It was a talent he learned in childhood, passed from father to son, and it came in handy at the moment. He knew by the time of the night and the positions of the stars which direction was southwest – and it was in this direction he led the caravan. They followed this path in silence, the only noise being the humming from their motors. Hours passed. Finally, the first rays of sun began to appear behind them, signaling the beginning of another day. They proceeded without sleep across the barren Mauritanian desert, progressing steadily to the south and west, through a vast, empty, space.

In a few hours the sun began to scorch his eyebrows and sweat started running down the side of his face. Salek had volunteered for the expedition, and now he drew his headscarf tighter around his head, until only a slit in the fabric remained to permit his eyes to see. He was used to the desert, but he remembered the saying, only "mad dogs and Englishmen" go out in the noon day sun. He chuckled to himself. How true it was! No self respecting Bedouin would venture into the 120 degree noon day furnace that was the Sahara in the summer unless it was absolutely vital. But they were on a mission – one that could not be delayed by a siesta under an accommodating acacia tree. So he took another sip of water -- oh so carefully, for it was a precious commodity -- and tried to imagine he was on a tropical island cooled by a soft sea breeze.

By the time the sun mercifully set beyond the horizon they were deep into Mauritanian territory, far from any outpost of civilization. They had managed to travel over 400 miles, most of it through the Mauritanian desert. Zouerate was not far off. The French had given the Mauritanians sophisticated satellite sensing equipment, and was monitoring the southernmost part of Western Sahara with their aircraft. Meanwhile, the Mauritanian troops were concentrating their efforts in territories to the north. No one expected the Polisario to attack positions deep within Mauritania itself. Accordingly the territory of Mauritania between the capital on the Atlantic coast, Nouakchott, and the Algerian border – a stretch of barren desert only sporadically visited by marauding Bedouins -- was only loosely patrolled, allowing the caravan to cover a huge distance – nearly the length of the east coast of the United States -- without meeting a soul.

It was not until the early morning of June 5, near Tourine, an area to the east of Zouerate, that an incredulous French pilot broke the revere.

This was his first sortie of the day, and he was tired. The night before, drinking with his comrades and playing poker had blurred his vision and rendered him slightly nauseous. What was he supposed to do in this god forsaken outpost? He conjured up images of the famed French Foreign Legion – rugged fighters withstanding terrible ordeals in the desert. Good for the movies, he thought -- they probably died of boredom not heroic exploits. He had been there for a week now. Part of a small contingent of French pilots sent by Valery Giscard d'Estaing to "train" the Mauritanians. Train them indeed! As if any of these barely literate semi-nomads could learn to fly a Mirage! This was no crop-duster, it was one of France's most sophisticated jets, and two of them had been sent to Mauritania to provide surveillance, and, if necessary to "engage the enemy." He knew what that meant. Bombing them to bits. Phosphorus bombs. Napalm. Secret stuff that they were not suppose to use. But who was to know? And who made these rules anyway? The same UN that turned a blind eye to the backdoor agreement to divide the territory between Morocco and Mauritania? These thoughts kept churning in his head, for to tell the truth, he felt a little guilty.

But there was little chance his conscience would have a chance to bother him with this assignment. There was a greater chance he would go mad with boredom – or drink. The same routine, day after day: one sortie in the morning, another at dusk. Nothing to see for miles but a few stray camels, the horizon blurred by the heated sand to form mock "oases" of water. Mirages, all of them, for there were no bodies of water for miles.

He had gone nearly the entire length of the border and was on his return leg when they appeared. Just a few dark spots against the sand. But they were moving. Probably camels, he thought at first, but he descended to take a closer look. What he saw jogged him to full alert. Land Rovers! And they had guns!

Back at his barracks, Lieutenant-Colonel Ahmed Ould Bouceif was enjoying his breakfast. Zouerate was no Nouakchott, but he managed to bring just enough amenities with him to this backward hole to provide some creature comforts. Heaven only knew how long he would have to stay. The Sahrawis – mostly deserters from the Spanish Tropas Nomadas – had been able to harass the Mauritanian forces with their ghazzi raids. They could not hold fixed positions for long. However, Bouceif knew that the Mauritanian army was weak, and Mauritania's hold on the southern portion of the territory and settlements within its northern border was precarious. The iron mines near Zouerate that supplied most of the foreign exchange for the country had been a particularly attractive target. The power station that fed the mines had been bombed in December, and in April a guerilla group raided the iron mining company's railways from Zouerate to the port at Nouadhibou.

To stop these attacks Ould Daddah had sent him to Zouerate.

However, it was June, in the first month of the hot summer, when not even cockroaches attempt to cross the burning sands of the Sahara. . . sands that can melt the soles of your shoes below a sun that can send you into delirium in a few minutes. There had been no enemy action in this area for weeks and he seriously doubted that the few straggling civilian Sahrawis who wandered near his camp would have the military experience, or the necessary equipment, to launch an offensive against his trained military unit, especially now that it had been fortified by Mauritania's French ally with sophisticated satellite communications equipment and aircraft. He had nearly 1,000 men under his command, and his major problem was how to keep them from going stir crazy.

He had just put the last morsel into his mouth and was preparing to wash it down with a sip of tea, when the officer appeared.

"Sir," the young man stammered, "we just received a communication from one of our pilots that he has spotted what appears to be a group of enemy combatants with weapons in the desert just east of Tourine and heading in our direction. . ."

It was now a few hours after that communiqué. Commandant Mohammed Khouna Ould Heydalla and his troops had just rounded the last dune when he saw the Land Rovers – five dots in the distance, travelling at top speed to the west. He had been dispatched by Boucief to investigate a possible sighting by a French pilot of enemy combatants. Probably headed for the rail line, he thought. His commander had been clear – he was to prevent them from sabotaging the railroad line at all costs. He was slowly gaining on them, almost within distance to fire, when they abruptly halted and aimed their machine guns in his direction. They managed to pierce one of the combat vehicles and kill the driver, but their guns were no match for the sophisticated armaments of his troops, and they were greatly outnumbered. One or two of them managed to escape into the desert, but he was able to disable two of the vehicles and forcibly eject its wounded occupants.

Back in Zouerate Boucief was pacing nervously. When his attache gave him the news his features began to relax. Good! It wouldn't do to have a successful sabotage of the rail lines blot his record. And there were prisoners. And he knew how to make prisoners talk. If there were any other guerillas in the area, he wanted to know.

He gave the command. Soon the bedraggled and bleeding prisoners were herded into a windowless room, with walls built thick to muffle any sounds

. . . .

It was 3 o'clock in the afternoon when his afternoon siesta was suddenly interrupted by a knock on the door. Ould Heydalla entered the room quickly, his countenance obviously disturbed. "Well, what is it," barked Boucief, slightly irritated at having his slumber interrupted.

" I think you should know . . . we questioned the prisoners. At first they wouldn't tell us anything, but they were finally "persuaded" to talk. But what they said . . ." his voice trailed off somewhat breathlessly.

Boucief stared at the officer. "Well, what is it . . . and it had better be important!"

"They claim that they are reinforcements for a Polisario column of 100 or more men who are heading to Nouakchott!"

Boucief could not hide his surprise. The Polisario would not dare attempt such a thing. Nouakchott was nearly 1000 miles from the Polisario controlled territory, and they would have to go right through the center of Mauritania. Besides, a column that large travelling through the middle of Mauritania would have been detected. It was most likely a clever ruse to divert needed resources

129

from the Zouerate area and permit their colleagues to cut the railroad lines. He was not going to fall for it, but he would report it back to headquarters just the same.

It was now 3:30 in the afternoon, and the charge d'affaires had just given the latest reports to Ould Daddah in the palace. One report in particular got his attention.

"A column of guerillas advancing towards the capital?" he exclaimed half surprised, half amused. "What do they take us for, idiots?" and with that exclamation he hurled the document contemptuously into the trash. He summoned his chief of staff and chief military officer in the palace. "What do you make of this?" he barked.

Neither official wished to contradict the leader. Besides, the report was incredulous – obviously a trick to get Mauritania to divert needed resources from the defense of the iron mines, or perhaps the route to Dakhla in the north. Ould Daddah knew full well that El Ouali was capable of such subterfuge, for without such tactics his ragtag army of misfits would never be able to persevere against the infinitely superiorly trained and armed Mauritanian forces – particularly with support from Morocco and France.

"El Ouali is probably trying to get you to postpone your trip to the Cape Verde Islands," ventured one of them.

"Well, it is not going to work," he replied, smiling. And with that last statement the subject was closed.

El Ouali had indeed sent the column spied by the Mauritanians at Tourine as a diversionary tactic, and it was not the only one. Other Polisario units had been dispatched to Zouerate, Atar, Ouadane, Chinguetti and even Tichit in southern Mauritania to divert attention from the main column. Meanwhile, as the hours slowly passed, the main column steadily pressed onward toward its destination.

June 6, 1976. The Dunes.

It was the morning of June 6. The little caravan had proceeded without rest for two days and nights and Salek could hardly keep his eyes open. The terrain up to the outskirts of Zouerate had been like the *hammada*, largely flat and rocky, through which they could make good progress, but once they approached Choum a sand dune appeared, quickly followed by another. El Ouali crawled up one of the dunes to survey the horizon. What he saw caused him to pause. Before him was an ocean of dunes, gently undulating as far as the eyes could see. "We won't be able to make much progress here," he said to his men. "We'll just have to make the best of it." He was right. As they proceeded forward every step became arduous. Vehicles quickly became swallowed by ravenous mounds of sand, spinning their wheels aimlessly.

Salek's Land Rover became stuck, and he and the other occupants spent nearly an hour extricating it from the sand pit into which it had descended. And his was not the only one – all around him vehicles stood motionless.

El Ouali shook his head. "I think we will have to carry the Land Rovers and push the trucks until we reach the end of the dunes." Salek looked at his companions. They had been without food and sleep for days and their eyes burned from the sand and glare of the sun. But within minutes they managed to hoist their vehicle over their shoulders and began to snake around the dunes in a slow procession, sometimes pushing, sometimes carrying the Land Rover on their backs in the blistering heat, all the while fighting the dust and sand carried by the wind into their eyes and nostrils, until they would reach a stretch of rocky terrain where they could heave a collective sigh of relief and loosen their burden. It sometimes took hours to advance a few hundred yards. Eating and drinking had become only a secondary consideration, but their supplies of both food and water were quickly being depleted. It was summer, and during the day undulating waves of heat would rise from the sands, scorching their feet. Yet they soldiered on.

It was then that they saw it – the unmistakable silhouette of a jet, streaking across the sky overhead. They were out in the open, nowhere to hide.

"Do you think they saw us?" one of them asked. El Ouali looked pensive. "Probably," he replied. "From here on we will have to assume that they know we are here and we will have to take diversionary measures."

Salek scanned the horizon. There was nothing but enormous mounds of sand for miles. He groaned slightly as he and his team shoved their Land Rover again with all their might and once again proceeded to inch their way through the dunes, sweat and sand blinding their eyes and filling their lungs, their hands raw and swollen from the sun, their feet covered with blisters.

It took them another two days and one night of excruciating pain to get through the dunes that stood like mountains in their path. When the dunes finally gave way to rocky terrain, they rushed at full speed through the desert, taking care to avoid any areas where people might congregate and only stopping to take water under cover of darkness.

Meanwhile, an incredulous Boucief had received yet another report of enemy combatants – this time a powerful military column fifty miles west of Atar. This finally got his attention. The next day he set out from Zouerate with four hundred men racing towards the capital, while farther west a second column of troops headed south from Awsard under Colonel Viah Ould Mayouf's command. Another smaller force was dispatched from the capital eastward. It would be a classic pincher movement, granting the guerillas no avenue of escape.

June 7, 1976. Nouakchott.

By the evening of June 7, oblivious to the forces which had been sent to intercept them, El Ouali and his men were able to reach Oum Tounsi, fifty miles east of Nouakchott. He had decided to use the tarmac road that connected Nouakchott to the copper mines at Akjoujat to speed up the rest of the journey. However, he was surprised to find a convoy of petroleum tankers also speeding their way to the capital. He ordered his men to destroy them, and soon the entire area was engulfed in flames and smoke. The exhausted

131

troops camped for the night a short distance away, out of food and water, with only enough petrol for the return trip to Bir Lehlou. However, their slumber was interrupted by a small troop of Mauritanian soldiers who had seen smoke from the fires and had come to investigate. Bullets started firing in all directions. After an hour or so most of the Mauritanian troops had fled into the desert, leaving behind eight prisoners, a Land Rover and a number of bodies in the sand.

But El Ouali would not let this minor skirmish divert attention from his mission. It was nearly dawn, and time for the *coup de grace*. He dispatched a small group with instructions to bomb a few places in the city and return. He would keep the rest of the soldiers with him about twenty miles west of Oum Tounsi, and order a few to seek some food and water so that they wouldn't die of thirst on the return trip.

Salek was confused. "I thought our mission was to bomb the city?" he said, wondering why his commander had not sent the whole contingent forward.

El Ouali placed his hand on his shoulder. "Look," he said, smiling, "we gain nothing by trying to storm the Bastille. We only need to show the Mauritanians that we are capable of storming the Bastille. It is more important that some of us get supplies for the return home." His mood was upbeat, but there were serious undertones. They very well could die in the desert if they didn't find supplies, and there was not one drop of petrol they could spare.

After a couple of hours blasts could be heard coming from the northern part of the city. Then the blasts stopped. One of the soldiers turned on his radio and heard reports that the palace had been attacked. El Ouali heaved a sigh of relief. Hours passed. The group that had been sent to attack the palace had not returned. Unbeknownst to him, they had been followed by a small Mauritanian force and rather than lead them to El Ouali's group, they had decided to retreat into the desert. After waiting a few hours El Ouali decided to dispatch another group. At first they shelled only the northern outskirts of the capital, but, finding scant resistance from the few local gendarmes who remained to guard the city, they proceeded farther. By 10 p.m. that evening they reached the walls of the palace. After a fifteen minute assault on the palace and a few neighboring embassies they retreated.

But they never reached El Ouali and the main force. Rather, by the time they had begun shelling the city a Mauritanian column had sneaked up behind them and fighting quickly escalated, with both forces firing aimlessly into the other's direction in near total darkness.

By 11 p.m., El Ouali had begun to pace nervously. Salek and the soldiers who had remained with him had managed to confiscate enough food and fuel for the return journey. The Mauritanians knew they were there somewhere and it was just a matter of time before their troops found them. It would be suicide to remain much longer.

When Salek saw the look on his leader's face he knew what had to be done. And without another word they began the long trek back through the desert to the Mauritanian border.

June 7, 1976. Ould Daddah.

Meanwhile, the scene in the sumptuous palace that housed the President of Mauritania was one of complete bedlam. When Ould Daddah had gotten the report of a column of guerillas heading for the capital, he quickly summoned the palace guard and the few soldiers who were there to provide protection. But the Mauritanian military had been stretched thin by the continuous assaults in the north, and thinking that no one in his right mind would attempt an attack on the capital – miles away from the border and protected by the sea in the west and an unforgiving desert in the east – most of the army had been sent north. He was vulnerable, and he knew it.

So, Ould Daddah locked himself in his office and prayed that Boucief and his forces would arrive in time. Then the assault began. First one, then a barrage of artillery blasts shook the palace. After fifteen minutes all was quiet. Ould Daddah heaved a sigh of relief. But then, later that day he heard blasts again – this time coming from the northern part of the city – and his aides rushed in with reports of guerillas roaming the city, shooting at will. There was nowhere to hide. He locked himself once again in his office and waited what seemed like an eternity, as the bomb blasts came nearer and nearer.

Then, once again, silence. It was nearly midnight before he emerged from his office, shaken but unharmed. Where the hell was Boucief, he wondered? But he could deal with that later, he thought. For the time being he was just glad to be alive.

June 8, 1976. The Desert Odyssey.

By sunrise the following day the column of guerillas led by El Ouali had reached Benichab, a place that held water tanks that served the copper mining city of Akjoujt. El Ouali asked Salek and two others to scale the tanks to fill their canteens with water. When they began their descent they spotted the plane that had passed and then circled around to get a closer look.

They hurried back to their vehicles. Once alerted to their presence Mauritanian troops would be sure to arrive within a few hours. Little did they know that a large contingent of Boucief's troops was already only minutes away. El Ouali ordered Salek and most of the group to proceed to Bir Lehlou as fast as they could. He and a handful of men would stay behind to sabotage the tanks to prevent the Mauritanian forces from using them.

Salek looked at the sky. The signs were ominous. Darkness on the horizon and a stiff breeze. The telltale signs of the irifi, the windstorms that frequently plagued this part of the desert in the summer months. If they didn't leave quickly they risked being engulfed in an envelope of dust and wind, obscuring directions, and making further travel treacherous.

The water towers were barely out of his sight before three Mauritanian columns appeared on the horizon, half obscured from view by the approaching wall of sand. The windstorm was fast developing. El Ouali and his group had managed to destroy one of the tanks and were waiting for two of the vehicles

133

at one of the other tanks to join them. However, one of these vehicles got stuck in the sand, unable to move. The driver of the other one raced back to El Ouali for help. Ouali told him and his companions to take two Land Rovers and catch up with the main force. He would stay behind to aid the one that was stuck in the sand.

By this time the desert had been transformed into a swirling mass of sand, darkening the sky and making it nearly impossible to see. El Ouali, clutching his headscarf tightly around his face, tried in vain to make out the outline of the Land Rover of his companions. He finally saw the silhouette of a man approaching him and, thinking it was one of his comrades coming to find him, moved towards him. But it was not one of his comrades. His Land Rover had been surrounded in the storm by the armored squadron led by Lieutenant Ney Ould Bah, one of Ould Boucief's deputies. Before he could decide where to turn the piercing shriek of gunfire shattered the silence, followed by an explosion. Then another, blanketing guerillas and Mauritanians alike in a carpet of sand. The Mauritians fired wildly, their eyes blinded by the pellets of dirt that rained down on them.

On a hill a few miles from the area, the occupants of the two Land Rovers sent ahead waited for El Ouali's group. However, when the dust cleared they saw only Mauritanian troops approaching from that direction. Instead of joining the main column they fled quickly through the desert and managed to make their way to a point 50 miles north east of Zourate. There, their luck ran out. They ran out of gas and after a few hours a Mauritanian unit spotted them. Shots were fired. After an hour half of them lay dead in the sand; the rest were taken prisoner.

Unaware of what had transpired for El Ouali and the troops that had remained with him, Salek and the main part of the Polisario force continued their retreat. After proceeding 15 milesor so they had stopped and waited for El Ouali and his men to join them. While they were waiting they were surprised to see Mauritanian troops accompanied by armored vehicles quickly approaching their position from the direction where they had left him.

They took cover and waited. When the Mauritanians were within range, they fired upon them. They were able to destroy one of the armored vehicles before fleeing into the desert.

They raced at top speed in the direction of their base camp. By nightfall they were tired and without food. They had managed to evade the Mauritanians but they were finding it difficult to navigate the sand dunes. They desperately needed some sleep, so they took the risk of stopping for the night.

At dawn they prepared to continue their journey. Salek cast a worried glance at his fuel gage. They would soon be out of fuel. They were still in the middle of the desert, far from their camp, trying to stay out of sight of the French-built reconnaissance aircraft. Zouerate was at least 100 miles to the north. When they had travelled a few more hours they spied a Mauritanian column coming from the north and knew that they had been discovered. However, much to their surprise the Mauritanians remained at a distance and they were able to continue on their way. When they came closer to Zouerate, the Land Rovers and trucks began once again to get stuck in the sand, and they were constantly pulling them out, only to have them get stuck again. They were rapidly getting to a point where the fuel for the Land Rovers would run out, so some people left to find a source of fuel.

Towards dusk Salek saw in the distance two of the Land Rovers that had belonged to one of the groups that had fired on the palace. However, instead of joining them, the vehicles remained at a distance. He found this strange and was just about to proceed towards them when he saw on the horizon a column of Mauritanian vehicles which seemed to be standing still. So that's why they were not approaching! The Mauritanians had obviously followed the two Land Rovers, thinking that they might lead them to additional units. Much later he found out that these were Viah Ould Mayouf's forces from Awsard. After waiting patiently a few minutes, one of the Mauritanian vehicles drove up to the Land Rover of the guerillas that was the closest, and he could see its occupants climb out, their hands held high in a gesture of surrender. However, by this time the sun had set and dusk had begun to cast shadows among the crevices and sand. Before they could capture the second vehicle, it managed to hide among the shadows and join the main force. The Mauritanians didn't even try to pursue it. Salek chuckled. They probably reasoned that they did not need to attack during the night and risk some casualties since our Land Rovers were nearly out of fuel and we could be more easily captured the following day.

The next morning the Mauritanian commander ordered his troops to proceed to the spot where the guerillas had been the night before. There they found a handful of Land Rovers, and some discarded blankets and spare parts scattered in the sand, but no men. Under cover of darkness the guerillas had simply abandoned the Land Rovers, taken all of the unnecessary equipment out of the trucks, put all of their soldiers into the trucks, and fled before dawn.

Salek and the others in his group spent the remainder of the night and the next day driving. By the next evening, however, the trucks were also running out of fuel. They abandoned one truck and proceeded with the other two until a second truck also ran out of fuel. Some of the men decided to stay with the truck while the remainder forged ahead with the other one. This third truck managed to reach a Polisario unit at El-Mreiti, 250 miles from the Algerian border, and vehicles were quickly dispatched to rescue the soldiers who had been left in the desert.

It had been a grueling journey and none of the soldiers who had straggled back from the expedition knew what had happened to El Ouali. Brahim Ghali had eagerly pumped the men who had been with him for information, but to no avail. El Ouali had been separated from the group that joined the main force, and no one who had stayed with him to sabotage the water tanks had returned. Only one week later did the guerillas learn of his fate.

The exploit had indeed achieved its objective. Within hours of the attack broadcasts of the event filled the airwaves of the Mauritanian and Moroccan capitals and newspaper accounts found their way to the capitals of most of the countries of Africa and beyond. For days incredulous pundits bantered about it and a rather shamefaced Ould Daddah was forced to give an explanation. The OAU's Liberation Committee, whose rather tepid recommendation in January that the organization recognize the Polisario as an African liberation movement had been shelved as "too divisive," gained the courage to recommend once again recognition of the Polisario at their June meeting, and diplomats throughout the continent held their breaths waiting to see what would transpire at the next month's meeting of the Council of Ministers.

However, this achievement on the political battlefield was bought at a price. After an hour, when the dust had finally cleared at Benichab, Ould Bah's men had surveyed the damage. There, at a spot near the water tanks were the burnt remains of two Land Rovers. Beside one of them lay the body of a tall, young man with bushy hair.

July 2, 1976. The Organization of African Unity.

The unfolding drama in the Sahara had not only attracted the interest of the United States. It had also been closely watched by the major Western power in the region -- France. By the time the inhabitants of Spanish Sahara had rebelled against the colonial rule of Spain, France had already lost its colonies on the continent, but not necessarily its influence. The King of Morocco had been allowed to return to his throne, but only under the careful eyes of the French, who continued to pull the strings of commerce in the kingdom. Ould Daddah had tried to wrest control of the resources of Mauritania from French rule by nationalizing the iron ore industry, but by the time of the Western Sahara conflict he, too, was forced to rely on the expertise, as well as the military might, of his former colonial overseer. The other countries – Mali, Senegal, the Ivory Coast – found themselves client states as well. Only Algeria had managed to escape the long tentacles of its former ruler.

Algeria! It had been the jewel in the crown of the French empire, not a mere colony, but a department of France itself, rich in oil, gas and fertile plains. Thousands of French citizens – some with illustrious names like Coco Chanel, Yves St. Laurent, and Camus – had been born there, and the Algerian capital Algiers was resplendent with the grandiose homes and buildings built by the French during their period of occupation. It was clear that they meant to stay. So, when after years of a bloody and grizzly war that left thousands dead, the French were summarily expelled from their African paradise, the scars ran deep and remain to this day.

Valery Giscard d'Estaing, the President of the Republic was just as intently interested in seeing to it that nothing destabilized the throne of the King of Morocco as were the Americans – perhaps even more so – and he had pulled a number of diplomatic strings to steer the United Nations and Spain on the right course. France had never been content to see a non-Francophone colony encroach upon what it considered to be its rightful sphere of influence in Africa, and when the King had laid claim to the Spanish territory – despite the ruling of the International Court of Justice denying his claim -- the French President had done nothing to dissuade him. He had watched with dismay the beginnings of the revolt among the Sahrawis and was determined to prevent them from amassing any diplomatic muscle at the United Nations or – just as important -- among their neighbors on the African continent. For the war that had developed between the Sahrawis and Morocco and Mauritania had not remained a matter of interest only to the Western powers, it was of grave concern to the other states on the continent of Africa as well.

On July 2, 1976, the 19th annual summit of the Organization of African Unity was convened in the Mauritius. The OAU, created by the states of Africa to push for the independence of the colonies on the continent, was still in its infancy, and already two of its members – Morocco and Mauritania – were testing its resolve on two of the principles it held the most dear: the right of the inhabitants of the colonies to self determination and the maintenance of the boundaries established by the colonial powers in order to avoid territorial conflicts.

On February 27, the same day as the SADR was proclaimed at Bir Lehlou, the OAU executive committee had held a conference to consider whether or not to admit the Polisario as a liberation movement. But once the Polisario had declared the establishment of the Sahrawi Arab Democratic Republic, the question had become whether or not to admit the SADR as a state. As the members of the organization took their seats on July 2 at the annual summit, El Ouali's Nouakchott expedition was still fresh in their memories, and it was clear that the courage and determination of the members of that expedition had not failed to make an impression on even the most hardened of diplomats. But the Western Sahara issue quickly led to turmoil within the organization. Both Morocco and Mauritania threatened to quit the OAU if its admission to the organization was ratified at that meeting. Most of the Francophone nations – bowing to pressure from France – stood solidly behind them. The threat was sufficient to cause the Chairman, Seewoosagur Ramgoolam, to postpone its consideration until an "extraordinary" summit could be convened. But such a summit was not convened. Instead, throughout the remainder of the year the organization careened rudderless through a political tempest, unable to steer a course in any direction.

August, 1976.   The El Ouali Offensive.

It was nearing the end of the long summer months. At Bir Lehlou a small group of men once again met under an acacia tree. But this meeting somehow lacked the joyful exuberance that had filled the previous ones. They were the same young men who had confidently defied the world and had brazenly declared war on their neighbors to the north and south just a few months ago, but somehow they seemed to have aged. It was if the breath had been kicked from their lungs.

"I told him it was too risky – that he should send someone else. I should have made him listen," said Bouhali, ruefully.

137

Bachir, El Ouali's brother, shook his head. "He would not have listened," he replied, "I spoke with him the night before he left. I asked him why he wanted to lead this mission himself – why he didn't leave it to the military people. He asked me how long could he expect to enjoy the respect of the soldiers if he was afraid to lead them in their battles?"

"Still," Bouhali answered, "His genius was on the political battlefield. He was the face of the Polisario – the one person everyone knew. We needed him to negotiate with world leaders, to represent our movement. . . and now that he is gone . . ."

"Now that he is gone," interrupted Ghali, "we need to show the world that our movement is greater than one man."

And so, in the meeting of Polisario officials in their Third Congress they held that August, they chose someone else to be the secretary general of the movement, Mohammed Abdelaziz, the man who had led their troops in some of the fiercest battles of the war, a man known for his meticulous planning, knowledge of enemy tactics, cunning, and ability to create a consensus among the fiercely independent leaders. At the same time they decided to expand the war to include other regions. They had already engaged the Moroccans in skirmishes as far north as the ant-atlas mountain range. Now they would expand their activities in the south and extend the war deep into Mauritanian territory as far south as its border with Mali.

After this Congress Sidi Hiduk took Abdelaziz' place as commander of troops in the north, but the territory was divided into the 1st and 5th military regions, with the commander of the 5th region responsible for much of southeastern Morocco. Bouhali remained the commander of troops in the central or 2nd military region, and Ayoub Lahbib remained in charge of troops in northern Mauritania and its portion of Western Sahara, in what was dubbed the 3rd military region. And a 4th military region, with responsibility for most of southern Mauritania was added to the list. Brahim Ghali, as Minister of Defense, remained the coordinator of all military units.

And instead of withering away, the movement seemed to be imbued with a greater sense of purpose – an even greater determination that their fallen heroes would not have died in vain. With even greater vigor, in a crusade they named the "El Ouali" offensive, the fighting quickly escalated in the last months of 1976 and spread to the farthest regions of Mauritania. Both Tidjikja and Tichit, outposts in the remote interior of Mauritania, were attacked in August, and Nema, seventy miles from Mauritania's southern border with Mali, was overrun in September.

And through it all Sidimi marched with the troops into battle . . . .

November 15, 1976.

The summer months were now a distant memory. It was now November, and Sidimi had been marching with Bouhali's troops for over half a year, accompanying their forays as far north as the hills of Hagunia and as far west as the beaches of Boujdour. One evening as the troops were preparing their evening meal nestled among the caves and crannies of Lemgassem, one of the scouts that had been positioned near Smara interrupted their meal with an important communiqué. A Moroccan column was on the move, traveling south. There was also a large Mauritanian force coming towards them from Bir Moghrein.

Sidimi knew what that meant. They would soon be moving out. She watched as Bouhali and a handful of his men climbed into their Land Rovers and drove at top speed westward to survey the scene. The sun had already set by the time they returned.

She raced through the camp to where Abdati was busy loading supplies into a truck.

"Where's Bouhali?" she asked, grabbing his arm. "Tell me what is going on!"

Abdati stopped for a moment what he was doing.

"The Moroccans and Mauritanians are approaching Amgala, and their troops extend for miles. Bouhali has gone to rouse the men in the hills. . . we will be leaving shortly." Then, giving her a brotherly pat on the shoulder, he added ". . . and I guess you had better get your things together, too!"

There was little time to plan. She hastily packed the medicines, bandages and other medical equipment she used and loaded the American jeep – graciously donated by the Moroccan army – that she had been given for her traveling "clinic." Within a few hours, with a large column of men following him, Bouhali proceeded to a hilly spot within a mile of the assembled enemy troops, ordered his men to hide their vehicles, and waited.

It was nearing winter, and the desert air in the evening had turned bitterly cold. Salek, who had returned from his mission in Mauritania, huddled next to his Land Rover, shivered and drew his worn out army blanket tighter for warmth. He had tried in vain to get some sleep and had watched the first rays of the sun rise over the distant hills. Shortly after the sun appeared he heard the distant rumble of engines that announced the approach of troops. Within an hour three Land Rovers appeared on the horizon, then a dozen, followed by tanks and troop carriers. Overhead jets buzzed menacingly. He counted them. 7, 8, 9, ten tanks, and as many troop carriers, all carrying heavy artillery. Following them at a distance of a mile was a column of infantry.

Bouhali waved and immediately a dozen or so men drove off in the direction of the column of infantry. Then he waited. Before long he heard the muffled sound of shots in the distance. That was the signal to move.

He shouted a command and the remaining guerillas mounted their Land Rovers and dove at the tanks at the head of the procession at lightning speed, from two directions, firing their weapons at full blast. The tanks swirled around in circles, firing aimlessly into the hills, creating huge craters in the rocky soil. But it was impossible for them to outmaneuver the Land Rovers that darted to and fro like a bevy of ants. The occupants in the three lead vehicles fought back, as best they could, but their guns were no match for the

139

machine guns carried by the guerillas in their Land Rovers. Within less than an hour the firefight was over, the guerillas vanishing into the wilderness as quickly as they had come.

A mile to the rear the column of infantry had found itself surrounded by attackers they could not see. They quickly took cover in whatever crevices they could find. Cut off from their command, in an unknown land and not knowing where they were headed, they became confused and disorganized. Some of them scattered into the desert, others tried to find the path back to Smara or Bir Moghrein, still others tried to forge ahead.

The sporadic attacks went on for days. If the troops found it difficult to move during the day, their nights were filled with terror. They formed a circle and surround themselves with land mines. But the guerillas found and removed these mines. While guerilla infantry harassed their troops at the perimeter, others in Land Rovers would bombard their central command.

Sidimi had found a crevice, hidden from the battlefield by a hill, and somewhat protected from the harsh night time winds, where she put the jeep that contained the medicine and other provisions she carried for the wounded. She covered herself as best she could with an old blanket. Then she waited. As the morning sun began to warm her hands and feet she could hear the muffled gun blasts in the distance, followed by the sounds of vehicles racing their engines. Then the whistle of rockets and the blasts of cannons. From where she stood she saw clearly the silhouettes of tanks swirling in the dust and the outline of cars racing to and fro. But she had no time to be a spectator. Casualties had begun to arrive – first one, then another, until there were a dozen blankets stretched on the sand, their occupants covered in blood.

She beckoned to one of her aides to help her with one of the wounded, but when she removed his shirt her aide gasped and turned away. The wounded man's left arm had been nearly severed at the elbow, and a naked and bloody bone was protruding from the torn flesh. Sidimi looked at her patient. Thankfully he had passed out. Without a word she took the large knife she carried with her and passed it through the flames – one, two, three times – until she was convinced that it was rid of any germs. Then, she quickly sliced through the flesh until the wasted limb fell to the ground. She beckoned for her assistant to retrieve it. At first he hesitated, thoroughly repulsed by the sight. She barked an order and the assistant quickly covered the limb with a cloth and carried it away. They would later bury it, with the other limbs they had removed and with the dead. Meanwhile Sidimi pressed the hot knife against the wound, awakening the soldier who screamed and tried to sit upright. She gently forced him down. It was all over. She would wrap the limb in gauze and send him to Tindouf to recover. His marching days were over.

She stopped for a moment at one of the blankets. It was a young man not too much older than her brother. She had tied bandages around his chest as best she could to stop the bleeding, but she knew it was no use. The bullet had penetrated his abdomen and thick black blood was oozing from the wound. She held his hand and tried to comfort him.

"Are you in pain?" she asked.

He looked at her with calm, clear eyes. "No, the pain has stopped. I just feel tired," he said in a whisper barely audible over the din of the battle.

As he gazed at her she could see tears slowly fill his eyes. "I am not afraid of dying," he said slowly, "But I left my son in Smara. He was only two years old. He will never know me. I will never see him grow." Then he looked into her eyes with a sadness that pierced her to her core.

"When you have a child, you will understand," he said, once again averting his eyes.

Sidimi paused for a moment. Then she reached for something she carried in a small pouch around her neck. It was a small, tattered photo. She placed it close to the soldier's eyes.

"This is a picture of my daughter," she said softly. "She was only three months old when I left her and her brother and sister in El Ayoun with my mother. I joined the men fighting in the north with Abdelaziz when the Moroccans invaded." She blushed slightly. "I was considered good with a rifle." She touched the picture tenderly and placed it back in her pouch. "The children were too young to make the trip through the desert, so they stayed with my mother in El Ayoun." She said those words as if trying to convince herself.

The soldier's face softened. "Have you been able to get any word of them?" he asked.

"No," she said.

After a pause that seemed like an eternity, the soldier again spoke. "I wonder if they will remember us?"

"They will remember us."

Those were the last words he said as he slowly drifted into the long black night that awaits us all.

December, 1976.

The military invasion of Western Sahara had eclipsed tribal rivalries and brought together the *Ahel es-Sahel* from all corners of their diaspora in a common cause. By the winter of 1976, in addition to the thousands of fighters from nearly all the Sahrawi tribes in southern Morocco who had joined them, several thousand more from northern Mauritania and almost all of the Reguibat who had settled in the Tindouf and Bechar regions of Algeria – numbering nearly 18,000 – had joined the defectors from the Spanish Tropas Nomadas and territorial police to swell the ranks of the Polisario.

At the beginning of the war, to play on tribal rivalries, Dlimi had created a number of small mobile units comprised of Sahrawis which accompanied Moroccan forces and roamed southern Morocco and the Saguia el Hamra region guarding the convoys of troops and supplies. Most of them were manned by Sahrawis from southern Morocco and were known by the names of their commanders: Salek Faitah, Aida Tamek, Mohammed Kheir, Mohammedi,

141

Deisch, Lahsen Moulid, Ahmed Moulay and Habouha. But many of these Sahrawis defected during 1976, and others refused to fight their brethren in battles. By 1977 these units were largely disbanded.

During the fall and winter months of 1976 skirmishes between guerilla forces and Moroccans as far north as the Atlas mountain range proceeded at regular intervals. Members of the 1st and 5th military regions attacked enemy forces at Housa, Farsia and Jdiriya and any supply caravan brave enough to try to traverse the Saguia el Hamra or Laayoune – Tan Tan corridors. Polisario troops never spent more than a few days at one spot. Scouts would monitor the movement of enemy troops and attacks by troops from these regions against convoys or major skirmishes would occur every 4 or 5 days.

Meanwhile troops in the 2nd military region constantly harassed Moroccan and Mauritanian troops in the Laayoune – Boujdour – Smara – Amgala – Bir Lehlou corridor. With their superior knowledge of the desert terrain and their ability to guide themselves in total darkness, they had been able to mount surprise attacks over long distances and evaporate into the night air as quickly as they had come. Troops from the region staged a ten day long attack against the Moroccans at Smara. After that they moved south to attack the Mauritanians at Bir Moghrein. There were attacks in Bir Lehlou, and near Lemgassem, and one against a convoy going between Mahbes and Bir Lehlou in which they were able to seize the entire convoy. Two weeks after that battle they attacked Moroccan troops at Mahbes and were able to occupy it briefly.

The battles between troops from the 2nd military region and the combined Moroccan-Mauritanian forces continued intermittently for weeks along the route from Gara Fouggar, Dara Khiba and Boudhair. Over a thousand Polisario fighters joined the foray. Some, in Land Rovers, pushed the enemy forces from the southern plains into the hills that stretched north of the plains, into the arms of waiting guerilla infantry. Others sniped at their positions under cover of darkness, retreating by day.

By the end of November the Moroccan and Mauritanian troops throughout the region were badly in need of supplies. However, the Mauritanians bore the brunt of the hardship. In a desperate move, Mauritanian troops stationed at Bir Moghrein started to march again towards Mheris to engage Bouhali's units. But before they arrived at the outpost they were ambushed by guerillas that destroyed their column, demolishing 3 tanks, 10 trucks and many other vehicles in the process. The following month they were again ambushed and two Mauritanian planes were shot down. They then called for help from Moroccan troops stationed at Smara and Guelta Zemmour. On December 19, Colonel Abdel Karim Khataby and his Moroccan troops marched towards their location but were intercepted by guerilla forces. Colonel Khataby was killed on the first day, and his troops, thoroughly demoralized, retreated after waiting ten days for reinforcements which never arrived. By the end of the year the Moroccans were forced to fly supplies to Bir Moghrein by air to relieve the beleaguered Mauritanian troops and the Mauritanians had refused to venture north from Bir Moghrein to Ain Ben Tili.

And the worsening situation in the Sahara became a thorn in the side of the rulers of the world.

Late December, 1976. Washington, D.C.

Henry Kissinger was sitting alone in his office in the State Department. It was a bright winter day in the Nation's Capital, but he was in no mood for looking at the sunlit sky. It was a month after the election that had determined that he would not remain at the helm of United States' foreign policy, and the future was looking grim. Gerald Ford, Richard Nixon's Vice President who ascended to the presidency when Nixon resigned over the Watergate scandal, had been battered by an unforgiving public, and before long a peanut farmer from Georgia, whose greatest asset was his lack of experience on the national stage, would take over the reins of government.

Kissinger was determined that if he was forced into exile it would not be without leaving a lasting mark. He had already laid the groundwork for a continued U.S. influence in South America, and now it was Africa's turn. Congress, in an uproar over unauthorized military support for pro-Western regimes around the world, despite their questionable records on human rights, had just passed the so-called "Clark Amendment" to the U.S. Arms Export Control Act of 1976 – named for its author, Democratic Senator from Iowa Dick Clark --which prohibited aid to private groups engaged in military or paramilitary operations in Angola.

As a result, Kissinger had been forced to find another way to advance his foreign policy agenda in the country. Simple. He would allow United States allies to act as U.S. "surrogates." So, he had contacted d'Estaing of France – always a reliable ally in such endeavors – and together they had concocted a strategy to maintain support for the UNITAs and other pro-Western regimes on the continent.

The French intelligence agency would organize in secret an alliance among an elite group of states – referred to colloquially as the "Safari Club"— that would include the U.S., France, Saudi Arabia, Iran, Egypt and Morocco – whose mission would be to counteract Soviet influence in Africa. The four Arab states would funnel military aid, or troops, to pro-Western forces, while the United States and France would act as "advisors." Israel would also intervene if necessary.

Already Hassan had indicated his willingness to participate – assuming he was still on the throne.

It was now up to Kissinger to see that he remained on the throne.

So when advisors from the Pentagon, the NSA, and the CIA met to discuss the issue, he came straight to the point.

"Moroccan and Mauritanian troops trying to consolidate control over the territory of Western Sahara ceded to them by Spain are meeting stiff resistance from a group of Bedouin guerillas calling themselves the Polisario. We have been giving King Hassan military support as has France, but so far this support has not been sufficient to thwart their raids. Hassan's regime is vital to U.S. interests and this Sahara campaign is vital to his regime. I want to hear your thoughts on how we can help him defeat these rebels. . . and why no one warned me about these guerillas before."

The room grew quiet for a moment, then a man in uniform with stars on his shoulder, after looking around the room in vain for help, spoke up, somewhat sheepishly.

"This group – the Polisario – was for the most part just a ragtag group of disgruntled students and former soldiers in the Spanish army who had been engaging in clandestine, small scale attacks against the Spanish. We never thought they would be able to muster the strength to engage in a war with trained Moroccan and Mauritanian forces."

"Well," said Kissinger sarcastically, "this 'ragtag group' as you put it has managed to successfully harass both the Moroccan and Mauritanian forces for nearly a year, and they were even able to cross nearly 1,000 miles of desert to attack the Mauritanian capital Nouakchott."

"Yes, I know," said the man in uniform, stifling a smile, "but their leader was killed and it didn't accomplish much militarily speaking."

Kissinger slammed his fist on the table. "They didn't need to accomplish anything militarily speaking . . . what they accomplished was far more important, they got pictures of themselves plastered across the newspapers and everyone started to pay attention to this war of theirs." He paused. "They may be ragtag, but they know how to use the media! What I want to know is why is it that the Moroccan army has been so ineffective in stopping their attacks?"

"The problem is that they employ classic guerilla tactics – striking targets quickly, usually at night and sometimes from far distances, then melting into the desert before they can be apprehended."

"Why can't they find their hideouts and attack them?" the man in the dark suit asked, "I would think they would stick out like a sore thumb in the desert!"

The man in uniform shook his head. "The territory they occupy isn't just sand dunes. There are a number of dried river beds, nooks and crannies where a small group can hide, and the Ouarkziz and Zuni escarpments are ideal guerilla territory."

One of the young aides raised his hand hesitantly. "Sir, isn't it true that the guerillas rely on support from Libya and Algeria to maintain their military operations? Is there any way we could place pressure on them to stop this support?"

The man in uniform again spoke up. "I think your assistant has a point. Isn't this conflict really between Morocco and Algeria? Is there any way we could put political pressure on the Algerians?"

Kissinger gave the man in uniform a withering look. Political pressure. When the military can't find a solution they toss the ball to us.

The man in the dark suit spoke up. "We know that Khaddafi has been giving them some weapons which they have been able to smuggle in through the desert and we are trying to close that route. As for the Algerians . . . well, we have threatened to help the Moroccans pursue any Polisario troops that cross the border from Morocco into Algeria, but so far we haven't found any evidence that they are doing this. Nor have we found any evidence that they are attacking Morocco from bases in Algeria. Look, here is a map of the area where Morocco intersects with Algeria, and here is the Algerian border with Western Sahara," he said, pointing to areas on a map.

"As far as we have been able to tell, all the Polisario troops are stationed either in Western Sahara, Mauritania or southern Morocco. They only go to their headquarters in Tindouf for supplies or medical treatment. . . and their attacks on targets in Morocco are from bases there, not Algeria."

"But can't we complain about the Algerians giving them support?"

"Of course we can – and we do – just as they complain about our giving support to the Moroccans. I'm afraid we are not exactly on the high moral ground here, especially after what we did behind the scenes to support the Madrid Accords and scuttle the UN plans for a referendum."

The room became quiet. "So, in other words we have nothing that we can use to put pressure on Algeria. The Algerians can continue to give arms and support to guerilla troops in Western Sahara as long as they do not themselves engage in any battles, and if the Moroccans bomb their headquarters in Algerian territory they would be killing for the most part women and children refugees – nothing we would like to see on the 6 o'clock news."

". . . besides committing an act of war!"

"And a war between Morocco and Algeria would be in no one's self interest," interjected Kissinger. "So what can we do?"

The room once again became silent.

"Well, the best we can do is give them some additional military aid and hope for the best," someone said.

And on that gloomy note the meeting adjourned, and the year 1976 faded quietly into the past.

CHAPTER 4
1977

Mauritania.

Although there continued to be battles between guerillas and enemy forces throughout the territory and beyond, in 1977 the main thrust of the guerillas' forces was in the south – within Mauritania itself – in a campaign that often utilized troops from more than one military region. Mauritania's northern border with Western Sahara, which ran parallel to the railroad lines which linked the iron ore mines of Zouerate to the Nouadhibou port, had become the staging ground for continuous assaults by groups of guerillas who would swoop from desert outposts, disrupt lines of communication, and overpower scantily defended garrisons. On three occasions guerillas had ripped up stretches of the track from the Zouerate iron mines to the port of Noudhibou, slowly bleeding the government of Ould Daddah of its export revenue and demoralizing its citizens.

However, the *coup de grâce* was the attacks on the trains themselves. With almost two hundred cars, pulled by four locomotives, they often stretched over a mile and would take almost a day to reach the coast. On February 20, 1977, guerillas in two Land Rovers with machine guns attacked a train for the first time, destroying three locomotives with rocket fire about sixty miles south of Zouerate. The trains then became a favorite target. Time and time again they were bombed, until attacks on the trains became routine news. At first the Mauritanian government did nothing to protect them other than posting a few, relatively inexperienced and thoroughly scared, soldiers in the cars. However, after months of attacks they started putting machine guns on the roofs of the cars. This did nothing to deter the guerillas who simply blasted the guns before they could be put to use.

Their plan was working. Now if they could only scare away the 280 or so Frenchmen working for SNIM, the Société Nationale des Industries Minières, and COMINOR, the Comptoir Miner du Nord, the government would be left without skilled workmen to work the mines and the mines would come to a complete halt.

It was time to plan a major assault.

April 30, 1977. Zouerate.

It was early spring in the desert and in a small enclave several hundred miles to the south of Bir Lehlou, Brahim Ghali called together the commanders of the 3rd and 5th regions for a high level strategy meeting, and together with Abdelaziz they decided on a plan.

Word was sent out to guerilla units in scattered locations throughout the southern part of the territory to begin a long march through the desert. At a rendezvous point about 200 miles east of Zouerate they met up with Salek and a group of about one hundred fighters who had marched south with Brahim Ghali, another fifty from the 3rd military region who had marched west under the command of Ayoub Lahbib, and several other *kateeb* from the 5th regional command under the direction of Hammada El Ouali, who had marched south from their hideouts deep in the Ouarkziz mountain range. They then followed the route through the desert taken by El Ouali the previous year until they reached the outskirts of Zouerate.

Meanwhile, Bouhali set up a blockade to the north of the town to prevent Mauritanian reinforcements from Bir Moghrein from coming to the aid of the Zouerate forces.

By the evening of April 30 they had reached their rendezvous point, and Salek could see in the distance the lights of the mining complex shining bright in the darkness. But directly in front of him was a dirt wall and the rim of what appeared to be a large ditch. He had heard that in response to the mortaring of the local power station that had taken place in the early days of the war, Ould Daddah had dug an enormous trench, thirty five miles long and eleven feet deep, around the complex to ward off invaders, liberally sprinkled with both anti tank and anti personnel land mines.

He said a silent prayer and gently lowered himself into the dark pit. So far, so good, he thought. But now the hard part would come. Squatting on his belly he slowly began inching his way through the trench in the direction of the faint glow that appeared above him on the far horizon, probing the earth before him gently with his fingertips for any sign of metal. He could hear the muffled sounds of comrades who were crawling on his left and right. He wondered who would reach the goal line first! No matter, as long as none of them was blown to bits. When he had proceeded no more than a few inches his fingers touched something smooth and hard. Ever so gently he dug the object out of the earth with his fingers, placing it carefully in a knapsack on his back. He crawled another few inches. Another object. For hours he crawled, slowly, inch by inch, covering every inch of the earth in front of him with his fingers. It was nearly daybreak when his fingers finally touched the wall at the other side of the trench. He could hear voices above him, the voices of sentries that were patrolling the complex. He froze. Someone asked for a cigarette. Someone was telling about his last leave. Someone laughed. Slowly the voices receded, and after waiting what seemed an eternity he began the slow crawl back through the trench along the path he had taken. It would take him the entire night to reach the other side to the safety of his comrades. But when he had finished a path through the trench had been cleared.

While Salek was in the trench Ghali's men were pushing the assorted Land Rovers and trucks slowly, inch by inch, towards the target -- at a snails pace, to eliminate as much noise as possible.

At the first glimmer of sunlight the infantry quickly scaled the embarkation, dove once again into the pit, and headed for the buildings. When the lone sentry saw the wave of guerillas approach, he quickly put up his arms in surrender. The Land Rovers and trucks raced through the trench onto the other side, their machine guns blasting. The fighters kicked in the doors to the barracks and the Mauritanian soldiers, still in their beds, offered no resistance. The other members of the fifteen hundred strong Mauritanian garrison, whose commander Ould Heydalla, was away in Nouakchott, also gave up without a struggle. It was not their fight. A useless strip of land in the desert was not worth sacrificing their lives.

Salek and his companions roamed through the complex unchallenged for two hours, demolishing railway installations, administrative buildings and the power station. Eventually they reached the airport. Two planes sat on the tarmac and they were quickly blown to bits. While the others were busy destroying the planes and equipment at the airport, Salek and two of his companions burst into the airport bar, Le Ranch, and discovered, to their surprise, a group of Frenchmen who had spent the night there drinking. Two of them fired at the guerillas and were gunned down. Six others – five men and one woman -- escaped through a rear door but were quickly captured.

By midday, after gathering up as much ammunition and supplies as they could, the guerillas started their long trek back to the desert. However, no sooner had they reached a point near Zadnas, 250 miles or so from the mining complex, then they saw columns of soldiers following them from two directions. A small contingent of fewer than 100 Mauritanian soldiers was approaching from the direction of Zouerate, but a much larger column of over 600 Moroccans was approaching from Bir Moghrein to the north.

Ghali surveyed the area around him. They were out in the open. They could either disperse and try to out run the troops in the desert, or they could hold their ground. He looked at the faces of the men who surrounded him. He had only 200 or so troops at his command, but each one was a seasoned desert fighter.

He turned and shouted an order, and within seconds the column of Land Rovers turned and at full speed began to race through the desert towards the approaching enemy lines, their machine guns blasting. The enemy troops stopped dead in their tracks, then they began to disperse, returning fire as they melted into the sand. After an hour all that remained of them were dots on the far horizon, receding into the distance.

The column of guerillas began again their trek eastward, toward the waiting *hammada*.

Within days of the attack the French citizens in Zouerate began to be evacuated and the operation of the mines grounded to a halt.

But the guerillas didn't stop there. One month after Ghali and troops from the 3rd and 4th military regions attacked Zouerate, Bouhali selected a number of fighters to go to the outskirts of the town. The idea was to prevent the troops from Zouerate from sending supplies to Bir Moghrein by ambushing caravans as they left the base. But after waiting a few days for a supply caravan to leave the enclave, they began to run out of water and decided to attack the town itself. They were not able to use their vehicles since the Mauritanians had made the berm surrounding the complex significantly higher, so they attacked on foot. Again they were able to overrun the town. Once inside they destroyed a number of installations, and in their retreat they were even able to shoot down the plane of the commander of the Mauritanian air force, Colonel Khaddar.

Four months later Bouhali's troops attacked a convoy of Mauritanian troops stationed at Bir Moghrein -- and the Moroccan troops sent to reinforce them -- in the salt pans adjacent to the outpost at a place called Aridal, and totally eliminated them.   Thirty-seven Moroccan officers and twelve Mauritanians were captured, as well as dozens of cars and other equipment, in one of the most devastating defeats of the year -- and the one road from Bir Moghrein to Zouerate had become impassable.

September 1, 1977. Lemgassem.

The soldiers who formed the nucleus of Bouhali's troops were a hardy bunch. They had become used to the constant marching and change of location. When one is constantly on the move it is difficult to maintain even a semblance of civilized life. So, they were relishing the small camp, nestled in the hills of Lemgassem that had become a makeshift base of operations. Here there was a tributary of the *wadi* close by for bathing and washing clothes. There were abundant caves that could shelter them from the heat, the wind, and the cold. They even dared to build small fires to brew their tea and cook their food.

However, their camp was just 25 miles from a Moroccan garrison that had been sent from Lebouirate at the end of June to establish a base at Tifariti – and the Moroccans knew where they were. Moroccan spy planes had located their camp and from time to time sent bombs their way -- but they dropped them from high altitudes so they caused little damage. The constant attacks on their troops and caravans had left the Moroccans wary of leaving the safety of their garrison to engage them -- but there was always the chance that some day some brave soul might try.

September 1, 1977 was one such day.

Bouhali had left with a handful of men on a scouting expedition, leaving another handful of men behind to guard the camp. The rest of his forces were sprinkled throughout the region, ready to relay information of any troop movements. Sidimi had just returned from a sojourn to Tindouf to stock up on additional medicines and supplies and was busy stacking vials and bottles

149

in the cave that served as her dispensary. In one of the hills surrounding the complex a sentry reclined on a boulder indolently smoking a cigarette. But his dreams were soon shattered by a noise that made him sit up and get his binoculars. What he saw caused him to scramble down the hill and run as fast as he could to the camp.

"Troops are coming!" he yelled, trying to catch his breath. Within a minute he was surrounded by men excitedly asking questions.

In her cave Sidimi heard the din and decided to investigate. "What is it?" she asked as she approached.

"There is a column of Moroccans coming our way . . . probably a unit of the 'rapid intervention forces' that Dlimi has created. They should be here within an hour," one of them responded. Then giving Sidimi a stern look he added "You should probably hide as best you can."

"What are you going to do?" asked Sidimi.

"We have sent someone to catch up with Bouhali and to spread the word to the troops scattered in the hills. In the mean time we will find places in the hills to hide. Hopefully we will be able to hold them off until Bouhali arrives," he said before running off.

Sidimi raced to the cave where she had stocked the medical supplies. There was no time to load the crates of medicine and other supplies in her jeep and take them somewhere safe, so she tried to cover the cave's entrance with brush and stones, and hid the jeep as best she could. Then she grabbed her gun, climbed one of the nearby hills, found a crevice to hide in, and waited for what seemed like an eternity.

But it was actually only a few minutes before the quiet that surrounded her was pierced by a shot. Then another. Then a barrage. Shots and blasts of artillery that were coming from the direction of the hills to her right.

She left her hiding place and climbed to the far side of the hill. Through the trees she could see a clearing below her, and in the clearing a number of vehicles – Moroccan vehicles – carrying light artillery. Crouched beside them were Moroccan soldiers, firing at the trees on the far side, their backs towards her. Above her she could hear the fierce whirring of a helicopter, raining bullets on the hillside where the guerillas lay. She took her gun, aimed, and fired – and one of the soldiers fell to the ground.   The others swirled around and started firing aimlessly in her direction. She waited a moment until the firing stopped. Then she crawled to another tree, aimed and fired again. She changed positions again before firing another round. Meanwhile, the helicopter swirled around, aiming its guns in her direction. One volley, then two. Bullets missing her by inches. She grasped her gun and fired a shot, aiming at the propellers, but the bullet missed, instead lodging in the pilot's door. The steel bird fired again, this time blanketing the ground around her and sending bits of earth and rock swirling in the air. But it had missed its mark, and Sidimi managed to fire another round, this time piercing the glass on the pilot's door. The helicopter shuttered for a second, then raised itself up and moved to the far side of the hill.

Not a moment too soon. Sidimi looked at her weapon. She had three rounds left, and the Moroccans were blocking her from reaching the spot where the additional ammunition was stored. From now on she could only pray that Bouhali would arrive soon with reinforcements. For nearly an hour her colleagues managed to keep the Moroccans pinned down with only their light arms. Then, to their great relief, they heard the sound of gun fire in the distance. Bouhali's troops! The Moroccans heard it too, and scrambled into their vehicles to beat a hasty retreat.

While on patrol with a handful of his men Bouhali had stumbled upon a Moroccan supply caravan being escorted by a platoon of soldiers. At the end of a long line of trucks they noticed one that was loaded to the brim with ammunition -- ammunition that they badly needed. So, instead of retreating, they had decided to ambush them. On foot they attacked, and within less than an hour had managed to chase the soldiers escorting the caravan into the hills. They were returning to their camp, with the truck of ammunition in tow, when they had gotten the message.

That evening, when peace once again descended on the camp, Bouhali took the men he had left there aside and praised them for their work. But he was puzzled. If all of them were in positions to the right of the Moroccans, who was firing on them from the left? And who was it who disabled the helicopter?

They shook their heads. No one knew.

For a long while it remained a mystery. When they finally realized it was Sidimi the troops started affectionately calling her Che -- as in Che Guevara, the Argentine Marxist revolutionary who was both a doctor and a guerilla fighter – a nickname that she found somewhat amusing, for in her eyes she hadn't done anything extraordinary at all.

September 1, 1977. Rendezvous with Destiny.

Back at his palace in Rabat, oblivious to the skirmishes that were taking place at Lemgassem, Hassan sat in his armchair contemplating his next move. In January a new President of the United States had taken office – Jimmy Carter – who had championed the principles of human rights and adherence to international law, neither of which would endear the Moroccan regime to him. Of course, politicians had espoused these principles before, and had abandoned them in a heartbeat when the pressures of *realpolitik* began to emerge. But that wily diplomat Kissinger had been replaced by a bunch of neophytes and Carter's administration seemed to be drifting rudderless through the treacherous shoals of international diplomacy. There was no telling what he might do. The King couldn't afford to lose the political or military support of the United States, and he had done everything possible – from supplying troops for their proxy war in the Congo to supporting the apartheid regime in South Africa and the UNITAS -- to win their favor. But so far that had not been enough to persuade the new President to cater to

Morocco's interests. No, something else was needed. Something that Carter would find irresistible. He needed a Plan "B".

In a few days one would be dropped in his lap. . . .

It was a sunny day in mid September, and the cafes in Casablanca were filled with tourists intently perusing their maps, planning their excursions to Fez or Marrakesh. A man in a tan safari suit with a patch over one eye stood out from the crowd. Perhaps a business man taking a brief respite from a long day's work. None of the tourists paid particular attention.

After a few minutes he was joined by another man, taller and thinner, with short, black curly hair and a greyish goatee. At another table sat two men in dark suits, wearing dark glasses, reading a newspaper, and glancing every now and then at the direction of the man with the patch. In a car parked a few yards from the café, two other men sat, eyes glued to the first pair, with cups of coffee perched perilously on the dashboard.

The man with the patch was the first to speak. "I am happy to have this opportunity to meet you. My Prime Minister would be quite happy to begin a dialogue with your President to discuss topics of mutual interest. I think we both know that the talks in Geneva are going nowhere." He took a sip of coffee and waited for the other man to respond.

The other man looked at him intently. He turned to a waiter and ordered an express, and when his eyes returned once again to his companion, his words were brief and to the point.

"My President has assured me he would be willing to meet your Prime Minister in person to discuss the return of our lands and an end to the conflict."

The man with the patch seemed to ponder this last statement for a moment. Then he spoke, in a quiet tone. "I think that could be arranged. . . do you have any suggestions about a location?"

The other man leaned back in his chair, his body suddenly relaxed. "He has told me he would be willing to meet anywhere . . . even Jerusalem!"

The man with a patch broke into a smile. Jerusalem! That would indeed be historic. "Let me see what I can arrange," he finally said, standing as if to leave. "In the meantime let us continue our discussions."

The other man also smiled. "Yes, Morocco is beautiful at this time of the year," he said, and then added, nonchalantly, ". . . and the Moroccan King is a gracious host." The man with the patch smiled again, nodded, and turned to leave.

As the man with the patch walked away from the café down the avenue, the two men in the car put down their cups and pulled away from the curb. In a few minutes the other man finished his coffee and walked in the opposite direction, followed at a discreet distance by the two men in the dark suits.

On November 9 a press release would announce that the President of Egypt, Anwar Sadat had declared his intention to visit Israel to address the Israeli Kniesset, at the invitation of Israeli Prime Minister Meachim Begin.

October 25, 1977. Final Straw.

During the summer and fall of 1977 guerilla attacks in Mauritania became both more numerous and more audacious. After the first Nouakchott campaign Ould Daddah had claimed that the Polisario would not dare attack Nouakchott again since they had lost El Ouali. In 1977 the guerillas decided to prove him wrong. From bases near Amgala, six dozen Land Rovers under the command of Ayoub Lahbib swept through the desert to the outskirts of the city, and on the afternoon of July 3rd once again bombed the presidential palace and the radio station. Although units from Bouhali's forces were positioned between them and Mauritanian units at Zouerate and Awsard for protection, they encountered no resistance, and on their return home Ayoub's troops were bold enough to take the tarmac highway to the north, under cover of darkness, before vanishing into the desert twenty miles from Akjoujt. They returned to their Amgala bases with almost no casualties. Two weeks later they repeated the raid.

As a further act of defiance, on October 25, they staged another attack on the railway, about thirty seven miles south of Zouerate, this time seizing two French technicians whom they held for political concessions. This was the last straw for COMINOR, which immediately suspended all rail service.

It was also the last straw for Giscard d'Estaing of France.

October 27, 1977. Operation Lamantin.

Giscard d'Estaing was frustrated. At a secret strategy session with his allies at the end of 1976 it had been agreed that he would take the lead in bolstering the Mauritanian forces, and for months he had been supplying Ould Daddah with arms and training. Scores of civilian "advisors" had been sent to ensure the supply of the one major Mauritanian product of any use to France – the iron ore produced at the Zouerate mines. None of these efforts produced the desired results, and the Mauritanian forces, like a bevy of bewildered children, seemed incapable of thwarting the advances of the Sahrawi guerillas in the sandbox that was the vast Mauritanian desert.

Now they had gone too far – captured additional French civilians in a raid on the Zouerate rail line and demanded concessions from France for their release. Just whom did they think they were dealing with? -- he thought, his blood pressure rising.

The day was October 27, 1977, two days after the attack. The place was the Elysee Palace. D'Estaing had summoned Louis de Guiringaud, Yvon Bourges, the Defense Minister, Robert Galley, the Minister for Cooperation, and General Guy Mery, the Chief of Staff of the Armed Forces, to an emergency meeting to plan a response, and he was in no mood for compromise.

Mery was the head of a permanent crisis command known as the Centre Opérationnel des Armée (COA), situated in a bunker under the defense ministry in Paris, which had been entrusted with strategic planning for French military intervention in Mauritania. It was he who spoke first.

"Monsieur le President, I know you are anxious to send the guerillas a message, but I strongly advise against an Entebbe style commando operation to free the hostages. Finding them in the desert would be like searching for a needle in a haystack, and, if they are being held in Algerian territory – which is entirely possible -- it would involve France in a direct clash with Algeria." He held his breath for a moment to let his words sink in and then continued. "I think we need to keep in mind the larger picture. This incident may have dropped into our laps the opportunity to buttress Ould Daddah's defenses directly without risking a public outcry."

D'Estaing's visage, at first noticeably disturbed by the sanguine tone of his top general's comments, began to soften as he pondered what he had heard. After a long pause he turned to face him. "What exactly do you have in mind?"

Thirty minutes later, a plan was agreed. Using the Ouakkam airfield on the Cap Vert peninsula at Dakar, only fifteen minutes' flying time from Nouakchott for a supersonic jet, the French air force would provide direct air support to the Mauritanian army, including sorties over Western Sahara territory to ferret out and destroy guerilla outposts. The plan was dubbed "Operation Lamantin."

One week after Operation Lamantin was hatched in the Elysee Palace, a special force of 185 elite troops flew out to Dakar under the command of General Michel Forget, to buttress the eleven hundred French troops who were already there. Forget, accompanied by sixty military specialists, then flew to Mauritania to establish a communications network to detect and destroy guerilla cells in the desert.

At the same time, in order to observe guerilla positions and photograph unmapped desert regions, French Breguet Atlantic aircraft began quietly flying over Mauritania and Western Sahara from the Ouakkam airfield in Dakar in coordinated sorties with Mirages, 4 long range strategic reconnaissance aircraft sent from Bordeaux. By the first week of December six Jaguars from the French tactical air command base at Toul had been stationed at Ouakkam, plus two KC-135F refueling planes, and four Noratlas transport planes, in addition to the two Breguet Atlantic aircraft.

The stage for what was to come had been set.

December 12, 1977. Revenge.

The men lay for hours in the sun drenched desert, their clothes soaked in sweat, hidden among the rocks and the crevices. As usual the train was arriving late, but they would wait, patiently and silently, for as long as it would take.

On November 21 Ould Daddah had announced the reopening of the railway, sending an open invitation to the guerillas. The very next day, when COMINOR sent its first train down the line from Nouadhibou they had attacked, capturing the engine driver and ten Mauritanian soldiers. It was now December 12, and Ould Daddah was trying again.

In order to deter the guerillas, the Mauritanians had placed small units of soldiers at intervals along the length of the rail line. The commander of a force of roughly 200 fighters in nine Land Rovers chose to attack one of these units at a spot about forty miles southwest of Zouerate called Tmeimichatt. After subduing the Mauritanian soldiers they waited. Finally the scout they had sent to test the rails waived his hands in the air. He had felt a slight tremor in the rails, a sign of an approaching train. He quickly resumed his position.

Within minutes the train arrived, passing at slow speed, a big, fat, undulating monster of over a hundred cars, each one loaded with iron ore bound for the coast.

As the train slowly passed their position, the commander gave the signal. The sound of a thousand thunder claps pierced the silence and the engine and the first two cars flew into the air and crash landed, crumpled in heaps of metal, like discarded children's toys, several yards from the track. The ensuing fire demolished another two cars, scattering bits of smoldering iron over the rocky terrain.

Salek and his companions quickly boarded the remaining cars and marched the Mauritanian soldiers, as well as the civilians who worked for COMINOR, to the side of the tracks. There were over 82 prisoners. In addition they confiscated 22 cars and 2 trucks. Their work done, the guerillas loaded the prisoners onto the trucks and hastily returned to the Land Rovers that had been hidden beneath camouflaged tarps under the sprawling acacia trees that dotted the landscape. From there they began the long procession back to their camp.

They were inching their way through the huge sand dunes that marked the approach to a place called Zug, just over the Mauritanian border in Western Sahara, only ten miles from the wreckage, when the assault began. From seemingly nowhere first one, then two Jaguars streaked across the sky, firing at their vehicles. Then the bombing began, and the desert began to be filled with craters from the explosives, sending enormous clouds of dust and sand whirling through the air, choking their throats and making it impossible to see. They had removed the windshields from their vehicles, to eliminate glare from the sun and make it more difficult for them to be spotted, but this had also eliminated any protection from the sand which now rained down on them. In the semi darkness they searched in vain for any familiar signs in the desert to show them the direction they should take.

Salek decided to take cover at the edge of one of the dunes and to wait until the dust had settled. The dust had also made it difficult for the pilots to identify their vehicles, and after a few more sorties, they abandoned the search and returned to their base. The sky gradually cleared, and Salek looked around for signs of his companions.

In the distance he saw the burnt remains of one of the Land Rovers, its inhabitants scorched beyond recognition. A little farther on he found the remains of one of the trucks, overturned and riddled with bullets, its occupants lying motionless a few feet away. As he proceeded, with grim determination, he counted the dead – over ten guerillas and dozens of Mauritanians – with another ten gravely wounded. Three of the nine Land Rovers that had set out on the mission and six of the Mauritanian cars were able to be salvaged. The other vehicles were damaged beyond repair or had simply been covered by the dunes.

There was no time to bury the dead in a proper ceremony. Instead, their bodies were gently placed in a gully, and covered with as much sand and rock as they could quickly muster. Salek recited a verse from the Koran. The cars and Land Rovers were now crowded with the wounded, as well as the frightened Mauritanians. Salek as well as several of his companions would have to take turns walking besides the vehicles. It would be a long, slow, sad march through the desert.

Two hours passed, then three. In order to accommodate the weight of the additional passengers they had to jettison many of their supplies. Only the water was conserved, and even this was beginning to run low. Two of the wounded had died, and had been left behind, hastily buried beneath the sand. The soldiers were now able to ride in one of the vehicles, allowing the pace to pick up slightly.

They had managed to traverse nearly fifty miles of desert when they heard the noise again. At first a faint but constant hum, like that of a bumble bee, a sound made ever more distinct against the backdrop of a silent desert. The hum grew louder until it was transformed into the whirr of an engine. They looked up and saw against the horizon the unmistakable outline of a plane. The French Jaguar, after refueling at its base in Dakar, had returned, following the tracks of the Land Rovers and the debris in the desert until the pilot could see clearly the outline of the remaining vehicles. Salek and his companions tried to run for cover, but there was scant cover in this part of the desert and their vehicles stood out like pimples on the face of the earth. One by one the vehicles were attacked, first by gunfire, then by bombs which exploded with terrific force spraying bits of metal and fire. Napalm.

The commander shouted for his comrades to disperse. It is easier to attack a group of vehicles in a convoy than a handful of cars scattering every which way in the desert. The ploy worked and for a few moments the French pilot did not know which vehicle to attack. So he chose one at random. The bomb shattered the Land Rover, scattering remnants of those who were in it and painting the desert floor red with blood. But the other vehicles were nowhere to be seen, having burrowed like serpents into the sand. After searching for a few more minutes he sighed and returned to base. Tomorrow would be another day.

Salek was lucky. He was alive. He looked around but could see no sign of his comrades. Just as well, he thought. He pondered his next move. He could crawl back to their base, but if the planes were able to follow his tracks, he would be leading them straight to the command cell they had so carefully hidden in the desert. No, he would hide in a gully somewhere and wait until the French were tired of the search. He had no food, and was nearly out of water, and his Land Rover carried several wounded comrades, as well as Mauritanians, but he had no choice.

That evening as he tried to get some sleep he thought of his days as a youth in El Ayoun. His mother, his father, and his two sisters. He wondered whether they were safe. He wondered whether they were still alive. He banished dismal thoughts from his head and tried to think only of the good times, the happy times. And despite all his efforts the image of Elena invaded his memories, the way her lips pouted when she pretended to be cross, the way her eyes sparkled when she was excited, the way she smelled when she brushed against him. . . No, he could not let himself think those thoughts. She was gone. That was the end of it. But try as he might, he could not banish the image of her from his mind.

The following day he waited. The desert was once again devoid of sound, save for an occasional crow that would mark his territory or signal his discontent at his intrusion. By this time there was no water left, and if he did not get the wounded some medical attention quickly they were sure to die. So, they moved, stopping from time to time to sweep the rocky soil behind them with cut branches to remove any tire tracks.

When the sun was at its zenith they heard it again. The Jaguar had returned, buzzing around them like an angry bee, searching for any remnants of their troops in the desert. They were out in the open, completely exposed. There was no place to hide.

Salek decided to make a run for it. He revved up his engine and shot into the desert at top speed, in a zig zag course to avoid the bullets that were streaming in his path. Somehow through skill, or luck, or simply the will of Allah, he and those in his car managed to survive. After a few sorties the Jaguar, tired of pursuing moving dots in the sand, gave up the chase and returned to its base.

They continued through the night. By daylight they were in sight of the camp. A sentry had noticed their approach, and they were met by three of their unit. Salek was escorted to a shelter where he was treated to tea and morsels of food and given some fresh clothing to wear. The wounded were taken to another area where soldiers who had been given some rudimentary medical training were waiting. The Mauritanians, exhausted, frightened and half starved, were herded into a third area, where they were fed by guards and allowed to sleep.

When Salek had rested he was taken to the commander of the unit. The news was grim. Scores of his comrades had been killed, or wounded, or simply unaccounted for. For two days the Jaguars had bombed and strafed anything they could find in the desert for miles around the point where the train had been ambushed – killing Mauritanian goat herders who had the misfortune of crossing their paths as well as scores of Polisario fighters, and at least half of the Mauritanian prisoners who accompanied them. The bodies of victims, often shattered into fragments and scattered by the wind, lay strewn across the desert for miles, their blood forming pools of red in the white sand. Bits of metal, the remnants of cars and weapons projected from the sand like some macabre form of modern art. Stragglers had been drifting into the camp with horrific stories, and wounds to match.

December 20, 1977. Achilles Heel.

It was nearing the end of the year and while there were no snow flakes to mark the passage of time, one could sense the difference in the the changing reflection of the sun on the sands of the Sahara and the subtle difference in hues of red and gold dispersed among the amber grains. There was also a subtle change in the direction of the wind and an increase in the thunderous storms whose rain and dust would sweep across the empty plains at night, tearing through the tents and leaving in their wake a blanket of sand. But most of all there was a change in temperature. Gone was the scorching heat of midday, when all you could do is enjoy the traditional siesta and wait for the cool relief of the evening. The days had become milder, bearable. But the nights! They had become progressively colder. Now they would pass the evenings huddled in their tents, covered in blankets for warmth. If they had tents. If they had blankets.

Early one morning in the Lemgassem camp the soldier nominated to be the camp's "cook" had built a big fire. It was a Friday, the Moslem holy day, and although war does not recognize holidays, he always tried to prepare something special to mark the day. Yesterday a slab of lamb had arrived – a rare luxury during the war -- and he looked forward to preparing a little rice and turning it into a type of stew favored by his countrymen.

Sidimi had also arisen early. She would wander down to the *wadi* to take a bath in the secluded portion of the riverbed reserved for her use before the others took their turn. By the time she returned to the tents the cook was already roasting the meat, and the sweet aroma was wafting gently through the campsite.

"Bachir, you are a wonder!" she said, squatting close to the fire. "I only wish I could cook like you!"

The man blushed slightly, the beginning of a smile appearing on his face.

Soon Bouhali had joined them and the cook poured each a cup of Sahrawi tea to help them start the day. Instead of lingering for a second cup . . . which was his normal custom . . . Bouhali quickly drank his tea and started to walk back to his tent. Sidimi put down her cup and followed him. They walked together a few paces in silence before she spoke.

"Something's up, I can tell," she finally said, looking him in the eyes. He smiled a half smile.

"You are beginning to know me too well!" he replied. Then, after taking a breath he continued. "Yes, I have received a communiqué from Abdelaziz. He has called a meeting of the top political and military leaders. I will be leaving for his base camp soon."

She was quiet for a moment. Then she turned to him again. "Is it the French?" she asked.

"I don't know," he replied, "but it must be something important."

They stood for a moment without speaking. Their thoughts, however, were soon interrupted by the sharp sound of an explosion. Then another. Looking at the sky they could barely see the outline of a small speck of silver.

"Oh, not again!" Bouhali exclaimed, a note of irritation in his voice. But almost before he could mutter another sound another bomb burst so close to them that tiny bits of shrapnel became imbedded in their pants and a cloud of dust enveloped them.

"Quick, climb in here," he cried, grabbing Sidimi and pushing her into one of the makeshift trenches the guerillas had dug for just these types of emergencies. Another bomb burst nearly knocked him off his feet as he fell in the ditch next to her.

All around them soldiers scrambled to grab belongings, to dive into ditches. After another minute or two it was quiet again. That is, it was quiet except for the cook who was running in the direction of the jet waving his fist in the air and shouting words not used in polite conversation.

The fire he had so carefully nurtured was demolished . . . and the charred remains of his dinner were scattered in the sand.

At the sight of the cook they burst into laughter. They had become used to the Moroccan bombing raids. The Moroccan aircraft based in Laayoune had been bombing their camp once or twice a month – usually on a Friday, the day that was supposed to be set aside for prayer -- but always from high in the sky, not wishing to face the guerillas' estrellas. So, the only thing they had managed to destroy was their dinner and the pots they used to brew their tea!

"So, I guess it will be back to rice and a few morsels of goat meat again," Sidi finally said through her laughter, making a slight movement, as if to get up.

Bouhali had already jumped out of the ditch and reached his hand towards her to help her up.

"Are you all right?" he asked, suddenly serious.

"Just a few bruises from the fall, and a few pieces of shrapnel in my clothing," she said, plucking a few slivers of metal from her pants.

They looked at each other, perhaps a second or two longer than was necessary. But before either of them could say anything else Abdati ran up to them. "Commander, the car is ready to take you to the President," he announced breathlessly.

"I will be ready to go with you in a minute," he responded, gruffly. Then, turning again to Sidimi, he said, in mock seriousness, "Take care of those bruises. It will not do for our chief medical officer to be out of commission." Then he turned and started walking briskly to his quarters.

Abdati looked at his sister, grinning.

"What are you smiling about?" she asked, slightly annoyed.

"Oh, nothing, sis. It's just that I have noticed that Bouhali spends more than a little time in your clinic. . . and you seem to enjoy making tea for him in the morning," he said, the grin returning. "Are you sure there is nothing going on between you two that I should know about?"

She stopped what she was doing and turned to him. "You have been reading too many romantic novels, Abdati," she said, shrugging her shoulders and beginning to walk in the other direction.

159

"Still, I wouldn't be surprised if one day . . ." he called after her. But before he could complete the sentence Bouhali emerged and Abdati quickly followed him. When they had gone a short distance Bouhali noticed that he was looking at him, the same grin on his face.

"What's so funny?" he growled.

"Oh nothing . . . really nothing," Abdati replied, quickly regaining his composure. The look on Bouhali's face told him that he had better not raise the subject, so for the rest of the journey he sat next to him in silence.

Back at the spot Abdelaziz had chosen as his base camp a number of the Polisario leaders were milling about, waiting to hear what he would say. He had called an emergency meeting to address the new developments. The fact that the Moroccans had surrounded the major cities with acres of land mines was bad enough. The fact that Hassan was in the process of acquiring more sophisticated aircraft from France – Mirage jets that were faster and could fly lower than the olds F-5s – was even worse. But the most serious problem was the direct intervention of French forces in the battles against Mauritania – a move that had already caused them a number of casualties and which fundamentally altered the pieces on the chess board.

"The French are no longer content merely to give weapons and military aid to Ould Daddah," he began, gravely. "They are now fighting his war for him. Their pilots are better trained than his, and their Jaguars are far superior to the F-5s that he had been using. They are faster and can carry up to ten thousand pounds of bombs and rockets . . . and they have two 30 mm guns. They are also equipped with electronic gear that can protect them from attack by surface to air missiles and can be refueled in mid flight so they can cover large distances." He stopped and looked intently at each one of them. "There are six of them. They are stationed at an air base in Dakar and they are using two Berguet-Atlantic reconnaissance aircraft to detect our locations and strafe our positions."

For a moment the commanders were at a loss for words. Finally, one of them spoke up. "What do you suggest we do?" he asked, somewhat hesitantly.

Abdelaziz looked at him with eyes of steel. "What we always do," he responded slowly, his voice firm. "Find their Achilles heel!"

CHAPTER 5
1978

With the commencement of Operation Lamantin France virtually took control of the Mauritanian defenses, deploying sophisticated electronic missile countermeasures and airborne detection equipment, and mapping Mauritania's Saharan desert and its portion of Western Sahara. The French secret service even began recruiting mercenaries to fight alongside Mauritanian forces.

But if d'Estaing thought that these maneuvers would dampen the guerillas' enthusiasm for attacks within Mauritania, he underestimated their resourcefulness. Instead of abandoning their campaign against the rail line the guerillas parried the air strikes by simply changing their strategy. Rather than mounting large scale attacks on the mining complex and the railway they simply staged a continuous stream of small scale *ghazzi* raids, swooping from nowhere, destroying the tracks, demolishing the locomotives, and then dispersing into small units before disappearing into the desert. If a plane approached they would seek cover in the sand dunes that dotted the landscape and cover their vehicles with tarps. Since the planes usually tried to follow their tracks they were careful to obliterate their traces in the sand. Also the Jaguars were less effective at night time than they were during the day, so they relied on night time raids, dispersing and disappearing before dawn.

They also learned that the Jaguars were used in conjunction with reconnaissance aircraft which would patrol the territory and send word to the Jaguar base in Dakar, Senegal, when they spied Polisario columns. The Polisario commanders were able to estimate the time that it would take for the Jaguars to be deployed to the area under attack so that they could retreat in safety.

As a result, despite Operation Lamantin, the attacks on the railway remained as frequent as ever. A train was derailed on December 27, 1977 at Inal, midway between Zouerate and Nouadhibou. On January 7, 1978 a train was attacked at Choum, a hill at the edge of the sand dunes, 110 miles south of Zouerate. Touajil, a station fifty miles to the north, came under fire on January 26. A month later, four locomotives were derailed, several hundred yards of track were destroyed, and the railway was closed for four days. When it reopened, on February 25, another train was derailed sixty miles south of Zouerate. And so it continued, month after month, well into the summer.

At the same time as the attacks against the rail lines, guerillas continued their onslaught against Mauritanian troops throughout both Mauritanian and

161

Western Saharan territory. In April of 1978 Tichla was overrun. Battles then followed at Argoub, Boulanour, Inal and Doutrain. Guerillas later occupied Tmeimichat, capturing 126 prisoners and a number of vehicles. At Glaibat Le Guelaya they were able to defeat a force led by Major Mayouf, commander of the northern Mauritanian regiment, and evacuate a number of civilians.

Despite the thousands of troops sent by Morocco to defend positions in the north of the country and the might of the French air force, Ould Daddah was unable to stem the constant hemorrhaging of his army throughout the country at the hands of the guerillas, and by the summer of 1978, the strain on the Mauritanian economy and on the morale of its citizens had reached the breaking point.

July 10, 1978. Presidential Palace, Nouakchott.

On the evening of July 9, 1978, Ould Daddah sat in his office nervously twirling his pen. He was exhausted and at his wits end. This was not the future he had pictured for his presidency when he had delivered a new nation into the arms of the world. He had fought so hard to wrest control from the French, and yet he had been unable to run the iron and copper mines without their help. And here they were again, giving him orders, controlling his armed forces. As for Morocco, all his carefully laid plans had backfired. He had not really wanted to assert a claim to Western Sahara, he did it out of necessity, out of fear that if he did not accede to Morocco's invitation he would face Moroccan troops within shouting distance of his major city, ready to reassert their claim to his territory. And yet that is exactly what he faced today. Too weak to repel the guerillas by himself, he had been forced to acquiesce in the aid Morocco was all too willing to provide, and now nearly 10,000 Moroccan troops were on Mauritanian soil, in addition to the thousands of Moroccan troops which had positioned themselves around Dakhla and other strategic positions in Western Sahara near the Mauritanian border, ostensibly to protect his government – but will they really leave once the war is over?

The war! He had never expected such a war. This was not in the rosy picture Hassan had painted when he asked him to join him in presenting their claims to the international court. No, it was all to be handled diplomatically, through negotiations with Spain. A simple transfer of territory from a colonial power to the African states to which it belonged. A *fait accompli* that would stop the pressure from the UN for "self determination" dead in its tracks. Instead he had been boxed into a war that was slowly bleeding the country, forcing him to institute a very unpopular war tax of three days' wages per month, and to enlist mercenaries from the south and children as young as 14 in the army.

And on top of that he had to face the constant grumbling of his troops. Mauritania was a country ripe with inter-racial and ethnic tensions. The ruling class was largely of Arab ethnicity, but there was a significant black population from the Wolf, Soninke, Peuls and Toucoulents tribes. A significant portion of the Mauritanian army and officer corps were from these groups. It was they, more than anyone else, who were risking their lives in the war. They chafed at his programs to turn the country into an Arab and Moslem state, and saw the attempted annexation of portions of Western Sahara as a plot to extend Arab rule over the region. The same policies that had won the support of Khaddafi had alienated many of his own people. But perhaps more important were their fears of the Moroccan troops that had now infiltrated the country, able to overthrow the government and annex the country at the whim of the Moroccan King. Accordingly, he lived in constant fear of a mutiny.

Now his Saharan campaign had turned Khaddafi against him and had deprived him of the support of even his close friend Boumedienne. He was isolated politically, a pariah among the African nations.

And so here he was, in the midst of a quagmire from which he could not extract himself, squirreled away in his quarters -- scarcely able to face his aides, not to mention his Generals.

So he was somewhat surprised when he heard the knock on the door. Someone coming to see him at this time of night? What could it mean?

On July 10, 1978, the President's chief of staff, Lieutenant-Colonel Mustafa Ould Salek addressed the nation. The President had been deposed and was under arrest, he announced. The Constitution had been suspended. There would be a new government, with a new Parliament. As he spoke the army took over the radio and government buildings, dismissing most top officials.

There was scarcely a peep of protest from the streets. Instead, one could almost hear a collective sigh of relief. Three days later several thousand cheering civilians marched through Nouakchott in a show of support. At his first press conference, on July 12, Ould Salek made the commitment that they were waiting for. He announced that his government would "set out a timetable, with Morocco . . . to lead us to peace. . . ."

Back at the newly built stucco building that served as Polisario headquarters in the camps, Abdelaziz sat at a desk surrounded by his political advisors and the top commanders in the field. It had been an extraordinary three days and the commanders were relishing every last moment, scarcely able to contain their joy.

All but Abdelaziz. For several weeks the man who had served as an unofficial liaison between the guerillas and the Mauritanian power brokers, Ahmed Baba Miske, had hinted that a move of some sort was forthcoming, and the guerillas had quietly lessened their attacks on Mauritanian garrisons. But now that it had taken place, he had to decide how to respond. "Let us give them some space to see what they will do," he finally said. "But what was it that that American ball player once said?"

Bachir smiled. I think you are referring to "The opera isn't over 'til the fat lady sings!"

"Yes," Abdelaziz said, looking at each one of them in turn. "We must wait until the fat lady sings to plan our next move. But let's give her some time to clear her throat!"

The next day Abdelaziz announced a "temporary" cease fire in Mauritania as a "gesture of good will" toward the new regime, and the guerillas began to put their long struggle with their neighbor to the south on a back burner and focus their eyes once more on their neighbor to the north.

July 11, 1978. Frustrations.

Back in Agadir a sullen figure sat in his armchair pondering his situation. The year 1978 had only increased Colonel Ahmed Dlimi's frustrations. By the end of 1976 Moroccan troops in the territory had been clearly on the defensive with losses as high as one to two hundred men a month. Guerilla units of 5 or 6 Land Rovers carrying machine guns had attacked convoys at random, usually under cover of darkness, interrupting supplies to such an extent that he had been forced to transport most supplies by air or sea.

By the summer of 1977 the guerillas could amass *kateebs* of up to 150 vehicles armed with heavy artillery to engage his forces. The Moroccan air force could offer little protection. By the time they received word of an attack and were authorized to respond the attack was usually over. Even if they did arrive in time it was impossible to attack the invaders without jeopardizing their own troops, and chasing them into the desert was like running after a skulk of desert foxes.

He had ordered Colonel Abrouq, the Moroccan regional commander, to move his command center from Agadir to Laayoune to be closer to the battle areas, and he had split several of his regiments into smaller mobile 'rapid intervention forces' of 250 to 300 men, armed with heavy machine guns, rifles, cannons and armored vehicles, to try to respond quickly to guerilla assaults. But nothing seemed to deflect their attacks.

Early in 1977 he had reached the decision to send forces to occupy the smaller outposts in the eastern part of Western Sahara – the area close to the border with Algeria -- in order to impede the Polisario's lines of communication and to intercept supplies coming from Algeria. He had established a logistics hub at Smara, and began building an air strip there to accommodate jet aircraft, and by May his troops had occupied Bir Lehlou and Ain Ben Tili. But he then faced severe problems trying to supply his troops in those remote outposts. By July of 1977 they had been badly in need of supplies. So at the end of July he had sent the Moroccan 6th military regiment from Lebouirate to Tifariti to occupy it and make it the base of supplies for the region. He had planned to send supplies from Smara to Tifariti and then from there to the outlying areas. But a column of Moroccan troops had been intercepted in a day long battle on the road between Smara and Tifariti that August, and after that the road between them had remained closed. Later that August troops from Tifariti managed to get to Smara by taking an 11 day long circuitous route through the flat highlands southwest of the outpost to Amat Elham in Mauritania and then north past Amgala to Smara. But the commander of the force had found this route so laborious that he recommended that it not be used again. He had continued for several months to try to supply Ain Ben Tili and Bir Lehlou from Tifariti, and thought that he might also supply Bir Lehlou through Mahbes, which got its supplies from the garrison at Zag.

But on October 11 when a column of "rapid intervention forces" from the 6th regiment tried to go from Tifariti to Bir Lehlou, they were ambushed, and the stragglers who had returned told their commanders in Smara that the overland route from Tifariti was too dangerous, then on the 14th of October another convoy leaving Mahbes for Bir Lehlou was also ambushed, and the road joining these outposts was closed.

By the end of the year he had been forced to supply Tifariti by air. He had even built a runway near the outpost for this purpose, and he had managed to get some supplies to the garrison there despite sniper attacks by Polisario units. But the smaller outposts continued to experience grave shortages of supplies.

And then there was the Mauritanian debacle. As a result of the attacks on Zouerate in May and Nouakchott in July, and the guerilla attacks deep within Mauritanian territory, Ould Daddah had been forced to do the unthinkable: sign a mutual defense pact with Morocco which would authorize the stationing of Moroccan troops in Mauritania. In July of 1977, Dlimi had been obliged to send 600 Moroccan paratroopers – members of the elite Green March Commando rapid intervention forces -- into Zouerate to reinforce the Mauritanian garrison there and to accompany the convoys of materials to the coast, and that was just the beginning -- in the succeeding months he had been forced to send thousands of additional Moroccan troops into the territory, stretching thin his reserves.

And once entrusted with the duty of defending Mauritanian positions, he had faced enormous logistics problems. In order to supply Mauritanian outposts such as Bir Moghrein, just over the Western Sahara border 150 miles southwest of Bir Lehlou, he had first attempted to use Zouerate as a supply center. However, guerilla attacks on the town and supply caravans had continued despite the heavy buildup of troops, and the attack in early October of 1977 that demolished a number of the Mauritanian troops stationed there, as well as the Green March Commando Parachute force sent to reinforce them, had eliminated this option.

He sighed as he reached for the bottle of scotch that always sat by his side and poured some into a glass. It had become clear to him that trying to supply garrisons in the outlying regions of the territory and Mauritania was more of a chore than it was worth, so he had made a tactical decision. He had withdrawn his troops from Bir Lehlou and Ain Ben Tili and the more remote outposts and had concentrated his manpower in Tifariti and the areas near the main towns, the Zouerate mine, and the "useful triangle" of Laayoune, Smara and Boujdour. Then he had amassed troops in a "mopping up" operation west of Tifariti for the purpose of eliminating the guerilla units near Lemgassem responsible for the attacks that had stymied his operations. But when they had attacked the guerillas his troops had met stiff resistance and had to retreat. When they had tried again they had been routed by a mere handful of men on foot and pursued through the hills. Several trucks and sixteen prisoners had been taken on that occasion and the Moroccan troops had begun calling that section of the territory the "region of ghosts."

165

And if all this were not enough, now there was a coup in Mauritania to contend with – a coup that would undoubtedly leave the guerillas free to intensity their attacks against Moroccan troops.

He took a sip from his glass and let the liquid warm his throat. He was quickly running out of options. He was gambling that in time another strategy would work. He had long recognized that the Achilles heel of the guerillas was their total lack of air power. So, beginning in 1976 he had pressed the King to improve and increase his air support. In January of 1976 the government had placed an order with Dassault for 25 Mirage F-1 combat aircraft, and a year later 25 more planes were ordered. Delivery of the Mirages was not expected until 1979 but in the meantime he had arranged for Moroccan pilots to be trained to fly them at the French air force base at Tours. In addition, by mid 1977 two hundred French military advisors had arrived in Morocco to provide additional training and to supervise the delivery of French planes and other weapons systems.

But he knew that no increase in equipment would provide adequate air support if the King maintained his stranglehold on the Air Force. After the previous attempts on his life by Air Force pilots Hassan was holding the commander of the Air Force, El Khabbaj, on a tight leash, refusing to allow him to send aircraft aloft without his personal approval. When he travelled abroad, the King would ground his Air Force entirely. The King's paranoia had effectively crippled the ability of the Air Force to provide cover for the troops, with devastating consequences, but all his attempts to convince him to loosen the reins had so far failed.

Rather than face his military defeats realistically, the King persisted in blaming all his problems on Boumedienne. It was the Algerians who were behind the guerilla attacks. It was the Algerians who were providing the weapons. It was the Algerians who were leading the troops. He seemed to view the war as a personal vendetta on the part of Boumedienne.

But on the ground Dlimi knew better. After the attack at Amgala he had tried in vain to capture additional Algerians to support the King's allegations. But he had failed. After months of fighting he had been unable to produce a single Algerian soldier among the dead, wounded or captured guerillas. And, much to his eternal chagrin, many of the weapons and vehicles used by the guerillas had once been part of his arsenal. It was not the Algerians who were masterminding the assaults. It was not the Algerians who were putting their lives on the line. It was not the Algerians who were fighting with a ferocity that could only stem from people defending their homeland. It was that motley crew of uneducated desert wanderers whom he had so cavalierly dismissed at the beginning of the war.

As he sat in his armchair sipping his drink and pondering his next move one thing seemed certain -- this war of Hassan's – the war that he had started for personal prestige rather than to satisfy the needs of his people -- was slowly bleeding the country to death and was likely to continue well into the future unless something was done quickly to turn the tide in Morocco's favor. What that might be he hadn't a clue.

<h3 style="text-align:center">July 13, 1978. Marrakesh.</h3>

It was the second week in July, three days after the Mauritanian coup, and far to the north the King was pacing nervously in his palace.

Normally Hassan enjoyed the opportunity to escape the concrete jungle of his offices in Rabat during the summer and cool his toes in one of the bright green pools that adorned his palace in Marrakesh, but not this time. The war in the Sahara – the war that he had never expected, the war that he had promised his subjects would be over in four weeks – was not going as planned. It was now in its third year. He had managed to obtain a few weapons and equipment from both the United States and France and a massive infusion of capital from the Saudi King, but still his troops had not been able to turn the tide against the insurgents. And now, despite all the money and manpower he had poured into bolstering his erstwhile ally to the south, Ould Daddah had been deposed and no one knew what the future would bring.

"Did you see the communiqué that was sent yesterday?" Hassan shouted. Then, reading from a paper in his hand he said, 'As a gesture of good will to the new regime in Mauritania, the Polisario will grant a temporary cessation of hostilities.' He then slammed the paper on his desk. "They obviously think that the new man . . . Ould Salek . . . will give in to their demands."

He turned to face the man sitting before him. Colonel Ahmed Dlimi had been summoned to an emergency meeting – the third time this year – and was trying to calm an increasingly irritated monarch.

"If he does he is a fool," he said, reaching for the paper. "We have over 10,000 troops stationed in Mauritania and the southern portion of the territory. He wouldn't dare do anything without our approval." Then, becoming more serious, he added, "Still, the situation is dangerous . . . this temporary cease fire will enable the guerilas to concentrate all their forces on Moroccan targets . . . and our troops are already stretched to the limit . . ." and in an even more serious tone he continued ". . . and if Mauritania withdraws from the war we will have the burden of trying to control another large swath of territory with guerila forces attacking us from enclaves deep within the Mauritanian desert. It will be a nightmare!"

The King listened intently to what Dlimi said. Then he walked slowly to the window and paused, deep in thought.

When he turned again his expression was serious. "I want you to go to Nouakchott to talk with this new man . . . to make sure that he knows our position and doesn't do anything foolish."

Dlimi put the paper down slowly and looked at the King. His small frame seemed to have shrunk even more, and the months of frustration had carved lines in his brow. "Of course," he responded. He rose and started for the door. But before he reached it, he turned again. "One more thing," he said, slowly. "Those new weapons and surveillance equipment we have requested from the Americans . . . have you gotten a response yet?" The King turned to face him again, the beginning of a smile crossing his face. "Don't worry about the Americans. They will come around in due course."

As Dlimi left the room he was puzzled. He knew his mission -- to keep the new Mauritanian leader in line. But something in the back of his mind disturbed him. A strange sense that something was afoot . . . that the King was up to something. There was something going on in his head . . . something he had not told him. But what?

And that question bothered him all the way back to his headquarters in Agadir.

Within a few weeks Dlimi's predictions came true. The July coup in Mauritania had freed the Polisario to direct the full force of their military might to defeating Morocco, which they began to do with gusto.   On the last day of September they again attacked one of the control stations of the Boucraa conveyor belt. Then they were bold enough to lob rockets into the capital – Laayoune. Meanwhile attacks on convoys and military outposts in the territory began to increase.

But the worse part for the King was that they were not content merely to attack targets within Western Sahara. No, beginning shortly after the coup in Mauritania they escalated their attacks on targets in Moroccan territory, with small units of guerillas, usually on foot, ambushing convoys traversing positions in the Draa Valley and Ouarkziz mountains, deep within the belly of Morocco.

On August 27 they even attacked a supply convoy of the Moroccan army at Sidi Amara, in the valley of the Oued Draa, far within Moroccan territory. And another convoy was ambushed in the last days of September as it tried to make its way to Guelb Ben Rzouk, a border post in the Draa Valley in northeast Morocco near the Algerian frontier.

And as the war entered this new stage the guerilla forces became more sophisticated. They still lacked heavy artillery – their forces were armed with no more than Land Rovers, trucks, light surface to air missiles and light artillery. But they had become a highly organized military machine and had mastered the art of using weapons positioned in the rear of moving vehicles to fire while moving at top speed towards their target.

During all of this period they patiently waited to see what Ould Salek would do. His dilemma was clear – end the conflict with the Polisario and ignite the wrath of Hassan, with his thousands of troops in the country, or continue the conflict and be blamed for the destruction of the country's economy at the hands of the Polisario. And for several months Ould Salek teetered on the precipice of indecision, unable to clear a path forward.

November 30, 1978. The OAU.

The long awaited day in November had now arrived. For two years the proposed "extraordinary summit" on the question of Western Sahara had been postponed because of major political differences among the members of the organization. France had exerted enormous pressure on its former colonies, many of whom for the preceding two years had found themselves politically tied to the Moroccan and Mauritanian cause. By the time the OAU held its ordinary summit in Khartoum in July of 1978, however, the government of Ould Daddah had collapsed and the political landscape had begun to change. The member states – in particular those outside the Francophone camp -- were more than ever resolved to end the conflict. However, instead of convening an extraordinary summit to tackle the issue, the Chairman, Gaafar Nimeiry, decided to take the politically less controversial route of appointing a committee composed of five heads of state – Mali, Nigeria, the Sudan, Tanzania and the Ivory Coast -- to examine the problem.

This "committee of wise men" – as it was dubbed – was holding its first meeting in Khartoum. As they assembled around the large conference table their faces were grim.

"My contacts tell me that Ould Salek had been running between Rabat, Algiers and Paris like a scared rabbit, trying to cement an end to the conflict in Western Sahara that would please all the major players," one of them announced.

"He would have more luck trying to reconcile the Israelis and the Palestinians," another said, with a note of sarcasm in his voice.

"I have heard that he is planning another trip to France . . . to seek d'Estaing's support for a new initiative. I think he desperately wishes to end the conflict. . . and will seek any way to do this," someone interjected.

"I have heard that too," another one answered, "I think d'Estaing is eager to repair France's tattered relationship with Algeria, and has been attempting to broker some sort of deal. . . but no one seems to be paying much attention to his suggestions."

"Yes, I hear that Hassan, as stubborn as ever, sent Ahmed Reda Guedira, to Nouakchott in August to reaffirm the King's position: no territorial concession would be allowed," someone remarked.

". . . and I have heard that the Polisario has also remained firm: Mauritania would need to withdraw from the territory, renounce any claim to it, and hand it over to Polisario forces," someone added glumly.

The room became quiet as everyone quietly assessed the situation. Finally, Olusegun Obesanjo, the Nigerian head of state, broke the silence.

"I understand there have been several meetings between Mauritanian officials and the Polisario, but nothing positive has developed," he proclaimed, hesitantly, looking in the direction of Moussa Traore, the President of Mali.

Traore looked at his companions for a moment, then cleared his throat. "Yes, there were a few meetings earlier this year, and just last month Ould Salek asked me to arrange a meeting in Bamako. It was supposed to be a secret, but somehow Hassan learned of it and, without waiting for an invitation, he sent Dlimi and Reda to join it. But when they arrived Bachir, El Ouali's younger brother who was heading the Polisario delegation, refused to meet them, and they had to sit out the meeting in another room with Khaddad, Bachir's assistant!"

"I imagine that didn't sit well with Dlimi!" one of them said, somewhat amused.

Traore paused for a moment remembering the tirade he had to endure at Dlimi's hands. Then he smiled. "No, I have never seen him so angry!" he said. "But I understand Bachir's reason – he didn't want to give the Moroccans a chance to disrupt an agreement with Ould Salek, which he knew was their intention."

"Were they able to come to any sort of understanding?" someone asked.

Traore again paused. Then he shook his head. "No, I had a feeling that the Mauritanians wanted to suggest something, but that the arrival of Reda and Dlimi intimidated them . . . even though they were not involved in the discussions. But they did agree to have another meeting in Tripoli – this time without the Moroccans. I understand that this was the first meeting between Ould Salek and Abdelaziz. But, again, nothing came of it as far as I know."

The room became silent. "What about this demand for a 'global solution'?" someone finally asked, "Is it just a ploy to drag out the discussions or do you think there is any chance that Hassan will agree to a compromise that would end the war?"

Traore reflected a moment before responding. Hassan had been insisting on a 'global solution' to the problem – one that would involve an agreement by Morocco – as an attempt to thwart a unilateral agreement between the guerillas and the Mauritanians. "Well, this is what Ould Salek has been advocating for a long time . . . something that would get him off the hook with both the Moroccans and the Polisario," he said, slowly. "However, Hassan seems to be only interested in a 'global solution' that would involve a complete capitulation of the guerillas . . . which he knows is not forthcoming." Then he sighed and shook his head again. "But I understand his position," he said slowly. "He would be risking political suicide at home if he backed away from his claim to the territory or permitted a Sahrawi mini-state to be established south of his borders. The opposition parties – especially the Istiqlalians – would crucify him. And he would risk stoking the flames of rebellion among the Sahrawis in his portion of the territory and Morocco . . . not to mention the Berbers." He sighed again. "No, if he is serious about extricating himself from this war he would need a graceful exit . . . and I don't see one on the horizon. On the other hand he is hemorrhaging badly on the battlefield . . . and he can't keep up the expenditures on the war indefinitely. Already he is in hock up to his eyeballs with the Saudis. And d'Estaing seems to be pulling back. The Americans . . . well, you can never predict what they might do. But unless someone comes up with a new strategy . . . and fast. . ." He shrugged his shoulders.

"I have heard rumors that Hassan has been trying to arrange a secret meeting with Boumedienne at his chateau in Belgium, but that Boumedienne has been putting him off. Any truth to that?" prompted one of them.

"I have heard the same thing," another chimed in, "and I have also heard rumors that Boumedienne has been secretly traveling to Moscow for medical treatment for some undisclosed ailment. He didn't look well to me at the last conference and he hasn't made an appearance in public for several weeks."

"But even if Hassan and Boumedienne were able to come to some sort of compromise, what could it possibly be?" a third person added, "Does anyone really think the guerillas would accept anything less than independence for the entire territory . . . especially now that Mauritania is on the verge of withdrawing from the conflict?"

The room became silent again as everyone was lost in thought. Finally Obesanjo looked around the room and spoke up.

"Look, everyone knows that the only way to resolve this conflict. . . and to uphold the principles our organization stands for . . . is to organize a referendum and let the people themselves choose which way they want to go. There is no mystery to this," he said firmly.

"Yes, if only Hassan wasn't so stubborn . . ." replied Traore.

"He is only being stubborn because he knows he will lose!" Obesanjo retorted. "The Sahrawis do not want to see the territory become part of Morocco. And considering the way he has been treating the people since he invaded it is no wonder. I would have thought he would have taken pains to win them over. But not Hassan!"

Traore laughed. "What do you expect? If he stifles dissent among his own people you expect him to be courteous to the Sahrawis?"

"Well, all I know is that there is no way we can give in to Hassan on this issue and consider ourselves a reputable organization. After all, he has transgressed two of our most important principles: the right of the people in African colonies to self determination and the sanctity of the borders established by the colonialists."

"Well, what do you suggest we do?"

Obesanjo reflected a moment. "Well, I think two of us should go and talk to Hassan, Ould Salek and Boumedienne to get the lay of the land. But in the mean time we should start thinking of how to organize a referendum, so when the time comes . . . ."

So, the meeting ended with the appointment of Obesanjo and Traore as delegates to visit the capitals of Morocco, Mauritania and Algeria, while, in the back rooms of the foreign ministries of five African states a bevy of young lawyers and diplomats began the task of putting together a plan to end the conflict in Western Sahara once and for all.

December 1978. The United Nations.

Meanwhile, the recent events in the Sahara had not gone unnoticed at the United Nations. The coup in Mauritania had been a wake up call for its delegates. For a number of years the members of the organization had been content to allow the OAU to take center stage in resolving the dispute, and the OAU's promise of an extraordinary summit had provided a convenient excuse to avoid confronting the problem.

After the coup, however, Morocco's political dominoes began to fall, and Hassan and his allies could no longer prevent the General Assembly from taking

171

a stand. Two rival resolutions were passed in December of that year. The first, drafted by Morocco and its supporters, merely continued to repeat support for the OAU's efforts. The second, however, backed by Algeria and most of the non-aligned nations, reaffirmed the right of the people of Western Sahara to self determination and independence and recognized the responsibility of the United Nations to supervise the decolonization of the territory.

The line in the sand had been drawn.

December 1978. Bouhali and Sidimi.

The ancient Chinese philosophers believed that since the beginning of time mankind has been split into two forces, male and female, yin and yang, with each individual only half of a complete unit, doomed to unhappiness unless he finds his other half. If that is true, they could have found no better example than Bouhali and Sidimi. From the first moment they met they seemed to be drawn together as if by some invisible force, some manifestation of fate. Both stubborn, both opinionated, both fearless, they were at the same time opposites and soul mates, and complemented each other in what seemed to be a seamless fashion. It was one of those rare unions in which the whole was greater than the sum of its parts, for in working together, they seemed to surmount every obstacle presented. And as the days passed, you could see them spending more and more time together. For a while they danced that funny little jig that couples do when they are not quite ready to acknowledge to the world – or to themselves – that they are destined to be together. But finally the dam broke, and they admitted what had been apparent to the others for a long time.

Their marriage ceremony was simple – as befitted one conducted in wartime on a battlefield – with no special preparations, only the required witnesses. For a while only their immediate entourage even knew of the marriage. But from that day forward it was a rare day when you would see one without the other. And once the news spread, the people in the camps had something besides battles to celebrate.

December 27, 1978. Hassan's Reprieve.

But the King had nothing to celebrate. The news he had been given upon the return of Dlimi and Reda from Bamako had caused him a few grey hairs. They had managed to prevent Ould Salek and the Polisario from reaching an agreement on anything, but the scoundrels had not only rebuffed his envoys, they had managed to arrange a follow up meeting in Tripoli that Ould Salek agreed to attend in person, ignoring him completely. The storm clouds were gathering over his head, as one by one his political chips began to disappear. First, the treachery of Ould Salek. Then, the rebellion at the OAU. And now the meddling of the UN. Even if his plan to woo more aid from the new United States President succeeded, his help might come too late to prevent a withdrawal of Mauritania from the conflict and the political and military repercussions that would inevitably follow.

It was now more vital than ever that he arrange a face to face meeting with Boumedienne.

To him the conflict had always been between him and Boumedienne. . . a personal feud between the leaders of two sister states. He had been holding discussions . . . in complete secrecy. . . with envoys of Boumedienne for months in an effort to woo him away from the guerillas. Nine months earlier he had sent his sister Laila on a secret mission to arrange a dialogue. This had been followed by no fewer than seven secret meetings between Boumedienne's envoys and his personal counselor, Ahmed Reda Guedira, accompanied by Dlimi. He had tried everything. He had assured them that he would not allow the dispute to evolve into a war between the two sister countries – despite the guerillas' incursions into Morocco proper. He had offered to put on hold his claims to Algerian territory. He had offered to allow them access to the Atlantic through the Sahara for their goods, if that was what they desired. But nothing seemed to work. Finally, this past May, he had suggested that he meet Boumedienne for face to face talks at his chateau in Belgium.

For weeks now Boumedienne had offered one excuse after the other why he couldn't accept. There were rumors that he was ill and constantly flying to the Soviet Union for treatment. Maybe the rumors were true . . . or maybe he was waiting to negotiate with Ould Salek without him. He could not let Ould Salek and Boumedienne come to some secret agreement behind his back.

For the first time in his life he felt helpless in the grip of events he could not control.

But just as he seemed resigned to enter into discussions to end the war, fate threw a curved ball, changing the diplomatic landscape in an instant from grey to cherry pink. For just as it seemed the darkest – just when the King finally faced the fact that he might not be able to hold onto the territory, just when the specter of defeat appeared before his eyes, just when escape seemed impossible -- something happened that would alter the figures on the chessboard once again, something that would breathe new life into the King's campaign.

On December 27, 1978, after falling into a coma, Huoari Boumedienne, the President of Algeria, passed away.

CHAPTER 6
1979

Boumedienne's death destroyed any chance that Hassan would come to the bargaining table. He remained convinced that Algerian support for the guerillas was primarily due to Boumedienne's influence and believed that a new government would be more amenable to a solution that favored Morocco—whatever that government might turn out to be.

For after Boumedienne's death Algeria plunged into chaos. For a while the government teetered on the brink of anarchy as rival factions jostled for power. Abdelazziz Bouteflika, the Foreign Minister and a pro-Western liberal, was widely favored to take the helm, but he faced stiff opposition from communist leaning Mohammad Saleh Yahiaoui. After a great deal of political wrangling, the rival factions settled on a compromise candidate, Chadli Bendjedid, the Minister of Defense.

Hassan, to his great dismay, soon learned that he would have no greater luck wooing Bendjedid to his side than he had had with Boumedienne. Algeria continued to support the guerillas both militarily and politically.

And as if to send a clear message to Hassan, in 1979 the Polisario began to engage Moroccan troops in some of the largest and bloodiest battles of the war. By the time of Boumedienne's death the guerillas had already managed to box the Moroccans into the main towns and a few isolated garrisons in the territory, and there had been a number of isolated skirmishes within Morocco itself. However, by the beginning of 1979 they were ready to intensify the war. In a push they named the "Houari Boumedienne Offensive" they amassed roving caravans of Land Rovers and vehicles equipped with a new weapon -- "Stalin Organs"-- multiple rocket launchers with a 12 mile range. Their attacks became more sophisticated, often involving advanced planning and coordination among three or four of the military regions, each assigned a specific task.

And they brought the onslaught deep into Moroccan territory.

January 16-17, 1979. Lamsayel.

It was a cold day in January, in an area just north of the Saguia el Hamra, a few miles from Laayoune, and Abdati rubbed his hands to keep warm. For weeks, from bases in the foothills of the Zini mountain range, guerillas had been attacking Moroccan convoys attempting to bring provisions from Tan

Tan to Laayoune. The previous day Ayoub and his troops had attacked a Moroccan convoy and had been able to capture a couple of vehicles and take 5 prisoners. Then earlier today Bouhali's troops had staged another attack on a convoy near the Ould Cheibeka. The troops were now carefully loading the supplies they had confiscated into trucks to be whisked away to their rear bases when a messenger arrived.

"What do you think it is?" Abdati asked the man helping him to load one of the trucks. Before he could answer one of their comrades approached them, an excited look on his face.

"We have just gotten word that Colonel Toubji has left Laayoune with his troops coming in our direction!"

Toubji was the commander of the 4th green march commandos, a unit of the Moroccan forces Dlimi created to specialize in rapid intervention and guerilla tactics.

"Bouhali has gone off in the direction of Laayoune to see the position of Toubji's troops," he continued.

Upon hearing word of Toubji's approach Bouhali had decided to see for himself where they were located. However, the winter rains had flooded the *wadi*, bringing with them a blanket of fog, cutting visibility to near zero. For nearly an hour he strained to see some sign of the troops through the haze. When the fog finally lifted, he frowned. They were close – perhaps no more than a couple of hours away from his men.

He quickly returned and gave orders.

Meanwhile, Toubji quickened the pace of his troops. As soon as he had gotten word of the attack on the convoy he had set out from Laayoune, determined to ambush Bouhali's forces before they could retreat back to the safety of their bases in the hills. He was now nearly at the point where the attack had occurred when the first shots were fired.

Bouhali's forces had surrounded him and were firing from all directions. First one, then two, then three of his vehicles were hit by the guerillas' machine guns and bazookas. Soon a half dozen trucks and Land Rovers were on fire. The assault lasted only a few minutes, but by the time the firefight ended and the guerillas retreated, Toubji had fewer than half his men guarding a heap of smoldering ruins.

He quickly got on his mobile device to call headquarters in Laayoune. "We've been attacked . . . . just north of the *wadi* . . . most of the vehicles are damaged. Yes, I need some mechanics . . . and reinforcements . . . fast!" He knew that he would be unable to move his troops until his vehicles were repaired. He also knew that in the meantime his troops would be sitting ducks for guerilla attacks. So he told his men to be on guard, sat down on a boulder to wait, and said a silent prayer that the reinforcements would come soon.

It was shortly before dusk when a few men arrived. A dozen or so. Not enough to buttress his troops, only enough to try to repair his vehicles.

"What can they be thinking?" he said to himself in frustration as he again picked up his mobile device. After a moment of shouting he put it down

again. A second, larger, heavily armed force would be sent from Laayoune, he was assured, and another from Boucraa. If they would only arrive in time
. . . .

By the time the moon arose that evening a column of several hundred men had marched north from Laayoune and were camped slightly south of Toubji's forces at a place called Lemsayal, a point in the *wadi* where several tributaries meet, about 25 miles north of Laayoune, and another Moroccan force had left its base near Boucraa.

Meanwhile, a few miles to the east Bouhali had called a hasty meeting with the commanders of the 1st and 3rd regions. Abdelaziz had transmitted a message he had gotten from one of his spies in Tan Tan. Besides the force that was camped at Lemsayal, and the troops that were advancing from Boucraa, a third Moroccan contingent had been sent from Tan Tan to sandwich them in from the north.

So now there were at least four Moroccan forces that were converging upon them. The commanders reasoned that Toubji's troops would be stuck where they were for some time, and that the swollen *wadi* would prevent the troops that came from Laayoune from advancing quickly to the north. And it would take time before the troops from Boucraa reached the area. So they devised a plan. Bouhali would move his troops north to intercept the troops from Tan Tan. Meanwhile, Ayoub would position his men so as to engage the troops coming from Boucraa in the event they tried to intervene, and Said Sgheir and the troops from the 1st military region would remain in the east to block any other troops that might come from the Moroccan base at Hagunia.

Abdati had been among the infantry who had led the charge that afternoon, and had been rewarded for his efforts by a piece of shrapnel that had lodged in his shoulder. In the hiatus of the battle during the evening his sister was carefully removing the fragment.

"It could have been worse," she said, extracting the piece of metal carefully with a set of tweezers and putting some disinfectant on the wound, "it could have lodged in your right shoulder, making it difficult for you to fire your weapon. You'll be good as new in a couple of days."

He had just begun to put his shirt back on when one of the older soldiers approached where he was sitting.

"I just got orders. We'll be moving out soon. You'd better get ready."

Sidi grabbed her brother gently by the arm. "Perhaps you should rest a few days and let that wound heal before joining the others," she said softly.

He smiled. "Its only a small flesh wound. I'll be all right!"

Sidimi looked intently at his face. However, she didn't see the chiseled features of a veteran of four years on the battlefield. No, she saw a boy of seven or eight happily playing stick ball with his cousins in the dusty streets of El Ayoun. She kissed him tenderly and watched as he disappeared with his comrade.

At around 11 p.m. Bouhali marched with his troops 45 miles to the north, quietly and without using their headlights. He then sent two cars ahead to survey the area and determine where the Moroccan troops were positioned. When he got this information he moved his men to that spot and waited.

At around 8 o'clock the following morning they were ready. The infantry advanced, paving the way for Land Rovers wielding machine guns and troops launching estrellas. A helicopter was hit and sputtered to the ground, as one or two of the Moroccan tanks burst into flame.

The Moroccans quickly retaliated. Aided by tanks and other heavy artillery, they bombarded the invading troops mercilessly. Fighter jets swooped over the area unloading bombs indiscriminately on friend and foe alike and blanketing the entire scene with craters. Helicopters buzzed overhead spitting bullets at anything that moved. Charred Polisario and Moroccan vehicles lay spewing fire in the dust, and the ground turned crimson. Meanwhile Ayoub and Sgheir got news of the battle and decided to abandon their defensive positions and bring their troops to join the fray. Bouhali's troops then joined with those of the 1st and 3rd military regions to surround the Moroccans on three sides. Then they advanced, the smoke of their weapons and those of the enemy canceling any brightness the helpless sun could provide.

Abdati manned a machine gun in the rear of one of the Land Rovers leading the assault while his companion, Omar, drove. In the dust and blackened sky that surrounded him, Abdati could barely discern the figures that moved a few yards away. They forged ahead with their Land Rover, almost by rote, in the direction of the Moroccan command center and the tanks that surrounded it.

Abdati had managed to lob a number of volleys in the direction of one of the tanks and heard the noise of an explosion, but he was unable to see clearly whether he had hit anything. As Omar turned in the direction of another tank, something ripped through their Land Rover from the sky. At once the vehicle lurched and shot into the air before turning on its side. Omar flew through the air before landing a few feet from the burning car. But Abdati was pinned down under the vehicle, unable to move his leg. When he had finally recovered from the shock of the blast he felt dizzy and he could feel something wet under his pants. A bomb fragment had lodged in his abdomen and blood was seeping steadily from the wound.

Omar managed to crawl to where he lay and began firing at the Moroccan lines with his AK-47. With his shirt he beat the flames into submission. Then he tried to lift the car to release Abdati's leg, but after a few tries he gave up and decided to creep back through the lines for help.

After a few minutes he saw a Polisario Land Rover in the distance.

"I need your help," he shouted, excitedly, when he reached the vehicle.

Salek, who was busy firing a machine gun didn't bother looking around. "What is it, Omar?" he shouted over the din, as he launched another blast.

"Its Abdati," he yelled, "He's pinned down under our Land Rover. I need your help to get him out."

When Salek heard Abdati's name he stopped what he was doing and turned to face the soldier. Without waiting for a response Omar blurted, "He's been wounded. I think it is serious."

Salek left his companions and swiftly followed Omar back to the area where he had left Abdati and surveyed the surroundings. The battlefield was filled with craters, smoke and the smoldering remains of upturned vehicles. Searching for him would not be easy. Finally, in the distance he was able to recognize the silhouette of an overturned Land Rover. On its far side, not more than 50 yards away, was an armored vehicle whose occupants were sending a steady stream of bullets in their direction. He fired back, running as fast as he could to the safety of the overturned car, with Omar a few feet behind. Underneath the car he saw a limp figure.

"Look, on the count of three help me lift it as much as you can," he said. The two of them pushed with all their strength and after a few seconds it moved, just slightly, but enough for Salek to reach down and drag Abdati a couple of feet. The shock of the movement caused him to groan, and he opened his eyes.

When he saw Salek, he smiled. "It is good to see you, *habibi*!" he managed to whisper.

Salek looked at him. Blood was seeping through his clothes and his legs were mangled.

"We'll get you back soon," he muttered softly.

Then, turning to Omar, he shouted "Can you cover me, while I take Abdati?"

Omar nodded, and without a further word Salek lifted Abdati carefully over his shoulder and the two of them began to run as fast as they could in the direction of their troops.

But they didn't get far. Before they progressed more than a few yards Salek heard another explosion and a groan. When he looked behind him he saw a body sprawled on the ground. He gently laid Abdati down and crawled to where Omar lay in the dirt, slightly groaning. A piece of shrapnel had lodged in his leg, another in his chest.

He crawled back to where Abdati lay. Abdati had been silent through the ordeal and only the slight rhythmic heaving of his chest confirmed that he was still alive. When Salek placed his face close to his, with every ounce of strength left in him, Abdati pulled him closer and whispered something in his ear.

Salek looked around him for any sign of help, but no one was near.

Abdati managed a weak smile, and a calmness seemed to come over his features, as if he could already see the world beyond. "It is my time," he whispered in a barely audible voice.

"Go!" was all he said before releasing Salek from his grip.

The guerillas were still blasting the Moroccan troops with their machine guns when through the dust a figure slowly approached, carrying something on his shoulders. . . .

"Quick, bring him here!" Sidimi shouted when she saw the silhouette approaching. When she saw who it was her eyes widened. Grabbing Salek by the shoulders she screamed "Where is Abdati?" The look on his face told her the answer.

She released him and started running in the direction of the noise and smoke. Salek grabbed her by the shoulders. "Wait, Sidi . . . wait until the planes leave!"

But she wouldn't listen and pushed him aside.

It was only a few minutes, but seemed like an eternity, before she saw, through the clouds of dust and smoke, the figure of a man sprawled in the sand. She rushed to the body. He was still breathing, and when he saw her a glimmer of recognition seemed to cross his face. His lips moved, as if he was trying to say something, and she leaned closer. But he made no sound, and soon his lips moved no more.

She felt a hand on her shoulder, and heard a voice urging her to leave. At first she refused to budge, but finally, half dazed, she obeyed Salek's command, and started the slow trek back to her jeep.

An hour later, when quiet finally descended on the battle field Said Sgheir, the leader of the 1st military region surveyed the scene. The bodies of over 600 Moroccans lay in the dirt. 250 more were wounded, and 51 were taken prisoners. They had been able to capture 4 armored vehicles and 60 cross country vehicles, and had destroyed 7 tanks and 96 trucks. In addition, they had managed to shoot down one F-5 jet and 4 helicopters. Two large Moroccan columns had been destroyed.

Commander Toubji, who escaped with 10 cars to Hagunia, was later to write a scathing expose of the incompetence of the Moroccan military commanders entitled "Les Officiers de sa Majesty."

Later that evening Omar began to regain consciousness. He was lying on a blanket near a Land Rover, his chest wrapped in bandages, the shrapnel in his chest and leg removed. A soldier was hovering above him and when he saw that he was awake, gave him some medicine to relieve the pain.

He grabbed the sleeve of the soldier's jacket and pulled himself up. "Abdati?" The soldier shook his head.

Omar slumped back onto the blanket, something moist in his eyes.

Bouhali had been busy planning the retreat, when news reached him of Abdati.

That evening he went to the makeshift operating enclosure where Sidimi was busy, as usual, removing fragments of shrapnel and bullets from the bodies of the wounded.

"Sidimi, . . . about Abdati . . .," he started.

But Sidimi didn't let him finish. "He was a brave soldier – my little brother!" was all she said.

Bouhali searched for other words he might say, but finding none that would mean anything, he turned around and quietly left.

He didn't see the tear that was slowly drifting down her cheek.

January 28, 1979. Tan Tan.

The battle of Lamsayel, where they were able to defeat a large, elite commando unit, emboldened the guerilla fighters. They considered it the

179

beginning of a new phase in the war, the prelude to the major battles to come. Ten days after the battle at Lamsayel their troops marched north, through the Zini escarpment, this time not to attack a convoy or column of troops, but to lay siege to a city -- the coastal city of Tan Tan.

Tan Tan was a provincial capital on the highway between Agadir and Laayoune in the part of southern Morocco that had been ceded to Morocco by Spain in 1958. It was the home of thousands of Sahrawis, some whose ancestral pasture lands were here, others who, like Ouali's parents, migrated northward from Spanish Sahara after the defeat of the Army of Liberation and the draught that killed almost half the Sahrawis' livestock in the late 50s. Prior to the war it had been just a dusty settlement of no particular importance. But following the outbreak of hostilities it was fortified by the Moroccan army and boasted an air base and a garrison of several thousand soldiers.

Following the battle at Lamsayel, Salek and a handful of guerillas had been sent north to survey the approach to the city. The Moroccans had spread their forces in a semicircle enclosing its southern and eastern access, the direction from which they expected any attack to occur. To the northeast was a paved road leading north towards Agadir. Approximately 80 miles to the south was a troop of mobile intervention forces, ready to protect the troops stationed in fixed positions around the city in the event of an attack.

Back at a point not far from Lamsayel the commanders of the 1st, 2nd and 3rd military regions, with a combined troop strength of several hundred men, Land Rovers fitted with machine guns, and a few small anti aircraft missiles, converged to plan the attack. Bouhali and his men would stay near Lamsayel to block any intervention from Moroccan forces in the south. Meanwhile, Ayoub Lahbib and Said Sgheir would take their troops north and attack the garrison and airfield. After that they would move their forces into the city.

On January 27, a column of fighters quietly moved northward. By that evening they had reached the outskirts of the city, so far undetected by the Moroccans. Shortly before the sun rose on the following day, Salek and a handful of his comrades left on a mission.

In the darkness they swiftly covered the distance between the Polisario forces and the troops that formed the Moroccan defensive line. In the semi dark Salek could see the lights of one of their positions no more than quarter mile away to his right. Another was an equal distance to his left. In his head he had mapped the terrain, noting every bush, every gully. He carefully navigated a path between the Moroccan positions until he could see the lights of the town before him. Now would be the tricky part. Abdelaziz had given him the name of someone in the town – a woman who, since the very beginning of the war, had been providing him information about troop and convoy movements, undercover and at great personal risk. He would contact this woman and help her and her family escape. Without making a sound he made his way through the empty streets, dodging a group of Moroccan soldiers who were just returning from a soiree in a nearby canteen. When he had located the address he knocked at the door, praying under his breath that she would be the one to open it. He knocked again. He could hear movement at the other side and after a few long minutes the large, wooden door opened a crack and the eyes of a young woman peered down at him.

"Lamira Hamdi?" he asked quietly. The woman looked at him intently for a moment. She didn't recognize him, but he was no Moroccan. Finally she opened the door, Salek slid into the room, and she quickly closed the door behind him.

"Who are you?" she demanded.

"My name is Salek, and I have been sent by Abdelaziz," he answered, quickly. "Polisario forces have surrounded the city and are preparing to attack. I have been sent to gather you and your family once the attack begins and to guide you through the Moroccan lines to safety."

The woman silently scrutinized the man. For years now the Moroccans had cast a suspicious eye on the Sahrawis in the town, noting their every move. As the daughter of one of the local traders, she was often aware when convoys were preparing to head south, and she had been allowed to travel to Las Palmas to buy provisions. It was from there that she had managed to ferry messages to Abdelaziz. But the others were not so lucky.

Finally she smiled. "Abdelaziz is kind to be thinking of me," she said, softly. "Please give him my regards when you return."

Salek was startled. "You mean you are not coming back with us?" he asked.

Lamira shook her head.

"I will stay here," she said.

"But why? We can get you to Tindouf safely!" Salek muttered, somewhat perplexed.

She took his hand and clasped it warmly. "I am more useful here," she replied, "But there are others who will want to go. Let me warn them."

He would have liked to argue with her but there was no time. In less than an hour the word had been spread, under the noses of the sleeping Moroccans.

At the crack of dawn the assault began. A massive column of infantry and Land Rovers approached from the tarmac road northeast of the city and from the direction of Lemseid to the southeast. They quickly overcame the few stationary troops that were in defensive positions facing those directions, and dispersed the others. Storming into the center of town they remained in the city for four hours, freeing Sahrawi prisoners and destroying military installations, the military barracks, oil depots, the power station and a local bank.

Meanwhile, Sahrawis began to pour out of their homes, filling the streets, joyously shouting Polisario slogans. Salek looked around him. Dozens of men, women and children had gathered around him, with what few possessions they could carry, eager to abandon their homes for the barren plains of Tindouf. He motioned, and they began to follow him.

As the long procession passed Lamira in the street he walked up to her and clasped her hand warmly. "Goodbye, Lamira," he whispered, "and may Allah be with you!"

She smiled. "Give Abdelaziz my regards," she said gaily. And while the Moroccan troops were busy trying to repel the guerilla invasion, Salek and a handful of his comrades quietly tiptoed with the civilians through the Moroccan lines.

The Polisario troops departed from Tan Tan as quickly as they had come, fading into the landscape like ghosts on a moonless night. But they remained close by -- ready to pounce on caravans and isolated garrisons southern Morocco -- and to plan their next bold move.

January 31, 1979. Hassan's Rage.

Deep in the bowls of the palace, an aide scurried hurriedly along the corridor. "The King is in a foul mood," he whispered to a colleague, "He just read an article by the leader of the Istalqalians about the attack on Tan Tan – and Dlimi, Basri and a number of other officials are in there with him."

A door to the large marble room opened and a thoroughly white faced servant emerged with a tray. Behind him they could hear the sound of shouts and raised voices. "Am I glad to be out of there!" the servant exclaimed, somewhat breathlessly, closing the door behind him. The aide shook his head. "I wouldn't want to be in Dlimi's shoes right now," he said in a low voice, "I don't care how wealthy he is!"

They proceeded quickly down the hallway, trying to get as far away as they could from the tempest that was brewing.

Inside the room, an ashen faced Dlimi stood facing the King. The attack on Tan Tan had unnerved the citizenry and had sent shock waves through the corridors of the palace. The opposition parties had gleefully begun to ask embarrassing questions about the wisdom of the King's policies, questions that Dlimi had tried to pari. But none of his excuses could explain why his forces had been unable to stem the guerillas' forays into Moroccan territory, or could placate the King, whose anger had been increasing daily.

Hassan, in full military uniform, was pacing to and fro in the room, waving a baton in his hand wildly and shouting at the top of his lungs. "Tan Tan!" he yelled. "One of our major cities!" And then, shaking the baton perilously close to Dlimi's nose, he added, "And they took the residents with them! Right through the army lines. And nobody stopped them!" He took a few more steps, and then, tossing his arms in the air in a gesture of utter bewilderment, he added "Unbelievable!"

Then, slamming the baton on his desk, he cast a contemptuous look at Dlimi and, in a voice seething with rage, growled, "Do you have any idea how foolish this makes me seem?" He tossed a rolled up newspaper at Dlimi and barked, "Here, read it yourself! My enemies are gloating! The Istalqalians are complaining – again – about the lack of security and inflaming the people against me!"

Dlimi was used to the King's tirades, and usually had a well-rehearsed response to toss back. But this time he was at a loss to find a suitable explanation for the direction the war was taking. It should have ended long ago, this insurrection. No one expected the guerilla campaign to last a month, and now it had been more than four years with no end in sight. First he had to withdraw his troops from the outlying areas of the territory because of the attacks on the supply caravans. And now he was facing a major onslaught within Morocco itself. Of course, it didn't help that he had been forced to deploy troops to aid the weak-kneed Mauritanians – troops that he should have been able to use to help secure Moroccan towns. . . and the King's stubborn refusal to allow the Air Force to engage the enemy without his approval didn't help either. But his forces still greatly outnumbered the guerillas – and they had better weapons at their disposal. He tried as best he could, but he could not come up with an excuse for the Tan Tan fiasco.

"Your Majesty, we were not expecting an attack so far to the north, and our forces are stretched to the limit buttressing the Mauritanians, but I have sent a regiment . . ."

But the King was in no mood to hear excuses. He marched to where a map hung on the wall, and with his baton pointed first to the town of Assa, then to Aka, Oum Lahsen and finally to Tan Tan – all towns in Morocco attacked recently by the guerillas, all in a line moving progressively northwest.

"How long do you think it will take them to reach Marrakesh?" he asked angrily. Then he pointed his baton again at Dlimi and Basri.

"You have been telling me that attacks on territory within Morocco are under control. . . that with the new planes, equipment and recruits I have given you, you would be able to stem the guerillas' attacks on our cities. Is this what you mean by 'under control'?" he yelled. Then in a voice low and menacing, he waved the baton close to their faces and growled, "It is dangerous to lie to the King! Heads can roll."

Finally, with a wave of his hand he dismissed the entourage. His army was useless. So were his advisors. He would have to look elsewhere for the answer.

As his advisors' footsteps receded down the hallway the King barked an order and a phone was quickly put before him. He dialed a number from memory and a voice at the other end answered "Pentagon. How may I direct your call?"

February 11, 1979. Pentagon.

In his office the man with stars on his shoulder stared out the window at a tree in the garden below. How he loved watching the tree bloom in the early spring, its branches gradually swathed in soft pink flowers which bathed the courtyard in a sweet fragrance. He sighed. When the cherry blossoms were in their splendor it was difficult to think thoughts of war.

But the cherry blossoms had not yet emerged, and he was facing a delicate problem. A week ago the King of Morocco had called him desperately pleading for aid. The guerillas trying to wrest control over the territory of Western Sahara had done the unthinkable – attacked a major city in Morocco – and there was no telling where their attacks might end. Not even Rabat was safe.

183

He had hurriedly called a meeting with top officials at State. He turned from the window. Three men in dark suits were sitting uncomfortably on the chairs that circled his desk, waiting for him to speak.

When he did, it was with a solemnity that befitted the occasion.

"All of you by this time have heard of the invasion of Tan Tan in Morocco by guerilla forces," he began. "We at the Pentagon believe that this has posed a serious problem for the King. His troops apparently have been unable to put an end to these incursions into Moroccan territory and we are worried that they may decide to go father – perhaps even to attack Rabat and overturn the King. We cannot let that happen. You all know how valuable the King has been recently . . ."

He didn't need to explain. They all nodded their heads.

"Last week the King telephoned me to request more military equipment," he continued. "He was particularly interested in acquiring some sophisticated surveillance equipment and ammunition. I have the list here." He passed around a few pieces of paper. Then he waited for a response.

He didn't have to wait long. One of the men tossed aside the paper that had been handed to him. "You know the President's position on this," he began to say in a similarly grave tone. "He refuses to allow United States military equipment be used in the Sahara campaign. And as for the ammunition he is requesting, well, you know full well that we cannot allow him to use it!"

The military man expected that answer. Drawing himself up to his full 6 foot 4 inch height, he responded, coolly, "But the attacks are no longer confined to the region of Western Sahara. The attacks are now occurring in Moroccan territory. We have a duty to help the King defend his territory."

The other man did not appear convinced. "I don't see how you can draw a line between the war in Western Sahara and the attacks in Morocco. They both stem from the same problem, Morocco's decision to annex the territory."

The military man leaned on his desk and gave the man a cold, hard look. "The guerillas have crossed the line here. It is one thing to initiate a fight in the territory. That poses enough problems. But to infiltrate Morocco itself!" Then he paused. "But all right," he said somewhat languidly, resting back in his chair, "Perhaps you would like to explain to the President why we decided to stand by and let the regime of one of our most important allies be toppled by a bunch of Bedouins with ties to Algeria."

The other man winced. Then, giving the man across from him a similarly cold, hard look he said, "OK, I'll request that we give him permission to buy a few more items." Leaning across the table, he quickly added, "But with a caveat that they can only be used in Morocco, not in Western Sahara."

The military man smiled. "Of course."

May 19, 1979. Marrakesh.

As Dlimi marched through the marbled halls of the palace in Marrakesh he went over and over again in his head how he would divulge the news to the King. The palace had barely overcome the shock of the guerillas' attack

in Tan Tan. Hassan had sprung into action quickly, leaning on his friends
the Americans for aid. "It was the least they could do," he thought wryly,
"after the King humiliated himself in order to help them." He had learned
what the King had up his sleeve last July, and why he was so confident that
the Americans would soon increase their aid – he had been acting as a go-
between in the talks between the Egyptians and the Israelis that led up to
the Camp David Accords. He hadn't approved of the King's overtures to the
Israelis, or the fawning posture Hassan had taken with the Americans. In fact,
he didn't approve of the Americans.

But their increased aid would come in nicely, he thought. He didn't mind
the strings that were attached -- no use in Western Sahara. Strings were made
to be broken.

But as soon as one fire was put out another one surfaced. Now the
King would have to face another problem with Mauritania. The King had
withdrawn 600 troops from Akjoujt and 1,200 troops from Nouadhibou to
placate Ould Salek, but had kept 6,000 troops in other parts of Mauritania and
the Mauritanian portion of the territory – 2,000 in Zouerate, 800 in the Atar
region, 800 at Bir Moghrein, and 2,500 at Dakhla and Argoub – despite Ould
Salek's demand that they be removed by March. Their presence had been
enough to keep Ould Salek in line. But Ould Salek was no longer in charge;
he had been replaced at the helm in a military coup in April by Lieutenant
Colonel Ahmed Ould Bouceif – the same Ould Bouceif who had routed El
Ouali at Nouakchott at the beginning of the war.

For a while it seemed that Bouceif might be willing to tow the Moroccan
line. But just like his predecessor he had started to demand concessions from
the King – concessions the King was utterly unwilling to contemplate now
that Boumedienne was dead.

And Dlimi's agents had just sent him word of a secret meeting between
Bouceif and the guerillas that would take place in Tripoli the following week.
Boucief had raised alarm bells in April when a joint communiqué issued by the
Libyan government suggested that in talks held in Tripoli Mauritania's Foreign
Minister had promised that Mauritania would hand over to the Polisario the
part of Western Sahara that it had annexed. Boucief had quickly backed away
from that statement, but just two weeks ago he had met with the leaders of
Nigeria and Mali – the co-chairs of the OAU committee of 'wise men' --and
again a rumor surfaced that Bouceif had tired of Hassan's unwillingness to
compromise, and was thinking of caving in to the guerillas' demands.

As Dlimi entered the marble ante chamber the King sat waiting for him.

"Well, what is it this time?" the monarch said in his usual weary tone of
voice.

Dlimi was nonplussed. "Your Majesty, I have just gotten word that Boucief
is planning a rendezvous with the guerillas next week . . . arranged by Khaddafi
. . ."

At the last remark the King straightened in his chair. He knew about the
earlier meetings between the Mauritanians and the Polisario. There had been

several in July and later in August.   Higher level talks had followed with Bachir Mustapha Sayed and Mahfoud Ali Beiba in Paris the second week of September. He knew all about those meetings. The Mauritanians – with the help of the French – had come up with the ridiculous idea of creating two states in the Sahara – one for the Moroccans and the other for the guerillas. This had pleased no one. He had rejected it outright, and had insisted on a 'global solution' to the conflict . . . on his terms. Then there was the meeting in Bamako. Even though the guerillas had rebuffed his envoys their presence had been enough to keep Ould Salek in line and to foil any agreement when he met Abdelaziz later in Tripoli. And before he could arrange another meeting he had been replaced at the helm by Boucief. But now another meeting? With Boucief? In secret? Without involving him?

"I thought Boucief had agreed not to hold any meetings with the guerillas without our presence," Hassan asked, a note of irritation creeping into his voice.

"He did," Dlimi responded quietly, "But apparently he has changed his mind."

Hassan sat quietly for a moment. "He wouldn't dare come to any accommodation with the guerillas without our consent, would he? After all we still have enough troops in his territory to overcome his forces if he gets out of line."

"I know," replied Dlimi, "But the economic situation in his country has become dire and he just might be desperate enough to throw in the towel." He paused. "Ever since the French decided to back away from the conflict his situation has gotten worse."

The King paused for a moment. The French! Yes, d'Estaing was running away like a scared rabbit . . . lessening his military support for Morocco as well as Mauritania. . . trying to negotiate a graceful way out for the Mauritanians. The Americans were made of stiffer stuff. Then he spoke slowly, measuring his words carefully.

"Do you think he is really serious about breaking ties with us? Just when I have been making headway with the Americans? If he would just wait a few more months . . . I don't think Chadli has the stomach for another year of fighting."

Dlimi remained calm. Bendjedid was not the only player on the field. There were powerful Generals in Algeria who were just as adamant about the Western Sahara issue as Boumedienne, and he doubted that Bendjedid would be able to withdraw his support from the guerillas even if he wanted to – and there was no sign that he wanted to. But no one could convince Hassan about that. And as for the Americans . . . the Americans were like a swarm of locusts, devouring everything in their way and spitting out the carcasses in the sand. When they had no more use for Hassan they would discard him like yesterday's newspaper. But he wouldn't say any of this to the King.

Instead, he simply said, "My feeling is that Boucief is trying to involve the Libyans in the negotiations in order to buy time. He is not eager to agree to the Polisario's terms . . . I have heard that he is desperate to keep his troops in the territory." He suppressed a smile and walked a few paces before continuing. "Of course, the French are pressuring him to withdraw from the alliance discreetly, if he must. They are trying to involve themselves in the negotiations. . . so far without much luck. Their latest suggestion is that we govern the territory in a tripartite administration."

"What nonsense!" Hassan interjected, waiving his hand in frustration.

"You needn't worry . . . there is no way the Polisario will accept that. But Boucief will have to make a move soon. The Polisario won't wait forever, and if he caves in . . ."

Before he could finish his sentence, the King snapped.

"We'll just have to see to it that that doesn't happen!"

May 27, 1979. Dakar.

On May 27, 1979 a large private jet sat patiently on the tarmac at Dakar's airport waiting for its passengers. The previous day it had brought the President of Mauritania, Ahmed Ould Boucief, to the city to engage in a furious round of talks with the Senegalese leadership. It was now preparing to take off, its destination unknown.

Crews on the ground were busy loading bundles into the jet's hold, while a handful of technicians checked the controls, and two Mauritanian soldiers stood nearby amiably chatting with a female attendant. Soon a truck carrying fuel arrived and started the process of loading its cargo into the plane. No one noticed when one of the men on the truck disappeared behind the rear of the plane and opened a side panel. Within a few moments he was back on the truck and the truck disappeared.

Later that day Bachir Mustapha Sayed and two of his colleagues sat in the spacious lobby of one of the finest hotels in Tripoli. They had been waiting for hours for the arrival of the man who had requested an urgent, private meeting to discuss the withdrawal of Mauritania from the conflict, and were growing impatient. Only the football match on the hotel's TV screen relieved their boredom. Suddenly the match was interrupted by a news flash.

Ahmed Ould Boucief, the President of Mauritania, had been killed in a crash of his private jet shortly after takeoff from Dakar airport -- his destination unknown.

June, 1979. Heydalla's Dilemna.

It was the beginning of summer in Mauritania, nearly a year after the coup that deposed Ould Daddah. The fat lady had cleared her throat, but so far had not begun to sing. Lieutenant Colonel Mohammed Khouna Ould Heydalla had been pacing back and forth in his office for so many days that the carpet was beginning to look worn. One of the last acts Ould Salek performed as leader after the coup that deposed Ould Daddah, was to request that Morocco withdraw its troops from Mauritania by the end of the following March – a bold step considering that at the time Hassan had stationed more than 10,000 Moroccan troops in Mauritania and the Mauritanian part of Western Sahara -- more than the entire Mauritanian army. Despite this request Hassan had kept 6,000 troops in the area. Just to make sure Ould Salek stayed on course.

But Ould Salek hadn't remained in power long. He had quickly been replaced by Heydalla's commanding officer, Lieutenant Colonel Ahmed Ould Boucief. And now Ould Boucief was dead. Killed in an airplane crash the previous month. It had become Heydalla's turn at the helm, but he was not enjoying the position.

He had inherited a quagmire. The war was costing a fortune – a fortune Mauritania did not have – and the people were grumbling. Even members of his troops had turned against it. The country's economic future hinged on the Guelbs Project – a project that would open up the 360 million ton iron deposits at El-Rhein that was scheduled to be financed by 15 foreign governments, companies, banks and aid agencies. The consortium had pledged to cofinance the project's $500,000 first stage, but only on the condition that Mauritania withdrew from the Western Sahara conflict and ensured security in its northern regions. He wanted desperately to find a way to exit this situation gracefully. If it were up to him he would sign a peace agreement with the guerillas tomorrow. There was only one problem – Morocco.

For months his predecessors had tried one diplomatic maneuver after the other – reaching out to Hassan to see whether some political compromise with the guerillas could be reached. And for a brief period it seemed that such a "global" compromise might be possible. But all that had changed with the death of Boumedienne in December. After his death Hassan had become adamant – no compromise could be reached that would affect the division of territory reached in the Madrid Accords.

So here he was, pacing back and forth in the presidential palace, caught between a Scylla and a Cerberus, unable to move in any direction and unsure how long the Polisario would wait before striking again.

The answer was not long in coming.

On July 12, 1979, after waiting a year in order to let the new regime find a way to exit the conflict gracefully, the temporary cease fire was suddenly lifted and Bana Baha, leading troops from the 4th military region, assembled from their outposts deep in the southern reaches of Mauritania, attacked and overran Tichla, a small settlement in the southern part of the territory. Scores of prisoners, including the local Mauritanian prefect, were captured. The government of Mauritania was rudely shaken out of its complacency.

And so was the OAU.

July 17-20, 1979. Monrovia.

As the leaders of the African states that had formed the OAU sat in the conference room of their hotel in Monrovia, Liberia, they waited anxiously for the report that was scheduled to be delivered. It was mid-July and the weather outside was steamy, almost as steamy as the heated conversations that had filled the halls earlier that day.

For years now they had been grappling with a conflict that had festered like an infected pimple upon the map of the region. The occupation of Western Sahara by two of its members -- Morocco and Mauritania -- ostensibly against the will of its inhabitants, had become a serious embarrassment to the organization. Although there were calls for an extraordinary summit to address the problem as early as 1976, for years they had hesitated, looking for a diplomatic way to address the problem without embarrassing two of their members. However, the coup against the President of Mauritania in 1978 – widely seen as a direct result of the conflict – had been the last straw. Intervention in the conflict had become a political necessity.

It was now July of 1979, just days after the assault on Tichla. The "wise men" who had been assigned the arduous task of finding a solution to the conflict at the previous summit in Khartoum had issued a report, and the members of the organization had met in Monrovia to address their findings.

As Olusegun Obesanjo, the chair of the ad hoc committee, prepared to speak, the room became deathly quiet.

"We have studied the issue carefully," he said slowly, casting a glance at the Moroccan delegate, "and we have come to the conclusion that the only way to end this conflict is to permit the inhabitants to decide for themselves whether they wish to join Morocco or become an independent state. We therefore suggest that there be an immediate cease fire and a withdrawal of all troops, followed by a referendum organized under the auspices of the United Nations and the OAU." He passed around a report, several pages thick, followed by a resolution that recommended an immediate cease fire and "the exercise by the people of Western Sahara of their right to self determination through a general, free referendum enabling them to choose one of the two following options: (a) total independence, (b) maintenance of the status quo." Then he waited.

He didn't have to wait long. The Moroccan delegate sprang to his feet, waiving the report over his head and then slamming it to the table. "This is unacceptable. We will never consent to this . . ." He was joined by delegates from two other countries. But their words were drowned out by shouts from other delegates, signaling their approval. In this way the conference continued, each side trying to out shout the other, until well into the night.

Finally, the Chairman, William R. Tolbert, Jr., put the measure to a vote. To Morocco's consternation the Mauritanian delegation voted in favor of this proposal and it was endorsed by 33 votes to 2.

When reports of the meeting filtered back to Hassan he remained undeterred. He treated the decision with contempt, and immediately threatened to seize the Mauritanian portion of Western Sahara if Mauritania should abandon it.

But the attack on Tichla had been the last straw for Heydalla. On July 30 he declared that Mauritania had no claims to Western Saharan territory and wished to resume negotiations with the Polisario "as rapidly as possible." Four days later, representatives of Mauritania and the Polisario met in Algiers, and put an end to a conflict that neither had ever really wanted.

August 7, 1979. Dakhla.

When he stepped off the plane you would have thought he was the King himself, all the attention he received. Dignitaries of all stripes came to meet him on the tarmac, a favored few were allowed to kiss the ring on the finger of his right hand – a show of obeisance in what was still a feudal state. And he bore himself with an air befitting the attention he received. Driss Basri, now appointed the Minister of the Interior, was one of the most powerful men in Morocco, and he knew it. At his side was Ahmed Dlimi, and behind him at a safe distance an entourage of followers.

The King had been furious when he heard of the total capitulation of his Mauritanian allies. He had done everything within his power to shore up their defenses and boost their military capabilities. He began to rue the day that he decided to solicit their partnership in the Sahara campaign, marring what had otherwise been a brilliant political strategy. And now, before the Polisario had a chance to take advantage of the situation, he would need to act. Within twenty four hours of the signing of the Algiers Accord he had sent five Hercules C-130 transport planes with troop reinforcements to Dakhla. Two days later he withdrew most of the Moroccan troops still in Mauritania, but not the twenty five hundred or so troops in the vicinity of Dakhla and the thousand at Bir Moghrein in northeastern Mauritania.

Now, on August 7, the final step would be taken.

Dakhla, known in Spanish as Villa Cisneros, was a tiny fishing village of white stucco houses and a decidedly Mediterranean air, that had been established by the Spanish as their one and only settlement on the southern coast of their colony. A day's drive from Laayoune on a dirt highway that paralleled the coast, it had always been a relatively quiet and serene oasis, where migrating Bedouins could be found mixing with fishermen and their families, exchanging animals and other goods found in southern lands for citified amenities. Even when occupied by Mauritanian officials it had managed to maintain its calm and pleasant aura.

But not today. The residents who lined the pavement had fear on their faces. It was only the Moroccans who smiled.

A giant podium had been prepared as befitted a dignitary of Basri's stature. The few Mauritanian officials who had remained in the city were quickly escorted to vehicles that would take them to the airport and to waiting transport to their home country, and a bevy of Moroccans replaced them at their desks.

With great fanfare Basri strode up the steps of the podium, flanked by Dlimi and a handful of other Moroccans, and made a short speech. The message was clear. Henceforth this was going to be Moroccan territory and its

190

inhabitants Moroccan citizens. He waited, but there were no ebullient cheers from the crowd, only grim silence. Embarrassed, the Moroccans in the crowd, including the soldiers who had mingled with the onlookers to ensure that there was no violence, began to clap. Seemingly undeterred, he went on to recount the territory's place in the history of Morocco – how it had been part of the state of Morocco since the time of the Sultans and would remain a part of Morocco until the end of time.

Then, with a flourish, he made a signal and the Moroccan flag was hoisted over the roof of the main government office, and he departed a happy man.

August 11, 1979 Bir Enzaren.

The small radio that had been the Polisario leaders' link to the outside world had blasted news of the triumphant Moroccan display at Dakhla for over a day. When Abdelaziz finally turned it off, he turned to his companions and said in a quiet voice, "We cannot let this challenge go unanswered!"

Brahim Ghali just smiled. He already had something in mind.

Basri had barely returned from his sojourn to the "southern provinces" when the retaliation began. Within four days after the ceremony Bouhali, Ayoub Lahbib and Bana Baha embarked on a joint expedition to attack the Moroccan base at Bir Enzaren, 60 miles northeast of Dakhla, with a combined force of several hundred soldiers.

The terrain surrounding the base was largely flat with nothing to provide any substantial cover. So the leaders relied on the element of surprise. For several days before the attack small units of guerillas would patrol the desert near the base, drawing fire and diverting attention from the main force that had approached quietly from three directions – north, east and southwest. During the evening of August 10 the commanders moved their troops to the edge of the base slowly and by increments, under cover of darkness, never moving more than two vehicles at a time to reduce noise. They had no heavy artillery, just Land Rovers equipped with machine guns and light surface to air missiles. Bouhali and his men were in between the two other units. In front of him was an area of trees and beyond that a contingent of Moroccans were camped on a slight ridge protecting the entrance to the town. During the evening, while it was still dark, he sent two men to the area of trees to survey the situation. When they had ascertained the best approach they signaled their comrades with special infra-red flashlights, whose beam could not be seen by the Moroccans. At their leaders' command they raced towards the Moroccans at full speed just before dawn, when it was still dark, and took them by surprise. The infantry entered into hand to hand combat with the Moroccan soldiers. At the same time, Land Rovers with machine guns broke into the camp shelling the inhabitants. After overcoming those troops they advanced towards the town itself and occupied it. Meanwhile, troops from the 4th military region were busy fighting Moroccan soldiers on the left while troops from the 3rd region had managed to cut through the enemy lines to the right.

At the sound of gunfire coming from all directions many of the startled Moroccans began to flee, seeking refuge among the civilians in the small village. Others fired aimlessly into the desert. The Moroccan troops stationed on the far side of the town tried to fire upon them, but it was difficult for them to determine which vehicles were Polisario and which were Moroccan so they finally stopped. When the firing stopped the guerillas took stock of their booty. They had been able to capture at least 175 prisoners, who were shown off to journalists visiting Tindouf on August 30, and they had acquired a number of vehicles. At least 82 Moroccans lay dead in the sand. The Moroccan air force, unable to fire at them while they were intermingled with the Moroccan soldiers, followed their retreat, and strafed their positions. However the F-5s merely dumped their bombs indiscriminately in the desert, causing few casualties.

The raid on Bir Enzaren had been successful. But the most audacious attack of the year was yet to come.

August 24, 1979. Prelude.

Throughout the spring and summer of 1979 attacks on Moroccan troops and caravans had also proceeded unabated in the northern part of the territory. In March troops from the 2nd and 4th military regions ambushed a Moroccan column of troops going between Laayoune and Smara. Later on in March, troops from the 2nd military region battled Moroccan forces and took its commander prisoner near Smara. At the end of April troops from the 1st and 2nd military region attacked a column of enemy soldiers near Elkhouloua and captured its commander, Captain Laroussi, as well as a number of trucks and other equipment.

In addition, guerilla units had stayed in southern Morocco, harassing Moroccan troops and caravans, long after the battle at Tan Tan. At the end of March troops from the 2nd and 3rd military regions attacked a convoy going between Tan Tan and Laayoune. Two months later a caravan traveling between Tan Tan and Tarfaya had been ambushed. The road south to Laayoune had become impassible, forcing the Moroccans to transport most supplies to the territory by air or sea. There had been new raids on Tan Tan -- one on June 13 and another on June 27 – and Assa was again attacked on June 14. By August southern Morocco was honeycombed with small groups of guerillas, reeking havoc on Moroccan troops on an almost daily basis.

Some of these guerillas were in the vicinity of Lebouirate.

Lebouirate was a small enclave of mainly Sahrawi civilians located in the valley that ran along almost the entire length of the northern border of Western Sahara, between the escarpment of the *hammada* high plains to the south, and the Ouarkziz mountain range to the north. The 1,200 troops of the 3rd mechanized infantry regiment of the Royal Moroccan Army were based at a garrison east of the town. Beyond the garrison farther to the east were a few hills, and a few miles beyond these hills, nestled at the far end of the valley was another Moroccan garrison which occupied the remnants of a fort built by the French or Spanish Foreign Legion near the enclave of Zag. Several miles north of Zag was the Lengueb pass through the Ouarkziz mountains – the only route from the eastern part of Western Sahara to Morocco. Two roads led to the pass, one from Lebouirate and the other from Zag.

The Moroccan garrison at Lebouirate was considered to be a difficult target because of the flat terrain that surrounded it – making a surprise attack difficult -- and the heavy artillery based there.

In early July, Mohammed Akeik, who had been appointed head of the 1st military region after the death of Seghir at Tan Tan a month earlier, was skirting the area of Lebouirate with his troops en route to the Lengueb pass -- his destination Assa -- when he reached for his binoculars and took a long look at the Moroccan position.

"Omar, come here for a moment," he said to one of his companions. "Take a look and tell me what you see." When Omar took the binoculars he focused on the closest Moroccan position and reported back, "I see some tanks on small mounds along the perimeter of the base. Nothing else."

"Exactly. It seems to me they are just begging for an attack. What do you think?"

Omar paused for a moment. "Well, we would have to cover the distance either in the dark or fairly rapidly because we would be in the open . . . but I think it could be managed!"

"Well, if we could manage to attack at least one of their positions successfully, it would be quite an accomplishment. They obviously think their garrison is impregnable or they wouldn't be leaving their tanks out in the open like this – either that or they are just plain stupid."

Omar couldn't help smiling at the last remark.

Akeik quickly assembled a few of his men. The plan was simple. A dozen or so soldiers on foot carrying bazookas would creep near the Moroccan positions at night and mount a sneak attack at dawn on one of them. After successfully breaching the perimeter of the base and neutralizing one or two tanks, their companions would follow with their Land Rovers, penetrating beyond the position and engaging the Moroccans beyond it in hand to hand combat. They would destroy as many tanks and artillery as possible, then they would quickly retreat.

Minutes before dawn Omar and a small group of his comrades crept silently over the flat plain towards the tanks on the hills that faced them. When silhouettes began to appear out of the darkness they climbed the hills, overcame the guards, and hurled anti-tank missiles at the tanks, immobilizing two of them. At the same time Land Rovers filled with their comrades streaked towards their position firing at the soldiers in the rear. The assault went as planned. By mid-morning they withdrew, having destroyed a couple of tanks and even taken a few prisoners.

After withdrawing to the safety of the escarpment, Akeik spent the next few hours deep in thought. The attack had shown that the garrison at Lebouirate was vulnerable. Why not mount another attack, this time with

193

a greater force? So, instead of proceeding to Lengueb he sent emissaries to Hammada El Ouali, the commander of the 5th military region, with a message. Then he waited. By August 11 two dozen men from Hammada's forces had joined his troops at the escarpment. Before dawn they approached the same position, destroying the newly installed tanks and lobbing rockets at the command center.

But this was just the beginning.

August 24, 1979. Lebouirate.

At first he didn't know what to think. When Akeik and Hammada asked for a meeting to discuss a proposed large scale assault, he hadn't thought of the Moroccan garrison at Lebouirate. Small hit and run strikes against one or two positions, sure, but a frontal assault on the main command center and one of the most heavily fortified garrisons in the region? That would be an audacious move! But if they could pull it off . . .

So, he listened intently as Akeik and Hammada unveiled their plan.

"You realize, that if this is to succeed we would need to amass a larger force than we have ever assembled," he finally said, doing some calculations in his head.

"Yes," Akeik responded, confidently, "But think of the message it would send if we were successful!"

Ghali hesitated for a moment, conflicting thought swirling through his head. It would indeed be a risky proposition. But, again, if they succeeded . . .

He quickly sent word to Abdelaziz, then to Bouhali and Ayoub. Once they were together he unveiled the idea. At first they were hesitant to respond. Then their enthusiasm began to mount, as one by one, they began to recognize the advantages such an attack would offer. Lebouirate was the sentinel at the eastern gateway to Morocco. Eliminate the forces at Lebouirate and the pathway to Zag and the pass through the Ouarkziz mountains would be wide open.

"It would have to be a surprise attack," Abdelaziz offered, after contemplating the strategic implications, "With the tanks they have at the perimeter, any forewarning would be suicide!"

"Agreed," said Ghali, "And we would have to use overwhelming force . . . the troops from at least four regions."

"Not to mention troops stationed between Lebouirate and Zag to prevent any reinforcements from arriving," added Bouhali.

Akeik and Hammada nodded their agreement.

And so, gradually, over many cups of tea, the outline of a plan began to emerge.

Within a week a long line of Land Rovers carrying bazookas, machine guns and a "Stalin Organ" began to creep silently across the *hammada*, from three different directions, their headlights dimmed to avoid detection. The stars studded the evening sky, blanketing nearly every inch with slivers of varying intensities. But the ground was pitch black with no electric lights or moon to guide the way.   Ever so slowly the two convoys coming from the east crept forward through the desert and through the passes through the escarpment until, once safely in the valley, they abruptly turned to the west. The one coming from the west followed the valley eastward from Lemseid. All three of them stopped when they were roughly three miles away from their target. Then they cut their engines, and for the rest of the journey they pushed their vehicles, so as to eliminate all noise of their approach.

Then they waited for the command.

It was the final day of Ramadan, August 24, 1979. Mohammed Azelmat, the commander of the FAR's 3rd Armored Squadron in Lebouirate had finished the evening meal that broke the day long fast and was sitting in his tent preparing a report for his superiors back in Rabat. The report did not take long – thankfully nothing of interest had happened. He and his soldiers had been forced to spend the month long Ramadan fast in the hottest month of the year in the middle of one of the hottest regions of the world, where the temperatures could reach 120 degrees Fahrenheit during the day. To make matters worse, they were constantly on edge. They had been attacked twice by the guerillas, and although the skirmishes were brief and small scale, they were enough to rattle his nerves. He had sent messages to Abrouq, his superior, in Laayoune asking for reinforcements, but his pleas had been summarily dismissed. Wasn't he in charge of one of the largest and best fortified garrisons? Abrouq was busy fighting commando units along the Tan Tan – Laayoune corridor and could not spare any units to buttress his defenses. Thankfully, no one would be stupid enough to attack in such heat! Or so he told himself. So, besides sitting around or sleeping all day, there had been nothing to do for nearly a month during the days, and all they could look forward to was a brief respite during the evening hours.

He fell asleep dreaming of the nightlife in the cafes of Casablanca. But his revere was rudely broken shortly before dawn by a sharp noise. He looked up, ran to the door of his barracks, and reached for his binoculars. He strained to see something, anything, but all he could see was the blackness of night. Soon peals of thunder were accompanied by flashes of lightning. The Polisario infantry were decimating the tanks one by one with their anti-tank bazookas, while their Land Rovers, headlights turned off, were racing towards the garrison at top speed from all directions, firing their automatic weapons and launching rockets. The noise was infernal. It was terrifying. The troops in the garrison quickly sprang into action, grabbing their rifles and running to the tanks that were perched indolently along the perimeter. But before they could even reach them they were mowed down by machine guns and grenades. A few managed to man their artillery, but most did not have time to fire them before being felled. There was carnage everywhere. The guerillas – numbering in the hundreds -- made their way to the bunkers in which the majority of the Moroccan troops had taken cover -- and then to the command center.

Azelmat at first did not know what to do. He had been taken completely by surprise. He ran to one of the bunkers and ordered the soldiers to take defensive positions as best they could. Although his men could not reach the tanks that were positioned at the perimeter of the camp, they had stores of ammunition and weapons scattered throughout the garrison that could serve as their defense. But their weapons were no match for the grenades and rockets being hurled at them at lightning speed by the ever approaching vehicles. Nor could they withstand for long a bombardment from their own artillery, now in enemy hands.

Azelmat reached for his phone and before long Moroccan F-5 jets appeared, but they remained at a high altitude and the bombs they dropped scattered over the area without inflicting much damage. A unit was dispatched from Zag to bring relief, but Hammada El Ouali's men had stationed themselves in the area east of the garrison to intercept any forces coming from this direction. Instead of joining the battle the units from Zag panicked and broke ranks, attempting to flee back to their fortress, but the guerillas pursued them, picking off isolated groups of vehicles one by one.

The assault lasted that day until sunset, when quiet gradually descended on the plateau. Azelmat began to realize that further resistance would mean almost certain death. With a few hand-picked men he hastily retreated in the darkness to a point on the northernmost outskirts of the compound and waited. After a half hour a vehicle approached – one of the few Moroccan Land Rovers still intact – and he quickly fled northward through the hills towards the safety of Assa.

The following morning the Polisario commanders surveyed the grounds. They had lost a number of good men, but the Moroccan troops had been decimated. At least 37 tanks had been destroyed and the bunkers and structures were in flames. They counted 111 prisoners, most of them itinerant Berbers from the Atlas region pressed into service. Many of them seemed to be relieved. At least they were alive.

By noon news of the battle had spread to the countryside surrounding the compound and a number of Sahrawi inhabitants in the surrounding area approached the Polisario leaders with cries of joy. For days they trickled past the guerillas, giving them food, telling stories of atrocities and pledging their allegiance.

The Moroccans did not attempt to re-establish a garrison at Lebouirate, and the area around it remained in Polisario hands for nearly five years. When the guerillas finally retreated, the settlement's entire civilian population went with them.

The battle of Lebouirate finally got the attention of the international press. A year later, a documentary producer for Hungarian television, Alajos Chrudinak, produced a film about the battle that won an award at the 1980 Film Festival in Venice. Unfortunately, this film never reached an audience in the United States or most other countries in the West, and the citizens of those countries remained for the most part blissfully unaware of the drama that was taking place in the North African desert.

September 17, 1979. Lengueb.

After the battle of Lebouirate troops from Polisario's 1st, 2nd and 5th military regions stayed in the area to plan an incursion into southern Morocco to attack Assa and other positions. However, by the beginning of September, the rainy season had already started, turning much of the terrain to thick mud and granting the soldiers a brief respite from the battlefield. On September 15, Hammada El Ouali and some of his men were enjoying an early morning cup of tea in a camp hidden among the escarpment crevices, when one of his scouts entered, an excited look on his face.

"Sir," he began to say, somewhat breathlessly, "for the past day a Moroccan column from Zag has been proceeding to the pass. It looks as if they were intending to meet up with a column coming through the pass from the north with supplies. However, the rain has flooded the tributaries of the *wadi* and the Zag force is now stranded between the two of them. The supply caravan from the north will be unable to reach them through the pass because of the floods to the north. "

Hammada immediately sent a message to Bouhali, who was camped with some of his troops nearby. Bouhali thought for a moment. The image of a hundred men and vehicles stuck in the mud, immobilized, flashed through his mind. He sent the scout with a message for the commanders of the other nearby units. Before long a handful of soldiers crowded into his tent. After a few moments they decided on a plan, and within a day Hammada, Bouhali and a few dozen men from the 2nd and 5th units began a six mile trek to a position just a mile south of where the Moroccans were trapped, while Akeik and some of his men took positions between them and Zag. There they set up camps, and waited.

By this time the rains had stopped and the waters of the river began slowly to recede. Bouhali could see with his binoculars the Moroccans, busily extracting their vehicles from the mud. On September 17, when they started to move, he gave the order to attack. Immediately the guerilla hoard ran towards the Moroccans strafing them with their AK-47s and lobbing grenades and rockets at their vehicles. Before long the Moroccan air force attempted to intervene and blanketed the earth with bombs – at times hitting their own tanks – but for the most part their bombs missed their targets.

Meanwhile, the commander of the Moroccan garrison at Zag decided to view for himself what was going on at Lengueb. He took a couple dozen men and Land Rovers and struggled up a trail leading to the crest of the *hammada* escarpment – a place where he could get a panoramic view of the surrounding countryside. While he was climbing the escarpment he heard the sound of gunfire in the distance. He quickened his pace. When he reached the summit he grabbed his binoculars. What he saw made his heart skip a beat. Puffs of smoke from exploding grenades and gunfire were clouding the landscape. He barked an order and his men quickly began to move back to Zag and from there down the escarpment in the direction of the pass. However, it took

197

hours for his troops to descend to the valley below, and when his men reached the level plain they were ambushed by Akeik and his troops and quickly overcome.

Five Moroccan tanks managed to escape the ambush but five others were captured intact and many others were destroyed. When the remnants of the Zag forces retreated they left behind 175 vehicles, including 80 new Land Rovers, as well as a number of cannons.

After the battle the Moroccans did not dare to leave the safety of Zag, and the Polisario forces stayed in the area, surrounding Zag and controlling access to the Lengueb pass for months.

September 25, 1979. The Jewel of the Sahara.

It was the final week of September, the best time to be in their hideout among the caves that dotted the area near Tifariti, a time when the temperature was neither too hot nor too cold, and the men of Bouhali's unit were resting, enjoying the cool autumn breeze. But not Bouhali. It was now a month after the successful campaign at Lebouirate. Akeik and a smattering of troops from several regions had remained in the area to blockade the Moroccan outpost at Zag and control the eastern pass through the Ouarkziz mountains. Already supplies to Zag were being airlifted. But after remaining a few weeks in the vicinity, the commanders of the regions and most of the troops had returned to their bases.

It was time to plan their next move. Lebouirate had shown them that with sufficient force, and a bit of cunning, the guerillas could mount a successful campaign against any target. It was time to focus on a target in the territory. And Bouhali knew just the target -- a target that would hold a significance for the people in the camp, a target that would put a nail in the coffin of the King's ambitions.

Bouhali had done his homework. He had assessed the troop strength and its weaknesses. He had studied the terrain. He knew the location of the heavy artillery and the command center. All that remained was to convince the others that it was time for them to strike. So when the President and Minister of Defense arrived for a meeting, he came straight to the point.

"Smara," he said. "I suggest that we attack Smara."

Abdelaziz and Ghali exchanged glances.

"You think that our next target should be Smara, rather than Mahbes?" Abdelaziz asked, taken by surprise. "The troops at Mahbes are hindering our access to the territory from our camps as well as our access to eastern Morocco. Some of the men have been suggesting that the Moroccan base there be our next target."

"I know," Bouhali replied, "but Smara would be a much more important target. "

The others were silent for a moment.

"What would you need in terms of troop strength?" Ghali finally asked, intrigued by the idea.

Bouhali stifled a smile. Interesting Ghali in the idea was half the battle. "It would have to be a coordinated attack," he responded quickly. "We would need the help of Akeik as well as Ayoub."

Ghali reflected for a moment. Then he faced him. His eyes were serious. "A frontal attack on a stationary, fully armed battalion, with reinforcements only miles away, would be a risky business anywhere. But against the troops at Smara . . . protected by at least four circles of troops . . ." He shook his head, solemnly.

Bouhali was aware of the risks. "But think of what it would mean to our troops if we succeeded!" he said, forcefully. "Besides which, we managed a frontal attack at Lebouirate didn't we?"

"Yes, but they weren't expecting us to attack Lebouirate . . . we took them completely by surprise." Ghali quickly interjected. "But this is a different matter. They have prepared themselves for an attack on garrisons in the territory. The garrison at Smara is surrounded by land mines and heavily fortified."

"Exactly why they wouldn't expect us to attack it!" Bouhali quickly replied.

Ghali hesitated for a moment staring off into the distance. "How many men do you estimate are there?" he finally asked.

"Roughly 5,400."

The two men looked at each other, each one buried in his thoughts. Finally, Abdelaziz, who had been quietly listening to the interchange, broke the silence.

"If we decide to do this it would have to be planned down to the smallest detail. We couldn't afford to make a mistake!" he said, slowly.

Bouhali turned to look at him. "There won't be," he said, his tone firm, "I have studied their defenses and I have a plan."

"Good," said Abdelaziz, rising to his feet, "I will call a meeting of the other commanders so that we can discuss it." And with a few parting words he exited the cave, followed by Ghali.

As the two men walked back to the Land Rover that would take them to their respective headquarters each man was deep in thought. Finally, Ghali turned to Abdelaziz and said with a grave voice, "You know, even if an attack on Smara succeeded we would not be able to retain control of the area. Dlimi would send his whole army, if necessary, to dislodge us. We would have to retreat almost immediately."

Abdelaziz smiled. "Yes, I know, but think of the message it would send!"

At a meeting of the commanders the plan was approved. They would attack the Moroccan garrison at Smara. For a week following this meeting they met each day to discuss preparations for what was to be their crowning achievement that year. Every inch of the terrain, every tree, every nook was mapped and logistics discussed. Within a fortnight the guerillas were ready.

October 6, 1979. Smara.

Smara, the city of learning established by Sheikh Ma el Ainin, was nestled in a plain that was protected to the north by hills and escarpments which made

199

an approach from that direction difficult. To the southwest was a tributary of the Saguia el Hamra *wadi* that went diagonally through the environs of the city.

The Moroccans had established a camp near the tributary, protected by several units of mobile forces. The camp, as well as the town itself, was circled by troops positioned along the small hills that dotted the landscape. Protecting the units to the east were land mines.

In the early hours of October 4, hundreds of guerilla troops from the 1st, 2nd and 3rd military regions sped silently through the desert in the direction of Smara from three directions. The plan was that Bouhali's troops would attack from the southwest, while Ayoub's troops would approach from the east and Akeik's troops would attack from the northeast. The infantry from all the units would attack the Moroccan positions during the night and the troops in Land Rovers would then proceed at full speed through those troops in the early morning. But during the afternoon Brahim Ghali arrived with additional recruits from the 4th military region, so the attack was delayed for a day while these men familiarized themselves with the terrain and integrated themselves into Bouhali's forces. Then it was decided that Brahim Ghali would be in charge of three Stalin Organs, which would lob rockets into Moroccan positions in the north of the city, in order to destroy the stores of ammunition and incapacitate the airport that was located there. By the evening of October 5 they were ready to move.

It was now just before dawn on the morning of October 6, and Salek waited in his Land Rover for the signal to attack. The *wadi* was normally dry at this time of the year. However, during the evening of October 4 it had rained, swelling the tributary with water and mud, making their approach to the city from that direction more difficult. It was nearly daybreak before he and the others had managed to get their vehicles through the mud and reach their positions.

The infantry from the 2nd military region had already engaged the troops stationed southwest of the town while it was still dark and they could approach without being seen, and he could hear the blasts of gunfire in the distance. Now it was the time for the men in Land Rovers to join the battle. Salek revved up his motor and charged in the direction of the Moroccan troops at full speed. The fighting quickly grew more intense. At daybreak Mirage jets – newly arrived from France -- streaked through the sky, showering bombs indiscriminately on guerillas and Moroccans alike. But the guerillas pressed on. The infantry had forged a wedge through the southwestern flank of the Moroccan defense forces, allowing a stream of vehicles to pour through, and within minutes the Moroccan units guarding the perimeter of the city began to disperse, fleeing in all directions, allowing the Polisario forces to pour into the city.

But not all of them. One of the Moroccans had found cover behind an overturned vehicle and was firing round after round at the oncoming troops. Salek looked to his left. The men in the Land Rover were slumped over and the vehicle had come to a dead halt. To his right another Land Rover was riddled with bullets, the men in it flung to the earth. He aimed his car in the direction of the shots, lowered himself below the rim of the dashboard, and put his hand firmly on the gas pedal. At once the Land Rover lurched forward and proceeded at top speed toward the overturned vehicle, ramming into it and forcing the soldier to run out of its path. Salek leapt onto him and for a minute or two they rolled on the ground, throwing punches, each one trying to get one of the guns that had fallen nearby. Then it was over. Salek looked at the figure that had slumped at his feet. On his shoulder was the insignia of an officer – a colonel in the Moroccan army.

While Salek and the other troops were embroiled in the battle, Bouhali turned to one of his comrades.

"Where are Ayoub's men?" he shouted. "I don't see any of them . . . nor Akeik's!"

He sent a soldier to where Ghali was busy directing the men firing the Stalin Organs. After a few minutes he returned.

"They had problems with the land mines and the infantry were not able to proceed during the night," he shouted. "They are starting the approach now . . . but the Moroccans are putting up stiff resistance. He said you should do what you can without them!"

By this time Bouhali's men had reached the city. What they saw was a ghost town. The streets were empty. The residents had hidden themselves to escape the bombs and napalm raining down on them from the passing aircraft. As Salek made his way slowly to the center of the town, eyes began to peer at him from cracks in doorways and windows. Finally, amidst shouts of joy, hundreds of men, women and children began streaming into the street surrounding and hugging him and his comrades. One of them, an elderly man with a distinguished air, made his way through the crowd and kissed him in the traditional Sahrawi greeting.

It was the Sahrawi sheikh who had been appointed the representative of Smara in the Moroccan parliament, Mohammed Ali Ould Sid el-Bashir. He looked at Salek with tears in his eyes. "We have been waiting a long time for this day!" he finally said, with a voice full of emotion.

Within an hour troops from the 1st and 3rd military regions began to filter in. They were quickly surrounded by joyous Sahrawis, waiving and shouting, and climbing into the trucks and Land Rovers. It was sheer bedlam.

In the midst of the clamor a guerilla approached Bouhali, an agitated look on his face.

"What are we going to do with all these civilians?" he shouted breathlessly. "They refuse to get off our vehicles . . . they want to go with us to the refugee camps!"

Bouhali looked around him at the crowd. "How many Sahrawis are here?" he shouted back, trying to be heard above the din.

"Several thousand at least," he yelled.

"We don't have enough vehicles to take them all," Bouhali shouted. "We'll

201

take as many as we can. The others will have to stay."

Then, casting a glance at the sky, he added "And be quick about it. Tell them we'll be leaving in twenty minutes. . . before the Moroccan jets have time to return. Quickly . . . go!"

Word quickly spread among the crowd and soon the streets of the town were filled with men, women and children bidding a sad farewell to others perched upon the Polisario vehicles. Within less than a half hour the caravan was ready. With troops carrying bazookas walking alongside as an escort, one of Bouhali's men led a long procession in a perilous trek eastward through a gauntlet of Moroccan snipers and land mines. As the procession left the environs of the city, troops from Akeik's and Ayoub's command forged westward through the *wadi* to route the Moroccans trying to escape to the garrisons at Laayoune or Boucraa.

The next few hours were tense. By nightfall the convoy of civilians had reached a point only 80 miles from Smara with headlights turned off to avoid detection by any Moroccan aircraft that might be in the vicinity. At the first crack of dawn they stopped again and covered the vehicles as best they could in ravines and under acacia trees. There they waited patiently until the sun set once again. It took them three nights to reach their destination.

When the residents of the Tindouf camps glimpsed the first truckload of civilians bedlam broke out, as refugees ran, crying and shouting, towards the vehicles to hug long lost relatives. Soukeina, in charge of logistics, quickly mobilized the leaders of each wilaya to distributed food, tents and other necessities. It was a massive effort – over 760 men, women and children had been evacuated from Smara.

And the celebrations continued for several days.

But there was no celebration in Rabat. In a news broadcast the day after the battle the Moroccan government admitted losing 121 dead, among them one of their most renowned army commanders, Colonel Driss Harti.

October 23, 1979. Mahbes.

It was the third week of October, and in the open Land Rover the woman sitting in the passenger seat was trying unsuccessfully to keep the dust out of her mouth and eyes. It was nine days after she had gotten word that Polisario guerillas had attacked and decimated a Moroccan garrison at Mahbes, and her editor was hungry for details. So, she had made the long trek from Algiers to the guerilla camps. There she had been taken on a whirlwind tour through nearly 800 miles of territory, stopping at the Western Sahara outpost Jdiriya, then crossing the Moroccan border into Lebouirate and finally settling on a hill top overlooking Zag – along a route littered with the carcasses of hundreds of Moroccan tanks, troupe carriers, Berliot trucks and cars, as well as the scattered remains of hundreds of soldiers.

And now she was going to her final destination, Mahbes. She learned that after escorting the civilians from Smara safely back to the Tindouf camp after the battle there, soldiers from four of the military regions -- over a thousand in all -- had descended upon Moroccan units at Mahbes, a town 30 miles from the Algerian border, and had killed more than a fifth of the battalion stationed there. The rest were forced to flee. This had followed the attack in August at Lebouirate and the decimation of one of the largest Moroccan garrisons in the vicinity, and a guerilla blockade of the Moroccan garrison at Zag and control of the Lengueb pass that left the guerillas in control of the entire northeast quadrant of the territory. Suddenly this little conflict had sparked her editor's interest.

For over an hour the car had barreled through the open desert at top speed, its driver impervious to the wind and sand that assaulted their faces through the empty windshield. At first she had strained to note the details of the passing landscape, but soon she wearied of the attempt. For miles it had been the same – nothing but flat, barren rocky soil only occasionally punctuated by a small acacia tree. She wondered how long it would be before she saw anything else – a sand dune, a hill, a crevice, anything to break the monotony.

In the seat next to her was a tall, thin man wearing camouflage fatigues, a green turban and a face worn and grizzled by the sun – the poster image of a guerilla warrior. Nestled behind him within reach was an AK-47, just in case. Behind his seat was Bachir, the interpreter cum escort, a fresh faced kid with a hippie hairdo who seemed more suited to the hallowed halls of a university than the present surroundings. Bachir spoke several languages and was fond of relieving the boredom by subjecting his companions to a constant banter on international political affairs. Yes, these guerillas were an eclectic bunch she thought.

After what seemed an eternity Bachir tapped her on the shoulder. "We are close to Mahbes now. We'll be there in a few minutes," he whispered in her ear. But the announcement was unnecessary. For several miles now the fresh, clean air of the desert had given way to a vile odor. The stench of death. As they grew closer to the battlefield the stench increased until her handkerchief was used to do more than repel the sand.

And then she saw it, sticking out of a trench. A human hand, or what was left of it. She asked the driver to stop and she slowly exited the car, somewhat fearful of what she would find. There, in the trench, was not one, but a dozen or so remains of men in the uniform of Morocco's 14th battalion, riddled with bullets.

"We are trying to bury them . . . but it is taking a while . . . there are so many," Bachir said in a low tone. She walked a few yards to where part of a blackened and twisted vehicle jutted from the sand.

"These were the ones who fell first, their first line of defense," Bachir informed her slowly. "It only took our fighters four hours to overcome them and head for the main garrison and the town. The assault began at dawn. By noon it was over."

She began to walk slowly towards the walls of what had been a fortress of the Spanish Foreign Legion in the colonial days. Beyond that were a few hovels,

203

the abandoned domiciles of Sahrawis who had fled the Moroccan invasion, confiscated by Moroccan troops when they swept the area at the beginning of the war. Everywhere she turned he saw the remnants of the battle. The Moroccan prisoners she had interviewed back in the Tindouf camps had recounted it in great detail – how on October 14 the guerillas had launched a surprise attack at dawn from three directions, with their Land Rovers descending upon them at full speed, bombarding them with bullets. Some of them had sought refuge in the buildings near the fort, others tried to escape on foot into the desert, but had been rounded up by the guerillas after 70 or so miles. A few of the officers – including Captain Mohamed Sakka, who was in charge of the garrison in the absence of Colonel Mohamed Chamsseddin – had taken armored vehicles and had fled towards the fortress at Zag. Most of their comrades, however, lay in the trenches.

Bachir stopped to take a closer look at one of the dead. The features of his face had not yet been obscured by decay and he could see that he had been young – perhaps no more than 18 years old. "I feel sorry for these guys," Bachir said with a sigh. "None of them really wanted to be here. I can show you letters we found, letters in which they speak of their disillusionment . . ." Bachir reached for a few papers tucked away in a portfolio.

But the visitor didn't need to see the letters. She had already seen the logbook kept by the commander of the Moroccan garrison at Lebouirate in which he wrote that his soldiers were "traumatized and demoralized" and that a "catastrophe of no uncertain proportions is likely to occur if the enemy decides to attack again." And she had already spoken to the prisoners. In fact, she had spoken to a number of Moroccan soldiers in the part of the territory occupied by Morocco who had told her in confidence the same thing. The war was going badly. The soldiers felt hamstrung by the fact that no major move could be made without approval from Rabat. They had no confidence in their superiors and were tired and afraid.

And she had been taken to the little enclave of Jdiriya – or at least what was left of it after it had been dynamited by the Moroccans before they retreated. Amidst the rubble she had seen something written on a wall by a soldier – a sad inscription to his daughter that read: "To Fatiha, I know you are waiting for me to return. Your unlucky father."

After wandering through the desolated remains of Mahbes for an hour she had had enough. She signaled that it was time to begin the trek back to Tindouf and from there back to Algiers and then onto the waiting arms of her editor back in the United States. But she still had a few questions to ask.

"Bachir, one thing still puzzles me. Mahbes is in the middle of nowhere . . . there are no hills or crevices for miles that could provide cover. I understand your reputation for long distance surprise attacks, but Morocco has something you do not – air power. Here, out in the open, I would think your men would be sitting ducks for their F-5s, not to mention the new Mirage jets they have just gotten from France."

Bachir smiled. She was not the first journalist to ask that question.

"They try to bomb us, but it is not as easy as you think. Just ask the French. If we were able to survive the attacks of the French Air Force with Jaguars, do you think we would have a problem with Moroccan pilots? It is not easy to catch a fox in the desert!"

". . . and you are fighting the Moroccans yourselves . . . without any Cuban, Soviet or Algerian troops or 'advisors' helping you?"

Bachir's demeanor suddenly changed. "We do not need others to fight our battles for us," he said in an emphatic tone. "We have gotten some equipment and training from the Algerians and others, but that is all."

The visitor shook her head, and as she settled back into her seat for the long, dusty journey back to the camps she wondered what Sun Tsu would have thought of this situation. This was indeed a crazy war and everything she had ever learned about warfare seemed to be turned upside down. Only one thing seemed certain. Despite all the arms and equipment both the United States and France had given the King, and despite his huge army, the war was in its fifth year, Mauritania had been forced to withdraw, and Morocco had still not been able to crush this little band of Bedouins. It was David versus Goliath – that old biblical tale – come to life here in the Sahara sands.

And before it was over the bones of countless young men would lay in the ground. She wondered whatever possessed her government to back Hassan's gambit in the first place. The Cold War, she thought ruefully. Goliath is our 'friend' so David must be our enemy. Its either black or white. Nobody cares whether the Sahrawis'struggle for independence was legitimate or not, whether they were intent on destroying the United States or not, whether our 'friend's' actions were legitimate or not. Especially since the debacle in Iran.

She heaved a sigh. She had long ago become disillusioned with the arguments that had underpinned US foreign policy since she was old enough to vote. First it was the so-called 'dominoes theory' that had propelled the United States into the disastrous Vietnam war -- the theory that 'communism' was a monolithic force intent on destroying Western democracies and that once one country in a region fell to 'communism' the others would quickly follow. Once Vietnam fell to communism -- so the story went -- it would soon be taken over by 'Red China' – who, everybody knew, was the mortal enemy of the United States – and it would lead to the collapse of Thailand, Cambodia, Burma, the Philippines and Indonesia -- the entire southeast Pacific.

Only it hadn't turned out that way. Vietnam had indeed fallen, and so did its neighbor Cambodia. But none of the other countries had followed suit. And instead of joining in some monolithic force to invade their neighboring countries, Vietnam and Cambodia had quarreled, and just this past Christmas Vietnam had invaded Cambodia expelling its government, the Khmer Rouge – prompting China to retaliate two months later by invading Vietnam – and the Vietnamese to respond by expelling the Chinese! Behind it all a simmering feud between the Soviet Union and its Chinese neighbor. And to top it all, we had now opened our doors to trade with China . . . which was quickly embracing the evils of capitalism. I wonder what those men and women who died in Vietnam would think of all this, she thought, suppressing a sigh. All right, it is not fair to judge policies from the advantage of hindsight, she admitted to herself. But if hindsight has any value at all, it is that we should never fear questioning the wisdom of the "best and the brightest."

And now this wisdom was telling us that we must prop up regimes 'friendly' to United States' interests regardless of what they do at home – and brand as our enemy any group that tries to change the status quo.

But she didn't believe in labels – and she had taken a good look at the people huddled in their hovels in Tindouf and their leaders. Nothing she had seen suggested that they were enemies of the United States. She suspected that once again United States foreign policy may have been led astray. No, she had no use for bullies, regardless of how useful they were to her government. Her editor was expecting a story that would extoll the Moroccan cause – that would brand the guerillas ignorant dreamers manipulated by their communist overseers to serve their interests, too backward to fight their own battles. She would have none of it. She would write the truth, and let the political chips fall where they may.

For, although she would not admit it, she couldn't help but feel a tinge of admiration for this small band of nomads who dared to defy the powers-that-be, and hoped that, just as in the story of David, justice might for once prevail.

Ohoud.

The year 1978 had not been a good year for the King, and the year 1979 was becoming even worse. The coup in Mauritania altered the political and military landscape, and the rebels' cease fire with Mauritania had freed their mobile units for attacks against Moroccan forces, which they had proceeded to undertake with gusto. At every turn Moroccan forces and convoys between Laayoune and Tan Tan had been harassed and decimated, never knowing when to expect an attack in the dark. By mid 1979 the road to the north was so dangerous that trucks carrying foodstuffs and other supplies were being escorted by armed soldiers, and even then they were not safe.

Attacks on major Moroccan garrisons within Western Sahara had been swift and bold, forcing the King's forces to retrench. They had already been forced to withdraw from Bir Lehlou and Farsia by the end of 1977. By mid 1979 they had been expelled from Tifariti, Amgala, Jdiriya and Housa as well. When the King had sent troops to occupy Dakhla after the Mauritanian capitulation, they had responded by attacking Bir Enzaren. Just a few weeks ago they had decimated a Moroccan garrison at Mahbes, and there had been additional battles near Boucraa. And, worst of all, in October they had managed to overrun the garrison at Smara – and to take over 700 of the inhabitants of that town – including a representative in his Parliament – with them to Tindouf, much to Hassan's chagrin. His troops had quickly re-occupied Smara, but Moroccan forces in the territory east of the "useful triangle" were now restricted to a single garrison at Guelta Zemmour.

As if that were not enough, they had intensified their attacks in Morocco itself, decimating the garrison at Lebouirate and even managing to invade Tan Tan. And after they decimated the troops at Mahbes they moved north to attack Tan Tan again and shot down a Mirage plane killing the pilot. Then there was a battle near Zag where another Mirage plane was shot down and the pilot taken prisoner. And now they were laying siege to the garrison at Zag and controlling the Lengueb pass.

His commander, Dlimi, had tried every military maneuver to destroy them, but nothing had worked. They had spread themselves like cockroaches across the vast desert, burying into the sand during the day, swarming over isolated outposts during the night, and then scurrying back to safe havens with the rising sun. And, just like cockroaches, they had been almost impossible to wipe out.

He took out his frustration on his officers. They were shiftless, they were incompetent, they were disloyal. Some found themselves facing a firing squad. Others died in mysterious accidents. Still others were banished from the realm. The lucky ones were merely stripped of their rank or fled. There were murmurs of discontent among the ranks – the kind that could get you killed. Dlimi was the fall guy for most of it.

The diplomatic "war" had been even worse. He was not adverse to the use of threats to get his way, and had reminded Heydalla on several occasions of the number of Moroccan forces stationed a stone's throw from the Mauritanian capital, ready to pounce at his command. He was also no stranger to intrigue, and had carefully nurtured a nascent pro-Moroccan resistance movement within the country. For a while these tactics had managed to keep the coalition intact, but when the Polisario attacked Tichla – and had displayed their captured prisoners for all the world to see -- his diplomatic pieces started to fall.

Heydalla's capitulation had forced him to take swift action to prevent being checkmated. He now had troops throughout the region of the territory formerly ceded to Mauritania. But now he risked losing not only the territory he had taken over from Mauritania, but the territory within Western Sahara he had initially occupied – and perhaps his crown as well – if he failed to stop the constant hemorrhaging of his forces in the territory and the infiltration of the guerillas into Morocco.

So he had once again summoned Dlimi to his palace to discuss a strategy to counter the Polisario's moves – this time in the presence of a guest from Washington, a man wearing a uniform with stars on his shoulder.

"It is rather simple," the man said, after patiently listening to the King's tirade. "You are far better equipped than they are . . . and with the new jets you have just gotten from France your forces will be far less vulnerable to guerilla attacks. The guerillas cannot keep and defend any territory for long. The attacks on Tan Tan and Smara – although devastating from a public relations standpoint -- were hit and run. Your commanders quickly regained control and fortified your defenses. I doubt that they will try an attack on these targets in the future. Moreover, without the element of surprise they find it difficult to confront your forces in a headlong battle, so for the most part they use the age old guerilla tactic of nipping at your heels and bleeding you to death. And this has worked as long as you kept your troops thinly scattered through the territory. And since you cannot patrol the vast expanse of desert that exists between your outposts, they are free to move at will, as long as they keep their commando units small and movable. And, I should add, they know the desert far better than you do – after all, it is their home!"

The King looked at his guest with eyes that betrayed a sense of frustration. "I know all that," he finally said, "But how are we to defeat them? My commanders have tried everything they could think of, and nothing has worked!" With that last remarked he looked at Dlimi with the kind of glance that would have withered a less stoic soul, and Dlimi wished with all his heart that he could for once tell the King what he really thought of him. But he kept his silence as the King's guest continued.

"The guerillas only attack you where you are weak. If you are to defeat them you need to make your forces as strong as possible."

"And how do you suggest we do that?" asked the King, slumping into his chair.

The man in the military uniform smiled. "For one thing, you should concentrate your forces into units of at least two battalions each."

Dlimi gave the guest a sharp look. Then, casting caution to the wind, he cleared his throat. "Concentrating our forces is a strategy that might help, but It would also help if the United States would let us have the weapons we ordered last year and more sophisticated surveillance equipment . . . and would remove the restriction on their use in the Sahara."

For a moment the two men just stared at each other in silence. The Carter administration had allowed Hassan to buy a number of weapons and sophisticated surveillance equipment, but had canceled a planned sale of twenty four OV-10 "Broncos", low flying aircraft designed by Rockwell International in the sixties for counterinsurgency operations in Vietnam, and twenty four Bell Cobra helicopter gunships, and the President had demanded that the Moroccan government stop using its Northrop F-5 aircraft and other military aid in Western Sahara. Of course, Dlimi had completely ignored this restriction, but his use of American armaments – as well as the phosphorus bombs and napalm prohibited by the international community – was getting more difficult to conceal.

The man in the military uniform smiled, and turned to the King. "Your Majesty, I will of course convey your request to the White House. I am sure that the President will give you whatever aid you will need to stem the incursions of the guerillas into Morocco. We do not wish to see your throne threatened by insurgents . . . that would be in no one's interest."

And with those last words he took his leave. As his footsteps receded down the long corridor, Dlimi turned again to the King.

"You know that we need that new equipment," he said in a cool voice.

"Yes, I know, I know, you have told me before," the King said, somewhat exasperated, "The problem is Carter and that Secretary of State of his. They are squeamish about our use of their weapons in Western Sahara . . ."

"Despite all the help you have given them?" Dlimi asked, wryly.

The King gave him a sharp look. It was no secret that Dlimi had opposed his overtures to Israel. But he chose to ignore it.

"Diplomacy sometimes takes time, Dlimi," the King said in a condescending tone, "but, of course, that is something you know nothing about."

Dlimi managed to control his temper once again and continued. "Well, do you have any idea how long it will take for your diplomacy to work, Sire?" he asked with a smile, a note of condescension creeping into his voice.

The King faced him again, with that same withering look. "Let us just say that I am working on it," he said in an irritated tone which suggested that the subject was closed. "For the time being just put into effect the suggestions of the American."

The King then rose from his chair and started to walk towards the door.

Dlimi hesitated for a moment. He wished to say something, but what he wanted to say would raise a delicate subject, one that he didn't want to discuss while the King was in a bad mood. But these days the King was always in a bad mood. So he took a long breath.

"There is one more thing, Your Majesty, as I have said before, I think you should reconsider your policy about the Air Force," he began. "Your requirement that the commanders obtain your personal permission before dispatching any aircraft has seriously compromised our ability to give air cover to our troops. By the time you give your permission the guerillas have long since departed, and when you are out of the country we cannot get any air support at all. We are handing victories to the enemy. Now that we have gotten these new Mirage jets . . ."

But before Dlimi could get any further the King silenced him.

"You know my answer to this," he growled in a low, menacing voice, staring at Dlimi across the room. Then he added, "I am beginning to lose patience with your ideas. You know, of course, that there are others who would like to be the commander of my forces!" With those last words he walked through the door, slamming it behind him.

By the time Dlimi reached his car his blood pressure had risen considerably. He was no miracle worker. It was getting harder and harder to deal with the old fool, he thought to himself. King indeed! Suddenly he remembered a fable he had heard as a child . . . about a King who had been convinced by his courtiers that he was wearing a splendid coat when all the while he was naked. He began to wonder how long it would take for the King to realize that he was naked.

Les Auxiliaires.

The prisoner with the long black hair and beard groped for the small carved indentations on the wall that would tell him what day it was. It had been more than three years since he had been captured by the Moroccans and

209

thrown into the cell that was now his home. In the cold, damp dungeon that was the black dungeon of Laayoune he could barely tell night from day. Only a sliver of light that managed to escape from a crack in the concrete high above his head would bear witness to the passing of days.

Suddenly the door opened and a blinding stream of light poured over his body. Someone called his name, and his body lurched forward, his knees buckling under the weight. A hand grabbed his arm and ever so slowly he rose upright. As if in a trance his mind struggled to control the legs that were flailing in every direction, unaccustomed to movement. First one, then two steps. Finally he was in control again and his legs made the long journey through the halls of the prison, up the steps to the courtyard and into the van.

It took them more than an hour to reach the impressive military compound. On the journey his eyes, for so long deprived of even the most minimal pleasure, lapped up the scenery – the glorious sun, the green grass, the sights and smells of civilization. It was just an ordinary day in the ordinary life of ordinary people, but for him it was one of the most glorious days of his life.

It did not last for long. Once inside the compound he, Mouloud and two other inmates were quickly shuttled out of the room, down a long passageway and outside into a courtyard. There he expected to see a line of soldiers with rifles, for death by firing squad was the preferred method of dispatch in the Moroccan army. But the courtyard was empty and he and the others were shepherded into a building at the far end where men in white coats greeted them. They were ordered to strip, and the men in white started probing and punching them as if they were examining sheep. After a few moments they were told to put on their clothes and a man in military attire walked into the room.

He looked at them closely before he spoke.

"You men are lucky," he said in a tone that suggested he was about to do them a favor. "You are being given the chance to get out of prison and fight for your country."

Hamed was about to speak out in protest when Mouloud put his hand over his mouth. "You mean join the Moroccan army?" he asked.

The man in uniform smiled. "Yes. His Majesty has graciously decided to forgive his subjects their youthful transgressions if they agree to enlist in his army. He has even created auxiliary units made up solely of Sahrawis to help repel the foreign invaders. If you agree your offenses will be pardoned and you will join this unit."

"May we have a minute to discuss it," Mouloud said, smiling.

The man was slightly irritated. Any sane man would have jumped at his offer. But he decided to be gracious.

"Yes, of course. Talk it over. When you are finished knock on the door and a sentry will bring you to me," he said, walking swiftly from the room.

Once he had gone, Hamed could no longer restrain himself. "Are you crazy, Mouloud? Fight in the Moroccan army? Against our countrymen?"

Mouloud gave him a long, hard stare, then spoke in a firm, deliberate voice. "Look, we are no good to anyone dying in that hell hole. Once we are out of it and on our own on the battlefield . . . well, you know, anything can happen in a battle . . . Think about it!"

Hamed started to quiet down as he thought about the various possibilities. Mouloud was right. First they needed to get out of that dungeon, and then . . .

In a few minutes they knocked on the door. A sentry retrieved them and brought them to the room where the man in uniform was waiting. A few moments later they were newly enlisted members of the "Auxiliaries of the Gendarmerie Royale".

November, 1979. Dlimi at Dakhla.

The new military strategy that Dlimi unleashed at the end of 1979 was simple. Bowing to the advice of the American he would counter guerilla tactics by the use of overwhelming force. Instead of spreading his forces thin within the entire territory he would assemble large units that would bolster the defenses of the main towns and be large and equipped enough that the guerillas would think twice before attacking.

So, following his discussion with the King, he amassed at Benguerir, near Marrakesh, a thirty five mile long column of troops, numbering six thousand men and fifteen hundred vehicles, which would reinforce the three thousand Moroccan troops which had remained in Dakhla and Argoub after Mauritania's withdrawal. In November this force, code named "Ohoud," began its epic journey to Dakhla, with Dlimi at the helm.

The huge armada inched its way at a snails pace, taking days to cover the few miles between Tan Tan and the Oued Chebeika. Dlimi had sent scouts ahead – from one of the few units of Sahrawis from southern Morocco that remained intact – to ferret out any guerillas. Nothing for miles!

As his troops began to cross the river bed he held his breath. During the night of May 30 a Moroccan convoy traveling between Tan Tan and Tarfaya had been ambushed and 23 soldiers had been killed. So many convoys had been ambushed in this spot that they had long ceased trying to send convoys over this route. His force would be the first Moroccan force to risk crossing the Oued Chebeika for many months. He passed over the bridge and waited at the other end until the last truck safely passed. Again, nothing!

He quickened their pace slightly as they reached the outskirts of Laayoune. Here they could bivwac for a night or two to rest and reassemble their supplies. The garrison stationed at Laayoune would offer additional protection.

After a few days he recommenced the journey. Slowly traversing the road south from Laayoune, constantly sending scouts ahead to survey the desert for any signs of guerilla presence. Again, nothing. Another week passed. When he saw the white stucco buildings of Dakhla in the distance, he heaved a sigh of relief. The journey had taken more than three weeks, but to the great relief of Dlimi – and the jubilation of the King -- he had arrived.

211

November 21, 1979. The United Nations.

While Dlimi was inching his way toward Dakhla, a continent away diplomats were scurrying through the halls of the United Nations with a newly developed interest in the conflict in Western Sahara.

Support for Hassan's position – never strong to begin with – was further eroded by the Algiers Accord. This time the lobbying of the United States, France, and Morocco's other allies didn't work. On November 21, 1979, a resolution was adopted affirming the legitimacy of guerillas' struggle to secure self determination for the inhabitants of Western Sahara. The resolution hailed the Algiers Accord, and deplored the continued occupation of Western Sahara by Morocco and the extension of that occupation to the territory recently evacuated by Mauritania. It also recognized the Polisario for the first time as the representative of the people of Western Sahara, and, in an important political gain for the liberation movement, recommended that it "should participate fully in any search for a just, lasting and definitive political solution of the question of Western Sahara."

By the end of 1979 all the signs seemed to be in the guerillas' favor, and there were many who saw an end to the conflict just around the corner. But, just as with the death of Boumedienne, fate can sometimes throw a curved ball and turn history on its axis. And so it was with the Saharan conflict in 1979, for just as things seemed propitious for the guerillas the current of destiny was disturbed by events that had nothing do with Morocco or the Sahrawis, but had involved problems on distant shores – the fall of the Shah of Iran, the coup against Anastasio Somoza of Nicaragua, the Soviet invasion of Afghanistan earlier that year, and the Cuban intervention in Angola. These four events had sent shock waves through Washington – waves that would eventually wash ashore on the coast of the Sahara.

December, 1979. Carter.

President Carter sat in solitude on the verandah enjoying the total silence that enveloped him. It was 5 o'clock in the morning and he was enjoying his morning coffee and the only time of the day when he could be alone with his thoughts. It was nearing Christmas and already the White House was festooned with decorations, but no amount of holiday tinsel could lighten his mood. Today his thoughts were troubled. He had come to office with a promise that he would inject ethics and principles into an office that had been muddied by the Watergate scandal, and yet, try as he would, events had a way of forcing him to make compromises. He didn't like dealing with foreign policy matters – he would just as soon let the rest of the world take care of their own problems and concentrate on solving the problems of the United States. God knows there were enough of them! Yet here he was being thrust once again into a foreign policy quagmire.

He held none of his predecessor's admiration for King Hassan of Morocco, and held only distain for the Machiavellian machinations of former Secretary of State, Kissinger. So when Hassan had come begging for aid at first he had resisted. To be sure, Morocco was a strong ally of the United States and Hassan had made it clear that he was more than willing to do whatever the administration asked of him, but he found the subterfuge used by his predecessors to circumvent the prohibition of funds to the UNITAs and other foreign insurgents – and Hassan's role in it -- distasteful. Wasn't he the President who promised he would never lie to the American people? Besides which, Hassan's throne was shaky for good reason: he was one of the last of the feudal monarchs and had stubbornly refused to introduce even a semblance of democracy in the country. Here he was fighting a war to annex a territory that the ICJ said he had no right to annex, and asking him, the United States President who championed the right to self determination, human rights, rule of law and democracy in the world, to give him the arms to do it! He had been willing to let him buy *some* military equipment, but he had drawn the line at permitting him to use this equipment to crush the rebels in Western Sahara.

So, a year ago February he had cancelled a planned sale of a number of weapons and aircraft and he had demanded that the Moroccan government stop using United States military aid in Western Sahara.

But then, like some reliable Uriah Heep, along came Hassan with an offer he could not refuse. He had always wanted to be a President remembered by the world for at least one crowning achievement, and what achievement would be a greater tribute to his sagacity than to change the course of events in the Middle East? Hassan was willing to help arrange the unthinkable – a détente between the Israelis and the Arab community. Under his watchful eye – for nothing happened in Morocco without his knowledge – two years ago Moshe Dayan had secretly met with Hassan Tuhami, a prominent aide of the President of Egypt, Anwar Sadat. This had been followed in 1978 by a series of secret meetings in Morocco between Tuhami and the Mossad chief Yitzhak Hofi. The result? A few months later, on September 17, 1978 -- following 13 days of secret negotiations that he, the President of the United States, had managed to organize at Camp David -- a Framework for the Conclusion of a Peace Treaty between Egypt and Israel had been signed.

Yes, he owed him big time, and just what did he want in return for all this generosity? It was not hard to guess.

Darn it, he rationalized, it wasn't his fault that the entire political landscape had changed. Despite every effort on the part of the United States to buttress the Shah of Iran – another U.S. ally – his regime had been toppled early in the year, and Iran had been taken over by a hostile band of Neanderthals who wanted to turn the clock back to the eleventh century. Not only that, but they had recently taken American citizens hostage, parading them on television for the whole world to see, humiliating him personally, and brazenly proclaiming that they would not release them without significant concessions from his administration. The United States public was in an uproar. To make matters worse, the U.S. backed regime of Anastasio Somoza in Nicaragua had been toppled, threatening U.S. interests on the continent, subjecting the United

States to ridicule, and making him look impotent. Already the conservative Republican hawks in Congress were circling the White House. He could not afford to have anyone accuse him of abandoning another U.S. ally. Unless he did something fast he had might as well forget winning another term in office.

So, he had increased the sale of military equipment and authorized an increase of direct United States arms deliveries from $33 million to $133 million. He had also approved the plans of Northrop Page Communications, a subsidiary of Northrop Corporation, to sell Morocco a $200 million electronic "integrated intrusion detection system." He had maintained, however, the restriction on the use of military equipment in the Sahara.

But the reports he was getting now were troubling. After the coup in Mauritania and the succession of guerrilla victories in 1979, fears had mounted among his military advisors that the Saharan war was seriously undermining the stability of Hassan's regime. A report of the CIA, leaked to the press in October, cautioned that the King was likely to lose control of events, probably in the space of a year, and perhaps even his throne. In that same month the Policy Review Committee of the National Security Council had advised him to drop the restrictions on arms sales to Morocco. During the past few weeks Stansfield Turner, the Director of the CIA, Defense Secretary Harold Brown and National Security Advisor Brzezinski had all urged him to make the move. The neoconservatives were pressuring him to do it. His military advisors were pressuring him to do it. The Israeli lobby was pressuring him to do it. Even members of his own administration were pressuring him to do it.

It seemed, once again, that principle had to bend to necessity. The Greeks were right. We are all governed by three forces, *fatos*, *ubris* and *ananche*, and no matter what we try to do, we cannot escape them.

So, he sighed a little sigh of resignation and signed a few papers, and with a stroke of a pen helped to seal the fate of a quarter million refugees in the Sahara desert.

On January 24, 1980, the Pentagon announced plans to sell $232.5 million worth of aircraft to Morocco – twenty F-5E jets, six OV-10 Broncos, and twenty four Hughes 500MD helicopter gunships equipped with TOW missiles. In February of that year the United States permitted the delivery of a mobile version of the FAAR radar system and invited Northrop Page to go ahead with the construction of its Integrated Intrusion Detection and Communications System, a highly sophisticated electronic battlefield system using seismic and infrared detectors to spot troop movements in remote areas. The following March the Carter administration announced that it would sell 125 Maverick air to ground missiles for Morocco's aircraft. FMS sales rose to a total of $274.4 million in 1980, while licensed commercial arms exports totaled $17.4 million – and the restrictions on their use in the Sahara were loosened.

CHAPTER 7
1980

By the beginning of 1980 Polisario troops had surrounded Zag for several months. They had also managed to extend their reach beyond Tan Tan and the Ouarkziz mountains to the anti-atlas regions where they remained within striking distance of the main towns of central and northern Morocco.   In the waning months of 1979 the King had managed to persuade a reluctant President of the United States that he needed additional military and surveillance equipment to defend his kingdom – and to "loosen" the restriction on their use in the Sahara. Soon the equipment would arrive and he would be able to fortify his garrisons. But in the meantime his troops at Zag and in other outlying areas were badly in need of supplies, and he couldn't sleep at night knowing that the guerillas were within striking distance of his palace. So, he instructed Dlimi to strike . . . and to strike without delay.

January 1, 1980. Zellaka.

It was early in the morning on the first day of the first month of the year and Dlimi was enjoying a restful sojourn in Laayoune after his grueling march to Dakhla. The success of that venture had enhanced his credentials in Rabat, boosted the morale of his troops, and had convinced him that the American was right -- that the way to defeat the guerillas was through overwhelming force.

After the attack on Smara he had immediately moved several battalions to secure that area and now that the enclave of Dakhla was secure it was time to direct his attention to what had become a major political embarrassment for the King. Polisario troops had remained in the Lebouirate area after their defeat of the Moroccan garrison. They had captured a veritable arsenal of weaponry, and from their bases in the area around Lebouirate were able to raid the supply routes from Tan Tan to Laayoune on a constant basis and block supplies and reinforcements from reaching Zag. The airlift of supplies to the fortress could not continue indefinitely. The King had made it clear: they must be dislodged from Moroccan soil at all costs.

Standing before Dlimi was the man he had chosen to do this, the officer in command of the forces in Western Sahara, Colonel-Major Abrouq. Dlimi had placed several battalions of his troops under his command and had discussed the planned operation in detail. They would have four assignments.

215

First, they were to take much needed provisions to the forces at Zag, then they were to sweep through the Dra'a valley, dislodge the Polisario from the region Ammeti to Zag, secure the Lengueb pass, and break the blockade of Zag. After that they were to proceed west from Zag to Jdiriya and Housa and clear the Polisario from the Aidar region. Finally, they were to march from Smara to Lemgassem and Tifariti in the Zemmour region. They would then be met with reinforcements from another large unit to wipe out the guerilla stronghold.

To inspire the troops he chose a code name for them that was familiar to every Moroccan school boy -- Zellaka – the place where the Almoravids conquered the Castillians in the 11th century and solidified the Moslem conquest of southern Spain, and the entire operation was code-named Iman, meaning "faith."

"You understand the importance of this mission?" Dlimi asked in a solemn tone. "More than one career depends upon it!"

Abrouq stiffened. "Yes, sir, I understand," he responded gamely.

"Good," he said, "I have provisioned you with enough supplies to last a month, and with almost a third of the army." Then, staring at the officer, he added, "and you must not fail!"

With these words Abrouq left the room. Once he was alone, Dlimi slumped into one of his chairs, deep in thought. "This better not fail," he muttered to himself, glumly, and reached for his bottle of scotch.

Within a week a 7,000 strong armada set out on their mission. However, this time the Polisario didn't simply fade away.

January 4, 1980. Checkmate.

Brahim Ghali, the Minister of Defense, sat in his base camp staring at the chess board in front of him. He had studied intently the moves that Bobby Fischer had used in some of his more famous bouts with Boris Spassky, and was silently wondering what move Fischer would make. Suddenly inspiration found him, and he moved a piece forward. This move would not checkmate his opponent, but would set up the conditions for victory in three or four moves.

Chess was just a genteel form of warfare, Ghali mused, and he would apply the same techniques he used on the chess board to the battlefield.

Several months earlier Abdelaziz' spies in Tan Tan had told him of preparations up north for the deployment of a huge force, masterminded by his old nemesis, Dlimi, whose aim was to take control of the route between Tan Tan and Dakhla. Over 6, 000 troops he had been told. What was he planning to do?

The reply was simple: nothing. Ghali was no fool. He would not pit his men against Dlimi's forces in a frontal confrontation, on Dlimi's terms. Let them go to Dakhla, he had urged Abdelaziz – and in the meantime let them concentrate the majority of their forces in this "armada." There will be easier pickings elsewhere.

So when this week he got word of pending arrangements to amass another convoy with orders to dislodge Polisario safe havens around Lebouirate and reinforce the outpost of Zag, he smiled. This was a far better target, and more critical as well, for the route through the Ouarkziz mountains was one of the principal routes the guerillas used to attack outposts in Morocco and which the Moroccans used to send forces into Western Sahara. And the mountainous terrain offered abundant opportunities for hit and hide missions.

So, lifting a cup of tea high above his head, he had proclaimed a toast. "Here's to you, Dlimi, my old friend. This time it is our move."

By the end of February, the commanders of the 2nd, 3rd and 4th military regions had regrouped their forces. Two weeks after that toast they were directed to rendezvous on the *hammada* northwest of Mahbes, and several hundred men set off for the Ouarkziz range. There they met up with resistance units buried deep in the mountain crevices, and placed cells at strategic locations high up in the escarpment, capable of monitoring the terrain below. Then they waited.

March 1, 1980 The Ides of March Redux.

It was March and the coolness of the winter had already begun to give way to the warmth of spring. Colonel Abrouq and his large armada, three abreast, numbering in the thousands, had already passed from Goulimine past the Zini mountain pass to Lemseid and had now penetrated deep into the valley beneath the Ouarkziz mountain range. He, Colonel Loubariss, and the other officers in the middle of the column, had nearly reached the hills of Ammeti, so far without incident, and, if all went well, would reach the outskirts of Zag in another day. His troops extended for miles in front and behind him. If their luck held out, they would soon be able to begin the task of dislodging the Polisario guerillas who had been hiding in the hills, preventing for weeks any troops or supplies from entering or leaving the garrison or from traversing the pass through the mountain range at Lengueb.

But the closer he got to Zag, the more nervous he became. Every slight sound – the call of a bird, the snap of a branch – would cause him to jump and his heart to skip a beat. He knew the guerillas were out there, somewhere.

He was right. Hidden within the shadows and crevices of the hills, shadowy figures were following their progress, at a safe distance.

Abrouq had followed a certain pattern when moving his troops. The command center and heavy artillery would be in the center of a column of soldiers that would march three abreast for miles ahead and to the rear. Also, they followed a predictable pattern when camping for the night. They would surround themselves with land mines and they would put the command center of their forces and their most important supplies and equipment in the middle of the camp.

All of this was duly noted by the guerillas.

In the morning of March 1, troops from the 1st, 2nd, 3rd, and 5th military regions surrounded their southern flanks. As soon as Abouq's troops started

217

to move they were attacked by soldiers on foot and in Land Rovers. By noon the guerillas had inflicted heavy casualties and had retreated. The Moroccans regrouped and moved on. That evening they camped as usual, surrounded by land mines. But during the evening the land mines – newly planted and therefore easy to find -- were carefully and quietly removed. At the first light of dawn foot soldiers overran the guards stationed at the perimeter of the camp and attacked the command unit, while other guerillas took up stations nearby to prevent any Moroccan forces from escaping. Abrouq's forces fought back, and the guerillas eventually withdrew.

After regrouping his forces again, Abrouq decided to forge ahead and reach Zag as quickly as possible. But no sooner had he progressed a few miles than the attacks began anew. Guerillas in Land Rovers would attack the column from the south, forcing them into the hills. They would separate the rear force from the main force and then attack the main force, trying to eliminate, if possible, the units that contained Abrouq and the other commanding officers. For days the attacks continued. In order to bring provisions to the guerillas, each night when it was dark trucks carrying ammunition and supplies would navigate the narrow, winding paths down the escarpment. They could not use their headlights or motors for fear of being detected by the enemy sentries or the Moroccan reconnaissance aircraft that patrolled the area, so, with their motors off and unable to use their brakes -- with cigarette lighters guiding the way -- they barreled down the narrow passageways, avoiding as best they could the boulders that lined their path. In this way they were able to continue the battle for eleven days. Panicking, many Moroccan soldiers eventually abandoned their vehicles and fled on foot through the mountains, escaping through the Lengueb pass, with Polisario units on their heels.

Abouq managed to survive and eventually did likewise – leading the remnant of his forces through the mountains on March 11, and regrouping them near Assa, a small enclave just a few miles north of the Ouarkziz mountains.   Behind he left 137 new prisoners and an assortment of vehicles for the guerillas.

March 11 – 14, 1980.

After pushing the Zellaka forces north through the Lengueb pass, Ayoub and his troops, together with members of the 1st military region, camped near a hill south west of the pass called Amat Lakhal from which they could monitor the entire area. Bouhali and his troops, accompanied by Mehdi Zerga, the deputy commander, and other members of the 5th military region, camped a few miles south of a smaller hill north west of Zag, and stationed a sentry on top of the hill to monitor the area near the pass.

Late in the afternoon of March 11, Bouhali and his colleague drove to the hill to see whether the sentry had observed anything.

"Isn't that Ahmed running down the hill towards us?" the driver asked, straining to see a figure in the distance.

Bouhali took out his binoculars. "Yes, its Ahmed. He must have seen something." Without another word they sped in his direction.

He was nearly out of breath when they finally reached him. "Moroccans . . ." he gasped. "Moroccan troops are advancing from the pass . . . in our direction!"

"What do you think?" the driver asked, peering intently at Bouhali.

"I think that they are probably heading for Amat Lakhal," he replied, mounting the hill. He took out his binoculars and scanned the horizon. However, it was nearly dusk and visibility was becoming poor. It was difficult for him to see more than a few hundred yards.

He turned to the driver. "I can't make out where they are, so we'll just have to go where Ahmed saw them and hope for the best."

When he had returned to his troops he summoned them and together with the troops of the 5th military region they quickly advanced through the *wadi* in the direction of the pass. Soon they were able to see shadowy figures moving in the distance. They advanced, forcing the Moroccans who were there back through the pass and capturing a few stragglers. By the time they returned to their camp it was dark and they were obliged to use the headlights of their Land Rovers to find their way.

Meanwhile, from his camp at Amat Lakhal, Ayoub saw the lights and came to investigate.

"I am glad it is you," he said when he saw Bouhali, "I was afraid it might have been a column of Moroccans. I heard all the commotion . . . what's going on?"

"I don't know yet," Bouhali answered, "But I aim to find out!"

He then approached the prisoners he had managed to capture.

"Where are your troops headed?" he asked, gruffly. Thoroughly scared, they all tried to answer at once. Most of them denied knowing anything, but one of them muttered "the big hill to the west."

When pressed further the man told them that they were not the main column . . . that the main column had proceeded westward to occupy a strategic location in order to protect a convoy that was at the other side of the pass that was expected to pass through it in a few days.

They had no time to spare. Ayoub returned quickly to his troops while Bouhali and Mehdi Zerga gathered their troops during the night. At dawn they engaged the Moroccans approaching Amat Lakhal in a coordinated attack, forcing them back through the pass.

Then they waited.

March 15, 1980. Intervention.

The day was March 15. The bedraggled garrison of Moroccan troops at Zag had been prevented from moving for months and supplies to them had been airlifted by helicopter. To the north, on the other side of the Ouarkziz mountains, what was left of Abrouq's forces milled about aimlessly, stubbornly refusing Abrouq's commands to advance, unwilling to be sitting ducks for the guerillas who had positioned themselves in the escarpment and hills

219

overlooking the pass. Dlimi had sent reinforcements from his Ouhoud troops in Dakhla, which were expected to arrive within the next week. But he would not wait for them to arrive.

At 10 in the morning three helicopters appeared in the sky over Assa, and when they touched down a very angry looking dark haired man with a mustache appeared at the door.

"Where is Abrouq?" he yelled at the waiting entourage.

Colonel Abrouq stepped out of the crowd. Before he could even salute Dlimi let loose a scathing tirade. Why hadn't he been able to repel the guerillas at Ammeti? Why had he abandoned his artillery and vehicles? Why had they retreated to Assa? Why hadn't they engaged the guerillas at the pass?

Abrouq withstood the abuse stoically, but his junior officers were visibly shaken.

When he had finished with Abrouq he turned to the officers.

"What is this I hear that you refuse to obey orders to lead the men through the pass? Is it true?" he shouted.

"Colonel Dlimi, sir," one of them started to reply in a quivering voice, "it is not that we wish to disobey orders, but we have been unable to find a way to penetrate the pass without being slaughtered by the guerilla snipers in the hills. We have tried several times . . . and our troops have just been mowed down!"

Dlimi looked at him with contempt. "Are you all a bunch of cowards? Do I have nothing but cowards in my forces?" he screamed.

He grabbed the officer by his collar, ripped the insignia off his shoulder, and threw him to the ground. He took out his revolver and pointed it at his head. Then he raised his eyes to address the group again.

"I will not countenance cowards among my officers. If any of you do not have the stomach to lead my troops I will give the command to someone who does. And I will personally shoot any one of you who refuses to enter the pass. Is that understood?"

The men shook their heads.

"Good. Then I want to see you assemble your troops immediately. We march to the pass this afternoon."

After he stormed off the thoroughly shaken officers looked at each other in dismay. "He will not be content until he gets all of us killed," one of them whispered. "Better take our chances with the Polisario than face a bullet in the back from Dlimi," another replied. "Perhaps we will be lucky . . . perhaps the guerillas will take us captive," added another wryly.

By 11 a.m. that day the remnants of a once powerful armada had been assembled and began a march, slowly as if in a funeral procession, towards the gateway through the mountains to the south, Dlimi in the lead.

When they reached the mouth of the pass, Dlimi stopped to address them one more time. "I want you to go through this pass and not stop until you reach the barracks at Zag," he shouted. Then, waving his pistol in the air, he added, "And remember, I will personally shoot any of you who comes back through this pass!"

In the hills overlooking Lengueb, Salek had been enjoying the refreshing coolness of the mountain air, a luxury for those born in the desert. It had been two days since any Moroccan troops had been foolish enough to enter the pass. So, he was astonished when he saw, in the distance, a column of soldiers marching slowly, single file, towards him. "They must be crazy," he thought to himself. When they got closer he could make out the figure of a tall, dark haired man with a mustache at the head. When they had reached the opening of the pass, the man had stood aside as the rest of the column marched solemnly ahead.

He quickly raced to where the commanders were enjoying a morning cup of tea and told them what he had seen. They conferred briefly and then ordered the troops secreted in the hills to wait until the force passed through the *wadi* to attack. Within an hour the advance column of Moroccans had exited the *wadi* and was fast approaching them. Salek reached for his AK-47 and prepared to fire. As the column marched dutifully forward, the command was given. The blasts of his gun, and those of his colleagues, reverberated through the hills, and the men below began to fall like toy soldiers in the wind.

The Polisario forces were able to capture more than 40 South African made armored vehicles, as well as a number of trucks and Land Rovers. The remnants of the Moroccan force fled back through the pass and no Moroccan forces tried to enter the pass thereafter until the siege of Zag was lifted in May.

April 20, 1980. Washington, D.C.

At his desk on the 6th floor of the cavernous building that housed the principal offices of the United States State Department in Foggy Bottom, Washington, D.C. a worried looking official was chairing a meeting of several aides and envoys from the Pentagon. The King had followed the suggestion of the Pentagon and had amassed his troops into large units. At first the strategy had seemed to work – his troops had gone from the border to Dakhla without incident, fortifying the troops along the way and delivering much needed supplies. But then disaster struck. He turned to a large map spread on the wall behind him.

"Polisario guerillas appear to have been successful in blocking a major concentration of Moroccan troops in the mountains of southern Morocco near Zag and remain in control of the pass that leads from Western Sahara into Morocco. You know what that means – they are able to penetrate into Morocco at will and to prevent any Moroccan relief forces from entering Western Sahara from the eastern part of the territory." He paused to point at these locations on the map.

He turned once again to his audience. "The fact that the guerillas are in control of Moroccan territory is a great embarrassment to the King and may lead to some significant political problems. I also understand from briefings at the Pentagon that control of the pass through the Ouarkziz mountains is also

221

significant from a military standpoint. In fact . . ." He stopped to emphasize his last words. ". . . it may allow the guerillas to overrun Morocco and force the King to abdicate."

He walked to his desk and sat on it, facing his audience.

"I cannot emphasize too greatly the danger this poses," he finally said, looking intently at the faces before him. "The area controlled by the guerillas is close to the Algerian border. There have been tensions between the Algerians and the Moroccans at this border area for years, and Morocco has recently fortified its army units there . . . leading the Algerians to follow suit and fortify their garrisons in the Bechar region. The area is a tinderbox . . . all they need is a match . . . and there will be a full scale war between the two countries . . . a war that we will be powerless to control once it is started. We need to find a way to diffuse the situation . . . and get the guerillas out of this territory . . . and fast!"

The military men in the room nodded their heads in agreement. Finally, one of them spoke.

"Now that they have forced Mauritania out of the war the guerillas have gotten bolder," he began. "The fact that they have been able to attack successfully major cities in southern Morocco like Tan Tan has caused an uproar among Moroccan citizens. Concentrating their forces, as we suggested, seemed to have worked when the King's troops went south to occupy Dakhla, but the force he sent to supply and relieve the garrison at Zag suffered terrible losses and hasn't yet been able to break the guerillas' siege." He stopped for a moment, looking at the others in the room. "I understand that Dlimi has ordered additional troops from the Dakhla detachment to reinforce the troops at Zag, but it is unclear whether they will have any greater success. It is the considered opinion of the staff at the Pentagon," he continued, somberly, "that we cannot depend on the Moroccan army to oust the guerillas." He looked around the room again. They were all nodding in agreement. "The problem is, we cannot send troops to aid the King," he added, shrugging his shoulders. "So we are looking into other military options."

The State Department official sighed. It was the waning months of the Carter administration, a new presidential election was looming on the horizon, Carter was facing stiff opposition, not only from the Republicans, but from Senator Kennedy in his own party, and soon he and many of the people on the 6th floor might be walking the pavement, looking for jobs in the private sector. He had no stomach for any last minute intrigues. But it had only been one year since the Shah of Iran had been deposed, and Iranian militants were still holding Americans hostages, to the great humiliation of the President and his office. Whatever happened, he couldn't allow another Shah debacle to mar his record, much less a full-scale war in the Maghreb.

"What other military options?" he asked, tentatively.

"Well, advising them on a more efficient use of their air power for one. Hassan recently took delivery of some Mirage jets from France and with the equipment that Westinghouse sold them, help from our "Blackbird" spy plane, and our satellite imagery we believe that their air and ground forces will be able to intercept Polisario communications and locate guerilla troops when they try to assemble for an attack . . . but locating them is one thing and defeating them is another."

"I understand that Hassan has been meeting with d'Estaing to beg for more aide," a young man sitting in the back interjected after a pause.

The older man stopped, then shook his head. "More aid? What he needs is a new army . . . or a miracle. . . and I don't believe in miracles!"

After a few minutes the meeting was adjourned and one by one the visitors filtered out of the room. All except one -- a skinny young man fresh from a university somewhere.

"I've been thinking," the young man said, slowly, "that perhaps there might be another way to solve this problem."

The older man stared at him, somewhat startled. "What do you mean?" he said, drawing closer.

The young man smiled. "Oh, just that there is more than one way to skin a cat, as the saying goes. . . and sometimes when bullets fail, other types of weapons succeed!"

The older man drew closer still. "Just what do you have in mind?"

A continent away a nervous looking slightly built man sat in an ornately carved arm chair at the Elysees Palace smoking his fifth cigarette and glancing from time to time at the portraits of stern looking men in ermine robes that peered down at him. When he was finally ushered into the chambers of the President of the Republic, a tall, distinguished looking and elegantly dressed man approached him.

"Your Majesty, it is always a pleasure to meet you!" the tall man said in a pleasant tone. He knew fully well why Hassan was there – the Polisario were on the brink of overrunning his country and he needed help. Noblesse oblige, he thought. It wasn't the first time, and it probably wouldn't be the last, that a client state of the Republic turned to him for aid.

Hassan sat down, the nervous look replaced by one of calm detachment. D'Estaing, after all, had been a friend of his for a long time and had a vested interest in helping Morocco to remain stable. After all, French investments constituted a huge bulk of the Moroccan economy.

"My friend," he started, "My country is in grave danger. The Algerian supported guerillas have managed to gain control of the eastern pass into Morocco from Western Sahara and have surrounded my garrison at Zag. But, of course, you know that!"

D'Estaing did know that, and he also knew of the Polisario attacks on Tan Tan and other towns in Morocco, and that despite a massive concentration of troops, and the deployment of his elite regiments, Hassan's forces had not been able to reach Zag. Moreover, his intelligence operatives had told him that Hassan's troops were afraid to confront the guerillas, that they had deserted battles *en masse*, that there were rumors that Dlimi had to force them into battle at the point of a gun – and that Hassan in a fit of anger had ordered the

223

execution of several of his officers. But he would not mention any of this to the King.

"Yes, I know that," was all that he said. Then, after a pause, he added. "And how can I help you?"

This was the invitation Hassan was waiting for. For the next twenty minutes he criticized his officers, his advisors, his troops – they were all useless. He needed French advisors on the ground, French forces in the air.

D'Estaing listed to all of this politely, and when the King paused to get his breath, he spoke with a clear, calm voice.

"My friend, I sent French military advisors, French planes and French pilots to help Ould Daddah, and it proved to be a catastrophe. I do not dare attempt another armed intervention in this conflict, the French public would not accept it, and I am having trouble enough as it is with public opinion." He was not lying. His popularity had plummeted after the economic downturn in France that followed the 1973 energy crisis, and he was facing stiff opposition from two political rivals, Francois Mitterrand on the left and Jacques Chirac on the right, who were just waiting for the chance to replace him at the top.

"Well, what about more military aid?" Hassan said, obviously disappointed.

"Do you really think more military aid is the answer?" d'Estaing shot back. "We have already given you substantial military aid and now you are getting additional aid from the Americans. It seems to me that what you need is not more military aid, but a new military strategy. . ."

"But we have tried everything! We have withdrawn our troops from the outlying areas and concentrated them in huge armadas, and they are still having trouble defeating the guerillas!" Hassan responded, becoming obviously more agitated. When he looked at d'Estaing again he was no longer the king of a great country, but a tired, old man with defeat staring him in his eyes. He slumped farther in his chair.

"If I do not find an answer soon, it will be too late!" he finally said, reaching for his handkerchief and dabbing his eyes. "The Algerians are behind it all . . . I know it!" he said vehemently. "I will not let them get away with it. They think they can fight a proxy war with my kingdom . . . they are mistaken. I will take the war to them, mark my words!" he shouted. "They are not safe . . . not at Tindouf . . . not at Bechar . . . not even in Algiers!" he growled menacingly.

Then, reaching for d'Estaing's arm, he pleaded, "I know I must negotiate with them to end this, but I need to negotiate from a position of strength . . . I have tried everything I know. Please tell me what I can do!"

D'Estaing smiled. "Perhaps you have not tried everything. I know some people who are known for. . . what is that English expression? 'Pulling rabbits out of a hat.' Let me get in touch with them."

Hassan gave him a puzzled look. What could he possibly mean? But he knew enough not to question a man who was nearly as adept in political intrigue as he was. So, he sat back in his chair and merely said, "I will, of course, welcome any suggestions you may offer."

With those last words the King was ushered out the door. Once he was gone d'Estaing settled back into his armchair and called for his assistant.

"Get me a telephone!" he said in a cool, clear voice.

April 20, 1980. Prince Fahd.

In his office in Algiers, Bendjedid eyed his visitor suspiciously. He had been surprised when he had received a call requesting a face to face meeting from the de facto leader of what many considered to be the most influential country in the Arab world – certainly the richest and the most conservative. A Prince among Princes. Prince Fahd of Saudi Arabia. At first he had been flattered by his request – even though he suspected that it would be a blatant attempt to bolster the regime of his royal cousin, King Hassan of Morocco. And now he had come, ostensibly to try to smooth tensions between Bendjedid and Hassan over their border dispute – at least this is what he had said.

The dispute over the border between the two countries had festered for as long as he could remember. It was the French who had initially established the line of demarcation, during the period in which Morocco was considered a "protectorate" and Algeria a full fledged department of France. Naturally they had drawn it in favor of Algeria – designating a huge swath of territory encompassing Tindouf and Bechar as Algerian. But they had come to rue that decision when Algeria expelled the French from its shores and Morocco became the darling child -- and some of the maps they had drawn were just different enough to lead to confusion. When the Istiqlalians, pouncing upon these discrepancies, embarked upon the "Greater Morocco" crusade – demanding that the Bechar/Tindouf region be returned to the Kingdom – the French were quite happy to encourage Mohammed V's claim to the disputed areas. In 1963, shortly after Hassan succeeded his father as King, he had embarked on an ill-fated attempt to wrest Tindouf from Algeria by force. Although mediation by the Arab League in the so-called "Sand War" quickly resulted in a cease fire and a de-facto boundary, a final demarcation in the Tindouf area was not reached until arduous negotiations between 1969 and 1972, and Hassan had still not ratified the results by the time of his attempted annexation of Western Sahara. As a result, friction between the two countries continued and there had been a massive buildup of the troops of both countries along the border.

And now that the Polisario had infiltrated the eastern part of Morocco and were in control of the Lengueb pass and the region of Zag – within spitting distance of the Algerian border – this buildup of troops had intensified. To make matters worse, Hassan had begun sabre rattling – threatening his neighbor with all out war if they continued to back the guerilla forays into his territory.

The Prince, who had been observing his host from the arm chair in which he sat, quietly put down his cup of tea and smiled.

"My friend," he began, "this friction between you and my brother Hassan is in no one's interest. And this war in the Sahara . . . ." He shook his head gravely. "I am afraid that it might spill over into an armed conflict between the two of you if you are not careful!" Then, drawing his face closer, he whispered, "You are walking on egg shells. Hassan has already convinced the President of the United States to authorize additional arms . . . ."

"arms that you will be paying for, no doubt!" Bendjedid interjected, wryly.

The Prince sat back in his chair and smiled. "Well, be that as it may, he *will* be getting more weapons, and I have it on the highest authority that the Western powers will allow him to pursue the guerillas into Algerian territory . . . all the way to Tindouf if necessary . . . even if it means confronting your troops!"

Bendjedid leaned across his desk, smiling, his eyes riveted on his guest. "You know as well as I do that the guerillas do not attack Moroccan positions from camps in Algeria. There can be no "hot pursuit."

The Prince also leaned forward, meeting his gaze.

"That may be the case," he began slowly, "but all it would take is one incident . . . a pretext . . . and you know how adept they are at creating pretexts!"

Bendjedid paused, then sat back in his chair, the smile disappearing. "They wouldn't dare risk a war between Morocco and Algeria!"

"They are desperate to save the throne . . . and desperate men do desperate things. Is it a risk you are willing to take?"

While Bendjedid was deep in thought Fahd leaned closer. "Do you really want Hassan to get more weapons from the Americans? Weapons that he might be tempted to use against you eventually? Right now he wants these weapons for his war in the Sahara, but after that? And if he should suffer an humiliating defeat by the guerillas what would be a better way to placate his enemies than to take back Morocco's historic lands from Algeria? And he will have an arsenal of weapons with which to do it! Think about it . . . an escalation of the arms race between the two of you is not in Algeria's interest."

With that last remark he settled back once again into his chair eyeing Bendjedid, who walked again to the window, not saying a word. He stood there for a moment, gazing through the window at the horizon, deep in thought. Finally he turned to face his guest again.

"What do you suggest I do?" he asked slowly.

The Prince began fiddling with his prayer beads, his eyes downcast. "The guerillas are your friends . . . they will listen to you. I am sure you can convince them that a war between Algeria and Morocco will not be in their interest. I am sure you can convince them to choose more suitable targets for their campaign . . . I am sure you will find a way!"

That was all he said, or needed to say. Within a few minutes he bade his host goodbye and departed as quickly as he had come, leaving Bendjedid staring out the window again pondering the situation he . . . and his country . . . were in, and trying to plan his next move.

May, 1, 1980. Retrenchment.

By the beginning of May soldiers from the Ouhoud detachment finally reached the beleaguered Moroccan troops attempting to infiltrate the Lengueb pass and the guerillas who had surrounded Zag for months suddenly were nowhere to be found. Some say that the Polisario -- whose forte had never been the defense of fixed positions -- facing a massive Moroccan troop buildup, had simply decided to retreat to their safe havens in Western Sahara, leaving behind a skeleton of troops to harass the enemy. Others say that their leaders had obtained a secret report from a meeting of the King's advisors in Rabat that prompted them to move their forces farther west.

But there are those who claim that threats had been made by United States officials that if the guerillas remained on Moroccan soil they would lift the embargo on certain military equipment and might intervene directly to protect the King. According to these rumors the Americans had promised that if the Polisario withdrew their troops they would arrange a meeting between the Polisario and the King in Medina to negotiate the terms of ending the war – but that when the guerilla leaders went to Medina after the siege had been lifted the King never arrived. Still other rumors claimed that it was the Algerians who placed pressure on the Polisario to diffuse the escalating tensions that might result in an all-out conflict with the Americans and the French and possibly war with Morocco -- and that the Polisario leaders decided to acquiesce, judging that a war between Morocco and Algeria would marginalize their conflict and not be in their interest.

Whatever the reason – or reasons -- may have been, the guerillas simply shifted their focus to targets within the territory itself, unleashing a barrage of new attacks, and when it was once again safe to visit the area of Zag, a team of foreigners descended upon Lengueb to 'study' the situation.

And back in his palace, Hassan was able to sleep for the first time in months.

July 1, 1980. Sierra Leone.

But Hassan's peaceful slumbers did not last for long.

The date was July 1, 1980. The place, a sumptuous conference room in a five star hotel in Freetown, Sierra Leone. The weather was stormy . . . but not nearly as stormy as the discussion inside.

It was the annual meeting of the OAU and tempers were flaring. The proposal endorsed at the last meeting in 1979 -- that there be an immediate cease-fire and that the question of sovereignty over Western Sahara be settled by a referendum -- had been totally ignored by Hassan, who had proceeded to annex Mauritania's portion of the territory that August. Hassan's snub enflamed his fellow delegates. By the time of the next year's meeting in Freetown, a narrow majority of African states had recognized the SADR government and were proposing that it be admitted to the OAU as a full member. Facing them across the table like gunfighters at a shootout was the delegation from

Morocco and a few of its allies threatening once again to walk out if such a proposal were endorsed.

Saika Stevens, the Chair of the meeting, had expected as much. For weeks he had wrangled with the problem. A walkout by Morocco and its allies would tear the organization apart and any chance it had of representing the African continent on the world stage. Yet they couldn't simply ignore Hassan's intransigence. He turned to Olusegun Obesanjo, the Nigerian Head of State, and one of the chairs of the committee of 'wise men' who had drafted the earlier proposal.

"Olusegun, do you have any idea how to handle this problem?" he whispered.

Obesanjo thought for a minute. As much as he would have liked to uphold the admission of the SADR he, too, realized that a walkout by Morocco and its allies would sound the death knell for the organization. There must be a way . . .

Finally, facing the delegates on both sides of the table, he asked to take the floor.

"My fellow delegates," he began in a low, calm voice, "more than half of you have recognized the SADR and according to the rules of our organization, that should be sufficient for it to be admitted to our organization as its most recent member. However, at the same time you have appointed a committee, which the President of Mali and I chair, to study the conflict over the territory and to propose a plan to end it. We made a series of recommendations at our last meeting. I believe that we should be given the time to develop these recommendations further, and, hopefully, find a peaceful and lasting solution to this conflict, before taking the step of admitting the SADR to our ranks. So, I propose that we temporarily shelve the proposal to admit the SADR until our next summit meeting when we will be in a better position to discuss the ad hoc committee's further recommendations."

Then, casting a glance at the Moroccan delegation, he added, " I am assuming, of course, that the Moroccan government will be willing henceforth to cooperate with the ad hoc committee in coming to a solution to this crisis."

The Chair issued a sigh of relief. "I propose that we endorse the delegate from Nigeria's suggestion and give the ad hoc committee time to work with the parties to arrive at a peaceful and lasting solution to the crisis. All in favor say 'ay.'" A chorus of approval issued from the hall.

He then turned to the Moroccans and added in a solemn voice, "I must warn you, Dr. Reda, that if you make this commitment we will take it seriously, and if your government does not abide by it, we will have no choice but to take up this resolution once again at our next meeting. Do we have your agreement?"

The stately gentleman representing the Moroccan government paused before responding. He knew that the King had no intention of compromising on his stand, but an agreement to "cooperate" with the ad hoc committee didn't entail any real concessions and would buy valuable time – and time was what the King needed to put into use the reconnaissance aircraft and surveillance equipment he had just received from the Americans. More importantly, time was what he needed to put into effect a new plan that he had been working on for months in secret meetings behind the palace gates with a cadre of advisors from a foreign land -- a bold plan that was intended to checkmate the guerillas for good.

So, with an engaging smile, he responded, "Of course we will agree to cooperate with the committee!" and to the great relief of the majority of delegates, the topic turned to less contentious matters.

July 15, 1980.

It was a beautiful summer day and the man sitting in the car that was winding through the streets of Tan Tan wished that he could trade his uniform for bathing trunks and enjoy the cool ocean breeze. But that would have to wait. Today he had a chore to perform.

As his driver passed the stucco buildings he couldn't help thinking how the town had changed since he first laid eyes on it, ten years ago, on a vacation to the "south" with his parents. Then it was just a small coastal hamlet, an obscure little dot on the map with little to brag about. But when the war started everything changed. Troops started pouring in and with them new construction, new commerce, and thousands of young men, lonely and far from home, yearning for some distractions – preferably the two legged kind.

But they had found little comfort here. The town and the surrounding area was largely inhabited by members of Sahrawi tribes, who followed their own customs, their own dress, their own food – even their own language – much like the Berbers of the Atlas region, and for the most part kept their distance from the Moroccans from the north.

But she was different. She had smiled at him when he had first come to order provisions for the garrison and was glad to chat with him each time he came. Last year, when hundreds of her fellow Sahrawis had followed the guerillas to Algeria after they had attacked and sacked the city, she had stayed, earning her his respect. She had proved herself to be a loyal subject. He had begun to look forward to the days when he was sent to order more supplies, and this was one of those days.

As he approached the store where she helped her father, he could see her through the window, on a ladder, placing cans on a shelf, her back turned towards him. She was not wearing the traditional robes of Sahrawi women, she was dressed in jeans and a loosely fitting sweatshirt, leaving what was beneath to the imagination. Her hair lay in long, soft, dark ringlets cascading indolently down her back almost to her waist. She wore little makeup, but her lips were the color of ripe strawberries.

"Lamira, I have come to order new provisions," he said, standing in the doorway.

When she heard her name she turned to face him and smiled.

229

"New provisions already?" she asked, climbing down the ladder. "Your soldiers must be very hungry . . . either that or they are planning to march somewhere!"

The soldier laughed. "You guessed it," he said in a jovial voice, "A whole battalion will be heading out soon."

"Laayoune again?" she asked in an indifferent tone.

"No, not this time. Somewhere else. Somewhere special," he replied, drawing closer to her. Then, after looking around to make sure they were alone, he whispered in her ear "Something is brewing . . . something special in the south. I heard the commanders talking about it the other day."

"Oh, really!" she exclaimed, smiling. "Do you have any idea what it is?"

The soldier, quite happy to impress her with his knowledge, leaned closer.

"It seems that a couple of months ago the King was visited by some foreigners who gave him a report with suggestions on how he could improve his campaign against the guerillas, and the King has decided to follow their suggestions . . . something about building a barrier . . . that's it . . . a wall of some kind . . . from somewhere in the northern hills to Smara." He then straightened himself before adding, "And I have been told that engineers are expected to arrive to build this wall next month . . . and that our troops will be among those protecting them!"

For a moment she was startled. But she quickly recovered, and smiling in her most gracious manner asked the soldier for his list of provisions. After finishing the transaction and waving the soldier good-bye she slumped into a chair, her thoughts whirling in her head.

A wall? A wall in the desert? It can't be true!

August 1980. The Technocrats.

It was one of the hottest days of the year, at the beginning of August. When the dozen or so Westerners in their khaki suits descended from their plane at the airport in Rabat, they couldn't wait until they reached the air conditioning inside. They were used to such temperatures, and the vicissitudes of the desert, in their own country, but in North Africa it somehow seemed hotter and drier. And in their home country they would not have the *irifi* winds to contend with, or the freezing temperatures at night in the winter months. They shuttered to think of what they were in for where they were going, far to the south, in the belly of the beast called the Sahara.

They grabbed their suitcases and sent porters to retrieve the cartons of equipment that had accompanied them. They had chosen a spot on a hill at a strategic point south of the Zini mountains to begin their work, and they were anxious to begin.

After a few moments they were loaded into cars to begin their trek to the palace to greet the King, and from there to the location that would be their home for the foreseeable future.

Hamed's Plot.

By the time the Polisario had withdrawn from Zag, Hamed had been marching along side Moroccan troops for several months, under the watchful glare of the commander of his "special" unit of Sahrawi soldiers. Perhaps slaves would be a better term, for, like Hamed, they had traded freedom from the brutal confines of Moroccan prisons for slavery on the battlefield. They were the first to be sent into battle, the first to be forced to perform the arduous tasks – a gun always pointed at their heads.

The commander of their unit was a Moroccan regular – a craggy faced lieutenant with a crescent shaped scar on his cheek obtained in a knife fight with guerilla forces in one of the early battles at Farsia. Ever since that battle he had harbored a deep seated hatred of the insurgents which manifested itself in the grueling tasks he forced his captives to perform – and the punishment he meted out for any infraction of his rules.

Many of the former prisoners were reluctant to fire upon their countrymen and during an attack they would often raise their weapons over their head in a silent signal to their brethren that they would not shoot, careful to avoid the watchful eye of their commander. For their part, the guerillas would avoid killing anyone they recognized as a Sahrawi, bypassing them in hand to hand combat and when attacking convoys.

And so it was that Hamed and Mouloud managed to survive the Moroccan military for several long months without being killed or killing.

Towards the middle of 1980, while their unit was stationed at the garrison near Smara, a tall, distinguished looking older man visited their commander and engaged him in a long discussion. Hamed and the other members of his unit were then herded into the commander's barracks for an important announcement.

"Men, " he announced, "This is Colonel Kashdami, and he has an important task for you."

Kashdami leaned against the commander's desk and surveyed the room. He knew full well that none of these men were eager to serve the Moroccan army and that he was taking a chance employing them in this project. But the continuous sniping of the guerillas had depleted his forces considerably, the engineers were seriously behind schedule, and he needed bodies to perform the manual tasks so that his soldiers would be free to guard the compound. In any event they would be closely supervised. It was a risk he had to take.

"Men," he started to say, "I have been placed in charge of an important construction project. And I need you to help complete it. So, I have requisitioned your unit and for the next six months you will be under my command."

And so, without further ado, the small band of Sahrawis were herded onto a truck, their destination unknown.

"What do you think this is all about?" asked Hamed when the truck had started to move.

"I don't know," Mouloud replied, "but whatever it is at least we will be away from the commander."

For an hour the two of them peered out the window trying to figure out where they were going. "It looks like we are headed north," Mouloud said, "Maybe they are taking us to Lemseid."

"But why would they take us there?" Hamed remarked, "Kashdami said something about a construction project. What could they be constructing at Lemseid?"

But they were not going to Lemseid. Instead when the truck stopped they were able to see a large conglomeration of tents just a few miles south of a place called Ras el Kanfra. The following day they were put to work carting soil, laying barbed wire, placing land mines, all under the watchful eyes of Moroccan sentries.

At night, while lying on the blankets that served as their beds, they would talk.

"What do you think they are building?" asked Mouloud in a low voice, once the others were asleep.

"It seems like some sort of wall to block our troops," Hamed responded.

"But that is crazy," said Mouloud in a puzzled tone. "They would have to build a wall the entire length of the Sahara to have any effect!"

"Yes, I know. But that seems to be what they are building," Hamed replied with a shrug.

Mouloud was silent, thinking. "Whatever it is, they are afraid of being attacked," he finally said. "Did you notice the number of guards they have posted along the perimeter? And the surveillance equipment in the command center? And I have noticed that each night before he goes to sleep Kashdami surveys the horizon with some special binoculars – I hear they are equipped with infra-red sensors that can detect the movement of troops in the dark."

"Do you think our comrades are out there somewhere, waiting to attack?" he added in a whisper.

"I wouldn't doubt it," answered Hamed. Then, after a moment, he added, "Just in case they are out there, perhaps it is time to look for a way to escape. If an attack comes the guards will have no time to worry about us."

And that night each of them lay awake for hours thinking of a plan that would set them free.

The next morning, as they prepared their rounds, they paid special attention to the position of the troops at the perimeter of the compound and the place where the guards stashed their weapons. Hamed managed to pilfer from the storage unit some provisions that he carefully hid beneath his blanket. As the days passed, and the procession slowly moved in the direction of Smara, they repeated their escape plan in their minds over and over, patiently waiting for the magic day.

It was the dog days of August and for days scouts had come to Abdelaziz with news that the 6th Moroccan regiment was on the move and was proceeding to an area just south of the Zini mountain range. Something was afoot, and he needed to know what it was. So he dispatched Salek to find out. Salek loaded his Land Rover, and with a single companion began the journey from where he was camped westward, under cover of darkness. When he had reached a point slightly south of a hill called Ras el Kanfra, he stopped and peered into the distance with his binoculars.

Handing the binoculars to his driver, he said "Ahmed, tell me what you see."

Ahmed took the binoculars in his hand, and a minute later responded, "I see what looks like a camp . . . a large camp . . . with soldiers and tanks and . . ." he hesitated for a moment, then continued ". . . and what looks like bulldozers!"

"Yes, exactly." Salek replied.

The driver looked at him in amazement. "But what can this mean?" was all he could blurt.

Salek took another look. "They are obviously building something, but just what it is is anyone's guess. And whatever they are building they think deserves the protection of a full regiment."

He quickly sped back to the place where Abdelaziz and Ghali were camped.

Reports of a troop buildup in the west had been trickling in for days. Moreover, their spies in Tan Tan had told them of unconfirmed rumors that Western intelligence services had advised the King to block off the route from the northern foothills to Smara with a sand barrier, and that a crew of foreign engineers had recently arrived to help him do it.

It began to make sense.

Bouhali, Akeik, Hammada, Ayoub and the other commanders were quickly assembled.

"How many men do you think they have there, Salek," Ghali asked after the others had joined them.

Salek thought for a moment. "At least a regiment . . . with a number of tanks and other heavy artillery." He paused a moment before continuing. "And they seem to be well prepared for any attack."

Abdelaziz, who had been deep in thought, raised his eyes.

"We heard rumors that the King's Western advisors had suggested building some sort of barrier between the northern hills and Smara. This must be it. But I don't think they will stop at Smara," he began slowly, "It can only be for one purpose -- to cut off our access to Smara and points west and restrict our ability to infiltrate Morocco from the coast. If he doesn't extend it beyond Smara he would leave his western flank open for attacks on Laayoune and Boucraa, and if he encloses those towns it would only make sense to try to enclose Boujdour."

Bouhali shook his head. "A wall enclosing the so-called "useful triangle" of the territory? It would take months, years . . ."

"Yes, I know," Abdelaziz answered, "But if they succeeded . . . just think . . . They have already regained control of the Lengueb pass, if we let them block our access to the north through the coast and the Zini mountains we will find it difficult to attack their troops in southern Morocco."

". . . or convoys coming from Tan Tan south," added Akeik.

"And who knows?" added Hammada, "If he succeeds in cordoning off the northwest quadrant, maybe he will try to protect Dakhla as well."

The others paused. "You don't think he would be crazy enough to try to build a wall through the whole territory?" asked Bouhali incredulously.

"I don't know. With Hassan anything is possible. One thing is certain . . . we have to stop him . . . and stop him now!" Abdelaziz replied.

The group became quiet as each one of them mulled over the implications of Hassan's venture. Finally, Ghali spoke up. "We must attack them quickly, before they are able to make much progress in the construction, because it will be much harder to attack them once they are behind a barrier."

The others nodded, and when they exited the campsite it was with a clear plan in mind. The troops from all four regions would combine forces and mount a sneak attack within the next few days.

As they were leaving the meeting Abdelaziz took Bouhali aside. "By the way," he said, trying to suppress a smile, "I forgot to mention that Salek told me that the regiment at Ras el Kamfra is the 6th, led by your old friend, Kashdami."

He knew that this would get a reaction, and he was not disappointed.

Colonel Kashdami was a Berber from the Rif region of Morocco who was considerably older than the Polisario commanders and had served a long time in the army by the time the war had started. Most of the Moroccan army consisted of young men from the ghettos of the northern cities or the poor areas of the Atlas and semi-Atlas regions trying to escape poverty the only way they knew how. They were massed together in poorly equipped squadrons, without even a tent to provide cover on the cold winter nights, and fed food that not even rats would enjoy. However, among the various regiments there were two that were given the best equipment and food, the most seasoned recruits, and the most experienced leaders. The 6th Moroccan regiment was one of them, and in 1979 Kashdami was appointed its commander.

He was one of only a handful of Moroccan commanders whom Bouhali respected. Initially he was stationed in Tifariti where he had been engaged in a number of skirmishes with Bouhali's forces, and there had been clashes in other locations as well. But there was one incident in particular that stood out in everyone's memory.

This was in February when Bouhali's troops were near Boujdour. The Moroccans knew that Polisario forces were in the vicinity and Kashdami's forces were sent to reinforce the troops positioned near the city. At first, because of the fog that had covered the area, the Polisario did not know of the arrival of Kashdami's forces and were enjoying a welcome respite from their constant marching. After a few days the commander at Boujdour thought the guerillas may have departed. However, fog from the nearby ocean was still covering the landscape and he could not see more than a half mile into the distance. So, Kashdami decided to leave with some troops to investigate. But as quickly as it had descended the fog lifted and Bouhali's men were spotted by the Moroccans' reconnaissance plane that was hovering above. Moroccan Mirage jets soon intervened, shelling his troops. When Kashdami heard the bombs he knew that guerilla forces were still there. Bouhali's troops were able to shoot down one of the Mirage jets, and although the pilot ejected and fell in the midst of Moroccan forces, a guerilla Land Rover was able to penetrate the Moroccan lines to capture him. When he heard this Kashdami was rumored to have told his forces that it must be Bouhali.

Kashdami and his forces were out in the open and after capturing the pilot Bouhali had the intention of ambushing them at dawn. But during the night, taking advantage of the noise of the ocean and the strong wind to disguise the movement of his troops, and without using their headlights, Kashdami was able to sneak away. Bouhali awoke only to find an abandoned campsite. Kashdami and his regiment were miles away, running as fast as they could in the direction of Boujdour. "Coward!" he had screamed – as well as a number of other epithets – before mounting a fast pursuit through the desert. They raced at breakneck speed, past a trail of cars and equipment abandoned by Kashdami in his mad dash for safety. In the hope of catching him they had followed him to the very perimeter of the Moroccan garrison at Boujdour where he had taken cover. But then they had wisely turned back, lest they, themselves, be lured into a trap.

The tale of the duel between Bouhali and Kashdami quickly became the stuff of folklore among the guerillas, who were waiting eagerly for the next encounter. And it was now drawing near.

August 20, 1980.

It was early in the morning of August 20. The Moroccans had started building the wall on August 18, under the direction of Colonel Ben Othman, with a small detachment of troops from Ohoud and Zellaka and Kashdami's regiment, and had just reached a point a few miles south of Ras el Kanfra where a ravine had cut through the landscape. Bouhali and Ayoub had sent word for their forces to reassemble in the ravine. Akeik and his forces would join them from their northern hideouts. All in all, more than 500 guerilla troops waited for the signal to attack.

Although the reconnaissance aircraft dutifully patrolled the sky, it was unable to detect the small units of guerillas squirreled away in the nooks and crannies that dotted the landscape. And it was difficult for it to patrol at night. So the Polisario troops moved about in the darkness with relative ease, just far enough away to be out of reach, but close enough to monitor every movement of the Moroccan troops.

The night before the attack guerillas had positioned themselves all along a

235

mile long stretch of the ravine, waiting for the signal to advance.

Meanwhile, in their bunkers, the men in Kashdami's forces had bedded for the night. It was a hot, breezy evening, and although there was no moon, the stars had enveloped the sky in a soft haze. Hamed couldn't sleep. He had bummed a cigarette from one of the guards and was sitting quietly a few steps from where his comrades lay, staring at the empty desert. When Mouloud noticed his blanket was empty, he rose and quietly joined him. They sat together for a moment in total silence. The camp was quiet now – the machines had stopped humming and, except for the sentries posted along the perimeter of the compound, the men were all asleep.

"What is it, Hamed?" Mouloud asked softly.

"I don't know – I have this strange feeling that something is out there."

Mouloud looked in the direction of the hills beyond the camp. There was nothing. Not a light. Not a sound. Just an enormous black void.

"Kashdami would have doubled the guards if he had seen something with his goggles. It is just your imagination – or wishful thinking," he said.

"Maybe," Hamed responded. Then, putting out his cigarette, he returned to where the others were sleeping and lay on the ground, covering himself as best he could with his worn blanket. "But all the same, I don't think I will sleep soundly tonight," he said quietly.

Neither would Kashdami. When Ben Othman told Kashdami that two days earlier guerilla troops had been spotted moving in the direction of their location, his blood froze. The guerillas might be within less than a day's march from his troops, and here he was stuck like a sitting duck, unable to move, babysitting a bunch of engineers with bulldozers. This time he couldn't flee -- he would have no choice but to wait until they came to him . . . and he knew they would.

He doubled the sentries on watch, and in the hours before dawn, while the engineers were safely sleeping, patrolled the perimeter of the camp himself . . . and waited.

He didn't have to wait long.

It was nearly dawn before Hamed was finally able to doze off. However, no sooner had he surrendered to sleep than his slumbers were rudely interrupted by a sharp blast. First one, then two, then a whole barrage of gunfire coming from the perimeter of the base.

Mouloud had heard it too. They quickly scrambled to where they could get a better view and witnessed a scene of utter confusion. Men were running in every direction, some to grab weapons and others to man positions along the trench that separated the camp from the open desert. Kashdami was standing in the middle of the compound barking orders.

The guerillas had descended, like a swarm of ants, upon the sleeping Moroccan troops, under cover of darkness. But Kashdami had been waiting for them, and had circled his wagons with heavy artillery, which began to send fireballs in every direction.

No one was paying the slightest attention to them. Together, without uttering a word, the two of them began to follow the plan they had rehearsed over and over in their heads the previous days. First Mouloud ran to the place behind the nearest guards' tent where they stored their weapons and grabbed two of them. Then he rushed past Kashdami's tent to the side of the compound opposite the one where the wall was being built, to a point where Hamed was waiting with the supplies he had managed to pilfer. Their plan was simple. Kashdami had surrounded the compound on three sides with guards and minefields, leaving only his southwestern flank – the one where the rapid intervention forces from Smara were expected to intervene – exposed. While everyone was congregating along the sand barrier and the directions where the guerillas would most likely attack, they would go in the opposite direction, to the southwest, and once in the open desert would try to bypass the rapid intervention forces and circle around to the south to rejoin their comrades in the eastern desert.

Together, on foot, they began to race through the open desert, their path partly illuminated by the periodic blasts of cannons and mortar that filled the sky. So far their plan was working. But no sooner had they turned south than they heard a loud "Halt!" from behind them.

"Let's run for it," shouted Mouloud, as he began to run. Hamed scrambled as best he could as bullets began to whiz past his ear. Suddenly he heard a groan and Mouloud slumped to the ground, blood seeping from the top of his leg. Hamed tried to put his arm around his shoulder to help him to his feet, but it was no use.

"Go, Hamed. Run for it. I will hold them off as best I can," Mouloud said, placing his weapon on his shoulder and aiming it at the direction the shots were coming from. Then, in a tone so soft it was barely audible he whispered "I will not go back to that prison."

Hamed froze. "I can't leave you here like this, Mouloud," he said, crouching near his colleague. "I will stay and together we will fend them off."

"Don't be silly," Mouloud shouted. "The best thing you can do for me is to find our troops and lead them here!" Then he smiled. "I will be all right . . . go!"

Hamed hesitated for an instant. Then he grabbed his gun and darted off. As soon as he was out of sight Mouloud struggled to his feet and began firing wildly at shadows in the distance.

Hamed ran as quickly as he could. Behind him he could hear a volley of shots coming from where he had left Mouloud, then a few from the direction of the Moroccans. Then a few more from both directions. Then silence.

He ran for several minutes, but in the confusion of the attack he had lost his sense of direction, and he hoped and prayed that he was on the right track. Behind him he could hear the rumble of canons and artillery in the distance.

It was now shortly before dawn, and the silhouettes of hills and bushes began to emerge slowly from the purple shadows.

Suddenly shots rang out again, and he took cover in a ravine. Reinforcements from Smara, he thought to himself. He would wait until they came closer, until they exposed themselves, until he could see better through the semi-darkness. But no sooner had he aimed his rifle in the direction of the shots then someone behind him shouted "halt!" Almost from instinct he turned around and aimed his rifle in the direction of the voice, when suddenly he stopped, dropped his weapon, and raised his hands in a gesture of surrender. "I am a Sahrawi!" he shouted to the figure emerging from the shadows.

The man, covered in khaki fatigues with a green scarf tied around his head, stopped and stared at Hamed.

"My name is Hamed El Ouali Mustapha Brahim," Hamed shouted, quickly. "I am the son of El Ouali Mustapha Brahim of El Ayoun."

The man looked at him somewhat quizzically. He was dressed in a Moroccan uniform, but his accent was hassaniya, the Sahrawi dialect.

"If you are Hamed, tell me your sister's name!" he barked.

Hamed smiled. "Soukeina."

A broad grin began to creep over the attacker's face. "Well, I guess miracles do happen!" he said, putting his weapon aside. "We thought you were dead!"

The fighting that night had been fierce, but after the initial onslaught the guerillas quickly withdrew. They had made only a dent in Kashdami's forces, but they had managed to halt the construction and disable a number of the bulldozers. It would take the engineers over a week before they could proceed.

Throughout the final days of August the attacks continued. As soon as the engineers seemed poised to advance after the first attack the Polisario attacked again, and they were able to prevent them from completing more than a few yards of wall. When the Moroccans had progressed another mile the guerillas attacked them a third time and burnt much of their equipment, including 3 of the bulldozers. When they resumed work and had completed 6 miles of the wall the Polisario resumed the attacks and shot down 2 airplanes. Colonel Ben Othman at that point concluded that without reinforcements he would be unable to deflect the constant guerilla attacks. So, he reached for the phone.

And by the end of August the construction of the barrier came to a grinding halt, as Othman waited for reinforcements to arrive. Dlimi did, indeed, send reinforcements. The Moroccan 10th regiment was sent from Tarfaya to supplement the troops at Ras el Kamfra. But they never got to their destination. They were intercepted by some of Akeik's units in early September and dispersed before they could reach their colleagues.

So, by mid September, the huge armada of engineers, bulldozers and troops remained bottlenecked, withering in the desert, unable to move in any direction, while back in his palace, Hassan placed a number of frantic calls to capitals around the world.

September 15, 1980. Algiers.

It had turned to autumn in Algiers, and Chadli Bendjedid was enjoying the cool breeze that flowed from the Mediterranean through the large windows that filled his office. He had just had another visit from Prince Fahd of Saudi

Arabia. It seemed that Hassan wanted him to agree to a temporary truce on the border issue.

He knew what was really behind this sudden peace overture. The past year witnessed Polisario attacks as far north as Ouarzazate, close to the border with Algeria and just a stone's throw from Bechar. This had forced Hassan to build up his troops in the area to prevent further forays into Moroccan territory. And those troops were still there, just a stone's throw from the Algerian border. In response he had had to reinforce the Algerian troops at Bechar and points north.

But now Hassan needed his troops elsewhere. He thought back to the plan that General Khalid Nazar, who was in charge of the Tindouf-Bechar region, had suggested six months earlier after he had learned that certain of Hassan's allies had advised him to build this dirt wall. Urge the guerillas to intensify their campaign to target positions deep within Morocco, Nazar had said, thereby obliging the King to keep his troops in the north and frustrate his plans to build the wall in the south. He had told Nazar at the time that he approved of the plan, but then he had had that visit from Fahd . . . It would have been a good idea . . . if it would not have prompted the Americans to heap even more military aid on the King – military aid that he would be forced to counter with additional troops – and perhaps risk their direct intervention in the war.

He shook his head and walked slowly back to his desk. Perhaps it was not the time to escalate tensions with the Americans.

And now the Prince had arrived for another meeting. "At least let me arrange a meeting, so you can discuss the situation face to face with Hassan," Fahd had said.

All he wanted was a promise that Algeria would not attack Morocco . . . "that is all," the Prince had emphasized. Well, he had no intention of attacking Morocco, so if that was all that was needed to get Hassan to de-escalate tensions at the border . . . .

When he got the phone call from Prince Fahd, Hassan's countenance began to relax. He would arrange a secret meeting with Bendjedid -- and promise him whatever it would take.

On September 23, 1980 the Moroccan commanders of troops stationed at Rachidia and Ouarzazate near the Algerian border received a communiqué. They were to re-deploy quickly to Ras el Kanfra -- one brigade equipped with anti-tank artillery and one regiment with troop carriers, both supplied with massive amounts of heavy equipment, including tanks, artillery, and anti-tank weapons.

This started a chain reaction.

In response to Hassan's troop movements, Abdelaziz withdrew nearly all the troops from the 1st and 5th Polisario military region from the south of Morocco and sent them to Ras el Kanfra, which in turn permitted Hassan to send the remaining Moroccan troops in southern Morocco to that area.

The tiny hill of Ras el Kanfra had become the center of the universe.

239

October 15, 1980. Kashdami.

Meanwhile, on October 15, in the cave that served as the headquarters of the commander of the 2nd military region, Bouhali was sharing an early morning tea with Sidimi when one of his scouts appeared at the entrance way.

"Sir, a detachment from Dlimi's force has left Zag. We think it is Kashdami," he said quickly.

At the sound of that name Bouhali put down his cup, and Sidimi turned away, trying to suppress a smile.

"I want to know where he is every minute of the day," Bouhali ordered, "and I mean *every* minute!"

With that command the scout disappeared and Bouhali returned to his tea. But he didn't rest for long. Within a day he had sent word to the various units squirreled among the hills and crevices to mass for an upcoming battle. And he watched. And he waited.

Kashdami and his 6th regiment had left Ras el Kanfra in September, when construction on the wall was halted, and had gone to reinforce the troops of the 3rd regiment stationed at Zag. Later the following month he had gotten orders to try to intercept the guerilla units that were on their way to Ras el Kanfra from the north and had decided to camp on the *hammada* near a hill called Bou Gouerba. The northern slope of this hill merged into the escarpment leading to the valley between the *hammada* and the Ouarkziz mountain range and contained the one path for several miles that would lead down the escarpment. After getting word that Kashdami and his forces were camped at this site, Bouhali and his men quietly surrounded his troops under cover of darkness. They would attack at dawn. There was only one escape route – down the narrow path descending the escarpment -- and this time there would be no ocean to mask the sound of any troop movements.

Nevertheless, Bouhali spent a restless night. He could hear the constant hum of engines coming from the direction of the hill. All night long the noise continued.

"What do you think they are up to?" he asked one of his men.

"I don't know," the soldier responded, somewhat at a loss for words. Then he added, "They are there, doing something. That's all I know."

The next morning they found out. They were gone. All that was left of Kashdami's camp were three trucks with large stones depressing their accelerators. Somehow Kashdami had become aware of Bouhali's presence and during the night had led his vehicles quietly one by one down the path leading to the valley in the direction of Ras el Kanfra, their departure masked by the noise of the stationary trucks.

Once again the slippery eel had avoided a confrontation and the troops accompanying Bouhali found it difficult to stifle their laughter at the way he had managed his escape. Bouhali shook his head. Crafty bastard he said to himself. "I'll get you one day, Kashdami," he shouted from atop the hill, his words echoing down the valley, "You cannot escape forever!"

But if Kashdami ever heard his words, no one ever knew.

240

December 7, 1980. Tindouf.

Soukeina was busy at the entrance to her tent washing the cups from the morning tea when the tall figure approached her. When she turned to face him the cups fell from her hands. It was as if she had seen a ghost, for that was how he appeared -- a skeleton of a man whose withered features bore only a scant resemblance to the brother she had left behind in Dakhla five years ago. She touched him cautiously, afraid that he might vanish into the air, the way ghosts often do. But his flesh was warm. He was alive. Suddenly an uncontrollable surge of emotion swept through her and she flung herself at him, nearly pushing him to the ground.

"Hamed!" she exclaimed through her sobs, "I thought you were dead!"

He held her gently, and a few minutes later, after her crying stopped, they entered her tent where she hurriedly prepared some tea and sat by his side, eager to hear the stories he would tell – and what stories they were! . . .how he had been wounded and captured by the Moroccans, how he had managed to survive the years in prison, how he had been forced to join the Moroccan military, and how he had escaped.

"Were you able to rescue Mouloud?" she asked, after hearing about the man who had been her brother's helpmate through the long, dark years.

Hamed grew silent. "No," he began slowly, his eyes cast down. "We went back to look for him, and we found him a few yards from where I had left him, but he was dead, his body riddled with bullets, with the bodies of three Moroccans close by. He had managed to hold them off long enough for me to escape."

Soukeina grew quiet for a moment. "What did you do after our troops found you?" she finally asked in a gentle voice.

"Oh, after I joined the troops we attacked the Moroccan forces who were guarding the southern flank and managed to destroy a number of them as well as two of their bulldozers and a lot of other equipment. By the time troops from Smara reached the scene we had left." He stopped for a moment and smiled. "We never succeeded in destroying Kashdami's regiment, but we destroyed enough of their equipment and artillery that it will be months before they are able to proceed any farther with the construction of their wall."

When he had relived every minute of the battle in graphic detail she finally let him sleep – and sleep he did, as if he hadn't slept for months – or years.

A gentle tap on his shoulder finally awakened him. Peering down at him was the soldier who had accompanied him to the camps.

"I hate to interrupt your rest," he said, softly, "But Abdelaziz is in the camps and would like to speak with you."

He struggled to his feet, and was quickly taken to a tent where the Polisario leader sat, surrounded by three men. When he saw the lean young man at the entry way, Abdelaziz stood up and, putting his arms around him, warmly greeted him in the Sahrawi fashion.

"I understand you escaped from Kashdami's forces," he began, once the formalities were over. "I would be interested in knowing what you were able

241

to observe. Any detail, no matter how small, might be important."

Hamed unleashed a torrent of information – the number of troops in Kashdami's regiment, the number of guards that were stationed along the perimeter, the position of their heavy armaments. . . .

"Did you happen to observe any surveillance equipment?" Abdelaziz interjected after a few moments.

Hamed knew what he was talking about. "They have something that communicates with the C-130 reconnaissance plane and that tells them where troops are positioned and the plane sends information to the Mirage jets, and I heard rumors about something they got from the United States . . . a company called 'Westinghouse', although I never saw it."

Abdelaziz mulled over this information for a moment. Then he changed the subject. "Have you heard what their plans are . . . where they are going with this dirt wall?" he asked.

"I overheard one of the engineers the other day talking about their plans," Hamed said, slowly, a serious note in his voice. "They expected to be in the desert for months . . . maybe even a year . . . and I don't think they intend to stop at Smara." Hamed paused for a moment, then continued, in a low voice, " I once heard one of the guards mention that Hassan was able to wrangle several million dollars from the Saudi king for a project . . . a project to build a wall through the heart of the Sahara!"

The men in the tent exchanged glances but said nothing. Finally, Abdelaziz stood, turned to his guest with a smile, and thanked him for the information. The others took their cue and followed him from the tent. When Abdelaziz was alone, he slumped back on his cushion. And there he remained, deep in thought, until well into the night.

CHAPTER 8
1981

No one knows who first raised the idea. The French boast that it was theirs. The American CIA, not to be undone, claim a role. Some say it was planned by Israeli technicians, with financial aid from apartheid South Africa and Saudi Arabia. Even Driss Basri, the infamous Moroccan Minister of the Interior, got into the act.

All we know for sure is that in the autumn of 1980, under the tutelage of Ahmed Dlimi, construction began on a large wall that ultimately undulated its way through the heart of the Saharan desert, colloquially called "the berm."

The berm was actually a series of embankments, initially just a few feet of sand but later growing to more than ten feet in height, fortified with stone, and crowned with barbed wire. It was built in sometimes overlapping stages, linked together, and guarded in the later years of the war by an estimated 100,000 to 180,000 Moroccan soldiers. At regular intervals along this barrier were surveillance stations manned by a small stationary force. The command center as well as the bulk of the forces ready to intervene in event of an attack were stationed in garrisons at intervals a few miles behind the wall. The troops along the wall, as well as each garrison, were protected by installations of sophisticated radar equipment of various ranges, generously supplied by Westinghouse and other international corporations, which could detect the movement of a mouse in the desert beyond. Immediately preceding the berm, buried just below the surface of the earth along its entire length and extending at times to a radius of 300 yards or more, were anti tank and anti personnel land mines. It was to become the largest installation of land mines on earth.

The idea started initially as a means to supplement the hills that formed natural barriers around the enclave of Lemseid at the base of the Zini mountains so as to cut off the guerillas' ability to wage surprise attacks and restrict their freedom of movement. Small walls of sand were erected to link the hills together. From that plan sprang the idea of cutting off the ability of the guerillas to attack Moroccan territory through the coastal route and to attack the main population centers in Western Sahara -- Laayoune, Boujdour, Smara, and the Boucraa mine and conveyor belt to the coast – and the initial segment of the berm by the end of 1982 extended just that far.

The hill of Ras el Khanfra was chosen as the place to begin construction, and when Moroccan forces congregated in huge numbers there in the summer of 1980, that had been their objective. A wall would first be built between Ras

243

el Khanfra and Smara. Then it would be extended to Boucraa where it would link up with an existing defensive line to the beach near Laayoune. From there it would be extended from Boucraa to encircle Boujdour on the coast. But, of course, none of these plans were made public – and the guerillas could only watch and wonder as a steady stream of engineers and bulldozers made their way south during the summer of 1980.

From the winter of 1980 onward Polisario forces expended enormous energy trying to prevent the erection of the berm, confronting the Moroccan forces in headlong battles as well as cutting off their supply lines, and as a result the construction of the initial 60 mile segment between Ras el Khanfra and Smara took six months. But their artillery, Land Rovers and small surface to air missiles were no match for the massive concentration of forces, heavy armaments and tanks – protected by Hercules C-130 reconnaissance aircraft and Mirage jets -- that accompanied the juggernaut of engineers and bulldozers that slowly inched their way across the desert.

After Dlimi announced the completion of the first segment of the berm on March 2 of 1981, a Moroccan force left Smara to begin the next step -- extending the wall to Boucraa -- and members of Polisario's 1st and 2nd military regions engaged them in battle as usual. But by mid-March the leaders decided that they should not spend all their time trying to fight the forces building the berm. There were easier targets elsewhere. By March the only Moroccan forces in Western Sahara outside the area enclosed by the berm were at Boucraa, Bir Enzaren, Dakhla, and Guelta, and by far the majority of Dlimi's forces were in the northwest quadrant, leaving the southern regions vulnerable.

So, the guerillas made the most of the situation. On March 24, 1981 they went south to attack two of the most elite regiments in the Moroccan army – at Guelta Zemmour.

March 24, 1981. Guelta Zemmour.

It was the evening of March 23, 1981. Hamed, fully recovered from his ordeal at the hands of the Moroccans, had been asked to join the infantry of the 2nd military region, and together with his companions had driven through the night from where they had been stationed. By the hour before dawn they had reached the gradual incline that announced the approach to the hilly region that surrounded the largest oasis in the territory – Guelta Zemmour. Guelta was nestled within the Zemmour massif, in the central part of the territory, within spitting distance of the Mauritanian frontier. Its proximity to the Boucraa mines made it a prize coveted by both sides. And the hills and gullies that surrounded it provided good guerilla cover. So it had become a favorite target and had already been attacked several times in the war.

In the morning of March 24, 1981 it was to be attacked once again.

The guelta that morning was eerily silent as befitted the graveyard of hundreds of civilians and soldiers on both sides of the war cut down in the numerous battles that had taken place in the surrounding hills in the six years since its beginning. How fitting, Hamed thought, his mind racing back to the image of Dlimi on television, gloating with self importance, announcing the completion of the first stage of the berm a few days ago. Decimating the largest garrison in the territory will wipe that smile off his face, he thought, as he proceeded to the rendezvous point.

The Moroccan garrison at Guelta Zemmour, housing the 3rd and 6th regiments, was built near a well in the *wadi*, protected by hills. On top of each one of these hills was an installation of heavy artillery. Surrounding the garrison on the top of the hills was a liberal sprinkling of land mines.

Nih Lahbib had ordered the troops in the 1st regional command to take up their positions in the hills just beyond the scope of the Moroccans' radar. A few miles to the south Ayoub and his men took up similar positions. They would lead the assault and later be joined by units of the 4th military command who would help ferry captured materials and prisoners to bases in the rear. Bouhali and his men would be to the northwest of the guelta, blocking any intervention by forces from Smara and Boucraa.

A small path leading to the garrison had been cleared of land mines the night before. At the first sign of the sun the commanders gave the signal and the guerillas leapt into action. Leaving their Land Rovers behind, they climbed through the hills and approached quietly on foot to within a few feet of the soldiers in the hillside protecting the garrison before unleashing their weapons. Within seconds explosions ripped through the campsites engulfing them in flames. Streams of guerillas dispersed to the left and right, engaging in hand to hand combat with the Moroccan defenders, while others sped towards the central garrison and the command center.   The assault was so quick that many of the Moroccan soldiers asleep in their blankets didn't have time to dress or load their weapons.

Within minutes Moroccan soldiers were running in every direction, some charging the Polisario fighters, others fleeing towards the command center or the hills.

The battle raged for hours. By nightfall the guerillas were in control of one of the Moroccan positions in the hills. The following morning the fighting continued. The commanders were expecting reinforcements from the 4th military region to arrive, but upon getting word that Moroccan detachments from Smara and Boucraa were fast approaching, they decided it would be prudent to withdraw. The troops were ordered to regroup and pick up as many rounds of ammunition and weapons they could carry on their backs. They left the scene the same way they had come. When they reached the vehicles they had left behind they quickly loaded them, and a few of the soldiers took off in the direction of their hideaways in the eastern desert. The rest pursued the fleeing Moroccans towards Boucraa for an hour or so before they, too, retreated.

Meanwhile members of the 4th military region were attempting to approach the area to reinforce the troops and help with the evacuation of materials. By the time the hills of the guelta were in view the sun was squarely in the sky. No sooner had the hills appeared, however, than the commander saw something else in the sky. Something that was streaming in their direction, flying low. They had not yet reached the crannies of the guelta that might provide cover, so all they could do was disperse and race at top speed in different directions. Then the firing began. Bombs created pot holes in the desert floor, enveloping them in clouds of dust, making it difficult to see. One, two, three Land Rovers burst into flames, their occupants reduced to dust. Then silence as the plane flew into the distance. But their retrieve was short lived . . . within minutes the planes returned, showering them with another round of bullets and napalm.

It was the Mirage F-1 fighter jets. After firing a few additional rounds into the fleeing vehicles they proceeded onward to attack the main column. But by the time they reached the guelta the majority of the guerillas' main force had already vanished.

Late that afternoon Sidimi drew her scarf tightly around her head, trying her best to shield her face from the scorching sun, as she tiptoed through the hot sands. Bouhali and his men had taken cover in whatever nooks and crannies they could find to the northwest of the guelta. After hiding her jeep full of medical supplies as best she could she decided to pass a canteen of water around to the thirsty troops. The desert around them was quiet, blithely unaware of the holocaust that would envelop it shortly.

She was far from the location of her jeep when the jet appeared. First one, then another, streaking across the sky at supersonic speeds, so close to the ground you could almost see the glint of the pilots' eyes, leaving bombs and napalm in their wake. After following the trail of the main guerilla force for several miles the Mirage jets had turned west, heading for home, and had stumbled by accident into Bouhali's troops. At first the guerillas simply stopped and stared. Then they quickly manned their estrellas and aimed volley after volley at the swift moving objects.

Sidimi covered her eyes from the cloud of dust that had quickly enveloped her. The sound of gunfire, men shouting and men crying out in pain swirled in her head and the pungent smell of gunpowder filled the air. Stray bullets streamed in her direction, ricocheting off the stones that littered the ground. She instinctively fell to the ground.

But then something caught her attention. Someone close to her had cried out in pain. She crawled to a point where she had a better view of her surroundings. Through the dust and flying debris she could just barely make out the silhouette of a body propped against the burnt out hulk of a Land Rover.

She lurched forward. But an arm restrained her.

"Sidi," a voice said, "Go back to your jeep and take cover. You won't be able to help him. The jets are returning. We have to wait until the firing stops . . ." She recognized the voice. It was Omar, her brother Abdati's former partner.

"By then it may be too late!" she shouted, as she wrested free of his hold and darted towards the spot where the body lay. Omar hesitated for an instant, and then ran after her.

"You won't be able to carry him by yourself. Let me help you," he said, as he caught up with her. They managed to proceed several yards before he pushed her to the ground. The jets had returned, showering the area with bullets and bombs that blanketed the earth with slivers of shrapnel and napalm. When she tried to get up she felt a sharp pain in her arm. A piece of shrapnel had grazed her arm and a spot of blood had begun to form. Omar pulled her to the ground again.

"Keep your head down!" he barked, pulling her closer.

"Are you hit?" he asked, noticing the blood on her arm.

"I'm all right. I've been hit but it is only a flesh wound." she replied calmly.

After waiting what seemed like an eternity for the jets to pass, they crawled to where the man lay. Sidimi tore open his shirt and looked at his chest. It was no flesh wound. Blood was oozing from a large gash.

"Do you think you could let us lift you?" she quickly asked.

"I think so," he responded, gamely. She grabbed his weapon and quickly slung it over her shoulder, while Omar gently lifted him to his feet. Then they half carried, half dragged him slowly in the direction of her jeep. At first the jets were nowhere to be seen, but their reprieve was short-lived. Before they could advance more than a few yards one of them returned, showering the area once again with bullets and bombs. They managed to crawl into a nearby gully, pulling the limp figure in with them, and waited until the jet disappeared once again over the horizon. By this time he had lost consciousness. But Omar had been hit, with blood oozing from his thigh.

She peered at the sky. The jet was nowhere to be seen. She decided to make a run for it. "Stay here, in the gully, until I can return with help," she shouted, clambering out of the ditch and beginning to run. She managed to advance a few additional yards before being spotted by one of the guerillas. He shouted something and within less than a minute he and some others came to her rescue.

Not a moment too soon, for the jet had decided to make another sortie and was fast approaching. Bombs and bullets started to descend again, but before it could escape an estrella managed to hit a wing, and the long, grey bird slowly spiraled to the earth.

When Sidimi had gotten the two men behind the boulder that sheltered her makeshift clinic, she looked around her. There was devastation everywhere, and scores of men were being brought to her, most bleeding from shrapnel and bomb fragments. She had no time to dress their wounds properly. That would have to wait until they reached their safe havens in the hills. All she could do was march . . . and pray that she would see nothing but birds in the sky.

March 25, 1981. U.S. Congress.

It was a blustery day in the nation's capital. Morris Draper, the Deputy Assistant Secretary in the State Department's Bureau of Near Eastern and South Asian Affairs -- oblivious to the fighting that was occurring in the desert a continent away -- found himself sitting for over an hour, impatiently waiting for the Chairman of the African Affairs Subcommittee of the House International Relations Committee to call the meeting to order. He was there to put a positive spin on what was quickly becoming a fiasco. The war in the Sahara had not been going well for the King, and the U.S. needed the King more than ever to act as its surrogate in Africa and to perform those messy little tasks that the U.S. government wouldn't – or couldn't – do. Twice in the late 1970s Moroccan forces helped to suppress uprisings against the pro-Western dictator Mobutu Sese Seko of Zaire which threatened European mining operations. By using Moroccan troops the United States had also been able to arm a rebel movement in southern Angola without violating the prohibition on direct military involvement.

However, it was Morocco's support of United States' interests in the Middle East peace process that had been its most valuable contribution. Ever the wily diplomat, Hassan knew just what buttons to push to cement his relations with the United States, at times even jeopardizing his relations with fellow Arab states. By the time Ronald Reagan was inaugurated as President of the United States in 1981, Hassan had become one of Israel's closest go-betweens in the Moslem world. Rumor had it that Western Sahara was the price that the United States had to pay in return for this support.

But, despite ever increasing military aid Hassan seemed incapable of winning the war against the guerillas, and some within Congress had begun to question the very premise of United States aid. Behind closed doors liberal Democrats had begun to express doubts about the legitimacy of buttressing a regime in its attempt to annex territory that it could not rightfully claim. Stephen Solarz, the Democratic chairman of the House Subcommittee on Africa, had openly argued that by arming Hassan the United States was feeding his illusion that he can win an unwinnable war, and diverting his attention from the real threat to his Kingdom – the festering problems within Morocco itself.

Draper knew that this wasn't the first time Congress had raised questions about the policy of the United States. During Carter's tenure the same Subcommittee had held a joint hearing on the issue of Western Sahara with the Subcommittee on International Organizations, and an entourage of congressmen, liberal professors and members of NGOs had paraded before the cameras, accusing the administration of denying the Sahrawis their "right" to self determination. One or two congressmen even decided to visit the Polisario camps for discussions. Later, when it had been made public that the administration was planning to permit the sale to Morocco of OV-10 armed reconnaissance planes – known to be the deadliest light strike counterinsurgency aircraft in the world – as well as Cobra helicopter gunships, and that there was evidence that Hassan planned to use this equipment in Western Sahara in contravention of the 1960 military agreement which banned the use of U.S. equipment outside the Kingdom, the plan had met stiff opposition in Congress. During the debate that took place in the

Senate Foreign Relations Committee in January of 1980, both the Chairman of the Committee, Senator Frank Church, and Congressman Stephen Solarz lambasted the administration's professed rationale for the sale -- that it would enable Morocco to negotiate a peaceful settlement of the dispute from a position of strength, and that the sale was tied to an obligation on the part of Hassan to cooperate with the OAU and the UN in these negotiations. Despite the deft maneuvers of Harold Saunders, spokesman for the Carter administration, skepticism among certain members of Congress had remained high, and now Draper would have to explain why the new administration had changed course and had withdrawn the link between the arms sales and the negotiations.

And on top of all of these problems with the U.S. Congress, there were the thorny diplomatic problems on the international front. The OAU seemed poised this year to admit the pseudo "state" established by the guerillas as a member, further complicating efforts to resolve the dispute behind closed doors. And the UN, which had remained relatively docile for the last few years, was beginning to sharpen its claws. Unless Morocco did something fast to stem the hemorrhaging support for its position, Draper believed, it would be impossible to stem the growing tide of dissent. It was clear that a new strategy was in order, and four days earlier Vernon Walters had met with the King to discuss such a strategy.

Draper's mission, however, was not to warn Congress of impending doom – they would get enough of that from the newspapers. His mission was to impress upon its members the importance of supporting an important ally despite it all.

So, mustering all the bravado he could summon, he began. "It is the prevailing view of this administration that America's allies and close associates should expect understanding and reliable support," he explained, surveying the crowd. "It would not be in the spirit of this administration's policy if support for America's traditional and historic friends – to meet reasonable and legitimate needs – were to be withheld or made conditional other than under extraordinary circumstances." He paused to let his words sink in. Then he continued.

"Morocco is important to broad American interests and occupies a pivotal strategic area. We intend to maintain and reinforce our historically close relationships with reliability and consistency as our watchwords."

The gaggle of congressmen who attended the session asked the predictable questions, for which he was well prepared. He favorably cited Morocco's concern over "the challenges posed by the Soviets and their surrogates and client states," Morocco's opposition to the Soviet presence in Afghanistan, its help in defeating the Shaba rebels in Zaire, "its pragmatic policies as regards the Middle East issues" and its willingness to allow U.S. warships to call at its ports. He ended on a triumphant note. "For all these reasons, and others, we intend to carry out a relationship that assures Morocco that it will be able to count on the United States as a steadfast and reliable ally."

249

June 1, 1981. All The King's Men.

Draper's rosy words before the United States Congress, however, could not mask the discontent in high circles that was bubbling to the surface, and a continent away cracks in the relationship between the King and his allies began to emerge.

The place was the sumptuous summer retreat of the King in Marrakesh, the day was the first day of June, and as the King prepared to welcome the trio of important guests who had made the long pilgrimage to greet him, he was not in a happy mood.

The war was still not going as planned. By this time the rebels should have been thoroughly routed. Practically his entire army had been sent to secure the towns and villages of Western Sahara, at a cost of millions of dollars each year. The American's idea of concentrating troop strength had had some success – he had been able to secure the corridor to Dakhla after the withdrawal of the Mauritanian forces. But the campaign of Zellaka had failed miserably, and it was only because of his deft political maneuvering and the increased support given to him by his allies – both militarily, politically and financially – and his newly acquired Mirage jets, that his troops had finally managed to break the guerilla siege of Zag and gain control of the Lengueb pass. Following the advice of his allies, he had begun this massive project to build a defensive barrier in the desert to eliminate the ability of the rebels to attack the major population centers at will. But it had taken his troops half a year to build fortifications along a mere 60 mile stretch of land.

And all of this had not come cheap. To be sure, the allies he had carefully cultivated over the past decade – the French and the Americans – had provided technical assistance and equipment, but not for free. The cost of the war had strained the coffers of the Moroccan state beyond endurance, forcing him to humble himself before his cousins, the princes of Saudi Arabia and the other Gulf states, and beg for their aid. And there were other costs even more humiliating – he had done everything but lick the boots of the Israelis in order to curry favor in Washington, risking public ridicule at home, the disgust of his fellow Arab leaders, and the ire of his top Generals.

And now he feared he would be asked to jeopardize all he had gained by caving in to the demands for a referendum – a referendum that would permit the people he had strafed with napalm, tortured, and forced into exile to vote whether to become Moroccans! Absurd! He had promised that he would "cooperate" with the committee that was preparing the groundwork for a referendum, but promises rolled easily off his lips, and he had no intention of following through.

But he feared that following through with the OAU proposal was now what they would ask him to do. One by one the delegation arrived. First, the American, followed by the Frenchman, with the Spaniard taking up the rear.

After the usual pleasantries, the King bade them to sit down. It was now time for business. The American was the first to speak.

"Your Majesty, I want to make it clear that the United States government fully supports your government and that we are prepared to do whatever is necessary in order to ensure its stability. That is precisely why we need to have a discussion about how to move forward with the Sahara campaign." The American paused in order to permit his counterparts to interject a comment, but they seemed perfectly content to let him do the talking for the time being.

He continued, "As you know, for some time we have been able to convince the United Nations to refrain from any action because of the OAU initiative. But we cannot pursue this strategy much longer, especially now that the OAU has put a concrete proposal on the table."

The King, well versed in hiding his emotions, nevertheless winced at the last remark. He had tried by every maneuver in the book to thwart the OAU's plans. He was prepared to abandon the group entirely if they persisted in meddling in his affairs. What was the OAU anyway? A group of puny leaders of puny countries . . . tom tom drummers . . . most of them dictators bloated with self importance. Who were they to dictate terms to the King of Morocco, a direct descendant of the Prophet? The OAU was not important to him.

But it seemed to be important to the United States, and to other Western nations who saw the organization as a buffer between themselves and the anarchists who threatened the region. They liked the organization's essentially moderate stand on most issues – and were particularly pleased with their policy of upholding the state boundaries established by the former colonists on the continent – regardless of how absurd – in order to reduce potential armed conflicts.

The Frenchman – an envoy from the newly elected President of France, Francois Mitterrand --decided to speak. "Your Majesty, as you know the French government considers you to be one of our most important allies, and we are fully aware of how important the Sahara campaign is to your government. But after the debacle in Mauritania we need to reconsider our strategy. It does not seem that you will be able to win a decisive military victory against the rebels in the near future – even if France decides to intervene directly, which it is not currently prepared to do." He shuttered thinking about the failed attempt to buttress Ould Daddah in Mauritania by intervening militarily. It would be a long time before France tried *that* again. "The members of the UN are getting impatient and calling for some action, and it seems clear that if nothing is done immediately to stop it, the Sahrawi Arab Democratic Republic will be admitted as a member of the OAU at its summit in Nairobi this year." With those words he paused to let the gravity of the situation sink in.

Before the King could speak the American chimed in, "Your Majesty, it would be a major diplomatic victory for the Polisario if the SADR were to be admitted to the OAU. Already there are over 50 countries that have recognized the SADR as the legitimate government of Western Sahara. Admission of the Polisario would complicate our efforts to encourage a settlement, for it would confer at least qualified legitimacy on the Polisario as the spokesman of the people of Western Sahara. It would also give them a stepping stone to recognition at the UN."

251

The last words made the King fall back into his seat. He could handle the SADR's admission to the OAU, but its admission to the UN was a different matter entirely.

After a long pause as he carefully considered his options, he spoke. "What would you have me do?"

The Spaniard, who had been quiet during the interchange, finally mustered the courage to speak. "Your Majesty, the only way to forestall the admission of the SADR to the OAU, in the opinion of my government, is for you to agree to the OAU proposal at its next meeting and work with the OAU to implement it."

The King was slightly irritated. Just like the Spanish, he mused, always ready to cave in to pressure.

He turned to the American. "I already informed the UN that I would cooperate with the committee, didn't I? And didn't I send two representatives to its meeting last September?"

The American smiled and took a long puff on his cigarette. "Yes, we know, Your Majesty," he said in a low voice. "And we also know that your representatives continued to insist that the problem was due to Algerian aggression and that there was no need to hold a referendum since the people of Western Sahara had already expressed their wish to be integrated with Morocco in the 'traditional' manner. It's all in the committee's report. This hardly constitutes the type of cooperation that is needed!"

The King rose from his seat and started to pace the room, raising his arms in a gesture of frustration. "I cannot go any further. I simply cannot risk having the future of the territory decided by a referendum, especially a referendum of the very people I have been fighting for the past six years."

The American cleared his throat and then spoke again. "We know it is a risk, but the risk of letting the SADR be admitted to the OAU is even greater. Besides, you might actually win a referendum, that is, if it is organized in a proper manner."

The King gave the man a long, cool look. He was smiling. He didn't need to explain. He was no fool, and political intrigue was the air he breathed. He fiddled for a moment with his pen before speaking. "So, you advise me to agree to the OAU plan, is that it?" he finally said, looking at each one of his visitors in turn.

"Yes, that is it," they said, and one by one they took their leave.

When they had left, Hassan sat in his arm chair smoking a chain of cigarettes and thinking about what his visitors had told him. Yes, perhaps they were right, perhaps it was important to stall the admission of the SADR at the OAU until this defensive barrier was built and he could boast of some military gains. And perhaps some sort of gesture would do the trick . . . after all, his promises had worked before . . . and no one had ever forced him to keep any of them! And he could always find some excuse to withdraw from a referendum at the last minute.

So, he put out his cigarette and called for his assistant. He would retire for

the night. Tomorrow he would prepare one of his carefully crafted speeches –
the kind dear to every diplomat's heart -- promising everything and nothing
in the same breath.

June 26, 1981. Nairobi.

The day was June 26. Hassan had announced his decision to attend the
OAU conference in Nairobi and there were rumors that he would finally
pledge his support for the suggestion of the "wise men" that the conflict over
Western Sahara be settled by a referendum. As the delegates assembled one
could hear a pin drop as everyone held his breath to hear what Hassan would
say. When the King finally took the rostrum he looked in the eyes of each of
them in turn. Then he smiled.

"My brothers," he began in a soft, languid tone, "I want first to give thanks
to those of you who have worked so tirelessly to find a political solution to the
dangerous situation which now engulfs my country." He stopped to nod his
head in the direction of the delegates from Nigeria and Mali and the others
on the committee of "wise men." "I appreciate your efforts and I wish to state
for the record my willingness to accept a referendum, that is, a controlled
referendum whose modalities would give justice simultaneously to the
objectives of the committee, that is to say the committee of wise men, and to
Morocco's conviction regarding the legitimacy of its rights."

Olusegun Obesanjo, a frown coming over his face, looked at the man sitting
next to him. "What exactly is he pledging?" he whispered, "a 'controlled'
referendum? What is that supposed to mean?"

Moussa Traore smiled. "Well, if his speech leaves his intentions ambiguous,
the statements he has made during the weeks preceding the summit make his
position quite clear. I have them written here." He unfolded a piece of paper and
began reading. " 'The recovery of our Sahara is well and truly accomplished,'
-- this is in a broadcast on the third of March -- 'This Sahara is ours. We are
not prepared to give it up, and though we are in favor of any agreement that
can put an end to the conflict, we cannot allow any such agreement to be made
at the expense of an integral part of our national territory.' And this is what
he said on the eve of his departure for the summit, and I quote: 'We will not
renounce a single grain of this Moroccan Sahara for which so many of us have
sacrificed our blood and which has cost us so much money.' "

"So, all this is just window dressing, is that it?" Obesanjo whispered,
shaking his head.

But before Maore could respond, Daniel Arap Moi, the President of Kenya,
himself no neophyte in the political arena, took the rostrum. During the
King's speech he had remained calm. He now turned to his guest and said
in a slow, clear voice, "Your Majesty, we appreciate your pledge to support
the work of the committee. In order to expedite the work they have started
it is my intention to introduce a resolution establishing an "implementation
committee" whose task will be to put together, with your assistance, the details
of the plan suggested by the committee." Then, fixing the King with a steady

253

gaze, he added, "and we will expect that the details of this plan will be finalized by the end of this year!"

With these last words the delegates from Gabon and Zaire rose from their chairs as if to speak. With a wave of his hand Hassan silenced them. As he turned to look at Arap Moi, he seemed to have lost stature, and had become just a small, tired man grappling with a problem beyond his control. He started to talk about the political situation in his country – about the pressures that were on his shoulders to recapture the lands of his ancestors, about the long, illustrious history of the Alawite kingdom, about the disastrous consequences that would evolve if he relinquished the territory. After a moment he got up from his seat and stood staring out a window, a handkerchief in his hands and a tear in his eye. When he returned to his seat he turned his eyes once more to those of the delegates.

"I beg you to give me more time – time to prepare my subjects for the possible loss of the territory, time to assuage my political opponents," he pleaded. "If you do not give me time to pave the way for what you are asking me to do, the result might be the downfall of my government, and chaos and anarchy in my country. Is that what you really want?"

The assemblage was dumbfounded. The members of the Moroccan delegation, which besides Reda and Basri included the leader of the Istiqlal party, squirmed nervously in their seats. President Bendjedid of Algeria later remarked that it was one of the most extraordinary exhibitions he had ever witnessed. For a moment no one spoke. Then, regaining his composure, the Chair quietly put the matter to a vote. The delegates voted to put aside for the moment the question of the SADR's membership in the organization. However, they adopted an eight point resolution – along the lines of the proposals made by the "wise men" -- that laid down the broad guidelines for an internationally supervised cease-fire and a truly democratic referendum. An "Implementation Committee" that included the presidents of Kenya, Guinea, Mali, Nigeria, Sierra Leone, Sudan and Tanzania was approved and mandated to work with the United Nations in supervising the referendum. The King was applauded for his magnanimity and asked, once again, to work with the implementation committee, and to the great relief of everyone present, the meeting finally turned to other items.

July 1981. The Dilemma.

Over the following weeks the Polisario pressed Hassan to work with this "Implementation Committee" and accept direct negotiations over the organization of the referendum, but he demurred, demanding to discuss the matter only with the Algerians.

Meanwhile, the guerillas were grappling with new threats on the battlefield.

The King had finally bowed to pressure from Dlimi and others to loosen his grip on the Air Force, and for several months his Hercules C-130 reconnaissance aircraft, combined with Westinghouse's sophisticated tracking devices, had enabled his newly acquired Mirage jets to pinpoint guerilla targets and conduct a series of deadly strikes. Unlike the old F-5s that had to fire from a high altitude in order to be accurate, the Mirage jets were able to fly low and take pictures of the terrain so as to pinpoint their targets, making them far more useful in attacks against small moving targets. They had first used their Mirage jets in December of 1979 against the troops blockading Zag. During battles at Akka and Housa in 1980, pilots flying Mirage F-1 aircraft had flown 10 sorties a day and had operated at altitudes and speeds that had neutralized the SAM 7 and SAM 9 light surface to air missiles of the Polisario. They had followed and bombed Polisario forces on a daily basis and had used French cluster bombs, which would scatter small pieces of napalm within a large radius upon impact, to inflict maximum damage. The previous March, at the battle of Guelta Zemmour they had intercepted the reinforcements from the 4th military region before they could reach the scene and forced them to disperse besides wreaking havoc on the troops from the 2nd military region in their retreat. And the increased sophistication of the surveillance equipment and weaponry of the Moroccan forces had prevented the guerillas from reaching their command center.

The increased efficiency of the Moroccan air force, combined with the increased size and sophistication of the troops and weapons that they faced, were bad enough. But the wall that Hassan was building imposed an even greater obstacle. No longer could the guerillas rely upon rapid, mobile assaults with no more than Land Rovers equipped with machine guns and infantry. These new obstacles led the Polisario, by the spring of 1981, to adopt a new strategy. They would mechanize their troops - starting with the men of the 2nd military region. After the battle of Guelta Zemmour, Bouhali was given a new mission – prepare his troops to used armored vehicles, tanks and troop carriers.

It was now the beginning of July. The temperature near Tindouf had reached 120 in the shade, if you could find any shade. A handful of men had gathered in the stucco building with a round dome that had become the Polisario's headquarters. Their mood was solemn.

Brahim Ghali didn't mince words. "We cannot go for long just nipping at the heels of the Moroccans. By the end of summer Bouhali's men will be ready. But we will need the right equipment if they are to be effective. We will need to use tanks – and troop carriers -- if we ever want to engage in a major assault against their positions behind the berm. "

Abdelaziz spoke up. "The tanks will not be a problem. We already got a few from Libya. . . and last spring I talked to Nazar about acquiring some more. At first he didn't think it would be a good idea for us to acquire armored vehicles . . . that it would inhibit our ability to wage hit and run missions. But now that Hassan has started building this wall he has changed his mind. He agrees that we cannot continue to fight a Goliath with sling shots. At some point we need to counter force with force. And we cannot fight forces behind a wall without better equipment. He is sending us some tanks and personnel carriers."

"But armored vehicles will not help us to repel the jets," said Bouhali, shaking his head. "Our anti aircraft artillery is second or even third generation. SAM 9's cannot be expected to be effective against Mirage jets. We cannot repel them without more powerful equipment."

" Preferably SAM 6s," Nih Lahbib interjected. "There is no other way."

The room became quiet. All of them had heard about the Soviet made SAM 6 surface to air missiles that were the state of the art anti aircraft weapons, capable of downing the most sophisticated aircraft, but reputedly complicated to handle.

Abdelaziz shook his head. "There is no way Nazar will help us get SAM 6 missiles. They cost a fortune and not even the most elite troops in the Algerian army have them. Besides which, the Algerian Generals are convinced that we don't have the expertise to use them."

"Is there anywhere else we can get them?" Bouhali asked.

Nih Lahbib paused. "The Soviets might be willing to part with some if we asked, but that would involve us in the Cold War quagmire. . ."

". . . not to mention make us another of their puppet states," added Abdelaziz quickly. "No, we cannot do that. " The others nodded in agreement, and for a few moments the room was quiet again as everyone present mulled over their predicament.

Finally, Brahim Ghali spoke. "I understand that the Libyans have ordered some new equipment from the Yugoslavians. Khaddafi wants to build up his arsenal for his dispute with Chad . . . and in case any of the Western powers decide to retaliate. His troops are being trained to use anti aircraft missiles by the Soviets, and this will undoubtedly include the new equipment." He paused for a moment. "We have already persuaded the Libyans to include some of our men in the program . . . without the Soviets' knowledge, of course. I have been told that this new shipment includes some state of the art anti-aircraft missiles . . . including the newest generation of the SAM 6."

"But even if they did agree to include some of our men in their program, training us to use the new equipment and giving them to us are two different things," Nih Lahbib interjected. "It won't be easy to persuade Khaddafi to part with any of them."

They all knew what he meant.

Khaddafi! the *enfant terrible* of the African continent. A man who had to be handled with kid gloves. El Ouali had impressed him with his revolutionary zeal and in the early days of the movement he had offered his support. But that didn't prevent him from sending a delegation to march at Hassan's side in the Green March after Hassan convinced him that it would be in the cause of "Arab unity." He just as quickly turned around when El Ouali pointed out Hassan's treachery and refusal to uphold the principle of self determination. El Ouali seemed to know what buttons to push to stay on his good side, but after his death it had taken Abdelaziz and the other leaders months of careful cultivation to woo him back to their fold. But he was as fickle as he was stubborn, and after the Nairobi OAU summit had suddenly extended an olive branch to Hassan, restoring the diplomatic relations with Morocco that had been severed upon Libya's recognition of the SADR in April of 1980. Abdelaziz had just returned from a trip to Tripoli to seek a clarification of the leader's position, and had been assured of Libya's continued support. But no concrete aid had been promised . . . and now there was no telling what he might do. He had become alarmed to the point of paranoia by Washington's moves to squelch his regime and Reagan's promise of military aid for any country threatened by his "adventurism." He had greatly reduced the military aid he had given them recently, and it was doubtful that he would now give them any sophisticated weapons that could be traced back to him.

"Even if Khaddafi did give us some additional weapons we would have to find a way to get them without letting anyone know. If word got out Khaddafi would face problems and we would lose the element of surprise," Nih Lahbib added.

". . . and if the Americans find out they will try to stop us. They are desperately trying to block any movement of arms from Libya," Akeik interjected.

"Yes, the only way it would work is if it were in complete secrecy. We couldn't even tell the Algerians," Bouhali exclaimed.

"We can't lie to Chadli . . . or Nazar," Brahim Ghali said, "If they ask, we must tell them. But no one else would need to know . . . including our own men!"

"Well, all this discussion is well and good," Abdelaziz remarked, shaking his head, "but we don't even know for sure whether Khaddafi has received any of these weapons yet, let alone whether he would think of letting us have a few."

Silence again. A few minutes later the meeting ended and the room quickly emptied. A man in the far side of the room sat for a moment alone and in silence. He had been listening intently to the discussion, without saying a word. Then he walked out the door and quickly caught up with Abdelaziz. The two marched together in silence. Then, when he was sure that they were alone he looked at him intently, flashing a broad grin.

"Let me find out," was all he said.

August, 1981. Libya.

As Bachir Mustapha Sayed stepped from the Land Rover that had traversed over 500 miles from Tripoli through the blistering heat of Libya's southern desert, he couldn't help wondering what he would find at his destination. His host – Libya's quixotic head of state – was as unpredictable as he was stubborn. Here he was, chest deep in a conflict with his neighbor, Chad. He smiled at the irony. Khaddafi, the great proponent of Arab unity, seemed to quarrel with every Arab leader he met—not to mention most other leaders. His dislike for Hassan of Morocco had even been greater than Boumediene's. He was angry with Anwar Sadat for his overtures to Israel. He was behind a coup attempt against the President of Tunisia. The monarchies of the Gulf hated his guts.

257

And now he was at the border of Chad, leading his troops in a campaign against his southern neighbor.

But he had money – and arms. And today the Polisario needed his help. So, when he agreed to meet him, Bachir, the younger brother of the man he had fondly considered his protégé, held his breath, and assumed his most diplomatic and ingratiating demeanor.

In the middle of the desert Khaddafi had set up a command post – an assortment of huge tents erected Bedouin style. There, like some medieval desert potentate, he welcomed Bachir. As he looked at the tall, dark haired young man entering his tent, he couldn't help noting the resemblance to his brother. For a moment his thoughts wondered to that day almost a decade ago when he had first set eyes on the scruffy kid who was to become the leader of a great movement. El Ouali had traveled to Tripoli for a meeting with the official in his government responsible for coordination with liberation movements and had been given a room in one of the classier hotels in the city. The following morning he could not be found. The official searched frantically throughout the hotel and finally found him, sleeping on a worn blanket in the garden. "Why have you slept here," he asked, astonished, "and why have you not eaten a meal at the hotel?" "I came to bring back something in my hand, not my stomach," the youngster had replied. When he had heard of the incident, he had asked that the youth be brought to his office. Standing before him had been a tall, bushy haired young man wearing shaggy fatigues and worn out shoes. "We are desert people," he had said, "and we are fighting for our home!" There was something about the youngster that touched him . . . a certain insolence, a certain honesty. He had decided to give him some military aid, channeled first through Timbuktu, then Nouakchott, and when the war started, through Algeria. And now he was facing his brother.

For an hour or so the conversation was consumed with the pleasantries that were *de rigeur* for such meetings in this part of the world – neither party wishing to venture too quickly into matters that might be considered sensitive. It was nearly dusk before Bachir turned the conversation to what mattered most.

"My friend," he started, "You know that the Americans and the French have been giving weapons to Hassan, including fighter jets and reconnaissance aircraft – and now they, and the Israelis, are helping them to build sand barriers to prevent our troops from attacking the garrisons near our main towns and entering Moroccan territory. You know that we do not have any planes or helicopters, and our anti-aircraft missiles are useless against their modern aircraft. I implore you, as our friend and benefactor, to give us access to more sophisticated weapons," he said in a solemn voice. Then in a lower voice he added, "It would teach the foreigners a lesson and greatly help the cause of Arab unity."

He watched Khaddafi's face closely. He knew the last words would get a response.

Khaddafi indeed had turned pale. The idea of the Americans, the French, and the Israelis meddling in what should have been an Arab solution to an Arab problem infuriated him. Earlier he had been inflamed by the pictures the French jaguars had taken of their attacks on the guerillas. More recently he had seen the pictures of the attacks on guerilla troops, taken by the Moroccan Mirage jets, that had been plastered in the newsreels by the Moroccan propaganda machine. And then another thought crossed his mind. The chairmanship of the OAU was scheduled to rotate to him in 1982 and already the Americans had begun to lobby its members to boycott any conference he chaired. The last time he was scheduled to be chairman, one year ago, not enough delegates attended to reach a quorum. Many of the members were sympathetic to the Polisario cause. Helping the Polisario now might have its political advantages . . . . and he had an arsenal full of weapons that would no longer be needed once he got a shipment of newer weapons from Yugoslavia that was scheduled to arrive any day now.

He turned to Bachir with a smile. "My friend, I have amassed a large stockpile of weapons which I will not need. Go to the director of my arsenal, with my blessings. He will be able to supply you with something." And the conversation once again turned to the price of eggs and butter.

The Arsenal

It was a hot day outside, and the temperature seemed even hotter in the cavernous enclave that housed many of the weapons that Khaddafi had stockpiled as insurance against an attack by Western forces – or an insurgency at home. As Bachir and his colleagues strolled through the dusty complex, at the side of Abu Bakr Zaber Unis, the Minister of Defense, they couldn't help but be impressed by the enormous supply of crates, filled with every sort of weapon, that were stacked in piles reaching the ceiling. The Minister, obviously proud of his collection, was eagerly describing the firepower and capabilities of each weapon.

As his colleagues busied themselves looking over the other armaments, Bachir's attention was drawn to a handful of enormous crates – more than 20 feet long -- in the corner, separated from the others and covered with a tarp.

"What's in those crates?" he asked the Minister.

The Minister's eyes beamed. "Those are missiles we just received from Yugoslavia last week. The newest version of the SAM 6 and 8s. We haven't had a chance to test them yet, but we have been told that they have twice the range of our other missiles. Of course, they are more difficult to use. I don't think anyone else in Africa has them."

Bachir stopped for a moment. "May I take a look?" he said, rather nonchalantly. His host was thrilled to be able to show off his latest prize, and called two of his attendants to open one of the crates. When they had removed a layer of straw, Bachir peered inside. There, side by side, were two large objects of different sizes. Bachir examined them intently. When he had finished his examination and the Minister's aides were putting the lid back

259

onto the crate, Bachir turned to him, and with the broad smile that was his trademark, said, "Well, sir, I think these are the weapons we want."

The Minister's smile suddenly turned to a frown. "Are you sure Khaddafi has authorized me to give you some of these?" he asked hesitantly. He knew full well Khaddafi's quixotic nature. He was capable of agreeing to anything. But this . . . .

Before he could utter another word he stopped and turned around. A third man had entered the arsenal and been quietly listening to their discussion.

"What do you think, Abdelslem, do I have your permission to give the Polisario any of our anti-aircraft missiles," he said in a deferential tone.

Abdelslem Jaloud, the second most powerful man in Libya, smiled. "Let me see what you want," he said. Bachir quickly pointed to some of the weapons in the crate, then, with Abdelslem at his side, he moved on to the other weapons neatly stacked in rows. When he had ended his tour of the arsenal, Abdelslem turned to him, again smiling, but with a serious look in his eyes.

"Well, we can't give you any of the anti-aircraft missiles we just received from Yugoslavia – Khaddafi would throw a fit," he said, " but some of the earlier generation SAM 6 missiles we can probably manage." Then he moved closer to Bachir and whispered in his ear, "as for the other weapons and equipment . . . I suggest that you ask for anything you want now. . . . Khaddafi might not always be so generous!"

When Abdelslem had departed, the Minister turned to Bachir with a puzzled look on his face. "Well, I guess you can have some of these missiles. But do you know how to use them?"

Bachir smiled. "We will learn."

August, 1981. Tindouf.

While the Polisario leaders were busy trying to acquire the weapons and training that would enable them to counter Morocco's new aircraft and surveillance equipment, the residents of Tindouf were busy trying to mold a new society.

When Soukeina wrote that "a" in the sand in 1976 she had begun one of the most ambitious campaigns of self education of women, by women and for women seen in modern times.

Without books, teachers, or supplies of any sort, using the sand as a writing tablet, and a branch of a bush as a pen, the women in the camps organized daily sessions in which the few women who had any knowledge of a subject, and the even fewer men who were present in the camps, would teach what they knew to any women who were interested. Many women managed to put aside their chores and travel great distances from their wilayas in order to attend. After these sessions the women would return to their wilayas and instruct the women and children there on the lessons they had learned. In this way, slowly over a period of many months, many of the women and children in the camps learned to read and write, add and subtract. Some even learned a few details about history and geography.

Each day brought a new challenge – and a new triumph – to the women in the camps, far from their homes and families, their men gone to war. They would not wait to return to their homeland to build the type of society they wanted. And they would not stick to the old ways. Ouali had opened their eyes to a new world, and once opened they would never shut again. So gradually, over a period of months, the fabric of a new society – a society based on democratic principles, equality, and a thirst for knowledge – began to emerge from the sands of the desert.

So, when Sidimi returned to the camps in the summer of 1981 with members of the 2nd military region, she saw a place that bore little resemblance to the one she had left. No longer did tents dominate the landscape. The tents were still there, but adjoining many of them were tiny stucco buildings, and in each wilaya stood large structures with imposing names painted over their doors. An administrative office building, a police barrack. A domed shaped stucco building called "Rabouni" housed the SADR main offices, and clustered nearby were huge stucco edifices, some surrounded by high stucco walls, dedicated to the army, the legislature and other important organs of government.

By 1981 the organization of the SADR had become substantially more sophisticated. The wali, or governor, of each of the three wilaya would preside over a People's Council composed of the officials administering the wilaya's districts. Each district encompassed approximately five thousand inhabitants, divided into eleven member cells. On the district level a kind of direct democracy was practiced. Meetings of the Base Congresses would be held in each district every one or two years, and at these assemblies elections would be held for delegates to the General People's Congress. The General People's Congress would elect a political bureau which would coordinate the policies of the Executive Committee.

In this government the women ruled. They controlled the leadership of the wilayas and districts. They controlled the Base Congresses. They were governors of wilayas. And a few of them had been elected to the Political Bureau. And it was the women who greeted Sidi as a returning battlefield hero.

No sooner had she stepped from the Land Rover that had escorted her from the field than she was whisked away by a bevy of brightly clad women to a stucco building in the center of the largest of the wilayas. It was a huge building, built "Arabic" style with a number of adjoining rooms surrounding a small, gravelly courtyard, adorned with a few small, well nurtured palm trees.

She was impressed. It was the building that the women in the camp had begun to build during her last visit in 1978, carving blocks of stucco bricks from mud with their bare hands, carefully placing them in rows, and covering the rows with a thick mud layer. They christened the building the February 27 School, after the date of the establishment of the SADR. It was there that classes specifically geared to women were held. As Sidi walked from room to room she was amazed to see women and girls of all ages, sitting side by side, listening to lectures in Arabic, history, mathematics, law, given by other

261

women with at most one textbook to share. In a corner of the building a group of young mothers, their babies in their arms, were listening to a lecture on hygiene and infant care. In another corner, a group of young women were practicing rolling bandages. Adjacent to the school was a minicamp where men and children could join their daughters, sisters, or mothers while they attended or taught at the school. The school had been such a success that they had achieved a near universal literacy in Arabic among adult women.

But as impressive as the school was, Sidi was anxious to return to the hospital that had also been built in her absence. There she found rows of blankets or cots where men wounded in battle lay. Women scurried to and fro carrying buckets of water, bandages and utensils. As she surveyed the scene she recognized several of the men she had cared for on the battlefield, who cried out greetings as she passed, and a short distance away another figure she recognized.

"Soukeina!" she shouted. The woman, who had been giving orders to someone, turned to look at her. She was still dressed in the khaki shirt and pants worn by the soldiers, and her hair was still in a boyish cut, making her stand out among the brightly robed women in the camp, but she was unmistakably the same Sidimi she had known since childhood. She dropped what she was doing and ran to greet her, embracing her and clasping her arm.

"I had heard that you were in the camps," she began to say, excitedly. "Here, let me look at you." She stood a few feet away and gave her friend a going over. "You look great! I see that being in the front lines agrees with you . . . you have even gained a little weight!"

Sidimi laughed. Taking her friend's arm again she started walking. "I understand you have been quite busy since I have been gone," she said gaily.

Soukeina blushed slightly. "Yes, I am now the wali of the Smara waliya and a member of the Political Bureau as well as being on the committee that deals with negotiations with relief agencies and the distribution of food in the camps. It keeps me busy . . . which is just as well, since Hamed is busy with the troops, and I have no other family here. But what are you doing here? I saw Bouhali the other day, and a couple of the soldiers in his unit. It is unusual to see him back in the camps. I figured something is brewing."

After taking a few more steps Sidimi turned to her. "Yes, something is brewing. For the past few months Bouhali has been training the members of his troops on how to use the more sophisticated equipment we are getting from the Algerians and Libyans." Then in a hushed voice she added, "I think they will be giving us tanks and other heavy artillery."

"Tanks!" blurted Soukeina, stopping in her tracks, somewhat astonished. She was no military expert but she had seen tanks in action, and the destruction they could cause.

"Yes, tanks . . . troop carriers," Sidimi repeated, "and something else . . . I don't know what it is – they are keeping it all top secret -- but whatever it is, it has made Bouhali quite excited."

Soukeina walked silently for a moment, mulling over the implications of what she had just heard.

"And will you be going through this training?" she finally asked.

"No," Sidimi responded, slightly blushing. "Abdelaziz asked me to take over as the director of the hospital here in Tindouf . . . and in charge of training medical officers to send into the field. While Bouhali's troops are all being trained there won't be much for me to do in the field . . . and most of the seriously wounded are here, anyway. It makes sense."

Then she put her arms around her friend in a joyous embrace as they walked side by side.

All at once Soukeina stopped walking and turned to her friend, a serious look on her face.

"When they get these tanks, what do you think they will do with them?" she asked, pensively.

Sidimi returned her look.

"I don't know . . . but they are planning something . . . something big!"

End of September, 1981. The Voyage.

It was the last week of September when a long convoy of trucks, numbering over 80, loaded to the brim with what appeared to be sacks of rice, grain and other foodstuffs, made its way slowly south from Tripoli past the Al Hamada al Hamra and through the Sawda Mountains to the tiny enclave of Dabdab. Then it turned to the west. By noon it managed to reach the place where the main road stopped and the giant sand dunes, which would stretch to the Algerian border, would dominate the landscape. This was Tuareg territory, and the driver of the 50th vehicle in the line instinctively reached for his rifle and placed it behind his seat.

"Do you think we will have any trouble?" he asked the passenger sitting beside him.

The tall man, dressed in black, with a black turban wrapped around his head covering everything but his eyes, had already placed his rifle beside him.

"I don't think so. There haven't been any attacks for a while. But it pays to be cautious," he said, quietly.

For the next two hours the caravan proceeded at a snail's pace along the tiny road leading to the border, stopping at times to shovel the sand blocking the road that had drifted from the dunes on either side. It was eerily quiet, as befits one of the most desolate spots on earth. At last the convoy reached a sign of civilization -- a small hut manned by a sole sentry a few miles south of the town of Zaizaitine.

There it stopped. The sentry gave the caravan a disgruntled look before ambling slowly towards the lead truck. It was the third such convoy that year. He was used to the long line of trucks that brought food and other necessities to the refugee camps at Tindouf three or four times a year through the so-called "Khaddafi trail". . . and was not inclined to spend a lot of time in the hot sun asking questions. He approached the driver of the first truck, asked a few questions, glanced at the provisions he was carrying in the back, and waived him through. He repeated this exercise for each truck in turn. When

263

he got to number 50 he stopped it briefly, and uncovered the sheet that lay atop its load.

"Rice?"

"Yes," answered the driver. "The settlement at Tindouf is low on supplies." The guard poked at the canvas sacks. Yes, it seemed to be rice. So he waived the truck on.

Once he could no longer see the sentry in his rear view mirror, the driver nervously took a cigarette from a pack that lay on the seat beside him and wiped a drop of sweat from his forehead. Yes, it was hot. The end of September in the desert was almost as hot as mid summer. But that was not why he was sweating. He had just passed the first hurdle on what was going to be a long, hazardous journey.

The passenger sitting beside him unloosened the scarf around his head and smiled.

"Relax, Moulay," he said. "We have nothing to worry about."

Moulay gave him a weak smile in return.

Once in Algeria the convoy followed the road north past Ain Amenas, a tiny dot on the map 18 miles west of the Libyan border, before turning due west on the road to Ohanet. It was now nearly dusk and purple shadows had begun to fill the crevices in the rocky terrain of the Plateau du Tinghert, an elevated plain that forms the southeastern border of the Grand Erg Oriental. The word is a Berber term for "field of sand dunes," and the Grand Erg Oriental – also known as the Eastern Sand Sea – is well named. Enormous dunes 2 to 5 yards high cover much of the landscape. The remainder is a flat, stony *hammada*.

The passenger in the 50th car had relieved Moulay as driver and the latter was taking a well earned nap when he was suddenly jolted by the sound of a horn. At once the truck in front of them stopped and the driver waived to the one ahead of him to stop. In a few minutes they had all stopped and the man in black got out of the truck.

"I think we should stop for the night here, before we reach Hassi Bel Guebbour," he said. "I don't think it is a good idea to drive through the dunes at night."

The others obeyed his command and soon blankets were unrolled, and fires lit for tea and the evening meal. They needed no coaxing to sleep that night.

Moulay was weary, and as he lay on his blanket drifting off to sleep his mind wandered to the events that had brought him there. In the middle of the summer he had gotten a call. He was needed on a top secret mission. He and a handful of his comrades were to be sent to Libya for training. In secret.

When he arrived in Libya he learned that the Libyan leader, Khaddafi, had become so incensed at the interference of the Western powers in the war over Western Sahara that he had agreed to train a select group of guerillas in missile defense techniques, and he had agreed to give the guerillas some of his arsenal of anti-aircraft missiles. But it had to be in secret. For weeks he and the others, pretending to be Libyans, had trained along side Libyan commandos in Soviet run classes.

And now it was time to return. There was only one problem. Khaddafi could not risk having any of the weapons traced to him. If the Polisario were to get their hands on this equipment it would have to be in complete secrecy.

He was now in the heart of the Algerian desert. Except for a handful of wandering Bedouins he had not seen anyone for hours. Nor was he likely to. For miles there was nothing but sand and rock. A good place to camp for the night, in the middle of the desert, far from any prying eyes, he thought. The heat of the day was gradually replaced by a cool stillness as both he and his passenger -- and the desert around them -- fell into a deep sleep.

He was still fast asleep when a noise close to his ears caused him to sit up abruptly. A sliver of light had just appeared on the eastern horizon. In the semi darkness he could see a shape moving a few yards from where he stood. An Algerian patrol? He froze. The figure moved closer. Then he relaxed. A camel. In the distance he could make out the forms of an additional three. Four camels in the middle of the desert. A Bedouin camp must be nearby.

When the sun had finally made its appearance he decided to look around. In the far distance he could make out the outline of a tent. The Bedouins had noticed the caravan too, and one of them was coming his way.

His greeting showed him to be from the Ould Jrir tribe, a tribe of Algerian Bedouins friendly to the Sahrawis.

By the time he arrived the others in the group had begun to rise, and the man in black was giving orders to one of them to prepare tea. The Bedouin eyed him for a moment before speaking.

"Good morning," he said, extending him a warm greeting. "Are you the leader of this group?"

The man hesitated for a moment, looking him over carefully before replying. "Yes."

"I would like to invite you and your companion to join my family for tea before resuming your voyage," the visitor said, smiling.

Moulay and his companion exchanged glances. Such an invitation would have been inhospitable for them to refuse. So, they left the truck behind and followed their host on foot to his tent.

Once inside, they were introduced to the other men and women of the family. The man who had come to great him was Ahmed, and he and his family had just come east, through the desert, and, together with their camels, goats, and sheep, were on route to better pasture lands in the south for the winter months. They offered their guests several cups of tea, which they were grateful to receive.

Then Ahmed could not restrain his curiosity. Who were they. . . and where were they going?

For a moment neither of them answered. Finally, the man in black smiled.

"We are Sahrawi, and we are taking supplies back to our camp in Tindouf," he said, nonchalantly, handing his cup back to his host.

265

"Supplies from Libya?" Ahmed asked, equally nonchalantly, pouring some more liquid into the cup.

"Yes"

Ahmed stopped pouring for a moment, fixing his gaze on his guest. Then a smile gradually crossed his face, and he handed the cup back to him.

"You are Polisario," he said in a matter-of-fact tone.

"Yes"

He smiled again, and quickly changed the subject. After making sure his guests were well fed, Ahmed walked them back to their truck. He glanced at the sacks stacked neatly in the rear.

"Rice?" he asked.

"Yes," the man next to him replied, a certain firmness in his voice.

"I see," Ahmed muttered slowly. Then, in a hushed tone he added, "You might be interested to know that a troop of Algerian soldiers has been patrolling the area around El Menia to the west for the past couple of days, searching every vehicle on the road. I think they are looking for smugglers . . . or the bandits from Mali who robbed a couple of oil field workers last week. We passed them on our way east."

The man in black paused and looked at him.

Ahmed was smiling. He didn't say a word. He didn't need to. His eyes said it all.

"Thanks," the man said as he climbed into the truck.

By noon the caravan reached Hassi Bel Guebbour, a tiny transit stop in the east-west Sahara route, strategically located about a hundred miles into the Grand Erg. So far the terrain had been largely barren rock, similar to the *hammada* surrounding Tindouf, but shortly past the outpost huge dunes of sand began to emerge – sometimes reaching heights of six feet or more – enveloping the road, the vehicles on it, and the passengers in the vehicles, in fine particles of red dust. This was the Sahara of lore – miles of undulating waves of sand as far as the eyes can see, whipped into a frenzy by the wind, topped by a scorching, unforgiving sun.

Moulay drew the scarf he wore tightly around his face until only his eyes were left to battle the dust.

"How long will it be before we reach the end of the dunes?" he asked.

"I don't know . . . it changes with the season. At least we probably won't have to face a sand storm," his passenger replied.

Moulay grunted. He was thankful that they were not attempting this journey in the spring time, when ferocious sand storms would roar through the erg, sometimes blocking passage for days. This was bad enough.

For five hours the troupe dragged themselves through this vortex. Finally, the bedraggled crew saw signs of civilization – an oil well, then another, and soon a dozen or more, and a road sign announcing the approach to the town of Hassi Messaoud.

Hassi Messaoud, or "Messaoud's well" in Arabic, was an oasis in the midst of the vast erg desert, and the sleepy little town surrounding the water hole had been an important stop along the ancient caravan route. However, life in the small settlement changed dramatically in 1956 when oil was discovered in the region. By the time Moulay and his companions passed by, a refinery had been built which supplied nearly half of Algeria's total oil production.

"Sonatrach owns this town," the man in black said, matter-of-factly. And who could disagree? The streets were filled with neatly dressed men with European haircuts and the establishments that would cater to them. The long line of dusty trucks, driven by equally dusty men, wound its way through a gauntlet of stares as it proceeded down the main street. They would first replenish their supplies and refuel, then they would be quickly resuming their voyage. It would take them a couple of hours to reach the major town in the area -- Ouargla.

Ouargla was the site of an ancient Berber settlement and souk that had become a major tourist attraction, as well as a famous 'hang out' for the hippie generation – made even more famous when Memphis Slim dedicated a song to it. It was now the most important commercial center in the region. Moulay would have loved to linger in the souk – to drink some coffee in one of the sidewalk cafes and buy a few trinkets for his family. But there was no time to dawdle. It was getting late. They needed to reach the outskirts of Ghardaia before resting for the night. So the caravan whisked past the town and took the road to the west.

It was now after dusk, and only the moon and the stars illuminated the desert terrain. Before long they saw gleaming lights in the distance and knew that they must be close to the city of Ghardaia. Ghardaia was built almost a thousand years ago on a hill in the M'Zab valley by an Ibadi sect of non-Arabic Moslems . . . and the area surrounding it was where Algeria's famous *degat nour* dates were grown. Its colorful white, pink and red houses rose in terraces and arcades, leading French philosopher Simone de Beauvoir to describe it as "a Cubist painting beautifully constructed."

Ghardaia was also the eastern gateway to the Grand Erg Occidental – the Great Western Sand Sea – and it was on the outskirts of the city that the caravan would camp for the night before attempting the arduous trek across it.

In the morning, Moulay had just finished re-packing his gear in the truck when his companion took him aside.

"I have told the others that we should take the northern route. I know that it is longer, but there is more traffic and we are less likely to meet up with robbers . . ."

". . . or Algerian patrols looking for them?" Moulay added, grinning.

The tall man in black stifled a smile.

Before long they were on the road again, this time heading north on the highway that would take them through the erg to the high plateau in the foothills of the Atlas mountains and the ancient oasis city of Laghouart.

Laghouat, which sits atop two hills which are extensions of Mount Tizigarine, guards the entrance to the Atlas steppes and the northern perimeter of the desert. It can trace its history as far back as the 11th century, when the Banu

Hilal invaders from Arabia, supported by the Fatamids of Egypt, crossed the area. Now it lay on the major route between Algiers and central Africa. Once they reached Laghouat the caravan would follow the road south through the high plateau all the way to Bechar, and from there to their camps in Tindouf.

Moulay was resting now. His passenger had taken the wheel. The terrain was now largely flat and rocky – with a slightly cool breeze – a delightful change from the hot, arid desert air. When he awoke, shortly after noon, he could see in the distance the top of Mount Issa, one of the highest mountains in the Saharan Atlas range. They could drive faster now, and at this rate they would reach Bechar before dusk.

A few hours later the road took them to within hiking distance of the Moroccan frontier and the small Moroccan enclave of Figuig. Here the rocky highlands to the north would give way to the flat and level *hammada* that would extend all the way to Tindouf and beyond. But they had made good time, and before long signs announcing the approach to Bechar began to be seen along the road.

Bechar was known primarily for its military history – during its colonial days it was the site of an outpost of the French Foreign Legion. More recently it was one of the prizes Morocco sought in the 1963 Sand War. To fend off any similar Moroccan campaign it was now the location of a major military base.

"We need to be careful when we go past Bechar," the man in black said to the driver. "We don't want to raise any suspicions."

Moulay nodded. The caravan bypassed the town – and the major military installation – and quickly headed in the direction of Abadla, a town on the *wadi* Saoura, where they would camp for the night. They chose a secluded place a few miles out of town, close to where the N50 highway branched off the N6 highway and would take them the remaining 500 miles to Tindouf.

By the evening of the following day they had reached the outskirts of Tindouf. The Polisario camps were located south of another main Algerian military installation, within a high security zone. Luckily, the Algerian government had been content to allow the Polisario to provide security for its own camps, and by the time the sun set on the fourth day of the caravan's voyage, the trucks finally reached the Polisario security patrol. When the sentry saw the man sitting next to Moulay in the 50th truck he waived the truck through without stopping. Most of the trucks proceeded to the spot in the camp where supplies were unloaded, but the truck that Moulay was driving, and the three trucks that followed him, veered off in the opposite direction --- toward the courtyard behind the headquarters of the Minister of Defense.

Abdelaziz was waiting at the door of the building, and when he saw the headlights of the trucks, walked briskly to the first one.

"Thank you, Moulay, well done," he said after the customary greetings. Then he turned to Moulay's passenger and embraced him warmly.

"Were there any problems?" he asked in a hushed tone.

"None," the man responded, smiling.

Without saying another word, they walked, side by side into the building.

The sacks of rice were carefully unloaded and after a quick inspection the man in black, who had now changed into a military uniform, summoned one of the soldiers and whispered something in his ear. Within a few minutes the four trucks were refueled and began their next journey, to an isolated spot a few miles south of Tindouf where a handful of strange looking objects were unloaded and quickly covered with tarps. There they would wait . . . but not for long.

October 13, 1981. Guelta Zemmour.

It was the first week of October, 1981. A long line of vehicles was slowly inching its way southwest from a starting point slightly south of Tindouf, headlights off, with only the moon and the stars as guides. There were 8 Toyotas with 23 mm machine guns, 2 vehicles equipped with light, shoulder held SAM9 missiles, various vehicles carrying ammunition, fuel and food -- and at the head of the line two tracked lorries and two trucks carrying large objects covered by a tarp. Nearly forty vehicles and two hundred people in all.

The caravan first passed north of Ouad Nassar, then, navigating a path carefully through the acacia trees and bushes that provided cover, it proceeded south of Tifariti and skirted Amgala before stopping 60 miles northeast of Guelta Zemmour, all the while traveling only after dusk. Then the vehicles proceeded south, until they reached a flat area 15 miles northwest of the guelta.

When they reached that spot, a tall man dressed in a military uniform got out of the first vehicle and surveyed the scene.

"Do you think this is a good spot, Moulay?" the man asked his companion.

The driver of the vehicle looked around. There were trees, crevices and hills for cover, and it was probably as close to the guelta as they could get.

"Yes, Brahim, I think it will do," he replied.

They motioned to the others. Soon the vehicles were scattered in the area, covered with tarps and hidden beneath the trees. Then they spread their blankets and sat down to wait.

A little farther to the east Bouhali and the members of the 2nd military region had also been crawling slowly through the desert at night, in small groups, coming from different directions, bringing with them 7 tanks, 30 armored vehicles with cannons, 20 BMP troop carriers, and 30 BTR troop carriers, aiming for a rendezvous with Ayoub's infantry at a point just northeast of the guelta.

They intended to attack Morocco's 4th infantry regiment. The regiment -- one of the larger units containing at least 4,000 soldiers – had been reinforced by two other battalions and was installed in an armed camp built by the Moroccans in a circular complex on a plateau in the guelta overlooking the southern territories, surrounded on three sides by hills. Atop the hills were heavy artillery, pointed at the desert beyond, ready to repel the approach of any attackers.

The plan was to have an elite squadron of Bouhali's men with 3 tanks, 3 troop carriers, 3 BTR troop carriers and two of Ayoub's infantry companies

269

lead an assault on the regiment's command center, while Ghali neutralized any Mirage jets that tried to intervene with his missiles, and forces shelled the Moroccan positions on the hills surrounding the command center with their artillery. They had decided that the elite unit would attack from the north through a ravine called Chalkhat Alban, which was a difficult approach through the hills and a direction that the Moroccans would not expect.

While the assault by the troops from the 2nd and 3rd military regions was going on, the commanders of the 1st and 4th military regions would take up positions in the north and west to intercept any aid coming from Moroccan units stationed near Boucraa or Smara, while Abdelaziz would stand by to coordinate the attack.

They were nearly ready. . .

It was now the morning of October 13, 1981, the time just before dawn. During the previous evening the infantry units had crept close to the hills where Moroccan 120 millimeter mortar installations had been established, carrying their own mortar on their backs. Special units among them had scoured the area for land mines which they carefully removed. The mechanized units had taken positions in crevices in the *wadi* to the east.

After having spent four days in their camp to the northwest of the guelta, Brahim Ghali and his men had also moved during the evening, creeping towards their destination inches at a time, one by one, to eliminate as much noise as possible. He had chosen a spot that would be away from the path of any intervention forces from Smara or Boucraa, within the range of the missiles, and devoid of obstacles. By midnight his troops had reached their goal.

"Moulay, I want the soldiers to place the vehicles carrying the larger missiles over there," Ghali said, pointing to an area close to where they had parked, "and to place the vehicles carrying the machine guns and the lighter missiles in a circle around them. Then I want you and the technicians to assemble and test the launching bases and the controls."

Moulay quickly complied. But when the technicians began to uncover and assemble the objects covered by tarps one of the technicians ran to him.

"There is a problem – the tube through which gas is introduced into the missile system is broken and we don't have a replacement!" he cried.

"Can you fix it?" Moulay said, fear starting to swell in his breast.

"We are trying," the man said nervously.

For what seemed an eternity the technicians frantically searched for a way to fix it. Nothing seemed to work.

Then Moulay's blood froze. He heard the slight buzz of the Moroccans' C-130 Hercules reconnaissance aircraft as it passed above them in the dark. No one moved. But it only passed by once.

It was 4 o'clock in the morning. Soon it would be daylight, and if they didn't have the missile fixed . . .

In desperation he grabbed one of the soldiers.

"I want you to get me a piece of tubing from one of the vehicles . . . any vehicle . . . that would fit this opening," he said, pointing to the opening in the missile,   ". . . and hurry!"

In a few minutes the soldier returned with something in his hand and gave it to him. He said a silent prayer as he pushed it into the opening – it fit! The technicians quickly filled the system with fuel and tested the instruments -- and not a moment too soon!

For no sooner had a sliver of the sun appeared over the horizon then something else appeared in the sky. The Moroccan's reconnaissance aircraft, its silver body illuminated by the sun, had returned. Moulay then asked for the order. Ghali nodded and Moulay quickly adjusted some measurements and pushed a button. On a nearby vehicle, in the semi darkness, one of the technicians adjusted the buttons on a strange looking device with four prongs protruding, each one tipped with three missiles. When he pushed a button a missile ejected with enormous force, nearly pushing him to the ground. Within a few seconds there was an explosion in the sky. The plane had been hit. It sputtered for an instant, then burst into flames and fell to the ground, scattering pieces of metal for nearly a mile.

Miles from where they stood, the guerilla troops, dumbfounded, stopped in their tracks and gazed at the sky. No one had told them that their leaders had been able to acquire a SAM 6 missile system. It had been kept top secret – only the leaders and the few troops trained to use it knew. When they first saw the missile racing towards the sun they thought it was a new Moroccan weapon. But when the reconnaissance aircraft burst into flames, their fear turned to joy. At once a tumultuous cheer surged forth, a cheer that reverberated in the hills and could be heard as far away as the Moroccan command center, as the troops, momentarily forgetting the assault, danced and joyously fired their weapons in the air.

In the midst of the commotion Bouhali, commandeering the troop carriers, raced to the walls of the garrison at top speed, followed by the tanks. The assault was quick and deadly.

The commander of the Moroccons' 4th regiment had been sound asleep when a sound that seemed like a hundred thunder bolts striking a steel wall, coming from all directions, awakened him. Outside his chambers he could already hear the shouts of men clambering in all directions. He quickly dressed and ran to the perimeter of the command center, and with his binoculars scanned the horizon. In the hills, where the heavy artillery had been stationed, flumes of smoke were visible. Hundreds of firecracker like blasts blanketed the sky. Through the smoke and dust he could barely make out the form of incoming vehicles, but the huge craters that had begun to appear around him convinced him that they were carrying more than just housers.

His men were already manning their artillery, firing repeated rounds at the oncoming silhouettes. But the cannons he had so meticulously placed on the hills surrounding the base were silent.

Slowly the rising sun began to lift the canopy of darkness and the commander was able to see what he was up against. What he saw made him stare in amazement. On the horizon, surrounding his garrison in every direction, was the heavy array of the Land Rovers loaded with machine guns that he expected. But interspersed among them was something he did not expect, something the guerillas had never used before, something that would change the dynamics of this, as well as every other future engagement. Tanks. T-55 tanks to be more precise. Tanks that were constantly firing hot balls of fire at his troops, decimating long rows of them with a single blast. And troop carriers and other armored vehicles.

He would need reinforcements, and quickly. He raced to his communications bunker which, thankfully, had been spared bombardment, and reached his commanding officer in Laayoune. Amid the roar that enveloped him he found himself repeating over and over again, "yes, tanks. . . and troop carriers" into the phone, ". . . and something else that was able to shoot down our reconnaissance aircraft." When he was finally convinced that he had been heard he raced again to where his men were quickly loading more ammunition into their weapons. He and his men for hours tried desperately to repel the invaders.

While the battle was raging, from out of nowhere another aircraft appeared. No, two. Mirage jets from the Moroccan base at Laayoune. Streaking through the sky at supersonic speeds they began to bombard the fighters and whatever other guerilla targets they detected before disappearing over the horizon. But instead of attempting to flee, the Polisario forces continued their advance. When they circled back for another attack a streak of silver followed them. There was an explosion, and one of the jets began to waver, smoke oozing from its tail, before disappearing over the crest of a hill on the far horizon. When the jet's mate returned a few minutes later to revenge its partner, it, too, was quickly blown out of the sky.

The roar that accompanied the initial invasion of tanks and troop carriers was deafening. By the time the Mirage jets appeared, Bouhali and the forces that mounted the initial attack had begun to infiltrate the command center, and he returned to the troops he had left behind at Chelkhat Alban to lead them on attacks on the other Moroccan positions. Throughout the day Bouhali and his troops continued their assaults on the Moroccans' defensive lines with their heavy artillery, while Ayoub and his infantry accompanied them, fighting the Moroccans in hand to hand combat through a thick cloud of smoke and shattering debris, under a hail of bullets and flying missiles.

By 3 p.m. the guerillas had been able to penetrate the Moroccans' positions in the east and were in control of the area, forcing the Moroccan troops to retreat to the hills west of the guelta. The guerilla troops then continued to fight Moroccan forces along the western perimeter until nightfall. The evening was spent burying the dead, caring for the wounded, and repairing, as best they could, the weapons that had been damaged in the onslaught. Except for the Moroccan prisoners of war, none of the soldiers on either side had much time for sleep.

By nightfall of the first day the guerillas had occupied the only trail through the western hills, to block any means of escape. The commander of the Moroccans' 4th regiment had taken refuge on one of these hills. During the night he lowered his Land Rover by ropes over the far side of the hill, and raced towards Boucraa. In the morning, some of his soldiers followed suit, escaping on foot over the hills and into the desert. However, most of his soldiers remained and grouped themselves in the western hills, putting up stiff resistance. But by 11 o'clock in the morning they found themselves overcome, and scattered. Some tried to find refuge farther in the hills. Others escaped over the hills to the northwest to Boucraa on foot, leaving behind their cars and other vehicles. Later that day some of the Polisario infantry chased after them. For 11 days guerillas continued to pursue and capture Moroccan soldiers wandering in the desert – totaling more than two hundred forty, including three pilots.

By the third day scouts had warned the Polisario commanders of an approaching Moroccan relief unit that had departed their base near Boucraa and were now racing through the *wadi* towards them. So, with an entourage of over 200 prisoners and as much of the Moroccan equipment as they could load onto their trucks and other vehicles, Bouhali and Ayoub retreated with their troops into the hills surrounding the guelta, allowing the Moroccan reinforcements to approach to within 20 miles of the base.

However, before the Moroccans reached the guelta, they were attacked by infantry from the 1st and 4th military regions, who shelled their troops for another four days. The battle continued. By the tenth day the troops in the hills had shot down two more Moroccan aircraft, a Northrop F-5E jet and a Puma helicopter, and what was left of the Moroccan forces evaporated into the desert.

. . . and what was to become one of the most famous battles of the war passed into history.

The morning following the last day of the battle the Moroccans issued an alarming press release claiming that two of their Mirage jets, their Hercules 130 reconnaissance plane, and two other aircraft had been shot down near Guelta Zemmour by attackers using sophisticated Soviet made SAM 6 missiles – missiles which were too sophisticated for the guerillas to master and could only have been used by Cubans, Eastern Europeans or other foreigners helping them.

October 13, 1981. Madrid.

While the battle was raging at Guelta Zemmour, back in Madrid Elena was seated at an ornately decorated table listening to the polite conversation that surrounded her and trying not to reveal her boredom.

"I understand the Prince will be attending the horse show in Madrid this year," the young gentleman to her right was saying. "You know, of course, Donna Cartenas, that my horse will be competing. I hope you and your family will be able to join us." He smiled and looked at Elena.

"What an excellent idea!" her mother exclaimed. "Why we would love to

273

join you, wouldn't we, Elena," she added, also looking in Elena's direction.

Elena knew what her mother was up to. She was getting dangerously close to the age when finding a husband would be difficult, and for the past year her mother had paraded no fewer than six eligible bachelors before her. But somehow she had found it difficult to be interested in their vapid chatter about meaningless things. And the life that was planned for her – a life of domesticity with children and china and endless long, boring dinner parties – had suddenly felt like a sentence to life in prison.

"Miguel, I was wondering what your opinion is about women using contraceptives?" she asked, a seemingly innocent expression on her face.

The room suddenly became silent. Her mother shot her a worried look, and their guest, Don Miguel de Cardozo, shifted slightly in his seat.

"Well, Senorita Cardenas, I of course support the position of the Pope on this matter. The use of contraceptives frustrates the natural function of the act by which God creates the human race, and is an affront to Him," he said, proudly. "After all, bearing children is a woman's most blessed vocation."

"So, you don't think a woman should have the right to limit the number of children she has?" Elena asked, sweetly, ignoring the panicked look on her mother's face.

"I believe a woman's place is in the home caring for the children God gives her . . ." he replied, a slight edge in his voice.

"Oh, so you don't think women should be able to have a profession . . . to be lawyers or judges . . . or a member of the Cabinet?"

At the last question he laughed, settled back into his seat, and with a smile on his face, responded, "I know women in other countries have forced their government to give them these rights, but I think they will soon find that women are unsuited for such professions. They are too emotional. It takes a steady hand . . . and an equally steady mind to make wise decisions about laws and politics."

"Like the decisions that gave Spanish Sahara to the Moroccans and Mauritanians?" Elena retorted, sweetly.

"Elena!" her mother shouted, "That is enough!"

But their guest silenced her with a wave of his hand. "Let her ask her questions," he said, suddenly turning serious.

Turning to her with a cool, steady gaze, he said, "Senorita Cardenas, I believe that our government made the decision that was in the best interests of its citizens. After all, why should we care about what happens to a few thousand nomads in the desert a thousand miles away?" Then he turned to his host.

"Don Cartenas, I am sure you will agree with me that those nomads would be incapable of governing the territory wisely . . . they are nothing but a bunch of terrorists . . . why for years they have been attacking our vessels peacefully fishing in the waters off Dakhla! Three years ago they boarded a Spanish fishing boat, the Saa, and abducted three of the crew. They only released them when the Canaries fishermen's union intervened. Then they boarded another boat, Las Palomas, and seized eight of its crew. And this was only the beginning . . . eight more Spanish fishing boats came under fire that year. And just this past year they boarded three more vessels and took their crews prisoner. The government was finally forced to declare its support for their "right to self determination" to stop the attacks and get the release of our seamen."

Elena smiled when she thought of the words Salek had spoken 'They would get their rights . . . but not by asking nicely!'

"So, you don't believe that they have a right to self determination, Miguel?" she asked.

Miguel looked again in her direction with eyes that had turned to steel. "I believe that their so-called 'rights' are not what is important. What is important is that our government act in the best interests of its citizens," he said, in a low, serious voice.

"Even if it means reneging on our promises and ignoring their rights under international law?" she asked, equally serious.

The man smiled again and turned to his host. "Do you see what I mean, Don Cartenas?" he said, "Women are incapable of understanding the intricacies of international politics!" Then, turning to Elena once again, in a paternalistic tone, he said, "You should not worry about such matters, Senorita. In the real world it is not always possible to adhere to lofty principles. Sometimes sacrifices have to be made, as it was in the case of our former colony."

After their guest had departed that evening, Elena's mother turned to her, an exasperated look on her face.

"I simply cannot understand what has gotten into you," she said, shaking her head. "Insulting our guest that way. You have rejected all the young men we have arranged for you to meet." Then she gave her a stern look. "Don't you want to find a husband . . . to get married . . . to have a family?"

Her mother must have continued talking for at least ten minutes. But Elena heard none of it. All she could think of were the words he had uttered -- "it is not always possible to adhere to lofty principles" – as if that excuse could justify any action, no matter how despicable. She had tried for years to put the events of the past behind her and to go on with her life. But it was no use. She could not forget that her government had completely ignored the legal rights of the people of Spanish Sahara – worse, that it had betrayed them. And as far as the rest of the world was concerned, where were the cries of injustice? None of the big powers had lifted a finger to enforce their rights, despite the lip service they always gave to the 'rule of law' and 'the right to self determination.' And the international lawyers and professors were no better. There was one – Thomas Franck – who had condemned Morocco's actions, but he seemed to be a lone voice among a herd of sycophants. Well, if that is what realpolitik is, it can proceed without me – I refuse to be coopted into the system, she thought.

"Its that Spanish Sahara business, isn't it --- and that boy!" her mother exclaimed in an irritated voice.

275

Her father, who had been listening quietly to the tirade, turned to face his daughter.

"Elena, don't throw your future away on a dream," he said somberly, "I know that what happened in the territory hurt you greatly – I wasn't too pleased about it myself – neither was Colonel Salazar and De Viguri, but there is nothing you can do to change things. We tried a couple of years ago to have the Cortes revoke the Madrid Accords, but it was useless." His mind traveled back to the hearings on the Madrid accords that were held by the Congress of Deputies in 1978, when the three of them had spoken out against the government's Saharan policy. Then he looked at his daughter, his eyes clouded by sadness. "The Sahrawis cannot win this battle. The major powers will not let them. Oh, they can win a few skirmishes and humiliate Hassan, but as long as he has the backing of the United States and France there is nothing any one of us can do. Even if they win on the battlefield, they couldn't win at the UN. The cards are simply stacked against them."

Elena listened patiently, but the more he talked the angrier she got. Perhaps it was the romantic in her. Perhaps it was Salek. But the more that people told her that she was powerless to change the course of events in the world -- the more that people told her that she could not change the destiny of people who had every principle of justice and international law on their side -- the more determined she was to fight for them.

That evening she lay quietly in her bed, her thoughts swirling. But she couldn't sleep. For the next week she moved zombie-like through her chores, never a smile on her face. Then one day, shortly before dawn, she packed her belongings, left a note for her parents, and took a taxi to the airport. Before boarding the plane she turned to take one last look at her country, at the life she would be leaving behind. Then she turned and quietly passed through the door.

October 24 , 1981. Tindouf.

Salek lay on a cot in the stucco building that served as the camp's hospital drifting in an out of consciousness, reliving the moment the troops had fired at the plane and he saw it hurl to the ground in a ball of fire, the moment he had advanced with the troops towards the northeast perimeter, the moment he heard the bomb blast . . .

"Take cover!" he yelled as he struggled to sit up.

A strong arm restrained him. "Relax, Salek, it is all over," he said as he gently pushed him back.

Salek, jolted back to consciousness, looked around him. He was in a room with stucco walls. He remembered the room . . . yes, it was part of the building used in the camps to care for the wounded. He had been wounded at Guelta and had been brought to Tindouf. . . and standing next to his cot was Hamed.

"How are you feeling?" his visitor said, smiling.

Hamed looked at him. Salek was still the same Salek, if somewhat thinner and a little worse for wear. Hamed had heard that after clinging to life by a thread after the recent assault on Guelta he had gradually recovered at Tindouf -- no doubt due to Sidimi's constant attention. Hamed had been with the troops for months, unable to see him, and now he was overjoyed to have the chance. Salek warmly grabbed his hand and tried to sit up, but a sharp pain in his chest forced him down.

"You are still pretty weak. Sidi had to operate to remove the piece of metal that had lodged near your heart. She gave you some morphine to relieve the pain," Hamed said, matter-of-factly. "So, you have been drifting in and out of consciousness for a while." Then he smiled. "But you are as strong as a camel, you will recover."

"Can you tell me . . . was it a success?" he asked his visitor, trying to hide his anxiousness to hear what happened at Guelta after he was wounded.

Hamed bent over him. "It was a great success! The Moroccan garrison at Guelta is gone . . . wiped out . . . as well as a number of their jets and aircraft . . . and . . . best of all . . . we won't have to worry about that reconnaissance plane anymore!" he said smiling.

Salek began to relax a little, but when he once more tried to sit up the pain in his chest forced him again to lie down.

"It will be a while before you will be up and about," Hamed said, placing his hand on Salek's shoulder, "You have to give that wound some time to heal! And I don't think you will have too much of a problem occupying your time," he added, a mischievous note entering his voice.

When his visitor had departed he closed his eyes again, the hole in his chest beginning to ache. And soon, tired from the exertion, he fell into a deep sleep.

That evening as he lay on the cot in the hospital, eyes closed, trying desperately to banish the sounds and smells of the battlefield from his mind, a figure appeared. She walked silently to where he lay and searched his body with fearful eyes. Finally she sighed a long, deep sigh of relief. "I was worried about you," she started to say, her words faltering, "I was afraid you had been seriously hurt." She quickly averted her eyes.

The sound of her voice slowly brought his mind back. He looked at the figure as if he had seen a ghost, for that was what she had been, a spirit wafting through his dreams. Was he dreaming now, he wondered? He reached out his hand to touch her and felt warm skin at his fingertips. He slumped back on his blanket, too astonished to speak.

Elena!

October 25, 1981. Elena.

When Salek finally got over his shock at seeing her, he bombarded her with questions. When did she get to Tindouf? How did she get there? What was she doing there? She told him that she had traveled to Algiers and had finally persuaded the Algerian Red Crescent to allow her to join some volunteers coming to Tindouf with supplies – that she couldn't stand by and watch the

277

fighting in the Sahara without doing something to help. They were glad to find someone who spoke fluent Spanish to join them.

"You know, Salek, several of the officials from the territory have spoken out against the Madrid Accords. The war has become an embarrassment for Juan Carlos. Salazar and my father have been urging the government to come to your aid, but so far no luck," she said, shrugging her shoulders.

"But at least they have recognized our right to self determination," he replied.

"Yes," she said, mischievously, "but not because you asked nicely!"

Salek started to laugh, ignoring the pain it caused in his chest.

"And the other countries?" he finally asked. "We don't get much news in the front lines."

Elena turned away. It had been frustrating to read the newspaper articles and to hear the speeches concerning the war in the Sahara. "It's the same old story," she began, slowly. "France has been against you from the start. My father says the French never wanted to see a non-Francophone territory in the region . . . that they had designs on the Spanish colony as far back as the turn of the century. He thinks that they were behind Hassan's plot to annex the territory. . . that Hassan would never have tried it without their encouragement. But I think its because of Algeria. France has never forgiven the Algerians for tossing them out of the country, and you, in their eyes are just an extension of the regime. They have managed to block everything at the United Nations. . . and now they are trying to block everything at the OAU."

"And the Americans?" he asked pensively. "I still cannot understand how a country that could produce an Abraham Lincoln. . . a John F. Kennedy. . . could just turn its eyes from this injustice."

A sadness seemed to come over him.

"It's still the same old story. . . the 'Cold War.' It permeates everything. You are aligned with Algeria. Algeria receives weapons from the Soviet Union. Ipso facto, all of you must be communists . . . or worse, terrorists," she said slowly.

"Well, I guess we are in good company," he said ruefully, shrugging his shoulders. "I hear that they also consider Nelson Mandela at the ANC a terrorist . . . and it is ironic, isn't it, that the reason why the Spanish Socialist Party has not endorsed our movement is because we are not 'communist' enough?" He laughed. But there was bitterness in his voice. Then he looked at her and smiled. "Another lesson in realpolitik!"

She decided to change the subject. "You know, this battle of yours at Guelta Zemmour has made headlines in all the European papers. My father was astonished . . . he told me that it was a battle that will be mentioned in army textbooks for years to come. No one imagined that you could have had the expertise to use those missiles . . ."

"Yes," he smiled, his mood beginning to lighten. "They all think that we are a bunch of ignorant camel herders without a brain in our heads manipulated by the Algerians. I've heard it all before."

She laughed and drew closer to him. "Well, I know it is not true," she whispered in his ear.

He looked into her eyes and wanted to say something, but the words wouldn't come out. After a moment, she drew back and turned to where a package leant against the wall.

When she returned to his side she was carrying a large object covered by a canvass cloth. She gently removed the cloth and placed the object at his side.

"I saved this for the time I would see you again," she said, quietly, as he took Esmeralda in his arms.

October 25, 1981. Esmeralda.

Salek lay on his blanket in the tiny hospital, the guitar next to him. The sun had set hours ago leaving only the stars to illuminate the darkness. There was no electricity, only a few forlorn kerosene lamps to light a path through the camp. It was the waning days of autumn and already the evening air had a certain crispness to it. During the long, hot, summer days the life of the camp had been turned upside down. The residents would escape the heat of the day by nestling in their tents and emerge from their cocoons only after the setting of the sun had cooled the sand under their feet. It was then that that they would gather to chat, spreading blankets on the sand outside their tents, the women scurrying to prepare the evening meal in what served as makeshift kitchens. By 10 o'clock in the evening plates of food would be spread on the blankets – the ubiquitous rice or couscous donated from afar, mixed with whatever supplies had reached them that day. If they were lucky – or if it was a grand occasion like a wedding – one of the few goats or sheep they possessed would be slaughtered and bits of fresh meat would be mixed with the concoction and offered to an assortment of guests. There they would sit for hours discussing the events of the day, which during these times meant the events on the battlefield, until the wee hours of the morning. But now it was nearly winter and the long, leisurely soirees of the summer had been put aside for more mundane evenings in the tents and the few stucco buildings that had been built to complement them. It was late in the evening and long ago the women had washed the dinner utensils and put the children to sleep, and but for the rustling of an occasional sheep or camel, not a sound could be heard.

In the stillness his fingers reached out to touch the guitar, tenderly, as if he were greeting an old friend. They were not the same fingers that had played it so joyously in El Ayoun, nor was he the same boy who had eagerly joined the call to fight for his country a few short years ago. The baby fat had disappeared from his face, to be replaced by the craggy features of one who had spent months in the desert battered by the sun and wind. And the changes in his body reflected the changes in his soul. He had killed, and had watched his friends be killed. He had heard of friends and neighbors in El Ayoun carted off to prisons in Morocco. He had heard rumors of whole families who had simply disappeared. Including his own.

He took the guitar in his hands and slowly managed the few steps that would take him out of the stucco building into the night air. A cool breeze was whistling through the camp and brushed against his cheek. He crouched on a mound of sand and began to play, the notes carried by the wind.

The strumming on his guitar could be heard throughout the camp, like some eerie dream penetrating the stillness, and one by one the inhabitants of the camp awoke from their slumbers and, still half asleep, strained their ears to hear the tune. As he played he conjured up memories of days gone past, memories of loved ones left behind, of loved ones dead. Elena was the first to hear it. It was the tune that he had played in El Ayoun, the first tune she had heard him play, the tune that had drawn her to him. In the tent she shared with the other foreign aid workers she lay on a blanket remembering that day, and soon every day they had spent together flashed through her mind in a flood of joyful memories. Then a sadness came over her and she wondered whether she would ever enjoy such days again. Sidimi, unable to sleep, had been wrapping bandages on the other side of the hospital when she was surprised by what seemed to be chords of music intertwined in the whistling of the wind. Yes, she was not mistaken, it was music, the notes of a guitar somewhere in the distance. Music! It seemed an eternity since she had heard music. She thought of the times she had listened to her uncle's radio, at the broadcasts from Spain, at the notes that had seemed to brighten even her darkest moods. Her thoughts wandered to the people she had left behind in El Ayoun – her mother, her two small children, her baby only a few months' old. She tried to imagine what they would be doing at this moment. Sleeping? Reading? Her baby would no longer be a baby. She would be six years old by this time. What would she know of her mother? What would they tell her? A moan of the patient who lay in a cot beside her brought her thoughts back to her surroundings. Would she ever again enjoy such moments of pleasure? Her thoughts continued in a reverie that for one brief moment cancelled the pain and suffering that surrounded her in the hospital ward. Soukeina also heard the music. She lay in her tent, her thoughts escaping to the past, thinking about her mother and great-grandfather, and wondering whether she would ever see them again. Then her thoughts turned to her aunt, buried in the sand with so many others at Mudraiga, and for the first time since she arrived in the camps she cried.

After a few moments Salek stopped playing and sat for a long time thinking, thinking about the plans he had had to be a musician, the life he had envisaged, a life he knew he would never have. Then his thoughts turned to Elena – Elena who had become the one bright spot in his life – and he wondered what would happen at the end of the war. But all this thinking is nonsense, he told himself. He had might as well wonder whether the seas would dry up or whether people would ever learn to live in harmony. We are all pawns of destiny, enslaved by the times in which we live. There was only one purpose to his life, one goal that gave his life meaning, to fight for the freedom of his country.

He thought of a speech he once heard. The man had warned "A revolution is coming – a revolution which will be peaceful if we are wise enough, compassionate if we care enough, successful if we are fortunate enough – but a revolution which is coming whether we will it or not. We can affect its character; we cannot alter its inevitability." What was he referring to? The revolution that would free all people from the scourge of discrimination because of race or religion? Or the revolution that would free all people from the scourge of tyrannical rulers? Or was he referring to the revolution that would finally force governments to adhere to the principles of democracy and self determination that they espouse so freely in speeches and so rarely in practice? Or aren't they all part of the same revolution?

He wished he could have been there to ask Robert Kennedy what he meant.

And with that thought he gathered up the guitar and entered the building for the night.

November 10, 1981. The King.

Back in his palace in Rabat, the King slammed the phone down and fumed. He had just finished another exasperating call with Dlimi. The man was either stupid or incompetent. The guerilla onslaught at Guelta Zemmour – and the weapons they had acquired -- had taken him completely by surprise, and he had no new strategies to offer. He had also finished a heated exchange with the commander of the air force in Rabat. He had finally caved in to Dlimi's plea to loosen his reins on their activities, but it didn't seem to help. They were now refusing to have their planes used for target practice. Their pilots did not have training in how to outmaneuver such sophisticated weapons he had been told. They would keep them in their hangers – or fly high enough to be out of range -- until Dlimi found a way to neutralize their new missiles.

And his prize C-130 reconnaissance aircraft had been blown to smithereens. So, after all the strings he had pulled to get the sophisticated Mirage jets from France he would be left without adequate air reconnaissance. Without such support the other surveillance and radar equipment he had gotten from the Americans would be of little use and his troops would remain easy prey for the guerillas. And although Dlimi had finally been able to wrest the Lengueb pass from the guerillas and impede their access to the Kingdom from the Zini mountain range, he still had not been able to prevent all attacks within Morocco. The guerillas were proving to be as slippery as eels, he thought, as he downed another scotch.

Several hundred miles away, a glum looking commander of the armed forces was also sitting in his office, deep in thought. He glanced at the new stars on his shoulder – stars that had required years of sweat and blood – and wondered how long they would remain there, or, indeed, how long he would be alive if he didn't do something quickly to counter the guerillas' advances. The wall . . . . the barrier that was supposed to deter their attacks once and for all . . . was taking forever to build, and in the mean time everything outside the wall was vulnerable. The guerillas were determined . . . and smart, he thought grudgingly. The attack at Guelta had been masterfully planned and executed – one that had caused even seasoned warriors at the Pentagon to pay homage, not to mention the press, which was totally agog at the news. So the Algerians had provided them with tanks at last, he mused. They were obviously willing to escalate the war. But where on earth did they get SAM 6 anti aircraft missiles? His own army didn't have them and none of his soldiers had been trained to use them. With those new weapons in their arsenal it had become far too risky to maintain outposts in the eastern part of the territory, outside the wall. So, a few days ago, he had informed the King that he would not attempt to reoccupy Guelta Zemmour. Two days later he had evacuated the 1500 troops at Bir Enzaren, 60 miles northeast of Dakhla.

These bases had been the only Moroccan positions in the eastern part of the territory. Now the only garrisons left were those behind the berm and the units stationed along the coastal towns -- Laayoune, Boujdour, Dakhla and Argoub. The vast expanse of desert beyond these towns – five sixth of the territory -- was left to the guerillas. He would have to get equipment to counter their tanks and new weapons -- and fast, before they grew any stronger.

And by the end of the day the two men, miles apart, had both come to the same conclusion: they would go once more to the Americans.

November 20, 1981. Reagan.

Reagan was a cowboy, and proud of it. His psyche was inextricably bound to the handful of movie roles in which he played one, and to the persona created by such models of American strength, tenacity and courage as John Wayne. He viewed events in the world through an actor's eyes, as one long drawn out grade B movie, with him in the starring role. For him foreign policy was easy – the good guys wore white hats and the bad guys black. And King Hassan of Morocco wore a white hat.

He had been the President of the United States for only a month when he had unveiled his foreign policy agenda. He believed that his predecessor's concern for human rights had strained relations with America's staunch allies and had weakened their ability to subdue threatening elements within their borders. He would have none of that.

It was now the third week of November in the first year of his presidency, only a few weeks after the debacle at Guelta Zemmour. The director of the CIA, William Casey, had personally delivered to him an urgent request for support from the King of Morocco. As he surveyed the group of advisors around the conference table, he was satisfied that they shared his philosophy. Grabbing a jelly bean from one of the bowls that always adorned the table, he began to speak.

"Gentlemen, I want your thoughts on how to proceed with the Morocco situation." One by one they spoke. The CIA, the Pentagon, the State Department had all agreed that they had underestimated the tenacity of the guerillas, and Algeria's resolve to support them. The Mauritanian fiasco had greatly humiliated d'Estaing, and it was unlikely that he would risk another overt incursion into the battle. The prolongation of the war – now in its sixth year -- had greatly weakened the King. The Moroccans had been unable to stop the rebels' incursions into Morocco itself, let alone defeat them in the Sahara, despite the significant aid that Ford and Carter – not to mention d'Estaing -- had given the regime. The King had nearly bankrupted the country, and had been forced to turn to Saudi Arabia and the other Gulf states for the funds to finance the thousands of troops he had stationed in the Sahara, and this new gambit – building a wall in the desert -- was taking forever to complete. Meanwhile, the citizens were growing restless.

As soon as he had taken office, Reagan had greatly increased the military assistance given to the King, and had removed any obstacles to its use in the Sahara, including any requirement that the aide be tied to Hassan's cooperation with attempts by the international community to find a political solution to the crisis. But this seemed insufficient to turn the tide of the war. And now there was this debacle at Guelta Zemmour and Hassan had come running to the White House for more aid. Unless the U.S. stepped up the aid that it provided there was a good chance that the regime would fall.

After all of them had had their say the room became silent. Finally, one of the advisors, a military man with stars on his shoulder, spoke up. "As you know, in order to deter the guerilla raids the Moroccans have built a small dirt wall beginning slightly north of Smara enclosing within it Smara as well as Boujdour, Laayoune and the Boucraa mines. It has been tough going . . . the guerillas have been putting up stiff resistance . . . but at least the guerillas have been forced to choose other targets . . . and I believe they are now thinking of erecting a wall in other areas of the territory. They have also gotten some Mirage jets from France, and that has allowed them to improve their air capabilities. They have begun to put these jets to good use – I understand they were able to inflict heavy casualties on guerilla forces in the previous battle at Guelta Zemmour in March. But now that the guerillas have acquired SAM 6 missiles . . . well . . . it's a new ballgame."

"Don't forget the tanks," spoke up another, "They have begun to use T-55 tanks. This alters the dynamics of the war considerably."

A man at the far end of the table interjected a question. "Does anyone know where they got these tanks and missiles from? The Soviets? The Cubans?"

The man with stars on his shoulder shook his head. "No. We think they got the tanks from the Algerians. So far, there are no indications that they are getting any direct military assistance from the Soviets or Castro. As for the missiles . . . we have no idea. We have been carefully monitoring the routes through Algeria, Mauritania and Mali, for any movement of weapons and have turned up nothing."

"Well, the important thing is that they have them," interjected the President. "So, do you advise stepping up our military sales to Morocco?"

The military man hesitated for a moment. "Yes, I think we will have to increase our military aid. But in addition to the weapons they have requested there is something else that we might suggest . . . something that we have been developing that might enable them to use their air power more effectively

283

. . . to be able to destroy their troops without fear of their SAM 6 missiles.
. . . a new weapon that we have been testing for a while, and that seems to be
very effective."

The President was intrigued. "And do you think this new weapon will
enable them to eliminate the guerilla threat?"

The military man hesitated for a moment. "It is not the whole solution, but
it will help!" he finally replied.

The room became quiet. Then a young man at the end of the table cleared
his throat to speak. He had waited dutifully while those who were senior
to him had their chance. Now it would be his turn. Unlike Kissinger, who
was ever the pragmatist, he believed that the future of a country depended
upon its ideals, and he was willing to fight for his. But his ideals were not
the murky hypocritical ideals of the far left, but rather the conviction that the
United States must always keep itself strong and be prepared to support its
allies whatever the cost and whatever means are employed to do it, if it is to
survive. The ends would justify the means.

The President was interested in what he would say. He was a useful ally, if
a little on the cocky side. Harvard's answer to Yale's Bill Buckley – only more
so. With strong connections to AIPEC and the Jewish community and even
stronger connections to Israel.

"Mr. President," he said, "I am not a military man, but it seems to me that
just giving them more sophisticated military equipment is not enough. We
need to teach them how to use this equipment to their best advantage, and
have the CIA and Pentagon help them with intelligence operations. Also, it
wouldn't be a bad idea to ask some of our allies to help them devise a better
military strategy then just sitting on their duffs in the desert waiting for the
rebels to strike, which is apparently how Hassan is conducting the war. And
if all else fails, we shouldn't hesitate to place some "advisors" on the ground in
the Sahara."

The President recoiled somewhat at the last suggestion. "You know, of
course, that we are prevented by law from sending troops to fight in the
Sahara."

"Yes, I know." he replied, "that's why I used the term 'advisors.'. . . and I
think before we rush into anything we should send a high level team to assess
the situation."

The room had become silent. The President smiled and considered this
last interjection for a moment and then, after devouring one last jelly bean,
thanked the participants for attending and adjourned the conference.

November 25, 1981. The Tourist.

As the stern-faced official from the Department of Defense took off in
a helicopter in the early hours of November 25th to survey the territory of
Western Sahara, he didn't know quite what to expect. He had been rushed
there, with no fewer than 23 other officials from the State Department, the

Pentagon, and the CIA, to get a first hand impression of the problems that had led to the debacle at Guelta Zemmour the previous month.

The King had lost no time running to the President for help. The guerillas' acquisition of tanks was a major escalation in the war. But armored vehicles are a two edged sword. Sure, they might enable them to blast through Hassan's defenses, but will they be able to disappear quickly into the desert once they have? With Land Rovers, maybe, but with tanks? The American shook his head. They had made themselves vulnerable to commando type search and destroy operations. No, it was the SAM 6 missiles – the missiles which had effectively grounded the Moroccan air force – that was the greatest threat. No one knew where these missiles came from, and Hassan was arguing that they were being used by Cuban or East European mercenaries, not Sahrawis. . . proof that the communists were behind the plot.

Hassan's accusations had sent shockwaves through the Pentagon elite. According to one senior official, the Moroccans "ran to us shouting for help." Help that the President was all too willing to provide.

The shuttling between Washington and Rabat began to take on a frantic undertone. Vernon Walters flew to Rabat for a meeting with Hassan on October 29. On November 5, Reagan's new ambassador to Morocco, Joseph Vernon Reed, took pains to assure the King that the United States was a "true friend." And like any true friend it would be "helpful."

And now he, plus a twenty three strong delegation of other officials, had begun a tour of Western Sahara to assess the Moroccan forces' requirements.

Sitting next to him in the helicopter, the person in charge of the Moroccan army, General Ahmed Dlimi, explained the situation.

"We have started to build a wall to protect the major towns in the territory from guerilla assaults. There, if you look to your right you can see where it starts." He then pointed to an area near the horizon where a small embankment was visible. "Despite constant attacks from the guerillas we have been able to extend the wall past Smara to Boujdour and the coast. We believe that the wall will prevent the guerillas from engaging in surprise, hit and run, attacks within the enclosed area, and that will permit us to reopen the Boucraa mine and establish better control over the main settlements."

The American looked to where he had pointed. There appeared to be a bump in the sand and gravel – a long bump extending for miles in either direction.

"The people in the settlements . . . do any of them support the guerillas?" he asked, somewhat innocently. The briefing papers he had received from the CIA had told him that support for the Moroccans was strong among the locals. His experience in Vietnam as a member of the Marine Force Reconnaissance team that initiated "Operation Stingray" -- small unit attacks behind enemy lines -- told him that the support of the civilian population was crucial in any effort to repel a guerilla insurgency.

Dlimi paused before responding. "The government in the territory is composed primarily of Sahrawis themselves who are fully supportive of their

285

integration with Morocco," he finally said. He chose to leave out the fact that the Moroccans had had to post guards to ensure that no Sahrawis could leave their enclaves. He wondered what the official sitting next to him would say if he knew that the Mayor of Smara and hundreds of its citizens had chosen to flee the town and join the camps in Tindouf in 1979 when the guerillas attacked. He was glad when his guest changed the subject.

"I hope to see this area – Guelta Zemmour – where the attack occurred," the American said, peering out the window at the vast expanse of empty land that reached to the horizon.

"That would not be advisable," Dlimi responded quickly. "The guerillas have taken over that area and with their SAM 6 missiles they could down our helicopter. It is best that I take you back to our positions farther north." He shouted something to the pilot and the helicopter swerved in a circle heading north.

"But General Dlimi," the American began to protest, "I haven't seen more than a few miles of the territory!"

"We'll arrange to take you later to Dakhla on another route," Dlimi responded, trying to disguise his discomfort with a smile. "In the meantime I can show you our defenses along the Zini perimeter and the Lengueb pass through the hills north of the Ouarkziz escarpment that we have finally been able to wrest from the guerillas."

With a lot of political pressure on Algeria and the guerillas from the United States, he thought to himself. "But is there some reason why we can't go there now?" he asked. *There is something he is not telling me*, he thought.

Dlimi smiled again. He had might as well know the truth. "The area between Boujdour and Dakhla is dangerous. The guerillas have been known to infiltrate it. Even the sea around Dakhla is dangerous. The guerillas have launched attacks on Spanish fishing vessels near Dakhla."

"You mean they are able to penetrate the territory as far as the Atlantic ocean? Why can't you stop them?" his passenger asked somewhat incredulously. "You far outnumber them in troops . . ."

Before he could finish, Dlimi interrupted. "They know the desert better than we do and are able to conduct surprise attacks and vanish into the desert before our troops can intercept them."

The American pondered this for a moment. "And there is no way you can tell where their positions are located. I mean, they have to be able to establish bases of operation somewhere?"

Dlimi, wishing he could change the subject once more, forced a reply. "Oh, some times we are able to listen in on their communications and discover where they are hiding, but they move constantly, and our pilots refuse to fly low enough to bomb them accurately – especially now that they have the SAM 6 missiles. So if they go out to intercept them at all, they simply dump their bombs as quickly as possible and return to base."

The American paused a long time before speaking again. He had always believed that only warriors defeat other warriors – and if the members of the armed forces don't have the will to fight, no insertion of weapons or intelligence will help.

"Tell me about the insurgents, General. I have been led to believe that this war is really between Morocco and Algeria. Is that true?"

Dlimi paused before responding. When he did, his words were carefully measured. "The guerillas would not have been able to prolong the war as long as they have without the arms and assistance they have received from Algeria."

"But the fighting – are Algerian troops involved in the fighting? Have the Cubans and the East Germans become involved?" he insisted.

Dlimi paused again. "That is what the King believes."

"And you?"

Dlimi looked at his guest and smiled. His mouth said "I believe what the King believes" but his eyes said something else.

The American stared at him for a moment. Then he slumped back in his seat. When he spoke again his voice was calm. "You say that the guerillas are able to come and go at will through the majority of the territory?"

Dlimi turned away. "Yes", is all he said.

When the official from the Department of Defense returned to Washington he immediately proposed training elite Moroccan troops to launch mobile commando style operations beyond the defense perimeters to force Polisario onto the defensive.

And within days elite U.S. commandos began to be assembled in barracks across the United States for deployment overseas.

But privately he had begun to wonder whether anything the U.S. could muster would enable Hassan to win this war.

CHAPTER 9
1982

By the time the official from the Department of Defense had surveyed the territory, despite constant attacks by the guerillas, the berm had been extended to 250 miles and had reached as far as Boujdour. It enclosed about one sixth of Western Sahara's total land area, all of the so-called "useful triangle" of the territory, and all the major towns except for Dakhla and its surroundings.

But the rest of the territory had been totally abandoned to wandering caravans of Polisario troops. The guerillas felt free to use the tarmac roads and did not hesitate to build campfires at night or use the headlights of their vehicles. At times the Moroccans were able to intercept their communications and zero in on the location of their bases. However, the few Moroccan aircraft that would dare to invade their territory on bombing missions were useless at night, and during the day were careful to fly high above the range of their SAM 6 missiles, seldom hitting their targets with their bombs.

Following the ejection of Moroccan troops from Guelta Zemmour and Bir Enzaren in the last few months of 1981 there was a slight lull in major military engagements as the guerillas once again shifted their battles to the halls of the OAU and the UN, and the big powers, behind the scenes, tried to whip Hassan's military apparatus into shape.

And all the while life in the camps went on as usual.

April 26, 1982. Letters.

Soukeina walked with a joyful gait through the tents and mud huts of the camp spreading the news: a relief worker had arrived with another two letters. Ever since residents of the towns and villages of the territory had escaped the onslaught of Moroccan and Mauritanian troops and settled within the confines of camps at Tindouf news of those left behind was sporadic and delivered primarily through letters, or cassettes disguised as music, smuggled into the Canary Islands by the few native traders trusted – or needed -- by the invading armies. These letters and cassettes often found their way – after weeks or some times months – in a circuitous route through the hands of sympathetic Algerian civilians, or the relief workers from the Algerian Red Crescent or the other international groups that provided the camps with the means to lead a meager existence.

As one of the highest ranked camp leaders – and the official responsible for overseeing the food distribution – Soukeina was often the glad recipient of these correspondences, which she would hasten to deliver to their addressees. Some times, as a result of the education courses that had been introduced when they first arrived, the elderly women and men of the camps would proudly read them to an eager audience. But more often Soukeina would need to read them, which she was preparing to do this day, for the letters had been addressed to the elderly matriarchs of the Boukhari and Ould Salek families.

The tent of Embarka Mint Salek was overflowing that day with visitors eager to catch any news of home. As she passed around cups of tea, Soukeina began to read one of the letters, the longer one addressed to Fatma Boukhari.

"My dear sister," she began, *"I hope and pray each day for your health and safety, and for the health and safety of your sons."* Soukeina paused a moment. It was difficult to get news to the people in the territory. Letters addressed to them might land in the hands of the Moroccans, which might lead to their imprisonment – or worse. Fatma's sister did not know that one of her sons had died at Ras el Kamfra. She went on. *"Zemla has been abuzz for a week now over the news about the battle at Guelta."* Soukeina paused to look at the date on the letter. It had been written in October of 1981 and it was now April of 1982. Still, old news is better than no news, she thought. *"The King came on television last night screaming that his "sons" had been brutally attacked by a guerilla force containing communist mercenaries from Eastern Europe and Cuba, with weapons supplied by the Soviet Union. We all had a good laugh. We are all so proud of our sons on the battlefield! Of course, we dare not celebrate. Moroccan police patrol the streets arresting anyone they suspect of collaborating with the Polisario. We try to go about our daily lives but it is like being in a prison camp. How I wish I had taken your advice and escaped when you did! The Moroccans have tried to create the illusion of normalcy by placing puppets in administrative positions. But we ignore them, and after Mohammed Ali Ould Sid el-Bashir defected two years ago with over 700 residents of Smara, they don't even trust their puppets! I wish I had some good news to tell you. If you see Sidimi, please tell her that her daughter is becoming a precocious little six year old and that her mother sends her love. I have lost touch with your cousins in Smara. The Moroccans have prevented us from leaving Laayoune and, as you know, we have been afraid of trying to send letters lest they be intercepted. I have heard rumors that now that they have enclosed Smara and Laayoune behind a wall they may allow us more freedom of movement. If I manage to get any news I will write. Dear Sister, I must end this letter now because Ibrahim is about to leave for Las Palmas. I long to see you again. With all my love. Embarka.*

When she had finished she handed the letter to the elderly lady at her side, who folded it neatly and placed it carefully in a small leather pouch in which she kept her valuables.

Then she opened the other letter. It was short.

"My dear cousin," it began, *"I have tried once again to get some news about your brother and his family. Since they disappeared no one has heard from them and the Moroccan police refuse to give any news about their whereabouts.*

They neither confirm nor deny that they have been arrested. Sahrawis who have managed to be released from Moroccan prisons say they have not heard or seen them. I will keep trying, but I fear the worst. Hundreds of our brothers and sisters – even small children – have been taken by the Moroccans or have simply "disappeared" without a trace, and there are rumors of mass graves in the desert. Be brave, cousin! If I get any news I will smuggle a letter to you somehow. With all my love, Layla."

The tent became as quiet as a cemetery. An ashen faced elderly women, struggling to keep back a tear, reached for the letter, which she placed in a crease in her *mefhla*. The silence persisted for well over a minute. Everyone in the tent had a relative or friend in the territory who had either been imprisoned, killed or simply "disappeared."

Finally, a young woman spoke up. "I have heard a rumor that our leaders have been meeting secretly with the Moroccans . . . is that true?"

All eyes turned to Soukeina. Soukeina hesitated for a moment.

"I have been told that the Algerian Minister of Foreign Affairs has arranged a meeting between Bachir and the Moroccan Minister of the Interior, Driss Basri, in Lisbon. I think Bachir wants to arrange a meeting with the King to discuss what the OAU has proposed to end the war," she began slowly.

"You mean the referendum?" one of them asked.

"Yes," Soukeina replied. "The King promised to cooperate with the OAU's plan in the meeting they held last year, and I understand that Bendjedid submitted detail guidelines for an internationally supervised cease-fire and referendum at the meeting of the Implementation Committee last August in Nairobi . . . but Hassan didn't send a delegate to this meeting and so far has not done anything else to keep his promise."

"Bachir would have a better chance meeting with a scorpion," one of them sneered. "Now that Hassan has managed to create this wall of his, do you think he will sit down and discuss the possible transfer of the territory to us?"

"Yes," another one added, "and I hear he is building a new wall. Its hopeless trying to reason with him!"

". . . and why is the OAU letting him get away with this," one of them said, angrily. "In fact, why have they not admitted us to their organization . . . we have been recognized by enough of their members!"

"Well," one of them added, "I heard a rumor that following the meeting in Nairobi last year, the OAU's Secretary General, Edem Kodjo, wrote to Abdelaziz to inform him of the SADR's admission to the OAU as its fifty first member. Is that true?"

Soukeina shook her head. "Yes, it is true," she said slowly, "but when the next session of the Council of Ministers was convened in Addis Ababa this past February, and a delegation from the SADR arrived to take its seat, the Moroccan delegation stormed out of the conference -- with representatives of eighteen other states in tow -- causing the meeting to end without reaching a quorum."

She sighed. "The OAU leaders are now begging our leaders to stay away."

"Well, why doesn't the United Nations do something about this?" another one asked.

Soukeina looked around her. She could see the frustration and sense of betrayal on their faces. "I don't know," she said, quietly. "I just don't know."

April 26, 1982. Fez.

Meanwhile, back in Morocco, the King was in a good mood as he prepared to welcome some important guests.

It was nearing the end of April, and as he entered the limousine which would take him on the two hour journey from his palace in Marrakesh to the ancient city of Fez he turned to the young man who was carrying his briefcase with a question.

"Have you made sure that the Americans have been escorted to all the historic sites in the city?" he asked without looking up.

The young man stiffened. "Yes, Your Highness, they were taken on a tour yesterday, and last night they were treated to a feast of Moroccan dishes, and some dancing and other entertainment."

"Good, and what about their rooms?"

" I have made sure that they have fresh flowers and sweets every day, and the valet service is at their service 24 hours. Oh, and yes, I have placed complimentary bottles of scotch in the rooms of the diplomats and the Generals, except for the one who likes bourbon. The brands you selected, Your Highness."

"Good," he replied settling into the car. "They must be treated like kings, which in a way they are."

A few miles away a group of men in dress uniform were milling around the lobby of one of the city's finest hotels, speaking jovially to each other and to the handful of men in dark suits who had joined them. Before long a Moroccan official ushered them into a conference room where they took their seats at a long, elaborately carved table. When they were all seated a short man wearing a gold embroidered cap entered the room.

They all stood to greet the King of Morocco.

He looked at the faces of his guests. No fewer than eighty U.S. officials, including eight Generals, an Assistant Secretary of State and both Assistant Secretaries of Defense were there with one objective in mind: devising a strategy to prevent the guerillas from invading Moroccan territory and to defeat their insurgency once and for all. He knew many of them. Indeed he had worked closely with a number of them on campaigns to eliminate radical elements in Mozambique, Angola, Guinea Bissau and the Congo. He knew their wives' names and what they drank. Others were newcomers. But he would get to know them as well.

Dlimi and Basri were there as well. Watching. Listening. But this would be the King's show.

After the normal pleasantries he got straight to the point. "Gentlemen,

291

you have had a chance to review our military situation with General Dlimi. I am eager to know what further steps you would recommend."

A grey haired man in a dark suit cleared his throat. "Your Highness, I first want to reassure you that the President and his administration is committed to helping you combat the radical elements in your kingdom." Then, shooting a glance at a man sitting across the table with stars on his shoulder, he added "I will let our military experts discuss the precise nature of our aid."

With that last comment, the other man turned to the King. "Your Highness, building a defensive barrier is a good idea, but is not enough. It is our belief that you need to go on the offensive, to ferret out the guerillas' hiding places. With your permission, we will send some of our military consultants to help train commando units within your armed forces. . . ."

"and our intelligence experts can give you satellite imagery of Polisario positions on a daily basis," added another man at the table.

"Of course, the defensive barrier will continue to be important," interrupted the grey haired man, "and we understand that you have made arrangements with Westinghouse for more sophisticated infra-red detection equipment. That is good. Matt, do you have any comments?"

A man farther down the table in a blue uniform began to speak in a soft southern drawl, "Your Majesty, you will need to improve your air cover. I understand your pilots are reluctant to confront the guerillas' SAM 6 missiles. We will have to give them training in counter offensive maneuvers . . . and, of course, the new bombs we have been developing, which we believe will be highly effective."

"We can leave the details to be ironed out between your men and ours. But I believe we are all in agreement about the overall strategy," said the grey haired man.

The King smiled and rose from the table. "Yes, I think we are all in agreement. Why don't we adjourn now. I believe lunch is being prepared."

As the King left the room the grey haired man quickly walked to his side. In a tone too low for others to hear he whispered in the King's ear, "The President wanted me to tell you that he is grateful for the help you have offered in the past. He is especially grateful for your promise in February to grant us transit facilities at Moroccan air bases in Casablanca and the Sidi Slimane military air base for our Rapid Deployment Forces."

The King smiled. "Tell President Reagan that I also appreciate his support, and that I look forward to a long and mutually beneficial relationship!"

May 26,1982. Somewhere in the Desert.

It was only spring in the Sahara, but already the soles of his shoes had begun to melt from the heat of the sand as he marched with the troops, and a sandstorm had smothered the sky the previous evening, clogging his sensitive equipment and blanketing everything with a thin film of red dust. The U.S. army commando had arrived in the desert, just south of Smara, only a week earlier and was still having difficulty acclimating himself to the extreme heat

and inhospitable climate. He could not imaging a more forlorn place on earth
– nothing but rock and gravel interspersed with a few hardy shrubs and the
occasional acacia tree for as far as he could see, where torrential rains could
wipe out settlements one day and enormous sandstorms bury what remained
the next.   It was here that he would have to transform a bunch of young and
inexperienced Moroccans into an elite commando unit capable of ferreting
out and destroying the guerillas who had mastered the art of desert warfare
and proved to be an illusive enemy for the past seven years.

He was in the first phase of their training, getting them in shape physically
and accustomed to the strict military discipline that was his bread and butter.
They were far from desert fighters. In fact, the majority were kids from the big
cities who were just as uncomfortable as he in these forbidding surroundings.

He, and twenty five of his comrades in the intelligence squad, had been
sent there to implement a new Saharan strategy concocted by the top brass
in Washington. They would train an elite squadron of Moroccan troops to
launch mobile commando style operations beyond the defense perimeters to
force the Polisario onto the defensive.

His mission was to shape this elite unit out of the army regulars. His
colleagues in the intelligence unit would provide Morocco with technical
assistance so that they could ferret out Polisario movements and bases in the
desert. Others from the Air Force were training pilots in ways to locate the
position of SAM 6s operated by Polisario and destroy them. The United States
military was using all the technology at its disposal to mold the Moroccan
forces into a sleek, effective military machine.

It was now an early morning in May and twenty five trainees had lined up
for his inspection.

"I am here to instruct you on United States Army counterinsurgency
techniques," he barked. "The training will be grueling, but by the time I am
finished with you, you will be able to fight the guerillas on your own terms,
find their locations, destroy them, and take back the territory that they have
managed to infiltrate."

One or two of the cadets managed a weak smile, but the others stood
motionless.

"Are there any questions?"

The cadets stood still for a moment. Finally one of them raised a hand.
"How long will the training be, sir," he said.

The soldier stared at him. "As long as it takes!" he barked.

Again, silence. The soldier looked at their faces, one by one. Then he sighed.

After he dismissed the unit he took one of the cadets aside.

"Where are you from, son," he asked in a pleasant tone.

"Casablanca, Sir," he replied.

"And how long have you been in the Army?"

"Just a few months, Sir."

The soldier looked closely at the recruit. He couldn't have been much older
than 18.

"Why did you enlist" he asked.

The young soldier seemed to be nervous.

"Don't worry, son," the soldier said, softly. "This conversation is just between you and me."

"Well, Sir," he began, "It is difficult to find work in Casablanca. In fact, it is difficult to find work in any city in Morocco. The economy is not good, and the King is putting all the government revenue into the Sahara campaign. So, I thought the best thing to do would be to join the army. Here at least we have something to eat . . . even if the food isn't very good." He hesitated for a moment, and then added, "I think most of the soldiers here joined up for the same reason."

"And the campaign to recover the Sahara . . . how do you feel about that?"

The young recruit seemed nervous again. "Well, you see, sir, that is the King's campaign. Most people in Morocco have never been to the Sahara and, sure, it would be great to recapture Morocco's ancient lands . . . but I'm not sure it is worth dying for!" He said the last words with some emotion.

The commando hesitated for a moment, then dismissed the boy.

He walked slowly back to the sprawling stucco building that was to serve as his headquarters.

"What's the matter, Sargeant," a voice from inside the building called out. "You look worried!" It was one of his comrades, a fresh faced green beret from the Indiana cornfields.

The commando stared at him for a moment, then shook his head.

"These kids don't really want to be here," he said. "That is going to be a problem. A successful commando is a risk taker, and in order to be a risk taker you have to believe in what you are doing. In fact, you have to believe in what you are doing so strongly that you are willing to put your life on the line for it. All the training in the world would not transform a soldier without the will to fight into an effective member of a special forces unit."

"Well, all we can do is train them . . . the rest is up to them!" the kid replied. Then he handed his comrade a cool drink. "Don't worry," he said, grinning, "the top brass must know what they are doing!"

The commando turned to the window. Outside were columns of young men marching in the sun to the orders of another fresh faced green beret from New Jersey.

"I hope so," he muttered.

As he put his glass down he sighed. He had hoped that this deployment would be over by Christmas. Now he was wondering whether he would return home in time to see his twelve year old graduate from high school.

August 15, 1982. Agadir.

As the tall, dark haired man with a mustache got off the plane a blast of hot air greeted him, and he looked forward to the air conditioned car that had been sent to greet him. It had been a nerve-wracking trip, even for someone used to the intrigues that inevitably filled the corridors of the palace, and he would be glad once he was back in the cool confines of his office in Agadir.

When he reached his office he shut the door behind him and sat quietly in his armchair. It was nearing 5 o'clock in the afternoon, and a half filled bottle of scotch sat on the little table near his arm, extending an invitation. He poured himself a drink, and sipped it slowly, allowing its warmth to fill his chest. Then he rose and looked out his window. Below him he could see a column of troops marching in an exercise, led by a tall blonde officer wearing a foreign uniform. It was now summer, and for months now he had watched from the sidelines as foreign advisors marched through his district, shouting commands.

"Good luck to them," he muttered to himself, returning to his chair and pouring another drink. For nearly seven years, as a loyal servant of the King, he had tried to put down the guerilla insurgency, using every means at his disposal, but nothing had worked. And throughout all this period he had to withstand the withering criticism of the King, who would blame everyone but himself for the army's woes. And now, in a desperate move, the King was relying on a wall – a wall to keep the rebels out.

Where will it all end, he thought to himself? The King has already strained the country's coffers to such an extent that the economy is in tatters, and he will need more money – a lot more money – if he intends to extend this wall of his beyond the 'useful triangle.' He has already had to beg the Saudis for more aid. But worst of all, he has had to prostitute himself to curry favor with the Americans. In February he had granted the Americans transit facilities at Moroccan air bases for Reagan's Rapid Deployment Force, and the CIA had established its African headquarters at Casablanca -- and now American faces and uniforms were a frequent sight at the restaurants and cafes in Agadir.

He slumped into his armchair, staring aimlessly at the ceiling. He had gradually begun to see Hassan in a different light – not as a stately leader but as a foolish, supercilious despot, oblivious to the woes of his people. The final straw had been that exhibition of his at the OAU meeting.

He shook his head, sadly, at the image of Hassan in tears, and how humiliated it had made him feel when he had heard of it. Any respect he had had for the Monarch, any belief that he was capable of leading the country in the right direction, had evaporated in an instant. What was left was just a grim sense of duty.

And now that sense of duty was driving him in another direction. When the war had first started he had welcomed it as an opportunity for glory. But as it dragged on, with no clear victory in sight, his initial enthusiasm had begun to sour. Are the sacrifices worth it, he had asked himself? Do the Moroccan people really want this piece of land that much, or is the war just a desperate ploy to keep the King from losing his throne?

And then the purges had begun. He had a feeling that he was walking on egg shells. It was only a matter of time before he would join them. His visits to the palace had become nightmares. And now that the King had sold his soul to the Americans and the Israelis and had no further use for him he was doubly afraid. He felt betrayed, and betrayal did not sit well with his temperament.

So he sat, the feelings that he had hidden so well from those around him bubbling to the surface. And when he finally left his office that evening, the path before him seemed clear.

November 15, 1982. The OAU.

A philosopher once said that diplomacy was just another form of warfare, and while the American and the French military were busy attempting to shape the Moroccan army into an effective military machine, a diplomatic war had been heating up within the capitals of Africa.

Hassan's performance at the Nairobi summit meeting in 1981 had not placated the organization for long. Delegates to the Implementation Committee meeting held in August of that year adopted detailed guidelines for a referendum. But the King ignored the guidelines, just as he had ignored every recommendation of the "wise men" before it.

But there was one thing that he could not ignore – the fact that the SADR had received the recognition of enough of the members of the OAU that it could be admitted as a member. The King's refusal to work with the Implementation Committee turned out to be the last straw for members of the organization. Following its meeting that August, the OAU's Secretary General informed the SADR of their state's admission to the OAU as its fifty first member.

This finally got the attention of the King. Considering this an affront, at a press conference in Paris on January 29, 1982, Hassan reaffirmed his refusal to negotiate with the Polisario, and refusal to cooperate with the Implementation Committee at its next meeting on February 8. So when the next session of the Council of Ministers was convened in Addis Ababa on February 22, and a delegation from the SADR arrived to take its seat, all eyes had been on the Moroccan delegation.

They didn't have long to wait. When the Polisario delegation walked into the room the Moroccan delegation stormed out of the conference as it had threatened – along with representatives of eighteen other states -- causing an abrupt ending to the meeting.

But it wasn't just the admission of the SADR that was causing problems for the organization. The next general OAU summit was scheduled to be held in Libya in August of 1982, with Mummar Khaddafi presiding. This did not sit well with American officials. Beginning in the spring the U.S. government began circulating a secret document to selected African governments, urging them to boycott the meeting, arguing that Khaddafi's "unprincipled" behavior would make it impossible for the U.S. to work with him as OAU chairman. On August 3rd, the states that had supported the SADR's admission to the OAU in the February meeting countered this move by issuing a proclamation, known as the Tripoli Declaration, reaffirming their solidarity with the SADR, and appealing to the member states to "adopt a constructive attitude in conformity with the OAU's traditions" by coming to the Tripoli summit "in a spirit of

African fraternity and solidarity." The plea fell on deaf ears. The controversy over the SADR's admission to the OAU was used by a number of Francophone states as a pretext to deprive Colonel Khaddafi of his opportunity to chair the organization, and the August summit collapsed, four short of a quorum.

Two months later, in order to permit a summit to be re-convened, the SADR announced that it would abstain from attending the next summit, and the organization hastily arranged for a truncated summit to be convened in November. However, a number of states still refused to attend and others walked out, this time in a dispute over the seating of a delegation from Chad.

The King and his allies had won another round. Khaddafi was snubbed once again and the SADR was deprived of its place in the limelight.

November 23, 1982. The United Nations.

But just as Hassan had managed to put out one diplomatic fire, another one burst into flames.

The members of the United Nations had for some time been more than willing to let the OAU take the lead in dealing with the Moroccan monarch on the thorny issue of Western Sahara. The King's pledge, however ambiguous, to permit a referendum decide the fate of the territory and the establishment of a committee at the June 1981 OAU summit to implement such a referendum, had raised the hopes of delegates to the United Nations that the issue might be able to be solved without their involvement. Hassan's subsequent refusal to cooperation with this committee dashed these hopes and finally forced the General Assembly to confront the problem.

On November 23, 1982 the corridors of the UN building in New York were bustling with unaccustomed activity. Moynihan had long ago departed his post as U.S. Permanent Representative to the UN to take on the responsibilities of Senator from New York, and Jeanne Kirkpatrick, his current replacement, was finding it difficult to keep the members in line on issues involving Western Sahara.

In an act of defiance aimed primarily at the United States, the General Assembly that day passed a resolution by 78 votes to 15 which reaffirmed "the inalienable right of the people of Western Sahara to self determination and independence," named Morocco and the Frente Popular para la Liberacion de Saguia el-Hamra y de Rio de Oro as the parties to the dispute, and declared that only negotiations between them could restore peace in northwest Africa and guarantee the fair conduct of a "general, free and orderly referendum on self determination in Western Sahara." The resolution appealed to the two parties to the dispute to start negotiations with a view to achieving a cease fire. Finally, the resolution affirmed "the determination of the United Nations to cooperate fully with the Organization of African Unity in the fair and impartial organization of the referendum."

The United States, which had abstained on all the resolutions adopted in 1979 and 1980, was the only Western power to vote against it.

And while everyone's attention was focused on the vote at the UN, a

continent away events were unfurling that would have a profound impact on
their plans.

End of December, 1982. Stockholm.

The tall, dark man with a mustache in the ubiquitous raincoat walked
quietly to the desk of the Grand Hotel in Stockholm and handed his passport
to the clerk. He was no one of any importance, just another one of hundreds
of lawyers who frequented the hotel on their business trips. Fashionably
dressed, but nothing ostentatious. Probably here for a convention, mused the
clerk with an indifferent air.

He took the elevator to his room, waited an hour, then descended and
headed for the restaurant where they were serving tea. Before long a short,
swarthy man, not as fashionably dressed, wearing a hat and sunglasses
approached his table and quietly sat down.

"You are looking well," he said, lifting his sunglasses.

The tall man smiled slightly in reply, and shot a glance at the two adjoining
tables. Sitting at one was an elderly lady and what appeared to be her
granddaughter, laughing and sharing a piece of cake. At the other were a young
couple immersed in intense conversation, oblivious to their surroundings.

The tall man began to relax.

"Things are getting worse," he finally said in a barely audible whisper. "The
King has nearly bankrupted the country with this Sahara campaign. I cannot
count the number of men we have lost. The men have no stomach for this
fight. The berm has been our salvation, but it doesn't keep the Polisario from
bleeding us to death, and as long as they are a threat we are forced to station
the bulk of the army in the Sahara. And in order to support this folly, the King
has made us virtual puppets of the Americans. It is disgraceful to see him
bowing constantly before the Americans – it turns my stomach." At these last
words the elderly grandmother at the next table glanced his way. He would
have to remember to lower his voice.

"He lost the respect of nearly every Arab leader for his support for Sadat,"
he said, once again in a scarcely audible tone, "and tried to make amends by
joining the boycott of Egypt after the Camp David Accords. But that hasn't
really fooled anyone . . . the only reason the Saudis are still supporting him is
because they fear that if he loses his throne they may be next! We have become
outcasts among our Arab brethren . . . pariahs to our own people . . . and
all for a worthless piece of desert that will cost us a fortune to maintain even
if the war ends. What for? Just to appease the fanatics? Just to show that the
King is more patriotic than his opponents?"

"Perhaps there is another reason," interjected the short man. "Perhaps he
is just doing it to keep the army occupied far away from the palace. Did you
ever think of that?"

"Yes, that could be part of the reason," the tall man said, with a slight laugh,
"He doesn't trust anyone --- and with good reason!"

He reached for the pack of cigarettes in his pocket, put it on the table and carefully lit one, relaxing in his chair. The short man reached for the pack and took another one. Then, as if an afterthought he asked under his breath, "Have you been able to reach the Algerians?" He knew full well that his companion had recently flown to the Canary Islands where he had met, in secret, with Lakhdar Brahimi, the Diplomatic Advisor to Bendjedid.

The tall man smiled and whispered in his ear, "The Algerians may not support us overtly but I do not think they will pose a problem." At this the short man smiled and leaned back in his chair once again. For a moment they were quiet, enjoying the sweet aroma of tobacco that warmed their lungs.

Finally the tall man turned to the short one and whispered, "What do your men think?"

The man paused slightly before answering. Then he leaned on the table and whispered, softly, "We can be ready as soon as next spring. All you have to do is give the word."

The tall man looked into the distance, as if pondering a great issue. When he turned once again to the short man his words were steady and deliberate. "We will have to plan this carefully. Already two attempts have failed, and you know what they did to Oufkir. . ." He didn't need to finish the sentence. They both knew the price they would pay if they failed. "From now on we cannot meet, even here in Sweden. I will have to think very carefully about the right time and the right place. When I have worked out a plan I will find some way to contact you. Until then, tell your men to be quiet. There must be no sign of discontent. You know that we are being watched."

The short man stifled a chuckle. Of all people he knew that they were being watched. All Moroccans were being watched, but especially ones who were known enemies of the King. After the last failed coup he had managed to escape to Sweden. He was the only one. The others were executed or simply "disappeared." Since then he had foiled two kidnapping attempts. His name was high on the hit list. Only by constantly changing his whereabouts, travelling under an assumed name, and wearing disguises had he managed thus far to escape the long tentacles of the Moroccan secret police.

With his last statement, the tall man stood as if to leave the table. Once again he shot a glance at the neighboring tables. The grandmother had left with the child and that table was empty. The young couple were still involved in heated amorous conversation. There was no one else in the vicinity. He hastily bade his companion goodbye and retreated to the anonymous safety of the hotel lobby.

The short man paused for a moment, then beckoned the waiter for the check. After leaving a few kroners on the table, he quietly got up and headed for a bank of telephones that were in the corridor adjacent to the restaurant. Once in a booth he dialed a number and a man answered. "It is set" is all he said, and placed the receiver back on the hook.

299

CHAPTER 10
1983

By the beginning of 1983 United States advisors in Morocco had become as thick as fleas, as the President of the United States poured all the military and diplomatic might of the country behind Hassan's venture, propping up his regime and removing any obstacle that stood in his way. And one by one dominoes began to fall . . . one in particular.

January 10, 1983. The CIA.

The U.S. Colonel sweated under the weight of his military uniform. No matter how the Army tried to fashion its uniforms to fit the climates of the various places around the globe it sends its troops, they are always either too warm or too cold. In this case even the summer weight uniforms issued to Army colonels could not protect them from the heat of the Moroccan sun – even in the winter months. And it was now well into the winter months.

So, he would be glad when this mission was over and he could return to the relative comfort of an Army installation in Germany.

As he walked through the corridors of the Royal Palace he could not help but be impressed with the grandeur of the place – marble and gold leaf wherever he looked, and huge windows overlooking well kept and beautifully flowered gardens. He owes all of this to us, he thought, wryly. If it were not for the military aid and support he gets from the U.S. he would be out on the street hawking tourist trinkets. He didn't have much use for kings, himself. He was raised on an Iowa farm where he had been thoroughly inoculated with the notion of democratic principles. But he understood fully well the value of a trusted military and political ally to United States interests around the world. And he knew full well the importance the military – not to mention the CIA – placed on keeping Hassan on the throne.

And they had concluded that the threat posed by the Polisario was not nearly as great as the threat posed by forces inside the country. Hassan had managed, with generous support from the CIA, to keep members of the opposition parties – the UNFP and Istiqlal -- in check. But they were not his greatest threat. No, his greatest threat was from the handful of Generals who controlled the massive military apparatus. They were powerful, and rich – indeed, the richest men in Morocco aside from the King himself. For years there had been plots against him by his most trusted aides. In 1970 he had narrowly escaped a coup, orchestrated by a handful of military officers. Then, in 1972 another group of military officers, calling themselves the "Free Officers Movement" had tried to shoot down his Boeing aircraft when he was returning from a trip to Paris.

And now unrest within the ranks of the military was beginning once again to pop up on the CIA's radar. The conservative Generals were not too happy about the war in the Sahara – not to mention the King's support for the United States – and by extension Israel – following Israel's invasion of Lebanon -- and there began to be more than usual rumblings in the military chatter monitored by the CIA. And now the Monarch had stoked the flames of revolt by purges that had shaken his officer corps and left many of them wondering, in private, whether it was time to increase democracy in a land ruled by one of the world's last absolute monarchs.

So, the CIA had cast a nervous glance at Hassan's top military operative, General Ahmed Dlimi. He played his cards close to the chest when the Americans were around so there was no knowing what was on his mind. But there were rumors that he had begun to question the King's policies and he was just proud, independent and arrogant enough to think of rebelling against him. This made him dangerous. So, for the past several months they had been discretely monitoring his actions. And finally their surveillance paid off.

So, it was important that the King got the information he was carrying.

When he crossed the threshold of the anteroom the King was waiting for him. It was not usual to be asked for a meeting on sudden notice, especially when he was vacationing at his Marrakesh retreat, so he was not just a little curious.

"Your Majesty, I thank you for agreeing to meet with me at such short notice," said the Colonel with a tone of gravity in his voice, "I can assure you that what I have to tell you is of the utmost importance." With that he glanced at the members of the King's entourage.

The King's curiosity grew. With a wave of his hand he dismissed his courtiers and beckoned the Colonel to sit.

As soon as they were seated the Colonel spoke. "Your Majesty, my contacts have given me some troubling information. It appears that General Dlimi has been in contact with Ahmed Rami in Stockholm." With that he shoved an envelope across the table. Hassan opened the envelope. In it were three pictures. One showed two men – a tall, well built, man who appeared to be in his late forties, with jet black hair and a mustache, and the other a portly, short, dark skinned man of a similar age – sitting at a table in what appeared to be a restaurant. The second photo was a close up of the shorter man. The third a picture of the taller man leaving a hotel with the words "Grand Hotel Stockholm" engraved on the wall. "There are others," the Colonel quickly added.

Hassan's face turned grey as he fingered the photos. He recognized the men. The short, burly man was the leader of the "Free Officers Movement", the group that had tried to assassinate him in 1972. He was the only member of the group that managed to escape and the Moroccan Secret Service had been trying to eliminate him ever since. The other man was his most trusted aide, the second most powerful man in Morocco, the man whom he had trusted to contain the Polisario.

"What would you like us to do?" said the Colonel, after a brief pause to let the gravity of the information sink in.

Hassan said nothing for a moment. Then he turned to the Colonel and in his most regal and hospitable manner, thanked him for giving him the information, implored him to thank his friend the President for his continued support, and bade him farewell.

As his footsteps along the marble corridor receded into the distance, the King gazed for a long minute out the window into the garden below and beyond.

He knew precisely what he would do.

January 24, 1983. The King's Palace, Marrakesh.

Dlimi fidgeted with his watch as the blue Mercedes passed the gate to the Royal Palace in Marrakesh. It was nearly 11 p.m. Before he had been able to finish his dinner he had been summoned unexpectedly to a late night meeting with the King and was wondering what had happened. A new Polisario attack? A diplomatic crisis? He was head of the security apparatus and should have known if something extraordinary had happened, but try as he might he could not pinpoint a reason for this unusual summons. Perhaps it had something to do with the visit of that American colonel a few days ago.

As he walked down the long corridor to the conference room an ever so slight shiver ran through him as if something were slightly out of place. It was quiet. Perhaps too quiet. If there were some sort of crisis there should be people shuttling around, commotion. But, no, the corridor was empty and silent enough to hear his heart beat.

As soon as he entered the room he knew. He could tell from the wooden gaze of the head of the King's personal security guard. He had been in that position several times himself. They led him to one of the underground chambers reserved for activities that were intended to be kept from the ears of any inquisitive staff, conveniently soundproofed. There he sat, waiting for the inevitable.

Hours passed. At 1:00 a.m. the door opened and the King entered the chamber followed by two tall foreigners carrying suitcases.

The door closed once more.

At 8 p.m. on January 25, 1983 the program of the state run Moroccan television station was interrupted with an important news bulletin. Over the newswire there had been an announcement: "The the horrible death of General Ahmed Dlimi in a car accident on the Marrakesh road."

But there was no state funeral or fanfare befitting one of his stature; and no one was allowed to see the corpse. And the repercussions of his death soon rippled through the officer corps, leaving many victims in its wake. One of

these was Bouhali's old nemesis, Colonel Kashdami. He had been a friend of
Dlimi's and after his death was stripped of his command and placed under
house arrest, where he stayed for a number of years until, old and gravely sick,
he was allowed to enter a hospital. He died soon after, in abject poverty, with
few Moroccans remembering his name.

May 31, 1983.

It was shortly after daybreak when Salek appeared at the door of the
hospital. Sidimi knew why he was there. For months now he had been
restless, wanting to join his comrades on the battlefield. His wounds had
healed nicely and he could have returned if there had been an urgent need for
his assistance. But there had been a lull in the fighting for a few months while
everyone waited to see whether Hassan would keep the promises he had made
at the OAU conference.

The night before, however, there had been a meeting of the top commanders
and today their wives were preparing special meals. It was clear that they
would soon be off again. Abdelaziz hadn't spoken a word, but she knew.

Sidi was busy giving a patient an injection of antibiotics mixed with
morphine to relieve the pain. The evening before she had had to remove a
portion of his leg that had become infected to prevent its spread and to save
what remained, and such an operation always left her emotionally drained.

"Sidi, he began," cautiously approaching the spot where she stood, "a friend
has told me that the commanders are planning something big – something
that will require the joint efforts of troops from several regions. Word has
gone out to the troops to mobilize. Hamed has already left and I want to join
him."

Sidi looked at him and sighed. Yes, it was time.

She took his hand and clasped it warmly. " Salek, you can go," she said,
"but you must promise that you will be careful – we cannot afford to lose our
greatest musician!"

He smiled, and then he was gone. After leaving the hospital he made his
way to a small clearing where a large black tent had been erected to house the
occasional foreign worker who would make a pilgrimage to the camps with
supplies. It was early in the day. Elena had just finished the tea that had been
prepared for her and was getting ready to make the trek to the February 27
school where, for the past few weeks, she had taught lessons in world history
to an eager audience of women, children and the occasional soldier. When
she saw him at the entrance way she smiled and reached out to greet him. But
there was no smile on his face, and slowly hers began to melt.

"You are leaving, aren't you?" she managed to say, slowly, her eyes cast
down.

He held her hand. "Yes, it is time." His words were soft and low.

They stood like that for a moment, frozen in time, neither one of them
wishing to speak.

When she looked up at him her eyes were moist. She put her arms around

303

him and rested her cheek on his shoulder, holding him close.

He stood motionless for a moment looking down at her. Then he drew her closer to him and kissed her tenderly on her forehead, then on the bridge of her nose, then softly against her cheek.

"I'll come back, Elena, I promise," he said softly as he withdrew from her embrace. And without another word he walked from the tent into the sun. She watched quietly as his figure receded into the distance.

And within the next two days the camp once again became the domain of women, children, and old men.

June 11, 1983. Resolution AHG 104.

By the time of the OAU summit meeting in Addis Abba on June 11, the SADR had gained the recognition of over 50 third world states, including most of Africa, and had won the sympathy of a number of recognized international leaders. Once again, however, in order to forestall a procedural impasse, the members of the OAU begged the leaders of the SADR to abstain from attending the annual meeting.

But this time they would offer them something in return. Abdou Diouf, the President of Senegal, a member of the ad hoc committee studying the Western Sahara issue who had supported Morocco in the previous OAU sessions, had become miffed that the meetings between the guerillas and Moroccan envoys in Portugal had been held without his knowledge. So, he promised the leaders of the SADR that if they stayed away from the June meeting he would see to it that a resolution was passed in support of their cause.

True to his word, when the delegates were seated around the table, Diouf surprised the Moroccan delegation by tabling a proposal -- and the organization quickly passed Resolution AHG 104, placing itself on record for the first time in support of direct negotiations between Morocco and the Polisario on the implementation of the OAU's long stalled plan for a cease fire and referendum. Two years later Diouf would shepherd a similar resolution through a session of the General Assembly of the United Nations.

The Polisario had won a round at the OAU and the UN, and its cause was quickly gaining political momentum among the sub-Sahara African states. Its progress on the African continent, however, was not duplicated in other parts of the world. Ironically, the SADR was least popular among its fellow Arab countrymen. Libya and Algeria had supported the SADR from the beginning. However the oil rich monarchies of the Gulf had stood solidly behind the King of Morocco, offering enough financial support to enable him to maintain his long, intractable, Saharan military campaign. Even Iraq supported the Moroccan position. Most astonishing of all, Yassar Arafat, instead of supporting another group of refugees fighting to regain their land, threw the weight of the PLO behind the Moroccan king.

And, ironically, even though it was constantly accused of being a "communist" regime, the SADR neither requested nor received the recognition or support of the Soviet Union or China.

The Polisario leaders, meanwhile, knew that their hard won political achievements throughout Africa would soon evaporate if they failed to keep up their pressure on the battlefield. It was now time to act.

June, 1983. Return to Arms.

By the beginning of 1982 the guerillas had managed to acquire a number of rather sophisticated armored vehicles and anti-aircraft missiles. They were to spend the remainder of the year trying to figure out what to do with them. Bouhali had been removed as commander of the 2nd military region and assigned a new task: train all the troops in the use of their new equipment. There were still attacks on outposts and caravans outside the berm – especially in the Dakhla region – and the attacks on the troops building the berm had continued, but both had been at a slower pace as they waited for the results of some of their diplomatic initiatives. In 1982 Bachir Mustopha Sayed had met with Driss Basri, the Moroccan Minister of the Interior, in secret in Lisbon, Portugal, where he had asked him to arrange a face to face meeting with the King. That meeting never took place. Instead, other meetings with Moroccan officials took place in the earlier months of 1983, all of which went nowhere.

By mid-1983 it had become abundantly clear that Hassan's pledge to support the OAU referendum plan was a ruse to lull the Polisario into a false sense of hope and quiet their military campaign for a sufficient time to allow him to re-invigorate his army, expand the berm, and conduct the behind the scenes maneuvering for which he was justifiably famous.

So, when the leaders of the Polisario met again in a strategy session in May of that year, they decided to renew the military onslaught, and through the wee hours of the night discussed troop movements, potential targets and logistics. They decided, for the time being, to avoid a frontal attack on troops behind the berm, and instead chose for their target the elite Moroccan garrison that had assembled to protect the access to the western pass through the Zini mountains in what was to become one of the bloodiest and most protracted battles of the war – the siege of Lemseid.

July, 1983. Lemseid.

It was the middle of the summer, and the heat was causing undulating waves to appear along the desert horizon. Hamed and his comrades had just left their command post and were traveling in a long convoy of troops of the 1st military region westward in the *wadi*, carefully avoiding the berm which was protecting Smara and Boucraa. At the head of the convoy, marching with the troops, was Abdelaziz -- Nih Lahbib at his side -- followed by a mile long train of Land Rovers, tanks, troop carriers, heavy artillery and SAM 6 surface to air missiles. They were planning a rendezvous with troops from the 2nd and 5th military region who had installed themselves in the vicinity of Lemseid.

Lemseid was a small settlement in southern Morocco situated between the escarpment to the south and the Zini mountain range to the north at the gateway to the one western pass through the Zini mountains. It had become a pivotal point in the Polisario's forays to the north, particularly after the berm cut off their ability to circle around Smara, Boucraa and Laayoune and attack positions in Morocco from the coast. The civilian population – mostly ethnic Sahrawis -- had earlier been evacuated by the Moroccans to Tan Tan to prevent their collaboration with the guerillas, and a large garrison with an airstrip had been built near the town, protected by hills on three sides. On the top of these hills the Moroccans had placed heavy artillery. It hadn't been an easy task – to place artillery on the highest of these hills, called Housinera, they had to put the weapons on the backs of donkeys. Between the hills the Moroccans had built small defensive barriers. The Moroccan defensive line was in the shape of a crescent wall behind this barrier. Nestled behind this perimeter was the command center.

Salek had joined the troops of the 2nd military region and as he approached the area he could see that because of the barriers and the proximity of the hills the garrison presented a difficult position to attack.

The commanders spread their forces about a mile from the hills that protected the garrison and prepared for the assault. The first objective would be to disarm as many of the cannons and artillery on the hills as possible. Squadrons of infantry were chosen and given orders. Hamed, and five of his unit, were told to neutralize the weapons on a hill just north of the garrison. Shortly before daybreak they took off, on foot, carrying mortar on their backs.

They decided that the best approach was from the north side of the hill, in the opposite direction of the troops. By this time the Moroccans would probably be aware of the presence of the guerillas and would have turned their cannons in their direction, exposing their flank.

But they were finding the climb over rocky crevices difficult, especially in the darkness of night, and more than once had to stop to regain their breath. It was essential that they be as silent as possible. Only with the element of surprise would their attack work. Slowly and carefully they crawled up the steep mountainside. When they reached the summit they could make out the outline of a rudimentary bunker. Two soldiers sat on a rocky ledge, smoking cigarettes, weapons in their hands, their eyes glued to the southern horizon.

Within a flash they were upon them, grabbing them behind their backs, by their necks. It was over in an instant. They set the explosives and scurried quickly down the embankment. After a hundred yards an explosion behind them sent rocks and gravel hurling towards their backs and its force knocked them to the ground.

By the time they reached their unit, explosions could be heard from all directions as one by one the mountain tops burst into flames.

Back with the troops, Abdelaziz was busy directing the positions. They had orders to move out at dawn, the infantry leading the way. While he and the foot soldiers surrounded the enclave on the north side, Nih Labib and the tanks would break through to shell the defenses along the garrison's perimeter. Troops from the other regions would take positions along the south and east approaches. Gradually they would form a complete circle around the garrison, firing upon them from all directions. Once they had broken through the defensive perimeter the infantry would swiftly charge the command center.

At the sound of the first explosion the attack began. Abdelaziz led the infantry charge. But the land mines managed to prevent a rapid advancement. For hours the tanks bombarded the Moroccans' defensive line, and at last it seemed to be crumbling. But the Moroccans put up stiff resistance and reinforcements quickly breached the gaps.

The battle seesawed back and forth for days. The guerillas managed to destroy the Moroccans' defensive perimeter three times -- and three times it was reinforced. Casualties on both sides began to mount. The troops sent from Moroccan positions to the north and south were not able to penetrate the guerillas' defensive lines, and the troops in the Moroccan garrison remained immobilized – unable to move in any direction – and blasted huge craters in the sides of the hills with their artillery in frustrated attempts to break the guerillas' hold.

The Moroccan air force, still wary of the SAM 6 missiles, would not fly into their range. But they were now armed with a formidable weapon – cluster bombs.

A cluster bomb is a device that contains several submunitions. They can be dropped from aircraft or fired from the ground. Either way they open up in mid air to release tens or hundreds of projectiles, capable of saturating a territory as large as several football fields, killing or severely wounding any person or animal in their way. They had been developed by the Americans and the Russians during the Second World War and had been extensively used by the U.S. military in Vietnam. After the battle of Guelta Zemmour in 1981, the U.S. Army had provided the Moroccans with BLU-63, M42, and MK118 cluster bombs, which had by the time of the battle at Lemseid already been used by them to bomb Bir Lehlou, Tifariti, Mehris, Mijek and Agwanit. They would later be banned in the 2008 Convention on Cluster Munitions, but in 1983 were considered standard equipment by the U.S. military.

And now they were raining down on the guerilla forces, causing extensive injuries.

But the guerillas held firm. And so the impasse continued.

August 1, 1983.

Nestled among the hills that surrounded Lemseid, Salek was enjoying his morning cups of tea.   It was now the 10th day of the battle. Fighting had become sporadic. Now and again the Moroccans would try to venture from their cage, only to be forcefully turned back by unseen assailants in the hills. Soldiers sent from Moroccan bases near Tan Tan and Assa would try to come to their rescue, but would not be able to penetrate the Polisario positions that surrounded the area, and would be forced to turn back. Supplies had to be airlifted, the roads were impassable. From time to time Polisario forces would

307

attack the Moroccan defensive positions, but they, too, found it impossible to penetrate their lines. The attacks went on for days, but there were also intervals of quiet. It had quickly turned into one of the longest sieges of the war.

Salek was now visiting the camp where Hamed and some of the troops of the 1st military region were camped. Hamed had become a close friend, and he enjoyed comparing notes about their life in El Ayoun and the events that had caused them to join the guerilla movement.

Today Hamed seemed pensive and Salek, quick to recognize his friend's moods, asked him if something was troubling him.

"Oh, nothing much," he responded, his eyes downcast, "It is just that last night I had a dream – or should I say, a nightmare – that I was back in that Moroccan prison. It was dark and the dampness of the dungeon was chilling my bones. All at once I looked up, and I saw Miriam's face – just as I had first seen her in her tent – looking down at me. Then, as quickly as she had appeared she was gone, and I was left in the dark." He stopped for a moment, then turned to face his comrade. "I often wonder what has become of her – and her father – and if I will ever see them again."

Salek was quiet. His thoughts wandered to Elena.

"Do you think we will ever be able to live a normal life?" Hamed murmured, peering far into the distance with large, sad eyes.

But Salek had no time to reply, for a messenger had quickly approached them. Moroccan troops had advanced towards their position from Tan Tan and they were expected to join the forces sent to repel them.

They quickly grabbed their weapons and joined the march north to where the other troops were camped. As they approached their position they could hear the sound of gunfire in the distance. Moroccan troops, advancing from the north with tanks and heavy artillery, had reached within striking distance of their troops and the guerilla forces were returning fire. Hamed and Salek quickly joined their comrades, manning some of the heavy artillery the commanders had brought with them. The firefight lasted several hours. Huge craters were dug from the earth spewing dust and dirt into the sky until the air was cloaked in a dull grey powder. Through the fog Hamed could barely make out the silhouette of a tank. The Moroccans were trying to cut a wedge through the guerillas' defensive line. He grabbed a grenade and lurched forward. When he was close enough he hurled the grenade at the tank. Within seconds an explosion ripped through the steel frame, sending huge splinters in every direction. Hamed tried to flee, but his knees buckled under him. A fragment of steel was lodged in his thigh, making it excruciatingly painful to walk. After a few seconds he dropped to the earth, dizzy from the loss of blood. After a few seconds more everything turned black.

August 5, 1983. A Camp Near Lemseid.

Salek approached the lanky soldier who was leaning against a boulder smoking a cigarette. It was two days after the latest skirmish with the

Moroccans, and, after forcing them to turn back, most of the troops had returned to their bases in the surrounding hills. But Salek had stayed behind, anxious to learn the fate of Hamed, who had not yet returned.

"Do you know where I can find Brahim Ghali?" he yelled. The soldier turned to face him, and broke out in a smile, revealing two rows of crooked and missing teeth. "He's over in that clearing," he managed to say, gesturing to a place on the far side of one of the hills, "and Abdelaziz is with him."

Salek thanked the soldier and walked in the direction he had indicated. He soon recognized the figures of Ghali and Abdelaziz, engrossed in conversation.

"Our scouts have reported that Benani has ordered several regiments – nearly a third of the Moroccan forces – to gather at Tan Tan for an assault on our troops surrounding Lemseid," Abdelaziz was saying to a stone faced Ghali. "The troops that were sent a few days ago were only a scouting party – sent to assess our strength. The main force is due to march in six days."

Salek had heard that name before. Colonel Benani, an officer better known for his business acumen than his military prowess, had been appointed the new commander of the southern region after Dlimi's mysterious death.

"We can't go on like this," he continued, "Our casualties are mounting and we have yet to penetrate the defensive perimeter, and if we stay any longer we risk being surrounded ourselves. It is time to retreat."

Then, in a barely audible voice, he added "There is something else . . . our ambassador in Algiers has told me that Mitterrand is threatening Bendjedid with retaliation if we continue the siege."

Ghali had been walking quietly by his side, but at the mention of Mitterrand's name he stopped. "What kind of retaliation?" he asked, wryly.

"I don't know, but his threats have made the Algerians nervous . . . they have had experience with the kind of tricks the French are capable of playing."

"Well, I think that they are just empty threats . . . a lot of hot air," Ghali said, shaking his head. "But it would be wise for us to retreat in any case. Our strength is in rapid assaults and quick retreats . . . relying on the element of surprise. If we try to hold onto territory we will be playing the game by Moroccan rules . . . not ours . . . and if we stay too long in any fixed positions we are inviting disaster."

Abdelaziz smiled and put his arm around Ghali's shoulder. "Yes, my friend," he said, softly, "but the others may not agree. You know how they feel about retreating from strategic locations . . . especially after Zag."

Ghali shook his head. "Bravado won't win this war . . . strategy will," he said, slowly. "I'm reminded of a story I once heard . . . about a commander of a small group of men fighting for the liberation of their land against a much larger, well equipped army. This commander refused to engage the enemy for weeks, always retreating when they advanced until his men rebelled, calling him a coward. But one day the leader of the large army decided to split his troops, and the commander saw his chance. He sent some of his men to blockade the road between the divided troops and attacked the troops that were the closest. Within 15 minutes it was over. He forced the army leader to surrender and his men won their independence." Ghali put his arm on Abdelaziz' shoulder. "The moral to this story is that we must not be afraid to retreat. There are always other targets. . . and we can always return to Lemseid when the time is right."

The two men looked at each other for a moment, then Abdelaziz smiled. "Brahim, I know you are right," he said, before turning to leave. But in a moment, he turned again.

"By the way . . . what ever happened to that commander?" he asked, somewhat curiously.

"Oh, they named a town after him. I think it is called Houston," Ghali replied.

After Abdelaziz was out of view, Salek cautiously approached Ghali.

"Sir, is there any word yet about Hamed," he said, hoping against hope that the answer would be yes.

Ghali had been deep in thought, unaware of the other's presence. Salek's words, however, jolted him back to reality. He looked at the man standing next to him for a moment, and then shook his head. "He isn't among the dead or wounded," he began to say, in a low voice, "and he has not returned to his troops. We have scoured the area where he was last seen to recover anyone who may have been wounded, and we found nothing." Then he paused, a grave look on his face, before continuing. "I have been told that the Moroccans may have captured some prisoners . . . besides Hamed there are three others who are missing."

These last words made Salek's heart sink. He thought of the stories Hamed had told him of life in a Moroccan prison. Better off dead, he said to himself. He thanked Ghali and took his leave, and as he walked slowly back to his post in a half daze a nagging feeling in the back of his head told him that he would never see his friend again.

September 7, 1983. Tindouf.

Back in the camps the intake of the wounded at Lemseid had filled the tiny rooms of the hospital to overflowing, and Sidimi was working around the clock directing the small cadre of nurses she had trained to handle the minor cases while handling the seriously wounded herself. It was 10 o'clock in the morning, and she had already completed two operations and was sipping a cup of tea to fortify herself for the third. She wondered how the Moroccans were doing. She had heard rumors that the Moroccans had had to empty the hospitals in Tan Tan, Smara and Laayoune to care for the wounded. When she looked up she saw a familiar figure walk into the room. The figure walked hesitantly to where she sat. Then, she bent down and kissed her cheek in the familiar Sahrawi greeting between two women.

For a moment Elena was silent, and Sidimi wondered why she had come to the hospital. Then she broke her silence. "Sidimi, I want to work with you . . . to help . . . to care for the wounded" she said in halting tones.

Sidimi paused for a moment.

"I thought you were helping Soukeina at the school," she said, quietly. "Don't you think you would be more useful there?"

"I think I could be of more help here. . . helping you with the wounded," Elena said quietly, "and helping in the field. You know you will need people to help the soldiers on the battlefield!"

Sidimi rose from where she sat and placed an arm on her shoulder.

"Elena, you shouldn't risk your life. This is not your fight," she whispered.

"Isn't it?" Elena replied, gazing firmly at her.

Sidimi gave her a long, appraising look.

"Elena, you have led the pampered life of a Spanish lady," she said, raising her voice. "Have you ever worked in a hospital? Have you ever tried to dress a wound? To assist at an operation? To care for the injured?" She then lowered her voice. "You do not know what a battle is like. . . the suffering. . . the pain . . . the death all around you. Do you really think you can take it?"

"Of course I can!" Elena said, a note of determination creeping into her voice. She would not admit that she became nauseous at the sight of blood.

Sidimi wasn't so sure, but she admired Elena's guts and determination. She reminded herself of someone she knew.

She turned once again to her and said, with mock seriousness. "All right, I will make a deal with you. I will let you assist me on my rounds for a week, and if you can take it . . . and if you still want to be trained as a nurse . . . I will allow it. But only here in the hospital . . . "

Before she could finish, Elena flung her arms around her. "Thank you, Sidi," she murmured in her ear, "You won't be sorry!"

And a day later she arrived at the hospital at the crack of dawn, ready to begin a new chapter in her life.

September 8, 1983. Smara.

By the end of summer the siege of Lemseid had been lifted and Salek and the other soldiers were itching for action. The commanders had withdrawn to their base camps to plan their next move. They wanted a target that would serve a political as well as military purpose, and, in a bold decision, chose to attack once again the garrison that guarded the town that was the heart and soul of the Sahara.

The day was September 8. From atop a hill Salek could see beyond the valley below to the rim of another hill to the west. Smara, the ancient seat of learning built by the great Sheikh Ma al Ainen, lay just over that rim. Protecting its eastern flank was the same wall of sand – now fortified with stone and several feet higher -- that also encircled Laayoune and Boucraa. But since the successful attack of 1979 the Moroccans had placed no fewer than seven dirt and stone berms, protected by land mines, around the perimeter of the town, and had placed heavy artillery at intervals along the innermost wall. And standing between the berms and Smara was a large garrison of Moroccan troops. From his vantage point he could see the sentry posts, the artillery, and the buildings that housed the command post and barracks. The "intervention "forces" that were prepared to descend upon any invaders were located a few hundred yards to the north and south. He estimated at least 3,000 men.

Abdelaziz had sent the troops of the 1st military region south where they now positioned themselves in a thirty mile wide arc along the defensive perimeter, waiting for the signal to attack.

When the sun had finally sunk below the horizon, Abdelaziz gathered the troops for some last words before their mission. There was no moon out that night, and except for the canopy of stars that watched them from afar and the faint glow of a light from a sentry tower in the distance, there was total darkness.

They made their way slowly, using the gullies and acacia trees that covered the landscape to mask their approach from the radar, then they dispersed themselves along the berm's perimeter. When they were about 300 yards from the outer embankment they fell to the ground and waited.

At the first glimmer of light over the horizon the invasion began.

The infantry, followed by troop carriers and Land Rovers, dashed towards the berm firing their artillery at the Moroccan installations along it. But no sooner had they reached within a few yards of the wall when explosions began sending clouds of sand and debris into the air. The land mines! Try as they might they hadn't been able to remove all of them. The troops were being battered badly, and after the first assault Ghali was seriously thinking of advising a retreat when he noticed a Land Rover, abandoned by its occupants, whose brakes had failed and was slipping down a hill directly into the land mine field. In a moment there was an explosion that cleared a path through the mines. He quickly ordered all his troops to empty their Land Rovers and push them into the field, creating wedges through which the infantry and armored vehicles could pass safely.

Once they were able to pass through the land mines the infantry swarmed like ants over the outer embankment, and began hand to hand combat with the Moroccan soldiers and the intervention forces that had quickly assembled to protect them, dodging the artillery that was being fired at them by Moroccan forces in positions well behind the berms, while the armored vehicles showered the compound with blasts of machine guns and cannon fire.

Day after day they repeated their attacks along the entire thirty mile long stretch of the berm that protected the approach to Smara.

When dusk had fallen on the seventh day, Abdelaziz called together the other commanders. From where he sat, applying an ointment on a scratch he had received in the battle, Salek could hear bits of the conversation. There were too many barriers, too many land mines. It would take too long to penetrate the walls. There would be too many casualties. Already they had suffered the loss of many men due to the land mines that surrounded the area. To try to advance farther towards the command center or the city might permit Moroccan forces from Laayoune or Boucraa to cut off their retreat. It was time to leave.

Salek sighed in frustration. It was Lemseid all over again. The berms had made a quick attack almost impossible, and the longer they lingered in the area, the more vulnerable they became. For the first time he was afraid.

They were losing the upper hand in the war, and he knew it. And this thought followed him all night as he and the other guerillas retreated, under the cover of darkness, as quickly, and silently, as they had come.

September 8, 1983. Prisoner.

When Hamed was finally able to open his eyes he found himself in a room that was white – white walls, white ceiling, white bed sheets, and looking down at him a woman dressed in white. "Here, this should relieve some of the pain," she said, nonchalantly as she stuck a needle into his arm. He tried to sit up, but a searing pain in his thigh forced him onto his back.

"Where am I?" he managed to ask.

"Near Tan Tan," the woman said curtly, writing something on a chart and not bothering to look at him. "You are lucky . . . the commander wants you fit to answer some questions. Some of the others . . . well, we usually don't have space for prisoners of war!" With that last remark she left the room.

When he was alone he tried to remember what had happened to him at Lemseid. He remembered being hit by a fragment of the tank he had blown and being unable to walk. Then everything went blank. The next thing he remembered was pressure on his chest and finding it difficult to breath. When he opened his eyes he could see that his face was half smothered by the corpse of a rather corpulent Moroccan, and that the bodies of other soldiers were heaped around him on a truck that was slowly moving. He strained and finally was able to move the bodies so that he could breathe, but he felt dizzy and was quickly losing consciousness. The truck finally stopped and he thought he heard someone say "This one's alive" before he passed out. The next thing he knew he was in this room.

Outside his door he could hear the sound of voices and soon a tall, dark haired man in a uniform entered the room.

"I am glad to see that you are finally awake," he said, smiling. "You are lucky. That piece of shrapnel missed your artery by less than an inch. In a few months you will probably be able to walk as good as new." Then, lighting a cigarette and offering one to Hamed, he continued. "In the meantime you will be our guest. . . and if you are willing to cooperate . . . well, your time here need not be unpleasant!"

Not again, he thought, glumly. He remained silent, refusing the cigarette, his eyes betraying no emotion.

The dark haired man put the cigarette back in its pouch and continued. "There are several questions that I want to ask you." Then, drawing a chair closer to Hamed's bed, he leaned over him and whispered, "We know that the Algerians are behind all this. That they are calling the shots . . . that they are supplying you with the weapons . . . the tanks . . . and, we're guessing, the SAM 6 missiles as well." Then he leaned back and took a drag on his cigarette before continuing. ". . . and we suspect that you are infiltrating our eastern areas through our border with Algeria." He then discarded his cigarette in an ashtray beside the bed and looked intently at Hamed, this time without a smile. "In fact, we believe that you have Algerian troops aiding you. I want you to confirm this and to tell me where your bases in Algeria are located!"

Hamed stared at him for a long moment. Then, gradually he began to smile. "We don't need bases in Algeria to attack Moroccan cities, and as for the Algerians commanding our troops, well, have you been able to capture one of these Algerians on the battlefield?"

The dark haired man frowned, then drew his chair closer. "Our commanders have reported seeing the mangled corpses of several men who did not appear to be Sahrawis after the battle of Guelta Zemmour in 1981. In fact, according to them they did not even appear to be Arabs. . . perhaps Cubans or Eastern Europeans. Are these the men who fired the SAM 6 missiles?"

Hamed tried, unsuccessfully, to stifle a laugh. The Moroccans still cannot believe that the Sahrawis are bright enough to learn how to use the SAM 6 missiles. Good. He remembered what Ghali had told him 'Let them think we are ignorant nomads. It is a major tactical error to underestimate the intelligence of your enemy.'

"Are these the same commanders whose troops were decimated?" he replied. "Do you think they would like to admit that they were defeated by a bunch of 'ignorant nomads'? We used the missiles ourselves. We didn't need any help from outsiders."

"And Mauritania? Has Heydalla been supplying you with troops and permission to establish bases in Mauritanian territory?"

Hamed smiled. "After trying desperately for two years to extricate themselves from the war, do you think the Mauritanians would be crazy enough to supply us with troops? Or to give us permission to stage attacks from their territory?" he said, slowly.

The dark haired man stood up and began pacing the room. "Well, you must have gotten help from somewhere!" he shouted. "Ignorant Bedouins would not be able to defeat a modern, sophisticated army . . . . not on their own!" He turned and gave Hamed a long, cold look. "Perhaps a few months in one of our cells will refresh your memory!" With those last words he left the room, slamming the door behind him.

Hamed remained alone with his thoughts in the hospital ward for several hours. Then a group of men entered, ordered him to his feet, and escorted him through the hospital to a waiting van. There a scarf was tied around his eyes and his hands were tied behind his back and he was dumped into the rear of the van. After an hour or so the van stopped, and two men grabbed his arms and led him through a courtyard to a thick steel door that guarded a large stone building. Inside the building was damp and the echoes from the men's voices reverberated through the walls. When they had walked a few feet he heard the sound of metal creaking and another steel door was opened. When his blindfold and handcuffs were removed he could see that he was in the hall of a large, dark and damp building made of stone, with enormous walls only partially illuminated by light from slits high up, near the ceiling. Before him was a tiny cell, no more than two yards wide, with what appeared to be a rug on one side and a bucket on the other. The two men pushed him unceremoniously into the cell and when they closed the door behind him he sat on the rug in nearly total darkness, the silence of the walls breathing down on him.

CHAPTER 11
1984

Thomas Paine once wrote "These are the times that try men's souls. . . Tyranny, like hell, is not easily conquered; yet we have this consolation with us, that the harder the conflict, the more glorious the triumph. What we obtain too cheap, we esteem too lightly; it is dearness only that gives everything its value. Heaven knows how to put a proper price upon its goods; and it would be strange indeed if so celestial an article as FREEDOM should not be highly rated."

Paine wrote these lines on December 23, 1776 . . . in the midst of the darkest days of the American Revolution. Someone could well have written those same lines in 1983, for that year had been such a time for the Polisario. There had been a stalemate on the political front, as a newly confident Hassan, buoyed by what seemed to be the success of the berm and other fortifications in repelling the guerillas' attacks, refused all overtures for a peaceful solution to the conflict and, instead, began extending the berm to other regions. What was worse, there had been heavy losses on the battlefield. The berm had changed the dynamics of the war and countering it had thrown the Polisario leaders into unfamiliar territory. They were now equipped with armored vehicles and sophisticated anti-aircraft missiles. But learning how to use them effectively against Morocco's newly designed defense system was proving to be a problem.

For the "berm" was not merely a wall, it was an entire defense system, including land mines, barbed wire, radar installations, troops positioned along it and rapid intervention forces at intervals behind them. And it was protected by aircraft ready to pounce on any invading forces with cluster bombs.

By the end of 1983 there had been two months of intense resistance against the troops building the 3rd extension of the berm, which started southwest of Boucraa and extended eastward to Amgala, then north to Smara. The guerillas suffered a number of casualties during these battles. The *coup de grace*, however, had been the battle in December against forces along a section of the berm between Boucraa and Amgala in which Hammada, the commander of the 4th military region, as well as his second in command and the commander of the reconnaissance unit, were all killed, along with scores of other fighters.

By the beginning of 1984 Abdelaziz called a halt to large scale military operations while the leadership determined how to best address the new battlefield dynamics.

Months of heated discussions followed. Some argued that they should halt military activities for a while and instead explore ways to neutralize the land mines and radar before plunging ahead with attacks. Others argued that they could not let the Moroccans believe that the berm had been a successful deterrent and they should attack immediately, day and night, exploding the land mines, demolishing the radar and breaching the berm with their armored vehicles. Some believed that they should forge ahead on their own. Others believed just as strongly that they should turn to their allies for help and advice.

Finally Abdelaziz made his decision. They would plan a large scale attack against a position behind the berm – but only after they had identified a suitable target, studied the berm and its defenses at that location thoroughly, and formulated a detailed plan of attack.

September 15, 1984.

It was early in the morning. The time when the incoming wounded – those for whom the prophylactic treatment they received on the battlefield was not enough – would be transported back to the tiny hospital in the refugee camps. As usual Elena was there, holding her breath, hoping against hope that she would not see Salek's face.

The first few weeks as Sidi's assistant had been rough. On more than one occasion she found herself running from the building to relieve her stomach, hopefully without anyone noticing. The men could talk all they wanted about the glory of the battlefield, but there was no glory in the amputated limbs and the maggot infested wounds she saw each day. She and the other women working in the hospital saw a true picture of the war, and it was not a pretty sight.

But it was now the middle of September, 1984. She had been at the hospital for nearly a year, and each day she had heard of another skirmish, sometimes two or three.

For months now the casualties that had trickled into the hospital had been from these battles, and from these casualties Sidimi was able to get a clearer picture of how the war was progressing than most of the commanders. She knew, for instance, that try as they might, they were finding it impossible to prevent the gradual mushrooming of the wall. By August a wall had nearly enclosed the outposts of Amgala and Housa in the north and another was encircling the city of Dakhla along the southern coast.

Salek had been among the troops leading these attacks, and for months he had not been seen in the camps. Bouhali had been reappointed commander of the troops of the 2nd military region in January, but the program for commanders and selected members of the forces Ghali had inaugurated in 1981 had continued, and from time to time a contingent of unwashed and battle weary veterans would find their way to selected training campsites in Western Sahara near the Mauritanian border where they would undergo intensive instruction in how to use the tanks, personnel carriers, anti-aircraft missiles and other artillery the guerillas had acquired.

The wounded that had arrived that morning had now been transported to the bunks at the hospital that would be their home for a while, and Elena was able to relax. By mid morning they had finished the major operations and would be able to grab a cup of tea. This was the time Elena looked forward to – the time she could pump Sidimi for the latest news.

Before she could open her mouth, however, Sidimi spoke. "No, there is no news about Salek. He is still with the forces up north." Elena looked so despondent that Sidimi felt obliged to take her hand. "In these times no news is good news," she said, gently. "He is not listed among the dead or injured." Then, turning once more to her work she added, "But I don't think he will remain up north for long. I have heard that Abdelaziz is planning another large maneuver against a position along a berm – with all our new artillery."

"Do you know where they plan to attack?" Elena asked without attempting to hide her interest.

"I have heard that it will be a segment of the berm near Mahbes," she responded. "I think they call it Zmoul Niran, "the mounds of fire."

October 1984. Zmoul Niran.

By the summer of 1984 the guerillas had waged small attacks against Moroccan positions around Dakhla and Argoub, not yet behind a berm, and there was intense fighting near Zag. For months the troops had battled the construction of the 4th extension of the berm, which extended from Lengueb in the north past Jdiriya, Housa and Smara. But their tanks and troop carriers had remained idle, and they had not yet attempted to breach the berm. This was all to change that autumn.

It was October, 1984, and in the flat pancake area west of the outpost of Mahbes three columns of guerillas, with Land Rovers, troop carriers and tanks, their headlights turned off, were creeping slowly through the desert from three directions towards an area slightly east of the area they had named Zmoul Niran, or "mounds of fire." They were careful to move slowly so as to eliminate as much noise as possible. It was crucial that the Moroccans would have no notice of their approach. A few miles in the distance was the berm, manned by Moroccan soldiers, and protected by land mines and radar. When they had reached a point just slightly beyond the reach of the radar they stopped. They had spent months studying the Moroccan forces and the defenses along this area of the berm and were able to select a point where there was a radar dead zone. This is where they would attack.

Salek and a small unit of demolition experts had been sent ahead the night before by Bachir Mustapha Sayed, who was in charge of the operation. Two evenings before the attack they had begun their slow crawl through the minefields. They had discovered that the Moroccans were inspecting the land mines twice daily to ensure that they hadn't been removed. So, this time, instead of removing the mines during the night, they simply removed the

317

triggering device in the mines and carefully replaced them.

At dawn the attack began. The mound of dirt and gravel did not prove to be much of an obstacle – guerilla infantry simply shoveled through it at three access points to make way for the Land Rovers and troop carriers, while the tanks remained outside the berm shelling its defenders.

For hours the guerillas battled the forces along the berm, eventually managing to penetrate several miles beyond it. By mid day the majority of the Moroccan forces along the perimeter had been killed, captured or scattered. But before the troops could reach the Moroccan garrison's control center, which lay several additional miles in the distance, they were intercepted by rapid intervention forces and Mirage jets began to shell their positions with cluster bombs. They decided to retreat. Mirage jets followed them, shelling them from on high, but, as usual, they refused to fly low enough to encounter the SAM 6 missiles, and many of the bombs that fell failed to hit their targets.

The guerillas hadn't been able to accomplish much militarily – they were not able to destroy the Moroccans' command center or penetrate deeply within Moroccan-controlled territory. But the psychological effect of the battle was tremendous – they now knew that the defensive barrier was not an impenetrable obstacle -- that with enough strategy and preparation the berm could be breached and the forces behind it decimated. It would take time – and preparation – but it could be done.

October 30, 1984.

While the battle of Zmoul Niran was raging, the thin man in rags etched another line in the wall of his cell with his fingernails. It was the only way he could keep track of the passing days, the passing months. By his count he had been in this cell nine months to the day. Each day it was the same routine. Twice a day a plate of some sort of gruel would be pushed under the door of the cell. He would eat it hurriedly. He had long since gotten used to sharing it with the cockroaches and flies. Once a week – in a macabre celebration of the holy day – he was given four olives and a piece of La Vache Qui Rit cheese in addition to the gruel. When he had arrived at the prison his clothes had been taken and he had been given some torn rags to wear – old uniforms no longer fit for the soldiers. He didn't mind the holes, but the lice were a bother, and he was constantly rubbing them against the hard, stone floor in a somewhat futile attempt to remove them. He would sit in his chamber day after day with only the occasional rat to relieve his loneliness.

From time to time he would hear noises outside his door – the sound of voices – as a new inmate would arrive, but most of the time he spent in eerie silence. After he had spent a week in his cell a guard had taken him to a small courtyard where he was allowed to exercise for fifteen minutes, alone. After a few months other prisoners were permitted to join him, and he counted among them two Sahrawis he knew, but he was never allowed to speak to them and all they could do was smile when they passed.

He tried to figure a way to contact the other prisoners. Finally, one Friday he placed the tiny morsel of cheese he had been given into his mouth and crumpled its paper wrapper in his hand as usual. But before he could toss the tiny ball of paper away he stopped and stared for a moment at his hand. Could it work, he thought to himself? He carefully unwrapped the paper. Then he looked around for the olive pits he had discarded. One of them was still moist. He carefully inscribed a message onto the wrapper with the tip of the pit and crumpled it again. The following day, as he passed one of his comrades he dropped the small wad of paper at his feet. The prisoner looked startled but made no sound. He looked around, and when the guard was not looking stooped to pick up the object. Each week Hamed would pass crumpled wrappers to the other prisoners in the courtyard, and they in turn would pass tiny wads of paper to him. He learned that there were at least 50 prisoners in the camp – mostly Sahrawi soldiers. It wasn't much, but it was enough. And gradually the heavy veil of loneliness began to be lifted.

November, 1984. Ethiopia.

It had been four years since the "wise men" at the OAU had published their recommendation that the conflict over Western Sahara be settled by a referendum, and even though the SADR had been admitted -- theoretically at least -- as a member of the organization in 1982, Hassan had managed to keep its delegates from attending OAU summit meetings for two years, with the Moroccan delegation threatening to render any session inquorate that involved the participation of the Sahrawis.

But this year was different, and as Mengistu Haile Mariam, the chair of the OAU's summit in Ethiopia, in November of 1984, searched the faces of the seated delegations, he recognized Mohamed Abdelaziz, President of the SADR, and a number of Polisario leaders. Sitting opposite him was Ahmed Reda Guedira, the leader of the delegation from Morocco. When the meeting was called to order Guedira read the assemblage a letter from the King, and he and his entourage, as expected, walked out of the room. This time they were not followed by their familiar entourage, this time only one other delegation – the delegation from Zaire – joined them. But the Moroccan government had not merely withdrawn from the meeting, it had withdrawn from the organization -- the first state to have done so in the organization's history.

The Chairman was calm. The long struggle was over and the die had been cast. It was now up to the remaining members of the organization to push forward. Fingering the microphone at the dais where he was seated, he cleared his throat and welcomed the delegates, extending a particularly strong welcome to the delegation from the organization's fifty first member.

The SADR had won a significant political coup – but it was at a price. Khaddafi, in a pique over having been denied his summit in Tripoli the year before, had begged Abdelaziz to stay away from the Addis Ababa meeting and to convince the states that supported the SADR to do likewise. This created a showdown between Khaddafi and the Algerians. The Polisario was placed in the difficult position of having to choose between their two closest allies,

319

and for weeks there had been heated debates among the guerilla leaders. But, after having waited so long, the SADR could not refrain from finally taking its seat in the organization. Following the meeting Khaddafi left immediately for Saudi Arabia. From there he traveled to Morocco, where he embraced Hassan in a short lived détente, and turned his back once and for all on the Sahrawi cause.

December 20, 1984. Lemonade.

It was late in December, and Abdelaziz had called together all the commanders for a strategy meeting. They had won a hard fought battle for admission to the OAU, but faced new challenges on the ground. Try as they might, they had not been able to prevent the Moroccans from extending their huge sand barrier through most of the territory.

And fighting the Moroccan forces enclosed within the berm had proved to be difficult. At Smara they had had to dig through at least seven defensive barriers surrounded by land mines, making it impossible to launch a surprise attack on the command center before reinforcements arrived. At Zmoul Niran their forces had been able to penetrate roughly 5 miles beyond the barrier, attacking and destroying Moroccan forces in defensive positions along the wall and some of the mobile intervention forces that had come to their rescue. But they had not been able to penetrate as far as the Moroccans' command center which was situated over 10 miles behind it, and had found it difficult to retreat quickly and escape bombardments by Moroccan jets with the slow moving and unwieldy tanks.

Their large scale assaults on targets outside the berm had fared little better -- they had been forced to abandon their siege of Lemseid without destroying the garrison's command center, despite blockading the garrison for weeks and destroying the Moroccans' defensive line seven times. And they were quickly running out of targets outside the berm.

Abdelaziz shook his head solemnly. "We can't go on like this," he said, casting a glance at each one of them in turn. "It is too difficult to penetrate beyond the berm, and by the time we are able to get beyond their defensive positions we have lost the element of surprise. Also, our tanks are useful to break through the walls, but are difficult to maneuver once we are beyond the perimeter, and too slow moving for a quick retreat. And to get them close to the wall without being detected well, that takes a logistics genius!"

"Well, we managed to do it at Zmoul Niran, so it is not impossible," said Bachir.

"Yes, but we will not always be able to find a radar dead zone," he replied, "and we won't be able to simply dig our way through the walls much longer, already the Moroccans are beginning to increase the height of portions of the berm and fortify them with stone. In the future we will have to get close enough to blast through the walls. We need to find some way to neutralize their radar and their surveillance capabilities before we launch any more large scale attacks."

The room became silent, each one of them deep in thought.

Finally, Bachir raised his voice. "Let's look on the bright side. There is no doubt that the berm presents a logistics problem. But the Moroccans are concentrating nearly all their forces along it – nearly 180,000 men as far as I can tell – and the cost of maintaining them there cannot be borne forever – even with Saudi money."

". . . and most of them are in fixed positions," added Akeik, "They can't go beyond the berm to chase our forces without running into their own land mines, and even with their sophisticated surveillance equipment it is difficult for them to detect our positions as long as we keep moving . . ."

". . . and their pilots are still afraid of our missiles, so they don't fly low enough to do major damage even when they do intercept us," added Bachir.

"So, we still have the freedom to roam at will beyond the berm," noted Akeik.

". . . and in the meantime, their troops are like sitting ducks," added Bouhali, "Never knowing when . . . or where to expect an attack."

Abdelaziz paused for a moment, deep in thought. "Yes, there must be some way to turn all of that to our advantage," he finally said.

Ghali, who had been quiet during the conversation, looked at each one in turn. "I think that before we plan our next major assault we should spend a little more time probing the Moroccan defenses, finding their weaknesses."

'I don't know," Bouhali said, shaking his head. "It would be a mistake to let the Moroccans think that we are being deterred by their wall."

"But it would be a greater mistake to rush into new attacks before we have fully mastered their defensive system!" Ghali quickly retorted.

"I think Brahim is right," Abdelaziz answered. "We have nothing to lose, and everything to gain by taking our time to make sure we are thoroughly prepared." Then turning to Bachir, he queried, "What is that English saying you mentioned to me the other day, Bachir?"

Bachir thought for a second, then smiled. " 'If life gives you lemons, find a way to make lemonade!' "

"Well, that is just what we need to do . . ." Abdelaziz said, "We need to find a way to make lemonade!"

CHAPTER 12
1985

The year 1984 had ended with a political stalemate in the Sahara. The King had gained a new ally, but the SADR had become a full fledged member of the OAU. And on the ground Moroccan troops found themselves sequestered behind an ever expanding series of walls that would eventually bisect the territory.

The initial walls were built of sand, no more than three feet high, with Moroccan troops positioned at irregular intervals along them. As the war progressed, so did the sophistication of the berms – and by 1985 most of the walls were made of stone as well as sand, high enough to shield an individual from view, topped with the latest radar equipment provided by corporations in the United States and other major Western suppliers. Along the entire length of the berm in the later years were army installations at regular intervals, and behind them at the same regular intervals, barracks and a command post manned by several hundred soldiers. Protecting the berm were land mines so sensitive that the touch of a camel's hoof would result in a blast heard for miles. By 1984 satellite images of Polisario troop movements were being sent to the commanders of these posts at least once per day, courtesy of the United States CIA. If there was an attack at any point along the berm, reinforcements from surrounding "rapid intervention forces" would immediately scramble to its defense.

By 1984 the initial wall surrounding Smara, Boucraa and Laayoune had been extended from a point southwest of Boucraa past Smara to Amgala, with a tiny, separate section surrounding the town of Dakhla. Then, later that year, the northern segment had been expanded to enclose Farsia, Jdiriya and Housa and reach as far as Zag. By the end of the year only the Guelta Zemmour oasis, the small outpost of Awsard, the wells of Mudraiga near the Zemmour massif, and the region of Mahbes close to the Algerian border, would be beyond the enclosures.

But beyond the walls the guerillas roamed at will.

. . . and they began to make lemonade.

The year 1985 saw a number of battles between Polisario forces and the Moroccans trying to build the 5th extension of the berm -- the one that would enclose the southern regions -- as well as several other battles near Dakhla. However, within months they had ushered in a period they called the "War of

Attrition," a period spent probing the Moroccan defenses to determine their weak points and developing measures to exploit them.

The guerillas first employed some of the tactics they had used in their previous battles to disarm the land mines. During the night specially trained troops would crawl on their stomachs, inch by inch, through the mine field, silently and gently feeling the ground around them. When they discovered a mine they would carefully dislodge it and place it in knapsacks on their backs, then cover its hole with sand once again. In this way, during a period of months, whole swaths of land mines would be removed without the Moroccans being any the wiser. When the Moroccans began to examine the mine fields every morning, instead of removing the entire mine the guerillas simply removed the firing pins and placed the inoperative object back where it belonged.

Next, they addressed the radar installations. Much of the radar equipment that had been supplied by the United States and other Western powers was not well suited to the sandstorms and extremely high temperatures of the Sahara, and was only sporadically operational. Indeed, the radar failed to operate so many times that at one point in the war the Moroccans turned to dogs to warn them of the guerillas' presence. When the radar *was* in operation, they found that it could not detect movements at a certain distance, or when units were in a "dead zone" protected by hills and gullies, so they would be able to approach the berm easily at these points. They would then use this knowledge to harass the Moroccan troops. At times they would avoid tripping the radar. At night individual guerillas would take turns approaching the berm through dead zones close enough to observe the movement of the soldiers and overhear their conversations. Then they would silently dig fox holes under the berm and from these positions hurl grenades into the camp before silently retreating. At other times they would take advantage of the radar. Small infantry units would quietly creep to positions camouflaged by hills or crevices and beyond the range of the radar at several points along the berm. Then they would conduct a "cat and mouse" game – approaching the berm quietly by foot at night, then appearing at dawn, tripping the radar and quickly scampering out of the reach of the Moroccan artillery. The Moroccans, in a futile effort to attack them, would waste round after round of ammunition. They would some times do this several times a night along the entire length of the berm.

Eventually the Moroccans would become so accustomed to their presence that they would not react when the radar sounded. In some cases, in order to get some sleep, they would even disconnect the installations. In these ways over time the Polisario were able to effectively neutralize the radar.

Most of the time during this period the guerillas would make no attempt to engage the Moroccan troops in battle. Rather, the warfare was psychological. The intention of the guerillas was to innerve them, drain their resistance, and deprive them of needed ammunition. They employed numerous methods. At times they would simply remove the barbed wire that was placed on top of the berm. On one occasion after the Moroccans had spent three months laying barbed wire, one day they awoke to discover that it had been removed overnight. On another occasion the guerillas, spotting a Bedouin family on the other side of the berm, waited until dark, sneaked through the berm at a point between two large Moroccan battalions, and quietly evacuated the civilians --camels, goats and all – to the great consternation of the Moroccan commanders the following day.

These constant and unpredictable harassments forced Hassan to deploy ever increasing numbers of troops along the berm, augmenting the cost of the war exponentially. Before long it became a question of the soldiers protecting the berm, not the other way around.

But attacks did occur. And the Moroccans, never sure whether these petty annoyances were the precursor of a major attack – or which part of the berm would be subject to such an attack -- spent their sleepless nights in nervous anticipation.

June 10, 1985 was such a night.

June 10, 1985. Somewhere Along the Berm.

It was June 5, 1985, a sultry summer evening, and a Moroccan sentry in an outpost near Housa had just finished the bottle of wine he took to accompany him as he manned one of the turrets that dotted the berm. He was not supposed to be drinking alcohol – not only was it against the Moslem religion but it was against Army regulations. But he was in the middle of nowhere, alone, on a sand wall, in the middle of the night, looking out on the vast desert, and he longed to be back in Casablanca with his young wife and child, far from the heat and the boredom that filled his days.

All at once, without warning a screeching wail pierced the calm. He shot out of his chair, his hands reflectively grasping his rifle, eyes fixed on the perimeter of the wall. Nothing. Around him he could hear the shouts of men aroused from their slumber, scrambling out of their barracks, searching for weapons in the darkness. The wailing lasted for a good three minutes before it ceased. By this time the entire platoon was up and at their positions along the berm, waiting, with eyes glued to the nothingness of the desert. Still nothing. After a tense few minutes the soldiers began to drift back to their enclosures, muttering under their breath. The sentry returned to his chair. Maybe it was a stray camel or even a fox, he thought, nervously.

An hour passed, or maybe two. The sentry was finding it difficult to keep from sleeping. One of the consequences of too much alcohol. Then, once again, the tranquility of the night was pierced by the wail. Once again the soldiers ran from their barracks to their positions on the wall. Once again, nothing.

In the morning, the platoon leader received a wire from the troop commandant. The same thing had happened during the night at Jdiriya and Smara. Soon other wires arrived, the problem was cited at three more locations along the berm. Commanders were ordered to check the radar installations. But the radar seemed to be working fine.

The next night, the same thing occurred. The radar suddenly started issuing warning blasts, but there were no troops to be seen or heard. Three times, four times during the night. The troops, already demoralized and bored, started to become irritable from lack of sleep.

It was now the 10th of June. Radar had been blasting on and off for five nights and the soldiers had begun to ignore the alarms. And that is when the guerillas struck.

Quietly, under cover of darkness, a handful of shadowy figures inched their way close to the perimeter of the berm. Using only their fingers they carefully sifted through the gravel and rocks before them, searching for the round metal that would indicate the presence of a land mine. When they found one they would ever so carefully dig around it with their fingernails, before extracting it and placing it in a sack on their backs. Following closely on their heels were commando units carrying heavy equipment. It took them more than two hours, crawling on their bellies, to traverse a distance of fewer than 100 yards. When they were within a few yards of the wall, the siren started to wail. Using this noise to cover their footpaths, they quickly scrambled up the embarkation, cut the barbed wire, and scurried to the other side. Between them and the garrison of sleeping soldiers were 300 yards of open desert. Quickly, and quietly they buried the land mines at strategic points and then retreated once again to the wall. At a pre-arranged signal they opened fire.

They quickly overcame the sentry guards who manned the outposts and from those outposts began firing at the soldiers stationed at fixed positions along the berm. After a few seconds, the soldiers from the garrison began to stream out of their bunkers. One by one the land mines began to explode. In the dust and confusion the Moroccans lost their sense of direction and began running in all directions. Those who advanced to the wall were met by the onslaught of guerilla forces; many chose to run into the desert. The commandos retreated as quickly as they had come, before the 'rapid intervention forces' could reach the scene. By morning there was nothing left of a quarter mile stretch but a few smoldering buildings, bits of bloodied clothing and an empty bottle of wine in a sentry turret.

November, 1985. The Diplomat.

It was a lovely autumn day in New York and the Secretary General of the United Nations, Javier Perez de Cuellar, was glad to be home after a grueling trip to some of the most remote regions of Africa. De Cuellar, a Peruvian born of aristocratic Spanish lineage, was a diplomat of the old school, when diplomacy was the second sport of Kings, and the destiny of millions was often settled in the parlors of grand mansions on Park Avenue, Berkeley Square and Avenue Foche. His career was fueled by a form of *noblesse oblige*, where undertaking the problems of the world was considered a sacred duty. By the time he became the Secretary General of the United Nations he had tried his hand at settling a number of intractable disputes. In 1974, as Permanent Representative of Peru to the United Nations, he had been that country's

325

representative on the Security Council when events heated up in Cyprus. In September of the following year he was appointed the Special Representative of the United Nations Secretary General for Cyprus – a post he held until the end of 1977. Then, in 1979 he was appointed Under Secretary General for Political Affairs, and, in 1981, while still holding this post, he became the Special Representative of the Secretary General for Afghanistan during the Soviet invasion. But despite his gallant efforts none of his interventions in these crises had been able to bring about the peaceful solution he desired. So, when he replaced Kurt Waldheim in 1982 as Secretary General, he was more determined than ever that when he left office he would leave behind him a positive legacy.

It was now 1985, his appointment as Secretary General would be up for renewal in one year, and he still had not made the impact he wanted. In 1982 his attempt to mediate a peaceful solution between Argentina and the United Kingdom over the Falklands had been futile, and his attempts to resolve other conflicts in the Americas had produced mixed results.

As the product of a former Spanish colony he exhibited a natural interest in the fate of sister colonies, and his attention gradually shifted to the former Spanish colony on the African coast, particularly after a meeting in 1982 with Olaf Palme, an influential member of the Nobel committee, who introduced him to the leader of the Polisario. Although most of his fellow diplomats had quickly turned to other matters when the fighting in North Africa de-escalated in 1984, the status of Western Sahara was still in limbo, and ending the intractable conflict over the territory quickly became somewhat of an obsession with him. . . a personal crusade. In order to better acquaint himself with the issues – and the protagonists – he had decided to take a whirlwind trip to the region, visiting the King of Morocco in 1985 and attending the OAU summit, which was held that year in Addis Ababa. What he had learned was not propitious. The King had no intention of relinquishing one inch of the territory, despite his promises to the United Nations and the OAU to permit a referendum to decide the territory's future. The members of the OAU – particularly Algeria, Nigeria, Zimbabwe, Angola, Tanzania and Mozambique -- were just as adamant about the right of the people of the territory to self determination. There was no way to reconcile the two positions. He would have to pull a diplomatic rabbit out of a hat to solve this one.

When he was back in his office he called for one of his aides, a quiet, dark haired young woman in her mid-30s, and handed her a fat dossier.

"Here," he said somewhat wearily, "I want you to take a look at these papers. They are a proposal drafted by a committee of the OAU to address the Western Sahara issue. I understand that many of the details were proposed by the President of Algeria himself. See what you think of them and report back to me as soon as you can."

The young woman sighed. She was familiar with the conflict. The OAU had for years tried to find a way to reconcile the positions of the parties without any result, and she doubted that the United Nations could do any better. But she would keep her opinion to herself – at least for the time being.

"Have you formed any impression of the parties?" she asked somewhat nonchalantly.

De Cuellar, who had started reading some papers on his desk, spoke without looking up. "I found the King to be charming . . . elegant . . . and quite shrewd, even if a bit stubborn," he said, "He made it quite clear that he would welcome having a referendum decide the status of the territory . . . as long as it was on his terms! As for Bendjedid . . . well, he did not seem to have any personal animosity towards the King . . . I think he would be glad to have the dispute handled amicably. But that guerilla leader . . ." He shook his head and looked up. "Don't you think it is ironic that the would-be leader of a former Spanish colony can't even speak decent Spanish!" he said with a note of sarcasm. "In any event I doubt I will have to deal with him too much," he added, returning to his papers and waiving his hand in a gesture of dismissal.

The aide took the papers and started for the door.

"Oh, by the way," de Cuellar called after her, "for the time being let us keep this matter just to ourselves."

The woman stopped and turned to face him. De Cuellar gave her a look that needed no interpretation. Like most diplomats he preferred to play his cards close to his chest, and laying the diplomatic underpinnings for an overture of this magnitude is best done in secret.

"Understood," the young woman said as she quietly closed the door behind her.

CHAPTER 13
1986

By 1986 most of the towns and army installations in the territory had been enclosed behind the berm, and the Polisario leaders intensified their "War of Attrition."

Brahim Ghali took all the fighters and trained them in the removal of land mines and the placement of them behind the berm, and in determining dead zones and vulnerable positions along the berm. The land mine campaign lasted months. As a result, the Moroccans gradually decreased the zone of protection of the land mines from 500 yards beyond the berm to 300 yards and eventually to only 50 yards. Moreover, they were forced to check the land mines daily. Instead of the land mines protecting them, they had to protect the land mines

In the first stage of the "War of Attrition" Polisario units had concentrated on finding ways of approaching the berm without tripping the radar or land mines to mount sneak attacks on Moroccan troops stationed along the berm before fading into the dust. When they did intentionally trip the radar – in order to strike fear into the hearts of the troops guarding the wall or lull them into complacency -- it was at three or four isolated positions.

But now the "War of Attrition" was in its second year, and they decided to adopt a new strategy. They mobilized hundreds of troops, as well as residents of the camps -- to race along the berm night and day in full view of the Moroccans, making as much noise as possible and deliberately setting off the radar, daring them to fire upon them. At times they would play peek-a-boo in the ravines and crevices that abutted the wall. At other times they would lob fire crackers into the air over the Moroccan troops. They would sometimes place aluminum in the trees for the Moroccan artillery to shoot at. On some nights the entire length of the berm would be ablaze.

Brahim Ghali even organized competitions among the troops of the various regions to see which one could wreak the most havoc – and awarded prizes at the end of the year for those who had carried out the most frontal assaults or the most assaults from the rear, for those who had removed the greatest number of land mines or discovered the most dead zones, or for those who had engaged in the greatest number of provocations!

And everyone joined the fray. . .

February 27, 1986. Sidi at the Berm.

Sidimi checked the engine of her jeep once again to make sure it would stand the rigors of tonight's escapade. Even though she realized that the others she had trained were fully capable of handling the wounded on the battle field and that her talents were needed at the hospital, her spirit had remained with those at the front lines, and she had been itching to join the fray for months. By the end of 1985 the southern segment of the berm had been extended to encompass Guelta Zemmour. Like a giant octopus it had gradually ensnared within its tentacles the major towns and outposts of the territory leaving only a narrow strip of land in the east and south outside its enclosure. While most of the troops were busy trying to impede its progress as best they could the residents of the camps had been mobilized to harass the troops along its entire length. And Sidimi was eager to join them.

It was now the 27th of February, 1986 – the 10th anniversary of the proclamation of the SADR – a particularly auspicious occasion for what she had planned. So it was with a sense of exhilaration that she loaded the jeep with the gear she would need – her trusty AK-47, binoculars, a flashlight, provisions for a night's escapade, and enough ammunition to last a several hours' shooting spree.

When she had just about finished a figure approached her tent.

"Sidi, I want to join you," she said, matter-of-factly.

Sidimi looked at the young woman in front of her and shook her head. "Elena, I can't bring you along. It will be too dangerous," she replied. "Besides which, you don't know how to use one of these," she added pointing to her weapon.

"But I know how to drive," Elena said in a firm voice. "None of the other women can drive and there are no men available to drive you . . . and you can't drive and shoot at the same time!"

Sidimi stopped for a moment. It was true. She couldn't drive and shoot at the same time. She had planned to stop, shoot, and then speed off . . . but stopping would make her an easier target.

"Elena, if anything happened to you I would never hear the end of it from Bouhali . . . not to mention Salek!" she finally said.

Elena smiled. "But if anything happened to me it would probably happen to you as well . . . and we would both be buried as heroes!" she responded, in a slightly amused tone.

Sidimi tried, without success, to stifle a smile. Elena had changed a lot since coming to the camp. She was no longer a teenager and the pampered daughter of privilege she had been back in El Ayoun. She had blossomed into a strong-willed woman in her late twenties and had withstood the rigors of the hospital. She had become one of them.

"All right, Elena," she finally said with a sigh, "but you will have to do exactly what I say. Your life . . . and mine . . . may depend on it."

And with those last words they took off.

The sun was just beginning to set. Soon nightfall would cover the desert with a rich, dark blanket. There would be no street lamps to pierce the darkness, only the twinkling stars to guide the way. Sidi was as familiar with the desert as Bouhali and deftly guided the vehicle through the *hammada* to its destination. Before them, in the distance, they could see the glimmer of lights sprinkled at intervals along a long chain that extended in each direction as far as they could see. Watch towers. Soon they saw the headlights of a vehicle approaching them from the south.

"Who's there," yelled the driver, as he came closer.

"Its Sidi," she responded.

Within another moment he had joined her. It was one of the soldiers she had treated at the hospital and after they had exchanged the obligatory greetings, he told her that he and a small group of soldiers had planned to patrol the berm to the south, and that others in his unit were even farther south.

"If you want to patrol the area to the north, that would be helpful," he added, giving Elena a quizzical look.

"Fine," Sidimi replied, ignoring the look, "and give my regards to Bouhali when you see him!"

The soldier grinned and departed.

When he had left, Sidimi got into the passenger seat and loaded her weapon.

"Elena, you must do exactly what I say," she started to say. "I want you to turn off the headlights and pull closer to the berm until we trip the radar. Then you should put your headlights on and drive away quickly in a course parallel to the berm. Try to keep the same distance away. Any closer and we might run into land mines . . . and any farther away and I might not be able to hit anything. . . and try not to hit any major holes, I don't want to have to repair a broken axle!"

"Any other orders?" Elena demanded, wryly, taking the steering wheel in her hand and turning off the lights.

Sidimi put her hand gently on her shoulder. "I know you are up to it," were her last words as they sped off.

After they had travelled another hundred yards or so the stillness of the night was disturbed by the wail of a siren and they could hear men shouting in the distance. As soon as she had heard the siren Sidimi aimed her gun at one of the lights that stood atop the closest tower. Shots rang out in both directions as Elena darted from the scene at full speed. Sidimi fired again, and then again. After the third shot she could see sparks flying from one of her targets. A radar installation had been damaged. They raced alongside the large sand snake for an hour, carefully keeping inches out of the range of the Moroccans' bullets. Sidimi had managed to place bullet holes in three of the radar installations, and once or twice a Moroccan bullet had managed to lodge itself in the side of her car.

Just as she had settled back into her seat a tremendous jolt sent her flying and the jeep teetered perilously on its side. She grabbed her flashlight and looked around to where Elena, slightly dazed, had begun to extricate herself from the driver's seat. "Are you all right?" she asked, in a low voice. Elena brushed away a lock of hair to reveal a trickle of blood. "I hit my head, but it is not serious," she replied, with a weak smile. Sidimi looked at the wound. "It didn't fracture anything. You are lucky," she said, "but you will probably have a large lump for a few days!"

Elena smiled. "What happened?" she asked, looking around her.

Sidimi pointed the flashlight at the ground. The front left tire had disappeared into a large hole. "Apparently we hit a ditch. Maybe the Moroccans are laying traps for us," she said after circling the vehicle.

"What can we do?" asked Elena, trying to hide her alarm.

"Well, we'll just have to push it out!" Sidimi exclaimed, calmly.

"That's easier said than done," replied Elena, for the first time in her life wishing that there was a man . . . preferably more than one . . . around.

Sidimi laughed. "We can do it, just wait and see! It is only a matter of leverage."

She took a moment to study the position of the wheel, then she told Elena to lean against the right rear axle with all her strength. The front wheel lifted a few inches. She quickly placed dirt and rocks under the tire. Then they started to push the vehicle over the rim of the hole. But before they were able to move it more than another inch, a blast of gunfire and the sharp whizz of a bullet caused them to take cover. Bullets were flying in their direction from the berm, and one or two of them had managed to reach as far as the car.

Sidimi raised her head just enough to see, in the distance, the outline of the berm, illuminated by lights. There, on a watch tower, beneath a radar installation that was piercing the night with a high pitched wail, was the shadow of a man . . . a lone sentry.

"I think he is the one firing at us," Sidimi announced. "We must have wandered too close to the berm and he saw our flashlight. We are not quite out of range."

Now Elena could not disguise her alarm.

"What can we do?" she asked, excitedly. "We can't move the jeep with him shooting at us!"

Sidimi thought for a moment. "There is only one thing we can do," she replied, "I will have to shoot him!"

"But how?" asked Elena, a note of apprehension in her voice.

"If we are in range of his weapon, he must be in range of ours," she said, matter-of-factly as she extinguished the flashlight and in the total darkness began to inch closer to the wall. She tried to sound calm, but her muscles tensed as she crept closer, feeling with her fingers for metal in the dirt before taking each step. If they were in range of the Moroccans' guns, they were in range of the land mines.

After a few hesitant steps she stopped and looked up. She could barely see the silhouette of the man's head and shoulders as he crouched in the turret.

I will have to aim this carefully, she thought as she rested the weapon against her shoulder. Then she slowly squeezed the trigger. At once the blast

331

of the gun reverberated in her ears and as she looked on, the figure of the man jerked and slowly slumped below view.

She backtracked quickly the way she had come to where Elena had crouched at the side of the jeep, and told her to move quickly. In the total darkness they heaved and heaved, and finally were able to push the vehicle onto the level ground. Then they pushed it a few yards away from the berm, out of the range of the Moroccans' guns, before finally starting the motor and racing away.

It was already 4 o'clock in the morning, long after the other guerillas had called it a night, and a very weary, but exhilarated duo ambled their way back to the welcoming embrace of their comrades.

February 28, 1986. Moroccan Command Post Laayoune.

It was 6 o'clock that same morning and Colonel Abdelaziz Banani, the commander of the Moroccan forces in the Sahara, had just finished his second cup of coffee in his office in Laayoune. By this time he had become accustomed to the early hours. And to the reports. For weeks now he had received the same reports, day after day. So, when a flushed faced lieutenant knocked on his door, he was not surprised.

"What is it now," he asked somewhat wearily.

The lieutenant started to read from a bunch of papers in his hands. "The commander of the 2nd regiment reported enemy presence 150 miles southwest of Amgala. The radar seemed to work but the enemy was able to get to the perimeter of the land mines before being detected. His troops were able to see headlights in the distance, and there was considerable commotion, but they were out of the range of his weapons. They remained in the vicinity all night, causing the radar to blast continuously until they decided to disconnect it. He also reported that a stretch of barbed wire along the berm in his district had been removed during the night. The 1st regiment reported enemy presence along a five mile stretch between Housa and Farsia. They could see enemy vehicles and hear the noise of their engines. They attempted to fire upon them, but they were moving too fast and they were slightly out of range. Their radar kept them up all night. The radar of the 3rd regiment's post at Amgala did not detect any movement, but the dogs they recently acquired barked continuously for two hours and they could hear noises and see lights in the desert. The commander of the 4th regiment near Zag reported seeing columns of guerillas at dawn and fired upon them. It is unclear whether any of them were destroyed since his troops were prevented from investigating because of the land mines." The lieutenant stopped for a moment to catch his breath. "Sir, we are still receiving reports. Do you want me to return . . ."

The commanding officer shook his head and dismissed him with a wave of his hand. "No, that will not be necessary," he finally said. And the lieutenant quickly made his exit.

He heaved a sigh. He had been assigned this command after the Dlimi debacle. At first he had relished the opportunities it offered – financial as well as military. By the time he had been promoted to the rank of colonel he had amassed a small fortune from business enterprises in his native city, Fez. And now he was doing the same in the Sahara. Already he was in control of the lucrative fishing trade off the coast of Dakhla and he was gradually consolidating his control over trade with the Canary Islands and establishing a number of other commercial ventures in the territory. Although the war was gradually bankrupting the country and causing severe economic hardship to most of its citizens, it had proved quite lucrative to him. His only problem had been placating the King.

He knew enough not to try to sugar coat matters with Hassan! He remembered what happened when Dlimi had tried to soft pedal the guerilla victory at Tan Tan. No, he would not try to sugar coat things. In the past year it hadn't been necessary. During the previous year the only serious encounters with the guerillas had been with the troops building the latest extension of the berm, and they had not been able to overcome the enormous buildup of troops he had assigned to protect the engineers. He had begun to think that the wall strategy was working. Then the harassment started. First it had been just some foolish pranks – removing the land mines at night, cutting the barbed wire, tripping the radar – just enough to rattle the nerves of his troops and cause them sleepless nights. But then the attacks had started. Nothing big – but enough to panic the troops. He had traveled to the field on more than one occasion to soothe their nerves, but nothing seemed to work. And now this new development – hundreds of guerillas patrolling the berm at night, tripping the radar, causing havoc – not at just one or two locations, but along its entire length.

He barked an order and soon another fresh faced lieutenant entered the room.

"I have just gotten another dozen reports of enemy activity along the line. Tell me, once again, why it is that we cannot use the satellite imagery and surveillance equipment the Americans have given us to pinpoint the enemy locations and destroy them," he growled.

The lieutenant -- the engineer in charge of the surveillance equipment -- blanched. "The radar, when it is working, only tells us that they are there, not their exact location, sir," he stammered, "and when we do see them they are always out of range of our weapons." He cleared his throat before continuing. "And we only get satellite images once or twice a day . . . and by the time we get them they have already moved on. The same with the Westinghouse equipment . . . they move too fast along the berm at night for it to be useful."

The General gave him a withering look. "You mean to tell me that with millions of dollars worth of sophisticated surveillance equipment we *still* cannot pinpoint their movements? What about their camps? They have to camp somewhere!"

The lieutenant shuffled his feet slightly.

"We have been able to pinpoint some of their camps in the desert from time to time, and we inform the commanders of the Air Force, but they don't seem to be able to neutralize them."

"Why not?" barked the Colonel, growing impatient.

"Well, sir, apparently the pilots are afraid to fly too low because of their anti-aircraft missiles, so they dump their bombs from a high altitude, and some times they hit their target . . . but most of the time they don't," he replied in a low voice.

"So, you mean there is nothing we can do but sit here and wait for them to attack?" the Colonel yelled.

The lieutenant, turning red, did not answer.

The Colonel waved his hand, and the lieutenant was dismissed.

When he was alone again, he thought of all the great military campaigns of history and wondered what Napoleon or Alexander or Julius Caesar would have done. Despite all the precautions he had taken – installing radar, fortifying the structures, placing barbed wire and land mines as protection, and placing practically the entire army in posts along the berm, he hadn't been able to stop the harassment of his troops – or the surprise attacks.

And what about these vaunted commando units that had been trained by the Americans? The few times they had ventured from the protection of the berm they had been mowed down like rabbits. No, venturing into the wasteland had proved to be no answer.

He sat at his desk mulling over the situation he was in. The harassment of his troops along the berm and the constant attacks by guerilla forces against the troops building the last sections of the berm had caused him headaches. But at least they hadn't been able to penetrate beyond the berm to attack major military installations or the troops in the main population centers, he consoled himself thinking. Let them wander in the desert, we have what we want – the phosphates, the fisheries, the main population centers – and already they have been put to use. The Boucraa mine was back in operation, adding much needed revenue to the depleted Moroccan coffers. And the government was awarding lucrative fishing licenses to companies eager to exploit the vast marine resources off the coast. And when the berm was finally completed . . . well, it would protect nearly 80% of the territory from guerilla attacks. It will all come to pass eventually, he thought to himself. All I have to do is wait.

And with that last thought he finished his report to the King, took an aspirin for his headache, and prepared to face another day.

October, 1986. Tindouf.

It was the middle of the night in the second week of October, and Soukeina was having trouble going to sleep. Thoughts of her great-grandfather swirled in her head, and he seemed to be calling to her from some faraway place. Ever since she arrived in the camps she had waited for some word, some slight news of whether he was still alive. And as the months and years passed, so did her hope of ever seeing him again. Tonight, like so many other nights, she spent the evening hours tossing and turning on the blanket that served as her bed. The winds had picked up, making an eerie howling noise as it rippled through the tents, covering everything with a blanket of fine red dust.

By this time Soukeina had grown accustomed to the piercing winds that could suddenly, without warning, turn the sky pitch black and topple the tents like match sticks. But tonight the winds had brought with them droplets of rain, first only one or two that would tap the canvass tent gently before rolling off nonchalantly towards the earth, but then a dozen more . . . and more still, until a steady tapping of water on canvass broke the silence of the night. Soukeina arose from where she lay and peered out of the tent. In the near total darkness she could hear the patter of raindrops glancing off the stones that littered the ground and when she extended her arm tiny pinpricks of water rolled off it. She hurriedly unfurled the canvass flap that exposed the entrance to the tent. But soon the flap began to quiver ominously and within minutes a strong gust of wind sent it flailing to the roof of the tent. She managed to grab it, but before she could fasten it to its stakes she heard a noise she had never heard before . . . a noise that sounded like the roar of an angry beast, and looking down she saw that her feet were covered in water . . . water that was quickly turning the winding footpath in front of her into a small stream. The water quickly started to penetrate the tent, and for the next few minutes Soukeina tried desperately to save the rugs that were strewn on the floor and keep the water from washing away the cups and kettles she used for tea. Outside she could hear shouts as other women, awakened by the rain, scurried about doing the same.

Sidimi, at the other side of the camp, heard the noise too. She peered outside her tent. The sand was drenched and sticky. She took large canvas bags of rice and shoved them against the walls of the tent. Then she quickly ran to the building that housed most of the critically wounded. The walls of the building were intact, and the floor was mostly dry, but small rivulets of water were slowly dripping from the roof, perilously close to the equipment, vials of medicine, and patients who lay helpless on mats and stretchers on the ground. She moved some of the wounded, slowly dragging their mats into a part of the building that the water had not yet penetrated, and hastily gathered the medicine and equipment and covered them with a tarp. Then she huddled near them, and prayed.

Soukeina, meanwhile, was battling what seemed like an avalanche of water. Within a few minutes the small stream outside her tent had grown into a fast moving rivulet, collapsing tents, turning the ground into quicksand, and washing away everything in its path. She waded through the water and mud to check on the animals. Three of the sheep – a ram, a ewe and its lamb -- were mired in the mud, unable to move, the water around them rising fast. With all her strength Soukeina grabbed the ram by his horns and pulled and pulled, falling several times in the water, and after several minutes finally extracted the beast from the mud. Then she went back for the ewe. She had lost her balance and lay on her side in the mud, the water nearly covering her. Her little lamb clung perilously to her, afraid to move. Soukeina pushed and shoved, but she couldn't dislodge her from the mud, and watched helplessly as the water began to cover her. She grabbed the lamb, who was bleating in protest, and waded through the stream to place it on dry land. In the semi-darkness she couldn't see more than a few yards in front of her. Rushing past her in the water were pots, utensils, anything movable, and the small gully in the wilaya that had been the location of several tents was now inundated with water, turning it into a small lake. She watched desolately as the posts of her tent began to crash under the weight of the water and one by one disappear down stream, carrying with them her waterlogged tent.

All at once she remembered the school -- the mud brick building that she and a dozen other women had so carefully built – and the small cache of books and writing utensils that were their prized possessions. Her heart seemed to race ahead of her as she scrambled through the mud and water towards the building, fearful of what she would find. The water had risen now to her knees, making each step arduous and hazardous. She drove herself through instinct – and sheer resolve – through the slippery mess for what seemed an eternity. Finally she reached the place where the path began that would lead to the entrance of the school. Caked in mud from the tip of her toes to her waist she began to extricate herself from the oozing mess when she felt a sharp pain in her head and everything went blank.

Mercifully, the rains of the Sahara are as quick to end as they are to begin, and within another half hour silence descended once more on the camp. The residents huddled together as best they could during the night, and at the first ray of sun began to survey the damage.

A half dozen refugees – the elderly, the young, the weak – had been killed, either drowning in the rushing rivulet or hit by the debris that followed it, and scores of animals as well. Many tents and mud brick buildings had been destroyed along with their contents. The domed shaped roof of the headquarters at Rabouni had caved in, smearing its halls with mud and brick.

Sidimi had been busy at the hospital giving first aid to the fallen when she got the news. She dropped what she was doing and rushed to the spot, a few yards from the schoolhouse, where the body of a woman lay sprawled on a blanket, half covered in mud, surrounded by women. She quickly kneeled beside her and placed her ear to her nose. She was breathing.

"Quick, help me get her to the hospital," she yelled, and together with two other women they half dragged, half carried the body.

It was an hour before she began to regain consciousness. The first thing she saw was Sidimi's face bending over her. She tried to move, but felt woozy.

"It's the morphine, Soukeina," Sidimi said in a soft tone. "You were hit by a piece of a tin roof that collapsed and we gave you something to reduce the pain."

Soukeina lay there for a moment, motionless. Then her eyes widened and she grabbed Sidimi's arm. "The school?" she cried in a worried tone.

"Relax, Soukeina, the school was not damaged," Sidimi responded, holding her hand.

Soukeina managed a smile and her body began to relax. The morphine was making her feel tired. In a semi-conscious trance scenes from her childhood drifted through her mind in an endless procession, and then images of the books she had read -- scenes of faraway places and the faces of the men and women she had read about. And then another figure – her great-grandfather, just like in her dreams, reaching out his arm as if to beckon to her. She could not follow him – not yet. With all her strength she willed her mind back. She grabbed Sidimi's arm once again, the muscles of her body tensing. "You must promise me that you will see to it that the school continues," she said looking deeply into Sidimi's eyes.

"Of course it will continue," Sidimi said, softly, "and it will grow until every last man, woman and child has an education! But now you must try to rest."

Soukeina's body became limp as she drifted once again into her dreams. She dreamt of the day she first wrote the letter "a" in the sand, the day the first handful of women carrying their babies sat beneath an acacia tree to begin the process of learning how to read and write, the day the women lay the first brick in what was to become their school -- and a smile inched across her face. And later that day, when her great-grandfather reached out and beckoned to her again, this time she gave him her hand and followed him quietly into the shadows.

CHAPTER 14
1987

At the beginning of 1987 the Moroccans were in the process of building the final segment of the berm. When finished it would effectively bisect the Western Sahara territory.

The guerillas had stalled its construction as much as they could. When Moroccan forces were concentrated in one region, they would attack positions in another region, forcing them to shift their forces to counter the attacks. They shelled their troops and attacked their supply caravans.

And the constant guerilla threats along the berm had caused the King to deploy ever increasing numbers of troops along its length, increasing the cost of the war to an estimated 1 billion dollars per year and sapping the Kingdom's coffers.

Throughout all this period the guerillas had refrained from launching large scale attacks on targets behind the berm. But after two years of studying and waiting they were finally ready to begin a new stage of the war.

February 1, 1987. A New Stage Begins.

At the beginning of the second month of 1987 -- the month in which the Moroccans started to build the segment of the berm in the south that would reach the Atlantic coast -- Abdelaziz called a meeting of the leaders to discuss strategy.

He came straight to the point. "I think the time has come to launch a large scale attack against the garrisons behind the berm," he said, carefully measuring each word. "By this time we know enough about the weaknesses in their defensive strategy to be able to use our weapons effectively . . . our decoy methods have been able to neutralize the biggest obstacle – their radar -- and we have been able to address the problem of their land mines. There is no longer any reason why we cannot launch a successful major attack on their garrisons." He paused. Then looking directly at the men who surrounded him, he added, "I think we've waited long enough!" The room became silent. During the past two years the guerillas had made important gains politically, becoming a member of the OAU and receiving the recognition of additional countries, but Abdelaziz was savvy enough to know that political gains are ephemeral and could be wiped away in an instant if the Polisario failed to maintain their pressure on the battlefield. Such has always been the way of politics. But he wanted to hear the assessment of the Minister of Defense and the opinions of his commanders.

After waiting a moment he turned to the man at his right. "Do you agree with me, Bouhali?" He needn't have bothered to ask. The leader of the 2nd military region had been waiting for such a decision to be made for weeks. He knew every inch of the berm in his district, and all of its weaknesses. His men were ready and itching for action.

When he spoke his voice was full of passion. "I think we are as ready as we will ever be, and I don't think we can afford to wait much longer before delivering a major blow. It is all well and good to bleed their resources and destroy the morale of their troops, but it may take years before their coffers really feel the effect, especially if they profit from the resources of the territory and the Saudis continue to foot their bills, and they seem to have an inexhaustible supply of young, green recruits to throw at us. And we can't let them build the final stage of the berm without giving them a message . . . a message that a wall will not deter us!"

Abdelaziz looked around the room. The others were nodding in agreement. "We need to show them once and for all that they cannot rely upon the berm as a defense," one of them said, emphatically. "Yes," another added, "we need to inflict the kind of wound that makes the King take notice. . . that scares the Moroccan people . . . and forces him to face the fact that the war will go on indefinitely unless he keeps the promise he made in 1981 to permit a referendum."

". . . or withdraws from the territory!" said another, vehemently.

A heated conversation ensued as one by one the leaders vented their emotions. The years of waiting patiently had been difficult. They were ready for action. Suddenly the group became silent, as all eyes turned to Ghali.

"We are ready," was all he needed to say. They were all in agreement. Good. Now for the second question. How should they proceed?

Abdelaziz took out a map and spread it on the table. On it were written notes indicating the positions and strengths of the Moroccan troops along the berm.

"We know that the bulk of Morocco's army along the berm has been divided into three sectors along geographic lines, each containing 4 or 5 regiments, each regiment containing two battalions," he said, drawing circles on the map to show the locations. "But the battalions are not evenly distributed," he continued, "In some areas there are nearly a thousand troops, in others only a few hundred. The areas on the map in red indicate the positions where the troops are the thinnest."

"Let me see that map," Bouhali asked, moving closer to get a better look. When he had spent a moment scrutinizing it, he pointed to an area near Farsia. "They have just finished constructing the wall in this area, " he said. "In the past we have been able to get within a few yards of it without being detected. . . despite the fact that their positions are elevated. Their commander, Abdelamen Marti, is currently away being treated for wounds he received in a battle two months ago, and his replacement isn't as experienced. . . and now

339

that the majority of their forces have been sent south to construct the berm near Guelta, their forces along the berm in this area are thinly spread out."

Abdelaziz looked at the spot where he was pointing. Yes, he remembered it from his forays with the troops from the 1st military region. It would not offer many areas to hide, but it was within easy reach of their outposts, and with the right preparations it just might work.

And the long awaited preparations for the onslaught began.

Abdelaziz called a meeting on the 16th of February with a majority of the central command to plan the attack in meticulous detail. Special emphasis was placed on engineering. . . how to neutralize the land mines, the barbed wire, the trenches, the radar defenses, and blast through the fortified entrances. It was decided to organize the training of soldiers in demolition techniques and to take them to inspect the area that would be under attack. The commander of the 6th military region, Mohammed Akeik, was placed in charge of the training program. Abdelaziz oversaw the other preparations. The attack would involve two battalions and one squadron of anti aircraft specialists from the 2nd military region as well as their mechanized units and SAM 6 missiles; 3 units of infantry and artillery from the 5th military region; 4 units of infantry from the 4th military region; and from the 6th military region, one unit of artillery of three different sizes, and some soldiers who would go behind the berm to place mines.

After a week of preparations they were ready.

February 17, 1987. The Serpent.

The long sand serpent bisected the desert until it disappeared over the horizon. On either side there was nothing but dirt, rocks and the occasional acacia tree for miles, finally melting into the undulating waves of heat that formed the horizon. Not a sound could be heard except the steady drone of the helicopter. The landscape had gradually changed from the craggy hills of the Ouarkziz range that protected the entry into Morocco from the south, past the gullies of the Saguia el Hamra, to the flat plains that linked the territory to the *hammada* wasteland surrounding Tindouf, past the rises of the Zemmour Massif to the oasis of Guelta, and beyond that to the flatlands and dunes leading to the ocean – an expanse of land that would engulf most of the eastern part of the United States.

It was the middle of February, 1987. Moroccan engineers had just started building the last section of the berm, and a new wall had just enclosed Farsia in the north.

They had been flying from dawn and it was now nearly four o'clock in the afternoon, and shadows had begun to infiltrate the landscape. This was not the empty sand dunes of the Arabian peninsula, but rather a terrain similar to what you might find in the Mohave desert, with nooks and crevices just big enough to hide a camel, a herd of sheep – or a band of guerilla fighters. As the lengthening shadows formed silhouettes against the sky he felt a tinge of apprehension.

"Any chance we might run into a guerilla unit?" the man said nervously, breaking the silence that had enveloped them for the past hour.

The pilot smirked under his breath. He knew how important it was to make a good impression on the man beside him, who, after all, was one of the most powerful Congressmen in the United States. Still, he found it difficult to be the diplomat. Hell, he was a soldier, not a babysitter! But he managed to force a smile.

"I doubt it," he said, not bothering to face his companion. "There are thousands of land mines placed along the entire length of the berm to discourage any attacks. They would be blown to bits before they could come close enough to attack, even with anti-aircraft weapons. Besides, our radar would detect them from miles away."

The man relaxed a little. He was well aware of the sophisticated electronic sensing equipment that companies in the United States had sold to the King and that was now employed throughout the length of the berm. As he looked down, he could see the barbed wire that topped the sand, dirt and stone embankments, and in the distance he could make out the silhouette of one of the guard posts that interrupted the edifice at various intervals.

"Besides," continued the pilot, "we have nearly 180,000 soldiers manning outposts along the berm. Almost our entire army."

The man gazed a long time into the horizon. He couldn't help but marvel at the sight. The berm was indeed impressive – a massive structure of dirt, rock and sand that according to rumor could even be seen from space. By its final completion it would be the largest functional military barrier in the world. Only the ancient Chinese had built one longer. And it was protected by the largest concentration of land mines in the world. He turned again to his companion.

"Just how long is the berm nowadays," he finally asked. This was his third trip to the area and each time the berm had enclosed more of the territory.

"Oh, 1500 miles, more or less," he replied, finally smiling, "and we are continuing to build it. In one year we will have enclosed Awsard and will have reached the coast, just above Nouadhibou." He was proud of his country's accomplishment, even if it did take the Israelis to plan it, the French and Americans to help build it, and the Saudis to finance it. The berm had changed the dynamics of the war, he thought. No longer were the rebels able to attack at random and retreat into the safety of the desert. The berm had enclosed more than 80 percent of the territory – including all of the major cities and outposts and the important phosphate mine. What was left to the rebels was mere sand and rock. And although they were a constant irritant they had been unable to launch major attacks against Moroccan garrisons or seriously breach the Moroccan defenses for over a year. He smiled again as he prepared to land. Yes, finally, after more than ten years of fighting, the war was going their way.

It was a week after the Congressman's visit, and two days before the 11th anniversary of the founding of the SADR. The 2nd 4th and 5th regional army units, bringing with them more than 30 tanks, 60 armored personnel carriers and vehicles carrying SAM 6 anti aircraft missiles, and dozens of Land Rovers, began their quiet march by night from their isolated outposts to a desert location along the berm south of Farsia. When they reached a spot several miles from the berm, they stopped and waited.

At that point behind the berm there was a garrison of the 8th Moroccan brigade with 4 battalions. The terrain was in favor of the Moroccans, whose troops were elevated on hills and could see for a long distance, and there were few places to hide or to escape the detection of the radar. So instead of attempting to hide, they did the opposite. For weeks prior to the assault small units of guerillas had raced their Land Rovers along an 80 mile stretch of the berm day and night, tripping the radar, but safely out of reach of the Moroccan artillery. The Moroccans initially spent sleepless nights firing back, thinking they would be attacked, but not knowing at which point. But after becoming used to these demonstrations, they became tired of wasting their ammunition – as well as their sleep -- shooting at ghosts in the desert. So on the evening of February 25, when they heard the alarm of the radar and saw the headlights of the Land Rovers in the distance, they just went back to sleep.

They never saw the heavy buildup of Polisario forces that lay just beyond the Land Rovers.

During the evening a handful of demolition experts crawled on their bellies through the mine field, carefully extracting the mines at three different access points to the wall along a 16 mile stretch and cutting through the barbed wire that surrounded it. Then, ever so carefully so as not to alarm the sentries who patrolled only a few yards away, they placed explosives and the mines along the rim of the berm and waited. Then it was Salek's turn. While their colleagues waited along the berm's exterior, Salek and a half dozen guerillas carrying land mines in sacks on their backs, approached the berm through the path they had made and, after waiting for the sentries to pass their position, scampered quietly over the wall. Salek could see several miles away the lights of the command center, and in the far distance the flickering lights of the 'rapid intervention forces' that lay a few hundred yards beyond it. His companion quickly dispersed to the left, and he to the right. But before he could progress more than a few yards one of the sentries turned and started to walk, nonchalantly, in his direction, lighting a cigarette as he moved. Salek froze. He pressed against the wall hiding himself as best he could in its shadow, and slowly drew out his knife. The sentry was getting closer, now no more than a few feet from where he stood. But, before he reached his position, he stopped, and turned again, his back towards him. There he stood, for what seemed an eternity, as the smoke from his cigarette filled his lungs. Then he tossed the cigarette aside and began to walk, in a slow gait, back in the direction from which he had come. When he had left the scene Salek quickly darted a few yards towards the command center, withdrew the mines he held in his knapsack, and planted them where they would impede the advancement of the garrison troops and the mobile intervention forces. Then he quickly retreated to the other side and waited.

By an hour before dawn, Polisario infantry had positioned themselves all along the 16 mile stretch of the berm at the points of attack, without being detected by the Moroccans. Then the assault began. After blasting through the berm at the three different positions along the wall where the land mines and explosives had been placed, guerillas in Land Rovers, troop carriers and tanks simultaneously sped towards the berm at full speed, their artillery blazing. Once they were behind the wall, Salek and the other Polisario infantry who had been waiting along the berm quickly scrambled into the vehicles and entered the compound where they engaged in hand to hand combat with the Moroccan forces positioned along it. At the same time, the larger artillery, including troop carriers loaded with machine guns, pushed through at the main point of attack towards the command center. They quickly disabled the communication equipment. The Moroccans, asleep when the attack began, were taken by surprise and barely had time to reach for their weapons before being assailed by the infantry. In the far distance the mobile forces could hear the noise of the battle, but when they tried to intervene they ran into the land mines and were mowed down by the foot soldiers. In the ensuing dust and confusion it was difficult for them to distinguish friend from foe. Many of them panicked and started to flee.

When the dust had settled the guerillas had been able to penetrate more than three miles behind the berm to destroy the Moroccan headquarters, artillery, and radar instillations. Sixteen tanks had been destroyed. A number of the forces along the berm, as well as the intervention forces, had been killed or had fled.

The Polisario troops quickly departed with 83 prisoners, as well as a number of vehicles, weapons, and two heavy tanks. Although Moroccan Mirage jets fired upon them during their retreat, they refused to get close enough to the guerillas' anti aircraft missiles to inflict much damage.

But this was only the beginning. Guerilla troops remained in the general vicinity for weeks. Between the end of February and the second week of March there were two other major battles in which they managed to destroy large segments of the berm, and the troops behind them, near Mahbes and again near Farsia.

Then their forces swept through the territory like a tornado, attacking targets at random and striking fear into the hearts of the Moroccan soldiers in the trenches. In July, forces in the south attacked positions near Tichla. The following day they moved north to attack the berm near Houza. Other battles followed that month against berm positions near Smara, Awsard, and Guelta Zemmour.

On May 8, the berm near Farsia was again attacked. Then the guerilla forces moved south again to attack positions near Mudraiga. Still farther south they attacked positions near Tichla in June and again in July.

On November 18 -- days after the Moroccan engineers had managed to refortify the berm near Farsia -- the Polisario destroyed it again. They did the same at Mudraiga, killing more than 300 soldiers. On the final day of the year a battalion behind the berm near Housa was attacked.

All tolled, in 1987 Moroccan forces along the berm suffered at least 16 major attacks.

The guerillas had delivered their message. The berm could no longer be considered a successful deterrent. By the end of 1987 the morale among Moroccan soldiers along the wall had reached an all time low, and their grumbling reached as far as the marble halls of the palace in Rabat.

December 1, 1987. Rabat.

It was early in the morning, and the courtiers of the King of Morocco were not accustomed to being summoned at this hour. But for days the King had wakened at dawn, and after pacing for two or three hours, would summon them to get the latest dispatches. It was never pleasant news.

The wall – the expensive wall – the wall that had taken his engineers seven years to build and was supposed to be the answer to further guerilla incursions into the territory, had not prevented a series of major attacks and setbacks and his commanders in the field were grumbling.

He had done everything his foreign advisors had told him to do – even going so far as to grant his Air Force pilots greater flexibility, at great risk to his personal safety. For two years their strategy had kept the guerillas at bay, although their constant small scale attacks had forced him to deploy an ever increasing number of troops to the region. But this year had been different, they had begun once again to launch major attacks. It was true that they had not been able to penetrate far beyond the berm, and he had been able to increase his stranglehold on the towns of the territory and the major resources it possessed. But most of his troops had been concentrated in fixed positions along the berm – sitting ducks for guerilla attacks. And the discontent among his troops had reached crisis stage.

When the King had read the early morning dispatches he slumped into one of the chairs that adorned his bedchamber, deep in thought.

The reports were nearly unanimous. The troops stationed along the berm were demoralized by the attacks that came without warning. The "rapid intervention forces" and air power that was supposed to give them support was not effective. They were spending their nights with one eye open, unable to sleep – and meanwhile the enemy had complete freedom to choose where to attack and when.

Such discontent was dangerous. On more than one occasion it had fomented an open rebellion. He wasn't worried so much about the foot soldiers – they could be kept in line, or so he hoped. But the top brass! It was only four years ago that his most trusted aide, Dlimi, had betrayed him. Something had to be done to make them content with his policies – and fast.

"Get me Benani on the phone!" he barked, sending a courier scurrying through the hallway. Within a few minutes an aide handed him a phone, and a voice at the other end extended him a hesitant greeting.

Several hundred miles away a harried Commander of the Southern Region attempted once again to answer the barrage of questions. Yes, he had read the latest reports. Yes, the guerillas had managed to capture some of the soldiers and escape with some of the equipment. No, the intervention forces had not been able to pursue them. No, the jets had not been successful in eliminating them. Yes, he had doubled the guards along the berm.

"Your Majesty," he started to explain for the hundredth time, "the problem is that we know they are out there . . . our radar detects them . . . but they position their troops all along the berm during the night, and we cannot tell where they will attack . . . and it is impossible to fortify the entire length of the berm . . . ."

After a few moments the tirade ended, and a weary commander sat back in his armchair. What was he to do? The guerillas were no longer content merely harassing his troops along the berm, now they had found a way to penetrate the berm's defenses and mount large scale attacks on targets deep within Moroccan held territory. And there was no way to tell just where they would attack.

He reached for a cup of tea that was growing cold on his desk. Perhaps that would soothe his queasy stomach. What could he do, he asked himself again? Sending troops into the desert to try to seek and destroy them wasn't the answer . . . it would be just what they would want. Fortifying the berm wasn't the answer . . . it had already been fortified with stone and cement and crowned with barbed wire, but that didn't protect it from their heavily armed troop carriers and tanks. He opened the bottle of aspirin that had become his constant companion. He was out of ideas, and slowly going out of his mind.

Meanwhile, the King crumpled the papers in his hand and threw them into the waste basket. Once again he needed to devise a Plan B – but what could it be?

December 10, 1987. Political Solution.

It was nearing the end of the year and the King had summoned a grim faced Minister of the Interior to his private quarters. If he could not find a military solution, he would have to find a political one.

"Have you been able to talk with the people at the UN?" Hassan asked, imperiously, standing at his window and looking down at the garden below.

Basri took a deep breath. He had been closely following events at the United Nations ever since they had passed the resolution calling for direct talks between the parties and – much to his displeasure – had named the Polisario rather than Algeria the other party. And he had been privy to the discussions between the King and the Secretary General on his several trips to Rabat when he had tried – without much luck – to persuade the King to go along with the idea of a referendum based on the OAU proposals. They are a bunch of imbeciles, he thought to himself. Don't they realize that the King cannot afford to lose face with his people . . . that it would be political suicide for him to give in to any plan that might result in the independence of the territory . . . even if it means continuing this costly war? But, no . . . they insist on the impossible! He was angry – and frustrated. But now that the guerillas had stepped up their campaign the King had asked him to contact de Cuellar to see if some accommodation could be reached -- and the Secretary General had tossed him a lifeline.

"Perez de Cuellar has suggested that a commission be sent to the territory to assess the situation – and the prognosis for peace," he started slowly to say.

". . . while the fighting continues?" the King interrupted, turning to face him.

Basri shook his head. "No, he has suggested that the parties agree to a temporary halt in military operations to allow the commission to do its work."

The King paused for a moment. "A cease fire, you say?"

"Yes, a cease fire."

The King turned his gaze back to the window and to the garden, still full of blooms. A commission and a report, he thought. That might take months . . . months that he could put to good use. And a cease fire would put an end to the guerilla attacks . . . at least momentarily. When he turned again to Basri he was smiling.

"Tell the Secretary-General that we welcome his suggestion, and will gladly welcome the commission . . . and agree to a temporary halt in military operations to permit them to visit the territory," he said. "But Basri," he added as the official started for the door, "I don't want a fiasco like the one that greeted the Spanish the last time a UN Mission visited the territory!"

Basri smiled. "Don't worry, Your Majesty," he said as he closed the door.

When Basri had left the room he turned again to the window, deep in thought. A cease fire to buy time to find a plan B . . . yes, that was exactly what he needed!

December 20, 1987. Laayoune.

In a back alley of the Zemla district of Laayoune, a slim figure dressed from head to tow in a long, flowing, brightly colored robe, darted quietly from building to building, stopping now and then to peer over her shoulder to make sure she wasn't being observed or followed. When she reached the door of her destination she tapped on it softly three times. She could hear a noise on the other side, and within a minute or two the heavy wooden door opened a crack and two eyes peered out at her. Then the door quickly opened and without a word she hurried inside.

There, huddled in the semi darkness, were the figures of a dozen men and women, sprawled on low lying couches. When she had entered the room one of them, a middle aged women dressed in a similar long robe, rose to greet her.

"Aminatou, welcome," she said in a soft whisper. "I hear that you have news!"

The newcomer smiled and turned to the others. "I have just heard that a delegation from the United Nations will be arriving in Laayoune next Thursday to assess the logistics for holding a referendum."

"A UN delegation . . . are you sure?" queried one of the men, a puzzled look on his face. "There hasn't been a visit by the UN here since the one they sent when the Spanish occupied the territory. The Moroccans have closed the borders and aren't letting any foreigners in. Are you sure your information is correct?"

"I read the announcement in the paper myself," Aminatou responded, "and Haddad just got back from a trip to the Canary Islands where he also heard the news. The King and the Polisario have agreed to a temporary halt in military operations to allow a commission sent by the Secretary General to visit the territory and the Polisario camps to prepare a plan for a UN sponsored referendum. According to the newspaper I read, the visit will be this Thursday."

"The last time a UN Mission visited us we were able to mobilize our neighbors to demonstrate in favor of independence," said an elderly man in the back of the room. "I remember it well . . . we lined the roads with thousands of Sahrawis carrying banners!"

Aminatou remembered it well herself. Although she had been young at the time, she remembered accompanying her mother through the district to the street that led to the airport in the early hours, carrying signs, and the commotion that had followed. The day's events had since become part of Sahrawi folklore.

"Yes, I know," she said softly, "and this time we must do the same." The others one by one nodded. They had been yearning for the opportunity to let the world know what was happening in their territory, but had been forced to keep silent during the years of Moroccan occupation, when any hint of opposition to the government policy invited torture – or worse. Yet they had managed to form clandestine cells through which they ferreted information and correspondence to the guerillas – at great risk to their personal safety. Now they would organize a demonstration, perhaps not as large as the one that greeted the first UN Mission, but large enough to show the world where their sympathies lay. Through an underground human chain word was quickly spread, and on the following Thursday morning several dozen Sahrawis hid in houses and businesses along the route the commission would take, ready to spring into action at a moment's notice.

At ten o'clock in the morning a fleet of black cars made their way from the airport through the streets of the capital. When they stopped in front of the Parador, a half dozen dignified looking men in tailored suits emerged from the cars and started to walk up the steps to the door of the hacienda. That was their signal to move. All at once dozens of men and women emerged from the doorways, carrying signs with pro-independence slogans on them. Almost immediately dozens of men in police uniforms began to race through the crowd with sticks, beating the protestors. The crowd tried to disperse, but it was no use – they were outnumbered by the Moroccans, and one by one they were hauled away.

At the police station Aminatou, her face covered in blood and her right eye swollen, stood defiantly. "You have showed the world your brutality," she shouted through teeth covered in blood. "The UN commission will tell the world about you!"

347

The police captain just smiled. "You mean *these people*?" And with a laugh he marched the dignified visitors through the room. "Let me introduce you to Mo Akhaloun, a grocer from Marrakesh – he does look quite distinguished in that suit, doesn't he?" The man turned slightly red and cast his eyes to the floor. "Oh, and here is Omar Benini, a lieutenant in our armed forces. He could pass for English, don't you think?" The lieutenant beamed as he stood at attention. "And as for the others, well, Driss, I understand, is a teacher of mathematics at a high school in Casablanca, and Omar here is a veterinarian. As for the others, well, let's just say we had a little help from our European friends." He bowed slightly in the direction of two slim, dark haired men in blue suits standing in a corner. Then he turned to her.

"You didn't really think the same trick would work on us that worked on the Spanish, did you?" He gave her a contemptuous look. Then he continued. "You see, we were expecting you to pull something like this. Basri simply publicized a false day for the arrival of the UN commission and asked some of our supporters to imitate them. Clever, eh?"

He laughed. "You see, the real commission is not due to arrive for another four days!"

Aminatou gave the policeman a defiant look. "You will not be able to stifle us forever!" she shouted. "Some day the world will know about what you do . . . and we will have our revenge!"

The police captain just smiled. "If you live to enjoy it!" he shouted as he ordered his men to take the prisoners away.

December 27, 1987. The Commission.

It was nearing the end of December when an assortment of officials led by a Somali diplomat, Abdelrahim Farrah, crept wearily out of the cars that had taken them on the long, dusty route from Zouerate in Mauritania to Agwanit in Polisario-controlled Western Sahara. In Mauritania they had spoken to several officials at the Foreign Ministry. They had already been entertained by the King at his palace in Marrakesh and had visited Laayoune in the territory occupied by Morocco. Their trip to the territory, for years off-limits to the outside world, had been the first visit of a foreign delegation since the one sent by the United Nations before the start of the war. They had thought that their visit might prompt demonstrations by the natives, but to their surprise the visit went smoothly, and they heard not a ripple of dissent from any quarter.

Now it was time to visit the territory controlled by the guerillas. Farrah already knew what to expect. For months the guerillas had launched major attacks on Moroccan troops along the berm from carefully concealed hideouts sprinkled through the portion of the territory of Western Sahara that was under their control. The delegation was swiftly taken on a tour of some of the southern military installations by the commanders of the region. Then it was back to Zouerate, where they took a plane to the tiny military airstrip at Tindouf to visit the refugee camps and later to confer with the Polisario leaders in a camp just north of Tifariti. From there it was off to Algiers, and then back to New York – where an anxious Peres de Cuellar was pacing the floor.

December 29, 1987. Kenatra Prison.

The end of the year was fast approaching. For over a year the tiny group of prisoners in Kenatra prison had managed to maintain contact with each other by passing messages written on wads of cheese wrappers surreptitiously under the noses of the guards who watched over them during their weekly exercise routines, and so far luck had smiled on them -- they had not been caught. But this day their luck abandoned them, for just as Hamed dropped his message on the floor the guard turned, and, spotting the crumpled paper on the ground, bent down to pick it up.

"We can't have you littering the floor with trash," he began to say. "Who dropped this?"

The group remained silent for a moment. Then Hamed spoke up. "I am sorry," he said, slowly, "it must have fallen from my pocket."

The guard gave him a stern look. "Well, you shouldn't be putting anything in your pockets anyway. Next time leave your trash in your cell." And with those words he made a movement as if to toss the object into a nearby bin. But before it left his hand he stopped and looked at it closer. There was something written on it. He spread the paper with his fingers. Then he looked again at Hamed.

"So, you thought you could send a message to your comrades, did you? Very clever! Let's see how clever you are when I bring you before our commandant!" And Hamed started the long walk through the dark, damp corridor, to an office at the other side of the prison, a rifle pointed at his head.

When he walked through the door his face suddenly turned white. There, sitting behind a desk ,was a face whose craggy features he knew only too well, a face that brought back memories he had tried for years to banish, a face that belonged to a man he hated with every fiber of his being – the Hyena.

CHAPTER 15
1988

It was early in the morning, an hour or so before the camp would spring to life. The celebrations ushering in the new year had barely finished and the weary inhabitants of the camp were catching a few last moments of sleep before facing a new day. But not all. A lone figure drew his cloak closer to his body for warmth in the chill morning air and walked briskly towards the domed shaped building that housed the Presidential office. As he approached it he could hear the muffled sound of raised voices inside.

"I tell you, it was a mistake to halt our attacks . . . even for a short period of time," Bouhali was saying, his voice dripping with bitterness. "We had the Moroccans scared . . . their troops were close to mutiny. It was time to press forward. I don't understand why we stopped!"

"It was just for a short period, Bouhali," said Bachir in a tone meant to soothe. "We need to cooperate at least to some extent with the Secretary General if he is ever going to be able to push the United Nations to action. Besides which, the fact finding mission gave us the chance to press our demands."

"Still, I don't like it . . ." Bouhali replied, shaking his head. "We've lost the psychological advantage and it gives Hassan just what he wants. It may take weeks   . . . months for those diplomats to write their report . . . time for him to redeploy his troops and do some political maneuvering."

"Well, we just won't give him that time," spoke a voice from the doorway.

All eyes turned as Abdelaziz entered the room. Two months ago he had agreed to cease military operations for a short period in order to permit the Secretary General of the United Nations to send a fact finding mission to the territory to "assess" the situation on the ground. This would enable the Secretary General to draft a proposal to end the conflict – or so he said. He had agreed, reluctantly, but his decision had not been popular – he had only managed to convince the others to go along with it by writing a letter to the Secretary General insisting that the members of the mission be impartial and that they take back with them a series of written demands. Now the diplomats had left, and it was time to discuss their next move.

"I agree with Bouhali," he continued. "We need to keep the pressure up. Hassan probably hopes that this cease fire will last long enough for him to beg for more aid from the Americans . . . or the Saudis . . . or both. We will not give him that breathing spell." Then, walking a few steps to his desk, he spread a large sheet across it. "Here," he said, looking around the room, "We need not wait until the report of the fact finding mission is published. For the past week I have been going over what I believe are weak points in the Moroccan defensive system. I have brought with me a map indicating the positions along the berm that I would suggest as a possible target. But I would like your input." He paused long enough to let his message sink in. "If we agree on a target there is no reason why we cannot commence another full scale assault by the end of the month . . . one that will give a message to Hassan."

". . . and to some UN officials as well!" someone added.

Abdelaziz smiled. "Yes, to some UN officials as well!"

The commanders one by one looked at the map. For two hours they discussed troop strength, compared notes on the Moroccan commanders, and assessed vulnerable points along the berm. Then they discussed logistics. By noon they had narrowed it down to two possibilities, and by the end of the day they had reached a decision.

And by the end of a fortnight they were ready to move.

January 31, 1988. United Nations Headquarters.

It was the last day of January. The Secretary General of the United Nations had awakened his aide at 5 o'clock in the morning to summon her to his office, and the bleary eyed young woman was sipping her third espresso in a futile effort to dislodge the cobwebs of sleep that had enveloped her head. But when she saw the worried look on her superior's face, the cobwebs were banished in an instant and replaced with a sense of foreboding.

De Cuellar looked tired. He had won a second term as Secretary General in 1986, but the strain of the office and his constant travels had taken its toll. In July of that year he had entered a hospital for a routine examination and had left it a week later after undergoing a quadruple coronary bypass operation. Although he had been pronounced fit to resume his duties, he had been warned to curtail some of his constant globe trotting. So, he had to rely on others for much of the diplomatic footwork. He had managed – after making a pilgrimage to Geneva to speak personally with Bachir Mustapha Sayed -- to convince the Polisario to curtail their activities for a few weeks so that he might send his chief assistant and a hand picked commission to North Africa to assess the situation on the ground.

But the previous day the Polisario had resumed the attacks – demolishing a section of the berm and decimating the soldiers protecting it near Mudraiga in a blitzkrieg assault that left several hundred Moroccans dead. The attacks would undoubtedly escalate unless he did something fast. When the door had closed behind his visitor he stopped his pacing for a moment and looked at her. "Tell me," he said, a slight weariness in his voice, "What is the status of the proposal for the Western Sahara thing?"

The young woman was startled. She hadn't yet heard of the Mudraiga incident and wondered why this matter all of a sudden had acquired a sense

351

of urgency. But, putting aside her puzzlement for the moment, she responded, calmly.

"Sir, it will be difficult holding a referendum in the territory under the best of conditions – there are inadequate facilities in place and we would have to provide everything we would need. Unless we obtained the full cooperation of the parties – particularly Morocco – it would be next to impossible. And even if we could surmount the logistics obstacles there would be other problems we would need to face – deciding who would be eligible to vote in the referendum, for one thing, and then trying to identify those voters – you know, of course, that most of the residents of the territory carried no identifying documents until the Spanish started giving out identification cards in 1974," she said in a voice barely concealing her exasperation.

De Cuellar was nonplussed. He had faced similar problems before. For several years now he had been trying to implement a similar plan for the cessation of hostilities in Namibia. It was never easy to administer a plebiscite in such regions – but it can be done. "And how did the OAU propose handling those problems?" he asked calmly.

"Well, it seems that before the Spanish departed they conducted a census of the population. The OAU has suggested using this as the basis for voter eligibility," she replied. "And they suggested using the tribal elders, the sheikhs, to help identify those people."

The Secretary General paused for a moment, considering the ramifications of the OAU proposal. The fact that it had already gained the approval of most of the African states would greatly help matters politically, he thought, so basing the UN proposal on their plan would be a good strategy.

"Well, it seems like a reasonable proposal to me," he finally remarked, "What's wrong with it?"

The young woman shook her head and managed a weak smile. "Nothing at all . . . in fact, since there are only 74,000 individuals on the Spanish census we could complete the identification process in a few months . . . if the parties would agree to it!" She paused before continuing. When she did her voice was low and serious. "It suits the Polisario fine. . . but the King! He demands that the natives who migrated to Morocco in the late 50s and their children be allowed to vote. He is adamant about it!"

A thought flashed through his mind as he recalled the meeting he had had with the King in 1985. Hassan had warned him then that determining who would be eligible to vote in a referendum would be . . . how did he put it? *problematic*   He had wondered at the time if Hassan had some secret plan in mind. Bendjedid had warned him that the King would try to load the dice in his favor. *Of course*, he thought with a smile. Of course he would!

He turned to face his assistant. ". . . and if we agreed to the King's demand?" he asked.

The young woman paused before replying. "Opening up the voters' list to the thousands of Saharans who emigrated would produce a logistics nightmare . . . and might take us years," she said in a low voice.

De Cuellar paused and looked out the window again. His suitcase was on standby, ready to go at a moment's notice. It was a beautiful sunny day in New York. He didn't relish the idea of leaving his comfortable surroundings to drag himself through the African continent, but if that was the only way he could get people to agree . . . He sighed.

After a moment he turned to his assistant with a final question. "Does anyone have any idea how the people of the territory would vote on this issue?"

The young woman reflected for a minute before responding. "The people in the camp will obviously vote for independence," she replied. "But no one can tell how the people who remained in the territory will vote. There is a total clampdown on interviews with the natives. When we were there we were only allowed to speak with a few of them in the presence of Moroccan officials. . . and, as I understand it, any expression of anti-Moroccan sentiment is treated harshly. The Moroccan officials claim that the people support integration with the "motherland." However, the only thing we know for sure is that a United Nations mission sent there in 1975 found overwhelming support for independence and against integration with any other country."

The Secretary General again paused. Then he began to mumble in a low voice, as if to himself, "Yes . . . *independence*, the Holy Grail . . . as if all problems would be solved by independence!" He turned abruptly and stared at his assistant. "Do you really think these people have the experience to manage a modern state? I wonder. . ." Then he turned again to his window, muttering again to himself.

The young woman stood, transfixed, not knowing what to say. But no reply was expected.

"Thank you. . . you may go now," de Cuellar finally sighed, mustering a brief smile.

When the young woman had left, de Cuellar sat behind his desk mulling over his next move. He shook his head. It would take every diplomatic fiber in his body to get the parties to agree to this, he said to himself. But, after all, he hadn't been elected the Secretary General of the United Nations for nothing. He would find a way.

He stood and looked out his window again. Small sheets of ice had covered the East River causing it to glisten in the morning sun. But the Secretary General hadn't noticed. There was a queasy feeling in his stomach. Would Morocco really ever give up this territory? And what would happen if it *did* become independent? A feudal Algerian puppet state? A failed micro-state governed by semi-literate nomads? Were the French right? And how would he be remembered if they were? That queasy feeling started again. He sighed, audibly, and shook his head. "I will get them to agree to this referendum," he muttered again to himself, "that will be the first step. . . but once they agree . . . ."

Staring out the window as if into the future the seeds of his own Plan B began to emerge, and after remaining transfixed for several minutes he smiled and quietly returned to his desk.

February 15, 1988. Judgment Day.

Hamed lay on the rags that served as his bed watching a solitary cockroach slowly navigate the wall. "Good luck finding any crumbs here!" he muttered to himself. He had been alone in the dark pit that served as his cell for weeks now, with only the cockroaches and an occasional intrepid rat as companions. From the marks he had placed on the wall he estimated that it must be some time in February. He remembered all too well the last time he had left his cell – that cold day in December. After he had gotten over his initial shock at seeing his old nemesis, he had stood silently facing him, trying to adopt a calm demeanor as the man got up from behind the desk and approached him, lit cigarette in his hand.

"So, you think you can disobey our regulations, do you?" the Hyena had asked, flashing a brief, menacing smile. "How many of your comrades are part of this plot?"

He doesn't recognize me, Hamed had thought to himself, facing him in silence.

The man casually approached him, flicking the ashes of his cigarette as he walked. When he was not more than a foot away he stopped and looked him squarely in the eyes. "Oh, I see, you don't want to get your comrades in trouble, is that it?" His voice was gravelly and somewhat distant. "Well, perhaps you need some help loosening your tongue!"

With that last remark he beckoned his aides to hold Hassan's arms and approached closer, the lit cigarette dangling menacingly from his fingers. He pulled back the sleeve on Hamed's left arm and froze, his eyes growing wider.

When he looked up again his eyes had narrowed to two slits. "You have been a prisoner before, haven't you?" he barked. "What is your name?"

Hamed had remained silent. *Perhaps he will not remember,* he had thought.

But luck was not on his side. The Hyena ordered his men to remove Hassan's shirt. His arms were full of round pot marks where flesh had been burned—the reminders of several past interrogations. *So, I've been a prisoner before,* he had thought. *Just one of many. It means nothing. . .* But something else had caught the man's attention. A scar on his shoulder where a bullet had been removed.

The man peered at him intently. Then a flash of recognition came over his eyes.

"I remember you," he began slowly. "You were one of the prisoners I sent to help Kashdami build the wall. A member of the Auxilleries!"

His heart had sunk, but he remained silent, his eyes silently glaring at the man.

A smile crept over the Hyena's face. "Well, this puts a different light on things," he said, gaily, waiving his arm in the air. "You are not a prisoner of war . . . you are a deserter!" Then drawing close, he growled in his ear, "And do you know what we do with deserters? We shoot them!"

The man barked an order and the next thing he knew he had been dragged once again down the long hallway to the pit that had become his home. There he had remained, just waiting as the days and weeks passed by. In the semi-darkness that enveloped him it was difficult to determine day from night. Only the appearance of trays of food told him of the start of a new day. And so the waiting continued, day after day.

But today the waiting would end. Just after sunrise a burly Moroccan soldier unlocked the door to his cell and unceremoniously ushered him through the cavernous labyrinth to an outside van, where he began a long drive to an impressive, ornate building festooned with flags. He was quickly taken to a wood paneled room and told to stand at attention. Facing him were three stern faced men in officers' regalia peering down at him from a desk set atop a wooden platform.

"You have been charged with desertion from the army of your king and your country. Do you have anything to say in your defense?" one of them growled.

Hamed looked at the man squarely in the eye. "I have no king," he said defiantly. ". . . and Morocco is not my country."

"But you admit that you joined His Majesty's forces, didn't you?" another one said, his voice exhibiting some irritation.

Hamed was silent.

A man with a craggy face and a moon shaped scar on his cheek, who had been sitting quietly at the back of the room, raised his voice. "Sirs, if I may be allowed to speak," he began. "This man was a prisoner in Laayoune who agreed to join the Auxilleries. He was later seconded to Colonel Kashdami, under my command, for help in building the berm at Ras el Kanfra. During a skirmish with the guerillas he and another member of the Auxilleries escaped and our forces recaptured this one during the battles at Lemseid, where he was fighting with the guerillas." Then he gave Hamed a look dripping with contempt. "This man is not only a deserter, he is a traitor!"

The third man – the one who had not said anything so far – smiled at the man. "Lieutenant, I understand your concern about this case . . . there is no question that this man deserves some punishment. But the Crown desires to be magnanimous towards its subjects. . . who have undoubtedly been subjected to false information promulgated by the leaders of this so-called 'liberation movement.'" Then he looked directly at Hamed, still smiling.

"The King is prepared to offer you clemency provided you appear on a television broadcast and admit that you have been brainwashed by the lies and false promises that the guerilla leaders have been spreading . . . that they are communists who are mere puppets of the Algerian government, and that it is the Algerian military and the Soviets who are directing the guerilla battles and supplying them with arms." He continued smiling. "If you are willing to tell the truth to the world, we might be willing to forget some of these earlier transgressions."

Hamed stared at the man, then in a low, steady voice he began to speak. "I would be more than willing to tell the truth to the world, but I'm afraid it is not *your* version of the truth. The truth is that I am a Sahrawi and my country

355

is the territory you call Western Sahara, not Morocco . . . and that this fight is and always has been a fight by my countrymen to free our country from the unlawful occupation and the slavery of our citizens by your King and to establish the kind of government *we* want – not what Algeria or any other country wants." He came closer to the officer and stared into his eyes. "I know you think that we are a small people . . . an insignificant people . . . a group of ignorant desert dwellers incapable of standing up to the mighty King of Morocco and the Western world. But there is one thing that we have that you do not . . . truth and justice on our side. We will fight our own battles . . . and we will continue the fight until every last inch of our territory is free!"

The man's smile disappeared. "You realize that your version of the truth will get you killed," he said, menacingly.

"At least I will die with honor," Hamed said in an even voice.

The man stared at him again. "So be it," he said, his voice low and somber.

The following morning, at dawn, the same burly soldier led Hamed to an outside courtyard. As he began the slow procession to the far side his thoughts turned to his life in El Ayoun, to his mother and sister and the other members of his family. But most of all his thoughts turned to Miriam and the image of her as she bent over him long ago in her tent. He saw her face as clearly as if she were standing there beside him, for in a way she was . . . she had always been.

When he got to the wall at the far side of the courtyard he turned to face the soldiers lined up in front of him. He turned his face to look at the sky. It was a beautiful shade of blue. He had never seen it look more beautiful. Then he looked again at the soldiers. He heard someone yell a command.

All at once he shouted "libertad!" . . . and then he was heard no more.

May 5, 1988. Rabat.

Three months after his discussion with his assistant in his office that blustery day in January, the Secretary General of the United Nations found himself sitting in a marble room at a palace in Rabat facing a King. On the table before them were several pieces of paper that the King was reading, nervously.

Finally, he put the papers down, pushed them across the table, and turned to face his guest. "These proposals of yours contain nothing new. . . It is basically what the OAU has been suggesting for years . . . and as I told you before, we cannot agree to them without some fundamental changes."

Perez de Cuellar was expecting this response. For months now his assistant had been fine tuning the proposal for a referendum that had been made by the OAU, trying to draft an agreement that would cater to the interests of both the Moroccan king and the Algerian government while remaining palatable to the members of the Security Council.

Morocco and Algeria -- these were the important stakeholders, he thought. Although he had paid lip service to the official position of the United Nations – as well as Algeria -- that the parties to the dispute were Morocco and the

Polisario, he had never considered the leaders of the guerilla movement more than actors playing a bit part in a drama in which the King of Morocco and the President of Algeria assumed the lead roles. In drafting the referendum proposal the wishes of the Sahrawis and the officials who represented them had been only secondary considerations, and though he had shuttled between Rabat and Algiers on several occasions in pursuit of a mutually acceptable solution, he visited the Tindouf camps less frequently.

And there was another player on the field – the United Nations – and de Cuellar knew, above all, that he had to draft a plan that would pass muster with its sometimes irascible members. He could find a way to compromise on the King's demand that his troops remain in the territory, but the option of independence had to remain on the ballot for the organization to be seen as upholding the principle of self determination, and basing the voters' list on the Spanish census would be the only way the process could be completed in a time frame – and at a cost – that would be acceptable to the Security Council. But he wouldn't tell that to the King.

"I know it will be difficult," he started to say, "but you must be prepared to make some concessions if there is to be an end to this war. And now that the guerillas have cranked up their attacks I am sure you will agree that it is even more important to find a way to resolve the conflict . . . and quickly!"

The King winced. The attacks that had resumed the previous year had destroyed his peaceful nights, although he wouldn't want his visitor to know it.

De Cuellar looked at him closely. Yes, the dart had hit its mark. Taking another sip of coffee, he continued "Think it over. I'm sure we can reach some sort of mutually acceptable agreement."

The King sat for a moment without saying a word. He had no use for United Nations bureaucrats, whom he considered to be mere servants of the great powers. Yet, it was true . . . he needed time to find a way to stem these attacks. The organization had at times been useful, and if he could manipulate the United Nations to do his bidding. . . or at least drag out negotiations long enough to find a way around his problem . . . well, he was prepared to be gracious.

He smiled. "Have you talked to the Algerians?" he said, offering his guest a piece of French pastry.

De Cuellar shifted in his seat. Yes, he had indeed spoken to the Algerians, and they had been adamant that any agreement would have to include the option of independence for the Sahrawis, and would have to be approved by them. Bendjedid had again expressed misgivings over the Moroccan's sincerity, warning him that Hassan would try to find some devious way to rig the vote. But, again, he would not tell that to the King.

"Yes, I have spoken to the Algerians, and they are willing to compromise on a few details if you are," he lied.

The King reflected for a moment. He had had no luck convincing the Algerians to abandon their opposition to his plans. Two years ago King Fayd, who had replaced Khalid as King of Saudi Arabia, had arranged talks between himself and Bendjedid, and formal relations between the two countries had just been reestablished. But they had not renounced their support for the guerillas. He had offered everything . . . a passage through the Kingdom to the Atlantic for their goods . . . a settlement of the border dispute on their terms . . . an attractive concession on trade . . . not to mention the generous gifts he had offered their top political and military leaders   . . . nothing had worked. Perhaps this UN flunky would have better luck, he thought. When he finally turned to address his guest his manner was gracious, befitting the monarch of a great nation.

"You can tell the Algerians that I will give due consideration to your proposals and give you a response shortly."

And after finishing his coffee and pastry, Perez de Cuellar was ushered from the room, into a waiting car that would whisk him to the airport.

Once inside the car he heaved a sigh of relief. Diplomacy is just a game, he thought. And truth is relative. Ten years from now no one will care if he had to bend the truth a bit to resolve this conflict. And as he headed off to Algiers he prepared in his mind another version of the truth to tell Bendjedid.

He had set the stage. And so the diplomatic dance continued, with de Cuellar's emissaries shuttling between Rabat and Algiers, Algiers and Madrid, Madrid and Paris, Paris and New York, New York and Tindouf, each time dancing to a different tune until they could barely differentiate truth from fiction.

August 10, 1988. The Pentagon.

By the time de Cuellar took up the Western Sahara gauntlet the cracks in Hassan's wall --- both militarily and politically -- had become glaringly apparent to officials in a large five sided building in Virginia.

"Confound it!" yelled a man with stars on his shoulders to a group of military and civilians in his office, "We've thrown everything at him . . . weapons, radar equipment, satellite tracking information, training for his troops . . . and still he has been unable to defeat a group of itinerant Bedouins. I don't care if they are being given weapons from Algeria. The Algerians are not fighting their war, despite what Hassan is saying, it is *their* troops on the ground! What's the matter with them, anyway?"

He looked around the room for an answer. Finally, a young officer at the back of the room spoke up.

"Sir, if I may comment," he began, hesitantly, "the Moroccan soldiers don't seem to have the stomach for this fight. I have spoken to several of them . . . they are tired of being asked to spend months . . . some times years . . . along a sand wall in the middle of the desert. All they want is to go home to their families."

"The guerillas have found ways to penetrate beyond the berm," added a senior officer, "and this has intensified the low morale among Moroccan units. They feel they are sitting ducks . . . cannon fodder for a cause they don't really care about."

"I thought they were all psyched up about regaining the lands that once belonged to the Kingdom," said the older man with a somewhat sarcastic sneer. "Well, if the army is not behind him, he is in trouble. Look what happened in '72 . . . and with Dlimi! One hundred eighty thousand angry young men . . ." and with that thought he shook his head.

After a moment's reflection he turned once again to the group. "The one thing that has always puzzled me is Algeria. What do they hope to gain from all of this? I could understand Boumedienne . . . to him this was just a continuation of the Algerian revolution . . . and, besides, he had no love for the King of Morocco . . . but now, what keeps them going?"

A civilian in the room cleared his throat. "Well, some people have said that the Algerians want an outlet to the Atlantic for their iron ore at Gara Djebilet. . ."

He gave the man a stern look. "Do you really believe that?"

The man looked a bit sheepish. "No, not really. There are easier ways to get an outlet for their iron. They already have access to the Mediterranean and before all this started they had reached an arrangement with Hassan for shipment of the ore through southern Morocco. In fact, this arrangement was scuttled because of Boumedienne's support for the Polisario. I understand that they are now claiming that they want to build their own steel plant and are planning to build a rail line to the Mediterranean coast to supply it. In any event, I am sure that Hassan would be more than willing to accommodate them with an outlet to the Atlantic – through southern Morocco, or Western Sahara if they prefer -- if they withdrew their support for the guerillas."

The senior officer raised his voice again. "I have heard that they are afraid that Hassan will use the same "Greater Morocco" argument he is using to claim Western Sahara to raise trouble again about the border between Moroccan and Algeria. You know he has never formally agreed to the de facto border between the countries."

The civilian again spoke up. "Yes, but we have tried for years to convince the Algerians that if they would just stop supporting the insurrection in the Sahara we would be willing to intercede on their behalf to smooth over this border issue. Hassan is a realist. He knows that is a lost cause. But . . . no dice."

The old man sighed. "Perhaps we will never know. In any event what matters is that they seem determined to support the cause of the guerillas . . . perhaps even more so now that they are on the brink of overcoming the defenses along the berm."

He paused again before addressing them. "What is important is that we figure out a way to extricate Hassan from the pickle he finds himself in. It is clear to me that unless some type of miracle occurs he will not be able to win a decisive victory against the guerillas . . . and I don't believe in miracles! And the longer this war is protracted the greater the chance that some disgruntled military officer will arrange a coup attempt . . . and this time it might succeed." Turning again to his audience he said, quietly, "So what do you suggest?"

The room once again became quiet as each member of the group struggled to find an answer. Finally, the civilian spoke up.

"Sir, I think our best bet is to convince Hassan to agree with the proposal that has been made by Perez de Cuellar at the UN. I understand that he has drafted something and given it to the parties with a demand that they give a response by the beginning of September. I suggest that we just hand the whole matter over to the UN and let it diffuse the situation."

"You mean, try to convince Hassan to permit a referendum?" The older man shook his head. "I know we arm twisted him before to cooperate with the OAU when they suggested a referendum, but that was before he withdrew from the organization . . . and, anyway, he never really kept his promise . . . and so far he is dragging his feet with the proposals of the UN." He turned to face the younger man. "What makes you think we could force him to accept the UN proposal?"

The young man shrugged his shoulders. "It is simple. He has no other choice."

August 10, 1988. The Wall.

Building the berm had seemed to be a brilliant military strategy – cutting off the ability of the guerillas to attack targets within reach of the major towns and outposts of the region and disappear into the hinterlands as quickly as they had arrived. But as any student of history would know, defensive lines rarely deter invading forces for long. The Ming emperors discovered this to their dismay after the Great Wall of China was penetrated by Manchurian barbarians in the 17th century, leading to the Qing dynasty and over 200 years of Manchurian emperors on the throne of the "Central Kingdom". The Germans eventually found a way to neutralize the Maginot Line built by France after the First World War to deter another invasion by that country. And the Bar Lev Line, a chain of fortifications along the eastern coast of the Suez Canal built by Israel after the Six Day War -- and hailed by many military experts as the ideal way to prevent an attack by Egypt -- was destroyed by Egyptian forces in fewer than two hours during the October 1973 War.

Besides being ineffective in the long run, defensive barriers are costly to maintain and require a huge investment in manpower. Manning, equipping and maintaining a 1800 mile long defensive position would drain the treasuries of most countries, and, indeed by 1988 it had already drained the resources of Morocco. By the end of 1982 the Moroccan troop strength in the Sahara had grown to eighty thousand men, most of them stationed in isolated garrisons along the wall. That number had more than doubled by 1988. It was only through the generous aid of the King of Saudi Arabia that Hassan had been able to maintain it. Indeed, Saudi Arabia had basically paid for the war, and no one knew how long the Saudis' patience with Hassan's Saharan policies would continue.

In addition, walls are just as effective in keeping a population confined as they are in repelling invaders, and for years now the Moroccan forces had been cooped up within their sand cage, sitting ducks ever fearful of an attack, with the guerillas free to roam the countryside beyond and strike at will.

And far to the north another berm that had divided peoples for generations had begun to crumble, with repercussions that reached to the distant Sahara and beyond – the Berlin Wall – releasing states from the ideological bonds that had tied them to the aspirations of an empire intent on dominating the world. The world that for years had been seen as a checkerboard of black and white squares was being gradually transformed into pockets of varying shades of grey. Michel Gorbachov was extending olive branches to the West. Red China was greedily absorbing the lessons of capitalism. Even Vietnam, after having fought a long and grueling war to impose its version of communism on the countryside, all of a sudden reached out to its mortal enemies for agreements on international trade.

One of the states that began to assume an aura of grey in the eyes of the Western world was Algeria. As long as it was deemed a client state of the Soviet Union, Algeria – no matter what its intentions towards the West – was a pariah in the eyes of governments such as the United States. However, when the Soviet Union began to falter and finally fall apart under the weight of its own economic and political strains, business interests in the United States began to cast an envious eye on the oil and other mineral riches of the country. Gradually the fingers of commerce began to reach across the divide, and with it an increased political rapprochement.

This was not good news for the King of Morocco, who saw his political hold on United States policy begin to weaken. As long as his good friend Reagan was President, he could relax. But his presidency was coming to an end, and after that? Already the Americans were pressuring him to cave in. Only the French, whose animosity towards the Algerians remained unabated throughout the years since the revolution, could be relied upon as an ally, and after d'Estaing's humiliating riposte by the Polisario in Mauritania it was doubtful if France would once again get directly involved in the military struggle.

As the King sat quietly in his garden, all these thoughts passing through his mind, he suddenly felt tired. It was August, and not even the cool shade of his prized palm trees could mask the summer heat. The Secretary General had just delivered to him the latest version of his peace proposal. He had been stalling for months . . . picking apart his several drafts and making numerous demands that would be impossible for him to meet. But de Cuellar had now set a deadline of September for a response. And he had just gotten off the phone with his contact at the Pentagon. They were demanding that he cooperate. All right . . . he would agree to this referendum business . . . but he would insist that they agree to his terms. . . and he reached for the phone.

August 10, 1988. The Proposal.

A thousand miles away, in Rabouni, a group of men were also contemplating events. The Secretary General had just sent the President the latest version

361

of his peace proposal, and Abdelaziz had called a meeting to discuss its terms.

When they had assembled he read from his notes. "They are suggesting that the question of sovereignty over Western Sahara be settled by a referendum in which the people of the territory could choose whether to form an independent state or be incorporated into Morocco. This referendum would be monitored by the United Nations and the OAU after a cease fire and the containment of all troops. The cease fire and containment of troops would be monitored by a UN peacekeeping force and the UNHCR would be responsible for repatriating the refugees in Tindouf." He put the paper down. "It is basically the OAU proposal -- minus a few important details."

"I don't like it," Bouhali announced, shaking his head. "It doesn't include a withdrawal of troops. There is no way that a fair referendum can take place while Moroccan troops are still in the territory . . . even if the UN tries to contain them. There is no way that a small troop of military observers would be able to control the Moroccan army . . . even if they tried, which I doubt they would in case of a problem!"

". . . and we can't send our civilians back into the territory without adequate protection!" added Akeik. "The only way this would work is if all Moroccan troops were forced to withdraw and the UN took over the administration of the territory."

". . . and if the borders were closed to prevent any additional Moroccans settling in the territory pretending to be native born Sahrawis," added Nih Lahbib, remembering Hassan's penchant for foul play. This last remark was followed by a chorus of approval on the part of all present as each thought of an incident of Moroccan trickery.

Finally, Bouhali gestured them to be quiet. "We told de Cuellar's fact finding mission our demands last December," he growled, obviously irritated. "Yet, he is still ignoring them!"

For a moment there was silence. Then Bachir shook his head. "De Cuellar knows our concerns," he began to say, showing signs of his own frustration. "I was hoping that they would be reflected in this latest proposal."

"But they aren't are they?" Bouhali shot back.

The room became silent again.

Abdelaziz listened to all of this carefully. He, too, had misgivings about the Secretary General's proposal, but they had waited so long for a referendum that would decide the status of the territory once and for all, legitimately, legally . . . .

"What do you think, Brahim?" he asked the man sitting to his right. Ghali thought for a moment before speaking. "I agree with all of your concerns," he finally said, carefully choosing his words. "The Secretary General has asked for a response by September. If we reject his plan outright it might scuttle the idea of a referendum for good. Perhaps we should let him know that although we accept his referendum proposal in principle, we have serious concerns about some of the details he has outlined that would have to be addressed before we would accept it formally and agree to a cease fire."

". . . and let him know that until and unless we *do* accept it formally . . . and Hassan agrees to our terms . . . we have no intention of letting up on the fighting," Bouhali added, forcefully, followed by cheers from the crowd.

"You know Hassan . . ." cried one. "His promises mean nothing and we can't afford to lose the military momentum. If Hassan agrees to this at all, it will only be if we are in a position of strength!"

Abdelaziz looked at the faces of the group. One by one, somewhat hesitantly, they indicated their approval.

Then he faced the group and added ". . . and in the meantime, Bouhali is right . . . we cannot afford to let up on our attacks . . . let us send another message to Hassan! We'll meet again tomorrow to plan the details."

At last the members of the group smiled, and one by one they left the cool confines of the building for the bright, hot August sunlight.

A written message was sent to New York that day. But there would be no let up on military activities. Rather, within a week of sending that message the guerillas readied themselves to give another message to Hassan – a message in the only language he seemed to understand.

August 18, 1988. Message to Hassan.

On the 18th of August, 1988, Bouhali and the commanders of the troops from the 1st and 5th military regions led their troops on what was intended to be a message to Hassan – a message that the guerillas were willing to continue their assaults indefinitely if he did not come to the bargaining table. They chose for their target the Moroccan forces behind the berm between Housa and Smara at a hilly place called Abrouma. The aim was to decimate the Moroccan intervention forces commanded by Colonel Loubariz that were located not far behind the berm at that point – and to keep the pressure on Hassan. They breached the berm through explosives and land mines that they had placed in strategic locations, and while the infantry of the 1st and 5th military regions were keeping the forces along the berm to the left and right of the breach occupied, the armored vehicles of the 2nd military region sped directly to the intervention forces, and attacked them before they were able to move. The guerillas were able to occupy their position within minutes, and took truckloads of equipment with them when they departed. This battle was the first time they used their newly acquired SAM 8 missiles – smaller, easier to use, and more effective than the SAM 6. Once they got a taste of their new weapons, the Moroccan jets refused to intervene.

The message to Hassan had been delivered, loud and clear.

September 1, 1988. The United Nations.

The two figures walked silently along the cavernous hallway inside the cavernous building that housed the United Nations in New York. One, a young dark haired woman in her mid 30s, carried a briefcase filled to the brim with papers; the other, an older, distinguished looking man with slightly greying

363

hair, merely a small file. Before making a grand entrance in the conference room they escaped to the 2nd floor and settled in two of the large, comfortable, white leather armchairs that adorned the North Delegates lounge. The man smiled as he drank an espresso. In a few moments he was expected to address the members of the Security Council with an important message – that the parties to the conflict over Western Sahara had agreed to his referendum proposal. It was the culmination of years of painstaking diplomacy, and he was proud of his accomplishment.

The young woman, however, nervously fidgeted with her pen. "Are you sure it is wise to tell them that they have agreed without noting their reservations?" she finally blurted. "The Moroccans are adamant that the voters should merely decide to accept or reject Moroccan nationality without the option of independence . . . and they continue to insist that the voters' list be expanded. And as for the Polisario . . . well, they refuse to consider anything that doesn't involve the complete withdrawal of Moroccan troops and the administration of the territory by the UN." She paused for a second. "All they have really agreed to is the *idea* of a referendum . . . nothing more. . . and the Polisario have made it clear that they will not stop their attacks until we agree to their demands. Why, just last week they staged another one!"

The man took one last sip of coffee. "Relax," he said in a low tone so that he could not be overheard. "Today I will not have to reveal any of the details of the plan. We will still have time to hammer out the details with the parties . . . but it is important to get the Security Council behind us. We need their imprimatur on our work . . . and it will make it more difficult for the parties to reject our proposals once they are on record as agreeing to the plan." With that last comment he rose and, with her trailing a few steps behind, they walked to the escalator that would take them to the conference room on the first floor.

As they entered the room the hustle and bustle of the delegates subsided, and when the Secretary General walked to the podium and took the microphone to announce that the government of Morocco and the Polisario had accepted his peace plan "in principle" -- with minimal remarks and comments – a round of applause greeted his words – a round of applause that reverberated throughout the room and into the hall. All around the room there were smiles, except on the face of a young dark haired woman carrying a fat briefcase. She just shook her head and quietly slipped away.

September 16, 1988. Another Message to Hassan.

It was two weeks after the Secretary General made that announcement that the guerillas unleashed their second message to Hassan.

The commanders had concluded that in order to wage assaults against Moroccan positions behind the berm it was essential that their troops were supported by armored vehicles, not merely Land Rovers equipped with machine guns. Although they had found their tanks unwieldy and slow, their troop carriers had proved to be ideally suited to carry heavy artillery and soldiers swiftly through the desert, and had been used successfully during the previous year's assaults. But in 1988 the only soldiers with troop carriers were the specially trained units of Bouhali's 2nd region that were stationed in the north. They needed to provide troop carriers for assaults in the southern region. Some of the commanders had suggested dividing the soldiers manning troop carriers into two units, one in the north and the other in the south, both under the same command, but they finally decided to create a second, independent unit that would coordinate its attacks with the commanders in the southern region. So before long an armored unit called the 7th regional command was formed, based in the south.

It was men from this unit, joined by troops from the 3rd and 4th military regions, that delivered the next message to Hassan.

The day was September 15. Three huge forces quietly began their march through the desert. They patiently waited until they were sure that the US satellite overhead had conveyed their positions to the Moroccan command and the CIA had shut down communications for the remainder of the day. Then, as darkness fell they raced through the countryside from different directions, covering miles of territory in the span of a few hours.

They had decided to attack the Moroccans' 3rd regiment -- one of two "elite" regiments that Morocco had organized in order to create better morale among the troops and assuage fears that had begun to surface among Moroccan civilians that the war was not going as planned. The commander of the 3rd regiment was Colonel Abdeslam Abidi, who was the most prestigious officer in the Moroccan army at that time.

The 3rd regiment was headquartered in the region of Mudraiga, not far from the point along the berm that the guerillas had attacked in the spring. There were between 100 and 200 Moroccan soldiers stationed in positions along the wall with roughly 50 of them placed at 5 mile intervals. Mine fields and barbed wire protected their positions. At a distance of a few miles behind the berm were the roving "rapid intervention" forces of the 3rd regiment, divided into 2 or 3 subgroups. The command post of the regiment was behind them.

Brahim Ghali had traveled south from headquarters with a few hand-picked men. At a point a few miles from the spot where they intended to infiltrate the wall they were met by Nih Lahbib, leading members of the 1st military region. Later, troops from the 3rd and the 7th military regions met them coming from the south.

The area near Mudraiga was under the jurisdiction of the Polisario's 3rd military region, whose commander, Ayoub Lahbib, was responsible for conducting reconnaissance and recommending a spot for the joint attack. He had chosen a spot that provided protection from the Moroccan radar instillations and cover for any attack by air.

During the night the specially trained infantry crawled to the berm and removed the landmines. They put the landmines and explosives on the point of the berm through which they planned to create a breach. Then they waited.

At roughly one hour before dawn the guerillas mounted their troop carriers and Land Rovers and slowly approached the wall. Every 25 miles there was one radar installation. Normally each Moroccan battalion had one. During the "war of attrition" the guerillas had become adept at detecting when the radar was working and when it was not. On this date, the radar installations along the berm were not working, but the bigger unit at the command post -- one that had a longer range -- was. However, the spot chosen by Ayoub provided cover for their movements, permitting them to move towards the berm quietly, headlights dimmed, without being detected, until they got very close. Although the Moroccans could hear their motors, they did not know precisely where they were or where they were going, and since the guerillas for the past two years had conducted decoy maneuvers all along the berm, they were accustomed to hearing these noises at night, and were not alarmed.

So, when the guerillas finally made a breach through the wall with their artillery, the Moroccans were taken by surprise. The infantry and soldiers on the troop carriers dispersed to the left and to the right, engaging the soldiers along the berm and surrounding the command post from the north and south, blocking the advance of the "intervention forces." At the same time the main guerilla force, with their artillery, passed through the breach and raced towards the command post. By this time the major radar installation was blasting, but the attack was so fast – it took only 10 to 15 minutes for the guerillas to reach the command post once they breached the berm -- that the Moroccan forces had no time to react. When the Moroccan soldiers along the berm heard the sounds of artillery blasts many of them panicked -- thinking that their comrades had fled and that they were left to face the enemy alone. Most decided to flee rather than fight.

Colonel Abidi, however, was one soldier who did not flee. He had grabbed a weapon and was shooting wildly through the clouds of dust before a guerilla reached him. He tried to fire again, but the bullet hit the barrel of the guerilla's weapon and ricocheted onto the ground. Then he started to fire again, but before he pulled the trigger the guerilla pulled his. He fell to the ground and his weapon fired harmlessly into the air.

After another few minutes the sounds of the battle grew fainter and eventually the only sound was the radar blaring. The commanders could be seen surveying the damage, and after a brief interval Ayoub ordered a retreat. Then prisoners, weapons and anything else movable, were loaded onto vehicles and the guerillas quickly dispersed through the breaches in the wall to their remote hideouts in the desert. Moroccan units from garrisons in Smara and elsewhere were quickly mobilized to attack the retreating forces, but by the time they reached the location of the battle, the guerillas, once again, were nowhere to be found.

CHAPTER 16
1989

De Cuellar's announcement that the parties had 'accepted' his proposal 'with minimal reservations' took both parties by surprise, and the Polisario, who had been kept in the dark about Hassan's demands, decided to take the initiative, and demanded that there be a face to face meeting with Hassan to discuss the important points that needed to be settled. For weeks the King demurred, maintaining his position that he would only negotiate with the Algerians. But at the beginning of 1989 something changed his mind, and the guerilla leaders prepared for what would be their first face to face confrontation.

January 5, 1989. The King's Palace.

It was January, 1989, and Bachir Mustapha Sayed, Mahfoud Ali Beiba, and Brahim Ghali were being escorted through the King's palace in Marrakesh by a trove of nervous and watchful guards. It was to be the first time they would come face to face with Hassan and they were more than a little curious. In November of the previous year, they had been startled when the King had announced to the world that he would accept the results of a referendum and that, if the people of the territory chose independence, "he would be the first to establish an embassy in Smara." The guerillas had quickly sent word to Rabat that they would be all too happy to sit down with him and discuss the organization of such a referendum. At first the King demurred, but after weeks of stalling, he had abruptly agreed to a face to face meeting.

They had a lot to talk about. Perez de Cuellar's referendum proposal was now on the table for discussion, and the Polisario leaders had debated for weeks the points they would raise.

As they walked down the gilt and marble hallway that led to the conference room they couldn't help but be impressed by the grandeur of their surroundings. Undoubtedly fit for a king. But they also couldn't help wondering how many ordinary Moroccans had had to toil in semi poverty to enable the King to enjoy all these trappings.

"Do you really think the King will be willing to give in to our demands?" asked Mafoud in a whisper, as they walked down the long hallway.

"Who knows?" Bachir replied. "But one way or another meeting him here as equals will serve our purpose. It will force his allies in the West to recognize that we are not mere puppets of the Algerians – or terrorists – or ignorant nomads – but people who deserve a seat at the table – whose opinions matter. . .”

“. . . and it won't be bad, either, to show our people that Sahrawis don't need to kneel before the King – or any other leader!” added Ghali.

They were led to a room adjoining one of the conference rooms and asked to be seated. The King would summon them shortly. An hour later an aide walked into the room and asked them to follow him into the conference room. There they sat again, waiting. After another thirty minutes a door at the far side of the room opened and a short, thin man wearing a heavy silk tunic and a cap embellished with gold thread walked into the room, followed by no fewer than six men in uniform.

He positioned himself at the head of an elaborate mahogany conference table and without speaking a word, gestured to the visitors to join him. After they were seated, Bachir gave him their credentials as representatives of the Sahrawi Arab Democratic Republic. The King winced as he took the papers in his hand. The contrast between the two couldn't have been greater. The King, nervous and pale as a ghost, appeared dwarf-like next to the tall, broad shouldered, desert fighter with jet black hair and piercing black eyes. *So this is Ouali's younger brother,* the King thought to himself. *A man who as a child was raised in Tan Tan, in my Kingdom. Who had attended a Moroccan school.* In his eyes he was simply a Moroccan. But Bachir's reputation had preceded him, and he would not do anything to offend him.

Then he stole a glance at the other two. Their faces were not familiar, but he had heard about them. The young, wiry man with the bushy black hair and a defiant air about him was from Laayoune and had been the principal culprit in the recurring sabotage of the Boucraa mines. The older one with a stately demeanor and eyes that seemed to miss nothing had been the guerillas' Minister of Defense for the past thirteen years and was rumored to have masterminded some of their most successful battles, including the recent attack on his 3rd regiment and the capture of its commander.

His face turned even whiter, and his fingers began to fidget nervously with his pen, but he said not a word. Instead, he beckoned to one of his entourage to bring him some cigarettes. At once a trolley appeared loaded with every type of cigarette and cigar. The King reached for a package of cigarettes and opened it. “Would you care for a cigarette?” he asked politely. They all shook their heads. He lit one and began nervously puffing on it, looking out the window, his thoughts wandering. The previous October he had attended the annual meeting of the Arab League in Algiers – one of the few occasions when he could meet the Algerian president face to face. During the meeting a group of leaders from the North African states had met to organize a union of the Maghreb countries – a union in which he wished to play a prominent role. They were planning to have their first summit early in the following year, and he was desperate to have that meeting held in Marrakesh. But he would need the approval of the Algerians – an approval that Bendjedid would never give while negotiations over the fate of the Sahara were stalled. So he had promised him that he would meet face to face with the Polisario leaders to iron out the details of de Cuellar's proposal. A promise that he was now forced to keep.

After a few moments he turned and focused his gaze on Bachir. He asked him if he was the leader of the delegation. After satisfying himself that he was the leader, he addressed all his remarks to him.

"You asked to have this meeting," he announced somewhat wearily. "Just what is it that you want to discuss?"

Bachir struggled to overcome his rising blood pressure. *You know damned well why we are here,* he thought to himself. *Did you or did you not agree to have direct talks with us to iron out the details of the UN proposal?* But instead of allowing the King to know precisely what he thought of him, he swallowed hard, put on his most ingratiating smile, and came directly to the point. "We want to discuss two matters. First, the type of economic, cultural and security relationship we can create with Morocco if Western Sahara becomes an independent state. Then the implementation of the United Nations proposals that you have agreed to . . ."

"Agreed to *in principle,*" the King interrupted, averting his eyes again and taking deep puffs of his cigarette. Without waiting for Bachir to continue the King began his monologue.

"I know we are both tired of this war . . . the bloodshed . . . the imprisonment of men, women and even children. I would like to see it all end, as I am sure you would. . . as the whole world would! I would gladly give you whatever I could to stop it . . . economic interests, political stature, a seat at my table . . . everything most dear to me. But you must understand. . . there is one thing I cannot give you . . . your independence!"

He rambled on and on. Talking about the history and grandeur of his Kingdom. About how he cared about his subjects. About how it pained him to see them suffer. About the suffering of the political prisoners and prisoners of war . . . both Morocco's and the Polisario's. About how he was the only one in the Kingdom who could solve this issue . . . no one else's opinion mattered.

The three guests exchanged glances. Finally Bachir cleared his throat.

"If you do not want to discuss the future relationship of Western Sahara and Morocco, perhaps it is best to discuss the implementation of the UN plan," he said, interrupting his speech.

The King became quiet, and turned to look at him. "What is it about the plan that you would like to discuss?" he said in a barely audible voice.

Bachir paused for a second, riveted his eyes on his host's, and then continued in a calm, determined voice. "We would like to agree on a format for determining eligibility to vote based upon the criteria suggested by the United Nations. We would also like to discuss the withdrawal of Moroccan troops . . ."

"I do not believe it will be necessary to withdraw Moroccan troops," the King said, quickly, putting his cigarette down and interrupting him in a voice that suggested that no further discussion was necessary. "As for these other

369

matters, my advisors are studying the UN proposals and I will inform you and the UN of my decision in due course."

Bachir held his breath for a moment before again addressing the King. "We are prepared to discuss all of these issues with you here . . . today."

The King turned away from the delegation and stared absent mindedly out the window. Then he began again his monologue.

"I have been on this throne since you were a child," he began to say, as if lecturing in a classroom, "and there are a few things I have learned. You can conquer a territory, but it is not the same as conquering the hearts and minds of the people in the territory. I know I have failed in that regard."

Then he turned to face Bachir, and again, as if lecturing a child, continued. "There is a fundamental difference between a King and an elected President – when a President leaves office another takes his place – perhaps even an opponent – and his work is finished. But a King! A King leaves a legacy to his son . . . and to his son's son . . . who carry his name. His country is his life." Then, turning once more to the window, he added, "and the leader of a country and a farmer have something in common. Political change is like a seed that you plant in the earth. A farmer plants a seed and waits for it to grow. He must harvest his crops at the right time. Too early and the fruit is bitter and falls to the ground, too late, and the fruit decays. So it is with political change . . . it must be harvested when it is ripe and sweet."

Then, with a grand, sweeping gesture he announced, "I am the father of all my citizens . . . . your father!"

"We already have fathers," Bachir quickly retorted. "We don't need another one!"

The King's smile disappeared. When he turned again to face Bachir his voice was calm. "I am not ready at the present time to discuss the issues you have raised," he responded, languidly. "But I will schedule another meeting in a couple of months where we can address all of these issues . . . and others as well."

Bachir again paused. Another ploy to buy time? *Does he take us for idiots !* he thought. But once again he put on a smile. Then, in a slow, deliberate tone with just a hint of menace, he said, "We will come back in two months. At that time we will expect that you will be prepared to discuss the details of the UN plan," and with these words the members of the delegation rose to their feet.

But before they had reached the door the King called out to them. "And one more thing . . . I would like you to stop that radio broadcast . . . you know the one. . . I find it insulting!"

Bachir stopped and smiled. Then, without uttering a word he left the room. When the three members of the delegation were half way down the hallway, Mafoud turned to him shaking his head. "Isn't it just like Hassan," he said in a whisper. "He showed no concern about the fate of the commander of his 3rd regiment, the only thing he asked is that we cancel a radio program broadcast from the camps that pokes fun at him."

Brahim smiled. "Yes, 'The King in Paradise and People in Hell,'" he said. "I hear it is very popular in Morocco!"

After they had departed, the King sat down once again in his armchair. It had been a disagreeable meeting . . . and he was glad that it was finished. He had no intention of participating in any other disagreeable meetings. Or fulfilling any of his promises. The Maghreb summit would be held in February in Marrakesh and after that, well, let them come, if they wish. I will let them speak to one of my assistants . . . one of my *junior* assistants, he thought. Meanwhile, he had another ace up his sleeve.

He called for his assistant. "I want you to arrange a meeting for me with Khaddafi as soon as possible," he said, the smile returning to his face.

And within a fortnight he was in Tripoli, where he arranged with Khaddafi the return of Libyan dissidents he held in Moroccan prisons in return for his pledge to halt any future humanitarian aid to the rebels.

March 15, 1989. The United Nations.

It was early spring, and already the crocuses were beginning to emerge from their winter slumber. In his elaborate rooms overlooking the East River, Perez de Cuellar sat with an exasperated look on his face.

"It looks like it will be up to me again," he blurted, heaving a sigh. "The King has postponed his meeting with the Polisario – this time without setting any future date." He shook his head. "I don't think they will take much more."

The young woman sitting across from him couldn't help chuckling beneath her breath. He should be used to Hassan's machinations by this time, she thought.

De Cuellar continued his monologue as if the other figure were not in the room. "If direct talks between them are not possible I will have no other choice but to spend another couple of months shuttling between the capitals of that god-forsaken part of the world . . ." He shook his head again. Then, remembering his assistant's presence, he turned to face her.

"How far have you progressed in getting an agreement on the details of the referendum?" he asked.

The young woman stopped to take a breath. "The problem is that they both still insist on terms that the other will never agree to." Then withdrawing two documents from a thick briefcase she shoved them across the desk. "Take a look for yourself," she said. "The King's letter makes it very clear. In our proposal we gave into his demand that he would not be required to withdraw his troops, but that is not enough . . . he continues to insist that the choice on the ballot be between becoming citizens of Morocco or the 'status quo' . . . whatever that means. He is also adamant that the criteria for eligibility be expanded to include the natives who migrated to Morocco and other states during the late 50s . . . not just the people on the Spanish census and their families. For their part, the guerillas maintain their insistence that the Moroccans withdraw their troops. They want the territory to be administered

371

by the UN . . . and for further settlement by Moroccan civilians to be prohibited. There is no way I can draft an agreement that would satisfy both of them!"

De Cuellar returned to his desk and sat in his chair for a long time, deep in thought. By this time he should be considered an expert in organizing plebiscites, he thought to himself, wryly. Hadn't he spent the last three years trying to get South Africa to agree to withdraw and implement the resolution for a plebiscite in Namibia that the United Nations had passed over a decade ago? There had been a number of obstacles to overcome in that case as well. Two years ago he had finally resolved the dispute over electoral procedures. Only South Africa's demand linking independence to a Cuban troop withdrawal in Angola had remained. Finally, the Americans had been able to negotiate a compromise on that issue, and last December a Tripartite Accord had been signed between Angola, Cuba and South Africa paving the way for the appointment of his representative and a UN peacekeeping mission – UNTAG – to implement the referendum. The starting date for the implementation of the UN plan was next month. UNTAG, with a military component of 7,500 supported by 2,000 international civilian and local staff would then supervise the withdrawal of all military forces in Namibia and begin the registration of voters. So far everything was going like clockwork. But this Sahara thing . . . well, that was another matter.

After a few moments of silence, he looked again at his assistant. "Has anyone else seen these letters?"

The young woman squirmed slightly in her seat. "No, only me, Diallo, De Soto, and the others on your staff." Then she paused before adding, "I thought you would have mentioned these reservations in your report to the Security Council . . ."

"The Security Council!" de Cuellar snapped, interrupting her, and gazing into space with a frustrated look, "They are the last people I want to know about these demands. I must convince them that the parties are in agreement on this proposal if we are to have any chance of getting their support!"

Then he fixed his gaze on his assistant. "I want you to keep these reservations to ourselves for the time being . . . until we can find a way to gloss over them," he said slowly and emphatically.

"What about the heads of the peacekeeping and political departments . . . they will surely want to be part of any negotiations!" the young woman said, nervously.

"Don't worry about them," de Cuellar snapped, with a dismissive flick of his hand. "I will take care of them. For now the negotiations will be directed by my office . . . and my office only! And I suppose I will have to start by taking another trip," he added, wearily.

And within a week his odyssey began once more. By the beginning of summer, the Secretary General had logged thousands of miles in an effort to shore up support for his nascent proposals and had organized a 'technical commission' of specially selected emissaries to visit the territory and hash out the logistical details – all under the watchful eyes of his assistants, who made sure that their contact with the parties – and other officials of the UN -- was closely monitored. And in this way progress in drafting a final set of proposals limped along through the summer months and well into the fall. The litany of concerns raised by each party was never revealed to members of the Security Council, nor to the special task force the Security Council created to draft the final referendum plan. By the end of the year the outline of a plan for a cessation of hostilities and a referendum was beginning to germinate. It would later be known as the Settlement Plan.

Autumn, 1989. Another Message to Hassan.

In the fall of 1989 all hell broke loose again. Just prior to a trip to Spain in September, the 'direct talks' that Hassan had promised were postponed by the King yet another time – and he was quoted as saying that "there is nothing to negotiate because Western Sahara is Moroccan territory."

The fury of the guerillas, that had been held in check somewhat by the appointment of de Cuellar's 'technical commission,' was suddenly unleashed in another series of violent attacks.

In April, Bouhali had been named Minister of Defense and Brahim Ghali had taken over the command of the 2nd military region. In September, Ghali led an attack on Morocco's 3rd Green March Commando Unit that was based near Housa, advancing 12 miles into Moroccan held territory, decimating the unit, destroying all Moroccan positions close to it, and taking 24 prisoners. After this battle his troops attacked a Moroccan position along the berm at the intersection of the Guelta-Amgala regions. In this last battle Ghali employed a new strategy. When they had attacked positions along the berm previously, they had chosen two or three positions as access points, and, after blasting through the wall with explosives at these points, rushed through the breach in their troop carriers, Land Rovers and other vehicles to engage the Moroccans in hand to hand combat and blast them with their artillery. But this time Ghali decided to do something more spectacular. He directed his troops to mount a frontal attack on the berm -- blasting it with the artillery that was mounted on their troop carriers in a lightning assault, and, after breaking through the wall, advancing quickly to pierce the heart of the regimental command with the full force of their arms. The new strategy was a success and they managed to take another 28 prisoners.

While Ghali was occupied in the north, Bouhali sent soldiers from the 1st and 7th military regions south to augment Ayoub Lahbib's troops in what was billed as a 'big operation.'

Ayoub Lahbib was known for his daring attacks – often against great odds. His dramatic flair was a counterbalance to the cool reflections of Ghali, the shrewd calculations of Bouhali, and the meticulous planning of Abdelaziz. On this occasion the baton had been passed to him, with Abdelaziz coordinating the troops from the various regions, and he decided to attack the troops behind the berm at the site of one of the guerillas' greatest victories – Guelta Zemmour.

But this time the attack would be on a grander scale than even the previous autumn's attack near Mudraiga. Early in the morning of October 7, Ayoub positioned his troops along a nine mile stretch of the wall. At the crack of dawn the assault began. Polisario infantry scurried over the entire nine mile length, overcame the stationary forces and waited for the "rapid intervention forces" to arrive. At the same time guerillas blasted large holes in the wall in several locations, through which troop carriers and Land Rovers armed with machine guns swiftly penetrated. The Moroccan mobile forces could not determine which way to go – the guerillas were to their left, to their right, everywhere they looked -- like a swarm of ants descending upon a locust.

The fighting was intense, but after four hours the mobile forces had either been dispersed or killed.   The guerillas had penetrated fifteen miles into Moroccan held territory. Over one hundred Moroccan soldiers had been killed. The Moroccan reconnaissance aircraft and planes that had tried to intervene had been effectively deterred by the guerillas' SAM 8 missiles.

By the end of the year, with no agreement on a referendum plan in sight, the war seemed to be heating up, causing Hassan once again to run to the United States for help, and raising the diplomatic stakes for de Cuellar to an all time high.

CHAPTER 17
1990

January 1990. The Beginning of the End.

It was the first week of the new year, and once again the leaders of the Polisario had been called to a meeting to discuss an urgent matter. They were not content – especially Bouhali.

After the battles in the fall of 1989, Bouhali, now the Minister of Defense, had decided to meet with the commanders of the troops in the southern region to plan another attack. But as soon as he reached the outskirts of Guelta Zemmour he had received a message from Abdelaziz that he should return at once to Rabouni. When he was alone with the President the latter told him that he should put the new attack on hold for the time being since the Polisario leadership was debating whether to agree to the cease fire that de Cuellar had been urging for the past several months. He had called a meeting of his military commanders and closest aides to discuss the issue.

It was now time for that meeting and as Abdelaziz looked around the room he saw a number of somber faces.

He decided not to mince words. "As you know, for the past several months the Secretary General of the United Nations has been urging us to cease the attacks on Moroccan positions so that he might be able to finalize the details of a plan to end the conflict. I know that there are some of you who believe that this would be a bad idea, but a number of our allies – including most of our allies at the OAU – are urging us to do it, and I have recently had a meeting with Bendjedid in which he also asked us to do it. So, I think we should give it serious thought and I want to know your opinions."

He didn't have long to wait. Almost before he had finished Bouhali raised his voice.

"You all know how I feel about the idea of a cease fire," he exclaimed, emphatically. "All it will do is give Hassan another breathing spell. We have got them on the defensive now. The Moroccan troops are thoroughly demoralized. They cannot take much more. It would be folly to stop our attacks now, just when we have demonstrated that they cannot rely on the berm as a defense."

"I agree," Ayoub shouted. "What do we gain by a cease fire? It only helps Hassan!"

375

"But if the United Nations can bring an end to the fighting and give us what we want . . ." Bachir began.

"The UN?" Bouhali sneered. "The same UN that has refused to support us for the past fifteen years?" He stopped for a moment and shook his head. "The Western nations -- the United States and France – have been against us from the beginning. Do you really think they are going to change their position now? We have managed to stay out of the cold war quagmire – we are neither pro-Western nor pro-Soviet. Our strength is only our military . . . we have no other cards to play. The Western powers will never sacrifice Hassan for us!"

"The Western powers are not the entire United Nations . . . we still have most of Africa on our side . . . as well as many other third world countries," Mahfoud responded slowly.

"But there is no one who supports us on the Security Council, and they are the ones who matter," Bouhali retorted. "I still say, if we press on we can win this war!"

". . . yes, perhaps we can win the war . . . eventually," Bashir replied, gazing directly at Bouhali. "We might win the battle on the ground only to lose it on the diplomatic front."

He looked around him to where the others were sitting, somber expressions on their faces.

"Look, right now we have the support of practically all of Africa and a lot of other countries as well. What do you think would happen to that support if we snubbed a UN brokered referendum. . . a referendum, I might add, that is based upon the plan suggested by our allies? Isn't a referendum what we have been fighting for all these years? And yes, if we want to continue fighting we might eventually be able to force Hassan to his knees. But how long would it take? Another two years? Another five?" He paused before continuing, and when he did he lowered his voice to a bare whisper. "And a lot can happen on the political front in five years."

He looked around him. They knew what he was thinking.

"Right now we have a UN Secretary General who wants to leave a mark on history by being the one to end this conflict. He supports having a referendum settle the issue. . . and he was able to implement one in Namibia that seems to be working. His term will be ending in 1991, and who knows who will replace him . . . and what his priorities will be. . ." Bachir stopped to let the message sink in.

"Look," he began again, "I have been consulting with the Nigerians and other African leaders. All of them . . . without exception . . . are urging us to grab this chance to legitimize our position in the eyes of the world. . . . a chance that might not come again!"

For a moment all were silent.

"He's got a point," Mahfoud finally said, shaking his head. "The political landscape can change in an instant . . . and with it the support of the UN and our allies. And without that support . . ."

"I still don't like it," Bouhali interrupted. "We all know what Hassan is like. He promises one thing and does another. He may not be good at waging a war on the battlefield, but he knows how to wage battles in the United Nations. Look how he manipulated the OAU for all these years!"

Mahfoud shook his head. "He could afford to rebuff the OAU. The United Nations is a different matter."

"Still, I don't trust him," Bouhali added. "I think it is just another ruse to buy time, to put us off guard. I say forget this referendum business . . . at least on de Cuellar's terms . . . but if we do consider it, at the very least keep up the military pressure."

There was silence in the room for a moment.

"Perhaps the best option, for the time being, is to continue our negotiations with de Cuellar . . . to see whether we can get him to agree to our demands," Mahfoud slowly said. "Once we know for sure what the UN will be offering we will be in a better position to judge whether it is in our interests to accept their plan. We don't need to agree to a formal cease fire in order to do this . . . but it might be wise . . . to show our good faith . . . to put on hold any major confrontations for a while. If we aren't able to iron out the details of a referendum plan in a few more months . . . well, the battlefield will still be there!"

Abdelaziz had been watching the interchange closely. When Mahfoud finished speaking he broke his silence.

"I wanted to hear your views, but I don't think the decision is ours to make . . . we need to see what the people want."

He stopped for a moment. Then, turning to Bachir he continued. "I would like you to put together a small group to study our various options . . . put together a list of the pros and cons that we can discuss with the people at a special meeting. Do you think you will be able to do this within a couple of months, Bachir?" he asked.

"I will start immediately," he responded.

"Good, then it is settled," Abdelaziz said, his voice firm, "and in the mean time we can continue our debate. Then, in a softer voice, looking at Bouhali and Ayoub, he added, "I know some of you would like to keep up the military pressure, but I think we can afford to put any major battles on hold until we see what the people want us to do."

And with those last remarks the meeting came to an end.

Soliloquy.

That evening, as she passed him a bowl of fresh camel's milk, which would precede the evening meal, Khadidja sensed that something was troubling him. These days he often looked worried, and she was accustomed to sitting by his side quietly until the mood dispersed and he once again joined her conversation. But today the mood seemed to linger longer than usual, and after a few moments she put her hand on his shoulder.

377

"Is there anything I could do to help?" she whispered, softly.

He turned to look at her. He was lucky to have married her, he thought. She was not only beautiful, she was wise.

"I was just thinking of the day Ouali asked me to join his movement," he began, slowly. "I had planned to be a doctor . . . to devote my life to saving lives. I had no political aspirations . . . I never expected to be asked to make the decisions that would decide the future of our people . . . that the fate of our people would be placed in my hands."

"Perhaps that is why you make such a great leader," she replied tenderly. "Perhaps it is because you never had political aspirations!"

He smiled slightly. "But it is difficult to know what to do at times!" he muttered, casting his gaze away. "This referendum proposal of the Secretary General . . . it is what we have always wanted. . . but can we trust him? Can we trust the United Nations to conduct the referendum fairly? Can we trust Hassan to adhere to its terms? And if we do win a referendum . . . as I am sure we would if it is done fairly . . . would Hassan really withdraw from the territory?" He returned his gaze to her face. She had been looking at him intently. She hadn't said a word, but he knew what she was thinking. He knew what they were all thinking.

"It is a gamble," he said, his voice grave. "We are getting pressure from some of our allies to go along with the proposal, but I don't know . . . de Cuellar has not said whether he will accede to our demands, and if he doesn't . . . well . . . I don't know whether we can risk it." After a pause he looked away again.

"And yet, I am worried about what might happen if we *don't* risk it."

Khadidja had been listening calmly to his speech, but at his last remark she felt a slight tinge of apprehension. She put down the bowl of milk.

"What do you mean?" she asked with some trepidation.

He looked at her again. "Did you hear the latest news about what is going on up north?"

She shook her head.

"The Islamic Salvation Front has organized mass rallies to demand early local elections in Algeria," he exclaimed. "The group has already gained widespread support among the masses of uneducated and unemployed Algerians. . . and if it manages to get any seats in the next elections . . ."

Khadidja was puzzled. "Why are you worried about them?" she asked, quietly. "They have nothing to do with us, do they?"

He shook his head. "Not so far . . . but they wish to make Algeria an Islamic state . . . and their version of Islam is not ours . . . already they are forcing women to wear veils and declaring that they should stay at home . . . and their interpretation of *sharia* comes from Saudi Arabia," he responded, frowning. "Their doctrines threaten our entire way of life. I am worried about what will happen in Algeria if they continue to gain political power. If they try to impose their doctrines on us . . . and if they gain control of the government . . . ."

He shook his head and turned once again to face her. His eyes reflected the worry that had been plaguing him.

"We need the support of the government of Algeria!" he exclaimed.

Khadidja took his hand. "Perhaps they won't succeed in winning any seats in the elections," she whispered softly. "Perhaps the Algerians will wake up an see them for what they are . . ."

She kissed him softly on the cheek and got up quietly to prepare the evening meal. When she had left and he was alone with his thoughts, memories of days long since past returned. Ouali. The university. Quiet days with quiet cares. But his mind quickly snapped back to the present . . . and to the decisions he was facing. He remembered something that Ouali had told him . . . that what scared him the most, what caused him the greatest worries, was not facing the enemy in battle. No, it was facing the Sahrawi women when they looked at him for answers. The eyes of the Sahrawi women. It was difficult to face those eyes . . . .

He knew he would soon have to face those eyes. . . as well as those of the men who had followed him into battle, and that night, when he finally managed to sleep, all he could see in his dreams were thousands of eyes peering at him through the darkness.

March 1990. The Settlement Plan.

It was March of 1990, and the Secretary General had embarked on yet another whirlwind tour of the African capitals, this time towing along his latest special representative for Western Sahara, the Swiss diplomat Johannes Manz. It was imperative that he show some progress in the negotiations. The war had heated up dramatically in the last few months of 1989 and the George H. W. Bush administration had started making noises about giving Hassan even more aid -- two full squadrons of F-16 fighter bombers and some of the M60 tanks that the United States was planning to withdraw from Europe as part of agreed force reductions between NATO and the Warsaw Pact. This, he knew, would prompt Algeria to follow suit and increase the aid it was giving to the guerillas. He had urged the parties to agree to a cease fire in order for him to put the final touches on a plan to end the conflict, but so far had received no response. At least there had been no guerilla attacks for the past few months, but he had no idea how long that might continue. If he didn't get an agreement fast the whole issue might blow up in his face.

Upon arriving back at UN headquarters he summoned a few close aides into his office. "Any developments?" one of them asked hopefully.

The Secretary General shook his head. "I had hoped that Manz would be able to help me persuade the Algerians to drop their opposition to Morocco's demands, but, no . . . they are being just as stubborn as ever. With all the problems they are facing in their country I would have thought they would be eager to mend their relations with Morocco. . . but no dice."

His aides knew what he was referring to. In October of 1988, in response to austerity measures that the Algerian government had been forced to take because of slumping oil prices there had been mass demonstrations that had been brutally put down by the army, plunging the country perilously close to anarchy.

"Is it true that Bendjedid has decided to permit other political parties to organize legally?" one of his aides, a young man carrying a fat briefcase asked, somewhat inquisitively.

De Cuellar frowned. "Yes, it seems that he has decided that the only way to stem the unrest is to loosen the reins. Already a handful of parties have begun to emerge . . . some with somewhat dangerous political agendas," he responded, gravely. He was thinking of a group intent on making the country an Islamic state.

"But this is not our worry . . . we have enough to worry about trying to fix this Western Sahara problem," he said, shrugging his shoulders and turning to face his assistant. "Have you been able to make any progress with the plan?

The young woman squirmed slightly in her seat. "I have put together something that I think will be the best we can do under the circumstances . . . but I don't think either party is going to like it much!"

De Cuellar turned to the window overlooking the river. When he turned once again to face the entourage he scowled. "I don't care if the parties don't like it much . . . it is about time they learn that this issue will never be settled unless they compromise. The Security Council is already asking questions. I want to put something on the table before the whole matter blows up in our faces!" Then drawing closer to his assistant and peering directly into her eyes he said, in a slow, firm voice, "I want you to have a final plan on my desk by June."

"Without getting comments from the parties?" she asked incredulously.

"Without even notifying them!" de Cuellar barked.

Three months later, on June 13, the Secretary General revealed his plan to end the conflict in the Sahara -- colloquially dubbed the "Settlement Plan" -- to the members of the Security Council and the stunned parties. It was immediately made public. Nothing was said about any reservations of the parties, and the plan was quickly approved and adopted by a Security Council whose attention by this time had been diverted by growing tensions in the Persian Gulf.

For on August 2 of that year – barely six weeks after the plan was announced --Saddam Hussein invaded Kuwait.

CHAPTER 18
1991

In the latter months of 1990 and the early months of 1991, while the eyes of the Security Council and the rest of the world were glued to the evolving saga of the invasion of Kuwait and the "Desert Storm" that followed it, de Cuellar shepherded his plan to end the conflict in Western Sahara through the corridors of the UN, turning a blind eye to the parties' cries of concern. After the publication of the draft Settlement Plan in June of 1990, the King of Morocco sent an angry letter to de Cuellar, which he then made public. The Polisario followed suit that August. Their grievances were ignored. Instead, in April of 1991 the Secretary General issued another report to the Security Council, enumerating some revisions to the plan and -- after secret talks with the Moroccans, but not the Polisario – set September 6, 1991 as the date for a cease fire to begin. A resolution was quickly passed creating a UN peacekeeping force with the acronym MINURSO to plan and supervise the referendum called for under the plan.

. . . and diplomats of all stripes at the UN and elsewhere began to heave a collective sigh of relief that this long, intractable conflict, may finally be reaching its end.

May 31, 1991. Rabouni.

But the sigh of relief of the international diplomatic community was not shared by the parties. On the last day of May, in the small room that served as the President's office in Rabouni, leaders of the Polisario gathered to discuss the latest developments.

"De Cuellar has made no attempt to address the concerns we expressed in our letter last August," one of them said, angrily. "His revisions to the plan he published last June still allows most of the Moroccan army to stay in the territory during the referendum process. I still cannot see why they cannot do what they are doing in Namibia. The South Africans were forced to withdraw their troops and there will be over 7,500 UN soldiers sent to keep the peace. Letting 65,000 Moroccan troops remain in the territory monitored by only 1,700 peacekeepers is a recipe for disaster!"

"And in Namibia the UN will take over the administration of the territory," another added. "I don't see why they can't do the same in Western Sahara!"

"Or if they don't want to have the UN administer it, they can arrange to have Spain take over the responsibility . . . didn't they allow Great Britain to administer the territory during the plebiscite in Zimbabwe?" asked a third.

"De Cuellar is just jerking us around," another said, pounding his fist on the President's desk. "How many times do we have to tell him that what he is proposing is unacceptable?"

The shouting went on and on, each member of the group venting months of pent up frustration.

Bachir, sitting quietly by himself, listened to the comments intently. When the room had once again become quiet, he calmly raised his voice. "Look, I am just as disappointed as you are that de Cuellar hasn't acceded to our demands – Moroccan forces should not be allowed to remain in the territory and the UN should take over the administration – but I have spent months trying to convince him that he would be courting disaster by letting the Moroccans remain in the territory." He sighed and shook his head. "Let's face it, its Hassan, not de Cuellar. . . de Cuellar's plan may be the most we can expect Hassan to approve. So, unless we want to forfeit this chance for a referendum and continue the armed struggle indefinitely, we might be forced to accept his terms."

Bouhali shook his head. "You know where I stand. Why should we agree to a referendum anyway – even if we *can* get them to agree to our terms? We can gain control of the territory without going through the UN."

"Perhaps. . .but we may all be dead by the time Hassan runs out of Saudi money and American arms!" exclaimed a voice from the rear.

The room once again became quiet.

Abdelaziz, who had been listening silently to the comments, finally decided to speak.

"Yes, it is true that de Cuellar has rejected some of our demands," he began, slowly, looking at a paper on his lap, ". . . but it seems that Hassan has demanded that the option of independence be stricken . . . and that the criteria for eligibility be expanded. De Cuellar has rejected these demands. The option of independence will still be on the ballot and the criteria for eligibility will still be based on the Spanish census. Frankly, I will be amazed if Hassan agrees to these terms. He must know that most of the people on the Spanish census will vote for independence . . . and many of them live in our camps." He stopped for a moment, deep in thought.

"Perhaps Bachir is right," he continued ". . . perhaps this is the best we can hope for from the UN. . . or Hassan. We may have to give up some of our demands to get the two demands that matter the most . . . and we may have no choice but to accept the plan proposed by de Cuellar if we want a referendum. . . or keep on fighting. And as far as the cease fire is concerned . . . well, there is no way the UN will send people to conduct a referendum while there is still fighting going on!"

Then he paused and looked again at the faces of the people surrounding him. They were ashen. Sullen. Not one of them smiled. "I will leave it up to you . . . should we recommend to the people that we agree to de Cuellar's plan?" he said, his voice steady.

". . . or at least abide by the cease fire while we continue our discussions?" Bachir interjected.

For a moment you could have heard a pin drop in the room. Then, one by one they slowly nodded their heads . . . all but Bouhali and Ayoub. Abdelaziz paused for a moment, then he took the two of them aside. "It is supposed to be over in six months. We can afford to put our army on hold for six months. If it doesn't work out we can always return to the battlefield."

Bouhali and Ayoub just remained silent, as one by one the leaders filtered out of the room. All but Bachir, who lingered behind to discuss the letter they would send to de Cuellar.

When they were alone together Abdelaziz turned to him. The calm demeanor was gone. Instead he looked tired, worried, as if he were grappling with a great burden.

"You have been leading the discussions with the Secretary General . . . do you really think he can fulfill his promises?" he asked.

Bachir was silent for a moment. It was a question that he had often asked himself. "I know he wants very much to solve this problem before he leaves office and I think he *intends* to fulfill his promises . . . whether he will be able to do so is another question!" he muttered. "But the important question is what Morocco's allies will do – especially France and the United States. Right now they are backing de Cuellar's proposal, and not Morocco's position, and that is something important. If we let this chance pass, who knows what their position will be in the future? And another thing . . . it is important that the world see what the people of the territory want. It is their future that is on the line, and they have the right to have their opinion known and be respected. The major reason why my brother wished to gather the leaders of the Polisario together in the first place was to give expression to the will of the people. Once the people have had their say, it will be difficult for Morocco or its allies to reject it. And right now we have the stage!"

Abdelaziz looked at him for a moment without speaking.

"I hope de Cuellar will succeed," he finally exclaimed, his voice grave, "for we may need to get this referendum plan put into action as soon as possible. I didn't want to mention it at the meeting, but I have been worried for some time about what is going on up north."

Bachir was not surprised. "You mean the Islamicists?" he asked.

"Yes, . . . while the FIS was a small, underground movement, I did not give them a second thought, but as soon as the government permitted them to organize legally I began to feel uneasy . . . and last summer when the they won 54% of the vote in the municipal elections I began to really worry!" He paused for a moment. Then he looked sharply at Bachir.

"Bendjedid has tried to stem them by redrawing the electoral districts. But I think this will backfire on him. They are calling for a general strike in protest and the demonstrations they have organized in Algiers have been huge." His

383

mind flashed back to the pictures of the mass sit-ins in one of Algiers largest squares that had been plastered on the news programs the previous week.

"I don't think the military will let them get away with much more," he said, shaking his head. "If they win a majority of seats in the national parliament elections this December. . . well, I don't think that will sit well with the Generals. Already there is animosity between Nazar and Bendjedid. . ."

The look he gave Bachir needed no interpretation. He slumped in his chair, wearily. "No matter what the outcome there will be problems. If the government is toppled and Algeria plunges into chaos . . . I don't think the problems of the Sahrawis will be high on their list of concerns! . . . and if the Islamicists get into power . . . you know as well as I do that they are not our friends."

He stopped for a moment, then looking directly into Bachir's eyes, continued in a low voice, "We can no longer rely on the support of Libya . . . and if something happens in Algeria . . ."

". . . I don't believe that anything will happen in Algeria that will alter their support, militarily or politically. . ." Bachir interjected quickly, trying as best he could to convey a note of optimism.

Abdelaziz looked at him, no longer trying to hide the anguish in his soul. "But can we bet the future of our people on that?" he asked, quietly.

Bachir stopped for a moment. Then, placing a hand on his friend's shoulder, he added, "Well, if this referendum process goes as planned, it will at least buy us some time to see how the political situation in Algiers resolves itself." Abdelaziz remained silent. After a moment of hesitation Bachir walked to the door.

"I will have a draft of a letter to send to the Secretary General on your desk tomorrow," was all that he said as he quietly left the room.

July 30, 1991. Rabat.

The man from the State Department was a seasoned diplomat, but the subject he had come to discuss was of a delicate nature, and he had spent some time trying to think of a way to approach it with the King. Finally, he decided it was best just to come straight to the point.

So he turned to the man sitting across the table from him, and said, matter-of-factly, "Your Majesty, the brass in the Pentagon and the State Department have come to the conclusion that it is not in your best interest to prolong this war in the Sahara any longer." He waited a moment before continuing. "For a long time we have doubted whether you would be able to win an outright victory against the guerillas – assuming, of course, that they continue to get help from Algeria – but we had thought that if we showed the guerillas and the Algerians that we would support you as long as it would take to defeat them, one or both of them would eventually cave in and sue for peace. Instead, the opposite has happened. Despite all our best efforts, they are now in a position to inflict heavy losses on your troops along the berm and you risk alienating your troops – with potentially dire consequences -- if you continue the conflict too much longer. And even if by some miracle you were to win a decisive victory over the guerillas, you would still need to find some way to legitimize your occupation in the eyes of the United Nations." He paused again. "You know that the administration is solidly behind you, and we are grateful for the help you gave us in Kuwait. But to be frank, Saddam Hussein's attack on Kuwait has presented somewhat of an embarrassment for the President. People are beginning to ask why the United States has opposed Hussein's rationale for annexing Kuwait while at the same time supporting you in your war effort to annex the Sahara. And your friends in the Gulf are too busy trying to save their own necks to continue their financial backing for this war. For all these reasons, we have come to the conclusion that the best course of action for you would be to go along with de Cuellar's plan for a referendum."

The King sat patiently through this long speech. This was not the first time an emissary from the State Department had tried to convince him to go along with the referendum proposal. But when Secretary of State Baker had begged him to help push through the UN resolution on Kuwait -- authorizing the use of force to expel Iraqi forces from the country -- and to contribute to the military coalition, he had required as a condition for his support that they stop pressuring him to introduce greater democracy into his country . . . and that they support his position on the referendum. Now, they seemed to be backsliding . . . at least when it came to the referendum.

After a moment he turned to his guest, and quietly, but firmly said, "I told your boss when he asked for my help in Kuwait that I would accept some sort of referendum, but I can't accept what de Cuellar is proposing. For one thing, he wants to limit the list of eligible voters to those on the census the Spanish took in 1974. But that will leave out thousands of people born in the territory who left during the 1950s – the majority of whom settled in southern Morocco. That I cannot accept."

The diplomat paused before speaking. "I know that limiting the voting to people on the Spanish census is not the optimum solution, but it is the only way they would be able to conduct a referendum in a reasonable period of time. Opening up the list to those who emigrated prior to 1974 would involve months of interviews not only in Morocco, but in Mauritania and Algeria and who knows where else. Not to mention the proof problems. It would escalate the cost of the operation considerably. The United Nations is currently suffering a financial crisis and the delegates would never approve a costly peacekeeping mission in the Sahara. Be sensible. Using the Spanish census as the basis for eligibility is the only way the plan would pass muster at the Security Council. And after it is approved . . . well we can always ask for some minor revisions."

The King paused for a moment, staring at the man next to him who was smiling and nonchalantly fiddling with his pen. Then he shook his head. "Even if we were able to get some 'minor revisions' after the plan is approved by the Security Council, I have repeated time and time again that I cannot accept a referendum with the option of independence. This is out of the question."

The diplomat leaned closer. "You realize, of course, that neither the Algerians nor the international community will accept a referendum that does not include the option of independence. That simply would not comport with the notion of self determination." Then, growing suddenly serious, he paused, leaned closer still, and whispered "But just because there is the option of independence does not mean that when the time comes they will choose independence." He leaned back again on his chair and gave the King a look – a look that spoke volumes. "And anything can happen when they try to organize a referendum," he continued. For a moment, neither of them spoke.

The King stared at the man again. He remembered the words Kissinger had spoken before the conflict started. And in his head the glimmer of another "Plan B" began to emerge. He drew his chair closer to his guest and said, "Let's discuss this further."

When his guest had departed, Hassan sat in his armchair and poured himself a double shot of Johnnie Walker Black Label. He had agreed – for tactical reasons -- to cave in to de Cuellar's demands and accept the Settlement Plan in order to have a much needed cease fire, but he was not finished yet. He would teach those rebels a lesson. He would fire one last volley.

August 17, 1991. The Final Days.

It was a sweltering day in the middle of August. After weeks of cajoling Sidimi, Elena was happy to have escaped the oppressive heat of the Tindouf camps and to have been permitted to join Salek and be the medic for the troops in the hills surrounding Tifariti. She had already been there a week, counting the supplies and making sure that there would be enough medicine to take care of any casualties. But no one expected there would be many more casualties. For weeks now the small makeshift infirmary she created hosted mainly civilians involved in accidents, or army men suffering from respiratory or other ailments contracted while they were in the camps, not in the battles, and a sort of calm had descended over the troops. Talks at the United Nations had now been going on for weeks, and since the Secretary General had announced the formation of MINURSO in April there had been a lull in the fighting, and rumors of an imminent breakthrough had circulated among the residents of the camps.

Salek had again taken Esmeralda into his arms and had been busy serenading the troops and civilians in the area every evening. Most evenings were spent laughing and singing around huge fires. There had not been a bombing raid for months. A few, brave, families from the camps had even pitched their tents in the craggy hills around Tifariti and Bir Lehlou, forsaking the harsh *hammada* summer.

Elena and Salek spent long hours just talking – talking about the future, about what they planned to do, what they planned to see. They were no longer the impulsive teenagers they were when the war started – they had spent the past seventeen years, almost half their lifetimes-- in a struggle that had consumed their hearts and souls. They were now in their mid thirties, and their dreams had become the dreams of adults – the simple desire to live in peace, perhaps raise a family, perhaps find a job somewhere. They realized that the El Ayoun they had both known no longer existed, that most of the people they knew had escaped or were dead. Moreover, when they looked around them they could see that the society in which they lived had changed as well. Oh, the Sahrawi women still wore the traditional long flowing, colorful robes, and the men sported the traditional *draa* on festive occasions. But the younger women could also quote Gloria Steinem and the young men were just as likely to hum to the tunes of the Beatles as to their traditional music. Moreover, there were legions of children in the camp – an entire generation -- who had never known life outside its confines. And the people had become so accustomed to the version of democracy in the camps they practiced that they couldn't imagine a life under any other system of government.

And the world outside had also changed. The rebellious fever that had imbued the 60s had been replaced by a more sober world outlook. Communism was gasping its last breath, and technology was now king. It was fast becoming the age of dot coms and computers. This change was reflected in Polisario leadership as well. No longer the brash youngsters barely out of college who had stepped hesitantly onto the world stage, they were fast becoming seasoned statesmen. So, as Elena and Salek looked over the horizon to the west, they couldn't help but wonder what the future would hold.

One day, as he was nonchalantly cleaning his weapon, Salek heard the hum of an engine – a hum that grew louder within minutes. He had heard that hum many times before. He looked up just in time to see a flash of metal streak by, uncomfortably close to the ground, closely followed by three others. Mirage jets! He instinctively ran for cover, but there was no sound of gunfire, no blast of bombs, only the muffled sound of an explosion in the far distance. Others had seen it too, and had run to where a small pile of estrella missiles had been gathered, ready to be transported to Tindouf. These were the only anti-aircraft missiles left in the camp. The sophisticated SAM 8 missiles had been sent back to Tindouf the preceding week. But the jets did not return.

"What do you think is going on?" he asked one of his companions, when he reached where they had taken cover.

"I don't know," the other said, somewhat nervously, "but I will report it to Rabouni and ask for instructions."

A few minutes later he returned, a grave look on his face. "There has been an attack near Tifariti by four Mirage jets, apparently trying to hit our fuel depots" he said grimly. "Luckily they missed! Our troops managed to down one and capture the pilot. He is being taken back to Rabouni for questioning."

"But why?" Salek blurted, thoroughly confused. "I thought they had agreed to this cease fire . . . the cease fire that is supposed to begin in less than two weeks! What do they hope to gain?'

The other shook his head. "No one knows," he began to mutter, "but if the

Mirage jets try to attack us we will be sitting ducks without our missiles."

Salek sat on the ground, trying to make sense of it all. But try as he could he could not find an explanation . . . at least one that made any sense. Did Hassan wish to provoke the Polisario for some reason? To scuttle the cease fire? Or was it a last minute gambit to acquire more territory before the cease fire went into effect? Did he expect that the Polisario would just stand by and do nothing if he resumed the battles? Only one thing was sure, they had to be prepared for whatever might happen. And then he thought of Elena . . . .

He quickly made way to where she was standing by the lean-to that served as the dispensary, still calmly counting bottles of medicine, stacks of bandages.

"Elena," he said quickly, "You must go back to Tindouf . . . at once!"

She looked at him, somewhat puzzled. "Why would I want to go back when it has taken me so long to convince Sidimi to let me join you?" she said, smiling, and giving him an affectionate pat on the shoulder.

"Elena, I am serious," he said, giving her a stern look. "It is not safe here . . . not now."

"Oh, you mean the jets," she said, shrugging her shoulders. "I heard them too   . . . but they didn't fire upon us, did they? It was probably just the Moroccans taking one last look. I wouldn't be too concerned about it, if I were you." And with that last remark she turned and picked up another package of bandages.

"Elena," he said softly, taking her by the arm. "The Moroccans tried to bomb our fuel depots near Tifariti. I tell you something is up."

She looked at him, still smiling, and tenderly pushed aside a lock of his hair that had fallen on his brow. "If something *does* happen, do you think I would want to be anywhere but with you?" she said softly.

He stood motionless for a moment, just looking down at her. Then, as if something inside him finally broke, he drew her close to him and kissed her passionately, and they stood in each other's arms oblivious to the bandages that had fallen from her hand and bottles of liquid that had scattered on the floor. There they remained for what seemed an eternity, blissfully unaware of the commotion that had enveloped the others in the camp. And they probably would have remained there even longer had someone not screamed his name.

"What is it?" he screamed back.

"Come quickly," was the reply.

He looked at her, struggling to say something. "Go, " she said, touching his arm, "I will follow you in a moment." He ran back along the trail to where the others had camped. Someone had arrived, and he was bringing something on a big truck.

"I have something for you," he said, and withdrew the tarp that covered the truck. He could see protruding from the rear of the vehicle several large projectiles. A SAM 8 anti-aircraft missile system.

"The Minister of Defense told me to bring these to you. He heard about the Moroccan attack and wants you to shoot down any jets that get too low."

"But do you have any idea what is going on?" Salek asked, hoping that at least someone knew.

"No one seems to know," was the answer. "But the President is trying to evacuate Bir Lehlou and the civilians from the surrounding countryside and wants all unnecessary personnel to leave Tifariti. That is all I know."

Elena stood there without uttering a word. She had arrived just in time to hear the messenger's last words.

The man looked at her. "I can take you back to Tindouf with me, if you wish, Elena," he said softly.

"No . . . I will stay!" she responded.

"But, Elena . . ." Salek started to protest.

". . . it is no use arguing," she said, grabbing his arm, "If there is some more fighting I will be needed here to care for the wounded. It is what Sidi would do!" she exclaimed, firmly.

That evening Salek played his guitar as usual and the skeleton of troops that had remained in the camp tried their best to resume their activities as if nothing had happened. But later that night, when all that could be heard was the rustling sound of the wind through the trees, Salek stayed awake, just counting the stars.

August 18, 1991.

It was early in the morning of August 18, and Sidimi had barely arrived at the hospital when two soldiers appeared at the door, carrying a stretcher with a man wearing a Moroccan uniform on it. When they saw her they hurriedly placed the stretcher at her feet.

"Who is this," she asked somewhat puzzled.

"A Moroccan pilot," one of them responded, trying to catch his breath. "We managed to capture him after his plane was downed. Abdelaziz wants to question him . . . after you patch him up."

Sidimi looked closely at the man. He had suffered a broken leg, several broken ribs, and probably a concussion, and was bleeding from a wound in his chest, but he would survive. She turned once again to the men who had brought him.

"Tell me what happened!" she asked.

"The Moroccans have bombed Tifariti . . . that is all I know," one of them blurted, trying unsuccessfully to remain calm.

Tifariti! she thought, her mind racing. *The hospital!* She left the man in the care of one of her assistants and raced to the headquarters. Rabouni seemed to be swirling with commotion, people excitedly shouting and running in different directions.

"Where's Abdelaziz?" she asked one of the guards.

"He's in there," he said, pointing to one of the rooms. "But you can't go in . . . he's busy with some of the members of the Executive Committee."

She looked around her. In the corner of the room a man, one of Abdelaziz' chief assistants, was speaking in hushed tones to a subordinate.

389

"Tell me what is going on," she shouted, as she grabbed his arm.

"All we know so far is that the Moroccans have bombed Tifariti, Lemgassem and Bir Lehlou in the north, and Agwanit and Doujit in the south . . . and now we are getting reports that Moroccan forces have made breaches in the berm at Legdaim . . . a little southwest of Farsia," he said, his voice quivering with emotion.

Sidimi stood for a moment not knowing what to say. Then her mind returned to the image of Tifariti . . . and the hospital that was being constructed there.

"Tifariti . . . the people . . . the hospital . . ." she blurted.

"Don't worry, no one was injured . . . and the hospital was not hit. Apparently they were aiming for the fuel depots . . . but missed," he replied, forcing a smile.

". . . and Bouhali?" she queried.

"He was in the south examining the troops when the bombing occurred, but he is now near Farsia," he shouted to her as he walked briskly down the corridor. "Ghali is still in Venezuela, so Bouhali has taken over command of the troops of the 2nd military region . . . and has mobilized them as well as the troops of the 4th and 5th military regions. I think he plans to intercept the Moroccan troops if they leave the berm."

There was little time to think. The little clinic in Tifariti was loaded with supplies . . . supplies that were needed . . . and she had just ordered some equipment to be sent to the hospital that was nearly completed.

The door to the room where Abdelaziz and the other leaders were conferring suddenly opened, and she could hear the high pitched tone of several voices, all talking at once. When the door closed again she ran to a soldier who had left the room.

"What has happened to all the supplies that were at Tifariti . . . the clinic . . . the hospital," she yelled, grabbing his arm.

He looked at her with a puzzled look on his face. "I don't know, Sidi," he muttered, before running off. "We're finding it difficult enough to get all the people out!"

Sidi stood for a moment in silence. She would have to make sure her supplies were brought back to Tindouf for safety. She ran back to get her jeep . . . and her gun . . . before setting off.

August 19, 1991.

On a hill halfway between Tifariti and Bir Lehlou, Bouhali sat with Mohamed Dadi, the commander of the 5th military region, in his Land Rover, thinking. Two days ago he had been peacefully observing the troops in the south, when a distraught soldier had reached him with news of the bombing at Tifariti. He had called Rabouni immediately and directed the soldier guarding the SAM 8 missiles to send 8 units to the troops in the hills near Tifariti. Then he had rushed back to Tindouf. On his way back he had passed some of the soldiers of the 4th military region squirreled away in the hills near Tifariti, and told them to shoot at any jet that passed low enough.

When he had finally arrived at Rabouni the following day, he found a scene of utter chaos. Abdelaziz told him that the Moroccans had bombed four different locations – all supply stations for weapons or fuel – and would probably try to destroy any buildings in the area. He had quickly decided to mobilize all units and sent a plan of attack to Ayoub in the south.

But then another message had arrived. It was from Dadi, the commander of the troops of the 5th military region near Farsia. Shortly after the bombings Moroccan forces had breached the berm at a point slightly south of Farsia and were headed in the direction of Bir Lehlou. It would be the first time the Moroccans had tried to infiltrate Polisario held territory for years. What was Hassan up to? He had had no time to think . . . he had to move quickly. He had loaded his Land Rover and rushed to join him.

It was now a day later, and before he had had a chance to plan a response, a soldier who had been stationed in the west with the troops of the 2nd military region had arrived with another message -- a message that had turned his face grey.

"What is it?" his companion him asked, hesitantly.

"Another column of Moroccans – the elite 6th regiment – has come through the berm near Smara and are headed in the direction of Tifariti," he managed to mutter.

For a moment there was silence.

"What do you intend to do?" Dadi finally asked.

"I don't know yet," Bouhali responded, slowly. "I will ask the troops of the 2nd military region either to join us here or to augment the troops of the 4th military region to block the troops coming from Smara." He paused, then continued. "Either way we need to be ready to block their advancement."

He fixed his eyes on his companion. Then with words made of steel he added "This may be what we have been waiting for . . . a final confrontation . . . a confrontation that will decide the outcome of sixteen years of fighting. If Hassan is willing to meet us on our ground we need to be ready . . . ready for anything he can throw at us." Dadi smiled and nodded his head. "We are ready!" was all he said.

That afternoon he rejoined the troops. They were prepared . . . and ready for action.

August 19, 1991.

Meanwhile a jeep was slowly making its way westward, through the *hammada* and into the hills that skirted the Mauritanian border. She had passed Bir Lehlou – and seen the craters left where the bombs had dropped – and was now only a few miles from Tifariti. That morning she had passed a family that had been camped in the hills near Tifariti that was moving with its tent and the rest of its belongings back to Tindouf. Abdelaziz had called for an evacuation of the region, she had been told, and all the families were moving towards the camps. As for the soldiers based around Tifariti and the clinic – well, there were still units of guerillas scattered in the hills but the town itself was deserted, as was the clinic.

Sidimi thanked them for the news and continued her journey. When she reached the outskirts of the town – the place where the fuel depots were stored – she saw the scorched trees and burnt sand – the telltale signs of the bombing that had taken place. But the structures that housed the fuel were still intact. When she reached the town itself she felt an eerie stillness. Not a soul moved – only the trees gently waving in the breeze. She made her way to the makeshift clinic that had served the troops in the area for a number of years. It was scheduled to be replaced by a shiny new hospital that had been nearly completed. As she rummaged through the structures she found boxes of medicines that had been left behind by the hastily departing inhabitants, as well as some equipment, both of which she loaded carefully into her vehicle.

As she was preparing to leave she heard the noise of another vehicle. It was a soldier from the troops of the 2nd military region – Bouhali's old unit – who was passing Tifariti en route to joining the troops in the hills.

"What are you doing here, Sidi?" he asked in surprise when he saw her.

"I came to get some of the supplies for the hospital that were left behind," she replied, matter-of-factly.

"Well, you had better hurry," he said, quickly. "Moroccan troops have come through the berm slightly south of Farsia and are headed towards Bir Lehlou. They must be halfway there by now. If you don't move quickly they will block your escape back to Tindouf."

The news hit Sidimi like a thunderbolt. Troops infiltrating Polisario territory?

"Where's Bouhali?" she blurted. "He won't let the troops reach Bir Lehlou!"

"He's up north near Farsia . . . look, all I know is that Abdelaziz has asked us to evacuate all the civilians in the region."

Sidimi smiled at the soldier. "All right," she said, softly, "I will be leaving now." And without another word she climbed into the jeep and headed off towards the east – in the direction of the *hammada* north of Bir Lehlou.

August 20, 1991.

Early in the morning of August 20, Sidimi was preparing for the last leg of her journey. She had stopped for the night and pitched a small tent in a place a few miles north of Bir Lehlou that she remembered from her days with the troops of the 2nd military region. It would offer shelter from the night winds and sand storms that frequently harassed travelers in the *hammada*. As she packed her tent she became aware of a noise – a slight rumbling noise in the distance to the north. She took out her binoculars and scanned the horizon. She could barely make out the image of a column of troops – and they were not far, perhaps fewer than two hours away. But were they Polisario or Moroccan? She couldn't afford to find out.

She hastily sped away to the east, leaving a trail of dust behind her.

Meanwhile, slightly to the west of where she stood, Bouhali sat in his Land Rover scanning the horizon. Everything was set. The troops had been placed in strategic places a few miles north of Bir Lehlou, waiting for the signal. Bouhali had found a spot with a view of the direction from which the Moroccans would come to use as an observation post. He could hear in the distance the low rumble and, through his binoculars, could see the small clouds of dust on the horizon that signaled their approach.

He hadn't noticed the Land Rover that had quietly approached his position from the east.

"Bouhali, I need to speak with you!" the occupant shouted, getting out of the vehicle.

He moved swiftly and soon was by Bouhali's side.

"I want you to pull back the troops," he said, quickly.

Bouhali stared at him in astonishment. Had Abdelaziz lost his mind?

"But if we pull back the troops they will reach Bir Lehlou within the next few hours!" he retorted when he had regained his composure.

"If they want to tire themselves in the sun, let them," Abdelaziz said, with a dismissive waive of the hand.

"I don't get it," Bouhali exclaimed, staring at Abdelaziz with eyes wide in amazement, "Don't you see . . . now is the time to attack them . . . now that they have left the protection of the berm and are vulnerable. It is the opportunity we have been waiting for! We can surround them while they are on the move and position ourselves so that there is no retreat and no opportunity for reinforcements!"

Abdelaziz returned his stare for a moment, then shook his head. "But a confrontation is just what Hassan wants!" he said in a calm voice. "There are only two reasons why Hassan is doing this . . . to scuttle the peace proposals of the UN and reignite the fighting or to gain more territory before the cease fire goes into effect. I don't intend to let him do either. . . but this is not the way!"

He moved a few inches closer and leaned forward.

"Look," he whispered, "de Cuellar called me last night. He was furious. He told me that he has demanded that the King withdraw his troops by September 6, and Bachir is in Geneva where he has been asked to attend an urgent summit. I have gotten other calls . . . from some of our allies . . . also urging us to back off and let the Secretary General diffuse the situation. They have promised me that the UN will force him to bring his troops back behind the berm . . . that he will gain nothing from this aggression. Bachir is already in a meeting with the Secretary General. Let's at least see what de Cuellar is able to do before rushing to attack." He stopped for a moment to catch his breath. "But keep the troops on alert in case Hassan doesn't heed his demand," he yelled, as he walked back to his Land Rover.

For a moment Bouhali just stood there, speechless.

393

At 1 p.m. that day, with Bouhali's troops watching in frustrated silence from the side lines, the Moroccan troops that had broken through the berm near Farsia marched into Bir Lehlou where they proceeded to destroy whatever buildings and shelters they could find. That afternoon they continued their march towards the northwest. By that time the force advancing from Smara had reached a point 80 miles east of the berm and was poised to reach its destination – Tifariti – the following day.

August 21, 1991.

By the morning of August 21 the Moroccans reached Tifariti, destroying a number of buildings, including the nearly completed hospital and the school. But that wasn't the end of Hassan's revenge . . . .

It was 1:00 in the afternoon, and in the hills near Tifariti the camp cook was busy preparing the mid-day meal. Elena had just finished her morning chores, and as she was gathering clothes to wash, the man in charge of the unit passed her in the clearing.

"You know, Elena," he started to say, his eyes smiling, "the war might be over soon. Have you given much thought to what you will do when it ends?"

Elena blushed and turned away. "I really haven't given it much thought, Yahya . . . I guess I will wait to see what happens when it ends." She then grabbed the basket full of clothes and walked through the clearing to the path leading to the area of the small stream near the base where the people washed their clothes.

A few minutes later Salek appeared. When he saw Yahya he stiffened and blushed slightly. The older man couldn't help smiling. Youth really is wasted on the young, he thought. "Elena isn't here," he said, matter-of-factly. As Salek walked out the door, he called after him, "You know, you really should marry that girl!"

Salek was preparing to give him a quick retort when something diverted his attention. It was just a slight buzz, but it made the hairs at the back of his neck stiffen. He froze, straining to hear. Then he shouted "A jet!" Within seconds the tranquility of the camp turned to commotion as men ran from their tents, carrying their rifles, and jumping into the long trenches they had established for cover. Other men scurried to the SAM 8 missiles that had been placed nonchalantly under accommodating acacia trees, and quickly removed their canvass covers. This time the jet didn't merely pass by. Out of nowhere bombs started raining down, their shrapnel spreading over wide expanses of the ground. Yahya, hit by some of the shrapnel, hobbled to a nearby trench. Salek grabbed his AK-47 and started firing blindly at the bird in the sky. A missile was launched, but the jet was now out of reach, circling back for another sortie.

On its second loop more bombs dropped, one shattering shrapnel within an inch of Salek's nose. Another missile was launched and this time hit the nose tip. But the great grey bird continued circling in the sky.

All at once he remembered. Elena! He crawled out of the trench he had buried himself in to the one where the Yahya lay. "Elena! Where is Elena?" he found himself shouting over and over again. The older man, bleeding from wounds to his leg, was busy trying to extricate himself from the pit, barely aware of what Salek was saying. Elena, he thought. Oh, yes, Elena.

He turned his head to look at Salek. "She went to wash clothes . . . by the stream."

When Elena first heard the heavy drone of the jet she was alone in the middle of the small stream that the camp used for bathing and washing clothes. She quickly looked around for any place where she could hide. The stream was wide at that point, and she was completely exposed. She decided to run to one of the acacia trees that stood at the riverbank, a few yards away. She barely made it to the shelter of its outstretched arms when the firing began. A hail of shrapnel missed her by inches. If she could only reach the crevices in one of the hills that surrounded the camp she would be safe, she thought. So, she waited until the plane had passed and began to run at full speed towards the nearest gully.

It was then that she saw Salek. He was running in her direction. A wave of relief spread over her. She would be safe. He would know where to go. But before she could finish that thought the plane returned, a hail of bullets spitting in her direction.

Salek had been desperately searching the landscape with his eyes when he saw her, crouching beneath an acacia tree near the stream. He rushed down the path to where the sand met the water. When he reached the spot where she was crouching he yelled out, "Elena come, follow me." But she did not answer. He took a closer look and gently touched her head. A small rivulet of blood trickled down his hand. He cried out again, "Elena! Elena!" and shook her. But still she didn't answer.

The jet had circled once again and was nearly over him. As It passed over his head he took his gun and began shooting wildly at its fuselage before a shower of bullets fell on him.

A few moments later the jet started to sputter. One of the missiles managed a direct hit and before long it crashed into a hillside, scattering bits of metal and fuel over the countryside.

When it was quiet again the soldiers began looking for survivors and counting the dead. Eventually they came to the stream. There, spread in the sand, was the body of a young woman, and nearby, with arms outstretched as if to touch her, the body of a young man.

September 5, 1991. Hassan's Last Stand.

In a desperate move to eject the guerillas from as much of the territory as possible before the UN mandated cease fire, two weeks before it was scheduled to take effect Hassan had unleashed a torrent of attacks. Bombs fell upon Tifariti, Lemgassem and Bir Lehlou in the north, and Agwanit and Doujit in the south. This was quickly followed by an invasion of troops, prompting a livid Secretary General to call for the withdrawal of the troops and to summon the parties to an emergency meeting in Geneva.

As the Moroccans marched to Bir Lehlou, a delegation, lead by Bachir, was in Geneva in a tense meeting with the Secretary General. Abel Latif Filali, Morocco's Foreign Minister, who was supposed to attend meetings to discuss details about the deployment of peacekeepers and details of the cease fire, hadn't come. By the end of the meeting – following a flurry of phone calls between the White House and Rabat -- the Secretary General assured Bachir that the King would withdraw his troops and respect the September 6 cease fire. On September 5 the Moroccan troops hastily withdrew to the safety of the berm. Except for the two planes that had been shot down and a brief defensive skirmish with the troops approaching Tifariti, the Polisario had simply melted away at the approach of the invaders.

And the following day an eerie calm settled upon the territory.

September 6, 1991. The Cease Fire.

Word quickly spread through the Tindouf camps. People ran from their tents shouting and hugging each other. Others immediately started packing their belongings for the trip back home. Even Sidimi stopped her work at the hospital to watch the parade of Sahrawis who had filled the streets. It was sheer bedlam.

In the towns of Western Sahara, Sahrawis braved the displeasure of the Moroccans by filing into the streets, hugging and kissing each other.

The long war was over, and finally the people would be able to choose their destiny.

Bouhali watched the commotion in silence. "You still don't believe it was the right move, do you?" Sidimi asked gently. Bouhali shook his head. "The only way we will ever get our land back is through the barrel of a gun. It was true in Algeria, it was true in Vietnam, and it will be true in the Sahara. I know I am right," he said slowly. "But I hope I am wrong!" Then, turning to her, he added, "Only time will tell," and quietly left the room.

A few days after the cease fire took effect Sidimi made a long, silent pilgrimage to Tifariti and the hillside location that the soldiers had chosen as a graveyard. She took something from a bag that she had carried. It was Esmeralda. There were no headstones to mark the graves, but Sidimi leaned the body of the guitar against the hillside and managed to dig a hole big enough to insert the neck of the instrument. Quickly she covered the neck over with sand and rock until it could not move.

When she was finished she stood looking down at it. "There, Salek. Now you can play for the stars."

Then she walked slowly away.

September 27, 1991. Marrakech.

Two weeks after the cease fire had begun Hassan was nonchalantly hitting golf balls on one of the luxurious courses that border the palace at Marrakech. Driss Basri, a puzzled look on his face, approached him quietly, so as not to disturb his concentration. When the King had managed to place his ball on the green at the next hole, Basri, perhaps the only Moroccan official who would dare question a policy of the King, spoke up.

"Your Majesty," he said, in a low voice. "I still don't understand why you have agreed to let the UN organize a referendum in the territory that uses the Spanish census to establish the voters' list and includes independence as one of the options. Do you really think that is wise? You know that we cannot count on the majority of the Sahrawis on that list voting for integration with Morocco. At least half of them are in the Polisario camps, and as for the others, well, despite all our efforts to persuade the Sahrawis in the territory to abandon this rebellion, I suspect that the majority of them still support it."

The King didn't even bother to break his stride. Instead, after climbing into his golf cart, he said in a calm voice, "Do you really think I would be foolish enough to agree to a referendum if I wasn't sure I would win it?" and turning to look at Basri, he smiled.

"There is always a plan B!"

EPILOGUE

That was in 1991. To date there has been no referendum.

MINURSO was sent to the territory, but it did not take six months for it to organize the referendum. Morocco successfully lobbied for the criteria for voter eligibility to be expanded and the process of creating a voters list dragged on for years. A number of officials resigned citing Morocco's unfair influence on the process as the reason.

At the end of 1999, after overcoming many problems, MINURSO finally published the list of Sahrawis eligible to vote. When Morocco saw that the list was not in its favor, it simply pulled out of the process.

So far, the UN has not put any pressure on Morocco to keep its promise. Nor has it stopped Morocco's exploitation of the resources of the territory.

The Moroccan government eventually admitted having orchestrated the "disappearances" of Sahrawi civilians and 100 of the missing were found in Moroccan prisons and released.

The majority, however, were never heard from again.

In 2013 several mass graves, containing the bodies of men, women and children, were found in the desert a few miles east of Amgala.

In 1991 Aminatou Haidar was released from prison and became the spokesperson on the world stage for the rights of the Sahrawis living under Moroccan occupation.

In 2003, without ever seeing her mother or her homeland again, surrounded by the remnants of her family, Sidimi died from breast cancer, and was buried with full military honors. In 2016, after a long illness, Abdelaziz, who had led the Polisario in war as well as peace for nearly half a century, lost his struggle with cancer and was buried in Bir Lehlou.

The February 27th School continued in operation, and by the time of Abdelaziz' death the literacy rate among women in the camp exceeded 85% -- the highest of any country in Africa.

The Polisario never recommenced the war. Instead, today the Polisario leaders continue to fight for the rights of their citizens at the United Nations.

. . . and the thousands of Sahrawis who fought in the war and the refugees who fled the territory remain to this day in the wind swept refugee camp in the *hammada* they established in 1975, waiting for the referendum they were promised by the international community over 40 years ago.

www.ingramcontent.com/pod-product-compliance
Lightning Source LLC
Chambersburg PA
CBHW081354090726
47908CB00011B/2675